TORCH OF FREEDOM

*For a complete listing of Baen titles
by David Weber and by Eric Flint
please go to: www.baen.com.*

TORCH OF FREEDOM

DAVID WEBER
& ERIC FLINT

A Baen Books Original

Baen Publishing Enterprises
P.O. Box 1403
Riverdale, NY 10471
www.baen.com

ISBN: 978-1-4391-3305-7

Cover art by David Mattingly

First printing, November 2009

Distributed by Simon & Schuster
1230 Avenue of the Americas
New York, NY 10020

Library of Congress Cataloging-in-Publication Data

Weber, David, 1952–
    Torch of freedom / David Weber & Eric Flint.
        p. cm.
    ISBN 978-1-4391-3305-7
    I. Flint, Eric. II. Title.
    PS3573.E217T67 2009
    813'.54—dc22

                                                    2009033466

10 9 8 7 6 5 4 3 2 1

Pages by Joy Freeman (www.pagesbyjoy.com)
Printed in the United States of America

To Lucille and Sharon,
for putting up with us . . . still.

PART I

*Late 1919 and 1920 Post-Diaspora
[4021 and 4022, Christian Era]*

Beyond the Protectorates, starting at a distance of 210 light-years or so from Sol and extending for depths of from 40 to over 200 light-years, was the region known as "the Verge." The Verge was very irregularly shaped, depending entirely on where and how colony flights were sent out, and consisted of scores of independent star systems, many of them originally colonized by people trying to get away from the Shell Systems, which could be considered the equivalent of what were called "Third World nations" in pre-Diaspora times. Individually, very few of them of them had populations of more than one or two billion (there were exceptions), their economies were marginal, and they had no effective military power. Many of them had all they could do to resist piratical raids, and none of them had the power to resist the Office of Frontier Security and the League Gendarmerie when it came time for them to slip into protectorate status. There was a constant trickling outward from the inner edge of the Verge to the outer edge, fueled more than anything else by the desire of people along the inner edge to avoid the creeping expansion of the Protectorates. Indeed, some people living in the Verge were the descendants of ancestors who had relocated three or four or even five times in an effort to avoid involuntary incorporation into the Protectorates. Their hatred for the Office of Frontier Security—and, by extension, the rest of the League—was both bitter and intensive.

From Hester McReynolds, *Origins of the Maya Crisis.* (Ceres Press, Chicago, 2084 PD)

CHAPTER ONE

"Welcome back."

Sector Governor Oravil Barregos, Governor of the Maya Sector in (theoretically) the Office of Frontier Security's name, stood and held out his hand with a smile as Vegar Spangen escorted the dark, trim man in the uniform of a Solarian League Navy rear admiral into his office.

"I expected you last week," the governor continued, still smiling. "Should I assume the fact that I didn't see you then but do see you now is good news?"

"I think you could safely do that," Rear Admiral Luiz Rozsak agreed as he shook Barregos' hand with a smile of his own.

"Good."

Barregos glanced at Spangen. Vegar had been his personal security chief for decades and the governor trusted him implicitly. At the same time, he and Spangen both understood the principle of the "need to know," and Vegar interpreted that glance with the experience of all those decades.

"I expect you and the admiral need to talk, Sir," the tall, red-haired bodyguard said calmly. "If you need me, I'll be out there annoying Julie. Just buzz when you're ready. And I've made sure all the recording devices are off."

"Thank you, Vegar." Barregos transferred his smile to Spangen.

"You're welcome, Sir." Spangen nodded to Rozsak. "Admiral," he said, and withdrew in the outer office where Julie Magilen, Barregos' private secretary, guarded the approaches like a deceptively demure looking dragon.

3

"A good man," Rozsak observed quietly as the door closed behind Spangen.

"Yes, yes he is. And yet another demonstration of the fact that it's better to have a few *good* men than hordes of not-so-good ones."

The two of them stood for a moment, looking at one another, thinking about how long they'd both been working on assembling the right "good men" (and women). Then the governor gave himself a little shake.

"So," he said more briskly. "You said something about having good news?"

"As a matter of fact," Rozsak agreed, "I think Ingemar's tragic demise helped open a couple of doors a little wider than they might have swung otherwise."

"Some good should come of any misfortune." Barregos' voice was almost pious, but he also smiled again, a thinner and colder smile this time, and Rozsak chuckled. There was something a bit sour about the sound to the governor's experienced ear, though, and he cocked an eyebrow. "Was there a problem?"

"Not a 'problem,' exactly." Rozsak shook his head. "It's just that I'm afraid Ingemar's brutal assassination wasn't quite as 'black' as I'd planned on its being."

"Meaning exactly what, Luiz?" Barregos' dark eyes hardened, and his deceptively round and gentle face suddenly looked remarkably *un*gentle. Not that Rozsak was particularly surprised by his reaction. In fact, he'd expected it . . . which was the main reason he'd waited to share his information until he could do it face to face.

"Oh, it went off perfectly," he said reassuringly, with a half-humorous flick of his free left hand. "Palane did a perfect job. That girl has battle steel nerves, and she buried her tracks—and ours—even better than I'd hoped. She steered the newsies perfectly, too, and as far as I can tell, every single one of them drew the right conclusion. Their stories all emphasize Mesa's—and especially Manpower's—motives for killing him after he so selflessly threw the League's support to those poor, homeless escaped slaves. The evidence could scarcely be more conclusive if I'd, ah, designed it myself. Unfortunately, I feel I can say with reasonable confidence that we've fooled neither Anton Zilwicki, Jeremy X, Victor Cachat, Ruth Winton, Queen Berry, nor Walter Imbesi."

He shrugged insouciantly, and Barregos glared at him.

"That's an impressive list," he said icily. "May I ask if there are any intelligence operatives in the galaxy who *don't* suspect what really happened?"

"I'm pretty sure there are at least two or three. Fortunately, all back on Old Earth."

The rear admiral returned Barregos' semi-glare levelly, and, gradually, the coldness oozed out of the governor's eyes. They remained rather hard, but Rozsak was one of the smallish number of people from whom Barregos didn't attempt to hide their hardness as a matter of course. Which was understandable enough, since Luiz Rozsak was probably the only person in the entire galaxy who knew exactly what Oravil Barregos had in mind for the future of the Maya Sector.

"So what you're saying is that the spooks on the ground know we had him killed, but that all of them have their own reasons for keeping their suspicions to themselves?"

"Pretty much." Rozsak nodded. "Every one of them does have his or her own motive for seeing to it that the official version stands up, after all. Among other things, none of them wants anyone in the Solarian League to think *they* had anything to do with the assassination of a sector lieutenant-governor! More to the point, though, this whole affair's offered us a meeting of the minds that, frankly, I never expected going in."

"So I gathered from your reports. And I have to say, I never would've expected Haven to play such a prominent role in your recent adventures."

As he spoke, Barregos twitched his head at the armchairs in the conversational nook to one side of an enormous floor-to-ceiling picture window. The view out over downtown Shuttlesport, the capital of both the Maya System and of the Maya Sector from the governor's hundred and fortieth-floor office was stupendous, but Rozsak had seen it before. And at the moment, he had rather too many things on his mind to pay it the attention it deserved as he followed the governor across to the window.

"Hell with Haven!" He snorted, settling into his regular seat and watching the governor do the same. "Nobody back in Nouveau Paris knew what was coming any more than we did! Oh, the Republic's signed off on it after the fact, but I suspect Pritchart and her bunch feel almost as much like they've been run over by a lorry as anyone on Manticore. Or Erewhon, for that matter." He shook his head ruefully. "Nobody's told me so officially, but I'll be very surprised if Cachat doesn't wind up running all of Haven's intelligence ops in and around Erewhon. After all, given his recent machinations, he's probably the only person who really knows where *all* the bodies are buried. I don't often feel like I've been caught in someone else's slipstream, Oravil, but he's got to be the best improvisational operator I've ever run into. I swear to you that he didn't have any more notion going in of where this was all going to come out than anyone else did. And like I say, unless I'm badly mistaken, no one in Nouveau Paris ever saw it coming, either." He snorted again. "As a matter of fact, I'm pretty damned sure not even Kevin Usher would've turned him loose on Erewhon if he'd suspected for a minute where Cachat was going to end up!"

"Do you think he's going to be a problem down the road?" Barregos asked, rubbing his chin thoughtfully, and Rozsak shrugged.

"He's not really a lunatic, or even a loose laser head, for that matter. In fact, I'd say our friend Cachat has a good bit in common with a warmhearted rattlesnake, if the simile doesn't sound too bizarre even for me. Although, to be fair, Jiri's really the one who came up with it. It's apt, though. The man tries hard to hide it, but I think he's actually extraordinarily protective of the people and things he cares about, and his response to any threat is to remove it—promptly, thoroughly, and without worrying all that much about collateral damage. If you convince him you're going to be a threat to the Republic of Haven, for example, it'll almost certainly be the last thing you ever do. The only thing likely to get you killed quicker would be to convince him you're a threat to one of the *people* he cares about. Which, by the way, is a very good reason we should never, ever, in even the remotest back corner of our minds, think about eliminating Thandi Palane just to tie up the loose ends of Ingemar's assassination. I'll admit, I wouldn't want to do it anyway, but it didn't take me very long to realize that bad as Cachat's reaction might be, he wouldn't be anywhere close to the only enemy we'd make in the process. Trust me on this one, Oravil."

His voice was unusually sober, and Barregos nodded in acknowledgment. Warnings from Luiz Rozsak were best heeded, as several no longer breathing people the governor could think of right offhand might have testified. Assuming, of course, that they hadn't been no longer breathing.

"On the other hand," the rear admiral continued, "if you aren't a threat to someone or something he cares about, he's perfectly prepared to leave you alone. As far as I can tell he doesn't hold grudges, either—which may be because anyone he'd be likely to hold a grudge *against* is already dead, of course. And he recognizes that sometimes it's 'just business' even if interests he does care about are getting pinched a bit. He's willing to be reasonable. But it's always best to bear that image of a rattlesnake basking in the sun in mind, because if he does decide you need to be seen to, the last thing you'll ever hear will be a brief—*very* brief—rattling sound."

"And Zilwicki?"

"Anton Zilwicki is just as dangerous as Cachat, in his own way. The fact that he's got even better contacts with the Audubon Ballroom than we'd thought gives him a sort of unofficial, 'rogue' action arm all his own. It's got a lot less in the way of a formal support structure than Manty or Havenite intelligence, but at the same time, it's less likely to worry about the sorts of constraints star nations have to bear in mind. It's a lot more likely to leave its back trail littered with body parts, too, and it's got one hell of a long reach. He's smart, and he *thinks* about things, Oravil—hard. He understands just how dangerous a weapon patience is, and he's got a remarkable facility for pulling apparently random facts together to form critical conclusions.

"On the other hand, our initial appreciation of him was considerably more thorough than anything we knew about Cachat, so I can't really say he threw us any surprises. And the bottom line is that even with his links to the Ballroom and people like Jeremy X, I think he's less likely than Cachat to reach for a pulser as his first choice of problem-solving tools. I'm not saying Cachat's a homicidal maniac, you understand. Or that Zilwicki is some kind of choirboy, either, for that matter. Both of them are of the opinion that the best way to remove a threat is to remove it *permanently*, but at heart, I think, Zilwicki is more of an analyst and Cachat is more of a direct action specialist. They're both almost scarily competent in the field, and they're both among the best analysts I've ever seen, but they've got different . . . emphases, let's say."

"Which, now that they're more or less operating in alliance, makes the two of them more dangerous than the sum of their parts. Would that be an accurate summarization?" Barregos asked.

"Yes, and no." Rozsak leaned back in his chair, frowning thoughtfully. "They respect each other. In fact, I think they actually like each other, and each of them owes the other. More than that, they have a major commonality of interest in what's happening in Torch. But at heart, Zilwicki's still a Manty and Cachat's still a Havenite. I think it's possible—especially if the Star Kingdom's and the Republic's foreign relations keep dropping deeper and deeper into the crapper—that the two of them could find themselves on opposing sides again. And that, trust me, would be . . . messy."

"You said 'possible,'" Barregos observed. "Is that the same thing as 'likely'?"

"I don't know," Rozsak replied frankly, and he shrugged. "What they have is a personal relationship and, I think—although I'm not sure either of them would be willing to admit it—friendship. And it's complicated by the fact that Cachat's hopelessly in love with Palane and Zilwicki's daughter's become Palane's unofficial little sister. So I'm guessing that the most likely outcome if the coin ever drops between the Republic and the Star Kingdom again would be that the two of them would give each other fair warning and then retire to their corners and try very hard not to step on each other. The wildcard, of course, is the fact that Zilwicki's daughter is also the queen of Torch. The man's a Gryphon Highlander, too. He's got all the ingrained Gryphon loyalty to the Manty Crown, but he's also got that personal, almost feudal loyalty to family and friends. It may well be he'd give his primary loyalty to Queen Berry, not Queen Elizabeth, if it came down to an outright choice. I doubt he'd ever do anything to *harm* Manticore's interests, and I think he's equally unlikely to stand by and allow something to damage those interests because of simple inaction on his part. But I also think he'd try to *balance* Manticore's and Torch's interests."

"Interesting."

It was Barregos' turn to lean back, and he clasped his hands in front of his chest, leaning his chin on his thumbs while he tapped the tip of his nose gently with both index fingers. It was one of his favorite thinking poses, and Rozsak waited patiently while the governor considered what he'd just said.

"The thing that occurs to me," Barregos said at length, eyes narrowing slightly as they refocused on Rozsak, "is that I don't think Elizabeth would've let Ruth Winton stay on as Torch's assistant chief of intelligence if she wasn't thinking in terms of establishing a sort of backdoor link to Haven. It's obvious she didn't exactly pick High Ridge as her prime minister, after all.

I'm not foolish enough to think she's feeling particularly fond of the Republic of Haven—especially since that business at Yeltsin's Star—but she's smart, Luiz. Very smart. And she knows Saint-Just is dead, probably along with just about everyone else involved in that whole op. I don't say I think knowing that's suddenly made her fond of Havenites in general, but I do think that, deep inside, she'd really like to see Pritchart and Theisman succeed in restoring the Old Republic."

"That's my read, too," Rozsak agreed. "However much she may hate 'Peeps,' she's enough of a student of history to know the Republic wasn't always the biggest, hungriest hog in the neighborhood. And however little some parts of her personality might like admitting it, I think she recognizes that seeing the Old Republic come back would be a lot less strenuous—and dangerous—than going back to hog-killing time. Not that I'm prepared to even guesstimate how likely she thinks it is that they *will* succeed."

"I imagine we're both rather more optimistic in that respect than she is." Barregos' smile was wintry. "Probably has something to do with our not having been at war with the *People's* Republic of Haven for the last fifteen or twenty T-years."

"That's true enough, but I'm also inclined to think there's some genuine principle involved here—in Torch's case, I mean—too," Rozsak said. "The one thing Haven and Manticore have always agreed on is how much they both hate the genetic slave trade and Manpower Incorporated. That's the only reason Cachat was able to put together his . . . energetic solution to the 'Verdant Vista Problem' in the first place. I think both Elizabeth and Pritchart have a genuine sense of having created something brand new in galactic history when they played midwife, whether they wanted to or not, to the liberation of Torch. And my impression from speaking to Prince Michael and Kevin Usher at the coronation is that both Elizabeth and Pritchart believe that even if relations break down completely again between the Republic and the Star Kingdom, Torch could provide a very useful conduit. Sometimes even people shooting at each other have to talk to each other, you know."

"Oh, yes, indeed I do." Barregos' smile turned tart, and he shook his head. "But getting back to Ingemar. You think his arrangement with Stein is going to stand up now that he's gone?"

"I think it's as likely now as I ever thought it was," Rozsak replied a bit obliquely, and Barregos snorted.

Luiz Rozsak had never had the liveliest faith in the reliability—or utility—of anyone in the Renaissance Association even before the assassination of Hieronymus Stein, its founder. And his faith in the integrity of Hieronymus' successors was, if anything, even less lively. A point upon which, to be honest, Barregos couldn't disagree with him.

There was no question in the governor's mind that Hieronymus had been considerably more idealistic than his daughter, Jessica, yet there'd been even less question, in Oravil Barregos' opinion, that his last name should have been "Quixote" instead of Stein. All the same, as the founder and visible figurehead of the Renaissance Association, he'd enjoyed a unique degree of status, both in and out of the Solarian League, which could not be denied. It might have been the sort of status which was accorded to a lunatic who genuinely believed idealism could triumph over a thousand odd years of bureaucratic corruption, but it had been genuine.

He'd also been the next best thing to completely ineffectual, which was one reason the bureaucrats who truly ran the Solarian League hadn't had him killed decades before. He'd fretted, he'd fumed, he'd been highly visible and an insufferable gadfly, but he'd also been a convenient focus for discontent within the League precisely because he'd been so devoted to the concept of "process" and gradual reform. The bureaucracy had recognized that he was effectively harmless and actually useful because of the way he allowed that discontent to vent itself without ever accomplishing a thing.

Jessica, on the other hand, represented a distinct break with her father's philosophy. She'd allied herself with the Association's hard-liners—the ones who wanted fast, hard action on "The Six Pillars" of its fundamental principles for reform. Who were so frustrated and angry that they were no longer especially interested in restricting themselves to the legal processes which had failed them for so long. Some of them were ideologues, pure and simple. Some were passionate reformers, who'd been disappointed just a few too many times. And some were players, people who saw the Renaissance Association's status as the most prominent reform-oriented movement in the Solarian League as a potential crowbar, a way those who weren't part of the bureaucracy might just be able to hammer, chisel, and pry their way into a power base of their own.

Just as Barregos had never doubted Hieronymus' idealism was genuine, he'd never doubted Jessica's was little more than skin deep. She'd grown up in the shadows of her father's reputation, and she'd spent her entire life watching him accomplish absolutely nothing in the way of real and lasting change while his politics simultaneously excluded *her* from any possibility of joining the existing power structure. His prominence, the way the reformist dilettantes and a certain strain of newsies—what was still called "the chattering class"—fawned on him, kept her so close to the entrenched structure which ran the League that she could literally *taste* it, yet she would never be able to *join* it. After all, she was the daughter and heir of the senior lunatic and anarchist-in-chief, wasn't she? No one would be crazy enough to invite *her* into even the outermost reaches of the Solarian League's real ruling circle!

Which was why she'd been so receptive to Ingemar Cassetti's offer to have her father assassinated.

Barregos rather regretted the necessity of Hieronymus' death, but it was a mild regret. In fact, what bothered him most about it was that it didn't bother him any more than it did. That it was never going to cost him a single night's sleep. It shouldn't be that way, but Oravil Barregos had realized years ago that getting to where he wanted to be was going to cost some slivers of his soul along the way. He didn't like it, but it was a price he was willing to pay, although not, perhaps, solely for the reasons most of his opponents might have believed.

But with Hieronymus gone, Cassetti—who, Barregos had concluded after mature consideration, had been the most loathsome single individual he'd ever personally met, however useful he might have proved upon occasion—had engineered a direct understanding and alliance between himself, as Barregos' envoy, and Jessica Stein. Of course, Cassetti hadn't been aware that *Barregos* was aware of his plans to quietly assassinate his own superior. Nor, for that matter, had Cassetti bothered to inform Barregos in the first place that Hieronymus' death was going to be part of the bargaining process with Jessica. Then again, there'd been several things he'd somehow forgotten to mention to his superior about those negotiations. Like the fact that while the alliance the lieutenant governor had concluded with her might have been in Oravil Barregos' name, *he'd* intended from the beginning to be the one sitting in the sector governor's chair when Jessica's debt was called in. It was evident from what Rozsak had reported from Torch that Cassetti hadn't even guessed Barregos had seen it coming from the outset and made his own plans accordingly.

Ingemar always was more cunning than smart, Barregos reflected grimly. *And he never did seem to realize other people might be just as capable as he was. For that matter, he was nowhere near as good a judge of people as he thought he was, or he would never have approached* Luiz, *of all people, about planting his dagger in my back!*

"I know you've never had much faith in the Association's efficacy," the governor said aloud. "For that matter, *I* don't have a lot of faith in its ability to actually *accomplish* anything. But that's not really the reason we want its backing, now is it?"

"No," Rozsak agreed. "On the other hand, I don't think Jessica Stein is an honest politician."

"You mean you don't think she'll stay bought?"

"I mean the woman's a political whore," Rozsak said bluntly. "She'll stay bought, sort of, but she doesn't see any reason not to sell herself to as many buyers as possible, Oravil. I just don't think there's any way for us to even guess at this point how many masters she's actually going to have when the time comes for us to . . . call in our marker, let's say."

"Ah, but that's when all that evidence Ingemar was so careful to preserve comes in," Barregos said with a thin smile. "Having her on chip planning her own father's murder gives us a pretty good stick to go with our carrot. And, when you come down to it, we really don't need that much out of her. Just the Association's blessing for our PR campaign when events out here 'force our hand.'"

"All I've got to say on that head is that it's a good thing we *don't* need anything more out of her," Rozsak said tartly.

"I don't disagree, but the truth is, Luiz," Barregos smiled at the rear admiral again, this time with atypical warmth, "that no matter how well you play the black ops game, at heart, you don't really like it."

"I beg your pardon?"

Rozsak's offended look was almost perfect, Barregos noted, and he chuckled.

"I said you play it well, Luiz. In fact, I think you play it better than almost anyone else I've ever seen. But you and I both know the real reason you do. And"—the governor met Rozsak's eyes levelly, and his own were suddenly much less opaque than usual—"the reason you were so willing to sign on in the first place."

A moment or two of silence hovered in the office. Then Rozsak cleared his throat.

"Well, be that as it may," he said more briskly, "and whatever possible problematical advantages we may be able to squeeze out of Ms. Stein at some theoretical future date, I have to admit that entire funeral charade on Erewhon and the follow-up on Torch has landed us in a situation that's significantly better than I ever would have predicted ahead of time."

"So I've gathered. Your last report said something about a meeting with Imbesi and Al Carlucci?"

Barregos raised his eyebrows again, and Rozsak nodded.

"Actually, Imbesi's main immediate contribution was to make it very clear to Carlucci that our talks had his blessing—and that Fuentes, Havlicek, and Hall were on board, as well."

It was Barregos turn to nod. The government of the Republic of Erewhon wasn't quite like anyone else's. Probably because the entire system was directly descended from Old Earth's "organized crime" families. Officially, the Republic was currently governed by the triumvirate of Jack Fuentes, Alessandra Havlicek, and Thomas Hall, but there were always other people, with differing degrees of influence, involved in the governing process. Walter Imbesi was one of those "other people," the one who'd organized the neutralization of the Mesan intrusion into Erewhon's sphere of influence. His decision to cooperate with Victor Cachat—and, for that matter, Luiz Rozsak—had gotten Mesa evicted from what had been the system of Verdant Vista and was now the Torch System.

It had also finished off, for all intents and purposes, Erewhon's alliance with the Star Kingdom of Manticore. Which, Barregos knew perfectly well, had been possible only because of the way the High Ridge Government had systematically ignored, infuriated, and—in Imbesi's opinion—fundamentally betrayed Erewhon and Erewhon's interests.

Regardless of Imbesi's motivations, he'd once again restored his family to the uppermost niches of power in Erewhon. In fact, he'd become for all intents and purposes the triumvirate's fourth, not quite officially acknowledged member. And in the process, he had

moved Erewhon from its previous pro-Manticore position into a
pro-*Haven* position.

"Is Erewhon really going to sign on with Haven?" the governor
asked.

"It's a done deal," Rozsak replied. "I don't know if the formal
treaty's actually been signed yet, but if it hasn't, it will be soon. At
which point Erewhon and Haven will become parties to a mutual
defense treaty . . . and Nouveau Paris will suddenly become privy
to quite a lot of Manty technology."

"Which will piss Manticore off no end," Barregos observed.

"Which will piss Manticore off no end," Rozsak acknowledged.
"On the other hand, Manticore doesn't have anyone to blame
but itself, and from Prince Michael's attitude at Queen Berry's
coronation, he and his sister Elizabeth know it, whether anyone
else in Manticore's prepared to admit it or not. That idiot High
Ridge handed Erewhon to Haven on a platter. And"—the rear
admiral's smile turned suddenly wolfish—"handed Erewhon over
to *us*, at the same time."

"Then it's settled?" Barregos felt himself leaning forward and
knew he was giving away far more eagerness and intensity than
usual, but he didn't really care as he watched Rozsak's expression
carefully.

"It's settled," Rozsak agreed. "The Carlucci Industrial Group is
currently waiting to sit down with Donald, Brent, and Gail to
discuss commercial agreements with the Maya Sector government."

Barregos settled back again. Donald Clarke was his senior
economic adviser—effectively the Maya Sector's treasurer. Brent
Stephens was his senior industrial planner, and Gail Brosnan was
currently the Maya Sector's acting lieutenant governor. Given the
peculiarities of Maya's relationship with the Office of Frontier
Security, Barregos was confident Brosnan would eventually be
confirmed by OFS HQ back on Old Earth. At the same time, he
was even more confident she would be the "acting" lieutenant
governor for a long, long time, first. After all, his superiors had
stuck him with Cassetti in the first place because they hadn't
wanted Barregos picking his own potential successor. The fact that
he trusted Brosnan would automatically make certain people back
in . . . less than happy to see her inheriting Cassetti's old position.
Those same people were undoubtedly planning on delaying her

confirmation as long as possible in hopes that Barregos might have a heart attack—or be hit by a micro meteorite or kidnaped by space-elves or something—before they actually had to let her assume office. At which point they could finally get rid of the entire Barregos administration . . . including Brosnan.

"Should I assume you've been invited to come along as an unofficial member of our trade delegation?" he asked.

"You should." Rozsak smiled again. "I've already had a few words with Chapman and Horton, too. Nothing too direct yet—I figured we'd better be sure we had the civilian side firmly nailed down before I started talking military shop. But from what Imbesi said, and even more from what Carlucci said after Imbesi was 'unexpectedly called away' from our meeting, the Navy's ready to sit down with me and start talking some hard numbers. Exactly what those numbers are going to be will depend on how much we've got to invest, of course."

He raised an interrogative eyebrow, and Barregos snorted.

"The numbers are going to be higher than anyone in Erewhon probably expects," he said frankly. "The limiting factor's going to be how well we can keep it under the radar horizon from Old Earth, and Donald and I have been working on conduits and pump-priming for a long time now. There's a hell of a lot of money here in Maya. In fact, there's a hell of a lot *more* of it than Agatá Wodoslawski or anyone else at Treasury back on Old Earth even guesses, which is probably the only reason they haven't insisted on jacking the 'administrative fees' schedule even higher. I think we'll be able to siphon off more than enough for our purposes."

"I don't know, Oravil," Rozsak said. "Our 'purposes' are going to get pretty damned big if and when the wheels finally come off."

"There's no 'if' about it," Barregos responded more grimly. "That's part of what this is all about, after all. But when I say we can siphon off more than enough, what I'm really saying is I can siphon off all that we dare actually spend. Too much hardware floating around too quickly, especially out this way, is likely to make some of my good friends at the ministry just a bit antsy, and we can't afford that. Better we come up a little tight on the military end when the shit finally hits the fan than that we tip off someone back on Old Earth by getting too ambitious too soon and see the balloon go up before we're ready."

"I *hate* balancing acts," Rozsak muttered, and Barregos laughed.

"Well, unless I miss my guess, we're getting into the endgame. I wonder if any of those idiots back in Old Chicago have been reading up on the Sepoy Mutiny?"

"I certainly hope not," Rozsak replied with a certain fervency.

"I doubt anyone has, really." Barregos shook his head. "If any of them were truly capable of learning from history, at least someone would have seen the writing on the wall by now."

"Personally, I want them to go right on being nearsighted as long as we can get away with," Rozsak told him.

"Me, too."

The governor sat thinking for a few more moments, then shrugged.

"Do we have a firm date for this meeting with Carlucci?"

"It's a week from here to Erewhon by dispatch boat. I told them I figured it would be at least ten days."

"Is three days going to be enough for you and your people?"

"My people are already two-thirds of the way into the loop on this one, Oravil. With the exception of that little snot Manson, most of them already know—or they've guessed, at least—exactly what's about to happen. I've already made arrangements to peel him off for a few days while the rest of us sit down and talk nuts and bolts and I think three days should be long enough for us to get most of the pieces lined up. Donald and Brent are going to have to be part of that, too, I suppose, but they'll be sitting in mostly as observers, to make sure they understand what it is we're trying to accomplish. It'll be time to get them involved in generating actual numbers after they're up to speed on the hardware side, and I'll have the transit time back to Erewhon to finish kicking things around with them. It'll do, I think."

"Good." Barregos stood. "In that case, I think you should probably head on off to your office and get started talking about those nuts and bolts."

CHAPTER TWO

A sizable percentage of the Maya System's original colonists had come from the planet Kemal. Like most of their fellow immigrants, they'd been none too happy with the planet and society they were leaving behind, but they'd brought their planetary cuisine with them. Now, four hundred T-years later, Mayan pizza—courtesy of the kitchens of Kemal—was among the best in the known galaxy.

That point had particular relevancy at the moment, given the clutter of traditional delivery boxes and plates littered with bits and pieces of pizza crust scattered around the conference room.

Luiz Rozsak sat in his place at the head of the table, nursing a stein of beer, and looked at his assembled staff. Captain Edie Habib, his chief of staff, had her head bent over a computer display with Jeremy Frank, Governor Barregos' senior aide. Lieutenant Commander Jiri Watanapongse, Rozsak's staff intelligence officer, was involved in a quiet side discussion with Brigadier Philip Allfrey, the senior officer of the Solarian Gendarmerie for the Maya Sector, and Richard Wise, who headed Barregos' civilian intelligence operations. *That* conversation, the rear admiral thought with an inward grin, would have caused an enormous amount of acid reflux back in Old Chicago if Watanapongse and Allfrey's ultimate superiors had been privy to its content.

Brent Stephens and Donald Clarke sat to Rozsak's left and right, respectively. Stephens was on the large size, seven centimeters taller than Rozsak's own hundred and seventy-five centimeters, with blond hair and brown eyes. He was also a direct descendent of the first wave of Mayan colonists, whereas the black-haired, gray-eyed Clarke had been five years old when his parents arrived on Smoking Frog as senior managers for the local operations of the Broadhurst Group. Most places in the Verge, that would have made him a very poor fit for this particular little get together, since Broadhurst was one of the Solarian League's major trans-stellars, but this wasn't "most places." This was the Maya Sector, and the rules here were a bit different from those by which the Office of Frontier Security was accustomed to playing.

And they're about to get a lot more *different*, the rear admiral thought coldly.

"Can I take my file copy of our notes home with me, Luiz?" Clarke asked now, and Rozsak raised an eyebrow at him. "I'm headed off-planet this afternoon," Barregos' senior economic adviser explained. "It's Dad's birthday, and I promised Mom I'd be there for it."

Rozsak grimaced in understanding. Michael Clarke was only ninety T-years old, which barely constituted middle age for a civilization with prolong, but he had developed a progressive neural disorder not even modern medicine seemed capable of arresting. He was slowly but steadily slipping away from his family, and he wasn't going to have very many more birthdays when he remembered who his son was.

"He's out on Eden, isn't he?" the rear admiral asked after a moment.

"Yeah." It was Donald's turn to grimace. "It's not like we can't afford it, but I don't think it's doing much good, either."

Rozsak nodded in sympathetic agreement. The Eden Habitat was a low-grav geriatric center in geosynchronous orbit around the planet of Smoking Frog. It offered the very best medical care—care as good as anyone could have gotten back on Old Earth herself—and the most luxurious, patient-friendly staff and quarters imaginable.

"If you take it with you, are you really going to get very much done, anyway?" he asked quietly.

"Of course—" Clarke began just a bit sharply, then cut himself off. He looked at Rozsak for a moment, then inhaled deeply.

"No, probably not," he admitted heavily.

"I'm not that worried about the security risk, Donald," Rozsak said, mostly honestly. "I know you've got good security, and God knows Eden's people are going to make damned sure no one invades *their* patients' privacy! But we're not on that tight a time frame. You can take a few hours to spend with your parents."

"You're sure?" Clarke looked at him, and Rozsak shrugged.

"Your part's either already done, or else it's mostly going to happen once we get to Erewhon. We're talking nuts and bolts here, not financial instruments or investment strategies. Go ahead. Don't worry about it. It's more important that you're as close to rested as you can get when we head out than that we squeeze every single moment of utility out of your time before we leave."

"I'll admit, I'd be happier leaving it under lock and key down here," Clarke confessed. "And you're right. Spending the time with them is important, too."

"Of course it is." Rozsak looked at his chrono. "And if you're going to go off and celebrate a birthday this afternoon, I think you should probably head on home and see if you can't catch a few hours of sleep, first."

"You're right."

Clarke rubbed his eyes with the palms of his hands, gave himself a shake, then pushed back his chair and stood, switching off his minicomp as he did.

"Of course I'm right. *I'm* a rear admiral these days, aren't I?" Rozsak grinned up at the standing financier. "Go ahead—go!"

"Aye, aye, Sir," Clarke said with a weary smile, nodded to Stephens, and left.

"You did good, Luiz," Stephens said quietly as his colleague departed. "It's always worse for him when his father's birthday rolls around."

"Yeah, sure. That's me. Philanthropist and general friend of mankind."

Rozsak waved it off, and Stephens let him.

"Well, if you don't want to talk about that, are you really confident that Carlucci's going to be able to come through on all this?"

"Yes," Rozsak said simply. Stephens arched one eyebrow ever so slightly, and Rozsak raised his voice. "Jiri, do you think you could tear yourself away from Philip and Richard for a few minutes?"

"Sure," Watanapongse said. He grinned at Allfrey and Wise. "All we're really doing at this point is making bets on the football championship while we wait for the rest of you people to call upon our incomparable services."

"I think that's one of the things I like best about both you spooks," Edie Habib put in, not even looking up from her conversation with Frank. "Your modesty. Your constant air of self effacement."

Watanapongse smiled at her, then crossed to Clarke's abandoned chair and sat back down, cocking his head inquiringly.

"Brent is a little concerned over Carlucci's ability to make good on our discussions, I think," Rozsak explained. "Care to reassure him?"

Watanapongse looked at Stephens thoughtfully for a moment, then shrugged.

"The Carlucci Industrial Group has the *capacity* to build anything we need," he said. "It's all just a matter of willingness, figuring out how to pay for it, and time."

"And how to *hide* everything," Stephens pointed out.

"Well, yes, and that," Watanapongse acknowledged.

"Frankly, that's what worries me the most," Stephens said. "I think I've got a better appreciation than most for the degree of expansion CIG's going to have to pull off to make all of this come together. If anyone's looking, it's going to be hard to cover that up. Shipyards aren't exactly unobtrusive."

"No, they aren't. And neither are starships. But the idea is that we won't be 'covering up' at all. Edie came up with what's probably the best description for what we're doing from one of those old stories she likes to read, something called 'The Purloined Letter.'" Watanapongse smiled. "Everything we're doing is going to be sitting right there in plain sight . . . we're just going to convince everyone that it's something else entirely."

"Something else?" Stephens repeated very carefully.

"Sure."

"And exactly how is all of this going to work out?" the industrialist inquired. "I've been concentrating on financing schedules and priorities from our end so far. I'm just taking it on faith that you guys are going to be able to use all of this at the other end. I know you've promised to explain everything on the trip, but I can't quite convince myself to stop worrying about it until we get there."

"It's not too complicated, whatever it may look like at the moment," Rozsak told him. "Basically, it's sleight-of-hand. The Maya Sector is about to begin investing heavily in Erewhon, which—as the governor will explain to anyone from back home who notices what we're up to—is not only practical but downright farsighted, given Erewhon's current estrangement from Manticore and the steadily worsening interstellar situation out here." He rolled his eyes piously. "Not only does it make sound economic sense for everybody here in the Sector, but it represents an opportunity to start wooing Erewhon—and its wormhole terminus—back into the loving arms of the League."

Stephens snorted caustically, and Watanapongse chuckled.

"Actually," Rozsak continued more seriously, "it really would make good economic sense, however you look at it. And Erewhon's in a logistical bind. After what happened on Torch, the Erewhonese have pretty much burned their bridges with Manticore. Well, actually, that's not really the best way to put it. I'm sure Manticore—or at least the Manties' *queen*—would be willing to welcome them back, but Imbesi and his friends dynamited the central span pretty damned thoroughly.

"Anyway, as I'm sure quite a few people back on Old Earth are well aware, Erewhon's never built its own ships-of-the-wall. For that matter, it's bought most of its cruisers from foreign suppliers, as well. Back before they joined the Manticoran Alliance, the Erewhonese bought most of those ships from Solarian builders; since signing up with Manticore, they've bought Manty-built. But that source is going to be closed, especially once they get around to signing that formal mutual defense pact with Haven. On the other hand, Haven's not really in a position to sell them lots and lots of modern wallers, and even if Haven were, the Havenites' general tech base isn't as good—yet, at least—as Manticore's. For that matter, it isn't as good as the sort of 'Manticore lite' tech Erewhon has available on its own.

"So it's going to make sense for Erewhon to begin expanding its own naval building capacity. They've built their own destroyers and other light units for a long time, so it's not as if they don't have the local expertise. They've just never felt able to justify investing in all the infrastructure that goes into building *capital* ships. Now, obviously, we'd *prefer* for them to buy Solarian for any wallers they might need." The rear admiral managed to sound as if he actually meant that, Stephens noticed. "Unfortunately," Rozsak continued, "we can't force them to do that, and I'm afraid they're not entirely happy about placing orders for such big-ticket items in Solarian yards. Some of them actually seem to cherish the dark suspicion that the League might hold up the delivery of their new ships in order to do a little judicious arm-twisting where the Erewhon terminus is concerned. Ridiculous, of course, but what can you expect out of a bunch of neobarbs?

"But if they're not going to buy Solarian, and they can't buy Manty or Havenite, then their only alternative is to finally bite the bullet and begin building up the yard capacity to build their own. Obviously, no single star system is going to be able to build a lot of wallers, and it's probably silly of them to invest so much capital in a capacity that's going to be so seriously underutilized. But if they're determined to go ahead and do it, then we might as well invest in the project and help them build it. They're going to be buying a lot of what they need from us, so it'll be a shot in the arm for the Sector's business community. It's going to show its investors a tidy profit, too, and, like I say, it's also likely to give us—'us' in this case being the League as a whole, of course, as far as Old Chicago knows anything about—a toe in the door later on."

"Okay." Stephens nodded. "So, as you say, it makes sense—or it's *plausible*, at least—for Erewhon to be expanding its naval building capacity. And I'm sure we can make our investment, or our *official* investment, at least, sound reasonable, too. But what happens when they start building ships for *us*?"

"There are actually three things to consider there," Watanapongse said calmly. "First, they aren't going to be building any capital ships for us. All of the wallers are going to be being built to standard Erewhonese designs for the ESN. *Surely* you don't think a loyal sector governor would even be contemplating acquiring unauthorized capital ships of his very own? I'm shocked—*shocked*—by the very possibility that you might entertain such a thought! Of course, if anyone actually runs the numbers, they're going to realize the Erewhonese are building more SDs than they could possibly pay for—or, for that matter, man!—but it wouldn't be the first time a third rate, neobarb Navy's eyes got bigger than its stomach. If anyone asks, they're planning on putting the excess units straight into mothballs as a mobilization reserve, to be manned only if their navy expands in the face of an emergency situation. Given Battle Fleet's mobilization plans, that should make sense to the geniuses back on Old Earth, for a while, at least. Hopefully, by the time we're actually sending crews out to take possession of our part of the building program, it's not going to matter all that much if someone notices. Don't forget, we're talking at least two or three T-years down the road, where wallers are concerned, even after the yard capacity is built. Probably more like four or five years, minimum, to the first deliveries.

"Second, we're going to bury a few 'official' light units of our own in the Erewhonese program." He shrugged. "Given how strapped for hulls Frontier Fleet always is, and given the worsening situation between Manticore and Haven, Governor Barregos obviously has legitimate security concerns. The Sector would make a pretty juicy prize, if any of the locals were gutsy enough—or crazy enough—to try to grab it. That's not likely to happen, of course, but it *is* likely that privateers and piracy are going to spill over onto our local interests. I mean, the Sector trades with Erewhon, Manticore, *and* Haven on a regular basis. Sooner or later, we're going to have to start thinking in terms of commerce protection."

Stephens looked a little dubious, and Rozsak shook his head.

"Trust me, Brent. When I get done writing my evaluation as Frontier Fleet's senior officer here in the Sector, everybody back on Old Earth's going to understand that we're critically short of the sort of light units—destroyers, maybe the occasional light cruiser—you need for commerce protection. Unfortunately, everyone's *always* short of light units like that. Most systems with the kind of economic clout we have are full members of the League, which means they can raise their own system-defense forces to provide that sort of protection. *We* can't; we're officially a protectorate. That means the only place we can get the escorts we need is from Frontier Fleet, but Frontier Fleet doesn't have them to spare. So, what I'll be doing is using discretionary funds, plus additional 'special subscriptions' the governor is going to screw out of the local merchants and manufacturers, to buy a few extra destroyers, which will then become the property of Frontier Fleet. They'll be integrated into my own squadrons out here, they won't cost the Navy (or any of the other bureaucracies back home) a single centicredit, and when the situation out here finally calms down, Frontier Fleet will cheerfully transfer them somewhere else.

"Or that's what they *think* will happen, anyway."

Stephens could have shaved with Rozsak's smile.

"And they're also going to think that what we're building are only destroyers," Watanapongse added. "The *'light cruisers'* are officially going to be Erewhonese units, not ours. We'll be 'borrowing' a few of them from Admiral McAvoy once the piracy situation starts getting out of hand out here. It'll be another example of how those silly neobarbs built more ships than they had the cash and manpower to keep operational, so in the interests of getting the League's hooks even more deeply into the Republic of Erewhon, we'll be providing naval assistance in the form of experienced officers to help the poor neobarbs find their way around. In the meantime, no one back home's going to realize that our new 'destroyers' are going to be the next best thing to the same size as our *Morrigan*-class light cruisers."

Stephens frowned, and the lieutenant commander laughed.

"Nobody back home seems to have noticed the . . . tonnage inflation that's been creeping into classes out here, Brent," he pointed out. "By this time, Manty and Havenite 'heavy cruisers' are damned near the size of small battlecruisers, and some of their light cruisers are closing in on the tonnage ranges for Solarian *heavy* cruisers. The same thing's been happening to their destroyers, too, for that matter. Well, obviously we have to be building ships that could face up to those outsized Manty and Havenite designs, don't we? Of course we do! Still, if no one back on Old Earth has noticed that sizes are creeping up amongst the local neobarb navies, I don't see any special reason why we have to tell them that *ours* are, do you?"

His smile looked remarkably like Rozsak's, Stephens thought.

"Edie and I are already working up the reports and correspondence," Rozsak said. "Officially, we're going to be describing our new units as 'modified *Rampart*-class destroyers,' for example. We just aren't going to get too specific about what the modifications consist of . . . or the fact that we're talking about destroyers fifty or sixty percent bigger than the original *Rampart*. I'm pretty sure the geniuses back at OpNav are going to assume that any modifications will result in *decreased* capabilities, given their view of Manty and Havenite technical capabilities. A view which Jiri's and my modest efforts have probably done just a *bit* to help shape. And since all of the official correspondence—governmental, as well as from the private builders and inspectors—from the Erewhon side is going to be understating tonnages by about, oh, forty or fifty percent, there's not going to be anything to tell Old Chicago differently. And the beauty of it is that we're not going to be falsifying any paperwork; we're going to be sending them file copies of the actual, official correspondence from Erewhon."

Stephens pursed his lips silently as he considered that. Rozsak was right about how it would help cover their own actions, but the industrialist wondered just exactly how the admiral had convinced Erewhon to run that kind of risk. Eventually, someone back on Old Earth was going to realize they'd been systematically deceived by the Erewhonese (and the League's own official intelligence apparatus here in the Sector, of course), and the consequences of that could be severe—for Erewhon, not just Maya.

On the other hand, if that sort of situation arose, it would mean all the rest of their plans had failed disastrously, so there probably wasn't a lot of point worrying about it. Although getting the *Erewhonese* to look at it that way must've taken some doing. . . .

"You said there were three things to consider," he said to Watanapongse after a moment, and the commander nodded.

"The third thing, maybe the most important one of all," he said, his expression much more somber, "is that four- or five-T-year window between now and the delivery of our first wallers. Even after the SDs start coming out of the yards, it's going to take a while for any sort of volume production to build up. We'll hide as many of 'our' wallers as we can in the flow going to Erewhon, of course, but the odds are good that we're going to have to start shooting at somebody before we have a real wall of battle of our own."

Stephens felt a distinct stir of alarm, but Rozsak flashed him the lazy, white-toothed smile of a confident tiger.

"Even with a four- or five-year delay to our own first waller, we're going to be ahead of the curve compared to the rest of the League, Brent. A *long* way ahead of the curve. Trust me, the 'not invented here' syndrome is going to kick in back home even after they begin to figure out just how screwed any SLN ship is going to be going up against its Havenite—or, even worse, *Manty*—equivalent. So, what we're really going to need to tide us over is something that can kick the shit out of anything Frontier Fleet's likely to be sending out towards us with unfriendly intentions. Right?"

"With the proviso that I think we need to do a little worrying about the Battle Fleet units that might be sent along behind that first wave," Stephens agreed a bit caustically.

"Well, of course." Rozsak chuckled. "And it just happens we've come up with something that should let us do that, at least as long as nobody back on Old Earth is paying any attention to all of those ridiculous rumors about how Manticore and Haven have been sticking multiple drives into their missiles. Nonsense, of course! I'm sure those reports are just as exaggerated as Commander Watanapongse's diligent staff has consistently reported they are! Still, it's occurred to us that if someone *were* building multidrive missiles, and if they happened to have themselves a couple of dozen freighters—freighters that might happen to have military-grade drives, and maybe even sidewalls—that could carry, oh, I don't know, three or four hundred missile pods at a time, then they could probably do a lot of damage to a fleet equipped only with *single*-drive missiles, don't you think?"

Stephens's eyes narrowed, and Rozsak chuckled again, more harshly.

"That's one of the things Edie and I have been kicking around when we started thinking about doctrine and ship designs. And it's the real reason we're going to be building that extra tonnage into our light combatants. Most of it's going into fire control, not extra weapons."

"And the beauty of it," Watanapongse said, "is that Carlucci already has a commercial design—they picked it up from some outfit in Silesia—for a freighter designed around plug-in cargo modules. It's one of those ideas that sounds really good on paper, but it hasn't worked out that well for the Sillies as a commercial proposition. It's actually *less* flexible, it turns out, than what you can do reconfiguring a standard cargo hold's interior. But that's not something that's going to be instantly evident looking at it from the outside, and the basic construction just happens to be something that's going to lend itself well to a 'merchantship' pod-carrier design. The Sector government is going to be buying quite a few of them—several dozen, at least—as part of our move to broaden our investment base in Erewhon. We've got a lot of short domestic cargo routes of our own, just like the Sillies, so if it works for them, it ought to work for us, right? And even if it turns out they aren't the most cost-efficient possible way to haul freight around, so what? It was still worth it just to get our toes further into the Erewhonese door."

"And," Rozsak said quietly, "if it just happens that our new ships' plug-in cargo modules just happen to have exactly the same dimensions as the missile pods the Erewhonese Navy is going to be building for its own new ships-of-the-wall, well"—this time his smile could have liquefied helium—"it's a big galaxy, and coincidences happen all the time."

CHAPTER THREE

Catherine Montaigne looked down at the very large suitcase on the bed. The look was not an affectionate one.

"Do you realize, Anton, what an archaeological relic this is? We're coming close on two thousand years since the human race left our planet of origin—and we *still* have to pack our own bags."

Anton Zilwicki pursed his lips. "This is one of those damned-if-I-do, damned-if-I-don't, and damned-if-I-try-to-keep-my-mouth-shut situations."

She frowned. "What is that supposed to mean?"

He pointed with a thick, stubby finger to the door which led to the personal services bay of the bedroom. "There is a household robot in there with a perfectly functional travel program. I haven't personally packed a bag myself in . . . oh, years. Can't remember how many, any longer."

She rolled her eyes. "Well, sure. You're a man. Three outfits to your name, leaving aside socks and underwear—*identical* socks and underwear—and the sartorial imagination of a pot roast. Meat, potatoes, carrots, what more do you need?"

"Like I said, damned any way I turn." He glanced at the door, as if seeking an escape route. "The last time I looked, our daughters Helen and Berry were both women. So is Princess Ruth. And not one of the three has personally packed a suitcase in years, either."

"Well, of course not. Helen's in the military, so willy-nilly she's been tainted by male attitudes. Berry grew up without a pot to piss in, and she still accumulates personal belongings as if she

28

had the budget of a rat in the Terran warrens. And Ruth is just plain unnatural. The only member of the royal family in . . . oh, hell, *ever*, who wants to be a spy."

She straightened up and squared her shoulders. "I, on the other hand, retain normal female customs and views. So I know perfectly good and well that no fucking robot is going to pack my suitcase properly. Being fair to the critters, I'm still making up my mind what to put in the suitcase until it's closed."

"You're also one of the richest females in the Star Kingdom, Cathy. Hell, the Star Empire—for that matter, the whole damn galaxy, since the wealth of the Manticoran upper crust matches that of almost anybody in the Solarian League, damn their black and wicked aristocratic hearts. So why don't you have one of your servants pack your suitcase?"

Montaigne looked uncomfortable. "Doesn't seem right," she said. "Some things a person has to do for herself. Use the toilet, clean your teeth, pack your own suitcase. It'd be grotesque to have a servant do that sort of thing."

She stared at the suitcase for a few seconds, and then sighed. "Besides, packing my own suitcase lets me stall. I'm going to miss you, Anton. A lot."

"I'll miss you too, love."

"When will I see you again?" She turned her head to look at him. "Best estimate. You can spare me the lecture about the temporal uncertainties of intelligence work."

"Honestly, it *is* hard to know. But . . . I figure a number of months at a minimum, Cathy, and it could easily stretch to a year or longer."

"Yeah, that's about what I figured. Dammit, if I could . . ."

"Don't be silly. The Liberals' political situation on Manticore is far too critical for you to leave the Star Kingdom again once you get back home. As it is, you probably stretched it by staying here on Torch for so many weeks after Berry's coronation."

"I don't regret it, though. Not for one moment."

"Neither do I—and, for sure, Berry appreciated it. But while I figure you can afford one extended vacation"—he smiled as crookedly as she had earlier—"given that the occasion was the coronation of your daughter—you can't really do it again. Not until the political mess gets straightened out."

"It'd be better to say, 'political opportunity.' The repercussions of that quick trip you took back home a few weeks ago will have had time to percolate, by now."

Between the time Anton had returned to Erewhon from Smoking Frog with the critical information he'd found concerning Georgia Young and the time he'd had to help with the liberation of Torch, he'd been able—just barely—to return to Manticore and, with Cathy, confront Young and force her into exile. They'd also forced her to destroy the notorious North Hollow files that had played such a poisonous role in the politics of the Star Kingdom, before she fled.

"So they will," he said. "So they will."

When Cathy was finally done packing the huge suitcase, Anton began to summon the household robot. But Cathy shook her head.

"Not a chance, buddy. I'm not about to risk my valuable possessions being hauled around by a mindless machine when I've got a personal weightlifter at my service." She gazed approvingly upon Anton's dwarf-king figure. He was a number of centimeters shorter than she was, and seemed to be at least a meter wider.

Cathy had once heard someone at a party remark that Anton's shoulders could double in a pinch as a parking lot for ground vehicles. Everyone present had disputed the statement, pointing out that it was absurd. But not before they'd spent several seconds studying the shoulders in question.

He picked up the suitcase by the handle on the end and lifted it onto his shoulder. The motion was as smooth and easy as if he'd been handling a broom instead of a valise that weighed well over fifty kilos.

Cathy slid her arm around his waist on the side opposite the suitcase. "Now let's be off—before our blessed daughter decides to launch yet another innovation in Torch royal custom. An eight-hour-long goodbye party for the royal mother, that'll leave me stuffed like a goose and wobbly with liquor."

On their way out the door, her expression became pensive. "I hadn't thought about it before now. According to Torch protocol, am I a dowager queen or something like that?"

"I doubt it, sweetheart. There's practically nothing yet in the way of royal protocol on Torch—and, given Berry, that's not likely to change much as long as she's still sitting on the throne."

"Oh, that's such a relief. The moment I spoke the word 'dowager,' I felt like I'd gained thirty kilos."

❖   ❖   ❖

In the event, the "official royal leave-taking" was as informal as Cathy could have asked for. There were only a handful of people present in Berry's audience chamber to see her off. Berry herself, Princess Ruth, Web Du Havel, Jeremy X and Thandi Palane. Web and Jeremy were old friends, and while Ruth wasn't—prior to this trip to Torch, Cathy had only exchanged a few words with her at royal functions on Manticore—she felt quite familiar because of Cathy's long-standing ties to the Winton dynasty. Those ties had become politically strained over the years, but they were still personally relaxed.

Thandi Palane was the one true stranger to her in the group. Cathy had never met her prior to this trip. She knew a great deal about the Mfecane worlds which had produced Palane, because of their relationship to genetic slavery. Manpower used a lot of Mfecane genetic stock to produce their heavy labor lines. But she also knew perfectly well that she had no real knowledge of what it must have been like to grow up on Ndebele.

She'd gotten to know the big woman to a degree, in the course of her stay on Torch following Berry's coronation. She still couldn't consider her a "friend," though, in any real sense of the term. Palane had been *friendly*, to be sure, but there had remained a certain tight reserve in all her dealings with Catherine Montaigne.

That hadn't upset Cathy. First, because she recognized the phenomenon. She'd encountered it many times with genetic slaves recently escaped or freed from Manpower's clutches. No matter how well recommended Cathy was by other ex-slaves, and no matter what her political reputation was, there was simply no way that someone who'd recently come from the depths of genetic slavery was going to feel at ease in the presence of a wealthy noblewoman. And while Thandi Palane hadn't come from genetic slavery, being born and raised on Ndebele as what amounted to nothing more than a peon was close enough to produce the same reserve.

But none of that mattered, anyway. The other reason Cathy had a very favorable attitude toward Palane, however the woman acted toward her, was that she figured Thandi Palane was the single person in the universe most likely to keep Berry Zilwicki alive and reasonably intact in the years to come. The woman was the head of Torch's fledgling military, she was closely tied to Berry, and . . .

Utterly ferocious, when she needed to be.

Cathy looked around the room. Berry's "audience chamber" was actually just a hastily remodeled office in the big building that Manpower had once used for its headquarters on Torch—"Verdant Vista," as it had then been known—and which the rebels had taken over and turned into a combination "royal palace" and government center.

"Where's Lars?" she asked.

Berry grinned. "He's taking his leave from his new girlfriend. Don't ask me which one. If he survives adolescence—and he's only got a few more months to go—he's got a surefire career ahead of him as a juggler."

Cathy chuckled, a bit ruefully. Once he got past puberty, Berry's younger brother Lars had turned into something of a lothario. The secret of his attraction for young women remained mysterious to Cathy. Lars was a pleasant looking boy, but he wasn't really what you'd call "handsome." And while he certainly wasn't bashful, neither was he particularly aggressive in the way he approached and dealt with teenage girls. In fact, he was considered by most people, including Cathy herself, as "a very nice boy."

Yet, whatever the reason, he seemed to be a magnet for teenage girls—and more than a few women several years older than he was. Within a week after arriving on Torch with Cathy, he'd manage to acquire two girlfriends his own age and had even drawn the half-serious attentions of a woman who was at least thirty years old.

"Let's hope we manage to get out of here without a scandal," Cathy half-muttered.

Jeremy X grinned. Impishly, as he usually did. "Don't be silly. All the females involved are genetic ex-slaves. So are what pass for their parents—none, in the case of two of them—and every one of their friends. 'Scandal' is simply not an issue, here. What you *should* be worried about is whether Lars can get off the planet without getting various body parts removed."

He'd barely gotten out the last words before the lad in question manifested himself in the chamber. Nobody actually saw him come in.

"Hi, Mom. Dad. Berry. Everybody." He gave them all some

quick nods. Then, looking a bit worried, said: "How soon are we leaving? I vote for right away. No offense, Sis—I mean, Your Majesty. I just don't see any point in dragging this out."

His stepmother gave him a stern look. "What *is* the problem, Lars?"

He fidgeted for a few seconds. "Well. Susanna. She's really pissed. She said she had half a mind to—" He fidgeted some more, glancing back at the entrance to the chamber. "It was kinda gross."

Cathy rolled her eyes. "Oh, wonderful."

Web Du Havel laughed softly. "The truth is, Cathy, I've never been one for drawn-out leave-takings myself."

"Me, neither," said Jeremy.

So, she hugged both of them quickly. Then, shook Thandi Palane's hand. Then, gave Ruth another quick hug, and then gave Berry a very long one.

"Take care, sweetheart," she whispered into her step-daughter's ear.

"You too, Mom."

At Cathy's insistence, Anton toted the monster of a suitcase all the way into the shuttle waiting to take her to her orbiting yacht.

There followed a very long hug, even longer than the one she'd given Berry, accompanied by the sort of intellectually meaningless but emotionally critical words by which a husband and wife—which they were, in reality if not in name—part company for what they both know is going to be a very long separation.

By the time Anton emerged from the shuttle, Susanna had arrived. She'd brought a bag of rocks with her.

Anton glanced back at Cathy's shuttle. Compared to any true starship, it was tiny, little bigger than a pre-space jumbo airliner, as most surface-to-orbit craft tended to be. It was a *bit* larger than many such, admittedly. It had to be to provide to the palatial—one might almost have said "sinfully luxurious"—accomodations one rightfully expected from a permanently assigned auxilliary of the yacht personally registered to one of the wealthiest women in the explored galaxy. Cathy had always referred to it as her "auxilliary bacchanalia pad," and Anton felt more than a bit wistful as he recalled some of the bacchanalia in question.

Despite its small size compared to a *starship*, however, it was still quite large (indeed, "huge" might not have been too emphatic an adjective) compared to any mere human. Even one so swelled and exalted by righteous adolescent fury as Susanna.

"His mother's stinking rich, you know, and that shuttle was built by the Hauptman Cartel's Palladium Yard," Anton said to the blonde teenager. She was quite attractive in a stocky and athletic way. "They build a lot of the Navy's assault shuttles and ground attack craft. Really knows how to armor a ship, does the Palladium Yard, and I doubt they spared any expense on *her* shuttle. As a matter of fact, I *know* they didn't, since I personally wrote up the design stats for it. The point being, I don't think those rocks are even going to dent the hull."

"Sure, I know that." Susanna dug into the bag. "It's the principle of the thing."

As Anton predicted, the hull wasn't so much as dented. Still, she managed to hit it twice. The girl had one hell of an arm.

CHAPTER FOUR

Thandi Palane closed the door of her suite in the palace behind her, and then moved over to stand next to the man sitting at a large table by the window overlooking the gardens below. He seemed to be studying the gardens intently, which was a bit peculiar. The gardens were practically brand new, with more in the way of bare soil than vegetation—and what vegetation did exist was obviously struggling to stay alive.

Most of the plants had been brought from Manticore by Catherine Montaigne. A gift, she said, from Manticore's Queen Elizabeth, plucked from her own extensive gardens.

Berry had appreciated the sentiment. Unfortunately, most of Torch's climate was tropical or sub-tropical, and the planet had its own lush and diverse biota, much of which was quite aggressive. Only the diligence of the palace's gardeners had managed to keep the imported plants alive in the weeks since Montaigne arrived. Now that she was gone, Thandi was pretty sure that Berry would quietly tell her gardeners to let the Manticoran plants die a natural death.

It was not a sight one would have thought would lend itself to the sort of rapt concentration the man at the table was bestowing upon it. But Victor Cachat's mind often moved in a realm of its own, Thandi had found. It was quite odd, the way such a square-faced and seemingly conventional man—which he was, in fact, in many respects—could see the universe from such unconventional angles.

"And what's so fascinating about those poor plants below?" she asked.

He'd had his chin resting on a hand, which he now drew away. "They don't belong here. The longer you study them, the more obvious it is."

"Can't say I disagree. And you find this of interest because . . . ?"

"Manpower doesn't belong here, either. The more I think about it, the more obvious it is."

She frowned, and began idly caressing his shoulder. "You're certainly not going to get an argument from me—anyone here— that the universe wouldn't be a far better place if we were rid of Manpower. But how is this some sort of revelation?"

He shook his head. "I didn't make myself clear. What I meant was that Manpower doesn't belong in the universe in the same way those plants don't belong in this garden. It just doesn't *fit*. There are too many things about that so-called 'corporation' that are out of place. It should be dying a natural death, like those plants below. Instead, it's thriving—growing more powerful even, judging from the evidence. Why? And how?"

This wasn't the first time that Thandi had found her lover's mind was leaping ahead of hers. Or, it might be better to say, scampering off into the underbrush like a rabbit, leaving her straightforward predator's mind panting in pursuit.

"Ah . . . I'm trying to figure out a dignified way to say 'huh?' What the hell are you talking about?"

He smiled and placed a hand atop hers. "Sorry. I'm probably being a little opaque. What I'm saying is that there are too many ways—way too many ways—in which Manpower doesn't behave like the evil and soulless corporation it's supposed to be."

"The hell it doesn't! If there's a single shred of human decency in that foul—"

"I'm not arguing about the evil and soulless part, Thandi. It doesn't act like a *corporation*. Evil or not, soulless or not, Manpower is supposed to be a commercial enterprise. It's supposed to be driven by profit, and the profitability of slavery ought to be dying out—dying a natural death like those plants down there. Oh," he shrugged, "their 'pleasure slave' lines will always be profitable, given the way human nature's ugly side has a tendency to keep bobbing to the surface. And there'll always be specific instances—especially for transtellars who need work forces out in the Verge—where the laborer lines offer at least a marginal advantage over automated equipment. But the market should be shrinking, or at best holding steady, and that should mean Manpower ought to be losing steam. Its profit margin should be lower, and it should be producing less 'product,' and it's not."

"Maybe it's just too set in its ways to adjust," Thandi suggested after a moment.

"That sounds like an attractive hypothesis," he conceded, "but it doesn't fit any business model I've been able to put together. Not for a corporation which has been so obviously successful for so long. No one's ever had the chance to examine their books, of course, but they've *got* to be showing one hell of a profit margin to bankroll everything they get involved in—like their operation right here on 'Verdant Vista,' for example—and I just can't quite convince myself that slavery should be that profitable. Or *still* that profitable, I suppose I should say."

"Then maybe what they were doing here was them starting to diversify?"

"Ummm." He frowned for a moment, then shrugged again. "Could be, I suppose. It's just—"

The chiming doorbell interrupted him, and Thandi made a face before she raised her voice.

"Open," she commanded.

The door slid smoothly aside and Anton Zilwicki came into the room, followed by Princess Ruth. In a shocking display of topsy-turvy royal protocol, Queen Berry tagged along behind them.

"You can come out of hiding now, Victor," said Anton. "She's gone."

Berry came to the center of the room and planted her hands on slender hips. "Well, *I* think you were rude, I don't care what Daddy says. Mom's a really curious person and it drives her nuts not to have her curiosity satisfied. She never stopped asking about you, the whole time she was here. And you never came out to meet her even *once.*"

"Curiosity may or may not have killed cats," replied Victor, "but it has certainly slaughtered lots of politicians. I was doing the lady a favor, Your Majesty, whether she wanted it or not and whether she appreciated it or not."

"Don't call me that!" she snapped. "I hate it when my friends use that stupid title in private—and you know it!"

Anton went over to sit in an armchair. "He just does it because for reasons I can't figure out—he's a twisty, gnarly, crooked sort of fellow—using flamboyantly royal titles in private scratches some kinky egalitarian itch he's got. But don't worry, girl. He doesn't mean it."

"Actually," Victor said mildly, "Berry's the one monarch in creation I don't mind calling 'Your Majesty.' But I'll admit I do it mostly just to be contrary."

He looked up at the young queen, whose expression was cross and who still had her hands on her hips. "Berry, the very last thing your mother needed was to leave herself open to the charge that she spent her time on Torch consorting with agents of an enemy power."

Berry sneered. Tried to, rather. Sneers were just not an expression that came naturally to her. "Oh, nonsense! As opposed to leaving herself open to the charge that she spent her time on Torch consorting with murderous terrorists like Jeremy?"

"Not the same thing at all," said Victor, shaking his head. "I don't doubt that her political enemies will level that charge against her, as soon as she gets home. It will get a rapt audience among those who already detest her, and produce a massive yawn on the part of everyone else. For pity's sake, girl, they've been accusing her of that for decades. No matter how murderous and maniacal people may think Jeremy X is, nobody thinks he's an enemy of the Star Kingdom. Whereas I most certainly *am*."

He gave a mildly apologetic glance at Anton and Ruth. "Meaning no personal offense to anyone here." He looked back up at Berry. "Consorting with Jeremy simply leaves her open to the accusation of having bad judgment. Consorting with me leaves her open to the accusation of treason. That's a huge difference, when it comes to politics."

Berry's expression was now mulish. Clearly enough, she was not persuaded by Victor's argument. But her father was nodding his head. Quite vigorously, in fact.

"He's right, Berry. Of course, he's also now exposed as a piss-poor secret agent, because if he'd had any imagination or gumption at all he *would* have spent time visiting Cathy, while she was here. Lots and lots of time, to do what he could to make Manticore's politics even more poisonous than it is."

Victor gave him a level gaze and a cool smile. "I thought about it, as a matter of fact. But . . ."

He shrugged. "It's hard to know how that would all play out, in the end. There's a long, long history of secret agents being too clever for their own good. It could just as easily prove true, years from now, that Catherine Montaigne being in firm control of the Liberals—and with an unblemished reputation—would prove beneficial to Haven."

Anton said nothing. But he gave Victor a very cool smile of his own.

"And . . . fine," said Victor. "I also didn't do it because I'd have been uncomfortable doing so." His expression got as mulish as Berry's. "And that's all I'm going to say on the subject."

Thandi had to fight, for a moment, not to grin. There were times when Victor Cachat's large and angular pile of political and moral principles amused her. Given that they were attached to a man who could also be as ruthless and cold-blooded as any human being who ever lived.

God forbid Victor Cachat should just say openly that the Zilwicki family were people who'd become dear to him, Manticoran enemies or not, and he was no more capable of deliberately harming them than he would be of harming a child. It might be different if he thought the vital interests of Haven were at stake, true. But for the sake of a small and probably temporary tactical advantage? That was just not someplace he would go.

She wouldn't tease him about it, though. Not even later, when they were in private again. By now, she knew Victor well enough to know that he'd simply retreat into obfuscation. He'd advance complex and subtle reasoning to the effect that retaining the personal trust of the Zilwickis would actually work to Haven's benefit, in the long run, and that it would be foolish to sacrifice that for the sake of petty maneuvering.

And it might even be true. But it would still be an excuse. Even if Victor didn't think there'd be any long-range advantage for Haven, he'd behave the same way. And if that excuse failed of its purpose, he'd think up a different one.

Judging from the Mona Lisa smile on Anton Zilwicki's face, Thandi was pretty sure he'd figured it out himself.

Anton now cleared his throat, noisily enough to break Queen Berry out of her hands-planted-on-hips disapproval. "That's not why we came here, however. Victor, there's something I need to raise with you."

He nodded at Princess Ruth, who was perched on the arm of a

chair across the room. "*We* need to raise with you, I should say. Ruth's actually the one who broached the issue with me."

Ruth flashed Victor a nervous little smile and shifted her weight on the chair arm. As usual, Ruth was too fidgety when dealing with professional issues to be able to sit still. Thandi knew that Victor considered her a superb intelligence analyst—but he also thought she'd be a disaster as a field agent.

Cachat glanced at Berry, who'd moved over to the divan next to Anton's chair and taken a seat there. "And why is the queen here? Meaning no disrespect, Your Majesty—"

"I really, really hate it when he calls me that," Berry said to no one in particular, glaring at the wall opposite her.

"—but you don't normally express a deep interest in the arcane complexities of intelligence work."

Berry transferred the glare from the wall onto Cachat. "Because if they're right—and I'm not convinced!—then there's a lot more involved than the silly antics of spies."

"All right," said Victor. He looked back at Anton. "So what's on your mind?"

"Victor, there's something wrong with Manpower."

"He doesn't mean wrong, like in 'they've got really bad morals,'" interjected Ruth. "He means—"

"I know what he means," said Victor. Now he looked at Berry. "And I hate to tell you this, Your—ah, Berry—but your father's right. There really is something rotten in the state of Denmark."

Berry and Thandi both frowned. "Where's Denmark?" demanded Thandi.

"I know where it is," said Berry, "but I don't get it. Of course there's something rotten in the state of Denmark. It's that nasty cheese they make."

CHAPTER FIVE

"So," Zachariah McBryde asked, watching the head of foam rise on the stein he was filling with the precision of the scientist he was, "what do *you* think about the crap at Verdant Vista?"

"Are you sure you want to ask me that question?" his brother Jack inquired.

Both brothers were red-haired and blue-eyed, but of the two, Jack had the greater number of freckles and the more infectious smile. Zachariah, six T-years younger and three centimeters shorter than his brother, had always been the straight man when they were younger. Both of them had lively senses of humor, and Zachariah had probably been even more inventive than Jack when it came to devising elaborate practical jokes, but Jack had always been the extrovert of the pair.

"I'm generally fairly confident that the question I ask is the one I meant to ask," Zachariah observed. He finished filling the beer stein, handed it across to Jack, and began filling a second one.

"Well," Jack gave him a beady-eyed look. "I am a high muckety-muck in security, you know. I'd have to look very askance at anyone inquiring about classified information. Can't be too careful, you know."

Zachariah snorted, although when he came down to it, there was more than an edge of truth in Jack's observation.

It was odd, the way things worked out, Zachariah reflected, carefully topping off his own stein and settling back on the other side of the table in his comfortably furnished kitchen. When they'd been kids, he never would have believed Jack would be

41

the one to go into the Mesan Alignment's security services. The McBryde genome was an alpha line, and it had been deep inside "the onion" for the last four or five generations. From the time they'd been upperclassmen in high school, they'd both known far more of the truth about their homeworld than the vast majority of their classmates, and it had been a foregone conclusion that they'd be going into the . . . family business one way or another. But Jack the joker, the raconteur of hilarious stories, the guy with the irresistible grin and the devastating ability to attract women, had been the absolute antithesis of anything which would have come to Zachariah's mind if someone mentioned the words "security" or "spy" to him.

Which might explain why Jack had been so successful at his craft, he supposed.

"I think you can safely assume, Sheriff, that this particular horse thief already knows about the classified information in question," he said out loud. "If you really need to, you can check with my boss about that, of course."

"Well, under the circumstances, partner," Jack allowed with the drawl he'd carefully cultivated as a kid after their parents had introduced them to their father's passion for antique, pre-Diaspora "Westerns," "I reckon I can let it pass this time."

"Why, thank you." Zachariah shoved a plate loaded with a thick ham and Swiss sandwich (with onion; they were the only ones present, so it was socially acceptable, even by their mother's rules), a substantial serving of potato salad, and an eleven centimeter-long pickle across the table to him. They grinned at each other, but then Zachariah's expression sobered.

"Really, Jack," he said in a much more serious tone, "I'm curious. I know you see a lot more on the operational side than I do, but even what I'm hearing through the tech-weenie channels is a bit on the scary side."

Jack regarded his brother thoughtfully for a moment, then picked up his sandwich, took a bite, and chewed reflectively.

Zachariah probably had heard quite a bit from his fellow "tech-weenies," and it probably had been more than a little garbled. Under a strict interpretation of the Alignment's "need-to-know" policy, Jack really shouldn't be spilling any operational details to which he might be privy to someone who didn't have to have those details to do his own job. On the other hand, Zachariah was not only his brother, but one of Anastasia Chernevsky's key research directors. In some ways (though certainly not all), his clearance was even higher than Jack's.

Both of them, Jack knew without false modesty, were definitely on the bright side, even for Mesan alpha lines, but Zachariah's talent as a synthesizer had come as something of a surprise. That could still happen, of course, even for someone whose genetic structure and talents had been as carefully designed as the McBryde genome's. However much the Long-Range Planning Board might dislike admitting it, the complex of abilities, skills, and talents tied up in the general concept of "intelligence" remained the least amenable to its manipulation. Oh, they could guarantee high general IQs, and Jack couldn't remember the last representative of one of the Alignment's alpha lines who wouldn't have tested well up into the ninety-ninth-plus percentile of the human race. But the LRPB's efforts to preprogram an individual's actual skill set was problematical at best. In fact, he was always a little amused by the LRPB's insistence that it was *just* about to break through that last, lingering barrier to its ability to fully uplift the species.

Personally, Jack was more than a little relieved by the fact that the Board still couldn't design the human brain's software reliably and completely to order. It wasn't an opinion he was likely to discuss with his colleagues, but despite his complete devotion to the Detweiler vision and the Alignment's ultimate objectives, he didn't really like the thought of micromanaging human intelligence and mental abilities. He was entirely in favor of pushing the frontiers in both areas, but he figured there would always be room for serendipitous combinations of abilities. Besides, if he was going to be honest, he didn't really like the thought of his theoretical children or grandchildren becoming predesigned chips in the Alignment's grand machine.

In that regard, he thought, he had a great deal in common with Leonard Detweiler and the rest of the Alignment's original founders. Leonard had always insisted that the ultimate function of genetically improving humanity was to permit individuals to truly achieve their maximum potential. Whatever temporary compromises he might have been willing to make in the name of tactics, his ultimate, unwavering objective had been to produce a species of *individuals*, ready and able to exercise freedom of choice in their own lives. All he'd wanted to do was to give them the very best tools he could. He certainly wouldn't have favored designing free citizens, fully realized members of the society for which he'd striven, the way Manpower designed genetic slaves. The idea was to *expand* horizons, not limit them, after all.

There were moments when Jack suspected the Long-Range Planning Board had lost sight of that. Hardly surprising if it had, he supposed. The Board was responsible not simply for overseeing the careful, continually ongoing development of the genomes under its care, but also for providing the Alignment with the tactical abilities its strategies and operations required. Under the circumstances, it was hardly surprising that it should continually strive for a greater degree of ... quality control.

And at least both the LRPB and the General Strategy Board recognized the need to make the best possible use out of any positive advantages the law of unintended consequences might throw up. Which explained why Zachariah's unique, almost instinctual ability to combine totally separate research concepts into unanticipated nuggets of development had been so carefully nourished once it was recognized. Which, in turn, explained how he had wound up as one of Chernevsky's right hands in the Alignment's naval R&D branch.

Jack finished chewing, swallowed, and took a sip of his beer, then quirked an eyebrow at his brother.

"What do you mean 'on the scary side,' Zack?"

"Oh, I'm not talking about any hardware surprises, if that's what you're thinking," Zachariah assured him. "As far as I know, the Manties didn't trot out a single new gadget this time around. Which, much as I hate to admit it"—he smiled a bit sourly—"actually came as a pleasant surprise, for a change." He shook his head. "No, what bothers me is the fact that Manticore and Haven are cooperating on *anything*. The fact that they managed to get the League on board with them, too, doesn't make me any happier, of course. But if anybody on the other side figures out the truth about the Verdant Vista wormhole ..."

He let his voice trail off, then shrugged, and Jack nodded.

"Well," he said, "I wouldn't worry too much about the Manties and the Peeps being in cahoots." He chuckled sourly. "As nearly as I can tell from the material I've seen, it was more or less a freelance operation by a couple of out-of-control operatives improvising as they went along."

Zachariah, Jack noted, looked just a bit skeptical at that, but he really didn't have anything like a need to know about Victor Cachat and Anton Zilwicki.

"You're just going to have to trust me on that part, Zack," he said affectionately. "And I'll admit, I could be wrong. I don't think I am, though. And given the . . . intensity with which the operatives in question have been discussed over in my shop, I don't think I'm alone in having drawn that conclusion, either."

He took another bite of his sandwich, chewed, and swallowed.

"At any rate, it's pretty obvious no one back home in Manticore or Nouveau Paris saw any of it coming, and I think what they're really doing is trying to make the best of the situation now that they've both been dragged kicking and screaming into it. Which, I'll admit, is probably easier for them because of how much both of them hate Manpower's guts. It's not going to have any huge impact on their actions or their thinking when we get them to start shooting at each other again, though."

Zachariah frowned thoughtfully, then nodded.

"I hope you're right about that. Especially if they've got the League involved!"

"*That*, I think, was also improvisational," Jack said. "Cassetti just happened to be on the ground when the whole thing got thrown together, and he saw it as a way to really hammer home Maya's relationship with Erewhon. I don't think he gave a good goddamn about the independence of a planet full of ex-slaves, at any rate! He was just playing the cards he found in his hand. And it didn't work out any too well for him personally, either."

Zachariah snorted in agreement, and Jack grinned. He didn't know anywhere near as much as he wished he did about what was going on inside the Maya Sector. It wasn't really his area of expertise, and it certainly wasn't his area of responsibility, but he had his own version of Zachariah's ability to put together seemingly unrelated facts, and he'd come to the conclusion that whatever was happening in Maya, it was considerably more than anyone on Old Earth suspected.

"Personally, I think it's no better than a fifty-fifty chance Rozsak would actually have fired on Commodore Navarre," he went on. "*Oversteegen* might well have—he's a Manty, after all—but I'm inclined to think Rozsak, at least, was bluffing. I don't blame Navarre for not calling him on it, you understand, but I wouldn't be surprised if Barregos heaved a huge sigh of relief when we backed down. And now that Cassetti's dead, he's got the perfect opening to repudiate any treaty arrangement with this new King-dom of Torch because of its obviously ongoing association with the Ballroom."

"Can you tell me if there's anything to the stories about Man-power having pulled the trigger on Cassetti?" Zachariah asked.

"No," Jack replied. "First, I couldn't tell you if I knew anything one way or the other—not about operational details like that." He gave his brother a brief, level look, then shrugged. "On the other hand, this time around, I don't have any of those details. I sup-pose it's possible one of those Manpower jerks who doesn't have a clue about what's really going on could have wanted him hit. But it's equally likely that it was Barregos. God knows Cassetti had to've become more than a bit of an embarrassment, after the way he all but detonated the bomb that killed Stein himself and then dragged Barregos into that entire mess in Verdant Vista. I'm pretty sure that at this particular moment Barregos views him as far more valuable as one more martyred Frontier Security com-missioner than he'd be as an ongoing oxygen-sink."

"I understand, and if I pushed too far, I apologize," Zachariah said.

"Nothing to apologize for," Jack reassured him . . . more or less truthfully.

"Would I be intruding into those 'operational details' if I asked if you've got any feel for whether or not the other side's likely to figure out the truth about the wormhole?"

"That's another of those things I just don't know about," Jack replied. "I don't know if there was actually any information there in the system to be captured and compromised. For that matter, I don't have any clue whether or not the Manpower idiots on the spot were ever informed that the terminus had already been sur-veyed at all. *I* sure as hell wouldn't have told them, that's for sure! And even if I knew that, I don't think *anyone* knows whether or not they managed to scrub their databanks before they got shot in the head. What I am pretty sure of, though, is that anything any of them knew is probably in the hands of someone we'd rather didn't have it by now, assuming anybody thought to ask them about it." He grimaced. "Given how creative its ex-property on the planet was, I'm pretty damn sure that any of Manpower's people answered any questions they were asked. Not that it would have done them any good in the end."

It was Zachariah's turn to grimace. Neither brother was going to shed any tears for the "Manpower's people" in question. Although they didn't talk about it much, Zachariah knew Jack found Manpower just as distasteful as he did himself. Both of them knew how incredibly useful Manpower Incorporated had been to the Alignment over the centuries, but designed to be used or not, genetic slaves were still people, of a sort, at least. And Zachariah also knew that unlike some of Jack's colleagues on the operational side, his brother didn't particularly blame the Anti-Slavery League, genetic slaves in general, or even the Audubon Ballroom in particular, for the savagery of their operations against Manpower. The Ballroom was a factor Jack had to take into consideration, especially given its persistent (if generally unsuccessful) efforts to build an effective intelligence net right here on Mesa. He wasn't about to take the Ballroom threat lightly, nor was any sympathy he felt going to prevent him from hammering the Ballroom just as hard as he could any time the opportunity presented itself. Yet even though one difference between Manpower and the Alignment was supposed to be that the Alignment didn't denigrate or underestimate its future opponents, Zachariah also knew, quite a few of Jack's colleagues did exactly that where the Ballroom was concerned. Probably, little though either McBryde brother liked to admit it, because those colleagues of his bought into the notion of the slaves' fundamental inferiority even to normals, far less to the Alignment's enhanced genomes.

"When it comes right down to it, Zack," Jack pointed out after a moment, "you're actually probably in a better position than me to estimate whether or not the Ballroom—or anyone else, for that matter—picked up a hint about the wormhole. I know your department was involved in at least some of the original research for the initial survey, and I also know we're still working on trying to figure out the hyper mechanics involved in the damned thing. In fact, I'd assumed you were still in the loop on that end of things."

A rising inflection and an arched eyebrow turned the last sentence into a question, and Zachariah nodded briefly.

"I'm still in the loop, generally speaking, but it's not like the astrophysics are still a central concern of *our* shop. We settled most of the military implications decades ago. I'm sure someone else's still working on the theory behind it full time, but we've pretty much mined out the military concerns."

"I don't doubt it, what I meant was that I'm pretty sure you'll hear sooner than I would if anybody comes sniffing around from the Verdant Vista side."

"I hadn't thought about it from that perspective," Zachariah admitted thoughtfully, "but you've probably got a point. I'd be happier if I didn't expect the Ballroom to be asking the Manties for technical assistance where the terminus is concerned, though." He grimaced. "Let's face it, Manticore's got more and better hands-on experience with wormholes in general than anybody else in the galaxy! If anyone's likely to be able to figure out what's going on from the Verdant Vista end, it's got to be them."

"Granted. Granted." It was Jack's turn to grimace. "I don't know what we can do about it, though. I'm pretty sure some rather more highly placed heads are considering that right now, you understand, but it's sort of one of those rock-and-a-hard-place things. On the one hand, we don't want anybody like the Manties poking around. On the other hand, we *really* don't want to be drawing anyone's attention any more strongly to that wormhole terminus—or suggesting it may be more important than other people think it is—than we can help."

"I know."

Zachariah puffed out his cheeks for a moment, then reached for his beer stein again.

"So," he said in a deliberately brighter tone when he lowered the stein again, "anything new between you and that hot little number of yours?"

"I have absolutely no idea what you could *possibly* be talking about," Jack said virtuously. "'*Hot little number*'?" He shook his head. "I cannot *believe* you could have been guilty of using such a phrase! I'm shocked, Zack! I think I may have to discuss this with Mom and Dad!"

"Before you get all carried away," Zachariah said dryly, "I might point out to you that it was Dad who initially used the phrase to me."

"That's even more shocking." Jack pressed one hand briefly to his heart. "On the other hand, much as I may deplore the crudity of the image it evokes, I have to admit that if you're asking about the young lady I think you're asking about, the term has a certain applicability. Not that I intend to cater to your prurient interests by discussing my amatory achievements with such a lowbrow lout as yourself."

He smiled brightly.

"No offense intended, you understand."

CHAPTER SIX

Herlander Simões landed on the air car platform outside his comfortable town house apartment. One of the perks of his position as a Gamma Center project leader was a really nice place to live barely three kilometers from the Center itself. Green Pines was a much sought-after address here on Mesa, and the town house didn't come cheap. Which undoubtedly explained why most of Green Pines' inhabitants were upper mid-level and higher executives in one or another of Mesa's many business entities. A lot of the others were fairly important bureaucrats attached to the General Board which officially governed the Mesa System, despite the fact that Green Pines was a lengthy commute, even for a counter-gravity civilization, from the system capital of Mendel. Of course, Simões had realized long ago that having the long commute's inconvenience to bitch about to one's fellow government drones actually only made the address even more prestigious.

Simões had very little in common with people like that. In fact, he often felt a bit awkward if he found himself forced to make small talk with any of his neighbors, since he certainly couldn't tell them anything about what he did for a living. Still, the presence of all of those business executives and bureaucrats was useful when it came to explaining Green Pines' security arrangements. And the fact that those security arrangements were in place was very reassuring to people like Simões' superiors. They could hide the really important citizens of Green Pines in the underbrush of all those drones and still be confident they were protected.

Of course, he reflected as he climbed out of the air car and triggered the remote command for it to take itself off to the communal parking garage, their real protection was no one knew who they were.

He chuckled at the thought, then gave himself a shake and opened his briefcase. He extracted the gaily wrapped package, closed the briefcase again, tucked the package under his left arm, and headed for the lift bank.

✧   ✧   ✧

"I'm home!" Simões called out five minutes later as he stepped into the apartment's foyer.

There was no answer, and Simões frowned. Today was Francesca's birthday, and they were supposed to be taking her out to one of her favorite restaurants. It was Tuesday, which meant it had been her mother's turn to pick her up from school, and he knew Francesca had been eagerly anticipating the evening. Which, given his daughter's personality, meant she should have been waiting right inside the door with all the patience of an Old Earth shark who'd just scented blood. True, he'd gotten home a good hour earlier than expected, but still. . . .

"Harriet! Frankie!"

Still no answer, and his frown deepened.

He set the package carefully on an end table in the foyer and moved deeper into the spacious, two hundred fifty-square meter apartment, heading for the kitchen. Herlander was a mathematician and theoretical astrophysicist, and his wife Harriet—their friends often referred to them as H&H—was also a mathematician, although she was assigned to weapons research. Despite that, or perhaps because of it, Harriet had a habit of leaving written notes stuck to the refrigerator rather than using her personal minicomp to mail them to him. It was one of what he considered her charming foibles, and he supposed he couldn't really blame her. Given how much time she spent with electronically formatted data, there was something appealing about relying on old-fashioned handwriting and paper.

But there was no note on the refrigerator this evening, and he felt a prickle of something that hadn't yet quite had time to turn into worry. It was headed that way, though, and he slid onto one of the tall chairs at the kitchen dining bar while he looked around at the emptiness.

If anything had happened, she would've let you know, idiot, he told himself firmly. *It's not like she didn't know exactly where you were!*

He drew a deep breath, made himself sit back in the chair, and admitted to himself what was really worrying him.

Like a great many—indeed, the vast majority—of the alpha line pairings the Long-Range Planning Board arranged, Herlander and Harriet had been steered together because of the way their genomes complemented one another. Despite that, they'd had no children of their own yet. At fifty-seven, Herlander was still a very young man for a third-generation prolong recipient—especially one whose carefully improved body would probably have been good for at least a couple of centuries even without the artificial therapies. Harriet was a few T-years older than he was, but not enough to matter, and the two of them had been far too deeply buried in their careers to comfortably free up the amount of time required to properly rear children. They'd planned on having several biologicals of their own—all star line couples were encouraged to do that, in addition to the cloned pairings the Board produced—but they'd also planned on waiting several more years, at a minimum.

Although the LRPB obviously expected good things out of their children, no one had pushed them to accelerate their schedule. Valuable as their offspring would probably prove, especially with the LRBP's inevitable subtle improvements, it had been made pretty clear to them that the work both of them were engaged upon was of greater *immediate* value.

Which was why they'd been quite surprised when they were called in by Martina Fabre, one of the Board's senior members. Neither one of them had ever even met Fabre, and there'd been no explanation for the summons, so they'd felt more than a little trepidation when they reported for the appointment.

But Fabre had quickly made it clear they weren't in any sort of trouble. In fact, the silver-haired geneticist (who had to be at least a hundred and ten, standard, Simões had realized) had seemed gently but genuinely amused by their apparent apprehension.

"No, no!" she'd said with a chuckle. "I didn't call you in to ask where your first child is. Obviously, we do expect the two of you to procreate—that *is* why we paired you up, after all! But there's still time for you to make your contribution to the genome."

Simões had felt himself relaxing, but she'd shaken her head and wagged an index finger at him.

"Don't get too comfortable, Herlander," she'd warned him. "We may not be expecting you to procreate just yet, but that doesn't mean we don't have a little something we *do* want out of you."

"Yes, Ma'am," he'd replied, much more meekly than he usually spoke to people. Somehow, Fabre had made him feel like he was back in kindergarten.

"Actually," she'd let her chair come upright and leaned forward, folding her arms on her desk, her manner suddenly rather more serious, "we really do have a problem we think you two can help us with."

"A . . . problem, Doctor?" Harriet had asked when Fabre paused for a handful of seconds. She hadn't quite been able to keep a trace of lingering apprehension out of her voices, and Fabre had obviously noticed it.

"Yes." The geneticist had grimaced, then sighed. "As I say, neither of you were even remotely involved in creating it, but I'm hoping you may be able to help us out with *solving* it."

Harriet's expression had been puzzled, and Fabre had waved one hand in a reassuring gesture.

"I'm sure both of you are aware that the Board pursues a multipronged strategy. In addition to the standard pairings such as we arranged in your case, we also work with more . . . tightly directed lines, shall we say. In cases such as your own, we encourage variation, explore the possibilities for enhancement of randomly occurring traits and developments which might not occur to us when we model potential outcomes. In other cases, we know precisely what it is we're trying to accomplish, and we tend to do more *in vitro* fertilization and cloning on those lines."

She'd paused until both Simões had nodded in understanding. What Herlander had realized, although he wasn't certain Harriet had, was that quite a bit of that "directed" development had been carried out under cover of Manpower Incorporated's slave breeding programs, which made the perfect cover for almost anything the LRPB might have been interested in exploring.

"For the past few decades, we seem to have been hitting a wall in one of our *in vitro* alpha lines," Fabre had continued. "We've identified the potential for what amounts to an intuitive mathematical genius, and we've been attempting to bring that potential into full realization. I realize both of you are extraordinarily gifted mathematicians in your own rights. For that matter, both of you test well up into the genius range in that area. The reason I mention this is that we believe the potential for this particular genome represents an intuitive mathematical ability which would be at least an order of magnitude greater than your own. Obviously, that kind of capability would be of enormous advantage to us if only because of its consequences for the sort of work I know you two are already engaged upon. Long-term, of course, the ability to inject it into the genetic pool as a reliably replicatable trait would be of even greater value to the maturation of the species as a whole."

Herlander had glanced at Harriet for a moment and seen the mirror of his own intensely interested expression on her face. Then they'd both looked back at Fabre.

"The problem in this case," the geneticist had continued, "is that all of our efforts to date have been . . . less than fully successful, shall we say. I'll go ahead and admit that we still don't have anything like the degree of understanding we wish we had where designed levels of intelligence are concerned, despite the degree of hubris some of my own colleagues seem to feel upon occasion. Still, we feel like we're on the right track in this instance. Unfortunately, our results to date fall into three categories.

"The most frequent result is a child of about average intelligence for one of our alpha lines, which is to say substantially brighter than the vast majority of normals or even the bulk of our other star lines. That's hardly a *bad* result, but it's obviously not the one we're looking for, because while the child may have an interest in mathematics, there's no sign of the capability we're actually trying to enhance. Or, if it's there at all, it's at best only partially realized."

"Less often, but more often than we'd like, the result is a child who's actually below the median line for our alpha lines. Many of them would be quite suitable for a gamma line, or for that matter for the general Mesan population, but they're not remotely of the caliber we're looking for."

"And finally," her expression had turned somber, "we get a relatively small number of results where all early testing suggests the trait we're trying to bring out is present. It's *in* there, waiting. But there's an instability factor, as well."

"Instability?" It had been Herlander's turn to ask the question when Fabre paused this time, and the geneticist had nodded heavily.

"We lose them," she'd said simply. The Simões must have looked perplexed, because she'd grimaced again . . . less happily than before.

"They do fine for the first three or four T-years," she'd said. "But then, somewhere in the fifth year, we start to lose them to something like an extreme version of the condition which used to be called autism."

This time it had been obvious neither of the younger people sitting on the other side of her desk had a clue what she was talking about, because she'd smiled with a certain bitterness.

"I'm not surprised you didn't recognize the term, since it's been a while since we've had to worry about it, but autism was a condition which affected the ability to interact socially. It was eliminated from the Beowulf population long before we left for Mesa, and we really don't have a great deal in even the professional literature about it, anymore, far less in our more general information bases. For that matter, we're not at all sure what we're looking at here is what would have been defined as autism back in the dark ages. For one thing, according to the literature we do have—which is extremely limited, since most of it's over eight hundred years old—autism usually began to manifest by the time a child was three, and this is occurring substantially later. Onset also seems to be much more sudden and abrupt than anything we've been able to find in the literature. But autism was marked by impaired social interaction and communication and by restricted and repetitive behavior, and that's definitely what we're seeing here.

"In this case, however, we think there are some significant differences, as well—that we're not talking about the *same* condition, but rather one which has certain gross parallels. It seems from the literature that, like many conditions, autism manifested itself in several different ways and in different degrees of severity. By comparison with what our research has turned up about autism, what we're observing in *these* children would appear to fall at the extremely severe end of the spectrum. One point of similarity with extreme autism is that, unlike its milder form and other learning disorders, new communication skills don't simply stop developing; they're *lost*. These children regress. They lose communication skills they already had, they lose the ability to focus on their environment or interact with it, and they retreat into a sort of shutdown condition. In the more extreme cases, they become almost totally uncommunicative and nonresponsive within a couple of T-years."

She'd paused again, then shrugged.

"We *think* we're making progress, but to be honest, there's an element on the Board which thinks we should simply go ahead and abandon the project completely. Those of us who disagree with that position have been looking for a potential means of breaking the existing paradigm. We've come to the conclusion—or, at least, some of us have—that what's really needed here is a two-pronged approach. We've very carefully analyzed the genetic structure of all of the children in the entire line and, as I say, we think we've made substantial progress in correcting the genes themselves, the blueprint for the hardware, if you will. But we're also of the opinion that we're probably dealing with environmental elements that affect the operating software, as well. Which is what brings you to my office today.

"All our evaluations confirm that the two of you are a well-adjusted, balanced couple. Your basic personalities complement one another well, and you're clearly well-suited to one another and to creating a stable home environment. Both of you also have the sort of affinity for mathematics we're trying to produce in this line, if not on the level we're looking for. Both of you have very successfully applied that ability in your daily work, and both of you have demonstrated high levels of empathy. What we'd like to do—what we *intend* to do—is to place one of our clones with you to be raised *by* you. Our hope is that by placing this child with someone who has the same abilities, who can provide the guidance—and the understanding—someone intended to be a prodigy requires, we'll be able to . . . ease it through whatever critical process is going off the rails when we lose them. As I say, we've made significant improvements at the genetic level; now we need to provide the most beneficial, supportive, and nurturing environment we can, as well."

And that was how Francesca had entered the Simões' life. She didn't look a thing like either of her parents, although that was scarcely unheard of on Mesa. Herlander had sandy hair, hazel eyes, and what he thought of as reasonably attractive features, but he wasn't especially handsome, by any means. One thing the Mesan Alignment had very carefully eschewed was the sort of "cookie cutter" physical similarity which was so much a part of the Scrags descended from the genetic "super soldiers" of Old Earth's Final War. Physical attractiveness was part of almost any alpha or beta line, but physical *diversity* was also emphasized as part of a very conscious effort to avoid producing a readily identifiable appearance, and Harriet had black hair and sapphire blue eyes. She was also (in Herlander's obviously unbiased opinion) a lot *more* attractive than he was.

They were very much of a height, right at one hundred and eighty centimeters, despite the dissimilarity in their coloring, but it was obvious Francesca would always be small and petite. Herlander doubted that she was ever going to be much over a hundred and fifty-five centimeters, and she had brown hair, brown eyes, and an olive complexion quite different from either of her parents.

All of which only made her an even more fascinating creature, as far as Simões was concerned. He understood that fathers were genetically hardwired to dote on girl children, of course. That was the way the species was designed, and the LRPB hadn't seen any reason to change that particular trait. Despite that, however, he was firmly convinced that any unbiased observer would have been forced to admit that *his* daughter was the smartest, most charming, and most beautiful little girl who had ever existed. It was self-evident. And, as he'd pointed out to Harriet on more than one occasion, the fact that they'd made no direct genetic contribution to her existence obviously meant *he* was a disinterested and unbiased observer.

Somehow, Harriet had not been impressed by his logic.

He knew both of them had approached the prospect of parenthood, especially under the circumstances, with more than a little trepidation. He'd expected it to be hard to risk letting himself care for the girl, knowing as much as they'd been told about the problems the Board had encountered with this particular genome. He'd discovered, however, that he'd failed to reckon with the sheer beauty of a child—*his* child, however she'd become that—and the complete and total trust she'd extended to her parents. The first time she'd had one of the childhood fevers not even a Mesan star line was totally immune to, and she'd stopped her fretful crying and melted absolutely limply in his arms when he'd picked her up, nestled down against him, and dropped into sleep at last, he'd become her slave, and he knew it.

They'd both been aware of the fact that they were supposed to be providing the love and nurture to help ease Francesca through the development process, as Fabre had put it. They'd been prepared to do just that; what they hadn't been prepared for was how inevitable Francesca herself had made it all. Her fourth and fifth years had been particularly tense and trying for them as she entered what Fabre had warned them was the greatest danger period, based on previous experience. But Francesca had breezed past the critical threshold, and they'd felt themselves relaxing steadily for the last couple of years.

And yet... and yet as Herlander Simões sat in his kitchen, wondering where his wife and daughter were, he discovered that he hadn't relaxed *completely*, after all.

He was just reaching for his com when it sounded with Harriet's attention signal. He flicked his finger to accept the call, and Harriet's voice sounded in his ear.

"Herlander?"

There was something about her tone, he thought. Something... strained.

"Yes. I just got home a few minutes ago. Where are you guys?"

"We're at the clinic, dear," Harriet said.

"The clinic?" Simões repeated quickly. "Why? What's wrong?"

"I'm not sure *anything* is wrong," she replied, but multiple mental alarms were going off in his brain now. She sounded like someone who was afraid that if she admitted some dire possibility it would come to pass.

"Then why are you at the clinic?" he asked quietly.

"They screened me just after I picked her up at school and asked me to bring her down. Apparently... apparently they picked up a couple of small anomalies in her last evaluation."

Simões' heart seemed to stop beating.

"What sort of anomalies?" he demanded.

"Nothing enormously off profile. Dr. Fabre's looked at the results herself, and she assures me that so far, at least, we're still within parameters. We're just... drifting a little bit to one side. So they wanted me to bring her in for a more complete battery of evaluations. I didn't expect you to be home this early, and I didn't want to worry you at work, but when I realized we were going to be late, I decided to screen you. I didn't realize you were already at home until you answered."

"I won't be for long," he told her. "If you're going to be there for a while, the least I can do is hop in the car and come join you. And Frankie."

"I'd like that," she told him softly.

"Well, I'll be there in a few minutes," he said, equally softly. "Bye, honey."

CHAPTER SEVEN

"I don't mean to sound skeptical," said Jeremy X, sounding skeptical. "But are you sure you're not all just suffering from a case of EIS?" He pronounced the acronym phonetically.

Princess Ruth looked puzzled. "What's 'Ice'?"

"EIS. Stands for Excessive Intelligence Syndrome," said Anton Zilwicki. "Also known in the Office of Naval Intelligence as Hall of Mirrors Fever."

"In StateSec, we called it Spyrot," said Victor Cachat. "The term's carried over into the FIS, too."

Ruth shifted the puzzled look to Jeremy. "And what is *that* supposed to mean?"

"It's a reasonable question, Princess," said Anton. "I've spent quite a few hours pondering the possibility myself."

"So have I," said Cachat. "In fact, it's the first thing I thought of, when I started reexamining what I knew—or thought I knew—about Manpower. It wouldn't be the first time that spies outsmarted themselves by seeing more than was actually there." He glanced at Zilwicki. "'Hall of Mirrors Fever,' eh? I hadn't heard that before, but it's certainly an apt way of putting it."

"In our line of work, Ruth," said Anton, "we usually can't see things directly. What we're really doing is looking for reflections. Have you ever been in a hall of mirrors at an amusement park?"

Ruth nodded.

"Then you'll know what I mean when I say it's easy to get snared in a cascade of images that are really just reflections of themselves. Once a single false conclusion or assumption gets itself planted in a logic train, it goes right on generating more and more false images."

"Fine, but . . ." Ruth shook her head. The gesture expressed more in the way of confusion than disagreement. "I don't see that as any kind of significant factor in *this* case. I mean, we're dealing with internal correspondence between people within Mesa Pharmaceuticals itself. That seems pretty straightforward to me." A bit plaintively: "Not a mirror in sight."

"No?" said Cachat, smiling thinly. "How do we know the person on the other end of this correspondence, back on Mesa"—he glanced down at the reader in his hand, then did a quick scan back through the report—"Dana Wedermeyer, her name was—"

"Could be a 'he,' actually," interrupted Anton. "Dana's one of those unisex names that ought to be banned on pain of death, seeing as how they create nothing but grief for hardworking spies."

Cachat kept going. "How do we know that she or he *was* working for Mesa Pharmaceuticals?"

"Oh, come *on*, Victor," protested Ruth. "I can assure you that I double-checked and cross-checked all of that. There's no question at all that the correspondence we dug out of the files came from Pharmaceuticals' headquarters on Mesa."

"I don't doubt it," said Victor. "But you're misunderstanding my point. How do we know that the person sending these from Pharmaceuticals' headquarters was actually working for Pharmaceuticals?"

Ruth looked cross-eyed. A bit cross, too. "Who the hell *else* would be sitting there but a Pharmaceuticals employee? Or high-level manager, rather, since there's no way a low-level flunky was sending back instructions like those."

Anton sighed. "You're still missing his point, Ruth—which is one I should have thought of myself, right away."

He looked around for someplace to sit. They'd been having this discussion in Jeremy's office in the government complex, which was quite possibly the smallest office used by a planetary-level "Minister of War" anywhere in the inhabited galaxy. There were only two chairs in the office, placed right in front of Jeremy's desk. Ruth was in one, Victor in the other. Jeremy himself was perched on a corner of his desk.

The desk, at least, was big. It seemed to fill half the room.

Jeremy leaned over and cleared away the small mound of papers covering another corner of his desk with a quick and agile motion. Barely more than a flick of the wrist. "Here, Anton," he said, smiling. "Have a seat."

"Thanks." Zilwicki perched himself on the desk corner, with one foot still on the floor, half-supporting his weight. "What he's getting at, Ruth, is that while it's certainly true that this Dana Wedermeyer person was *employed* by Mesa Pharmaceuticals, how do we know who he was really working for? It's possible that he—or she, damn these stupid names and what's wrong with proper names like Ruth and Cathy and Anton and Victor?—had been suborned and was *really* working for Manpower."

He pointed to the electronic memo pad in the princess's hand. "That would explain everything in that correspondence."

Ruth looked down at the pad, frowning, as if she was seeing it for the first time and wasn't entirely sure what it was. "That seems a lot more unlikely to me than any other explanation. I mean, presumably Pharmaceuticals maintains *some* sort of supervision over its employees, even at management levels."

Victor Cachat sat a bit straighter in his chair, using a hand on one of the armchairs to prop himself up enough to look over at the display of Ruth's pad. "Oh, I don't think it's all that likely myself, Your Highness."

She turned her head to glare at him. "What? Are you going to start on *me* now, too, with the fancy titles?"

Anton had to suppress a smile. Just a few months ago, Ruth's attitude toward Victor Cachat had been one of hostility, kept in check by the needs of the moment but still sharp and—he was sure the princess would have insisted at the time—quite unforgiving. Now . . .

Once in a while, she'd remember that Cachat was not only a Havenite enemy in the abstract but was specifically the enemy agent who'd stood aside—no, worse, manipulated the situation—when her entire security contingent had been gunned down by Masadan fanatics. At such times, she'd become cold and uncommunicative toward him for two or three days at a time.

But, most of the time, the "needs of the moment" had undergone the proverbial sea change. Cachat had been present on Torch almost without interruption since the planet had been taken from Manpower, Inc. And, willy-nilly, since she was the assistant director of intelligence for the new star nation—Anton himself was the temporary director, until a permanent replacement could be found—she'd been working very closely with the Havenite ever since. Of course, Victor never divulged anything that might in any way compromise the Republic of Haven. But, that aside, he'd been extremely helpful to the young woman. In his own way—quite different way—he'd probably been as much of a tutor for her as Anton himself.

Well . . . not exactly. The problem was that Cachat's areas of expertise were things that Ruth could grasp intellectually but probably couldn't carry out herself, in the field. Not well, certainly.

Unlike Ruth and Anton, Cachat was not a tech weenie. He was adept enough with computers, but he had none of Zilwicki or the Manticoran princess's wizardry with them. And while he was an excellent analyst, he was no better than Anton himself. Probably not as good, actually, push came to shove—although they were both operating on a rarified height that precious few other spies in the galaxy could reach to begin with.

Victor's greater age and much greater experience meant that he was still a better intelligence analyst than Ruth, but Anton didn't think that superiority would last more than a few years. The princess really did have a knack for the often peculiar and sometimes downright bizarre world of the aptly named Hall of Mirrors.

But Cachat's real forte was field work. There, Anton thought he was in a league of his own. There might be a handful of secret agents in the galaxy as good as Victor was in that area, but that would be it—a literal handful. And none of them would be any better.

Anton Zilwicki himself was not one of that theoretical handful, and he knew it. To be sure, he was very good. In terms of fieldcraft, as most people understood the term, he was probably even as good as Victor. Very close, at least.

But he simply didn't have Cachat's mindset. The Havenite agent was a man so certain in his convictions and loyalties, and so certain of himself, that he could behave in a crisis like no one Anton had ever encountered. He would react faster than anyone and be more ruthless than anyone, if he thought ruthlessness was what was needed. Most of all, he had an uncanny ability to jury-rig his plans as he went along, seeing opportunity unfold whenever those plans went awry where most spies would see nothing but unfolding disaster.

There was great courage there, also, but Anton had that as well. So did many people. Courage was not really that rare a virtue in the human race—as Victor himself, with his egalitarian attitudes, was quite fond of pointing out. But for Cachat, that level of courage seemed to come effortlessly. Anton was sure the man didn't even think about it.

Those qualities made him a very dangerous man, at all times, and a scary man on some occasions. With his now-extensive experience working with Victor, Anton had come to be certain that Cachat was not a sociopath—although he could certainly do a superb imitation of one. And he'd also come to realize, more slowly, that lurking beneath Victor's seemingly icy surface was a man who was . . .

Well, not warm-hearted, certainly. Perhaps "big-hearted" was the right term. But whatever you called it, this was a man who had a fierce loyalty to his friends as well as his beliefs. How Cachat would react if he ever found himself forced to choose between a close friend and his own political convictions was difficult to calculate. In the end, Anton was pretty sure that Victor would choose his convictions. But that wouldn't come without a great struggle—and the Havenite would demand complete and full proof that the choice was really inescapable.

Princess Ruth probably hadn't parsed Victor Cachat as thoroughly and patiently as Anton Zilwicki had done. There were very few people in the galaxy with Anton's systematic rigorousness. Ruth was definitely not one of them. But she was extremely intelligent and intuitively perceptive about people—surprisingly so, for someone who'd been raised in the rather cloistered atmosphere of the royal court. In her own way, she'd come to accept the same things about Victor that Anton had.

Anton had once remarked to Ruth, half-jokingly, that being Cachat's friend and collaborator was quite a bit like being an intimate colleague of a very smart and warm-blooded cobra. The princess had immediately shaken her head. "Not a cobra. Cobras are pretty dinky when you get right down to it—I mean, hell, a glorified rodent like a mongoose can handle one—and they rely almost entirely on venom. Even at his Ming the Merciless worst, Victor is never venomous."

She'd shaken her head again. "A dragon, Anton. They can take human form, you know, according to legend. Just think of a dragon with a pronounced Havenite accent and a hoard he guards jealously made of people and principles instead of money."

Anton had conceded the point—and now, watching Ruth's half-irritated and half-affectionate exchange with a Havenite agent she'd once detested, he saw again how right she'd been.

It's not that easy, all things considered, to hold a grudge against a dragon. Not for someone like the princess, at any rate, with her horror of appearing silly. You might as well hold a grudge against the tides.

"Just trying to stay in practice," Victor said mildly, "in the unlikely event I should be presented at the Manticoran court in Landing. Wouldn't want to fumble with royal protocol, even if it is all a bunch of annoying nonsense, because it would undermine my secret agent suavery."

"There's no such word as 'suavery,'" replied Ruth. "In fact, that's got to be the stupidest and least suave word I've ever heard."

Victor smiled seraphically. "To get back to the point, Ruth, I don't happen to think it's likely myself that this Dana Wedermeyer person"—he pointed to the pad—"is anything other than what she or he seems to be. Which is to say, a very highly placed Mesa Pharmaceuticals manager giving orders to a subordinate. Or, rather, ignoring a subordinate's complaints."

"But . . ." Ruth looked back down at the pad, frowning. "Victor, you've read the correspondence yourself. Pharmaceuticals' own field people out here were complaining about the inefficiency of their own methods, and this Wedermeyer just blew it off. It's like she—or he, or whatever—never even looked at their analyses of her own corporation's labor policies."

For a moment, the frown darkened into something very harsh. "The murderous and inhuman labor policies, I should say, since they amounted to consciously working people to death. But the point for the moment is that even their own employees were pointing out that it would be more efficient to start shifting over to increased automation and mechanical cultivation and harvesting."

"Yes, I know. On the other hand, despite their complaints, Pharmaceuticals *was* showing a profit."

"But only because Manpower was giving them a discount rate on their slaves—and pretty damned *steep* discount, too!" Ruth argued. "That's one of the points their own managers were making—that they couldn't count on that discount rate lasting forever." She grimaced. "If it went out from under them, if they had to start paying the full 'list price' for their slaves, then the inefficiencies their people here on Torch were pointing out would have *really* come home to bite them! In fact, there was this one—"

She paged through the documents on her pad for a moment, then found the one she wanted and waved it in triumph.

"Yeah, this one! From what's-his-name." She glanced at the display. "Menninger. Remember? He was talking about Pharmaceuticals' overall exposure. They were already leasing their entire operational site here from Manpower, but they were counting on Manpower's giving them preferred slave prices, as well, and let's face it, Manpower transtellars don't have a whole lot of fraternal feeling for each other. Manpower's eaten quite a few of its Mesan competitors along the way, and this guy was worried they were setting Pharmaceuticals up for their next sandwich by putting them deep enough in Manpower's pocket they'd have to accept an unfriendly takeover or go bust!"

Jeremy X cleared his throat. "Let's not forget how closely most Mesan corporations collude with each other, as well, though. Sure, they've demonstrated a huge share of shark DNA over the years, but they *do* work together, as well. Especially when they're engaged in something the rest of the human race isn't all that likely to want to invest in. Openly, at least. And you can add to that the fact that we're certain that many of them are actually owned, in whole or in part, by Manpower. Like Jessyk."

Anton pursed his lips, considering the point. "You're suggesting, in other words, that Manpower was deliberately accepting a loss in order to boost the profits of Mesa Pharmaceuticals—in which they possibly have a major ownership share, even if they don't control it outright."

"Yes."

"Which was part of my point about wondering if this Wedermeyer might be working for someone besides—or, in *addition* to, maybe—Pharmaceuticals," Victor said. "If Manpower does have a hidden stake in Pharmaceuticals, then they may have been in a position to go on offering their 'discount rate' forever. As long as they were charging enough to cover their bare production costs, at least. I mean, there's nothing in the correspondence from this end that's concerned with humanitarian considerations. They're simply saying they could squeeze their profit margins upward, in the long run, if they started switching over. Even by their own analysis, it would have taken quite a while to amortize the equipment investment, especially assuming their outlay for slaves stayed where it was. They were more concerned about the long-range consequences of losing that rate—of having Manpower yank it out from under them, or *threaten* to, at least, at a time when it would give Manpower the greatest leverage with them. But there's nothing in the correspondence from the Mesa end to explain why the locals' analysis was being 'blown off,' to use your own charming term, Ruth. Suppose Wedermeyer was quietly representing Manpower's interests? *Wanted* Pharmaceuticals deeper into Manpower's pocket . . . or simply knew there'd already been a quiet little off-the-books marriage between them? In that case, he or she could very well have been in a position to know they were worrying over nothing. That their 'discount rate' was grandfathered in and wasn't going to be going away anytime soon."

Ruth had her lips pursed also. "But what would be the *point*, Jeremy? Oh, I'll grant the possibility of Wedermeyer working for Manpower. I doubt her own supervisors would have missed it if she was doing it against their interests, though. I mean, *Pharmaceuticals* has been around for two or three T-centuries, too, so it damned well knows how the game is played. *Somebody* besides her had to be seeing at least some of these memos, given the extended period over which they were written. The fact that she didn't even bother to come up with an argument—not even a *specious* one—for her position suggests she was pretty damned confident, that she wasn't worried about getting hammered by one of her own bosses. That only makes sense if Manpower *does* own Mesa Pharmaceuticals, and what possible motive could they have had for hiding that connection, really?

"It's not like their position with Jessyk, where the legal fiction that Jessyk's a separate concern helps give them at least a little cover when they're moving slaves or other covert cargoes. There wouldn't be any point in maintaining that sort of separation from Pharmaceuticals, and there was certainly no *legal* reason they'd have had to hide that connection. And there are a lot of reasons why they shouldn't have bothered. If the two of them were already connected, they were at least doubling their administrative costs by maintaining two separate, divorced operations here on Torch. Not to mention everywhere *else* the two of them are doing business together. Why do that? Even assuming they *are* in bed together, and that Manpower *is* covering its production costs back home, despite the discounted rate, we're *still* looking at Peter robbing his own pockets to pay his flunky Paul. They were discounting their slaves to Pharmaceuticals by over twenty-five percent. Leaving aside all the other economic inefficiencies built into the relationship, that's a hell of a hit to the profit margin they could've made selling them somewhere else instead of dumping them here to subsidize Pharmaceuticals' inefficient—by their own *field managers'* estimate—operation!"

Victor nodded. "I agree, and that's exactly why I don't think there's any logical explanation except . . ."

"Except what?"

He shrugged. "I don't know. But we've already agreed that there's something rotten about Manpower that goes beyond their greed and brutality." He pointed to Ruth's reader. "So, for the moment, we can just add this dead fish to the smelly pile."

PART II

*1921 Post-Diaspora
(4023, Christian Era)*

Because the Beowulfers imported a full, functional technological base, and because they were within such close proximity to Sol that scientific data could be transmitted from one planet to another in less than forty years, they never endured any of the decivilizing experiences many other colonies did. In fact, Beowulf has remained pretty much on the cutting edge of science, especially in the life sciences, for the better part of two millennia. Following the horrific damage suffered by Old Earth after its Final War, Beowulf took the lead in reconstruction efforts on the homeworld, and Beowulfers take what is probably a pardonable pride in their achievements. Beowulf's possession of a wormhole junction terminus—especially a terminus of the Manticoran Wormhole Junction, which is the largest and most valuable in known space—hasn't hurt its economic position one bit. In short, when you arrive in Beowulf you will be visiting a very wealthy, very stable, very populous, and very powerful star system which, especially in light of the local autonomy enjoyed by members of the Solarian League, is essentially a single-star polity in its own right.

From Chandra Smith and Yoko Watanabe, *Beowulf:*
The Essential Guide for Commercial Travelers.
(Gonzaga & Gonzaga, Landing, 1916 PD)

CHAPTER EIGHT

Brice Miller began slowing the cab as he approached Andrew's Curve, often called Artlett's Folly by some of Brice's less charitable relatives. The curve in the roller coaster track was also a rise, which tended to fool the rider into thinking the centrifugal force wouldn't be as savage as it was if the cab went into the curve at full speed.

In the amusement park's heyday, the cabs had been designed to handle such velocities. But that had been decades ago. Age, spotty maintenance, and the deterioration brought on by the nearby moon Hainuwele's plasma torus had made a lot of the rides in the enormous amusement park in orbit around the giant ringed planet Ameta too risky for public use. Which, of course, just added to the downward spiral caused by the original folly of the park's creator, Michael Parmley, who had thought up this white elephant and poured both a fortune and his extended family into it.

Brice's great-grandfather, he had been. By the time Brice was born, the park's founder had been dead for almost forty years. The small clan he left behind in possession of the now-ramshackle and essentially defunct amusement park was presided over—you couldn't really use the term "ruled" to apply to such a contentious and disputatious lot as her multitude of offspring and relatives—by his widow, Elfriede Margarete Butry.

She was Brice's favorite relative, except for his two cousins James Lewis and Edmund Hartman, who were the closest to his own age. And, of course, except for his very very favorite relative, the same uncle Andrew Artlett for whom the curve or the folly—it had been both, really—were named.

Brice loved his uncle's curve, although he always approached it very carefully since the accident. He'd been with his uncle when Andrew gave the curve its name. Coming into that section of the giant roller coaster at a truly reckless velocity, both of them whooping with glee, Andrew had managed to break the cab loose from the tracks. Not from the magnetic track, of course—it would probably have taken a shipyard tug or a small warship to do that—but from the magnetic grips themselves. The metal must have gotten fatigued over the long years.

Whatever the cause, the two grips had snapped as neatly as you could ask for. And there they were, a forty-two-year-old-going-on-twelve uncle and his eight-year-old-and-aging-rapidly nephew, in a cab not more than ten meters in any dimension, tumbling through space. The proverbially "empty" space, except this portion of the universe contained a lot of ionized particles vented from Hainuwele and swept into Ameta's magnetosphere, along with gases from Yamato's Nebula. They had no source of propulsion usable on anything except maglev tracks, and with only the meager life support systems you'd expect for an amusement park roller coaster cab which had never been designed to be occupied for longer than a few minutes at a time.

Still, they managed to eke out the air and power long enough to be rescued by the clan's *grande dame*, who came after them with the somehow-still-functional yacht that had been one of the many follies left behind by her husband. Fortunately, Friede Butry had been a renowned pilot in her day, and the old lady still had the knack of flying by the proverbial seat of her pants. That was about the only way she could have managed to pull off the rescue before the cab's shielding was overwhelmed by the harsh and lethal radiation in Ameta's magnetosphere, given that the yacht's instrument systems were in the same parlous state of repair as just about everything owned by the clan of a material nature.

On the negative side, the same Friede Butry had an acid tongue that suffered no fools gladly and suffered downright screwballs not at all. As it happened, the com systems on both the yacht and the now-adrift roller coaster cab had been among the few pieces of equipment still functioning almost perfectly. Nor, alas, could the com system in the cab be turned off by the inhabitants.

It had been designed, after all, to pass on instructions to idiot tourists. So, the entire rescue was accompanied, from start to finish and with not more than four seconds of continuous silence, with what had gone down into the clan's extensive legendry as Ganny's Second-Best Skinning.

(The Very Best Skinning had been the one she bestowed upon her deceased husband, when she first learned that he'd died of a heart attack in the middle of attempting to recoup his lost fortunes in a game of chance—right at the point where he'd triumphed but before his opponents had turned over the purse. Leaving aside the expletives, the gist of it had been: *"Forty years living on the edge, you put me through! And you couldn't hold on for four more seconds?"*)

Fortunately for Brice, his age had sheltered him from most of the ferocious diatribe. Still, even the penumbra of the vitriol poured upon Uncle Andrew by Ganny El had scarred him for life.

So he liked to think, anyway. The incident was several years in the past, and Brice was now fourteen years old. That is to say, the age when all bright and right-thinking lads come to realize that theirs is a solemn fate. Doomed, perhaps by destiny, perhaps by chance, but certainly by their exquisite sensitivity, to the tormented life of the outcast. Condemned to awkward silences and inept speech; consigned to the outer darkness of misunderstanding; sentenced to a life of loneliness.

And celibacy, of course, he'd told himself until three days earlier—whereupon his uncle Andrew piled misery onto melancholy by explaining to him the fine distinction between celibacy and chastity.

"Oh, cut it out, Brice. You're just in a funk because—"

He held up a meaty thumb. "Cousin Jennifer won't give you the time of day, and for reasons known only to boys who have been turned into hollow mindless shells by hormones—yes, I knew the reasons myself way back then, but I've long since forgotten since I stopped being a teenage cretin—your 'affections,' as they are politely called, have naturally settled on the girl in your vicinity who is probably the best-looking and certainly the most self-absorbed."

"That's not—"

"Point two." The forefinger came up to join the thumb. "You have therefore persuaded yourself that you are bound for a life of solitary splendor. If you can't have Jennifer Foley, you'll have no lass for a bride. Not that you've got any business daydreaming about brides, when you've got Tempestuous Taub riled at you for your dismal performance in trigonometry."

Brice scowled. His much older cousin Andrew Taub was the very least favorite of his cousins, at the moment. It was preposterous to expect a fourteen year old boy gripped by life's great despairs to attend to the tedious—no, leaden—dullness of sines and cosines and such. Even a teacher as anal-retentive as Andy Taub ought to realize that much.

"That's not—"

Remorselessly, the middle finger joined its fellows. "Point three. You don't care about marriage anyway. You're only telling yourself that because you're still"—he paused for a moment, his heavy features disfigured by a caricature of thought—"at least four months away, by my best estimate, from the liberating realization that you don't need to be married to get laid—which is *actually* what your Mongol horde of hormones has got you worked up about, when it comes to Cousin Jennifer."

"That's *really* not—"

But it was hard to divert Uncle Andrew once he was on a roll. The ring finger came up to join the others. To add to the unfairness of the moment, despite Andrew Artlett's anything-but-gracile appearance, he was actually very well coordinated. Coordinated enough to be one of those rare people who could lift his ring finger while leaving the pinkie still curled in the palm of his hand.

"Point four. Once that realization comes to you, of course, the relief will be only temporary—since it will also become obvious to you the first time you attempt to act upon your newfound knowledge that Cousin Jennifer has no more interest in humping you than wedding you." He bestowed a cheerful smile upon his nephew. "Whereupon you will suddenly realize you are condemned to a life of chastity—that means not getting laid—*as well as* a life of celibacy, which merely refers to remaining single."

Despite himself, Brice had been intrigued. "I didn't know there was a difference."

"Oh, hell, yes. Ask any churchman. They've been parsing the distinction for eons, the lecherous bastids. And don't try to interrupt me. Because it's at *that* point—"

Inexorably, the pinkie took its place. "—point five, if you've lost track—when you'll go completely off the deep end of early adolescence and start writing poetry."

Brice's protest died aborning. As it happened, he'd already started writing poetry.

"Really, really *bad* poetry," his uncle concluded triumphantly.

Sadly, Brice had already come to suspect as much.

✧　　✧　　✧

Brice brought the cab to a halt at the very apex of the curve. He couldn't have done that with most of the roller coaster's cabs, of course. Even those which were functional—still more than three-quarters of them—had been originally designed for tourists. Tourists were a species of the genus imbecile. Hardly the sort of people any sane amusement park would allow to control the vehicles on the various rides.

However, despite the unfortunate results of Uncle Andrew's enthusiasm on that memorable day, Friede Butry had not tried to impose tourist rules on her family. She had not remained the undisputed head of the clan because there was anything creaky about the old lady's brain. She knew perfectly well that preventing recklessness altogether, in a clan which had as many children as hers did—not to mention the childlike nature of some of its adult members—was impossible anyway. Far better to provide suitable channels for excessive enthusiasm.

So, although she'd rendered most of the roller coaster cabs dysfunctional, she'd seen to it that three of them were brought fully up to snuff—which included turning Uncle Andrew's jury-rigged controls into something approximating a professional design. And she'd imposed no restrictions on their use, except for the obvious rule that no one was allowed to ride the roller coaster without someone else in the control room—and not more than one cab at a time was allowed on the track. She went even further and enforced that last rule by reengineering the track so that the power would automatically cut off if more than one cab entered it. Only the Mysterious Lord of the Universe knew how rambunctious teenagers could manage to stage races on a roller coaster, but Ganny El knew perfectly well that the youngsters in *her* clan would certainly give it a try if she let them.

She probably also knew that her great-great-nephew Brice Miller had managed, with his uncle's help, to circumvent the controls enough to allow the youngster to ride the track any time he wanted to, whether or not the requisite observer was present in the control room. But, if she did, she chose to look the other way. Friede Butry, being a wise old woman in fact as well as theory, had learned long ago that rules were meant to be broken, so the savvy matriarch always made sure to put in place a few rules for that very purpose. Let the children and would-be children break those rules, and hopefully the ones that really mattered would go untouched.

Besides, although she'd certainly never told him so and Brice himself would have been astonished by the news, the truth was that Brice was Ganny El's second most favorite nephew of all time.

Her most favorite was Andrew Artlett.

Brice spent perhaps twenty minutes just gazing at the splendid vista that his perch on the curve provided him. In the distance, serving as a backdrop, was Yamato's Nebula. It was actually a dozen light-years away, but it looked much closer. Most of Brice's attention, though, was given to the giant planet around which the station revolved. Ameta's cool blue-green colors belied the fury that swirled in that thick atmosphere. Brice had spent enough time watching Ameta to know that the cloud belts and the periodic spots in them were constantly changing. For some reason, he found that continual transformation a source of serenity. Watching Ameta could remove for a time almost all of the fourteen-year-old angst that afflicted him.

Not all, of course. His two efforts to transfer that ringed glory into rhyme and meter had been ...

Well. Disastrous. Truly putrid. Poetry so bad there was a good chance the spirit of ancient Homer had shrieked for a moment, back there on distant Old Earth.

About twenty minutes after arriving at the curve, all of Brice's momentary pleasure vanished. He'd finally caught sight of the vessel coming toward the amusement park's docking area.

Another slaver had arrived.

He'd better get back. Things were always a little tense when slave ships showed up to use the park's facilities. They had no legal right to do so, but there were no effective authorities out here in the middle of nowhere to enforce the law. Soon enough, anyway, to make any difference. The mining boom that Brice's great-grandfather had expected to develop on Hainuwele had never materialized, despite several false starts. The gas-mining operations that did take place in Ameta's atmosphere required far less labor than old man Parmley had counted on to keep his amusement park in business—and those miners were in no position to serve as the system's police force, even if they'd been so inclined.

Years back, the first two attempts by slavers to use the park's mostly-abandoned facilities as a convenient and free staging area and transfer station had erupted in pitched battles with the clan. The family had won both fights. But two of them were enough to make it obvious that they couldn't possibly survive many more—and they were now much too poor to abandon the park.

So, a combination truce and tacit agreement had developed between Ganny El and her people and the slavers. The slavers could use the park as long as they kept their activities restricted to specified areas, and didn't bother the clan. Or the tiny number of tourists who still occasionally showed up.

And the slavers paid something for the privilege. Fine, it was blood money, and if the Audubon Ballroom ever found out about it there'd probably be hell to pay. But the clan needed the money to survive. There was even a little bit left over after each transaction for Ganny El to slowly build up a kitty that might, some day, finally allow the clan to give up the park altogether and migrate somewhere else.

Where? Friede Butry had no idea. On the other hand, she'd have *plenty* of time to think of a destination, as slowly as the funds accumulated.

CHAPTER NINE

As he watched Parmley Station growing in the screen, Hugh Arai shook his head. The gesture combined awe, amusement, and wonder at the inexhaustible folly of humankind. Hearing the little snort he emitted, Marti Garner eyed him sideways, from her casual sprawl on the chair in front of the viewscreen. She was the lieutenant who served as his executive officer, insofar as the command structure of Beowulf's Biological Survey Corps could be depicted in such a formal manner. Even Beowulf's regular armed forces had customs which were considered peculiar by the majority of the galaxy's other armed forces. The traditions and practices of the Biological Survey Corps were considered downright bizarre—at least, by those few armed forces who understood that the BSC was actually Beowulf's equivalent of an elite commando force.

There weren't many of them. The Star Kingdom's Office of Naval Intelligence was probably the only foreign service whose officials really understood the full scope of the BSC's activities—and they kept their collective mouths tightly shut. The tacit alliance between Manticore and Beowulf was longstanding and very solid, for all that it was mostly informal.

The Andermanni knew enough to know that the BSC was not the innocuous-sounding outfit it passed itself off to be, but probably not much more than that. The BSC didn't operate very extensively in Andermanni territory. As for the Havenites . . .

It was hard to be certain what they knew or didn't know, although it hadn't always been that way. Indeed, there'd been a time when the Republic of Haven had been almost as well connected with Beowulf as Manticore, but that had ended over a hundred and forty T-years ago.

For the most part, Beowulfers had been less than overjoyed when Haven officially became the *People's* Republic after the Constitutional Convention of 1750, but it was the Technical Conservation Act of 1778 which had effectively put the final kiss of death on the once cordial relationship. By making it a crime for engineers or professionals to seek to emigrate from the Peoples' Republic for any reason, the Legislaturalists had pushed Beowulf's meritocracy-worshiping public opinion beyond the snapping point. The PRH had responded to Beowulf's highly vocal criticism by launching a vigorous anti-Beowulf propaganda campaign (Public Information had been an old hand at such tactics even then), and relations between the two star nations had nosedived.

Military cooperation between the PRH and Beowulf had been dwindling well before 1778, of course, but it had terminated completely after the Legislaturalists passed the TCA. By this time, the Beowulfers were pretty sure that the regular armed forces of the Republic of Haven thought the Survey Corps was exactly what it passed itself off to be: a civilian outfit, but one which, given that it often ventured into the galactic equivalent of rough neighborhoods, was pretty tough. Nothing compared to a real military force, of course.

But that might not have been true of Haven's State Security, back in the days of the Pierre Saint-Just regime. And just how much of StateSec's institutional knowledge had been passed on to the succeeding intelligence outfit—which had also been one of its executioners—was an open question.

However, it probably didn't matter that much. Beowulf's Biological Survey Corps had never spent much time in Havenite space.

First, because that had become . . . impolitic following the collapse of Haven-Beowulf relations. But, second, because there was no reason to, given Haven's longstanding hostility to genetic slavery. Say what one might about the Legislaturalists—and, for that matter, the lunatics of the Committee of Public Safety—their opposition to slavery had remained fully intact. Personally, and despite a personal partiality for Manticore, Hugh had always been prepared to cut Haven quite a bit of slack in other areas, given its aggressive enforcement of the Cherwell Convention. He was pretty sure most of his fellows in the BSC shared his opinion in that regard, as well, although certain *other* branches of Beowulf's military might feel rather differently. The Biological Survey Corps' primary mission could best be described as that of conducting a secret war against Manpower, Inc. and Mesa, however, which gave its personnel a somewhat different perspective. Theirs, after all, was a pragmatic, narrowly defined purpose—a point Hugh was cheerfully prepared to admit with absolutely no trace of apology. Beowulf's continuing galactic prominence in the life-sciences affected all aspects of Beowulfan culture, including that of its military, and that was especially true of the BSC. Assuming you could have gotten any one of the its combat teams to discuss their activities at all—not likely, to say the least—they'd have probably said something to the effect that a person shoots their own dog, when the critter goes rabid.

As the centuries passed, most of the galaxy had forgotten or at least half-forgotten that the people who founded Manpower, Inc., had been Beowulfan renegades. But Beowulf had never forgotten.

"What in the name of God was he *thinking*?" Arai murmured.

Marti Garner chuckled. "Which God are we talking about this week, Hugh? If it's one of the more archaic Judeo-Christian-Islamic varieties you seem to have developed a completely incomprehensible interest in lately, then . . ."

She paused and looked to the team member to her left for assistance. "What's your opinion, Haruka? I'm figuring the Old Testament maniac—excuse me, that's 'Maniac' with a capital 'm'—would have commanded poor old Michael Parmley to build the screwball station to demonstrate his obedience."

Haruka Takano—he'd have been described as the unit's intelligence officer in another armed force—opened his eyes and gazed placidly at the immense and bizarre amusement park that was continuing to swell in the screen.

"How am I supposed to know?" he complained. "I'm of Japanese ancestry, if you remember."

Garner and Arai gave him looks which might charitably have been described as skeptical. That was perhaps not surprising, given Takano's blue eyes, very dark skin, features which seemed more south Asian than anything else—and the complete absence of even a trace of an epicanthic fold.

"Spiritual ancestry, I'm referring to," Takano clarified. "I'm a lifelong and devout adherent to the Beowulfan branch of ancient Shinto."

The gazes of his companions remained skeptical.

"It's a small creed," he admitted.

"Membership of one?" That came from Marti Garner.

"Well, yes. But the point is, I have no idea what some deranged deity from the Levant might have said or done." He raised himself from his slouch to peer more closely at the screen. "I mean ... *look* at the bloody thing. What is it? Six kilometers in diameter? Seven?"

The fourth person on the ship's command deck spoke up. "'Diameter's a meaningless term. That structure doesn't bear the slightest resemblance to a sphere. Or any rational geometry."

Stephanie Henson, like Hugh Arai, was on her feet rather than sprawled in a chair. She pointed an accusing finger at the object they were all studying on the screen. "That crazed construction doesn't resemble anything outside of a hallucination."

"Not true, actually," said Takano. "When he built the station, over half a century ago, Parmley was guided by some ancient designs. Places back on pre-Diaspora Terra named Disneyland and Coney Island. There's nothing left of them materially except archaeological traces, but a number of images survive. I spent a little time studying them."

The station now filled most of the screen. The unit's intelligence specialist rose to his feet and began pointing to various portions of the structure.

"That thing that seems to loop and wind all over is called a 'roller coaster.' Of course, like every part of the station that isn't contained inside the pressure hull, it's been adapted for vacuum conditions. And, at least if I'm interpreting the few accounts of the station I could track down correctly, they incorporated a number of micro-gravity features as well."

He pointed to the one and only part of the huge structure that had a simple geometric shape. "That's called a 'ferris wheel.' Don't ask me what the term 'ferris' refers to, because I have no idea."

"But ... what does it do?" asked Henson, frowning. "Is it some sort of propulsion mechanism?"

"It doesn't exactly *do* anything. People climb into those pressurized cabs you can see and the wheel starts—that much of the name makes sense, at least—wheeling them through space. I guess the point is to give people the best view possible of the surroundings. Which, you have to admit, are rather spectacular, in orbit around Ameta and with Yamato's Nebula so close."

"And what's that?" asked Garner, pointing to yet another portion of the station they were approaching.

Takano made a face. "It's a grotesquely enlarged and extravagant, absurd and preposterous—the terms 'insensate' and 'ludicrous' spring to mind also—version of a structure that was part of ancient Disneyland. The structure was a very fanciful rendition of a primitive fortified dwelling called a 'castle.' It went by the name of 'Fantasyland.'" He pointed to a spire of some sort rising from the station. "That's called a 'turret.' In theory, it's a defensive emplacement."

The com beeped, announcing an incoming message. Arai made his own grimace, and straightened up from the chair.

"Speak of the proverbial devil," he said. "Wait . . . let's say seven seconds, Marti, and then answer the call."

"Why seven?" she complained. "Why not five, or ten?"

Arai clucked his tongue. "Five is too few, ten is too many—for a slovenly crew engaged in a risky enterprise."

"That took just about seven seconds," Takano said admiringly.

But Garner was already starting to speak. She didn't bother making any shushing gestures, though. Despite its battered and antiquated appearance, the equipment on the *Ouroboros'* command deck was like the rest of the ship—the product of up-to-date Beowulfan technology, beneath the unprepossessing exterior. No one on the other end of the com system would hear or see anything except Marti Garner's face and voice.

Her response to the signal would, needless to say, have appalled any proper military unit.

"Yeah. *Ouroboros* here."

A man's face appeared on the com screen. "Identify yourselves and—"

"Oh, cut the bullshit. Check your records. You know perfectly well who we are."

The man on the other end muttered something that was probably a curse. Then he said: "Hold on. We'll get back to you."

The screen went blank. Presumably, he was consulting whoever was in charge. In point of fact, there would be no records of the

Ouroboros on Parmley Station—for the good and simple reason that the ship had never come here before. But Arai's team had gauged that the erratic and unstable manner in which the slavers who used the station kept it staffed, insofar as you could use that term at all, meant that the absence of records would just be attributed by the current overseers of the operations there as the product of sloppiness on the part of their predecessors.

Parmley Station was a transshipment point of convenience for freelance slavers, not one of the depot ports Manpower itself maintained on a regular basis. That corporation, as powerful and wealthy as it might be, was still a commercial entity, not a star nation. Manpower directly managed the core portions of its operations, but its activities were much too far flung—not simply throughout the immense reaches of the Verge but even through large parts of the Shell—for it to personally supervise all of them. So, just as it often farmed out paramilitary operations to mercenaries, Manpower also farmed out many of the fringe aspects of the slave trade to independent contractors.

A few of the larger independent slavers maintained their own regular transshipment stations, here and there. But most of them relied on an ever-shifting and informal network of ports and depots.

Those weren't very hard to find. Anywhere in the Verge, at least. The accounts of human expansion into the galaxy related in history books made the phenomenon appear far neater and more organized than it really had been. For each formally recorded colonizing expedition and settlement—such as the very well documented and exhaustively studied one that had created the Star Kingdom of Manticore—there had been at least a dozen smaller expeditions that were recorded poorly if at all. Even in the era of modern electronic communication and data storage, it was still true that most of human history was only recorded verbally—and, as it always had, the knowledge faded away quickly, with the passage of two or three generations. That was still true today, even with the advent of prolong, although the generations themselves might be getting a little longer.

If anything, the records of Parmley Station were more extensive than the records for many such independently financed and created settlements. That portion of the galaxy which had so far been explored by the human race measured less than a thousand light years in any one direction. As tiny as it was compared to the rest of the galaxy—much less the known universe as a whole—the region encompassed was still so enormous that the human mind had a hard time really grasping its extent and everything it contained.

"Less than a thousand light-years" is just a string of words. It doesn't sound like much, to human brains which almost automatically translate the term into familiar analogs like kilometers. A person in any sort of decent physical condition could easily *walk* several hundred kilometers if they had to, after all.

Astronomers and experienced spacers understood the reality. Very few other people did. The rough and uneven approximation of a globe which marked the extent of human settlement of the galaxy, in the two millennia that had passed since the beginning of the human Diaspora, contained innumerable settlements that no one had any knowledge of beyond the people who lived there and a relative handful of others who might have reason to visit. And for every such still-inhabited settlement, there were at least two or three which were now either completely uninhabited or inhabited only by squatters.

Such obscure settlements were the natural prey of the independent penumbra of the slave trade. The slavers avoided any settlements which were heavily populated or possessed any sort of military force. But that still left a multitude which were either uninhabited completely or inhabited by groups small enough and weak enough to be exterminated or forced to cooperate.

Slavers preferred cooperation, though, for the same reason they generally stayed away from completely deserted installations. Such places deteriorated rapidly, once all humans abandoned them—and the last thing any slaving contractor wanted to be bothered with was repairing and maintaining what amounted to nothing more than a way station for them, especially since it could be temporary. Slavers often found it necessary to abandon such way stations, if they came to the attention of one of the star nations that took the Cherwell Convention seriously.

As best as Arai's team could piece together the fragmented data, it seemed that Parmley Station had fallen into the hands of the slave trade about three decades earlier. There had apparently been some initial resistance put up by the people who inherited Michael Parmley's foolish enterprise, but so far as Takano could determine, those people had either been driven off or killed.

"Is that turret the only place the slavers maintain operations?" Stephanie asked.

Haruka shrugged. "Your guess is as good as mine. I'd say . . ."

"Probably," Hugh concluded for him. "As far out into space as it extends, that turret is big enough to hold a large number of slaves."

Marti cleared her throat. "Uh . . . speaking of which, boss."

"What? *Already?*" He gave Garner's feet a glance. "You haven't even put on the spike-heeled boots yet."

"They're too hard to fit into a vacuum suit." She gave him a leer. "But I can certainly put them on after the operation, if you're in the mood."

Henson shook her head. "Don't tell me the two of you are back at it again. Isn't there something in the regulations about excessive sexual congress between team members?"

"No," said Garner. "There isn't."

She was quite right, as Stephanie knew perfectly well—given that she and Haruka were enjoying a sexual relationship themselves at the moment. The customs and traditions of Beowulf's military, especially its elite commando units, would have made the officers of any other military force turn pale. And, in fact, probably only people raised in Beowulf's unusually relaxed mores could have handled it without disciplinary problems. For Beowulfers, sex was a perfectly natural human activity, no more remarkable in itself than eating. The members of a military unit shared meals, after all, not to mention any number of collective forms of entertainment like playing chess or cards. So why shouldn't they share the pleasure of sexual activity also?

Their relaxed habits on the matter worked quite well, especially given the long missions which characterized the teams of the Biological Survey Corps. It did so because the Corps' teams also followed the Beowulfan custom of making a clear and sharp distinction between sex and marriage. Beowulfan couples who decided to marry—technically, form a civil union; marriage as such was a strictly religious affair under the Beowulfan legal code—quite often chose, at least for a time, to maintain monogamous sexual relations.

Neither Hugh nor Marti answered Stephanie's question, which was rhetorical anyway. She hadn't expected an answer. Not surprisingly, one of Beowulf's most ingrained customs was *thou shalt mind thine own damn business.* As it happened, Arai and Garner had stopped having sexual relations almost two months earlier. There had been no quarrel or hard feelings involved. The relationship had been a casual one, and they stopped for the same reason someone might stop eating steak for a while. It was quite possible they might resume again before too long, if the mood came upon them.

There had not, however, been any spike-heeled boots involved. Beowulfan customs wouldn't have found that abhorrent, assuming both parties were consenting adults. It just so happened that both Hugh Arai and Marti Garner had conventional tastes, when it came to sex. Conventional, at least, in their own terms. Plenty of other cultures would have been aghast at what passed for "normal sex" on Beowulf.

The com unit came alive and the same man's face appeared. "Yeah, okay. We can't—well, we figure you're okay. What do you got for us?"

"The cargo's not too big. Eighty-five units, all certified. Mostly heavy labor units."

"Pleasure units?"

"Just two, this trip."

"Male or female?"

"Both female."

The heavy face broke into its first smile. "Well, good. We can use 'em."

Henson rolled her eyes. "Oh, great. I've got to put on the act again."

"I'll pass the word to June," said Haruka.

Stephanie Henson and June Mattes were the two female members of the team who usually served as would-be pleasure slaves on these operations. Both of them, especially Mattes, had the sort of flamboyantly female physiological characteristics that suited the roles. For the same reason, Kevin Wilson and Frank Gillich played the roles when males were needed. The tactic worked because slavers receiving the cargo were almost invariably gripped by their own lusts, so they rarely thought to check the cargo's certifications until it was too late. A very attractive appearance was usually all that was needed.

The same was not true, on the other hand, for the team member who always played the role of a heavy labor unit. The moment any slaver's eyes caught sight of Hugh Arai, they wanted to see his tongue sticking out. The man was huge and so muscular he looked downright misshapen. There was no way they were going to let him near them, no matter how many chains he was laden with, until they saw the Manpower genetic marker. Even from a bit of a distance, that marker was effectively impossible to disguise or mimic.

Arai stretched. The small command deck seemed to get even smaller. He smiled at his comrades and, lazily, stuck out his tongue.

There was no need to fake a Manpower genetic marker. It was right there on the top of his tongue, as it had been since he came out of the Manpower process that substituted for birth.

F-23xb-74421-4/5.

"F" indicated the heavy labor line. "23" was the particular type, which was one designed for extremely heavy labor. "xb" instead of the usual "b" or "d" for a male slave indicated an experimental variety—in this case a genetic manipulation aimed to produce unusual dexterity along with enormous strength. "74421" indicated the batch, and "4/5" noted that Hugh had been the fourth of five male babies "born" at the same time.

"Which outfit do you want to wear this time, darling?" Marti asked. "Rags soiled, rags torn, or rags stained by unknown but almost certainly awful fluids?"

"Go with the fluids," said Haruka. He waved at the screen. They had almost arrived at the docking bay. Only a portion of Parmley Station could be seen any longer in the screen. That portion, not surprisingly, looked old and worn down. But it also looked just plain dirty, which wasn't at all common for vacuum conditions. That was probably a side effect of the nearby moon's plasma torus. "The damn thing looks like it needs a scrubbing."

The com unit squawked again. The squawk was a completely artificial effect, the product of Beowulfan electronic ingenuity. It would resonate back to the slaver's unit and make a suitably run-down impression.

"Use Dock 5."

"Right," said Garner. "Dock 5 it is." She switched off the com.

"And a scrubbing it's about to get," said Henson. "Fluids included."

Arai nodded. "The human body holds five to six liters of blood. Even slavers, who have no hearts."

CHAPTER TEN

Brice Miller worked the brakes, easing the cab to a gentle stop. The brakes were an antique design, relying on hydraulic principles, but they worked well enough. Brice was rather fond of them, in fact. Like much of the station's jury-rigged equipment, it took some actual skill to make it work.

There was a small group waiting for him at the terminus. He waved at his cousins James Lewis and Ed Hartman and tried not to scowl openly at the third and fourth members of the party.

Those two were Michael Alsobrook and Sarah Armstrong. They were in their twenties, not teenagers like James and Ed and Brice himself.

Twenties going on fuddy-duddy, Brice thought sourly. The cab came to a halt and he clambered out.

"Stop glaring at us," Sarah said. "You know the drill—and it's Ganny's drill anyway, not ours."

"'Course, I agree with her," added Alsobrook. "The last thing we need in a delicate situation is hormones running loose with pulse rifles."

"Easy for you guys to be so blasé about it," James said. Like Brice himself, he was looking enviously at the pulse rifles cradled by Alsobrook and Armstrong.

"Yeah," chimed in Ed. "We're the ones gotta crawl around in air ducts without so much as a pocket knife for self-defense."

"Self-defense against what?" said Michael, his voice edged with sarcasm. "Rats?"

A bit defensively, Brice said, "Well, there *are* rats in those air passages."

Sarah looked like she was about to yawn. "Of course there are. Weren't you paying attention to your biology tutor? Rats and cockroaches—humanity's inescapable companions in the Diaspora. By now, the relationship is practically commensal."

"For them, maybe," said Hartman.

In truth, the occasional rats he'd encountered in the vents had scurried away as soon as they caught sight of Brice. He imagined the rodents might pose a danger if someone was weak and incapacitated—but, in that case, what difference would it make if the person had a weapon or didn't? His real gripe was just that—that—

Teenage male hormones were practically shrieking that he needed a weapon! When he sallied forth against the foe. Dammit.

Alas, older if not wiser heads prevailed. Sarah reached into the small bag she had slung over a shoulder and began pulling out the com units. The units themselves were small enough she could have fitted all three into her hand, but the wire and clip they each came with made them quite a bit bulkier if not much heavier.

"Here you go, guys. I just tested them and they're working fine."

There being no point in further argument, Brice took one of them and stuffed it into a pocket. "Usual place?" he asked.

Alsobrook nodded. "Yeah, there's nothing fancy going on. Just another slave ship coming in to transfer the cargo."

Brice made a face. "The cargo." It was more than a little disturbing, the way familiarity with evil calloused the soul over time. Even the clan had fallen into the shorthand habit of referring to the hideous merchandise by the slavers' own parlance. Perhaps that made it a bit easier to just watch while dozens of human beings were forced from one set of shackles to another. Watch—and extend their hand for a pay-off.

He'd written a poem about it once. The fact that it was probably a really lousy poem hadn't made it any the less heartfelt.

But . . . there was nothing he could about it. Any of them could do about it. So he just headed off toward the air vent that led into the ducts they normally used for their lookout posts. His cousins James and Ed followed.

By the time all three of them were in place, they'd be able to provide the clan with direct observations of what was happening with the transfer. They used antique methods for their signals, attaching the clips to wires that the clan had painstakingly laid in many of the station's air ducts. That probably made their transmissions undetectable, at least with the sort of equipment slavers were likely to have.

If anything went wrong, their assignment was simply to flee the area after making a report. Older clan members with weapons would then move in to deal with whatever needed to be dealt with.

Nobody was really expecting any trouble. Brice had only been two years old the last time violence erupted between the clan and the slavers. Two slavers who'd been part of the station's staff, both male, had been irritated because the latest cargo to arrive had contained no pleasure units. No female units of any kind, in fact. So, after getting drunk, they'd decided to make good the loss by searching out a female from the clan.

It had all been over very quickly. The clan left the corpses in the same compartment that was always used for pay-offs, along with a recording from Ganny El demanding punitive damages. Well, punitive pay, anyway. You couldn't really call it "damages" since the only ones damaged had been the two slavers shot into barely-connected shreds.

The slaver who'd been the station boss at the time hadn't argued the point. Those two clowns had probably been a pain in the neck for him anyway, and the amount Ganny demanded was enough to make the point but not enough to be a real burden. After all these years, the slavers who used Parmley Station knew full well that it would take a major and costly war to exterminate the clan—and, short of that, the clan could make their lives very miserable indeed if they chose to do so. The station was enormous, labyrinthine, and nobody knew it the way Ganny's people did. After the first fight with slavers, Ganny had had all the schematics and blueprints in the turret erased, except for those relevant to the turret itself. Then she'd had all the schematics and blueprints *anywhere* in the station erased except for a small number which were hidden away—and the computers which held them couldn't be hacked into because they were kept entirely offline.

So, the slaver boss had paid the weregild, and there'd been

no further repetitions of the incident. Still, you never knew. The
only difference between the slavers and the rats and cockroaches
who also infested the station was that the rats and cockroaches
were smarter—shrewder, anyway—and had way, way higher moral
standards.

Alberto Hutchins and Groz Rada perked up when they saw
the two slaves following closely out of the personnel tube behind
three of the crewmen from the *Ouroboros*. Both were indeed
female—and both were just as good-looking as pleasure slaves
always were. One of them was downright voluptuous.

Their pleased expressions faded when they caught sight of the
slave following them. The creature's body exuded physical power.
Not menace, exactly, since he was festooned with chains and a
lifetime of hard labor and strict discipline would have certainly
made him docile. Still . . .

Rada cleared his throat and hefted his flechette gun slightly.
"The big one doesn't come any closer until—"

"Oh, for God's sake, relax," said the female crewman who
seemed to be in charge of the contingent from the ship. She
turned her head and looked at the crewman who was holding
the huge slave's chains. More to the point, since he couldn't possibly have restrained the brute with his own muscles, he held a
slave prod casually in his other hand. The device was a distant
descendant of the cattle prods used on Earth in pre-Diaspora
days. Far more sophisticated in its design and capabilities, if not
in its basic purpose.

The crewman gave the monster a casual jab. The heavy jaws
opened and out came his tongue.

Hutchins and Rada relaxed, and Rada's flechette gun lowered.
Hutchins had never bothered to unsling his in the first place.
While he did not possess unlimited faith in the goodness of his
fellow men's souls (since, after all, his own contained very little
of that quality), this was a routine operation. Something he and
Rada had both done at least two dozen times in the four years
since they'd come to the station. Besides, the tribarrel-armed
weapons turret on the cargo bay bulkhead, controlled from the
slavers' command center in the amusement park's turret, was a
far more effective deterrent than any mere flechette gun, in his
considered opinion.

"Okay, then," he said. "Let's make the transfer."

He gestured with a thumb toward the battle steel box mag locked to the bulkhead to one side of the tribarrel, and the *Ouroboros'* crew leader nodded. Normal electronic fund transfers were entirely out of the question for an illegal transaction like this one. Despite all the ingenuity and sophistication of the current generation's practitioners of the ancient art of "money laundering," normal fund transfers left too many electronic footprints for anyone to be comfortable about. Besides, slavers—like smugglers and pirates—were not natively trusting souls.

Fortunately, it wasn't always possible to rely on normal electronic transfers, even when both parties to the transfers in question were as pure as the new fallen snow. Which was why *physical* fund transfers were still possible. As the female crewmember stepped forward, Hutchins punched in the combination to unlock the battle steel box, and its lid slid smoothly upward. Inside were several dozen credit chips, issued by the Banco de Madrid of Old Earth. Each of those chips was a wafer of molecular circuitry embedded inside a matrix of virtually indestructible plastic. That wafer contained a bank validation code, a numerical value, and a security key (whose security was probably better protected than the Solarian League Navy's central computer command codes), and any attempt to change the value programmed into it when it was originally issued would trigger the security code and turn it into a useless, fused lump. Those chips were recognized as legal tender anywhere in the explored galaxy, but there was no way for anyone to track where they'd gone, or—best of all from the slavers' perspective—whose hands they'd passed through, since the day they'd been issued by the Banco de Madrid.

The crewwoman didn't actually reach for the credit chips, of course. That sort of thing simply wasn't done. Besides, she knew as well as Hutchins did that if she'd been foolish enough to insert her hand into that box, the automatically descending lid would have removed it quite messily. Instead, she produced a small hand unit, aimed it in the direction of the chips, and studied the readout. She gazed at it for a moment, making certain that the amount on the readout matched the one Hutchins' superiors had agreed to, then nodded.

"Looks good," she said, and held out her hand.

Hutchins laid the remote for the mag lock release in her palm.

With that in her hand, she unlocked the box—which closed again, automatically—from the bulkhead, then spoke into her mike. Rada and Hutchins couldn't hear the words, since they were shielded, but they knew she'd be confirming with someone still on board the *Ouroboros* that the funds were in her possession. She listened for a moment, then looked over her shoulder at her fellow crewmen.

"Okay, we're clear. Let's get them moved."

"Beginning with the two in front," said Rada cheerfully, and the crewwoman snorted in obvious amusement.

Rada and Hutchins both grinned at her, but, truth be told, their real attention was mostly focused on the two pleasure slaves. In its own way, the activities they'd soon be engaged in with those slaves was as routine as the transaction itself. But it was a lot more enjoyable than the rest of their work and was one of the real perks of being a slaver.

The male crewmen handling the two pleasure slaves poked them forward with his own prod. "Here you go, boys. And I can tell you from personal experience that they're just as good as they look."

The very buxom one turned her head to look at him. Hutchins thought for a moment she was actually going to glare at her handler, as unlikely as that was. Pleasure slaves were trained into even greater docility than heavy labor ones.

But then he realized that her look was simply one of intent focus, and was even more surprised. Because of that same training, pleasure slaves spent most of their lives in something of a mental haze.

The crewman from the *Ouroboros* wasn't looking at the slave, though. He'd lifted his prod and was studying the gauge on the handle. Catching sight of it for the first time, Hutchins was surprised again. Slave prod gauges were pretty simple things, as a rule. But this gauge looked like something that belonged in a laboratory.

"Hey, what—"

"Clear," said the crewman.

Hutchins started to frown, began to wonder what the man meant, but he never finished either process. Indeed, the few remaining seconds of Alberto Hutchins' life passed in something of a blur. Somehow, the other pleasure slave had her chains around his neck, the busty one kicked his legs out from under him, and on his way down the slender one used the chains and his momentum to crush his windpipe and break his neck.

Rada lasted a little longer. Not much. As soon as she kicked out his partner's legs, the buxom slave lashed his hands with her own wrist chains and sent the flechette gun flying. That hurt, and he yelped. The yelp might have alerted the command center and roused the defensive tribarrel turret . . . if, that was, every one of the compartment's cameras and sensors—and the ones in the passage beyond, for that matter—hadn't been spoofed by the various nonstandard items built into that complicated looking slave prod. Rada wasn't really thinking about that at the moment, however, and the yelp was cut short anyway by a paralyzing jab from the male crewman's slave prod. That *really* hurt.

By then, moving much faster than Rada would have thought possible, the heavy labor slave was there. Somehow, his chains had come off. He seized Rada by the throat—actually, the creature's immense hand wrapped around his whole neck—and slammed his head against the nearby wall. The impact would have been enough to render a gorilla unconscious. Rada's skull was shattered.

Perched in his hiding place in the air duct, Brice was shocked into paralysis for a few seconds. The mayhem in the corridor below had erupted so suddenly, and been so violent, that his mind was still scrambling to catch up.

In his earpiece, he heard James Lewis exclaiming—just a noise, wordless; he'd probably done the same himself—and, a moment later, what sounded like retching from Hartman. Ed's position placed him closest to the scene, which was horrid enough even from Brice's viewpoint. The slaver who'd had his head slammed against the corridor wall . . .

Brice closed his eyes for a moment. Some of the man's brains weren't in his skull any longer. The strength of the slave who'd killed him was incredible.

But this was no time for being muddle-headed. Brice gave Michael Alsobrook and Sarah Armstrong a very quick summary of what had happened, concluding with: "You'd better tell Ganny."

He heard Alsobrook mutter: "Hey, no kidding." But Brice wasn't paying much attention to him any longer. Having done his required duty by quickly and accurately reporting what had happened, Brice was now free to use his own judgment concerning what he should do next. So it seemed to him, anyway. He saw no reason to muddy the waters by asking older and supposedly wiser heads what *they* thought he ought to do.

He peeked through the vent and saw that the crewmen from the *Ouroboros* had moved down the corridor six or seven meters in the direction of the slavers' command center in the station's big turret. Which was to say, six or seven meters closer to Brice himself.

So much was cause for caution, but no more than that. Well, possibly a little more than that. Most of the crewmen were carrying flechette guns—the modern descendents of the ancient Old Earth shotgun—and they were specifically designed for use aboard ship, where pulsers' hyper-velocity darts' ability to punch right through bulkheads (and other things . . . like life support systems or critical electronics) was contraindicated. Flechette guns were unlikely, to say the least, to blow through the ceiling of the corridor and strike Brice or his two companions hiding in the air ducts above. The military-grade light tribarrel which had somehow appeared and found its way into the heavy labor slave's hands was another matter entirely, of course. *It* was designed to punch through armored skinsuits, and it would experience no difficulty at all in turning Brice Miller into finely ground hamburger.

It seemed unlikely to Brice that anyone was likely to begin blazing away with that sort of artillery inside any orbital habitat unless he absolutely had to, so its presence didn't really worry him that much. He told himself that rather firmly. What *did* produce some definite alarm, however, was that the people from the *Ouroboros* had stopped in order to inspect one of the maintenance hatches that gave access to the air ducts.

He heard the female crewman say: "I wish to hell we had schematics." In response, the heavy labor slave shrugged his massive shoulders. Well, he probably wasn't really a slave, in light of recent events. In fact, he seemed to be in command of the operation, from what Brice could glean from subtleties of the crewmen's body language.

"Even if we had them, we couldn't count on them," he said. "A station as immense as this one that's decades old is likely to have had a lot of modifications and alterations—damn few of which would have made their way into a new set of schematics."

The woman scowled. Not at him, but at the hatch above her. "At least there's nothing tricky about the latches. Just straightforward manual ones, hallelujah. Hoist me up, Hugh."

The huge "slave" set down his tribarrel, bent over, grabbed her hips, and lifted her up to the hatch as easily as a mother might lift a toddler. The woman fiddled with the latches for a moment, and the hatch slid aside. Somehow or other—he seemed to be able to move astonishingly quickly for someone with that gorilla physique—the "slave" now had her gripped by her knees and he hefted the woman halfway up into the air duct. From there, she was easily able to lift herself into it.

By the time she did so, Brice had quietly scurried around a bend in the duct, so he was out of her sight. He planned to get at least two more bends ahead of her before he stopped. Behind him, he heard some soft noises which he interpreted as the sound of another crewman being hoisted into the duct. And, very clearly, he heard the female crewman say: "Give us five minutes to get into position."

By now, Brice was pretty sure the people from the *Ouroboros* were planning to take out the slavers who currently occupied the turret. And given the ruthlessness with which they'd dealt with the first two slavers, he was also pretty sure that "take out" was a phrase which, in this instance, was not going to be combined with softhearted terms like "prisoners."

He didn't spend much time chewing on that issue, though. Brice didn't care, when it came right down to it, how ruthlessly the newcomers dealt with the people who currently controlled slaving operations on Parmley Station. The killing of the two slavers he'd just witnessed had been shocking, certainly, because of its violence and suddenness. Beyond that, however, it had no more effect on him than witnessing the slaughter of dangerous animals. Brice's clan maintained practical relations with the slavers, but they loathed them.

The really important issue, still unsettled, was: *who are these people, anyway?*

He reattached the com unit to the wire strung in the passageway. Ganny Butry's voice came into his ear. "Who are they, boys? Can you tell yet?"

Ed Hartman was the first to respond, not surprisingly. Brice liked his cousin a lot, but there was no denying that Ed had a tendency to go off half-cocked.

"They gotta be another slaver group, Ganny, trying to muscle in," he said confidently. "Poachers. Gotta be."

James's voice came next. "I wouldn't be so sure of that . . ."

Brice shared James's skepticism. "I'm with Lewis," he said, as forcefully as possible when you were trying to whisper into a com unit. "These people seem way too deadly to be just another batch of slavers."

He added what he thought was the clincher. "And one of them is a slave himself, Ganny. Well . . . was a slave, anyway. I saw his tongue markers."

"So did I," said James. "Ed, you had to have seen it too. You were the closest."

Brice wondered where Lewis and Hartman were right now. Like him, they would have scurried out of sight once they realized some of the people from the *Ouroboros* were coming into the ducts. Also like him, they'd be cautious but not overly worried about the matter. There were many kilometers of air ducts running all through Parmley Station—and the only blueprints and schematics still in existence were hidden away. If you wanted to pass through the ducts, you either had to move slowly and constantly check your location with instruments, as the crewmen from the *Ouroboros* were doing, or you had to have memorized the network—as Brice and his cousins had done, over the years. Even they only knew part of it. There was no way the newcomers could catch them, once they were in the ducts.

Ed's reply was a bit slow in coming. That would be caused by nothing more than Hartman's reluctance to tacitly admit that, once again, he'd used his mouth before his brain. "Yeah, okay. I saw it too."

"Well, ain't that sweet?" said Michael Alsobrook. "Ganny, we're screwed. They gotta be from the Ballroom."

Brice had already considered that possibility. And if so . . . The clan could very well be in serious trouble. Ballroom killers on what amounted to an extermination mission weren't going to look gently upon people who—at least, from their point of view—also profited from the slave trade, even if they weren't slavers themselves. And they'd have no reason to keep the facility intact, either, the way slavers did. Even assuming Ballroom killers would observe the Eridani Edict, it only applied to planets, not space stations. They could just stand off and destroy the place with nuclear-armed missiles. Or, for that matter, rip it apart with their ship's impeller wedge without even wasting the ammunition.

Brice heard Ganny mutter what he was sure was a curse, but in a language he didn't know. Ganny knew a lot of languages. Then she added: "That's the sixty-four thousand dollar question, isn't it?"

Brice frowned. Ganny also used a lot of ancient and stupid old saws. What was a "dollar?" And why did the number sixty-four thousand mean anything?

He'd asked his uncle Andrew about it, once, after the first time he'd heard Ganny use the expression. Artlett's explanation was that the expression dated from the days—way before the Diaspora— when the human race was still confined to one planet and mired in superstition. Dollars were maleficent spirits notorious for sapping the moral fiber of those foolish enough to traffic with them. The number sixty-four thousand had magical importance since it was eight squared—eight no doubt being a magical number in its own right—and then multiplied by a thousand, which, given the antediluvian origins of the decimal system, was surely a number freighted with mystic importance.

It was a theory. An attractive one, even. But Brice was skeptical. His uncle Andrew had about as many theories as Ganny had old saws, and plenty of them were just as silly.

Still . . .

"I'm not so sure, Ganny," Brice said. "There's something . . ."

"Yes?"

"I don't know. I've never actually seen Ballroom assassins at work, but—"

"Damn few people have, youngster," said Ganny. "At least, not ones who survived the experience."

Brice winced. Ganny sometimes also had the habit of rubbing salt into wounds. Did she *really* need to say that, to someone who was sharing an air duct with possible Ballroom maniacs?

"Yeah, well. Ganny, these people just seem too . . . I dunno. They seem more like a military unit, to me."

Alsobrook spoke up again. "Ganny, that just doesn't make sense. Who'd be sending a military unit to Parmley Station?"

"I have no idea, Michael," replied Ganny. "But don't be so quick to dismiss the opinion of somebody who's actually seen the people we're talking about. Which, being blunt about it, you haven't."

Now, Ed spoke up again. "Ganny, they're getting real close to the command center. The people from the *Ouroboros,* I mean."

Brice tried to figure out which of the adjacent ducts Ed had to be in, to have seen that. Probably . . .

What difference did it make? Brice had come to the same conclusion, anyway. Staying ahead of the two *Ouroboros* crewmen who'd come into the air duct, he was now himself positioned almost over the slavers' command center.

What to do? He was certain that all hell was about to break loose, and was torn between two powerful impulses. The first was simple survival instinct, which was shrieking at him to get out of the area *now.* The other was an equally powerful urge to observe what was about to happen.

After a mental struggle that lasted not more than five seconds, curiosity triumphed. With Brice, it usually did.

The question now became: From what vantage point could he watch the upcoming events without exposing himself too much?

There was really only one answer, which was the small maintenance compartment located in one corner of the command center. As was frequently the case with such maintenance stations, it was built directly into the air duct network.

There was a risk involved, though. Unlike the air ducts, that compartment was designed to be easily accessible. It wouldn't take more than a few seconds for anyone in the command center who was seized by the urge to open the access panel and climb in. There'd be no need for a hoist, either, or even a stepladder. The maintenance compartment wasn't elevated more than a meter from the deck of the command center.

So be it. Hopefully, in the event that happened, Brice would manage to scramble back into the air ducts in time.

When he got there, he was disgruntled to see that Ed had gotten there ahead of him. And disgruntled again, not more than thirty seconds later, when James piled in too.

Disgruntled, but not surprised. For Hartman and Lewis, as for Brice himself, the survival instinct was usually trumped by curiosity. Uncle Andrew said that was because they were teenagers and so part of their brains hadn't fully developed yet. Specifically, that part of the prefrontal cortex that gauged risks.

It was a theory. Plausible and attractive, like most of his uncle's theories—but, also like most of them, probably flawed. The flaw in this case was the theorist himself—Andrew Artlett, who was of an age where his prefrontal cortex should certainly have been fully developed but who was notorious for taking crazier risks than anybody.

With three of them in there, the compartment was packed tight. And their ability to observe what was happening in the command center was going to be impaired by all three of them having to squeeze next to the entrance panel. Fortunately, the panel was more sophisticated than a simple mechanical one. Instead of narrow open air slits, it had a much larger vision screen. And the screen's electrical shield, designed to keep insects from wandering into delicate equipment, also blurred anyone's ability to look into the maintenance compartment from the command center.

Unless, of course, they turned off the shield so they could look inside for a quick inspection of the compartment without having to open the panel. That was part of the design, too—and the screen could be turned off with a flick of a finger.

So be it. Life was never perfect. Which was no doubt the reason that evolution, in its cunning, had seen to it that the prefrontal cortex of adolescents was not fully developed. If you looked at it the right way, that was simply a necessary adaptation to the invariant cruddiness of existence.

Across the large command center and off to the side, Brice saw the entry hatch begin to open.

James hissed softly. "Showtime."

CHAPTER ELEVEN

Hugh Arai had seen no reason to dillydally about the business. They *had* to move quickly, in fact, or the simple and crude event-loop they'd reconfigured the camera and sensors to show would alert the slavers very soon, unless they were completely inattentive. So the BSC team went into the command center firing. Quite literally—Marti Garner, in the lead because she was the best marksman, had already shot two of the slavers in the center before she finished passing through the entrance.

Bryan Knight, coming right behind her, tossed flashbang grenades into the two corners of the large compartment that weren't in clear line of sight. Marti opened her eyes once the blast and flash were over, and quickly scoured the visible areas looking for opponents.

There was one woman behind a desk, looking very confused. She'd have been close enough to one of the grenades to be affected by it. Garner disintegrated her head—spectacularly—with a tightly focused burst of flechettes.

Hugh Arai was the third member of the team coming into the compartment. He was carrying a highly modified version of a tribarrel pulser. The weapon was as close to a pistol version of a tribarrel as Beowulf's military engineers had been able to design. It was a specialty gun, almost literally handmade. Only someone of Hugh Arai's mass and strength could hope to use it effectively—or safely, for those accompanying him—and its ability to shred bulkheads might have caused some to look upon it askance in what amounted to a boarding action. The BSC was a great believer in providing for all contingencies, however. It was always possible that even slavers might have armored skinsuits available, after all, and despite its drawbacks, the weapon provided the unit with a scaled-down approximation of the sort of heavy weapons that a regular Marine unit would have carried.

Arai took position in the center of the compartment, while Garner and Mattes and Knight quickly inspected every area where someone might have been able to hide. But the place was empty now, except for the three corpses.

While they went about that business, Stephanie Henson sat down in front of the command center's operations console and began bringing up the relevant schematics and diagrams. She was swift and expert at the work, and within thirty seconds, she'd found what they needed. Less than a minute later, she'd bypassed the security locks and keyed in the instructions.

She leaned back in her chair. "Okay, Hugh. The command center is now sealed off from the rest of the turret, along with all of the surrounding air ducts. The power source is independent already, so we don't have to worry about that."

Arai nodded. "What about slaves?"

Stephanie studied the console for a moment, and then shook her head. "There are no signs of any occupants within five hundred meters of this command center except the eight people—maybe nine, if two of them are copulating right now—shown in the living quarters. One or more of them might be pleasure slaves, of course. No way to tell."

"No internal cameras?"

"They've been disabled."

Hugh grunted. That wasn't surprising. Nobody except military forces under tight discipline were going to tolerate active cameras in their living areas. The slavers had probably disabled those sensors decades ago.

He wasn't happy about the fact that he couldn't absolutely confirm that there weren't any slaves in the living quarters. But . . .

It was unlikely, given the obvious eagerness with which the slavers had reacted to the news that the *Ouroboros'* nonexistent cargo had included pleasure slaves. And it was an imperfect universe. He wasn't about to risk getting any of his people killed in the course of a direct assault, on the off chance there might be a slave mixed in with the other occupants.

He spoke into his com. "Take out the living quarters. Stephanie will guide the shots."

They all turned to look at the screens above Henson's console which provided views of the turret from outside cameras. Stephanie began keying in locations. A short time later, the *Ouroboros'* concealed lasers began firing. It didn't take long before that area of the turret which contained the slavers' living quarters was blown to shreds. They were able to spot only two bodies being expelled by the outrushing atmosphere. But there was no chance that any of the slavers could have survived, unless they were already wearing skinsuits or battle armor—and Stephanie would have recognized those in her readings of the sensors.

"And that's that," said Hugh. He spoke into his com again. "Double-check the readings for any signs of life anywhere else in the station."

After listening for a few seconds, Arai nodded. "Okay, people. There doesn't seem to be anyone else alive in this place. So we can save ourselves a lot of work."

Knight grinned. "I love nukes. I swear, I do, even if I know it's wrong of me and I'm a bad boy."

Henson chuckled. "I can't think of any commando unit this side of an insane asylum that *doesn't* love nuclear warheads, Bryan—on those rare occasions they can use them."

Arai spoke into his com again. "Get the missile prepped. We'll be back aboard the *Ouroboros* within five minutes."

Inside the maintenance compartment, three teenage boys took a deep breath in unison. That was almost enough to suffocate them, right there, as small as the compartment was.

"Oh, shit," whispered Ed.

"Oh, shit is right," echoed James.

Brice's mind was racing. There was no way to get in touch with Ganny without scrambling back through at least fifty meters of air duct. Their com units were designed for wire transmission, and the clan had never wired this maintenance compartment or any of the surrounding ducts. There'd been too great a risk of being spotted by the slavers.

It was probably a moot point, anyway, since they had no way of knowing where the commandos had sealed off the ducts from the rest of the turret. And even if it could be done, it couldn't possibly be done in time. Everything Brice had seen about this commando unit—whoever they were, which was still undetermined—indicated that they moved very quickly. In less than ten minutes, Parmley Station was going to be destroyed by a nuclear-armed missile.

He wasn't surprised that the *Ouroboros'* sensors hadn't picked up any signs of life in the station beyond the turret used by the slavers. The clan had spent decades carefully and systematically making sure that their whereabouts were kept completely hidden from any slavers who might be tempted to eliminate the need to pay the clan by launching a surprise attack on them. The *Ouroboros* probably had better sensors than anything the slavers possessed. But unless the people staffing those sensors had reason to think there was something to find, they weren't likely to have done the kind of careful cross-checking of data that would have been necessary to detect the clan.

In short, they were all going to be dead soon . . .

Anyway.

Brice decided he had nothing to lose. He started unsealing the panel.

"Hey, don't shoot!" he yelled. Yelped, rather. "We're just kids!"

Ed and James would probably ridicule him for that later, assuming they survived. It would have been a lot more dignified to have called out something on the order of: *Hold your fire! We are not your enemy!*

But Brice had a dark suspicion that top-of-the-line military units were prone to shoot enemies first and determine who they were later. Whereas even hardened commandos might hesitate before shooting kids.

It was a theory, anyway. Best he could come up with on such short notice.

By the time Brice came out of the compartment, more-or-less spilling onto the floor beyond, all of the commandos had gathered around.

Well, not quite. *One* of them had "gathered around"—that was the one with the slave markings—while the others had their weapons trained on him from various positions of cover.

On his hands and knees, he looked up at the huge commando. He didn't really see him at first, though, because his gaze was immediately drawn to the barrel of the man's weapon. Tribarrel, rather.

The clan possessed exactly two tribarrels. Ganny kept them under lock and key. She'd only let Brice even look at them once.

Abstractly, Brice knew that pulser barrels were actually quite small in diameter. But these looked huge. It was like staring at close range into three barrels of the sort of ancient gunpowder weapons Brice had seen in history books. Four thousand caliber, or something like that. He'd swear that small rodents could set up house in there.

The sight was enough to paralyze him for a moment. The commando reached down, seized Brice by the scruff of the neck, and hauled him onto his feet. The sensation was more akin to being lifted by a power crane than a human being.

"Okay, kid. Who are you?"

Oddly, the monster's voice was a rather pleasant tenor. From his appearance, you'd have expected a basso profundo with an undertone of gravel being poured down a chute.

The expression on his face was a surprise, too. There was more than a hint of humor in those heavy features. Relaxed humor, at that. Brice would have expected something more along the lines of what he thought a troll probably looked like, while glaring in fury.

"I'm, uh, Brice Miller. Sir. The two guys—kids—with me are James Lewis and Ed Hartman."

"And where did you come from?"

"Uh... Well. Actually, we live here, sir."

"Not *here!*" yelled Ed. Yelped, rather. He and James had come out of the compartment also, by then.

"No, no, no," Brice hastily agreed. "I didn't mean we live *here*. With the slavers."

"The stinking dirty rotten slavers." That was James's contribution, spoken in a rush.

"We live... well, somewhere else. On the station, I mean. With Ganny Butry and the rest of our people."

"And who's Ganny Butry?"

"She's, uh, the widow of the guy who built Parmley Station. Michael Parmley himself. He was my great-grandfather. She's my great-grandmother." He hooked a thumb at James and Ed. "Theirs too. We're all pretty much related. Except for the people we adopted."

"Those were slaves we rescued," added Ed.

"From the stinking dirty rotten slavers," said James. Again, in a rush.

One of the female commandos rose from her crouch. She was the buxom one who'd been passing herself off as a pleasure slave. Somehow or other, she'd gotten her hands on a flechette gun and looked like she knew how to use it. Raging fourteen-year-old hormones be damned. Brice wasn't even tempted to stare at her bosom. The last two males who'd behaved offensively in her presence were now dead-dead-dead.

"Talk about the well-made plans of mice and men ganging aft agleigh," she said. "What do we do now, Hugh?"

To Brice's relief, the giant commando in front of him had lowered his weapon.

"I'm not sure yet," said the man. He spoke into his com. "Hold off on the nukes, Richard. Turns out we got civilians aboard the station, after all."

Brice couldn't hear the reply. But a few seconds later the commando—Hugh, apparently—shrugged his shoulders. "Got no idea. I'll ask him."

"How many of you are there, Brice?"

Brice hesitated. "Uh . . . about two dozen."

Hugh nodded and spoke into the com again. "He claims two dozen. Seems like a good kid, loyal to his own, so he's almost certainly lying. I figure at least three times that. You ought to be able to find them with another search, now that you know there's something to be found. And before you start whining, no, that's not a reprimand. If the kid's telling the truth and these are Parmley's own descendants, they've had decades to conceal themselves. Not surprising we didn't spot them with a standard search."

Brice took a deep breath. He didn't see any point in delaying the inevitable.

"Ah . . . Mr. Hugh, sir. Are you folks from the Audubon Ballroom?"

A smile spread across the commando's face. It was a big smile, and it seemed to come very easily.

"No, we're not—and that must be a relief." He shook his head, still smiling. "Come on, Brice. Do we look stupid? There's no way a whole tribe of you has been living here for more than half a century unless you worked out some sort of accommodation with the slavers. Probably took bribes from them to keep you from being a nuisance. Maybe did some of their maintenance work."

"We never did a damn thing for them!" said Ed.

Hugh swiveled his head to look down at him. "But you took their money, didn't you?"

Ed was silent. Brice tried to think of something, but . . . what was there to say, really?

Except . . .

"Unless we were going to die, we didn't have any choice," he stated, in as adult a manner as he could manage. "We're broke. Have been since way before I was born. We had no way to leave and the only way we could stay was by making a deal with the slavers."

"The stinking dirty rotten slavers," added James. Brice thought that was probably the most useless qualifier uttered by any human being since the ancient Hebrews tried to claim the golden calf was actually there as a reminder of the evils of idolatry. And Yahweh hadn't bought it for one second.

The commando just laughed. "Oh, relax. Even the Ballroom . . ." He cocked his head slightly and glanced at Ed. "Did I understand you right, earlier? That you've adopted slaves into your group. And if so, where did they come from?"

"Yeah, it's true. There's about . . ." He paused, while he did a quick estimate. "Somewhere around thirty, I figure."

"Thirty, is it? Out of twenty-four total."

Brice flushed. "Well. Okay, there's maybe more than just two dozen of us, all told. But I'm not fudging about the thirty."

"It's thirty-one, actually," said James eagerly. He seemed to have become addicted to useless qualifiers. "I just did an exact count."

"And where'd they come from?"

Brice raced through every alternative answer he could think of, before deciding that the truth was probably the best option. The commando questioning him might be built like an ogre, but it was obvious by now that there was nothing dull-witted or brutish about his mind.

"Most of them come from way back—I wasn't even born yet—before we'd, well, worked out our arrangement with the slavers. There were a couple of big fights then, and we freed a bunch of slaves both times. Since then, of course, some of them have had kids themselves, but I wasn't including them in the thirty figure since they weren't born slaves."

Hugh scratched his heavy chin. "And who'd they marry? Or whatever arrangements you folks have. What I mean is, who are the other parents? Other slaves, or some of you folks?"

"Both," said Brice. "Mostly some of us, though. Ganny encouraged it. Said she doesn't want any more in-breeding than necessary."

The commando nodded. "That'll help. A lot, in fact. And where'd the rest of the slaves come from?"

"People who escaped later. There aren't many of them, though."

"Sure there are," insisted James. "I count four, all told. That's actually a lot, when you think about it."

It was, in fact. There shouldn't have been any at all, except the slavers who'd operated at the station were pretty sloppy about their work.

But Brice was intrigued by something the commando had said. "What did you mean? When you said, 'that'll help.'"

Hugh's grin was back. This time, though, Brice didn't find the sight all that reassuring. There was something about that cheerful-looking grin that was . . .

Well. Wicked-looking, actually.

"Haven't you figured it out yet, Brice? The only way you folks are going to get through this is by cutting a deal with the Ballroom. Sorry, but there's no way we're going to allow this station to fall back into the hands of slavers. And there's no way you people can stop that from happening on your own, is there?"

Brice stared up at him. Maybe the guy was joking . . .

Alas, no. "And we're not going to take it over ourselves," Hugh continued. "Not alone, anyway."

"And who exactly are you?" asked Ed.

"I'll leave that question unanswered for the moment," said Hugh. "Just take my word for it that we've got no reason to take on the headache of keeping this white elephant intact and running. But I'm thinking the Ballroom might. More precisely, Torch might."

"Who's Torch?" asked Brice and James simultaneously.

The commando shook his head. "You folks *are* out of touch, aren't you?"

The female commando named Stephanie supplied the answer. "Torch is the planet that used to be called Congo, when Mesa owned it. By everybody except them, anyway. They called it

'Verdant Vista' themselves. The swine. But there was a slave rebellion assisted by—oh, all kinds of people—and now the planet's called 'Torch' and it's pretty much run by the Ballroom."

Brice was wide-eyed. "The Audubon Ballroom has its own *planet*?"

"Oh, wow," said Ed. "I can see why they might want this station, then." Stoutly: "Every planet should have its own amusement park."

Hugh laughed. "It's a bit far away for that! Still, I'm thinking . . ." He shrugged again. "Something Jeremy X mentioned to me, the last time I saw him. It's a possibility, anyway."

Brice was wide-eyed again. "You know *Jeremy X*?"

"Known him since I was a kid. He's sort of my godfather, I guess you could say. He took me under his wing, so to speak, after my parents were killed."

Brice felt a lot better, then. The idea of cutting a deal with the Ballroom still sounded dicey to him. Kind of like cutting a deal with lions or tigers. On the other hand, Hugh seemed pretty nice, all things considered. And if he had a personal relationship with Jeremy X himself . . .

"Did he really eat a Manpower baby once, like they said he did?" asked Ed.

"Raw, they say. Not even cooking it." That contribution came from James.

And if Brice—no, it'd probably take Ganny—could keep his idiot cousins from opening their fat mouths again . . .

CHAPTER TWELVE

It took no more than three days in the presence of Elfriede Margarete Butry for Hugh Arai to figure out how the woman had managed to keep her clan together for half a century, in the face of tremendous adversity. Not just intact, either, but reasonably healthy and well-educated—so long as you were prepared to allow that "well-educated" was a broad enough phrase to include very uneven knowledge, eccentric methods of training, and wildly imbalanced fields of study.

Ganny El's clan were probably the best practical mechanics Hugh had ever encountered, for instance, but their grasp of the underlying theory of some of the machines they kept running was often fuzzy and sometimes bizarre. The first time Hugh had seen one of Butry's many grand-nephews sprinkle what he called an "encouragement libation" over a machine he was about to repair, Hugh had been startled. But, some hours later, after the mechanic finished with the ensuing work, the machine came back to life and ran as smoothly as you could ask for. And however superstitious the notion of an "encouragement libation" might be, Hugh hadn't missed the underlying practicality. The "libation" was actually some homemade alcoholic brew that hadn't turned out too well. Unfit for human consumption, even by the Butry clan's none-too-finicky standards, the fluid had been set aside for the "encouragement" of cranky machinery.

Hugh had asked the nephew—Andrew Artlett was his name—whether the "encouragement" was because the machine viewed the rotgut liquor as a treat or because it was an implied threat of still worse liquids should the machine remain recalcitrant. Artlett's snorted reply had been: "How the hell am I supposed to know what a machine thinks? It's just a lot of metal and plastic and such, you know. No brains at all. But the libation works, it surely does."

Ganny Butry would have made a pretty good empress, Hugh thought, if one given to some odd quirks. She'd have made a pretty good tyrant, for that matter, except she had an affectionate streak about a kilometer wide.

There wasn't any sign of that affection right now, though.

"—still don't see why you"—here came a word Hugh didn't know, but it didn't sound affectionate at all—"can't just go on your way and leave us alone. It's not like we asked you to come here. What happened to respect for property rights?"

"Parmley Station hasn't really been your property for a long time, Ganny," Hugh said mildly, "and you know it as well as I do. If we just leave, it won't be more than six or eight months—a year, tops—before another gang of slavers has set up shop here and you have to accommodate them. Whether you like it or not."

Butry glared at him. It was an impressive glare, too, for all that it came from a woman not much more than a hundred and forty centimeters tall. What made the glare all the more impressive was that, somehow, Butry managed to convey the sense that she was a tough old biddy despite—going simply by her physical appearance—looking like a woman no older than her late thirties or very early (and well preserved) forties.

That was the effect of prolong, of course. First generation prolong, that was, which stopped the physical aging cycle at a considerably later stage than the more recent therapies. Hugh knew that Butry's own family had been quite wealthy to begin with and her husband Richard Parmley had made his first fortune as a young man. So, even with the expense involved in those early days of the treatment, they'd been able to afford prolong for themselves and their immediate offspring.

But after her husband's last financial debacle—it had been the third or fourth in his career, Hugh wasn't sure which—and the long isolation of Butry's clan here on Parmley Station . . .

For all that it was generally a blessing, prolong could sometimes produce real tragedies. And Hugh knew he was looking at one, right here—with quite possibly a still greater tragedy in the making.

Ganny El, the matriarch of the clan, would live for centuries. So would the two dozen or so relatives on the station who were her siblings, cousins or children, and who'd gotten the treatments before the clan fell on hard times. But the *next* generation in the clan, people of an age with Ganny's great-nephew Andrew Artlett—there were at least three dozen of them—were simply going to be a lost generation, as far as prolong was concerned. Even if the clan could suddenly afford the treatments, they were already too old. Their parents—even their grandparents—faced the horror that they'd outlive their own offspring.

And the same fate would fall on the next generation, if the clan's fortunes didn't improve. And they had to improve drastically, and most of all, *quickly*. People like Sarah Armstrong and Michael Alsobrook were already into their twenties, and twenty-five years of age was generally considered the outside limit for starting prolong treatments.

If there was no real sign of Butry's age in her face, there was in her eyes. Those weren't the eyes of a young woman, for sure. They were colored a green so dark they were almost black, and when Ganny was in a temper they looked more like agates or pieces of obsidian than human eyes.

Hugh had gotten to know her fairly well over the past several days, though, and he didn't think Butry was really in a temper today. She was just putting on an act. A very well-done performance, true—she'd have made as good an actress as an empress—but still a performance. There was a practical streak in the woman that was even wider than affection, and a lot harder than any mineral. If Butry hadn't been able to accept reality for what it was, her clan never would have survived at all. As it was, at least within the limits given, you could even say they'd prospered.

A very scruffy sort of prosperity, granted, and one that couldn't afford anything like prolong. But the absence of prolong had been the standard condition of the human race throughout its existence until very recently. All Hugh had to do was look at the little mob of enthusiastic and self-confident great-great-nephews and nieces who were always in attendance on Ganny to recognize that these were hardly people who'd been beaten down by hardships. Some of them, like Brice Miller and his friends, carried that self-confidence into outright brashness.

"—so fine," she concluded the little tirade she'd been on. "I can see that you're not giving me any choice. You"—here came another word in a language Hugh didn't know. It sounded like a different language altogether than the one from which she'd extracted a curse just a couple of minutes earlier. Ganny was an accomplished linguist, among her other skills. Hugh was a good linguist himself, but Butry was in a different league altogether.

"You're always welcome to cuss me in a language I know, Ganny," said Hugh. "I'm really not thin-skinned."

"No kidding. You're a troll."

She went back to glaring, but now at some of her great-great-grandchildren. "There's no way I'm letting anyone else except me dicker with the Ballroom. If the murderous bastards are going to kill anyone, they can kill an old woman. And her most problematic offspring."

Her little forefinger started jabbing at the crowd. "Andrew, you're coming. So are you, Sarah and Michael."

The finger moved on to point to a pleasant-looking young woman named Oddny Ann Rødne. She was the offspring of a marriage between one of the Butry clan's women and an ex-slave who'd been freed in the first battle between the clan and the slavers, decades earlier. "Oddny, I'll need a sane female to keep me from going batty myself. Stop pouting, Sarah, you're already batty and you brag about it. And . . ."

The finger moved on and settled on a tightly clustered trio. "You three, for sure, or there won't be a station left when I get back."

Hugh did his best not to wince. Brice Miller, Ed Hartman and James Lewis were not people *he'd* have chosen to include on a chancy mission to negotiate with the galaxy's most notorious assassins. Less than a day after making their acquaintance, Marti Garner had bestowed upon them the monicker of "the three teenagers of the Apocalypse." Nor would Hugh have included Andrew Artlett, whom Marti had singled out as the missing fourth disaster.

Apparently, Butry was confident enough that she'd been able to cut a deal with the Ballroom that she was more concerned with removing the most rambunctious members of her clan from whatever havoc they could wreak in her absence, than she was about how Jeremy X would react to them. Although . . .

With Ganny El, who knew? She might have learned enough about Jeremy to realize that he was more likely to be charmed by such as Brice Miller than he was to be offended by him. It was not as if the words "brash" and "impudent" had never been bestowed on him too, after all.

But all Hugh said was: "Okay, then. We'll leave in twelve hours. That should give you enough time." He used his own forefinger, which was almost half the size of Ganny's entire hand, to point to two of his crewmates. "June and Frank will stay behind."

"Why?" demanded Butry. "You think we need watchdogs?"

Hugh smiled. "Ganny, your negotiations might actually succeed, you know. In which case, why waste time? While we're gone, June and Frank can start laying the basis for what follows. They're both very experienced engineers."

June and Frank looked a bit smug. The reason wasn't hard to figure out. Judging from the way most of the Butry clan's unattached men and women were gazing enthusiastically upon their very comely selves, neither one of them was going to be suffering from unwanted chastity over the course of the next few months until their crewmates returned.

To some degree, Hugh had chosen them for that reason. In point of fact, both June Mattes and Frank Gillich *were* experienced engineers, and they'd do a good job of laying the groundwork for modifying Parmley Station as needed, in the event Hugh's scheme came to fruition. But he figured the process would be helped along by what you might call a lavish display of goodwill.

A Manticoran wit had once commented that Beowulfers were the Habsburgs of the interstellar era, except that they didn't bother with the pesky formalities of marriage. There was enough truth in the remark that Hugh had laughed aloud when he heard it. He wasn't a Beowulfer himself, by birth. But he'd lived among them since he was a boy and had adopted most of their attitudes.

All of them, really, except for their indifference to religion. There, although he professed no specific creed himself, Hugh retained the convictions of the people who'd raised him.

When he was very young, barely out of the vats, Hugh had been adopted by a slave couple. The adoption had been informal, of course—as, for that matter, had been the couple's own "marriage." Manpower didn't recognize or give legitimacy to any relationship between slaves.

Still, there were practicalities involved. Even from Manpower's viewpoint, there were advantages to having slaves raising the youngsters who came out of the breeding vats instead of Manpower having to do it directly. It was a lot cheaper, if nothing else. So, Manpower was often willing to let slave couples stay together and keep their "children." With some lines of slaves, at least. They wouldn't allow slaves destined to be personal servants—certainly not pleasure slaves—any such entanglements. But with most of the labor varieties, it didn't much matter. Those slaves would be sold in large groups to people needing a lot of labor. It was usually possible to keep the families of such slaves more or less intact in the course of the transactions, since both the seller and the buyer had a vested interest in doing so. Having slaves raising their own children was cheaper for the buyer of the labor force, too.

Like most labor slaves, the couple who adopted Hugh had been deeply religious. Also like most labor slaves, the creed they adhered to was Autentico Judaism. Hugh had been raised in those customs, beliefs and rituals. And if he no longer maintained most of the customs and rituals and had his doubts about most of the beliefs, he'd never been able to shake the conviction that there was a lot more to it all than just superstition left over from humanity's tribal ancient history, as many (although by no means all) Beowulfers believed.

"I'm ready to go right now!" exclaimed Brice Miller. "Me, too!" echoed his two companions.

Ganny glowered at them. "Is that so? You *do* know the voyage is going to last weeks, right?"

The three boys nodded.

"And you *do* know that although the *Ouroboros* was designed to look like a slave ship, even to someone who came on board and gave it a casual inspection, our friends here who still insist on keeping their identity unknown even though it's blindingly obvious didn't bother to disguise their own living quarters? On account of they're a bunch of sloppy Beowulfers."

Seeing Hugh's attempt to keep a straight face, Butry curled her lip. "Think I was born yesterday?" She looked back at the kids. "You know all that, right?"

The three boys nodded.

"Right. So now I find out some of my great-great-nephews are morons. Where do you plan to sleep, night after night after night?"

The three boys frowned.

Hugh cleared his throat. "We're not set up to accommodate guests, I'm afraid. And although June and Frank's quarters will be available, that'll hardly be enough for all of you. So you'll have to clear out the supplies we've been keeping in some of the other sleeping compartments. That'll take a while, on account of . . . well . . ."

"Like I said," interjected Ganny, "a bunch of sloppy Beowulfers."

"Why don't we just move into the slave quarters?" asked Andrew Artlett. "Sure, they'll be awfully Spartan, but who cares? It's only a few weeks."

June Mattes shook her head. "There's a difference between 'Spartan' quarters and bare decks. There was no way we'd let anybody who wanted to inspect us to get that far, so we never bothered to set them up. All we ever let anyone see were the killing bays, since that was all it took to establish our identity as slavers."

The "killing bays" referred to the large compartments where slaves would be driven by nauseating gas, in the event a slave ship was being overtaken by naval forces. Once there, the bays would be opened to the vacuum beyond, murdering the slaves and disposing of their bodies at the same time.

It was a tactic that didn't work if the overtaking naval forces were Manticoran or Havenite or Beowulfan, since those navies considered the mere possession of killing bays to be proof that the vessel was a slaver, whether there was a single slave on board or not. In fact, quite a few captains of such ships had been known to summarily declare the slaver crews guilty of mass murder and have them thrown into space without spacesuits right then and there.

That had been the fate of the crew of the slave ship Hugh himself had been on when he was rescued, in fact. The Beowulfan ship which captured the slaver had gotten there quickly enough to stop the mass murder before it was finished, so Hugh and some others had survived. But his parents had died, along with his brother and both of his sisters.

"Okay, then," said Artlett. "Ganny can have one of the staterooms being vacated by June and Frank, and Oddny and Sarah can share the other. The rest of us will set up wherever you want us."

Artlett now bestowed a very stern look on Brice, Ed and James. "One thing needs to be made clear, you ragamuffins. No stunts.

No japes. We've got no guarantee these Beowulfers-pretending-to-be-whoever won't jury-rig our living quarters with the same gas mechanism to drive us to the killing bays. Then the ogre here"—he hooked a thumb at Hugh—"can just push a button and out you go into the wild black yonder. Which would be fine, if you went by yourselves, except that me and Alsobrook will get sucked out with you."

Miller and Hartman looked suitably meek. The third of the trio, though, looked unhappy.

"It sounds like it's going to take us all twelve hours just to get ready," said James Lewis. "When are we supposed to sleep?"

"On the voyage, dummy," came his uncle's reply. "You'll have days and days and days with nothing to do except sleep or get into trouble. I vote for sleep."

"We ought to bring along plenty of sedatives," said Michael Alsobrook. He bestowed his own stern look on the three teenagers. "You know damn good and well they're not going to sleep."

"Sure we will," said Ed Hartman. He made a flamboyant show of stretching and yawning. "Look, I'm tired already."

Whatever else, it would probably be an interesting trip. Hugh got up and stretched also. Not because he was tired, but because a Hugh Arai "stretch" was something that, as a rule, really intimidated people.

The three boys made a flamboyant show of cringing and looking deeply worried.

Hugh sighed. He hadn't thought it would work.

CHAPTER THIRTEEN

"Welcome to Torch, Dr. Kare."

"Why, thank you, ah, Your Majesty."

Jordin Kare hoped no one had noticed his brief hesitation, but despite all of the briefings he'd been given before heading off to the Torch System, the obvious youth of the star system's ruling monarch still came as something of a surprise.

"We're *really* glad to see you," the monarch in question said enthusiastically, holding out her hand to pump his. She rolled her eyes. "We've got this wonderful resource here in the system, and none of us have a clue what to do with it. I sure hope you and your team can fix that for us!"

"We'll, um, certainly try, Your Majesty," Kare assured her. "Not that this is the sort of thing anyone can give hard and fast time estimates on, you understand," he added quickly.

"Believe me, Doctor, if I'd ever thought it was, my 'advisors' here would have straightened me out in a hurry."

She rolled her eyes again, and Kare found himself hastily suppressing a smile before it could leak onto his face. Queen Berry was a healthy young woman, quite obviously, if perhaps a bit below average height. She had a figure that was slender without being skinny, and a long dark hair that was quite striking and attractive. He'd been warned before he ever departed Manticore that she was also what one of the Foreign Ministry types had described as "a free spirit . . . a *very* free spirit," and nothing he'd seen so far seemed to suggest that description had been in error.

From the sparkle he'd detected in her light brown eyes, she was fully aware of her reputation, too.

"But I'm forgetting my manners," she said, and half-turned to face the trio of people behind her. "Let me make the introductions," she said, either blithely unaware or uncaring that ruling monarchs were supposed to have other people make introductions for them.

"This is Thandi Palane," Berry said, indicating the tall, very broad-shouldered young woman who'd been standing directly behind her. "Thandi is in charge of sorting out our military forces."

Palane had a very fair, almost albino complexion, with kinky silver-blond hair and beautiful hazel eyes, and although she was in civilian attire at the moment, she managed to make it look as if it were a uniform. Kare had been thoroughly briefed on *her*, too, although now that he'd laid eyes on her, he didn't really think the warnings about her lethality had been necessary. Not because she wasn't lethal, but because he was pretty sure only an idiot would have failed to figure that out on his own. Her carefully moderated grip was like shaking hands with a cargo grapnel. It could have picked up an egg if it had wanted to, or crumpled a solid block of molycircs like foil. She couldn't have looked more affable and friendly, either, but it was the sort of cheerful affability one would have expected out of a well fed sabertooth, and he definitely wouldn't have wanted to be around when she decided it was feeding time.

"And this," Berry continued, "is Dr. Web Du Havel, my prime minister. While Thandi takes care of the military, Web is in charge of sorting *me* out." The teenaged queen smiled mischievously. "I'm never sure which of them has the harder job, when it comes down to it."

Kare had seen HD coverage of Du Havel following his initial arrival in the Star Kingdom of Manticore two and a half T-years earlier. As a result, he knew all about the prime minister's academic credentials—credentials, in their own way, even more impressive than Kare's own. And he also knew that the stocky, physically powerful Du Havel was himself a liberated genetic slave who'd been intended by his Mesan designers as a heavy labor/technician type.

Just goes to show that you never want to piss off anyone who'd make a good engineer, Kare thought as he shook Du Havel's still powerful but considerably less scary hand. *Du Havel may be the head of the "process oriented" branch of the movement, but I'll bet there's a* bunch *of people like him in the Ballroom, too. Although, come to think of it, if I were Manpower, this is one guy I'd rather have designing bombs to throw at me, if that kept him from concentrating on what he* has *been doing.*

"It's an honor to meet you, Dr. Du Havel," he said.

"And an honor to meet *you*, Dr. Kare," Du Havel replied with a toothy grin.

"And *this*," Berry said, her mischievous smile turning positively wicked for a moment, "is the famous—or infamous—Jeremy X. He's our minister of war. But it's all right, really, Doctor! He's all reformed now . . . sort of."

"Oh, not so reformed as all that, lass," Jeremy said, reaching past her to offer his hand to Kare in turn. He smiled lazily. "I *am* on my best behavior at the moment, though," he added.

"So I've heard," Kare said with all the aplomb he could muster.

Aside from Berry herself, Jeremy X was the smallest person in the entire room. He was also renowned (if that was the proper verb) throughout the Solarian League as the most deadly terrorist, by almost any measure, the Audubon Ballroom had produced in many a year. Given the caliber of the competition, that was saying quite a lot, too. Like Du Havel, he was another example of Manpower having created a nemesis of its very own, although he and the prime minister had chosen very different ways to go about their nemesis-ing. Jeremy, who'd been designed as one of Manpower's "entertainer" lines, had the compact, small-boned frame and enhanced reflexes of a juggler or a tumbler. Although he was undoubtedly on the small side, there was nothing at all soft or frail about his physique, and the reflexes and hand-eye coordination Manpower had intended him to use for sleight-of-hand or juggling crystal plates made him one of the most lethal pistoleers in the galaxy. A point he had demonstrated with enormous gusto to his designers over the years.

Kare was well aware that, as the Kingdom of Torch's minister of war, Jeremy had officially renounced terrorism in the kingdom's name. As far as anyone back home in the Star Kingdom of Manticore was aware, he'd meant it, too. On the other hand, the man who'd planned and executed (Kare winced mentally at his own choice of verb) so many deadly and . . . inventive attacks on Manpower executives was still in there, just under the skin. One on one, Kare never doubted that Thandi Palane was more dangerous than Jeremy could ever be; as implacable forces of nature, though, he suspected there would be very little to choose between the two of them.

Which suits me just fine, given the people the two of them are likely to be going after, he reflected grimly. *Even if Rabbi McNeil does have a point about vengeance belonging to a higher power. After all, nobody ever said He couldn't use any means He chooses to execute judgment.*

"I suppose I should introduce my own associates," he said as he got his hand back from Jeremy, and indicated the tallish, undeniably shaggy strawberry-blond man to his left.

"Dr. Richard Wix, Your Majesty," he continued. "Who rejoices, for some reason I've never quite understood, in the nickname of the 'Tons of Joy Bear.'" He grimaced. "We usually shorten it to 'TJ,' but I understand you have a very efficient intelligence operation here on Torch. If you can pry the origin of his nom de party out of him, I'd be delighted to know what it is."

"I'm sure if anyone can figure it out, it'll be Daddy," the queen said cheerfully, offering her own hand to Wix.

"Forewarned is forearmed, Your Majesty," Wix said. "Besides, it's not really all that much of a secret. If Jordin here ever stuck his nose out of the lab, he'd probably have figured it out for himself by now." He gave the youthful monarch a conspiratorial look. "He doesn't get out much, you know," he added in a stage whisper.

"And *this*," Kare continued in the tone of a man rising above the slings and arrows of smaller-minded individuals, "is Captain Zachary, *Harvest Joy*'s skipper. She's the practical-minded sort who's going to keep us all straight while we get to work."

"I think you and Web are both going to have your work cut out for you, Captain," the queen commiserated as she extended her hand in turn to the dark-haired, dark-eyed Zachary.

"It's not like it's something I haven't done before, Your Majesty," Zachary replied with a slight smile, and Berry chuckled.

"Well!" she said as she released Zachary's hand and gestured at the comfortable chairs around the conference table in what had once been the office of the Mesan governor of what had once been Verdant Vista. "Now that we've got the introductions out of the way, why don't we all find seats?"

It was not, Kare thought, the sort of preplanned, carefully choreographed protocol one might have expected out of most people who ruled an entire star system. On the other hand, Queen Berry's realm wasn't quite like most other star nations, either. It was barely fifteen T-months old (counting from Berry's coronation), for one thing, and it had been born in carnage, bloodshed, and all too often bloodcurdling vengeance, for another. The fact that the liberation of the planet now known as Torch hadn't simply degenerated into a blood-soaked chaos of massacre, torture, and atrocity was mostly due to the teenaged girl settling into her own chair at the table, and Kare found himself wondering, again, how such a cheerful-looking slip of a girl had done it. There was no question, according to Admiral Givens' people at the Office of Naval Intelligence or their civilian counterparts that it had, indeed, been Berry who'd somehow convinced the liberated slaves to forgo the full, bitter dregs of the vengeance to which generations of savage repression and mistreatment had, by any fair measure, entitled them.

On the other hand, the fact remained that she'd had to do that convincing to bring the bloodshed to an end, and it was the atrocities which had already been committed, however merited they might have been, before she managed to intervene which explained why Kare and his mission were only just now arriving in Torch.

They all settled into their chairs around the circular table. Palane sat between Kare and Wix, and Du Havel sat between Wix and Captain Zachary, with Jeremy X between Kare and Queen Berry, going the other way. There'd been no formal seating chart, but Kare found himself rather doubting that that neat spacing had occurred totally by chance.

"First," Berry said, without even glancing at Du Havel or Jeremy, "I'd like to start by saying that we're all very grateful to Mr. Hauptman for assisting us this way. And to Prime Minister Grantville and Queen Elizabeth, of course."

Well, she's got her priorities right, Kare thought wryly. He and Wix were officially here as privately paid consultants, on leave from the Royal Manticoran Astrophysics Investigation Agency. If it had been solely up to Klaus Hauptman, the financial backer of this expedition, the two of them would have been in Torch before the smoke had cleared, too. Unfortunately, and despite the Star Kingdom's official recognition of the Kingdom of Torch, the "taint" of the Ballroom had forced the Star Kingdom to move rather more slowly, even after that idiot High Ridge's ignominious departure from the premiership, than Kare was confident Elizabeth Winton or her new prime minister would have preferred. The Star Kingdom of Manticore understood more about the genetic slave trade and Manpower, Incorporated, than most star nations did, but even Manticore had been shocked by some of the HD footage which had come out of Torch. It wasn't just foreign public opinion Elizabeth had been forced to worry about, either.

There were more than a few Manticorans, even among those bitterly opposed to genetic slavery, who nursed serious reservations where the Ballroom was concerned. In fact, if Kare were going to be completely honest, he had a few reservations of his own.

Even now, though, the Grantville Government hadn't *officially* signed off on the survey effort. For the record, it was a privately funded project, backed by the Hauptman Cartel, which was picking up the complete tab for it. As a matter of fact, Kare and Wix were both receiving comfortable—*very* comfortable—stipends from Hauptman, and although *Harvest Joy* was a Navy vessel, the Star Kingdom had "leased" her to Hauptman for the effort and Captain Zachary was officially on half-pay at the moment. Given what Hauptman was paying her, she was actually making close to twice what her salary as an active-duty Queen's officer would have been, although that had very little to do with her presence in Torch. As the officer who'd commanded the survey voyage that led to the successful exploration and charting of the Lynx Terminus of the Manticoran Wormhole Junction, she brought a unique level of experience with her. Besides, Kare had worked with her on that effort. When it had been made clear to him that the "private venture" in Torch was actually about as private as Mount Royal Palace, he'd known exactly who he wanted as his survey ship commander.

"We're delighted to be here, Your Majesty," he said now. "It's not all that often anyone gets to survey a wormhole. The number of people who've gotten to survey *two* of them—and do it in less than three T-years, at that—could probably be counted on one hand." He grinned. "Trust me, it's not going to look bad on our résumés!"

"No, I don't guess it is," she agreed with a smile of her own. Then she glanced at Du Havel and Jeremy before looking back at Kare.

"Obviously, we'd like to get started as quickly as possible," she said. "For one thing, we're not at all sure how much Mesa really does or doesn't know about the wormhole."

"You didn't find anything at all in their databases, Your Majesty?" Zachary asked.

"Nothing," Jeremy responded for Berry. Zachary looked at him, and he shrugged. "I'm afraid Captain Zilwicki isn't on-planet at the moment, but if you'd like to discuss our data search with Ruth Winton we'll be happy to make her available to you. For that matter, if you—or Dr. Kare or Dr. Wix—could provide any clues or hints that might help us spot something we've missed, we'd be delighted to hear about them."

He held Zachary's eye for a moment, waiting until she gave him an ever so slight nod, then continued.

"I don't know how familiar you are with Manpower's procedures, Captain," he continued, and his voice had assumed a slightly distant tone, almost a professional chill. "Especially since the Ballroom started successfully attacking their depots whenever we—I mean, whenever *it*—could, Manpower's gotten even more security conscious. By now, their practice is to restrict the data available to any of their operations to what they figure that particular operation is going to need—a strict 'need-to-know' orientation, you might say. And in the last couple of T-years, they've improved their arrangements for wiping data, as well."

He shrugged.

"Although the initial claim to 'Verdant Vista' was backed by the Mesa System's government, everyone knew it was actually a Manpower and Jessyk operation. Of course, everyone also knows that the Mesan 'government' is actually pretty much owned outright by the Mesa-based transstellars, so the Mesan Navy's involvement probably shouldn't have come as quite as much of a surprise as it did for some people.

"At any rate, the management here in-system handled their data storage in accordance with Manpower's established policies. I'm sure they never in their worst nightmares expected what Captain Oversteegen and Captain Roszak—excuse me, *Commodore* Oversteegen and *Rear Admiral* Rozsak—helped us do here, but we found several largish chunks of their computer banks slagged down when we finally got possession of them. So we don't really have any idea how much effort they put into studying the wormhole here."

"Jeremy's right about that," Du Havel put in. "What we *can* tell you, though, is that we haven't found anything outside the computers to suggest there was any ongoing survey effort. And none of the Mesan survivors who decided to stay on here ever heard anything about that kind of effort. In fact, several of them have told us they'd been specifically told by their superiors that it *hadn't* been surveyed yet." It was his turn to shrug. "Of course, none of them were hyper-physicists. Almost all of them were involved in pharmaceutical research, so it wouldn't have been their area of expertise, anyway."

"As far as we can tell, though, Captain," Thandi Palane said, "everything they've told us is the truth. We've got a few treecats of our own here on Torch these days, and they confirm that."

Zachary nodded, and so did Kare. That tracked with what his own briefings on Manticore had suggested. And he was relieved to hear the tone in which Du Havel and Palane had talked about the Mesan survivors in question. The fact that an entire research colony of Mesans—of scientists who weren't Manpower or Mesa Pharmaceuticals employees and who'd actually treated the genetic slaves assigned to their efforts like human beings—had been not only spared but actively *protected* by those slaves during the chaotic bloodlust of the system's liberation had been a not insignificant factor in the ability of Torch's friends in the Star Kingdom to get this effort cleared. And he found the fact that the Queen of Torch and her senior advisors clearly thought of those scientists as fellow citizens, not dangerously suspect potential enemies, personally reassuring.

"That's interesting," he said out loud. "Especially given the persistent rumors before the liberation that Torch was 'at least' a three-nexii junction. What you've just told us certainly agrees with everything *official* we've been able to find, but I can't find myself wondering where that specific number—three, I mean—came from in the first place."

"We've wondered the same thing," Du Havel replied. "So far, we haven't found anything to suggest a reason for it, though." He shrugged. "Given the fact that it really hasn't made any difference one way or the other as far as our decision-making priorities go, though, it's been mostly a matter of idle curiosity for us. We've been too busy clubbing alligators to worry about what color the swamp's flowers are."

He grinned wryly, and Kare chuckled at the aptness of the metaphor, especially given how well it suited Torch's biosphere.

The F6 star now officially known as Torch was unusually youthful, to say the least, to possess life-bearing planets at all. It was also unusually hot. Torch, the planet almost exactly twice as far from Torch as Old Earth lay from Sol, could be accurately described as "uncomfortably warm" by most people. "Hotter than Hell," while less euphemistic, would probably have been more accurate. Not only was Torch younger, larger, and hotter than Sol, but Torch's atmosphere contained more greenhouse gases, producing a significantly warmer planetary surface temperature. The fact that Torch's seas and oceans covered only about seventy percent of its surface and that its axial inclination was very low (less than a full degree) also helped to account for its rain forest/swamp/mudhole-from-Hell surface geography.

The star system's original survey team had obviously possessed a somewhat perverse sense of humor, given the names it had bestowed upon Torch's system bodies. Torch's original name—Elysium—was a case in point, since Kare could think of very few planetary environments less like the ancient Greeks' concept of the Elysian Fields. He didn't know why Manpower had renamed it "Verdant Vista," although it had probably had something to do with avoiding the PR downsides of turning a planet named "Elysium" into a hot, humid, thoroughly wretched purgatory for the hapless slaves it intended to dump there. Personally, Kare was of the opinion that "Green Hell" would have been a far more accurate name.

And it would have suited the local wildlife so well, too, he thought with a mental chuckle. The chuckle faded quickly, however, when he reflected upon how many of Manpower's slaves had fallen prey to "Verdant Vista's" many and manifold varieties of predator.

Another little point the bastards might have wanted to bear in mind, he reflected rather more grimly. *People who survive this kind of planetary environment aren't likely to be shrinking violets. Given where their settlement pool is coming from in the first place, the locally produced generations are probably going to be an even uglier nightmare for those bastards. Pity about that.*

"Well," he said after a moment, "TJ and the rest of the team and I have already taken a pretty close look at the data you people have been able to provide. Obviously, you didn't begin to have the instrumentation we've brought with us, so we weren't actually in a position to reach any hard and fast conclusions about what we have here. One thing we *have* observed, however, is that the terminus' gravitic signature is quite low. In fact, we're a bit surprised anyone even noticed it."

"Really?" Du Havel leaned back in his chair and crossed his legs. Kare looked at him, and the prime minister shrugged with a smile. "Oh, this certainly isn't my area of expertise, Doctor! I'm fully prepared to accept what you've just said, but I have to admit it piques my interest a bit. I was under the impression that ever since the existence of wormholes was first demonstrated, one of the very first things any stellar survey team's done is look very hard for them."

"That they do, Mr. Prime Minister," Kare acknowledged wryly. "Indeed, they do! But, as I'm sure all of you are aware, wormholes and their termini are usually a minimum of a couple of light-hours away from the stars with which they're associated. And what somebody who isn't a hyper-physicist may not realize is that unless they're particularly big, you also have to get within, oh, maybe four or five light-*minutes* before they're going to show up at all. There are certain stellar characteristics—we call them 'wormhole fingerprints'—we've learned to look for when there's a terminus in the vicinity, but they aren't always present. Again, the bigger or stronger the wormhole, the more likely the 'fingerprints' are to show up, as well.

"What we appear to have here, however, is a case of pure serendipity on someone's part. My team and I have looked very carefully at Torch, and we've determined that it really does have most of the 'fingerprints,' but they're *extremely* faint. In fact, it took several runs of computer enhancement before we were able to pick them out at all. That's not entirely surprising, given Torch's relative youth. Despite their mass, F-class stars are statistically less likely to possess termini at all, and when they do, the 'fingerprints' are almost invariably fainter than usual. That means nobody should have been looking for a terminus associated with this star in the first place, and, in the second place, that they shouldn't have been looking just sixty-four light-minutes from the primary. That's ridiculously close. In fact, our search of the literature indicates that it's the nearest any terminus associated with an F6 has ever been located relative to its associated primary. Coupled with how faint its Warshawski signature is, that suggests to us that whoever found it in the first place must have almost literally stubbed his toe on it. He sure shouldn't have been looking for it there, at any rate!"

He paused and shook his head, his expression wry. In a properly run universe people like Manpower wouldn't have the kind of luck it must have taken for them to stumble across a discovery like this one.

Although, he reminded himself, *I could be wrong about that. I'm pretty sure Manpower has to be gnashing its teeth over the thought that the goody they found has ended up in the clutches of a batch of anti-slavery "terrorists" like the Torches. So maybe what this really represents is the fact that God has a particularly nasty sense of humor where "people like Manpower" are concerned.*

That possibility, he reflected, was enough to warm the cockles of his heart.

"In addition to making it hard to find in the first place, the faintness of this terminus' Warshawski signature, coupled with its unusually close proximity to the primary, also indicates that it's almost certainly not especially huge. Frankly, despite the rumors to the contrary, I'll be surprised if there's more than one additional terminus associated with it—it looks a lot like one end of a two-loci system, what we call a 'wormhole bridge,' unlike the multi-loci 'junctions' like the Manticore Junction. Some of the bridges are more valuable than quite a few of the junctions we've discovered over the centuries, of course. It all depends on where the ends of the bridge are."

The Torches at the table nodded to show they were following his explanation. From their expressions—especially Du Havel's—the prediction that their wormhole was going to connect to only one other location wasn't exactly welcome, though.

"Even in a worst-case scenario, most wormholes are significant long-term revenue producers," Captain Zachary put in. Obviously she'd seen the same expressions Kare had.

"Unless the other terminus of this one is somewhere out in previously totally unexplored space—which is possible, of course—then it's still going to be a huge timesaver for people wanting to go from wherever the other end is to anything close to this end," she continued. "It's only four days from here to Erewhon even for a merchant ship, for example, and only about thirteen days from here to Maya. And from Erewhon to the Star Kingdom's only about four days via the Erewhon wormhole. So if the other end of your wormhole is somewhere in the Shell, anyone wanting to reach those destinations is going to be able to shave literally months off of her transit time. I'm not suggesting you're going to see anywhere near the volume of traffic we see through the Junction, of course, but I'm pretty sure there's still going to be enough to give your treasury a hefty shot in the arm."

"Maybe not a goldmine, but at least a silver mine, you mean?" a grinning Queen Berry asked.

"Something along those lines, Your Majesty," Zachary agreed with an answering smile.

"Which probably wasn't exactly a non-factor in Mr. Hauptman's thinking," Kare added, and chuckled. "From what I've seen and heard, he'd probably think backing this survey was a good idea even if it wasn't likely to add a single dime to his own cash flow. On the other hand, I understand he's going to be showing a nice long-term profit on his share of your transit fees."

"I think it's what's referred to as 'a comfortable return,'" Du Havel said dryly. "One-point-five percent of all transit fees for the next seventy-five years ought to come to a pretty fair piece of change."

Several people chuckled this time, and Kare nodded in acknowledgment of the prime minister's point. At the same time, the hyper-physicist really did feel confident Hauptman would have backed the survey effort, anyway. It was obvious to Kare that Klaus Hauptman regarded not making a profit for his shareholders whenever possible as a perversion roughly equivalent to eating one's own young. He supposed no one became as successful as Hauptman without that sort of attitude, and he didn't have any particular problem with it himself. But anyone who bothered to take a look around the Torch System would have been forced to concede that Hauptman also put his personal fortune's money where his principles were.

Anyone who knew anything about Klaus Hauptman and his daughter Stacey had to be aware of their virulent, burning hatred for all things associated with the genetic slave trade. By any measure one cared to use, the Hauptman Cartel was the Star Kingdom's single largest financial contributor to the Beowulf-based Anti-Slavery League. Not only that, the Cartel had already provided the Kingdom of Torch with well over a dozen frigates. No serious interstellar navy had built frigates in decades, of course, but the latest ships—the *Nat Turner*-class—Hauptman had delivered to Torch were significantly more dangerous than most people might have expected. Effectively, they were hyper-capable versions of the Royal Manticoran Navy's *Shrike*-class LAC but with about twice the missile capacity and a *pair* of spinal-mounted grasers, with the second energy weapon bearing aft. Their electronics were a downgraded "export version" of the RMN's (which was hardly surprising, given the fact that they were going to be operating in an area where the Republic of Haven's intelligence services had ready access), but the *Turners* were probably at least as dangerous as the vast majority of the .galaxy's destroyers.

According to official reports, the Hauptman Cartel had built them at cost. According to *unofficial* (but exceedingly persistent) reports, Klaus and Stacey Hauptman had picked up somewhere around seventy-five percent of their construction costs out of their own pockets. Given that there were eight of the Turners, that was a pretty hefty sum for even the Hauptmans to shell out. And according to the last word Kare had picked up before leaving Manticore for Torch, the Torch Navy had just ordered its first trio of all-up destroyers, as well. Even after they were completed, Torch would scarcely be considered one of the galaxy's leading navies, but the kingdom would have a fairly substantial little system-defense force.

Which just happened to be hyper-capable . . . which meant it could also operate in *other* people's star systems.

And the fact that Torch has officially declared war on Mesa isn't going to make those Manpower bastards feel any happier when they find out the sort of capability the Torches are building up out here, the hyper-physicist reflected with grim satisfaction.

When he'd mentioned that thought to Josepha Zachary on the voyage here, she'd nodded emphatically and added her own obser-vation—that Torch obviously had a well thought-out, rationalized expansion program in mind. It was clear to her that they were using the frigates as training platforms, building up a cadre of experienced spacers and officers to provide the locally trained (and highly motivated) manpower to systematically upgrade their naval capabilities as time, money, crewmen, and training permitted.

"At any rate," he said out loud, "and returning to my original point, that's why TJ and I were both a bit surprised that anyone ever managed to pick it up at all. Which, I suppose, could explain why Mesa apparently hadn't gotten around to surveying it yet. They may have had enough trouble finding it in the first place that they simply hadn't known it was there long enough."

"I hadn't realized it would have been so difficult for them to detect, Doctor," Jeremy said. "On the other hand, the fact of its existence had become sufficiently common knowledge that Erewhon, at least, knew all about it over two T-years ago. And, frankly, the Ballroom knew about it for at least six months before anyone in Erewhon realized it existed. Given what Captain Zachary's just said, I'm a bit surprised someone like the Jessyk Combine didn't get a survey crew in here sooner. If anybody in the galaxy would recognize the potential value to shippers, I'd think Jessyk would."

"Yes, TJ and I have kicked that around a good bit, too," Kare replied, "and he's come up with a theory for why they might not have surveyed it even if they'd known it was there all along, if anyone's interested."

"I don't know about anybody else, but *I* am!" Queen Berry said, and cocked her head at Wix.

"Well," Wix rubbed the mustache that was a couple of shades lighter than the rest of his rather unruly beard, "I hope nobody's going to confuse me with any kind of intelligence analyst. But the best reason I've been able to come up with for Jessyk and Manpower's trying to keep their little wormhole quiet is that they didn't want to draw any more attention to what they were doing here on Torch."

Faces tightened all around the table, and Du Havel nodded thoughtfully.

"I hadn't really considered that," he admitted, "and I should have. It's the sort of propaganda factor the ASL's tried to keep in mind for a long time. But you may well have a point, Dr. Wix. If this wormhole had started attracting a lot of through traffic, then there'd have been a lot more potentially embarrassing Solarian witnesses to the mortality rate among the members of their planet-side slave labor force, wouldn't there?"

"That's what I was thinking," Wix agreed. Then he snorted. "Mind you, that's a pretty sophisticated motive to impute to anyone stupid enough to be using *slave labor* to harvest and process pharmaceuticals in the first place! Completely leaving aside the moral aspects of the decision—which, I feel confident, would never have darkened the doorway of any Mesan transtellar's decision processes—it was *economically* stupid."

"I tend to agree with you," Du Havel said. "On the other hand, breeding slaves is pretty damned cheap." His voice was remarkably level, but his bared-teeth grin gave the lie to his apparent detachment. "They've been doing it for a long time, after all, and their 'production lines' are all in place. And to give the devil his due, human beings are still a lot more versatile than most machinery. Not as *efficient* at most specific tasks as purpose-built machinery, of course, but versatile. And as far as Manpower and Mesans in general are concerned, slaves *are* 'purpose-built machinery,' when you come down to it. So from their perspective, it made plenty of sense to avoid the initial capital investment in the hardware the job would have required. After all, they already had plenty of cheap replacement units when their 'purpose-built machinery' broke, and they could always make more."

"You know," Kare said quietly, "sometimes I forget just how ... skewed the thinking of something like Manpower has to be." He shook his head. "It never would've occurred to me to analyze the economic factors from that perspective."

"Well, I've had a bit more practice at it than most people." Du Havel's tone was dry enough to create an instant Sahara ... even on Torch. "The truth is that slavery's almost always been hideously inefficient on a production per man-hour basis. There've been exceptions, of course, but as a general rule, using slaves as skilled technicians—which would be the only way to make it remotely competitive with free labor on a productive basis—has had a tendency to turn around and bite the slaveowner on the ass."

He smiled again, chillingly, but then the smile faded.

"The problem is that it doesn't have to be efficient to show at least some profit. A low return on a really big operation still comes to a pretty impressive absolute amount of money, and their 'per-unit' capital costs are low. I'm sure that was a major element in their thinking—especially when you consider how much capital investment in slave-production facilities Manpower would have to write off if it were even tempted to 'go legitimate.' Not that I think it would ever occur to them to make the attempt, you understand."

"No, I guess not." Kare grimaced, then gave himself a shake. "On the other hand, whatever the Mesans' motives for leaving this particular wormhole unexploited, it gives me a certain warm and fuzzy feeling to reflect on the fact that when it starts producing revenue for you people, that cash flow's going to find itself being plowed into your naval expansion."

"Yes," Thandi Palane agreed, and her smile was even colder than Du Havel's had been. "That's a possibility I've been spending quite a bit of my own time contemplating. We've already managed a couple of ops I'm pretty sure have pissed Manpower off, but if we can get our hands on a few more hyper-capable ships of our own, they're going to be very, very unhappy with the results."

"In that case," Kare replied with a smile of his own, "by all means, as Duchess Harrington would put it, 'let's be about it.'"

CHAPTER FOURTEEN

"So what's on the agenda today?" Judson Van Hale asked cheerfully as he walked into the office.

"You," Harper S. Ferry replied repressively, "are entirely too bright and happy for someone who has to be up this early."

"Nonsense!" Judson gave him a broad, toothy smile. "You effete city boys simply have no appreciation for the brisk, bracing, cool air of dawn!" He threw back his head, chest swelling as he inhaled deeply. "Get some oxygen into that bloodstream, man!" he advised. "That'll cheer you up!"

"It would be a lot less strenuous to just kill you . . . and a lot more fun, now that I think about it," Harper observed, and Judson chuckled. Although, given Harper S. Ferry's record during his active career with the Audubon Ballroom, he wasn't entirely certain the other man was joking. *Pretty* certain, but not entirely. On the other hand, he figured he could rely on Genghis to warn him before the ex-Ballroom operative actually decided to squeeze the trigger.

Unlike Harper, Judson had never personally been a slave. Instead, he'd been born on Sphinx after his father's liberation from the hold of a Manpower Incorporated slave ship. Patrick Henry Van Hale had married a niece of the Manticoran captain whose ship had intercepted the slaver he'd been aboard, and, despite the fact that Patrick had been young enough to receive first-generation prolong after he was freed, he'd still had the perspective of Manpower's normally short-lived slaves. He and his new bride hadn't wasted any time at all on building the family they'd both wanted, and Judson (the first of six children . . . so far) had come along barely a T-year after the wedding.

Both Patrick and Lydia Van Hale were rangers with the Sphinx Forestry Service, and, although as a citizen of Yawata Crossing Judson had scarcely been the backwoods bumpkin he enjoyed parodying, he had spent quite a lot of his time in the bush during his childhood. His parents' employment explained most of that, and Judson had fully intended to follow in their footsteps. In fact, he'd completed his graduate forestry classes and his internship in the SFS when the liberation of Torch changed everything.

The fact that he'd never personally been a slave hadn't diminished his hatred for Manpower in any way, and he and his family had always been active in supporting the Anti-Slavery League. Judson's parents had never subscribed to the Ballroom's approach, however. They believed that the Ballroom's atrocities (and, even now, Judson figured there was no better word to describe quite a few of the Ballroom's operations) played into the hands of slavery's supporters. That wasn't a point on which Harper would have agreed with them, and truth to tell, Judson himself had always been a bit more ambivalent about that than his parents were. He'd wondered, sometimes, if that was because he felt as if he'd personally had a "free ride" where slavery was concerned. If he was more willing to see violence as the proper response because he felt hypocritical condemning those who resorted to violence against an abomination they'd experienced firsthand . . . and he hadn't. He'd escaped it before he'd even been conceived, after all, and the Star Kingdom of Manticore was one of the few star nations where no one really cared, one way or the other, if someone was an ex-slave or the son of ex-slaves. You were who you were, and the fact that you'd been designed as someone else's property was neither stigma nor a badge of victimhood.

In that respect, Judson knew he would never be able to fully share his parents' attitude. Both of them were fiercely grateful to the Royal Manticoran Navy for his father's freedom and equally fiercely loyal to the Star Kingdom of Manticore for the safe harbor and opportunities it had given him, but Patrick Henry Van Hale also remembered being a slave . . . and he'd been designed as a "pleasure slave." Even though he'd been only around nineteen T-years old when he'd been freed, he'd already undergone the full gamut of what Manpower euphemistically called "training." Lydia

Van Hale hadn't . . . but she'd been the one who'd spent years helping him deal with—and survive—the dehumanizing trauma of that experience. In ways they would never be able to escape, Patrick's slavery still defined who both of them were, and it was an experience Judson had never shared. They'd never harped on that, never indulged in the "if only *I'd* had it as good as you do" school of child rearing, yet he'd become only increasingly aware of that difference between them as he'd grown older. And as he'd also become increasingly aware of the lifetime scars they both carried with them from his father's experience, his hatred for Manpower and all things Mesan had only grown.

Which, he knew, was another reason he'd found it ever more difficult to shed crocodile tears for the Ballroom's "victims."

Yet he'd been his parents' son, and whatever he'd felt, he would never have been able to justify signing on with the Ballroom. Which was why the liberation of Torch changed everything.

His Forestry Service training had included eleven T-Months at the Royal Law Enforcement Center in Landing, which had given him a firm grounding in law enforcement and investigative techniques, and his childhood on Sphinx and the time he'd spent in the bush had accounted for his adoption by Genghis. As far as Judson was aware, only one ex-slave had ever been adopted by a treecat, but there were probably half a dozen *children* of ex-slaves who had been, and he was one of them. When the Kingdom of Torch had sprung into existence, Judson had realized immediately that it was going to need people with his skill set just as badly as it was going to need people with Harper's skills. In fact, Torch was probably going to need people like Judson even more, if only because there were so few of them.

When Jeremy X renounced the Ballroom's "terrorist" tactics on behalf of Torch, Judson's only qualm had evaporated. He'd been on the next ASL-sponsored transport to Torch, with his parents' blessing, and Jeremy and Thandi Palane had been delighted to see him . . . and Genghis.

He'd encountered a few ex-Ballroom types (and some he was pretty convinced weren't all that *ex-* about their relationship with the Ballroom) who seemed to regard him as some sort of Johnny-come-lately. Almost as a dilettante who'd sat around on his well-protected ass in his cushy Manticoran life while other people did the heavy lifting which had eventually led to Torch's existence. There weren't many of them, though, and as pissed off with them as Judson sometimes was, he didn't really blame them for it. Or he was at least able to maintain enough perspective to cope with it, at any rate.

He figured he owed a lot of that to Genghis' influence. The 'cat had been with him for over fifteen T-years, and he'd been Judson's best sounding board for that entire time. That had turned into an incredibly rich and satisfying two-way communication street since the two of them had mastered the sign language Dr. Arif had devised with the assistance of the treecats Nimitz and Samantha, and Genghis had stepped on more than one temper flare in the T-year they'd spent here on Torch. It was hard for a man to lose it when his treecat companion decided to smack him down for letting things get out of hand.

And it was Genghis' ability to communicate fully with Judson which made his telempathic abilities so valuable to Torch. At the moment, they were officially assigned to Immigration Services, although Thandi Palane had made it quite clear to Judson that that assignment was in the nature of a polite fiction. Their *real* job was to keep an eye on people who got close enough to Queen Berry to pose a potential threat to the teenaged monarch.

It'd help if Berry were willing to let us put together a proper security detail for her, he thought now, with a familiar sense of disgruntlement. *One of these days she's going to have to figure out that she's making it a hell of a lot harder to keep her alive by being so stubborn about it. And if she weren't such a lovable kid, I swear I'd snatch her up by the scruff of the neck and shake some sense into her!*

The thought gave him a certain degree of satisfaction . . . which was only slightly flawed by Genghis' bleeking chuckle from his shoulder as the 'cat effortlessly followed the familiar thought through its well-worn mental groove.

"Brooding about Her Majesty's stubbornness again, are we?" Harper inquired genially, and Judson scowled at him.

"It's a sorry turn of events when a man's own 'cat rats him out to such an unworthy superior as yourself," he observed.

"Genghis never signed a word," Harper pointed out mildly, and Judson snorted.

"He didn't have to," he growled. "The two of you have been so mutually corrupting that I think you're developing your own 'mind voice'!"

"I wish!" Harper's snort was only half humorous. "It'd make our job a lot easier, wouldn't it?"

"Probably." Judson walked across to his own desk and dropped into his chair. "Not as much easier as it'd be if Berry was only willing to be reasonable about it, though."

"I don't think anyone—except Her Majesty, of course—is likely to argue with you about that," Harper observed. "On the other hand, at least you and I have it easier than Lara or Saburo."

"Yeah, but unlike Lara we're both civilized, too," Judson pointed out. "If Berry gets too stubborn with her, Lara'll just sling her over a shoulder, unlike either of us, and haul her off kicking and screaming!"

"Now that," Harper said with a sudden chuckle, "is something I'd pay good money to see. And you're right—Lara'd do it in a heartbeat, wouldn't she?"

It was Judson's turn to chuckle, although he wondered if Harper found it quite as ironic as he himself did that the closest thing to a personal bodyguard the Queen of Torch would accept was a Scrag.

Well, an ex-Scrag, if we're going to be fair about it, he reminded himself. *And given that Lara's one of Thandi's "Amazons," I think it would be a very good idea to be as fair as possible in her case.*

Still, it was a bizarre sort of relationship, in a lot of ways. The Scrags were the direct descendants of the genetically engineered "super soldiers" of Old Earth's Final War, and an awful lot of them had found themselves in the service of Manpower or working as mercenaries for one or another of Mesa's outlaw corporations. Given the way most Scrags clung to their sense of superiority to the "normals" around them—and the reciprocal (and, in most cases, equally unthinking) prejudice most of those normals exhibited where the Scrags were concerned—it wasn't as if the majority of Lara's relatives found themselves with a lot of lucrative career opportunities. So, over the centuries, many of them had drifted into various criminal enterprises—which, of course, only strengthened and deepened the anti-Scrag stereotypes and prejudices. It had been only a short step from there to the role of Mesan enforcers and leg breakers, especially since Mesa was one of the few places in the galaxy where "genies" were regarded as an everyday fact of life. All of which meant that the Scrags and the Ballroom had shed an awful lot of each others' blood.

Yet, despite all that, here were Lara and her fellow Amazons, not simply accepted on Torch but full citizens trusted with the protection of Torch's queen.

And thank God for them, he reflected rather more soberly.

"Well," Harper said after several seconds, still smiling with the echoes of his mental vision of a squalling, kicking Berry tossed across Lara's shoulder and hauled off to safety somewhere, "I'm afraid that rather than giving our lives in the defense of our beloved—if stubborn—queen, our day is going to be one of those less scintillating moments of our life experience."

"I always get worried when you start trotting out extra vocabulary," Judson observed.

"That's because you're a naturally suspicious and un-trusting soul, without one scintilla of philosophical discernment or sensitivity to guide you through the perceptual and ontological shallows of your day to day existence."

"No, it's because when you get full of yourself this way it usually means we're going to be doing something incredibly boring, like counting noses on a new transport or something."

"Interesting you should raise that specific possibility." Harper smiled brightly, and Judson eyed him with a suspicion that rapidly descended into resignation.

"Oh, crap," he muttered.

"That's not a very becoming attitude," Harper scolded.

"Oh, yeah? Well, let me guess, O Fearless Leader. Which of us have you decided to assign as doorman this afternoon?"

"Not *you*, that's for sure," Harper said with an audible sniff. He watched Judson from the corner of one eye, timing his moment carefully. Then, the instant Judson started to brighten ever so slightly, he shrugged. "I've assigned the best qualified person to the job, and I'm sure *he* won't object the way certain other people might. Of course, despite all of his other qualifications, Genghis *will* need you along as interpreter."

Judson raised one hand in an ancient (and very rude) gesture as his traitor treecat's bleeking laughter echoed Harper's obvious amusement. Still, he couldn't fault the other man's logic.

Somebody had to be in charge of the reception, processing, and orientation of the steady stream of ex-slaves pouring into Torch on an almost daily basis. The news that they finally had a genuine homeworld to call their own, a planet which had become the very symbol of their defiant refusal to submit to the dehumanization and brutality of their self-appointed masters, had gone through the interstellar community of escaped slaves like a lightning bolt. Judson doubted that any exile had ever returned to his homeland with more fervor and determination than he saw whenever another in the apparently endless stream of ASL-sponsored transport vessels arrived here in Torch. Torch's population was expanding explosively, and there was a militancy, a bared-teeth snarl of defiance, to every shipload of fresh immigrants. Whatever philosophical differences might exist between them, they were meaningless beside their fierce identification with one another and with their new homeworld.

But that didn't mean they arrived here in a calm and orderly state of mind. Many of them did, but a significant percentage came off the landing shuttles with a stiff-legged, raised-hackle attitude which reminded Judson of a hexapuma with a sore tooth. Sometimes it was the simple stress of the voyage itself, the sense of traveling into an unknown future coupled with the suspicion that in a galaxy which had never once given them an even break, any dream had to be shattered in the end. That combination all too often produced an irrational anger, an internal hunching of the shoulders in preparation for bearing yet another in an unending chain of disappointments and betrayals. After all, if they came with that attitude, at least they could hope that any surprises would be pleasant ones.

For others, it was darker than that, though. Sometimes a *lot* darker. Despite Harper's deliberate humor, he knew as well as Judson that any given transport was going to have at least one "Ballroom burnout" on board.

Harper was the one who'd coined the term. In fact, Judson doubted that he himself would ever have had the nerve to apply it if Harper hadn't come up with it in the first place, and the fact that the other man had only made Judson respect him even more. Harper had never discussed his own record as a Ballroom assassin with Judson, but it wasn't exactly a secret here on Torch that he'd long since forgotten exactly how many slavers and Manpower executives he'd "terminated with extreme prejudice" over his career. Yet Harper also recognized that too many of his Ballroom associates had been turned into exactly what the Ballroom's critics insisted all of them were.

Every war had its casualties, Judson thought grimly, and not all of them were physical, especially in what was still called "asymmetrical warfare." When the resources of the two sides were as wildly unbalanced as they were in this case, the weaker side couldn't restrict itself and its strategies on the basis of some sanitized "code of war" or some misplaced chivalry. That, as much as the raw hatred of Manpower's victims, was a major reason for the types of tactics the Ballroom had adopted over the decades . . . and the revulsion of many people who rejected its methods despite their own deep sympathy with the abolition movement as a whole. Yet there were more prices than public condemnation buried in the Ballroom's operations. The cost of taking the war to something as powerful as Manpower and its corporate allies in ways that maximized the bloody cost to them was all too often paid in the form of *self* brutalization—of turning oneself into someone not only *capable* of committing atrocities but eager to.

The Ballroom had always made a conscientious effort to identify itself and its members as *fighters*, not simple killers, but after enough deaths, enough bloodshed, enough horror visited upon others in retaliation for horrors endured, that distinction blurred with dismaying ease. All too often, there came a time when playing the role of a sociopath transformed someone *into* a sociopath, and quite a few Ballroom fighters who fell into that category turned up here on Torch unable—or unwilling—to believe that a planet inhabited almost exclusively by ex-slaves could possibly have renounced the Ballroom's terrorist tactics.

Judson didn't really blame them for feeling that way. In fact, he didn't see how it could have been any other way, actually. And he'd come to feel not simply sympathy, but a degree of understanding for the men and women who felt and thought that way which he would flatly have denied he could ever feel before his own time here on Torch. He'd seen and learned too much from hundreds, even thousands, of people who—like his own father—had experienced Manpower's brutality firsthand to blame anyone for the burning depth of his hatred.

Yet it was one of the Immigration Service's responsibilities to identify the people who felt that way, because Jeremy X had been completely serious. And he'd been right, too. If Torch was going to survive, it had to demonstrate to its friends and potential allies that it was not going to become a simple haven for terrorism. No one in his right mind could possibly expect Torch to turn against the Ballroom, or to sever all of its links to it, and if Jeremy had attempted to do anything of the sort, his fellow subjects would have turned upon him like wolves. And rightfully so, in Judson's opinion. But the Kingdom of Torch had to conduct itself as a star nation if it ever meant to be *accepted* as a star nation, and a home for ex-slaves, built by ex-slaves, as an example and a proof of ex-slaves' ability to conduct themselves as a civilized society, was far more important than any open support for Ballroom-style operations could ever have been.

For all the vocal sympathy others might voice, from the comfort of their own well fed, well cared for lives, for the plight of Manpower's victims, there was still that ineradicable prejudice against slaves. Against anyone defined primarily as a "genie." As a product of deliberate genetic design. It wasn't even as if some genetic slaves didn't have their own variety of it, he thought, given the attitude of all too many of them towards Scrags. In his darker moments, he thought it was just that every group had to have *someone* to look down on. That it was an endemic part of the human condition, however that human's genes had come to be arranged in a particular pattern. Other times, he looked around him and recognized the way the vast majority of people he personally knew had risen above that "endemic" need and knew it was possible, in the end, to exterminate *any* prejudice.

But however possible it might be, it wasn't going to happen overnight. And in the meantime, Torch had to stand as the light for which it was named, the proof genetic slaves could build a *world*, and not just a vengeance machine. That they could take their war with Manpower with them and transform it in ways which proved that, in fact, they were not inferior to their designers and oppressors, but *superior* to them. And just as they had to prove that to the people whose support their survival required, they had to prove it to themselves. Had to take that ultimate vengeance upon Manpower by *proving* Manpower had lied. That whatever had been done to them, however their chromosomes had been warped or toyed with, they were still human beings, still as much heir to the potential greatness of humanity as anyone else.

Most of them would have been incredibly uncomfortable trying to put that thought into words, but that didn't keep them from grasping it. And so when someone who couldn't accept it arrived on Torch, it was Immigration's responsibility to recognize him. Not to deny him entry, or to threaten him with arbitrary deportation. The Torch Constitution guaranteed every ex-slave, and every child or grandchild of ex-slaves, safe haven on Torch. That was why Torch existed. But, in return, Torch demanded compliance with its own laws, and those laws included the prohibition of Ballroom-style operations launched from Torch. Despite everything else, Torch would not imprison people who refused to renounce the Ballroom's traditional tactics, but neither would Torch allow them to remain or to use its territory as a safe refuge between Ballroom-style strikes. Which was why the people whose own hatred might drive them to do exactly that had to be recognized.

And, as much as Judson personally hated the duty, there was no question that Harper was right. Genghis' telempathic sense, his ability to literally taste the "mind glow" of anyone he met, made him absolutely and uniquely suited to the task.

"All right," he said out loud, "be that way. But I'm warning you now, Genghis and I will expect tomorrow afternoon off."

He kept his tone light, but he also met Harper's gaze steadily. However well suited to the task Genghis might be, wading through that many mind glows, so many of which carried their own traumas and scars, was always exhausting for the treecat. He'd *need* a little time away from other mind glows, a little time in the Torch equivalent of the Sphinx bush, and Harper knew it.

"Go ahead," he said. "Twist my arm! Extort extra vacation time out of me!" He grinned, but his own eyes were as steady as Judson's, and he nodded ever so slightly. "See if *I* care!"

"Good," Judson replied.

Several hours later, neither Judson nor Genghis felt particularly cheerful.

It wasn't as if the arriving shuttles were steeped solely in gloom, despair, and bloodthirsty hatred. In fact, there was an incredible joyousness to most of the arrivals, a sense of having finally set foot on the soil of a planet which was actually *theirs*.

Of being home at last.

But there were scars, and all too often still-bleeding psychic wounds, on even the most joyous, and they beat on Genghis' focused sensitivity like hammers. The fact that the 'cat was deliberately looking for dangerous fault lines, pockets of particularly brooding darkness, forced him to open himself to all the rest of the pain, as well. Judson hated to ask it of his companion, but he knew Genghis too well *not* to ask. Treecats were direct souls, with only limited patience for some of humanity's sillier social notions. And, to be honest, Genghis had a lot less trouble accepting and supporting the Ballroom's mentality than Judson himself did. Yet Genghis also understood how important Torch was not simply to his own person, but to all of the other two-legs around him, and that much of its hope for the future rested on the need to identify people whose choice of actions might jeopardize what the Torches were striving so mightily to build. Not only that, Torch was his home, too, now, and treecats understood responsibility to clan and nesting place.

Which didn't make either of them feel especially cheerful.

<That one.> Genghis' fingers flickered suddenly.

"What?"

Judson twitched. So far, despite the inevitable emotional fatigue, today's transport load of new immigrants had contained few "problem children," and he'd settled into a sort of cruise control as he watched them filtering through the arrival interview process.

<That one,> Genghis' fingers repeated. <The tall one in the brown shipsuit, by the right lift bank. With dark hair.>

"Got him," Judson said a moment later, although there was nothing particularly outwardly impressive about the newcomer. He was obviously from one of the general utility genetic lines. "What about him?"

<Not sure,> Genghis replied, his fingers moving with unusual slowness. <He's . . . nervous. Worried about something.>

"Worried," Judson repeated. He reached up and ran his fingers caressingly down Genghis' spine. "A lot of two-legs worry about a lot of things, O Bane of Chipmunks," he said. "What's so special about this one?"

<He just . . . tastes wrong.> Genghis was obviously trying to find a way to describe something he didn't fully understand himself, Judson realized. <He was nervous when he got off the lift, but he got a lot more nervous *after* he got off the lift.>

Judson frowned, wondering what to make of *that*. Then the newcomer looked up, and Judson's own mental antennae quivered.

The man in the brown shipsuit was trying hard not to let it show, but he wasn't looking up at the crowded arrival concourse in general. No, he was looking directly at Judson Van Hale and Genghis . . . and trying to make it look as if he weren't.

"Do you think he got more worried when he saw *you*, Genghis?" he asked quietly. Genghis cocked his head, obviously thinking hard, and then his right truehand flipped up in the sign for "Y" and nodded in affirmation.

Now, that's *interesting*, Judson thought, staying exactly where he was and trying to avoid any betraying sign of his own interest in Mr. Brown Shipsuit. *Of course, it's probably nothing. Anybody's got the right to be nervous on their first day on a new planet—especially the kind of people who're arriving here on Torch every day! And if he's heard the reports about the 'cats—or, even worse, the rumors—he may think Genghis can peek inside his head and tell me everything he's thinking or feeling. God knows we've run into enough people who ought to know better who think that, and I can't really blame anyone who does for not liking the thought very much. But still . . .*

His own right hand twitched very slightly on the virtual keyboard only he could see, activating the security camera that snapped a picture as the brown shipsuit sank into the chair in front of one of the Immigration processors. However nervous the newcomer might be, he was obviously at least managing to maintain his aplomb as he answered the interviewer's questions and provided his background information. He wasn't even glancing in Judson and Genghis' direction any longer, either, and he actually managed a smile when he opened his mouth and stuck out his tongue for the Immigration clerk to scan its barcode.

Some of the ex-slaves resented that. More than one had flatly refused when asked to do the same thing, and Judson found it easy enough to understand that reaction. But given the incredible number of places Torch's new immigrants came from, and bearing in mind that the mere fact of ex-slavery didn't necessarily mean all of them were paragons of virtue, the assembly of an identification database was a practical necessity. Besides, the Beowulf medical establishment had identified several genetic combinations which had potentially serious negative consequences. Manpower had never worried about that sort of thing, as long as they got whatever feature they'd been after, and that lack of concern was a major factor in the fact that even if they were ever fortunate enough to receive prolong, genetic slaves' average lifespans remained significantly shorter than "normals'" did. Beowulf had devoted a lot of effort to finding ways to ameliorate the consequences of those genetic sequences if they could be identified, and the barcode was the quickest, most efficient way for the doctors to scan for them. There wasn't much that could be done for some of them, even by Beowulf, but prompt remedial action could enormously mitigate the consequences of others, and one of the things every citizen of Torch was guaranteed was the very best medical care available.

Given that no slaveowner had ever bothered to waste prolong on something as unimportant as his animate property, much less worry about things like preventative medicine, that guarantee was one of the kingdom's most ringing proclamations of the individual value it placed upon its people.

"Is he still nervous?" Judson murmured, and Genghis' hand nodded again.

"Interesting," Judson said softly. "You may just make him that way because he's one of those people who doesn't want anyone poking around inside his head."

This time, Genghis nodded his head and not just his hand. Treecats were constitutionally incapable of really understanding why anyone might feel that way, since they couldn't imagine *not* being able to "poke around" inside each other's minds. But they didn't have to be able to understand *why* two-legs might feel that way to grasp that some of them *did* feel that way, and if that were the case here, it would scarcely be the first time Genghis had seen it.

"Still," Judson continued, "I think we might want to keep an eye on this one for at least a couple of days. Remind me to mention that to Harper."

CHAPTER FIFTEEN

"You called?" Benjamin Detweiler said as he poked his head through the door Heinrich Stabolis had just opened for him.

Albrecht Detweiler looked up from the paperwork on his display and raised one eyebrow at the oldest of his sons. Of course, Benjamin wasn't *just* his son, but very few people were aware of how close the relationship actually was.

"Have I mentioned lately," Albrecht said, "that I find your extreme filial respect very touching?"

"No, somehow I think that slipped your mind, Father."

"I wonder why that could possibly be?" Albrecht mused out loud, then pointed at one of the comfortable chairs in front of his desk. "Why don't you just park yourself right there, young man," he said in the stern tone he'd used more than once during Benjamin's adolescent career.

"Yes, Father," Benjamin replied in a tone which was far more demure and chastened sounding than Albrecht recalled ever having heard out of him during that same adolescent career.

The younger Detweiler "parked" himself and folded his hands in his lap while he regarded his father with enormous attentiveness, and Albrecht shook his head. Then he looked at Stabolis.

"I'm sure I'm going to regret this in the fullness of time, Heinrich, but would you be kind enough to get Ben a bottle of beer? And go ahead and open one for me at the same time, please. I don't know about him, but I feel depressingly confident that *I'm* going to need a little fortification."

"Of course, Sir," his enhanced bodyguard replied gravely. "If you really think he's old enough to be drinking alcohol, that is."

Stabolis had known Benjamin literally from birth, and the two of them exchanged smiles. Albrecht, on the other hand, shook his head and sighed theatrically.

"If he's not old enough yet, he never will be, Heinrich," he said. "Go ahead."

"Yes, Sir."

Stabolis departed on his errand, and Albrecht tipped back his chair in front of the window with its magnificent view of powdery sand and dark blue ocean. He gave his son another smile, but then his expression sobered.

"Seriously, Father," Benjamin said, responding to Albrecht's change of expression, "why did you want to see me this morning?"

"We just got confirmation that the Manties' survey expedition got to Verdant Vista six weeks ago," his father replied, and Benjamin grimaced.

"We knew it was going to happen eventually, Father," he pointed out.

"Agreed. Unfortunately, that doesn't make me any happier now that it's gone ahead and actually happened." Albrecht smiled sourly. "And the fact that the Manties ultimately decided to let Kare head the team makes me even less happy than I might have been otherwise."

"One could have hoped that the fact that the Manties and the Havenites are shooting at each other again would have made them a little less likely to cooperate on something like this," Benjamin acknowledged dryly.

"Fair's fair—" Albrecht began, then paused and looked up with a smile as Stabolis returned to the office with the promised bottles of beer. Father and son each accepted one of them, and Stabolis raised an eyebrow at Albrecht.

"Go ahead and stay, Heinrich," the senior Detweiler replied in answer to the unspoken question. "By this time, you already know ninety-nine percent of all my deepest darkest secrets. This one isn't going to make any difference."

"Yes, Sir."

Stabolis settled into his usual on-duty position in the chair beside the office door, and Albrecht turned back to Benjamin.

"As I was saying, fair's fair. They aren't really *cooperating*, you know. They've just agreed to refrain from breaking each other's kneecaps where Verdant Vista is concerned, and we both know why that is."

"They do tend to hold their little grudges where Manpower is concerned, don't they?" Benjamin remarked whimsically.

"Yes, they do," Albrecht agreed. "And that pain in the ass Hauptman isn't making things any better."

"Father, Klaus Hauptman's been pissing you off for as long as I can remember. Why don't you just go ahead and have Collin and Isabel get rid of him? I know his security's good, but it's not *that* good, you know."

"I've considered it—believe me, I've considered it more than once!" Albrecht shook his head. "One reason I haven't gone ahead and done it is that I decided a long time ago that I'd better try not to get into the habit of having people assassinated just because it might ease my blood pressure. Given the number of unmitigated pains in the ass there are, I'd keep Isabel employed full time, and it would still be a case of weeding the tomato patch. However many weeds you get rid of this week, there's going to be a fresh batch next week. Besides, I've always felt restraint builds character."

"Maybe so, but I figure there has to be more to it than self-discipline were Hauptman is concerned." Benjamin snorted. "Mind you, I agree about the asshole quotient of the galaxy, but he's one asshole who's demonstrated often enough that he can cause us a lot of grief. And he's been so openly opposed to Manpower for so long that having him taken out in an obviously 'Manpower'-backed operation couldn't possibly point any suspicion in our direction."

"You've got a point," Albrecht agreed more seriously. "Actually, I did very seriously consider having him assassinated when he came out so strongly in support of those Ballroom lunatics in Verdant Vista. Unfortunately, getting rid of him would only leave us with his daughter Stacey, and she's just as bad as he is already. If 'Manpower' went ahead and whacked her daddy, she'd be even worse. In fact, I suspect she'd probably move making problems for us up from number three or four on her 'Things to Do' list to number one. An *emphatic* number one. And given the fact that she'd control sixty-two percent of the Hauptman cartel's voting stock outright, once she inherited her father's shares, the problems she could make for us would be pretty spectacular. This survey business and those frigates they've been building for the Ballroom wouldn't be a drop in the bucket compared to what she'd do then."

"So take them both out at once," Benjamin suggested. "I'm sure Isabel could handle it, if she put her mind to it. And she's Hauptman's only kid, *and* she doesn't have any children of her own yet, which only leaves some fairly distant cousins as potential heirs. I doubt that all of them share the depths of her and her father's anti-slavery prejudices. And even if they did, I imagine that spreading her stock around to so many people who'd all have legitimately different agendas of their own would end up with the family control of the cartel finding itself severely diluted."

"No," Albrecht said sourly, "it wouldn't."

"It wouldn't?" Benjamin's surprise showed.

"Oh, having both of them killed would dilute the *Hauptman* family's control, that's for sure. Unfortunately, it would only hand that selfsame control over to another family we have reason to be less than fond of."

"I'm afraid you've lost me," Benjamin admitted.

"That's because Collin just turned up something you don't know about yet. It would appear our good friend Klaus and his daughter Stacey don't want to see their opposition to Manpower falter just because of a little thing like their own mortality. Collin got a look at the provisions of their wills a few T-months ago. Daddy left everything to his sweet little baby girl, pretty much the way we'd figured he had . . . but if it should happen that she predeceases him or subsequently dies without issue of her own, *she's* left every single share of her and her father's ownership percentage—and voting stock—to a little outfit called Skydomes of Grayson."

"You're joking!" Benjamin stared at his father in disbelief, and Albrecht snorted without any amusement at all.

"Believe me, I wish I were."

"But Hauptman and Harrington hate each others' guts," Benjamin protested.

"Not so much anymore," Albrecht disagreed. "Oh, everything we've seen suggests that he and Harrington still don't really *like* each other all that much, but they've got an awful lot of interests in common. Worse, he knows from direct, painful personal experience she can't be bought, bluffed, or intimidated worth a damn. And, worse still, the daughter he dotes on is one of Harrington's close personal friends. Given the fact that he won't be around anymore for Harrington to irritate, and given the fact that he knows she's already using Skydomes' clout to back the ASL almost as strongly as he is, he's perfectly happy with the thought of letting her beat on Manpower with his money, too, when he's gone. Which"—he grimaced—"makes me wish even more that our little October surprise on her flagship had been a bit more successful. If we'd managed to kill her, I'm sure Klaus and Stacey would have at least reconsidered who they want to leave all of this to."

"Damn," Benjamin said thoughtfully, then shook his head. "If Hauptman and Skydomes get together, Harrington would have control of—what? The third or fourth biggest single individually controlled financial bloc in the galaxy?"

"Not quite. She'd be the single biggest financial player in the Haven Quadrant, by a huge margin, but she probably wouldn't be any higher than, oh, the top twenty, galaxy wide. On the other hand, as you just pointed out yourself, unlike any of the people who'd be wealthier than she'd be, she'd have direct *personal* control of everything. No need to worry about boards of directors or any of that crap."

"Damn!" Benjamin repeated with considerably more force. "How come this is the first I'm hearing about this?"

"Like I said, Collin only found out about it a few T-months ago. It's not like Hauptman or his daughter have exactly trumpeted it from the rooftops, you know. For that matter, as far as Collin can tell, *Harrington* doesn't know about it. We only found out because Collin's been devoting even more of his resources to Hauptman since his active support for Verdant Vista became so evident. It's taken him a while, but he finally managed to get someone inside Childers, Strauslund, Goldman, and Wu. Clarice Childers personally drew up both Hauptmans' wills, and it looks very much as if they decided not to tell even Harrington about it." Albrecht shrugged. "Given the sort of tectonic impact the prospect of what would be effectively a merger of the Hauptman Cartel and Skydomes would have on the entire quadrant's financial markets, I can see where they'd want to keep it quiet."

"And Harrington would probably try to talk them out of it if she did know about it," Benjamin mused.

"Probably." Albrecht showed his teeth for a moment. "I'd love to see all three of them dead, you understand, but let's be honest. The real reason I'd take so much pleasure from putting them out of my misery is that all three of them are so damned effective. And however much I may hate Harrington's guts—not to mention her entire family back on Beowulf—I'm not going to underestimate her. Aside from being harder to kill than an Old Earth cockroach, she's got this incredibly irritating habit of accomplishing exactly what she sets out to do. And while she may not be as rich as Hauptman is, she's already well past the point where money as money really means anything to her. From everything we've been able to find out, she takes her responsibilities as Skydomes' CEO seriously, but she's perfectly satisfied running it through trusted assistants, so it's not as if she'd be interested in adding Hauptman to Skydomes as an exercise in empire building, either. In fact, I sometimes think she's at least partly of the opinion that what she's got already represents too much concentrated power in the hands of a single private individual. Combining Hauptman with Skydomes would create an entirely new balance of economic power—not just in the Star Kingdom, either—and I don't see her wanting to stick her family with that kind of power."

"So he's planning on sneaking up on her with it and trusting her sense of duty to take it in the end?"

"I think that's what's going on, but I think it's really *Stacey* Hauptman who's doing the 'sneaking up' in this case," Albrecht said.

"Either way, it's a fairly unpalatable prospect," Benjamin observed.

"I don't think it's going to make the situation fundamentally worse," Albrecht replied. "It's not going to make it any *better*, but I don't expect it to have any sort of catastrophic consequences . . . even assuming Hauptman shuffles off before we pull the trigger on Prometheus."

Benjamin's expression turned very, very sober at his father's last seven words. "Prometheus" was the codename assigned to the Mesan Alignment's long awaited general offensive. Very few people had ever heard the designation; of those who had, only a handful realized how far into the final endgame of its centuries-long preparations the Alignment actually was.

"In the meantime," his father continued more briskly, "and

getting back to my original complaint, we've got to decide what we're going to do about Kare and his busybodies. It's not going to take them very long to complete their survey of the terminus. They're going to figure out that something's peculiar about it as soon as they do, and we really don't need them making transit and finding out where it goes."

"Agreed." Benjamin nodded, but his expression was calm. "On the other hand, we've already made our preparations. As you just pointed out, somebody like Kare's going to realize he's looking at something out of the ordinary as soon as he gets a detailed analysis. I doubt he's going to have any idea just *how* peculiar it is before they make transit, though, and once they *do* make transit, they're not going to be in a position to tell anyone about it. I agree with Collin, Daniel, and Isabel, Father. The survivors are going to conclude that whatever it is that makes this terminus peculiar is going to require a much more cautious—and time-consuming—approach before they try any *second* transit."

"I agree that's the most overwhelmingly likely outcome," Albrecht conceded. " 'Likely' isn't the same thing as 'certain,' however. And, to be honest, I expect someone like Hauptman to take his initial failure as a personal affront and push even harder."

"The only way to positively prevent that would be to take the star system back," Benjamin pointed out.

"Which we're already planning to do . . . eventually," his father pointed out in return, and Benjamin nodded again.

"Should I assume you want me to be thinking in terms of bringing that operation forward?" he asked.

"I'm not sure I want it brought forward yet," Albrecht said. "What I do want, though, is to make sure we don't fritter away our cover assets. Losing *Anhur* that way in Talbott last year was just plain stupid. And we're lucky that idiot Clignet and his 'journal' didn't hurt us any worse."

Benjamin nodded again. Commodore Henri Clignet's ex-State Security heavy cruiser *Anhur* had been captured with all hands—or, at least, all *surviving* hands—in the Talbott Cluster the next best thing to six T-months before. Benjamin wasn't going to shed any tears for Clinget and his fanatic cutthroats. In fact, he'd always considered the commodore one of the loosest of the loose war-heads among the ex-SS personnel Manpower had recruited. On the other hand, he was also aware that his personal dislike for the entire strand of the Alignment's strategy they'd been recruited to support might help to account for his less than hugely enthusiastic view of Clinget and his fellows.

"At least he didn't know who's actually pulling the strings where he and the others are concerned," he pointed out. "All he could really confirm is that Manpower's provided a home for several of the Peeps' waifs."

"True, but he confirmed that not just to the Manties but for Haven, as well." Albrecht shook his head with a smile of rueful, irritated respect. "Who would've thought the Manties would hand him and his entire crew back to Haven in the middle of a shooting war?"

"I wouldn't have," Benjamin admitted. "On the other hand, it was a damned smart move on their part. It left Haven with the responsibility of trying and executing them, which 'just happened' to wash so much of the People's Republic's dirty linen very much in public. And Pritchart and Theisman actually had to *thank* them for it." It was his turn to shake his head. "Talk about a win-win solution for the Manties!"

"Agreed. But it looks to us like neither the Manties nor the Peeps have any clear picture of exactly how many Clingets 'Manpower's' managed to get its hands on. So I think it's time for us to arrange a little discreet reinforcement for them. And I want to get Luff and all the rest of his 'People's Navy in Exile' pulled in where no one's going to be stumbling over any more of them."

"I'm not sure that's the best idea," Benjamin said, his tone thoughtful. "At the moment, Clinget's basically demonstrated that he and his friends have become pretty much garden-variety pirates who're simply being subsidized by Manpower. Everybody knows about the relationship now, but nobody's got any reason to expect that they're being recruited for a specific mission. For that matter, *they* don't know that, when you come right down to it. As far as they know, they are just doing what they have to do to survive, and they aren't looking more than a few months into the future at any given moment. They *aren't* going to be doing that until we offer them our little . . . inducement for Operation Ferret, either."

"And your point is?" Albrecht's question could have been irritated, angry, but it was merely curious, and Benjamin shrugged.

"I know we've planned all along on reinforcing Luff, but I've never been comfortable with the notion—not entirely. It's one thing for an 'outlaw transstellar' like Manpower to be subsidizing ships which more or less just fell into its lap; it's another thing entirely for that same 'outlaw transstellar' to be supplying those pirates with newer, more powerful ships. That's my first concern. The second one is that pulling them in from their independent operations is going to be an escalation. They're going to know that we—or Manpower, at least—really have something significant in mind for them to do. Some of them aren't all that tightly wrapped, as Clinget demonstrated. They may not like the idea of Ferret, and they may try to wiggle out of having anything to do with it. At least some of them are probably going to be opposed to the notion of attacking Verdant Vista, too. Collin and I both pointed out that possibility when the idea first came up, you know. Even the *People's* Republic of Haven took its opposition to the slave trade seriously, and some of these people are likely to do the same thing.

"And, finally, sooner or later, exactly how they prepped for any attack on Verdant Vista is going to come out. Somebody's going to be captured somewhere else and talk, or they're just going to drop a hint in the wrong place and it's going to get back to Manty or Havenite intelligence. And when that happens, people are going to start wondering, first, just how Manpower came up with the 'reinforcements,' and, secondly, why Manpower was willing to put a bunch like Luff's People's Navy in Exile 'on retainer'—and pay them well enough to keep them there—for however long it takes."

"Agreed. Agreed to all of it." Albrecht nodded. "On the other hand, if we actually mount the operation, then probably by the time anybody on the other side starts putting two and two together, they'll have other things to worry about. Don't forget that little surprise we're putting together for Manticore out in Monica right this minute. In other words, I'd say the chances are considerably better than even that 'Manpower's' relationship with this particular batch of 'pirates' isn't going to be of any great burning significance after the fact.

"Second, this wormhole survey expedition has me worried. If we wipe out the people mounting it, and turn the system into someplace that no longer has any habitable real estate, we should also reduce interest in a 'killer' wormhole that no longer goes anywhere interesting, anyway. Not to mention getting Jeremy X and his merry band of lunatics on Torch out of Manpower's hair—and ours—as permanently as possible. And clearing the way for us to reassert sovereignty—after a decent interval, of course—over the system for ourselves.

"Third, one way or the other, within the next few months, it's going to start becoming evident that the Monican Navy ended up coming into possession of over a dozen Solarian battlecruisers, courtesy of Manpower, Technodyne, and the Jessyk Combine. That being the case, I doubt anyone's going to be all that surprised if it turns out that we had—I'm sorry, that *Manpower* had—a handful of additional battlecruisers lying around and handed them over to a bunch of 'pirates' it could be pretty sure would use them against Manty interests somewhere else, maybe a little closer to home.

"And, fourth, if we keep them somewhere handy, where we can keep an eye on them and they aren't going to be flailing around the spaceways making potential problems for us, we remove at least one distracting element from the equation. And if it happens we decide never to mount the operation at all, then we simply detonate those little suicide charges none of them realize 'Manpower's' put aboard their vessels. They all blow up simultaneously in a star system where nobody else is going to know anything about it, and our potential security problem goes away. For that matter, I've been increasingly inclined ever since Clinget's journals surfaced to go with Wooden Horse anyway, if we do mount the operation."

Benjamin pursed his lips thoughtfully. The chance of any of their ex-StateSec puppets ever discovering the suicide charges which had been built into each of their ships during routine maintenance overhauls ranged somewhere between ridiculously minute and zero. Personally, if he'd been aboard one of those ships, he would have been going over it with a fine-toothed comb, given all of the many sets of circumstances he could think of under which it would be convenient for "Manpower" if their mercenary pirates simply . . . went away, as his father had put it. The fact that people who'd been StateSec officers didn't seem to be even considering the possibility was only one more indication, in his opinion, of how far they'd fallen since Thomas Theisman's restoration of the Old Republic had turned them into interstellar orphans.

But, as his father had just pointed out, the fact that those charges were there was the underlying premise of Operation Wooden Horse. Once the 'StateSec renegades' had attacked Verdant Vista and carried out a flagrant violation of the Eridani Edict, every space navy's hand would be turned against them . . . including that of the small Mesan Space Navy. On the other hand, the problem might never arise if a single Mesan vessel with the activation codes for those suicide charges should just *happen* to arrive at their post-Verdant Vista rendezvous and transmit them while all those nasty genocidal StateSec fanatics were in range.

"Let me see if I've followed your devious thinking properly here, Father," he said after a moment. "You're thinking that we go ahead and mount Operation Ferret and use our reinforced StateSec refugees to take out Verdant Vista. They go ahead and blow out the defenders, then take out the planet itself. As soon as they've done that, we deliver their severance checks and all their ships blow up. The planet is so wrecked nobody in his right mind would ever want to live there again, so the only inherent value the system has any longer is the wormhole terminus, which has just been demonstrated to be exceedingly dangerous. At the same time, we take out a huge chunk of the Ballroom's organized support and bodyslam its morale—and that of the ASL in general—throughout the galaxy. And because nobody's going to have any interest on living on the planet, most of the galaxy probably won't be too surprised—or get too worked up—if *Mesa*, not Manpower, presses its claim to what's left. Most folks will probably figure that it's just Mesa trying to recoup a little of the humiliation it suffered after being thrown out in the first place."

"More or less," Albrecht agreed. "And even if it doesn't work out with Mesa regaining formal sovereignty over the star system, it should throw things into confusion long enough for *nobody* to have possession of it—or be mounting any more survey expeditions—before Prometheus rolls over them."

"Neat," Benjamin said, his eyes slightly unfocused as he considered permutations. "There *is* the little matter of the Eridani violation, though."

"We've talked about that before, Ben," Albrecht pointed out. "Either there's going to be evidence it was the StateSec renegades—who don't have a star nation anymore—or else there are going to be too few survivors, if any, to identify the attackers at all. In the first case, obviously Manpower's going to come in for the lion's share of suspicion, especially after Clinget's confirmation that it's been recruiting StateSec mercenaries. That could be . . . unpleasant, but Manpower is only a transstellar corporation, not a star nation, and nobody's going to be able to *prove* Manpower gave the order, anyway. That's going to create enough ambiguity and confusion for our 'friends' in the League to derail any effort to apply the edict's penalties against the *star nation* of Mesa. There may be demands that Manpower be punished *by* Mesa, but those can be obfuscated and delayed for however long we need them to be delayed. For that matter, the *Alignment* doesn't really care what happens to Manpower at this point, and once a full-scale Prometheus is launched, punishing 'Manpower' isn't going to be especially high on most people's agendas anyway. And then there's the fact that the only actual star nation directly associated with these people, ever, is going to have been the People's Republic of Haven. I suspect Mesa's best tactic is going to be to argue that those nasty planet-killing renegades were initially created and enabled by *Haven*, and that Theisman's failure in letting them escape with the *Havenite* warships in their possession is the real ultimate culprit in this whole tragic affair."

Father and son looked at one another for a moment, then Benjamin shrugged.

"All right, Father. I'm still not sure it's a wonderful idea, you understand, but you've managed to deal with most of my reservations. And, for that matter, you've got a pretty good track record for spotting and backing operations against 'targets of opportunity' most of the rest of us hadn't noticed. I think we can go ahead and start organizing things, even if it turns out we never launch Ferret at all. Like you say, getting all of them into the same place will make cleaning up easier if we decide to just write the entire notion off, too. Before we actually start handing them modern Solly battlecruisers, though, I'd like to get Collin and Isabel's input."

"By all means." Albrecht nodded vigorously. "I'm inclined to think this is something we *are* going to have to take care of substantially sooner than we'd thought we were, but I'm not prepared to start rushing in without thinking things through first. We've come too far and worked too hard for too long to start taking foolish, unnecessary chances at this late date."

CHAPTER SIXTEEN

Luiz Rozsak felt his mouth watering in anticipation as he cut through the pastry "jacket" into the juicy center of the nicely rare Beef Wellington. Mayan "beef" actually came from "maya-cows"—locally evolved critters that looked sort of like an undersized brontosaurus crossed with a llama. Unlike the Old Earth animal from whom it had taken its name (more or less) the mayacow was oviparous, and quite a few of the local population were partial to mayacow omelettes. Those had never really appealed to Rozsak, but he'd decided over the past several T-years that he actually preferred mayacow beef to Old Earth beef. There truly were enormous similarities, yet he'd discovered some delightful, subtle differences, as well. In fact, he'd invested a modestly hefty percentage of his own income in backing a commercial ranching venture on New Tasmania, Maya's smaller continent. Unlike a great deal of the planet, New Tasmania was tectonically stable, remarkably lacking in volcanoes, and blessed with huge expanses of open prairie. Even today, there was plenty of room for operations like the Bar-R to grow and expand, and Rozsak was already showing a tidy profit on the new markets he'd opened up in Erewhon.

He put the bite into his mouth, closed his eyes, and chewed slowly, with a self-satisfied pleasure he didn't even try to hide from his dinner companion.

"This is delicious, Luiz," Oravil Barregos said from his side of the small dining table.

The two of them were seated in Rozsak's kitchen. Very few people realized that cooking was one of Rozsak's favored hobbies, and he

159

suspected that even fewer would have realized (or believed) that stern, driven, hugely ambitious Sector Governor Barregos actually enjoyed sitting down to an informal dinner, where he and his host served their own plates and poured their own wine, without hordes of servants hovering somewhere in the background. Or, at least, without hordes of supplicants plying him with food and wine in an effort to worm their way into his confidence.

"I think the asparagus might be just a little overcooked," Rozsak replied self-critically.

"You always think something's 'a little' something," Barregos retorted with a smile. "I don't think you've ever actually served me exactly the same dish twice; you keep fiddling with it so that there's always something different about it."

"Perfect culinary consistency is a bugaboo of small minds," Rozsak told him loftily. "And a bold spirit of experimentation shouldn't prevent a true chef from recognizing where his efforts fall short—*marginally*, mind you, only marginally—of his expectations."

"Oh, of course! And such monumental shortcomings, at that. Last time, if I remember correctly, the guacamole was a bit too thin to be perfectly satisfying."

"No," Rozsak corrected with a smile of his own. "That was time before last. *Last* time it was the Sauce Châteaubriand."

"Oh, forgive my faulty memory!" Barregos rolled his eyes. "How *could* I have forgotten? Something about the local shallots not measuring up, wasn't it?"

"Actually, it was my decision to experiment with that strain of shallots which has evolved on *Erewhon*." Rozsak's artful professorial manner would have fooled most people, since most people wouldn't have been able to recognize the gleam of humor in his dark eyes. "It *should* have worked," he continued, "but there was a degree of acidity I hadn't counted on. Oh, the meal was *satisfactory*, of course. Don't misunderstand me. Still—"

"Given the fact that you're the only person I know who makes Châteaubriand at all, and that your degree of fanaticism in the kitchen can be truly terrifying, I'm amazed to hear you saying something like that," Barregos interrupted. "'The meal was *satisfactory*'? You mean *you're* willing to *admit* that? Dear Lord, the end of the universe is at hand!"

Both of them chuckled, and the governor shook his head. It always amused him that Rozsak, supremely confident in so many ways, was never truly satisfied with his own culinary efforts. He truly was constantly experimenting, tweaking, tinkering with ingredients, and he was far and away his own sternest critic.

Of course, he doesn't have a lot of other potential critics, does he? Barregos thought. *It's not a side of him he shares with a lot of people, after all. I wonder why he keeps it so private? Because it's the one real escape he allows himself and sharing it would make it less of an escape somehow? Because the domesticity of it would be so at odds with his hard-as-nails, tough-minded, cynical admiral public persona?*

"Well," Rozsak said, almost as if he'd just read his guest's mind, as he reached for his wine glass, "given the way things are heating up, I've discovered that I need to relax in the kitchen just a bit more than I used to."

"If one of the side effects is producing meals like this," Barregos replied, keeping his tone light as he reached for his own wine, "maybe it's a pity I haven't kept you under more pressure all along."

"Oh, I think you've managed quite nicely in that respect," Rozsak reassured him, and the two of them snorted almost simultaneously.

"Speaking of Erewhonese vegetables—"

"Roots, Governor. *Roots,*" Rozsak corrected. "Like onions."

"Speaking of Erewhonese *plant life,*" Barregos said with a stern look, "how are our other Erewhonese ventures coming?"

"On the financial side, you really need to discuss that with Donald and Brent," Rozsak said rather more seriously. "My impression is that so far we've had enough cash to cover everything."

An arched eyebrow and rising inflection turned the last sentence into a question, and Barregos nodded.

"There's actually turned out to be even more cash in the till than I'd expected," he replied. "I don't think we can siphon any more out of our official budget without risking questions from Permanent Senior Undersecretary Wodoslawski's minions at Treasury, but it's rather impressive how much some of the transstellars' local management has been willing to kick into my 'discretionary fund' for those 'subscription ships' of yours. And even better, Donald's managed to arrange things so that a good seventy percent of our total costs look like—and are, for that matter—good, sound investment opportunities." He shrugged.

"We're still racking up a pretty impressive debt, but Donald and Brent are both confident we'll be able to service the interest and pay down the Sector's own public debt within no more than five to ten T-years."

"I'm glad to hear it." Rozsak cut another morsel of beef and chewed it slowly, then swallowed.

"I'm glad to hear it," he repeated, "but unless I'm pretty badly mistaken, our expenditure curve is about to start climbing steeply. Chapman and Horton are ready to start laying down their first locally designed SD(P)s. Which means, of course, that we're about ready to start doing the same thing. Discreetly, of course."

"Oh, of course," Barregos agreed. He smiled tightly. "The first half dozen of those were factored into the numbers Donald and Brent discussed with me last week, though."

"They were?" Rozsak sounded surprised, and the governor chuckled.

"Actually, we ended up owning a considerably larger chunk of Al Carlucci's new shipbuilding capacity than we'd anticipated." Barregos' chuckle segued into a grimace. "Having Pritchart and Elizabeth go back to shooting at each other hasn't helped the local economy. It probably wouldn't have helped things anyway, but I don't suppose anyone in Erewhon was really surprised when Manticore hammered them with that increase in transit fees." He snorted. "Actually, I'd imagine that if anyone in Maytag was surprised by anything it's that Manticore didn't smack them on the wrist even harder."

"A seven hundred and fify percent increase in Junction transit fees, a seventy-five percent duty on any Erewhonese product in the Star Kingdom, and a seventy percent capital gains tax on any Erewhonese investment in Manticore strikes me as a pretty substantial 'smack,'" Rozsak pointed out dryly. "Especially given the fact that Manticore's been Erewhon's biggest single trading partner for decades."

"Agreed." Barregos nodded. "And it's hammered the hell out of the Erewhonese economy, too. Produced its own little system-wide recession, as a matter of fact. On the other hand, I think even Imbesi would be prepared to admit that some sort of Manty retaliation for all the technology that got handed over to Haven was in order, and it could have been a hell of a lot worse. Of course, they've managed to pick up at least some of their losses from increased trade with *Haven*, but they're suddenly on the other end of the tech imbalance, which is kicking up more than a few problems while their industrial sector tries to retool and adjust. Not to mention the fact that they aren't any too fond of Haven at the moment, either, given who actually fired the first shot that landed them in their current mess.

"At any rate, right now, and not wanting to wish any additional unhappiness on our newfound friends in Maytag, it's offering us quite a few interesting opportunities we probably wouldn't have had otherwise. Among other things, CIG ended up needing a lot more capital investment from our side to get it up and running. That's why we floated that new bond issue back on Old Earth, which is also one of the reasons *we're* in better economic shape—and in a much better strategic position in Erewhon—at this point than we'd expected to be. Financially, the fact that the Sector was already so heavily invested in Erewhon gave us plenty of cover when the resumption of hostilities meant we had to raise additional capital from sources outside our immediate area. And Treasury was perfectly willing to sign off on the bonds—for the bureaucrats' usual cut, of course."

He smiled evilly, and Rozsak raised both eyebrows in silent question.

"Well," Barregos told him cheerfully, "those same bureaucrats back on Old Earth insisted—positively *insisted*—that the bond issue in question be underwritten directly by the Treasury instead of the Sector administration. I think it had something to do with . . . bookkeeping issues."

Rozsak snorted harshly in amused understanding. He wasn't at all surprised that the Treasury Department personnel in question wanted to handle the accounting as much in-house as possible, since it was so much easier to cook their own books (and hide their inevitable peculation) than it was to skim off of someone else's cash flow without detection. But that was merely the Solarian League's basic SOP, and he was still a bit puzzled by the governor's obvious amusement.

"And having *them* do the bookkeeping helps us exactly how?" the admiral asked after a moment. "Obviously it does, somehow, but I would've thought that having their fingers directly in the pie would be more likely to sound alarms at their end as we get further down the road."

"As long as the graft keeps rolling in, they aren't going to care what we're really doing with the money at this end," Barregos pointed out. "That's a given, and it's been part of our strategy from the very beginning. But what else it does for us is to make the debt a charge on the *Solarian League*, not the Maya Sector, and it never occurred to me or Donald that we might be able to get away with *that!*"

"And?" Rozsak asked.

"*And*, Luiz, if the day should ever come—perish the thought—when we good, loyal Solarians out here in the Sector should find ourselves in less than full accord with Frontier Security HQ or the Interior Department in general, *we* won't be the ones responsible for paying the bondholders off. As far as *we're* concerned, all that dreadful debt—close to sixty percent of our total investment in CIG, will be owed to Solarian citizens, not anyone out here. And the obligation to pay *off* those bonds, Donald tells me, will *also* belong to the League Treasury. Which means that as far as we're concerned it will just . . . go away. *Poof.*"

He smiled beatifically, and despite his own monumental aplomb and self-control, Rozsak's jaw actually dropped a half-centimeter or so.

"And," Barregos continued even more cheerfully, "I've just had a memo from one of Wodoslawski's senior aides. He wants to know if it would be possible to interest the Erewhonese directly in floating additional bond issues in the League to support their military expansion. It seems reports about Erewhon's concern—its worry about finding itself caught between its old allies and its new ones if things go really sour—has inspired certain individuals back on Old Earth to be thinking in terms of combining personal opportunity with foreign policy objectives. According to the memo, Treasury and State would like to acquire a bigger financial stake in Erewhon as a means of gaining additional leverage with the Republic down the road."

"Damn," Rozsak said mildly, and shook his head. "Those poor bastards. They don't even have a clue, do they?" Then he snorted. "Talk about history repeating! The whole thing reminds me of what Lenin had to say about capitalists selling rope to the proletariat!"

"I don't know about that," Barregos replied. "Frankly, you're a lot better student of pre-space Old Earth history than I am. If he meant those idiots in Old Chicago are stupid enough to be paying for the pulser darts likely to be coming their own way, though, yes. I'd say it does sort of . . . resonate."

"You know," Rozsak said thoughtfully, "I can't say I was especially delighted when the Manties and the Havenites started shooting at each other again. To be honest, it seemed likely to make a lot of problems for us. Oh, I figured there'd be opportunities in it, too, of course, but I was more worried about the probable economic dislocation and what might happen if Erewhon got sucked into the fighting and took our investment plans with it."

"That," Barregos conceded, "would really and truly have sucked from our perspective."

"Tell me about it!" Rozsak snorted. "Instead, it's worked out so much in our favor that I'm starting to wait nervously for whatever *bad* news the karma department is waiting to hit us with by way of compensation."

Barregos nodded. The Republic of Erewhon had been both surprised and more than mildly irritated by the Republic of Haven's decision to resume hostilities against the Star Kingdom of Manticore less than a T-month after Berry Zilwicki's coronation on Torch. In fact, Erewhon had been downright pissed off about it. There'd been just time enough for Maytag and Nouveau Paris to ratify the brand-new self-defense treaty between their two republics before the shooting started up all over again, and despite how severely pissed off the Erewhonese had been with the High Ridge Government, it hadn't cared at all for the position in which Eloise Pritchart's decision had placed it.

It was fortunate that the new treaty was *defensive* in nature, since, in light of the fact that Haven was clearly the aggressor this time around, that had at least obviated any requirement for Erewhon to sign on for active operations against its erstwhile fellow members of the Manticoran Alliance. On the other hand, as the Star Kingdom's new economic policies had made painfully evident to Erewhon, Manticore was less than totally pleased by the technology transfers which had been part of the Erewhon-Haven agreements. Personally, Barregos felt confident that the real reason Manticore hadn't been even less delighted (not to mention inclined to punish Erewhon even more harshly) was that the Manties were unhappily aware that Haven had probably captured enough even-more-modern Manty military technology in the course of Operation Thunderbolt to give the Republican Navy at least as much of a leg up as anything Erewhon could have handed over. It might have taken Shannon Foraker and Haven's revitalized R&D establishment longer to capitalize on what they'd captured without the starting point Erewhon had given them, but Foraker was dismayingly competent from Manticore's perspective. She'd have gotten there in the end on her own, eventually, and the Manties knew it.

And, he reflected respectfully, *Elizabeth Winton is smart enough not to forget that there's always a tomorrow. I'm sure she's pissed off as hell at Erewhon right now, but she also knows how much her own damned prime minister had to do with creating the new situation. And she's pragmatic enough to roll with the punch of Erewhon's tech transfers as long as Erewhon goes on refusing to participate in military operations against the Alliance. She doesn't want to do anything that's going to inflict irreparable damage on the possibility of* future *relations between the Star Kingdom and Erewhon.*

"It *has* offered us an even better opportunity to firm up our own relationship with Erewhon than I expected," he said out loud. "Completely irrespective of how it's helped our funding drives back on Old Earth."

"I'm afraid I'm a bit more focused on the hardware side of things," Rozsak said. "Having Manticore and Haven shooting at each other again's given Admiral Chapman and Glenn Horton the perfect pretext for expanding their wall of battle just as fast—and as much—as they possibly can. Which, of course, is going to expand our own strength right along with theirs. And, frankly, I'm more than a little impressed with some of the tech transfers flowing the other way. Foraker and her crew have obviously been working hard on catching up with the Manties. And from what Greeley is saying over in the ESN's Office of Research and Development, combining that with the Solarian tech *we've* been quietly feeding him is opening up some interesting possibilities of its own."

"Really?" Barregos looked thoughtful. "I hadn't thought about that possibility," he admitted after a moment, then shrugged. "I suppose I've been so well aware of how the Manties have been pushing the envelope that it didn't occur to me that the League might have anything significant to offer Erewhon."

"I'm not sure the League *would* have 'anything significant' to offer *Manticore*." Rozsak grimaced. "Even now, and even while I'm fully aware of how much that particular fact is likely to be working in our own favor in the not-too-distant future, I'm still a little pissed off—well, *irritated*, at least—by the thought that the Manties are so far out in front of the SLN. It's downright humiliating. Almost as humiliating as the realization that no one back on Old Earth seems to have the tiniest sliver of an awareness of just how bad things really are from their perspective. I'd like to think that someone in the Navy somewhere has at least the IQ of a gerbil!

"But Erewhon isn't Manticore," he continued. "The Erewhonese's tech base isn't nearly as advanced as the Manties' is, and I'd estimate that they're at least a generation or two behind the Manties' deployed hardware. How far behind the Manties' *R&D* they are is something I'm not even prepared to guess about at this point, but there are a lot of ways in which Solarian tech is letting them downsize and improve on some of the stuff they're getting from *Foraker's* teams. And," he bared the tips of his teeth, "under the circumstances and given the way Haven surprised them, as well as the Manties, with Thunderbolt, neither Greeley nor Chapman seems to feel any great need to fall all over themselves passing on their own improvements to Haven."

"I'm not really surprised to hear that," Barregos said.

"No, I'm not either," Rozsak agreed. Then he frowned.

"What?" Barregos asked, and the admiral shrugged.

"I've just been thinking about the other opportunities—and risks—involved in our current complicated little political calculus out this way. Admittedly, so far it's working out in our favor—in ways I never would have anticipated, as well as the ones we'd figured on all along. But the downside of it is, first, that despite everyone's best efforts, the fighting could spill over onto Erewhon after all, which wouldn't exactly come under the heading of a good thing from our perspective. And, second, that with Manticore and Haven so busy shooting at each other, we're right back to where we were when it comes to dealing with any little interstellar situations that crop up in our neighborhood."

"Such as?" Barregos gave him a quizzical look. "I mean, I'm certainly not disagreeing with you, Luiz. God knows I trust your instincts! But from where I sit right this moment, it looks like any 'little interstellar situations' that come up are more likely to play into our hands than to create additional problems. After all, the more potential hot spots we can point to out here, the less likely anyone in Old Chicago is to get all hot and bothered about our 'readiness campaign.'"

"Oh, from that perspective, I agree entirely. *That's* a win-win situation from our viewpoint. And Edie, Jiri, and I don't have anything more solid in the way of worrying about potential 'blow-up-in-your-face' hot spots than what Brigadier Allfrey and Richard Wise are reporting. It's not that I have any *specific* worries in mind, Oravil."

Rozsak didn't use the governor's given name very often, even in private conversation, and Barregos' eyes narrowed slightly at the indication that his admiral's concerns were serious.

"It's just that we're still at a vulnerable stage," Rozsak continued. "We've got a dozen of the new destroyers, and a couple of the new light cruisers, in inventory now, but we're still well short of any *significant* increase in our overall combat power. And we're also at a point where we can't call on anyone else—except for additional Frontier Fleet units, which we both know is the *last* thing we want to do—if something comes along that we end up needing backup to handle. I know that's not likely to happen, but one of my jobs is worrying about *unlikely* things, and I don't like the feeling of being spread too thin to handle all of our obligations if something does fall in the crapper."

"I can appreciate that," Barregos said after a moment. "At the same time, as you say, there doesn't seem to be anything looming on the horizon."

"Well, that's the problem with horizons, isn't it?" Rozsak smiled crookedly. "You can never see what's on the other side of one until it comes at you."

CHAPTER SEVENTEEN

"Come in, Jack. It's good to see you again. Have a seat."

"Thank you. It's good to see you again, too," Jack McBryde said, mostly honestly, as he obeyed the polite command and settled into what he privately thought of as "the supplicant's chair" in front of the desk in the office reserved for Isabel Bardasano's use whenever she visited the Gamma Center.

Bardasano smiled at him with an edge of sardonic amusement, almost as if she'd read his thoughts. Fortunately, telepathy was something even the Long-Range Planning Board hadn't yet scheduled for inclusion into its carefully managed genomes, and he smiled back at her. He was one of the people who'd figured out long ago that showing fear—or even nervousness—in Bardasano's presence, however reasonable those emotions might be, could be disastrous. Her own insouciance, even in the face of Albrecht Detweiler's occasional temper tantrum, was famous (or infamous) among the uppermost echelons of the Mesan Alignment, and she would not tolerate weaklings among her own trusted subordinates.

McBryde ranked high among those subordinates. He wasn't quite in the very uppermost tier, because he hadn't gone operational off Mesa, or even held supervisory authority over any off-Mesa operation, in over a decade. On the other hand, he reported directly to her (whenever she was in-system, at any rate) in his position as the Gamma Center's chief of security, which was probably one of the half-dozen most sensitive of the Alignment's security services' posts.

Personally, he was happier running the center's security than he'd ever really been operating off-world, and he knew it. Unlike Bardasano, who actively enjoyed what was still referred to as "wet work," McBryde preferred a position in which he was unlikely to have to kill people.

"It's good to be back," Bardasano said now, then shrugged slightly. "On the other hand, I've been out of touch too long. I've got a lot of catching up to do."

"Yes, Ma'am. I can see how that would be."

In fact, McBryde was more than a little surprised Bardasano was in a position to do any "catching up." She'd been back on Mesa for less than forty-eight hours, but rumors of how spectacularly her operation in the Talbott Cluster seemed to have blown up in everyone's face were already rampant within the Alignment hierarchy. The truth was that if anyone had asked him, this time around, and despite her impressive record of past achievements, he would have placed his own bet *against* her retaining her position as Collin Detweiler's immediate subordinate. For that matter, he wasn't sure he wouldn't have bet against her even surviving, given the apparent magnitude of the debacle.

Which would have been pretty stupid of me, now that I think about it, he admitted to himself. *Whatever else may be true about Albrecht and Collin, they don't throw away talent without a damned good reason. And while* this *operation may have gone south on her, her overall track record really is almost scary.*

"I've already viewed your reports on the Gamma Center," she continued, and gave him a less amused and more approving smile. "My initial impression is that everything seems to have gone just a bit more . . . smoothly here at home than it did in Monica."

"That, ah, was my impression, too, Ma'am, if you'll pardon my saying so."

"Oh, I'll pardon it." She snorted. "As far as we can tell so far, it was just one of those fluke things that pop up and bite field ops on the ass sometimes, no matter how carefully you prep ahead of time. But I've got to admit I hate investing that much time in an operation that comes apart quite as thoroughly as this one did." She shrugged. "On the other hand, sometimes shit just happens."

McBryde nodded, and he had to admit she'd always borne that same point in mind where others were concerned. If you screwed up because you were stupid, or failed to execute your part of an op—on time and as planned—because of something *you* did, she would very quickly make you wish you'd never been born. And in her public persona as Jessyk Combine's senior "wet work" specialist, she had deliberately cultivated a "mad dog" mentality where the operatives who had no clue they were working for the Alignment were concerned. That bloodthirstiness and obvious belief in the motivating power of terror were both significant parts of her cover, and the failures she eliminated to "encourage the others" were a completely expendable, easily replaced resource.

Still, there was an undeniably . . . vicious edge to her personality, one which enjoyed devising inventive punishments, even for Alignment Security personnel who screwed up too egregiously. But what very few people outside Security's upper echelons grasped was that it was an edge she had firmly under control. And he was willing to acknowledge that the fact that that edge existed—and was generally known among her subordinates—was an extraordinarily effective efficiency motivator.

"I don't think we're going to find any significant problems or necessary adjustments to your procedures," Bardasano continued. "There are a *couple* of things we may want to tweak a bit, because—just between the two of us, and despite what just happened in the Talbott Cluster—we're getting closer to Prometheus."

Her eyes, he discovered, were watching him very intently as she dropped the last sentence on him, and he felt himself stiffening. Only partly because of her suddenly closer scrutiny, too. Jack McBryde was one of the people who knew a great deal—almost everything, he suspected—about exactly what "Prometheus" implied, yet nothing had suggested to him that the culmination the entire Alignment had worked towards literally for centuries was as imminent as Bardasano seemed to be suggesting.

"We are?"

He made the question come out levelly, despite the undeniable, abrupt flutter of his pulse, and saw a flicker of approval in those intent eyes. Had she been deliberately probing to test his reaction to the news?

"We are," she confirmed. "In fact, my personal opinion is that we may well be closer to Prometheus than even Albrecht realizes at this point." Despite himself, this time McBryde's eyes widened, and she shrugged again. "I'm not talking about doing anything to jog his elbow, Jack! I'm simply saying my read is that events are accelerating—in some ways, along lines we hadn't even guessed might present themselves during our preliminary planning. You know we've always anticipated at least some of that."

"Yes, Ma'am," he agreed.

"From *your* perspective," she went on, "I think the most important implications are that it's going to become even more important that the Gamma Center completes its various projects on time. I know!" She waved one hand as McBryde stirred and began to open his mouth. "R and D isn't something that can be completed to a set schedule on demand. And even if it were, that's not your end of the Center's responsibilities. But what I'm going to need out of you is special attention to keeping those projects moving. Obviously, we need to go right on maintaining the highest possible levels of security, but at the same time, we have to be particularly aware of the need to avoid letting our security concerns get in the way of moving the various programs ahead."

"I see." He nodded in understanding.

"I know you've always tried to do that anyway," Bardasano said. "I imagine having Zachariah as a sounding board hasn't hurt in that respect, and I'm specifically authorizing you to go on doing that. I know the Gamma Center programs are only part of his responsibilities and that he's not directly involved in the nuts and bolts on any of them. Try to keep him in the loop anyway, though. Use him as a conduit to the research directors—a way for them to 'unofficially' vent about any problems to someone they know can play advocate for them with the big, nasty ogre in charge of all the security restrictions getting in their way."

"Yes, Ma'am." McBryde grinned crookedly. "I'm sure Zack will be just delighted to have even more of them crying in his ear, but he'll do it if I ask him to."

"Useful things, siblings. Sometimes I wish I had one or two." Bardasano might have sounded just a little wistful, although McBryde wouldn't have cared to wager any significant sum on the possibility.

"In the meantime," she continued, her tone shifting to something considerably more somber, "I think we have one particular problem I'm going to need you to spend some additional effort on."

"Problem, Ma'am?"

"Herlander Simões," she said, and he grimaced. She saw his expression and nodded.

"I know he's been under a lot of strain, Ma'am," he began, "but, so far, he's been holding up his end of his project, and—"

"Jack, I'm not criticizing his performance *so far*. And I'm certainly not criticizing the way you've handled him so far, either. But he's deeply involved in the entire streak drive improvement program, and that's one of our critical research areas. For that matter, he's got peripheral involvement in at least two other projects. I think, under the circumstances, it's probably appropriate for us to show a little additional concern in his case."

McBryde nodded.

"Tell me more about how *you* think this is affecting him," she invited, tipping back in her chair. "I've already read half a dozen psych analyses on him, and I've discussed his reactions—and his attitude—with Dr. Fabre. The people writing those analyses aren't in charge of directly supervising his performance, though. I know you're not either—not in the sense of being his direct superior—but I want your evaluation from a pragmatic viewpoint."

"Yes, Ma'am."

McBryde inhaled deeply and took a few moments to organize his thoughts. Bardasano's penchant for demanding operational evaluations on the fly was well known. She'd always believed that what she liked to call "snap quizzes" were the best way to get at what someone really thought, but she also believed in giving her unfortunate minions time to think before they started spewing less than completely considered responses.

"To begin with," he said finally, "I have to admit I never really knew Simões—either Simões—in any sort of social sense before all of this came up. For that matter, I still don't. My impression, though, is that the LRPB's decision to cull the girl really ripped him up inside."

My, he thought. *Isn't that a bloodless way to describe what that man has been going through? And isn't it just like those bastards over at the LRPB to have failed to consider all the unfortunate little social consequences of their decisions?*

Bardasano nodded, although her own expression didn't even flicker. Of course, she represented one of Long-Range Planning's *in vitro* lines, McBryde reminded himself, and one which had been culled more than once, itself. For that matter, at least one of her own immediate clones had been culled, and not until late adolescence, at that, if he remembered correctly. Still, while the culled Bardasano had been the next best thing to a genetic duplicate to Isabel (not quite; there'd been a few experimental differences, of course), it had scarcely been what the word "brother" or "sister" would have implied to a man like Jack McBryde. Like a lot—even the majority—of LRPB's *in vitro* children, she'd been tube-birthed and crèche-raised, not placed in a regular family environment or encouraged to form sibling bonds with her fellow clones. No one had ever officially told McBryde anything of the sort, but he strongly suspected that lack of encouragement represented a deliberate policy on the Board's part—a way to avoid the creation of potentially conflicting loyalties. So maybe this was simply too far outside her own experience for her to have more than a purely intellectual appreciation for Herlander Simões' anguish.

"I understand he tried to fight the decision," she said.

"Yes, Ma'am," McBryde confirmed, although "fight the decision" was a pitifully pale description of Simões' frantic resistance.

"There was never much chance he was going to get a reversal, though," he continued. "According to my information, the LRPB directors considered it a slam dunk, given the quality of life issues that reinforced the utilitarian ones."

Bardasano nodded again. Despite the qualifier on his own familiarity with the case, McBryde knew quite a lot about it. He knew Herlander Simões—and his wife, apparently—had lowered their emotional defenses when Francesca made it through the anticipated danger zone with flying colors. Which had only made the agony infinitely worse when the first symptoms appeared two years later.

Having them turn up on the very day of her birthday must have been like an extra kick in the heart, and as if that hadn't been enough, her condition had degenerated with astounding speed. On her birthday, there'd been no outward visible sign at all; within six T-months, the bright, lively child McBryde had seen in the Simões' security file imagery had disappeared. Within ten T-months, she'd completely withdrawn from the world about her. She'd been totally nonresponsive. She'd simply sat there, not even chewing food if someone put it into her mouth.

"I've read the reports on the girl's condition," Bardasano said dispassionately. "Frankly, I can't say the Board's decision surprises me."

"As I say, I don't think there was ever much chance of a reversal, either," McBryde agreed. "He didn't want to hear that, though. He kept pointing at the activity showing on the electroencephalograms, and he was absolutely convinced they proved that, as he put it, 'she was still in there somewhere.' He simply refused to admit her condition was unrecoverable. He was certain that if the medical staff just kept trying long enough, they'd be able to get through to her, reverse her condition."

"After all the effort they'd *already* put into solving the same problem in previous cases?" Bardasano grimaced.

"I didn't say he was being logical about it," McBryde pointed out. "Although he did make the point that because this child had made it further than any of the others had, she represented the best opportunity the Board would ever have—or had ever had so far, at any rate—to achieve an actual breakthrough."

"Do you think he really believed that? Or was it just an effort to come up with an argument which wouldn't be dismissed out of hand?"

"I think it was a bit of both, actually. He was desperate enough to come up with any argument he could possibly find, but it's my personal opinion that he was even angrier because he genuinely believed the Board was turning its back on a possibility."

And, McBryde added silently, *because those brain scans were still showing activity. That's why he kept insisting she was really still there, even if none of it was making it to the surface. And he also knew how little of the Board's resources would actually be tied up in the effort to get her back for him. He figured the return to the Alignment in general if they succeeded would hugely exceed the cost . . . and that the investment would keep his daughter alive. Maybe even return her to him one day.*

"At any rate," he went on aloud, "the Board didn't agree with his assessment. Their official decision was that there was no reasonable prospect of reversing her condition. That it would have been an ultimately futile diversion of resources. And as for the apparent EEG activity, that only made the situation even worse from the quality-of-life perspective. They decided that condemning her to a complete inability to interact with the world around her—assuming she was even still aware there *was* a world around her—would be needlessly cruel."

Which sounded so compassionate of them, he thought. *It may even have been that way, for some of them, at least.*

"So they went ahead and terminated her," Bardasano finished.

"Yes, Ma'am." McBryde allowed his nostrils to flare. "And, while I understand the basis for their decision, from the perspective of Simões' effectiveness, I have to say that the fact that they terminated her just one day short of her birthday was . . . unfortunate."

Bardasano grimaced—this time in obvious understanding and agreement.

"The LRPB goes to great lengths to keep its decision-making process as institutionalized and impersonal as possible as the best way of preventing favoritism and special-case pleading," she said. "That means it's all pretty much . . . automated, especially after the decision's been made. But I imagine you're right. In a case like this, showing a little more sensitivity might not have been out of order."

"In light of the effect on him, you're absolutely right," McBryde said. "It hammered his wife, too, of course, but I think it hit him even harder. Or, at least, I think it's had more serious consequences in terms of his effectiveness."

"She left him?" Bardasano's tone made it clear the question was actually a statement, and McBryde nodded.

"I think there were a lot of factors tied up in that," he told her. "Part of it was that she seems a lot more in accord with the Board's quality-of-life arguments. That's the way *he* sees her attitude, at any rate. So at least a part of him blamed her for 'abandoning' the girl—and *him*, in a sense—when she wouldn't support his appeals for a reversal. At the same time, though, my impression is that she wasn't really anywhere near as reconciled to the decision as she seemed. I think that deep down inside she was trying to deny how badly the Board's decision was hurting her. But there was nothing she could do about that decision. I think she admitted that to herself a lot sooner than he was prepared to, so she focused her anger on him, instead of the Board. The way she saw it, he was stretching out everyone's pain—and whatever the girl was enduring—in what he ought to have known as well as she did was obviously an ultimately useless crusade." He shook his head. "There's room for an awful lot of pain in that sort of situation, Ma'am."

"I suppose I understand that," Bardasano said. "I know emotions frequently do things, cause *us* to do things, when our intellects know better all along. This was obviously one of those times."

"Yes, Ma'am. It was."

"Is the wife's work suffering out of all this?"

"Apparently not. According to her project leader, she actually seems to be attacking her work with greater energy. He says he thinks it's her form of escape."

"Unhappiness as a motivator." Bardasano smiled ever so slightly. "Somehow, I don't see it being generally applicable."

"No, Ma'am."

"All right, Jack—bottom line. Do you think Simões' . . . attitude is likely to have an adverse impact on his work?"

"I think it's *already* had an adverse impact," McBryde replied. "The man's good enough at his job that, despite everything, he's still probably outperforming just about anyone else we could slide into the same position, though—especially given the fact that anyone we might replace him with would be starting cold. The replacement would have to be brought fully up to speed, even assuming we could find someone with Simões' inherent capability."

"That's a short-term analysis," Bardasano pointed out. "What do you think about the *long-term* prospects?"

"Long-term, Ma'am, I think we'd better start looking for that replacement." McBryde couldn't quite keep the sadness out of his tone. "I don't think anyone can go through everything Simões is going through—and putting himself through—without crashing and burning in the end. I suppose it's possible, even likely, that he'll eventually learn to cope, but I very much doubt it's going to happen until he falls all the way down that hole inside him."

"That's . . . unfortunate," Bardasano said after a moment. McBryde's eyebrow quirked, and she let her chair come back upright as she continued. "Your analysis of his basic ability dovetails nicely with the Director of Research's analysis. At the moment, we genuinely don't have anyone we could put into his spot who could match the work he's still managing to turn out. So I guess the next question is whether or not you think his attitude—his emotional state—constitutes any sort of security risk?"

"At the moment, no," McBryde said firmly. Even as he spoke, he felt the tiniest quiver of uncertainty, but he suppressed it firmly. Herlander Simões was a man trapped in a living hell, and despite his own professionalism, McBryde wasn't prepared to simply cut him adrift without good, solid reasons.

"In the longer term," he continued, "I think it's much too early to predict where he might finally end up."

Willingness to extend Simões the benefit of the doubt was one thing; failing to throw out a sheet anchor in an evaluation like this one was quite another.

"Is he in a position to damage anything that's already been accomplished?"

Bardasano leaned forward over her desk, folding her forearms on her blotter and leaning her weight on them while she watched McBryde intently.

"No, Ma'am." This time McBryde spoke without even a shadow of a reservation. "There are too many backups, and too many other members of his team are fully hands-on. He couldn't delete any of the project notes or data even if he were so far gone that he tried—not that I think he's anywhere *near* that state, at this point at least, you understand. If I did, I'd have already yanked him. And as far as hardware is concerned, he's completely out of the loop. His team's working entirely on the research and basic theory end of things."

Bardasano cocked her head, obviously considering everything he'd said, for several seconds. Then she nodded.

"All right, Jack. What you've said coincides with my own sense from all the other reports. At the same time, I think we need to be aware of the potential downsides for the Gamma Center's operations in general, as well as his specific projects. I want you to take personal charge in his case."

"Ma'am—" McBryde began, but she interrupted him.

"I know you're not a therapist, and I'm not asking you to be one. And I know that, usually, a degree of separation between the security chief and the people he's responsible for keeping an eye on is a good thing. This case is outside the normal rules, though, and I think we have to approach it the same way. If you decide you need help, you need an additional viewpoint, you need to call in a therapist, feel free to do so. But if I'm right about how imminent Prometheus is, we need to keep him where he is, doing what he's doing, as long—and as expeditiously—as we can. Understood?"

"Yes, Ma'am." McBryde couldn't keep his lack of enthusiasm completely out of his voice, but he nodded. "Understood."

CHAPTER EIGHTEEN

"Arsène, my man!" Santeri Laukkonen half-shouted (necessary, if anyone was actually going to hear him over the bar's background noise), and reached out to slap the blond, gray-eyed man on the shoulder. "Haven't seen you for a while! Business been good?"

Arsène Bottereau, late—*very* late, in his case—citizen commander in the service of the People's Republic of Haven's Office of State Security, tried not to wince. He was not outstandingly successful. First, because Laukkonen was a physically powerful man who hadn't pulled the blow in the least. Second, because Bottereau had been concentrating on keeping a low profile for a long time, now. And third, because he owed Laukkonen money . . . and wasn't there to pay it. Which was one reason he'd arranged to meet the fence and weapons dealer in a public bar rather than a quiet, discreet little office somewhere. Now he steered the other man to a corner booth—the sort of corner booth where waiters left one alone because they worked in the sort of bar where business discussions were likely to require an additional degree of . . . privacy.

Laukkonen's bodyguards were as accustomed as the bar's wait staff to keeping their noses out of their employer's business as much as possible, and they peeled off to flanking positions, close enough to hover protectively, yet far enough away to avoid overhearing anything which was none of their affair.

"Not so good as all that, Santeri, in answer to your question." Bottereau told him a small smile, once they were seated. "Now that people are shooting at each other out this way again, pickings are getting slim."

"I'm sorry to hear that." Laukkonen's tone was still genial, but his brown eyes had hardened noticeably.

"Yes, well, that's one of the reasons I wanted to talk with you," Bottereau said.

"Yes?" Laukkonen encouraged so pleasantly that an undeniable shiver ran down Bottereau's spine.

"I know I still owe you for that last load of supplies." The ex-Peep had decided going in that frankness and honesty were the only way to go. "And I'm pretty sure you've figured out that the reason I haven't come calling on you sooner is that I don't have the cash to pay for it."

"The suspicion had crossed my mind," Laukkonen allowed. His lips smiled. "I'm sure you wouldn't be thinking about stiffing an old friend, though."

"Of course not," Bottereau said, with total honesty.

"I'm relieved to hear it," Laukkonen said, still pleasantly. "On the other hand, I have to wonder exactly why you wanted to see me if it wasn't to *pay* me?"

"Mostly because I want to avoid . . . misunderstandings," Bottereau replied.

"What sort of 'misunderstandings'?"

"The thing is, I can't pay you right *now*, and to be honest, the way both the Manties and Theisman—and Erewhon, for that matter—are escorting their convoys in the area, things are getting too hot for *Jacinthe*. She's only a light cruiser, and we're beginning to see heavy cruiser escorts—even a couple of battlecruisers, out of Theisman." Bottereau shook his head. "I'm not going to get your money by ramming my head into that kind of opposition, and the stuff sailing independently around here right now is strictly low-end. It's not going to pay the bills, either."

"And this matters to me because . . . ?" Laukkonen's expression was not encouraging.

"Because I've got an . . . opportunity elsewhere. It's for a big paycheck, Santeri. Enough to let me finally retire, actually, as well as paying you everything I owe you."

"Of course it is."

Laukkonen smiled thinly, but Bottereau shook his head.

"I know. Everybody in my line of work is always looking for the big score."

It was his turn to smile, and there was absolutely no humor

in it. He hadn't seen a lot of options when the People's Republic went down with Oscar Saint-Just, yet if he'd realized then what he was getting into . . .

"I won't lie to you," he went on, looking Laukkonen straight in the eye. "There's nothing I'd like better than to be able to get the hell out, and this may be my chance to do just that."

"Unless, of course, something . . . unfortunate happens before you get to that retirement check," Laukkonen pointed out.

"Which is one reason I'm having this conversation with you," Bottereau said. "I know these people are good for the money. I've worked with them in the past, although I have to admit this time they're talking about a lot bigger paycheck than before." He grimaced. "On the other hand, what they're talking about sounds like a straightforward merc operation, not commerce raiding." It was interesting, a corner of his own mind noted, that even now he couldn't bring himself to use the word "piracy" in conjunction with his own actions. On the other hand, it never even occurred to him to mention anything about the People's Navy in Exile to Laukkonen. Mostly because he was certain it would absolutely convince the arms dealer he was shooting him a line of pure shit. "It's a single in-and-out op, and the amount they're talking about, completely in addition to anything we might . . . pick up along the way, would clear everything I owe you—and everyone else—and still leave me enough to set up somewhere else in something legitimate."

"And?"

"And I want you to understand that in order for me to get from where I am now to that paycheck—the one I'm planning to pay you out of—I'm going to need some time."

"How *much* time?" Laukkonen asked frostily.

"I'm not absolutely positive," Bottereau conceded. "Probably at least three or four months . . . maybe even a little longer."

"And just exactly what are you planning to operate on in the meantime?" Laukkonen's skepticism was plain.

"We're not going to *be* operating 'in the meantime,'" Bottereau replied. "This is something big, Santeri. To be honest, I'm not sure *how* big, but big. I do know they're going to be pulling in a lot more than just *Jacinthe* for this one, though, and it's going to take a while to get everything assembled. That's why I can't tell you exactly how long it's going to be. But they'll be picking up our regular maintenance and operating costs while we wait for the entire strike force to assemble."

Laukkonen leaned back on the other side of the table, regarding him thoughtfully, and Bottereau looked back as levelly as he could. For a change, just about everything he'd told the other man was true. Obviously he hadn't explained every single thing that was involved, but everything he had said was the stark, absolute truth. He hoped that unusual state of affairs was apparent to Laukkonen.

"You're not just trying to get a head start, are you, Arsène?" the fence/arms-dealer inquired finally.

"The thought had occurred to me, before this came along," Bottereau admitted. "On the other hand, I know all about your contacts. I figure there's no more than an even chance—if that—that I could stiff you and then disappear so completely nobody ever caught up with me. Frankly, I don't much like those odds, and even if I *could* pull it off, I imagine spending the next several decades wondering if I really had wouldn't he especially pleasant, either." He shrugged. "So, instead, I'm telling you ahead of time why you aren't going to see me for a while. I don't want you putting out the word so I get myself killed when I'm actually on my way back to Ajax to settle up with you."

Laukkonen still looked skeptical, but he folded his arms across his chest, frowning ever so slightly as he considered what Bottereau had said. Then he shrugged.

"All right," he said. "All right, I'll give you your three or four months—hell, I'll give you *six*! But the interest rate's going up. You do understand that, don't you?"

"Yes," Bottereau sighed. "How much did you have in mind?"

"Double," Laukkonen said flatly, and Bottereau winced. Still, it wasn't as bad as he'd been afraid it might be, and what Manpower was promising him would still be enough.

"Agreed," he said.

"Good." Laukkonen stood. "And remember, Arsène—six months. Not seven, and sure as hell not eight. You need longer than that, you damned well better get me a message—and a down payment—in the meantime. Are we clear on that?"

"Clear," Bottereau replied.

Laukkonen didn't say anything more. He simply nodded curtly, once, and walked out of the bar, picking up his bodyguards on the way.

❖   ❖   ❖

"Have a seat, Dr. Simões," McBryde invited as the sandy-haired man with the haunted hazel eyes stepped into his office.

Herlander Simões sat in the indicated chair silently. His face was like a shuttered window, except for the pain in those eyes, and his body language was stiff, wary. Not surprisingly, McBryde supposed. An "invitation" to an interview with the man in charge of the Gamma Center's entire security force wasn't exactly calculated to put someone at ease even at the best of times. Which these most definitely were not for Simões.

"I don't imagine it made you feel especially happy to hear I wanted to see you," he said out loud, meeting the situation head on, and snorted gently. "I know it wouldn't have made *me* happy, in your place."

Still, Simões said nothing, and McBryde leaned forward behind his desk.

"I also know you've been through a lot, these past few months." He was careful to keep his tone gentle and yet professionally detached. "I've read your file, and your wife's. And I've seen the reports from the Long-Range Planning Board." He shrugged ever so slightly. "I don't have any kids of my own, so in that sense, I know I can't really understand how incredibly painful all of this has been for you. And I'm not going to pretend we'd be having this conversation if I didn't have a professional reason for speaking to you. I hope you understand that."

Simões looked at him for a few seconds, then nodded once, jerkily.

McBryde nodded back, maintaining his professional expression, but it was hard. Over the decades, he'd seen more than his share of people who were in pain, or frightened—even terrified. Some of them had had damned good reason to be terrified, too. Security specialists, like cops the galaxy over, had a tendency not to meet people under the most favorable or least stressful of conditions. But he couldn't remember ever having seen a human being as filled with pain as this man. It was even worse than he'd thought when he'd spoken to Bardasano about him.

"May I call you Herlander, Dr. Simões?" he asked after a moment, and the other man surprised him with a brief, tight smile.

"You're the Center's security chief," he pointed out in a voice which sounded less harrowed than it ought to have, coming from a man with his eyes. "I imagine you can call any of us anything you want!"

"True." McBryde smiled back, easing carefully into the possible, tiny opening. "On the other hand, my mother always taught me it was only polite to ask permission, first."

A brief spasm of pain seemed to peak in a Simões' eyes at the reference to McBryde's mother. It obviously reminded him of the family he'd lost. But McBryde had anticipated that, and he went on calmly.

"Well, Herlander, the reason I wanted to see you, obviously, is that there's some concern about how what you've been through—what you're still *going* through—is likely to affect your work. You've got to know the projects you're involved in are critical. Actually, they're probably even more critical than you realize already, and that's only going to get more pronounced. So the truth is that I've got to know—and my *superiors* have to know—how well you're going to be able to continue to function."

Simões' face tightened, and McBryde raised one hand and waved it gently in a half-soothing, half-apologetic gesture.

"I'm sorry if that sounds callous," he said levelly. "It's not meant to. On the other hand, I'm trying to be honest with you."

Simões gazed at him, then shrugged.

"Actually, I appreciate that," he said, and grimaced. "I've had enough semi-polite lies and pretenses out of all those people so eager to 'save' Frankie from how terrible her life had become."

The quiet, ineffable bitterness in his voice was more terrible than any shout.

"I'm sorry about that, too," McBryde told him with equally quiet sincerity. "I can't undo any of it, though. You know that as well as I do. All *I* can do, Herlander, is to see where you and I—and the Gamma Center—are right now. I can't make your pain go away, and I'm not going to pretend that I think I can. But, to be brutally frank, the reason I'm talking to you is that it's my job to help hold the entire Center together. And that means holding *you* together . . . and recognizing if the time ever comes when we can't do that anymore."

"*If* the time ever comes?" Simões repeated with a heartbreaking smile, and despite his own training and experience, McBryde winced.

"I'm not prepared to accept just yet that it's inevitable," he said, wondering even as he did if he truly believed that himself . . . and doubting that he did. "On the other hand, I'm not going to lie to you and tell you I'm not going to be making contingency plans in case it does come. That's my job."

"I understand that." For the first time, there was a flicker of something more than pain in those hazel eyes. "In fact, it's a relief. Knowing where you're coming from, and why, I mean."

"I'll be honest with you," McBryde said. "The last thing I really want to do is to get close, on a personal level, to someone who's in as much pain as I think you are. And it's not as if I'm any kind of trained counselor or therapist. Oh, I've had a few basic psych classes as part of my security training, of course, but I'd be totally unqualified to try to cope with your grief on any sort of therapeutic basis. But the truth is, Herlander, that if I'm going to feel confident I understand you, and the security implications you present, you're going to have to talk to me. And that means I'm going to have to talk to you."

He paused and Simões nodded.

"I don't expect you to be able to forget I'm in charge of the Center's security," McBryde continued. "And I'm not going to be able to promise you the kind of confidentiality a therapist is supposed to respect. I want you to understand that going in. But I also want you to understand that my ultimate objective, however we got where we are, is to try to help you stay together. You can't complete the work we need completed if you fall apart, and it's my job to get that work completed. It's that simple. On the other hand, that also means you've got at least one person in the universe—me—you can talk to and who will do *anything he can* to help you deal with all the shit coming down on you."

He paused again, looking into Simões' eyes, then cleared his throat.

"On that basis, Herlander, let's talk."

CHAPTER NINETEEN

Rear Admiral Rozsak looked up as someone knocked lightly on the frame of his office door.

"I think I may have something interesting here, Luiz," Jiri Watanapongse told him. "Got a minute?"

"Just about," Rozsak replied with an undeniable sense of relief for the interruption as he looked up from the paperwork which obviously reproduced by cellular fission. He leaned back in his powered chair and beckoned for Watanapongse to step into the office and let its door slide shut behind him.

"And just what new interesting tidbit have my faithful espionage minions turned up for me today?" he asked after the commander had obeyed the silent command.

"I haven't been able to confirm this yet," Watanapongse said. "I know how much you just love hearing things that 'can't be confirmed yet,' but I think confirmation for this one's probably going to be a while coming. Under the circumstances, I thought you'd want to hear it anyway."

"And those circumstances are?"

"You remember Laukkonen?"

"How could I forget?" Rozsak said sourly.

Santeri Laukkonen was one of those unsavory sorts of people who were all too often involved in the basically unsavory sorts of business the Office of Frontier Security sometimes had to deal with. Not even Rozsak was positive where Laukkonen had come from in the first place, although if he'd had to guess, he would have put his money on an origin somewhere in the bowels of the Solarian League Navy's Office of Procurement. For a Verge gunrunner, the man was extraordinarily well tapped in when it came to "surplus" Solarian weaponry, at any rate. And not everything he handled came in the form of the legally licensed "export varieties" approved for extra-League sale, either. Not by a long chalk.

For the last several years, he'd been operating out of the Ajax System, whose proximity to the Maya Sector made it of more than passing interest to the people in charge of Maya's security. Over those years, he and Luiz Rozsak had found themselves involved in some extremely discreet—and very much arm's-length—transactions. The most circuitous of all had involved supplying munitions to a "liberation movement" in the Okada System. The order for that operation had come all the way from Old Chicago itself, and the liberation movement in question had provided the pretext for Frontier Security's urgent need to extend its benevolent protection to the unfortunate citizens of Okada.

And I still don't understand why the hell they wanted to do it, he thought sourly now. *It's not like it's the first time people got killed—in relatively large numbers—in the furtherance of some sort of half-baked strategy, but they didn't even hang on to the system afterward! Oravil's right—I really don't like black ops very much, but if I've got to carry them out for a bunch of Old Earth assholes anyway, I'd at least like for them to make some kind of sense afterward. It doesn't even have to be* good *sense.*

Actually, he'd come to the conclusion that Frontier Security itself had been played in this case. The "reform government" OFS had installed had just happened to be tailor-made to allow Admiral Tilden Santana to trade in his admiral's uniform for the presidential palace. And President for Life Santana appeared to be making some substantial contributions to the personal accounts of two senior bureaucrats back in Frontier Security's HQ.

"So, what about Laukkonen?" he asked, shaking himself back up to the surface of his thoughts.

"Well, he's in the favor-trading business, and he knows how we like to keep track of anyone whose ... operational interests might intrude into the Sector. In fact, I might as well admit that we went ahead and hinted as much to him."

"And just how much of an investment did we make in this 'hint' of yours?" Rozsak inquired dryly.

"As retainers go, it's not really all that much," Watanapongse replied. "Actually, it's pocket change for him, as well as for us. What he's really after is maintaining access, staying in our good graces, in case another instance of mutually advantageous back-scratching should arise."

"All right." Rozsak nodded. "I can understand that. So what tidbit has he thrown our way?"

"One of the points I've hinted to him we'd like to be kept particularly well-informed on is the operation of any StateSec holdouts in our area."

Rozsak nodded again. Any renegade StateSec ships had been smart enough to stay out of the Maya Sector, but he'd known at least some of them were operating just beyond the Sector's borders.

"Well, I'd say it's pretty obvious Laukkonen has been one of their suppliers. At any rate, it seems evident to me that he's got an even better feel for where they've been and what they've been doing than he wants to admit even now. But according to him, a 'very reliable source'—which I take to be one of his StateSec customers—has informed him that several ex-StateSec ships which have been working around this area of the Verge have been pulled off of active operations. Apparently, they're being concentrated for some sort of special op—something his 'reliable source' described as more of a merc operation than run-of-the-mill piracy."

"Really?" Rozsak's eyes narrowed. "I don't suppose our good friend Laukkonen was able to tell us exactly what the object of this hypothetical 'special op' might be?"

"No." Watanapongse shook his head. "On the other hand, it occurred to me that the evidence Manpower's been recruiting ex-StateSec units might suggest who was behind it. And if Manpower has an objective in this area, where do *you* suppose it might be?"

"Exactly what I was thinking," Rozsak said a bit grimly. "Did Laukkonen say anything which might suggest how soon the op's likely to kick off?"

"Nothing definitive. Probably not for at least another three or four months; that was the best estimate he could give us."

"If they're calling them in from individual operational areas, that's probably an underestimate of how long it's going to take to get them concentrated," Rozsak thought out loud. "And after operating solo for so long, even StateSec types are going to see the need for at least minimal training and drill before they try squadron-level operations again. Bearing that in mind, I'd say five months, maybe even six, would be more likely."

"I was coming up with the same guesstimate," Watanapongse agreed.

"All right," Rozsak decided. "I think we have to take the possibility that Laukkonen is onto something really serious. On the other hand, we can't start redeploying our available units on the basis of pure speculation. See what you can do about confirming this. I don't expect you to be able to nail it down absolutely, of course, but beat the bushes. See if we can shake out anything else to support Laukkonen's version of things. And do your best to get us some kind of realistic time estimate if it looks like there's really something to it."

"Yes, Sir."

Watanapongse nodded and turned back towards the office door, then halted and raised an eyebrow as Rozsak raised an index finger at him.

"I've been thinking," the admiral said.

"About—?" Watanapongse asked when Roszak paused.

"About Manson," his superior said, and the intelligence officer grimaced.

Lieutenant Jerry Manson was a fairly capable intelligence officer who, unfortunately, both thought he was much smarter than he actually was and possessed the loyalty quotient of an Old Earth piranha. Either of those failings might have been acceptable by itself; in combination, they were anything but.

Manson had been planted on them originally by Ingemar Cassetti—a fact of which, he undoubtedly believed, Roszak and Watanapongse were both unaware. They'd kept him in place because it was always easier and safer to manipulate the spy you knew about rather than inspire one's adversaries to plant spies you *didn't* know about, but they'd never entertained any illusions about his loyalty or lack thereof. He'd been quite useful on several occasions, too, yet that usefulness had always had to be balanced against the need to keep him completely in the dark where the Maya Sector's true plans were concerned.

That had still been manageable, if increasingly difficult, but now that Cassetti had been removed from the equation, there was no need to "manage" his chosen spy. And even if there had been...

"You've read my memo, I take it?" Watanapongse said aloud, and Rozsak snorted.

"Of course I have! And I agree. As long as he was just an orphaned little grifter, with no replacement master to call his own, the situation was workable. Now, though?" The admiral shook his head. "If he's sniffing around opening some sort of covert channel back to Old Earth, the time has come to cut our losses."

Watanapongse nodded. He was quite confident Manson didn't even begin to suspect how closely and tightly all of his communications had been monitored ever since he'd joined Rozsak's staff. If the lieutenant had ever suspected the truth, he would never have risked sending his own message back to Frontier Fleet HQ on Old Earth. It seemed evident that he'd finally come into possession of at least a few fragmentary clues about "the Sepoy Option," though. He'd been careful to keep them to himself when he drafted his message to Commander Florence Jastrow (who happened, herself, to be one of the more loathsome people Watanapongse had ever met, which undoubtedly explained why Manson would have thought of her), but he'd also made it clear to her that he suspected his superiors in the Maya Sector were up to something they shouldn't have been doing.

Unfortunately for Lieutenant Manson, his message had been not only intercepted but quietly removed from the queue. On the other hand, he was bound to start wondering about that in the next few weeks. At the moment, he was undoubtedly expecting a reply from Jastrow; when one never came, on the other hand...

"How do you want to handle it?" Watanapongse asked now.

"We're sure we've shortstopped all of his fishing expeditions?"

"As sure as you ever can be in this sort of game. Which is to say, almost certain."

"Then that'll have to do." Rozsak thought for a moment, then shrugged. "An accident, Jiri. Something as far removed from us or anything related to his official duties as you can manage."

"He's scheduled to go grav-skiing Friday," Watanapongse observed.

"Really?" Rozsak leaned back in his chair, expression thoughtful, then nodded. "I *do* hope he's careful," he said.

It was Watanapongse's turn to snort, then he nodded and headed back out of the office. Rozsak watched him go, lips pursed in silent thought for several minutes, then shrugged and returned to his unending paperchase.

✧   ✧   ✧

"Would you like some more potatoes, Jack?"

"Um? Ah, I'm sorry, Mom. What did you say?"

"I asked you if you'd like some more potatoes." Christina McBryde smiled and shook her head. "Your father and I are delighted your body could join us for dinner tonight, of course, dear, but it would be kind of nice if your brain could keep it company next time."

Jack snorted and raised both hands in chuckling surrender.

"Sorry, Mom—sorry!" He extended his hands in front of him, wrists together. "Guilty as charged, officer. And I can't even argue that my parents didn't teach me better when I was a sprout."

"I'd heard you'd had a proper upbringing," his mother told him, dark eyes glinting. "I have to admit, though, that until just a second or two ago, I would have found the rumor hard to believe."

"Ease up a little, Chris," Thomas McBryde intervened with a chuckle of his own. "The accused has admitted his guilt and thrown himself on the mercy of the court. I think a little clemency might be in order."

"Nonsense!" Zachariah put in from his end of the table. "Throw the book at the bum, Mom! Off to bed with no dessert!"

"Oh, I couldn't do that to him," Christina replied. "We're having carrot cake with butter cream icing."

"Oh, my. *Your* carrot cake?" Zachariah shook his head. "That *would* constitute cruel and unusual punishment."

"Yes, it would," Jack agreed emphatically.

"Why, thank you," his mother said with a dimpled smile. Then her expression sobered just a bit. "Seriously, Jack, you've been distracted all night. Is it something to do with your job, or can you talk about it?"

Jack's blue eyes warmed as he looked across the table at her. Christina McBryde was a sculptress and a painter, one whose light sculptures, in particular, commanded high prices not just here on Mesa, but in the Solarian League's art markets, as well. She'd never really wanted him to go into law enforcement, far less into Alignment Security. That was a job she knew someone had to do, but she'd been afraid of what a career in AS might cost her older son's soul along the way. She hadn't stood in his way, especially when all of the LRPB's aptitude tests confirmed how good he'd be at it, but she'd never liked it.

His father had been more supportive, although he'd had more than a few reservations of his own. He himself was a senior administrator in the Department of Education, and he'd never made any secret of the fact that he'd been both relieved and happy when his and Christine's oldest child, JoAnne, had decided to go into childhood education. Their second daughter—and their youngest child—Arianne had turned out (not surprisingly) to share Zachariah's scientific bent. She was a chemist, and despite her relative youth (she was only forty-nine T-years old) she'd recently become a scientific advisor to the CEO of the Mesa System government. The McBryde family could take solid, quiet pride in its contributions to the Alignment and to its homeworld (which weren't always the same things), yet there was no denying that both of Jack's parents worried about him.

And with good reason, he thought. He managed to keep his own expression light and semi-amused, but it was difficult. Just as it was difficult to realize that barely a T-month had passed since his first conversation with Simões. It didn't seem possible that he could have become so aware of—and oppressed by—the other man's pain and its inevitable final outcome in so short a period. Yet he had . . . and with the becoming, for the first time in a long time, he understood exactly why his mother had wanted him to do something else with his life.

"In some ways, Mom," he told her, "I really wish I could talk about it with you. I think you'd probably be able to help. Unfortunately, it does have to do with work, so I can't discuss it."

"You're not in any sort of . . . trouble?" she asked quietly.

"Me?" His laugh was at least three-quarters genuine, and he shook his head. "Believe me, Mom, *I'm* not in any kind of trouble. It's just—"

He paused for a moment, then shrugged.

"I can't really talk about it, but I suppose I can tell you it's just that one of the people I'm responsible for is in a lot of personal pain at the moment. It doesn't have anything to do with his job, or with me, really, but . . . he's hurting. And even though the reason he is doesn't have anything to do with his job, it's to the point where his emotional state could start affecting the quality of his work. And because of the nature of what he does and what I do, I'm one of the very few people he can talk to about it."

He glanced at Zachariah from the corner of one eye and saw from his brother's expression that Zack had realized exactly who he was talking about. Zachariah's blue eyes darkened, and Jack knew he, too, was comparing their family life with what happened to Herlander and Francesca Simões.

"Oh, I'm sorry to hear that!" Christina's quick sympathy was genuine, and she reached out to lay one hand on her son's forearm. "At least if he can only talk to a few people about it, I know at least one of them is going to have a sympathetic ear," she said.

"I try, Mom. I try. But it's one of those cases where there's not really much anybody can do *except* listen." He shook his head, his eyes shadowed. "I don't think this story's going to have a happy ending," he said quietly.

"All you can do is all you can do, Son," Thomas told him. "And your mom's right. If he's got you to talk to, then at the least this person, whoever he is, knows he's not all alone with it. Sometimes that's the most important thing of all."

"I'll try to remember that," Jack promised.

There was a moment of silence, then he shook himself and smiled at his mother.

"However, in answer to the missed question which started this entire conversational thread, if we've got carrot cake for dessert, then, no, I *don't* want any more potatoes. I'm not about to waste any space I could use on a second or third helping of carrot cake on mashed potatoes!"

CHAPTER TWENTY

Several hours later, as Jack let himself into his own apartment, his thoughts drifted back to what his parents had said.

The truth was, he thought, that even though they might have a point about the importance of a sympathetic ear, Herlander Simões desperately needed more than Jack McBryde—or anyone else—would ever be able to give him. And despite his own training, and despite how hard he tried, Jack's professional detachment wasn't enough to protect *him* from the fallout of Simões' despair.

He checked for any personal com messages without finding any and walked through the apartment's sitting area towards his bedroom. At the moment, it was a rather lonely bedroom, without female companionship, and he suspected his own reaction to Simões had a lot to do with that. His last relationship had been working its way towards an amicable parting for several months even before Bardasano had called him in, but he had no doubt his absorption with Simões had hastened its end. And he had even less doubt that it had a lot to do with why he'd found himself unable to work up much enthusiasm for finding a new one.

Which is pretty stupid of me, when you come down to it, he reflected wryly. *It's not like turning myself into a monk is going to help Herlander any, now is it?*

Maybe not, another corner of his brain replied. *In fact, definitely not. But it's a little hard to go leaping gaily through life when you're watching someone come gradually apart before your very eyes.*

He undressed, stepped into the shower, and keyed the water. Zachariah, he knew, preferred the quickness and convenience of a sonic shower, but Jack had always been addicted to the sheer, sensual pleasure of hot water. He stood under the drumming needle spray, absorbing its caress, yet this time he couldn't fully abandon himself to it the way he usually could. His brain was too busy with Herlander Simões.

It was the contrast between the barren unhappiness of Simões' current existence and his own family's closeness, he realized yet again. That comforting, always welcoming, nurturing love. Looking at his parents, seeing how after all these years their children were still their *children*. Adults, yes, and to be treated as such, but still their beloved sons and daughters, to be worried about and treasured. To be (although he suspected his mother would be more comfortable with the verb than his father) celebrated for who and what they were.

For who and what had been taken away from Simões.

He'd tried—and failed, he knew—to imagine what that had truly felt like. The pain of that loss . . .

He shook his head under the pounding water, eyes closed. Just from the purely selfish perspective of what had been stolen from Simões' own life, the anguish must be incredible. But he'd spoken with Simões several times now. He knew that part of the hyper-physicist's anger, his rage, really was the product of his sense that *he'd* been betrayed. That something unspeakably precious had been ripped away from *him*.

Yet those same conversations had made it clear to Jack that far more than his own loss, it was the entire lifetime which had been stolen from his daughter that was truly tearing the man apart. He'd seen the promise in his Francesca which Thomas and Christina McBryde had seen *realized* in their JoAnne, their Jack and Zachariah and Arianne. He'd known what that child could have grown up to be and become, all of the living and loving and accomplishments which could have been hers in the four or five centuries which the combination of prolong and her genome would have given her. And he knew every one of those loves, every one of those accomplishments, had died stillborn when the Long-Range Planning Board administered the lethal injection to his daughter.

That's what it really comes down to, isn't it, Jack? he admitted to the shower spray and the privacy of his own mind. *To the LRPB, Francesca Simões, ultimately, was just one more project. One more strand in the master plan. And what does a weaver do when he comes across a defective thread? He snips it, that's what he does. He snips it, he discards it, and he goes on with the work.*

But she wasn't *a thread. Not to Herlander. She was his* daughter. *His* little girl. *The child who learned to walk holding onto his hand. Who learned to read, listening to him read her bedtime stories. Who learned to laugh listening to his jokes. The person he loved more than he could* ever *have loved himself. And he couldn't even fight for her life, because the Board wouldn't let him. It wasn't his decision—it was the* Board's *decision, and it made it.*

He drew a deep, shuddering breath, and shook himself.

You're letting your sympathy take you places you shouldn't go, Jack, he told himself. *Of course you feel sorry for him—my God, how could you* not *feel sorry for him?—but there's a reason the system is set up the way it's set up. Someone has to make the hard decisions, and would it really be kinder to leave them up to someone whose love is going to make them even harder? Who's going to have to live with the consequences of his own actions and decisions—not someone else's—for the rest of his life?*

He grimaced as he recalled the memo from Martina Fabre which had been part of Simões' master file. The one which had denied Simões' offer—his plea—to be allowed to assume responsibility for Francesca. To provide the care needed to keep her alive, to keep private physicians working with her, out of his own pocket. He'd been fully aware of the kinds of expenses he was talking about—the LRPB had made them abundantly clear to him when it enumerated all of the resources which would be "unprofitably invested" in her long-term care and treatment—and he hadn't cared. Not only that, he'd demonstrated, with all the precision he brought to his scientific work, that he could have satisfied those expenses. It wouldn't have been easy, and it would have consumed his life, but he could have done it.

Except for the fact that the decision wasn't his, and, as Dr. Fabre had put it, the Board was "unwilling to allow Dr. Simões to destroy his own life in the futile pursuit of a chimerical cure for a child who was recognized as a high-risk project from the very beginning. It would be the height of irresponsibility for us to permit him to invest so much of the remainder of his own life in a tragedy the Board created when it asked the Simõeses to assist us in this effort."

He turned off the shower, stepped out of the stall, and began drying himself with the warm, deep-pile towels, but his brain wouldn't turn off as easily as the water had. He pulled on a pair of pajama bottoms—he hadn't worn the tops since he was fifteen—and found himself drifting in an unaccustomed direction for this late at night.

He opened the liquor cabinet, dropped a couple of ice cubes into a glass, poured a hefty shot of blended whiskey over the ice, and swirled it gently for a second. Then he raised the glass and closed his eyes as the thick, rich fire burned down his throat.

It didn't help. Two faces floated stubbornly before him—a sandy-haired, hazel-eyed man's, and a far smaller one with brown hair, brown eyes, and a huge smile.

This is stupid, he thought. *I can't change any of it, and neither can Herlander. Not only that, I know perfectly well that all that pain is just eating away at him, adding itself to the anger. The man's turning into some kind of time bomb, and there's not a damned thing I can do about it. He's going to snap—it's only a matter of time—and I was wrong when I downplayed his probable reactions to Bardasano. The break is coming, and when it gets here, he's going to be so damned angry—and so unconcerned about whatever else might happen to him—that he's going to do something really, really foolish. I don't know what, but I've come to know him well enough to know that much. And it's my job to keep him from doing that.*

It was bizarre. He was the man charged with keeping Simões together, keeping him working—*effectively* working—on his critical research projects. And with seeing to it that if the time ever came that Simões self-destructed, he didn't *damage* those projects. And yet, despite that, what he felt was not the urgent need to protect the Alignment's crucial interests, but to somehow help the man he was supposed to be protecting them from. To find some way to prevent him from destroying himself.

To find some way to heal at least some of the hurt which had been inflicted upon him.

Jack McBryde raised his glass to take another sip of whiskey, then froze as that last thought went through his mind.

Inflicted, he thought. *Inflicted on him. That's what you're really thinking, isn't it, Jack? Not that it's just one of those terrible things that sometimes happens, but that it didn't* have *to happen.*

Something icy seemed to trickle through his veins as he realized what he'd just allowed himself to admit to himself. The trained security professional in him recognized the danger of allowing himself to think anything of the sort, but the human being in him—the part of him that was Christina and Thomas McBryde's son—couldn't stop thinking it.

It wasn't the first time his thoughts had strayed in that direction, he realized slowly as he recalled past doubts about the wisdom of the Long-Range Planning Board's master plan, its drive to master the intricacies, shape the best instruments for the attainment of humanity's destiny.

Where did we change course? he wondered. *When did we shift from the maximizing of every individual into producing neat little bricks for a carefully designed edifice? What would Leonard Detweiler think if he were here today, looking at the Board's decisions? Would he have thrown away a little girl whose father loved her so desperately? Would he have rejected Herlander's offer to shoulder the full financial burden of caring for her? And, if he would have, what does that say about where we've been from the very beginning?*

He thought about Fabre's memo again, about the thoughts and attitudes behind it. He never doubted that Fabre had been completely sincere, that she'd truly been attempting to protect Simões from the consequences of his own mad, quixotic effort to reverse the irreversible. But hadn't that been Simões' decision? Hadn't he had the right to at least fight for his daughter's life? To *choose* to destroy himself, if that was what it came to, in an effort to save someone he loved *that* much?

Is this really what we're all about? About having the Board make those decisions for all of us in its infinite wisdom? What happens if it decides it doesn't need any random variations any more? What happens if the only children it permits are the ones which have been specifically designed for its star genomes?

He took another, deeper sip of whiskey, and his fingers tightened around the glass.

Hypocrite, he thought. *You're a fucking hypocrite, Jack. You've known—known for forty years—that that's exactly what the Board has in mind for all those "normals" out there. Of course, you didn't think about it that way, did you? No, you thought about how much good it was going to do. How their children, and their grandchildren and their great-grandchildren would thank you for allowing them* to share in the benefits of the systematic improvement of the species. Sure, you knew a lot of people would be unhappy, that they wouldn't voluntarily surrender their children's futures to someone else, but that was stupid of them, wasn't it? It was only because they'd been brainwashed by those bastards on Beowulf. Because they were automatically prejudiced against anything carrying the "genie" stigma. Because they were ignorant, unthinking normals, not an alpha line like you.

But now—now that you see it happening to someone else who's also an alpha line. When you see it happening to Herlander, and you realize it could have happened to your parents, or to your brother, or your sisters . . . or some day to you. Now you suddenly discover you have doubts.

He dragged in a deep, shuddering breath and wondered how the warmth and love and caring of his family could have crystallized this dark, barren night of the soul for him.

It's only fatigue—emotional and physical fatigue, he told himself, but he didn't believe it. He knew it went deeper and farther than that. Just as he knew that anyone who found himself suddenly experiencing the doubts he was experiencing, asking the questions he found himself asking, should immediately seek counseling.

Just as he knew he wasn't going to do anything of the sort.

CHAPTER TWENTY-ONE

In the event, the weeks that Brice Miller and his friends spent fretting over their upcoming encounter with the notorious Jeremy X proved to be pointless. When they were finally introduced to the feared and ferocious terrorist, after they arrived on Torch, it turned out that the reality bore no resemblance to the legends.

To begin with, he was not two hundred and twenty centimeters tall, nor was his physique that of an ogre. Quite the opposite, to Brice's surprise and relief. The former head of the Audubon Ballroom and current Secretary of War for Torch was no more than a hundred and sixty-five centimeters in height, and his build was wiry and slender rather than massive.

He seemed quite a cheerful fellow, too. Even puckish, you might say—at least if, like Brice, you had just recently encountered the term and been taken by it, but hadn't yet read enough literature to realize that "puckish" was by no means the same thing as "harmless."

Jeremy X didn't scowl, either. Not once. Not even after Hugh Arai—far more bluntly and precisely than he needed to, in Brice's opinion—explained the manner in which Brice's clan had stayed alive on Parmley station, for the past half century.

Unfortunately, while Jeremy X didn't scowl, someone else in Queen Berry's audience chamber—that was what they called it, anyway, although Brice thought it looked more like a big office with no desk and not very many chairs—most certainly *did* scowl. And she made up for everything Jeremy lacked, and then some.

Thandi Palane was her name. It turned out she was the commander of Torch's entire military. Brice had been surprised to hear that. If anyone had asked him to guess at the woman's occupation, he would have said either *professional wrestler* or *enforcer for criminal enterprises*. Uniform be damned. That woman was just plain scary. Even without the scowl.

Thankfully, the queen of Torch herself didn't seem to share her military commander's attitude. In fact, she seemed very friendly. And after a few minutes, Brice realized that Palane's scowl wasn't directed at him anyway. She was apparently just scowling at the general state of the universe, moral failings thereof.

By then, though, Brice had stopped caring what Palane thought or didn't think. In fact, he'd become almost completely oblivious to her existence—and even the existence of Jeremy X. That was because it hadn't taken more than five minutes in the presence of the queen of Torch before Brice had developed an infatuation for the young woman. A really, really powerful infatuation, the sort that drives all other thoughts from a teenage boy's brain like a steam cleaner scours all surfaces.

Also a really, really, really *stupid* infatuation, even by the standards of fourteen-year-old adolescent males. Brice wasn't so far gone that he didn't realize that, at least in some part of his brain. Big deal. He was providing neurologists with the most graphic evidence probably ever uncovered that the brains of adolescents—male adolescents, for sure—were not fully developed when it came to those portions that evaluated risks.

From the slack-jawed look on their faces, he was sure that his cousins Ed Hartman and James Lewis had been struck down by the same infatuation. And, alas—unlike Brice, who still had a few functioning neurons in his cortex—were now completely ruled by their limbic systems. You might as well have called them Amygdalum and Amygdalee. He could only hope they didn't do anything really foolish. Too much too hope, of course, that they wouldn't drool.

It was odd. Brice was already self-analytical enough to realize that his points of attraction when it came to girls were . . .

Being honest, not probably all that mature. Good looks came first, put it that way. And, prior to this very moment, he would have sworn that for his cousins Ed and James, good looks came first, last, and everything in between.

Yet the truth was that Queen Berry wasn't actually pretty. She certainly wasn't ugly, either, but about the best you could say for her thin face was that everything was in the right place, nothing was deformed, and her complexion was good in pale sort of way. She had nicely colored eyes, for sure. They were her best facial feature. A vivid blue that contrasted well with her long, straight dark hair.

True, also, that her slender figure—quite evident, in the casual clothing she chose to wear, even sitting on her throne (which was really just a big, comfortable-looking chair)—was unmistakably female. Still. Various secondary sexual characteristics that normally loomed large in Brice's assessment of female attractiveness and from what he could tell completely dominated that of his friends—big breasts, to name one—were markedly absent here.

So why was he smitten? What was it about the young queen's open and friendly countenance that seemed somehow dazzling? What was it about her certainly-healthy-but-that's-about-it figure that was producing hormonal reactions way more powerful than any he'd ever experienced gazing upon the voluptuous figure of Cousin Jennifer?

Part of the explanation was simply that Berry Zilwicki was the first unknown young woman that Brice Miller had ever encountered, aside from brief views of slaves being transported or the slavers overseeing the process, some of whom were also female. One of the many drawbacks of being raised as he had, part of a small clan of people very isolated from the rest of the human race, was that by the time boys reached puberty, they already knew every girl around. And vice versa, for the girls. There were no mysteries, no unknowns. True, the fact that some girls—for Brice, it has been Jennifer Foley—had suddenly developed in such a way as to stimulate new and primitive reactions from the opposite sex (or, sometimes, the same sex—Ganny's clan wasn't at all prudish or narrow-minded about such things) helped a bit. Still, while Cousin Jennifer's ability to stir up fantasies in Brice's mind was new, the cousin herself most certainly was not. He still carried a small scar on his elbow from the time she'd struck him there with a handy tool, in retaliation for his theft of one of her toys. And she was still holding something of a grudge for the theft itself.

They'd been seven years old, at the time.

The queen of Torch, on the other hand, was really *new*. Brice didn't know anything at all about her, except for the bare facts that she was several years older than he was—irrelevant, at the moment—and commanded legions of armed and dangerous soldiers. Also irrelevant, at the moment. Everything else was unknown. That, combined with her friendly demeanor, opened the floodgates of fourteen-year-old sexual fantasies in a way that Brice had never encountered and against which he had few defenses.

But there was more involved. Dimly, Brice Miller was beginning to grasp that sex was a lot more complicated than it looked. He was even verging on the Great Truth that most men were quite happy even when the Significant Other in their life was not especially good-looking. So perhaps Brice was not destined for a life of chastity after all. Given that his heretofore stratospheric standards seemed to be crumbling by the minute.

"—the *matter* with you, Brice? And the two of you also, Ed and James. It's a simple enough question."

The genuine irritation in Ganny El's tone of voice finally penetrated the hormonal fog.

Brice jerked. *What question?*

Thankfully, James played the fool, so Brice didn't have to. "Uh . . . what question, Ganny? I didn't hear it."

"Have you suddenly gone deaf?" Butry pointed at one of the men standing not far from the queen. He was on the short side, and so wide-bodied he looked a little deformed. "Mr. Zilwicki wants to know if you'd be willing to spend a few months—"

Zilwicki cleared his throat. "Might be as long as a year, Ms. Butry."

"Twelve counts as a 'few,' when you're my age, young man. To get back to the point, James—and you too, Ed and Brice—Mr. Zilwicki has a job for you." She gave Zilwicki a beady stare. "'Somewhat' dangerous, he says. A word to the wise, youngsters. This is one of those situations where the phrase 'somewhat dangerous' is a lot closer to 'a little bit pregnant' than it is to . . . oh, let's say the version of 'somewhat dangerous' that a conscientious playground attendant says to a mother when her child is heading for the seesaw."

That began dispelling the hormonal fog. For the first time since he'd laid eyes on the queen, Brice focused on someone else in the room.

Zilwicki. He was the queen's father, or maybe step-father. And his first name was Anthony, right? Brice wasn't entirely certain.

Good fortune struck again. Thandi Palane frowned—the frown helped clear away still more of the hormonal fog—and said: "Are you sure about this, Anton?"

"They're awfully young," added the queen doubtfully.

That was a dash of cold water. She'd said "awfully young" in the manner that a protective adult refers to children. Not, sadly, in the way that . . .

Well. That Brice imagined sophisticated older women spoke of young men to whom they were inexplicably attracted. Admittedly, he wasn't sure of that, either. Seeing as how the situation had never actually happened to him.

One of the other men in the room spoke up. He was a lot less striking than Zilwicki. Just an average-sized man, with a very square face.

"That's the whole point, Your Maj—ah, Berry. Add them into the mix, as young as they are, and with neither the ship nor anybody on it having any connection to either Torch or the Ballroom—or Manticore or Beowulf or Haven—and they'll be about as invisible as anyone can be, where we'd be going."

"And where is that, precisely?" demanded Ganny. "I can't help but notice that you've made no mention of that so far."

The square-faced man glanced at Zilwicki. "Mesa. To be precise."

"Oh, well. And why don't we sodomize all the demons in the universe, while we're at it?" Friede Butry glared at him. "What do you want us to do for an encore, Cachat? Circumcise the devil?"

Good fortune again. Brice had forgotten that man's name too. His first name was Victor, and he was from the Republic of Haven.

Ca-chat. Silently, Brice practiced the name a few times. It was pronounced in the Frenchified way that Havenites often spoke. KAH-SHAH, rhyming with "pasha," except the emphasis was on the second syllable instead of the first.

It finally dawned on him to wonder what a Havenite was doing as part of Queen Berry's inner circle. Especially given that Zilwicki—more memories came flooding back in, as the hormonal fog continued to lift—was from the Star Kingdom of Manticore. The somewhat haphazard and always intensely practical education given the clan's youngsters didn't spend much time on the fine points of astropolitics. But it wasn't so sketchy as to have overlooked the most hard-fought, bitter and longest-running war in the galaxy.

Haven. Manticore. And now . . . Mesa.

Suddenly, Brice was excited. Excited enough that he even forgot for a moment that he was in the presence of the universe's most wondrous female.

"We'll do it!" he said.

"Yeah!" and "Yeah!" came the echoes from James and Ed.

Ganny's shoulders sagged a little, but her glare at Cachat didn't fade in the least. "You *cheated*, you bastard."

Cachat looked more curious than offended. "How did I cheat?" Then, he shrugged. "But if it'll make you feel better . . ."

He looked now at Brice and his two friends. "The mission we'll be undertaking is in fact very dangerous. I don't think you'll be in much danger, yourselves, at least until the very end. You might not even participate in the 'very end' at all, for that matter, since you'll mostly be there just as a backup in case things go wrong. Still, it can't be ruled out—and the fact that something will have gone wrong if you do get involved means that it's likely to be pretty dangerous."

"And when he says 'pretty dangerous,'" Zilwicki chimed in, "he means 'pretty dangerous' in the sense that you've gone into the den of the most ruthless and evil people in the world and yanked on their collective beard, not 'pretty dangerous' in the sense that you've picked a fight in the schoolyard with some kids who are a bit bigger than you."

"So there's no hard feelings if you decline," concluded Cachat.

"We'll do it!" Brice said.

"Yeah!" and "Yeah!" came the echoes from James and Ed.

"You dirty *rotten* cheaters," hissed Ganny. She point a finger at the three boys. "You know perfectly well their brains haven't fully developed yet."

"Well, sure," said Zilwicki. He poked his forehead with a finger. "Cortex is still a little unshaped, especially in the risk-assessment areas. But if it'll make you feel any better, the same's probably true for me, even at my decrepit age." He hooked a thumb at Cachat. "For sure and certain, it's true for him."

"Oh, wonderful," said Ganny. Brice couldn't remember her ever sounding so sullen.

He, on the other hand, felt exuberant. He'd finally realized what was going on. The most wildly improbable fantasy, come true to life!

The *classic*, in fact. Young hero, sent out on a quest to slay the dragon in order to rescue the princess. Well, very young queen. Close enough.

The traditional reward for which deed of derring-do was well-established. Hallowed, even.

His eyes flicked right and left. True, in the fantasies there was only *one* young hero—it being a solitary quest, given the nature of the reward—but Brice was sure he'd outshine his friends. And Zilwicki and Cachat didn't count, because Zilwicki was the queen's own father and Cachat was apparently hooked up with Palane and no man, not even one with no frontal lobes at all, would be stupid enough to try to jilt *her*.

Then Ganny went and wrecked it all. "I'm coming too, then, Cachat, whether you like it or not."

Cachat nodded. "Certainly. The plan sort of depends on that, in fact."

"*And* my great-nephew Andrew Artlett." She pointed to the individual in question, who'd been standing against a far wall.

Cachat nodded again. "Makes sense."

Ganny now pointed to another person standing against the wall. A young woman, this time. "*And* Sarah."

"That'd be perfect," agreed Cachat. He nodded toward two others standing nearby. Oddny Ann Rødne and Michael Alsobrook. "They'd be handy, as well."

Ganny shook her head. "We'll need Oddny to take the news back to Parmley Station and help get everything organized. As for Michael . . ." She shrugged. "Where would he fit in the scheme? Which is pretty obvious, I'd say."

"Obvious, indeed," said Zilwicki. "You're the matriarch in charge, Andrew and Sarah are married, and the youngsters are their kids." He studied Brice and his friends for a moment. "Their ages don't match, unless they were triplets, which they very obviously are not. But given the somatic variation involved, you could hardly claim any of them except James were the natural offspring of Andrew and Sarah, anyway. So two of them have to have been adopted."

"Oh, that's *gross*," complained Sarah. She glanced at Artlett, half-glaring. "He's my *uncle*."

"Calm down!" barked Ganny El. "Nobody said you had to *consummate* the marriage, you nitwit. In fact, you don't even have to share a cabin with him." Butry's eyes got a little unfocussed. "Now that I think about it . . ."

"Good idea," said Cachat. He gave Sarah and Andrew a quick examination, his eyes flicking back and forth. "Given the age disparity, an estrangement would be logical. So if any Mesan customs officials decide to press a search, they'd discover a very good-looking young woman apparently on the outs with her husband. Even customs officials have fantasies."

"Oh, that is *so* gross," complained Sarah. "Now you're whoring me out to strangers!"

"I said, calm down!" Butry glowered at her. "Nobody's asking you to do anything more strenuous than bat your eyelashes. And as often as you do *that,* don't even try to claim you'll get exhausted in the effort."

Armstrong glared at her, but didn't say anything. But Zilwicki was now shaking his head.

"It's sad, really, to see such a crude resurgence of sexism."

Cachat and Butry stared at him. "Huh?" she asked.

"Not all customs officials are male, you know. Or, even if they are, necessarily heterosexual. If you want to create this little diversion—which I admit isn't a bad idea—then you really need a male equivalent for Sarah. Which"—he glanced at Andrew Artlett, and spread his hands apologetically—"I'm afraid Andrew is not."

Uncle Andrew grinned. "I'm ugly. Not that it gets in my way, much."

Zilwicki smiled. "I don't doubt for an instant that you're a veritable Casanova. But we don't actually want to get close to any Mesan officials, we just want to stir up their hindbrains."

Ganny was looking unhappy. "I don't care. I want Andrew along, if we're going to do this at all. He's . . . well, he's capable. Even if he is crazy."

A new voice came into the discussion. "Problem solved!"

Everybody turned to look at a young woman perched on a chair at the back of the room. Brice had noticed her, naturally, when they first came in. First, because she was an unknown young female; secondly, because she was attractive, to boot. But his attention had soon become riveted on the queen, and he'd almost completely forgotten the presence of the other young woman.

That was odd, in a way, because the young woman with the bright blonde hair sitting at the back of the room was quite a bit better-looking than the queen herself. Still not someone you'd call a beauty, true, but by any standard criteria of pulchritude she had Berry beat hands down.

What was her name? Brice tried to remember the initial introductions. Ruth, he thought.

"Problem solved," she repeated, coming to her feet. "I come along too—I might even help in the distract-dumb-males-or-lesbians department, although obviously not as much as Sarah—but I can pose as Michael Alsobrook's wife." She pointed at Brice. "We can claim him as a child, very plausibly, given his somatic features. Michael and I might be older than we look, given prolong. That only leaves James to be accounted for and that might even be an advantage even if it's necessary at all which it probably isn't because by now the human genome is so mixed up with so many recessive features that keep popping up that you never know what a kid might look like but even if somebody assumes there's no way that Michael could be the father I could certainly be his mother in which case"—here she gave Alsobrook a gleaming smile that was simultaneously fetching, amused and apologetic—"I've either been cheating on my husband or I've got loose habits, either of which might intrigue a nosy customs official—"

She hadn't taken a single breath since she started the sentence. It was pretty impressive.

"—although we've got to face the fact that if anybody does a DNA match the whole charade goes into the incinerator and it's the easiest thing in the world to gather DNA samples."

"Actually, it wouldn't," said Ganny, whose spirits seemed to be perking up. "It might even help. The fact is that all of us except you *are* related—too damn ingrown, to be honest—and while your DNA won't match, so what? There could any number of explanations for that. I can think of three offhand, two of which would certainly intrigue a nosy customs inspector with an active libido and an orientation toward females."

Zilwicki and Cachat practically exploded. "No!" they both said, almost in unison.

Ruth glared at them. "Why?"

Zilwicki's jaws tightened. "Because I'm responsible for your safety to the Queen, Princess. *Both* queens. If you get even hurt, much less killed, Berry's just as likely to skin me alive as Elizabeth Winton."

Princess, was it? Brice felt himself getting intrigued. That was less of a fantastical stretch than a young queen, after all—in fact, the more he thought about it, "queen" seemed rather stuffy—and the Ruth woman really was very attractive. Very talkative too, apparently, but that was okay with Brice. Seeing as how he'd probably be tongue-tied, anyway.

The princess jeered. "Don't be stupid, Anton! If I'm killed—even hurt—there's no way you're still going to be alive either. Not with this plan. So what do you care what happens afterward? Or do you believe in ghosts—*and* think ghosts can be subjected to corporal punishment?"

Zilwicki glared at her. But . . . said nothing. Brice began to realize that Cachat and Zilwicki hadn't been exaggerating when they said this mission was possibly dangerous.

Cachat tried a different tack. "You'll blow the mission." Sorrowfully but sternly: "Sorry, Ruth. You're a brilliant analyst, but the fact remains that you're not really suited for field work."

"Why?" she demanded. "Too jittery? Too jabbery? And what do you think these three kids are? Suave secret agents? Who just somehow can't keep their tongues from hanging out whenever they run into a female anywhere this side of nubile and short of matronly."

She flashed Brice and his friends a quick smile. "S'okay, guys. I don't mind and I'm sure Berry doesn't either."

Brice flushed. And made certain his tongue was firmly inside his mouth. He had just encountered the second of the Great Truths, which was that a female intelligent enough to be attractive for that very reason, no matter what else, was also . . .

Intelligent. Bright. Perceptive. Hard to fool.

He felt a profound wish that a dragon might show up. Frightening, taloned, clawed, scaled, to be sure. But probably not very bright, and certainly not able to read his mind. Well. Read his limbic system. Being honest, there wasn't all that much "mind" involved.

"Besides," Ruth continued, "you'll need somebody on Ganny's ship who's a computer and communications whiz. Anton, you can't be two places at once. If things do go into the crapper, probably the only chance you'll have of getting out is if somebody in the backup getaway ship can substitute for your skills manipulating God-knows-what in the way of Mesan security systems. 'Cause you're not likely to have time to do it, what with all the guns blazing in the getaway and probably having not much more than a tin can and some wires to work with even if you did. Have enough time, that is."

Now she flashed that same quick smile at Uncle Andrew. "Meaning no offense."

"None taken," he said, smiling back. "I'm a whiz with anything mechanical or electrical, and I'm even pretty good with computer hardware. But that's about it."

Ruth looked back at Cachat and Zilwicki, triumphantly. "So there. It's all settled."

"I'm for it," said Ganny forcefully. "I could give you all sorts of reasons for that, but the only really important one is that I'm getting even with you for playing tricks on my boys." She gave Brice and his friends a look that could best be described as disgusted. "Taking advantage of their stunted forebrains! Ed, put your tongue back in your mouth. You too, James."

She said nothing to Brice. He felt very suave, although he'd have to double-check the dictionary to make sure the word meant what he thought it meant. Now that Princess Ruth was coming along, he had a feeling he wasn't going to get away with his usual vocabulary habits. Use any long and/or fancy-sounding word you want, serene in the knowledge that your dummy cousins won't know if you got it wrong.

Didn't matter. What he was already thinking of as The Great Adventure would probably be better with a smart princess along. Even if such a fantastical creature was completely absent from the classics.

CHAPTER TWENTY-TWO

"I'm glad you decided not to get hardnosed about it, Jeremy," said Hugh Arai, as he lowered himself carefully into a chair in the war secretary's office.

Jeremy watched the delicate process with a sardonic smile. "You really needn't take so much care," he said. "If you crush the miserable thing, maybe I'll be able to get the State Accounting Office to authorize more suitable furniture. Not likely, though." He took a seat behind the desk. "I'm sorry to say that the anal-retentive manias of the SAO's officials is the clearest evidence I've ever seen that Manpower's genetic schemes actually work according to plan. Most of them are J-11s."

Now sure that the chair would hold his weight, Hugh looked up and gave Jeremy a smile. J-11s were the "model" of slave that was supposedly designed to handle technical work of an accounting and record-keeping nature. Like all such precise Manpower designations, it was mostly nonsense. Manpower's geneticists did breed for those skills, but genes were far more plastic than they liked to admit—certainly to their customers. There was no gene for "accounting," nor was there one for "file-keeping."

It was true that slaves designed for a certain task tended to do it well. But that was far more likely the product of the slave's training and—probably most important of all—the slave's own self-expectation, than any genetic wizardry on Manpower's part.

That said . . . In Hugh's experience, J-11s *did* tend to be anal-retentive. That manifested itself primarily in a certain sort of knee-jerk stinginess. *You might as well try to get blood from a stone as squeeze money out of a J-11* was a common wisecrack among genetic slaves and ex-slaves.

"As for the other," Jeremy continued, waving his hand in an airy gesture, "I am magnanimous by nature. It is well known."

"It most certainly is *not*."

Jeremy shrugged. "Those gypsies aren't the first people who've ever had to cut a deal with the devil in order to stay alive. Plenty of slaves and ex-slaves have done the same. But it was clear enough they didn't go any further than they had to, and . . . the fact that they adopted so many slaves spoke in their favor."

He gave Hugh a beady eye. "As you knew it would, so you can stop pretending you weren't trying to manipulate me."

"Manipulate the situation, it'd be better to say. I was just playing it by ear, so to speak. I wasn't actually sure what use we could get out of Parmley Station, but I had the sense that there had to be something."

He smiled, perhaps a bit ruefully. "Mind you, I wasn't expecting such an enthusiastic response as soon as we got here. Cachat and Zilwicki reacted like treecats discovering a bin full of celery."

Jeremy's smile was definitely on the rueful side. "I've sometimes regretted the way we let those damn spooks run loose among us. I'm not sure who's worse. Sometimes I think it's Cachat, sometimes Zilwicki—and in my darkest moments I think they're both playing a charade so I won't notice that Princess Ruth is the one really running amok."

"I'm a little astonished that the Wintons agreed to let her stay here."

"It's not really that odd, if you're willing to stretch the definition of 'public service.' The Manticoran dynasty has always had a tradition that its youngsters can't just lounge about idly."

Hugh shook his head. "In the nature of things, spying is hardly what you'd call 'public' service. And—being cynical about it—that's mostly the purpose of having young royals displaying their patriotic merits, isn't it?"

Jeremy pondered the question, for a moment. "Actually, no. Not with that dynasty, anyway. With most it would be, true enough. But I think the main concern of the Wintons is with maintaining their own . . . call it 'fiber,' for lack of a better term. The big problem with letting young royals spend their time loafing is that eventually they became *the* royals, and then it won't be long before the dynasty itself is a loafer."

He gave Arai another beady gaze. "I can tell you that our own founding dynast has stated any number of times that no kid of hers is going to be an idler."

Unwarily, Hugh said, "Well, good. But first she has to produce said kids."

Too late, he recognized the beadiness of the gaze. Jeremy hadn't become one of the galaxy's deadliest pistoleers if he hadn't known how to keep his eyes on the target.

"Exactly so. And for that, unless we opt for artificial insemination—and you really don't want to hear the Queen's opinion on that subject, trust me—we need a consort."

"Not a chance, Jeremy," said Hugh, chuckling. "Leaving aside the fact that I barely know the girl, having just met her, I have my own career plans."

Jeremy X had an impressive sneer. "Oh, right. I forgot. Hugh Arai plans to devote his life to the retail-trade slaughter of Manpower villains. 'Slaughter,' did I say? A better term would be 'pruning.' Very careful pruning, one tiny little slaver bud at a time. God forbid he should forego that grand opportunity in order to help forge an entire star nation of ex-slaves, which *could* actually do some 'slaughtering.'"

"We both agreed on my career, years ago," Hugh said mildly. "Godfather."

Jeremy glared at him. "I'm not your godfather, damn it! I'm your adviser—and my advice has changed. That's because the *situation* has changed."

"I'm still not playing Bachelor of the Week, Jeremy. For Christ's sake, I just met the woman! I've spent a total of maybe two hours in her presence, not one minute of which was taken up by a personal exchange between the two of us. Not even an exchange concerning the time of day, much less anything intimate."

Jeremy grinned impishly. "So? That's what dates are for, don't you know? Just say the word and I'll set one up."

Hugh shook his head. "I see your persistence hasn't changed any. Out of pure curiosity, though, where *does* a reigning queen go, on a date?"

Jeremy's grin was immediately replaced by a scowl. "With *this* queen? Damn near anywhere, the crazy girl. She has absolutely no sense of security, Hugh. I mean, none whatsoever."

Arai cocked his head. "This is coming from *you?* Mister I'll

Take Any Chance And Make Obscene Gestures At Security While I'm At It."

"It's not funny, Hugh. She's wide open for an assassination attempt—which you know, and I know, and everybody in the *galaxy* knows except her, Manpower would be delighted to carry out—and she refuses to take any serious precautions."

Hugh rubbed his chin. "None at all?"

"Not really. That gaggle of ex-Scrags she's had around her since the fracas on the *Wages of Sin* try their best to keep an eye on her. But you're a security expert—used to be, anyway, before you got started on this commando silliness—and you know perfectly well that jury-rigged protection's not really worth very much. The only way the Amazons can pull it off is by pretending they're just accompanying Berry whenever she goes out in public because they're devoted to her. Which is true enough that Berry's willing to look the other way, even if she does sometimes get grumpy about it."

The impish grin came back. "That's because she says having all those lady weightlifters around is scaring off potential boy-friends, most of whom are scared off anyway because of her silly titles. Her term, not mine—'silly.' But it occurs to me that you'd hardly be scared off by a bunch of genetically engineered female super-soldiers on account of Manpower already engineered you to bench press elephants."

"Very funny. I'll admit the prospect of facing down a bunch of ex-Scrags does not fill me with terror. I'm still not doing it, Jeremy." Hurriedly: "Even if I wanted to, there isn't time. If this scheme Cachat and Zilwicki cooked up is going to work at all, I've got to get back to Parmley Station."

"Why?" Jeremy demanded. "Your team can handle the work of getting that station fixed up without you, perfectly well."

"Maybe so—but they can't obtain the freighter. For that, we're going to need serious financial backing and that means I have to report back to Beowulf."

"Oh, that's nonsense. We're not talking about a warship, Hugh— hell, we're not even talking about a big freighter. Just something around a million tons. And as beat-up as we want it, we ought to be able to pick it up cheaply. Between them, Cachat and Zilwicki can come up with the money. Zilwicki could probably do it on his own, without even tapping into Havenite funds. His lady friend is one of the richest women in the Star Kingdom."

Hugh sat through the little speech with growing impatience. "Come on, Jeremy! Stop playing the innocent. You know perfectly well the issue isn't money as such—it's laundering the money so there'll be no trace of it for Manpower's agents to pick up. For that, nobody's as good as Beowulf's secret services."

Jeremy leaned back in his chair and bestowed a cool smile on Arai. "No, actually, they aren't the best. I admit Beowulf's very good at it—but you forget that we're less than a week's travel from the galaxy's champion money-launderers. Who happen to be on very good terms with Torch."

Hugh opened his mouth, and . . . closed it. Then opened it again, and . . . closed it.

"Ha!" Jeremy jeered. "Forgot about the Erewhonese, didn't you? They're not that many generations removed from outright gangsters, Hugh. And all that happened when they 'went legit' is that their money-laundering skills got even better. Had to, of course."

He looked out the window at the lush landscape three stories below. "All we have to do is set the problem before them—Walter Imbesi, that is, we don't even need to talk to the official triumvirate—and you'll have a tramp freighter delivered to you in less than two months with impeccable credentials—lousy ones, of course, but impeccable—and not a trace that any part of its origins had anything to do with either Torch or Manticore or Haven or Beowulf. Or Erewhon. And you've already got a crew that can't be traced."

Slowly, Hugh got up and went to the window, thinking as he went. The truth was that Jeremy's scheme was better than anything even Beowulf's secret services would be able to come up with. Assuming that Cachat and Zilwicki decided to undertake this very dangerous mission—that was still unsettled, as yet—then they'd have as good a backup escape route as you could ask for.

The Mesa System was home to a number of huge interstellar corporations, so it had a truly enormous amount of freight traffic coming in and out. Not as much as Manticore or Sol or a few of the other well-established old star systems in the League's core, but close.

True, Mesan security was pretty ferocious, but it was still forced to work within some limits. About thirty percent of Mesa's population were freeborn citizens, and they had a wide range of rights and liberties that were enshrined by law and even respected, most of the time. Mesa's government was not an outright dictatorship that could operate with no restraints at all. Like many rigid caste societies in history that had a large population of privileged free citizens—South Africa's apartheid system was a well-known example—Mesa's government was a mixture of democratic and autocratic structures and practices.

The same democratic liberties were not extended to the remaining seventy percent of the population, of course. Slaves constituted about sixty percent of Mesa's population with the remaining ten percent consisting of the descendants of slaves who'd been freed in the earlier periods of Mesan history.

In its origins, Manpower had claimed that genetic slavery was actually "indentured servitude." That fiction had been openly dispensed with centuries ago, when the Mesan constitution was amended to make the manumission of genetic slaves illegal. But that still left a large population of freed ex-slaves—legally second-class citizens ("seccies" was the slang term used for them)—inhabiting all of Mesa's large towns and cities, and even a number of villages in more rural areas.

Periodically, calls were made to expel all seccies from the system. But, by now, the seccies had become an integral part of Mesa's social and economic structure and provided a number of useful functions for the planet's freeborn citizens. As had been true throughout history, once a large class of ex-slaves came into existence, they were hard to get rid of, for the same reason that a large class of illegal immigrants was hard to get rid of. People were not cattle, much less inert lumps of stone. They were intelligent, self-motivated and often ingenious active agents. About the only effective way to just eliminate such a large class of people was to adopt a political and legal structure that was sometimes described as "totalitarian."

For a wide variety of reasons, Mesa was not prepared to adopt that option. So, Mesa's security forces simply kept a close eye on the seccies—insofar as they could. That wasn't as easy as it sounded, though, because seccy society was socially intricate, often shadowy, and intermixed with that of Mesa's freeborn citizens. Marriage was illegal, but despite all of Manpower's pretensions to creating new types of people, human nature remained pretty intractable. There were plenty of personal liaisons between seccies and freeborn, regardless of what the law said or official custom prohibited and frowned upon.

A large number of those liaisons were commercial, not personal. Mesa's huge population of slaves needed to be supplied, and—again, despite all official Manpower pronouncements—it often proved most practical to have those needs supplied by slave sutlers. And there were even some luxury goods, as well. "Luxury," at least, as slaves reckoned these things. Many of the slaves were allowed to work for themselves on the side, and use whatever income they garnered for their own purposes. That was a messy but useful way of keeping social antagonisms from becoming too explosive.

Seccies were very much what their name implied—second-class, or lower, members of Mesan society, thoroughly excluded from the "respectable" professions and employment generally. The majority of them eked out their existences doing casual day labor, and they were generally non-persons as far as Mesa at large was concerned. Some of them, however, had amassed considerable personal fortunes from their positions as slave sutlers—who frequently also served as loan sharks, drug pushers, etc., servicing the "gray economy" of the slave community. Some of these seccy sutlers, especially the richer ones, even had silent freeborn partners.

Naturally, some of the seccies had been co-opted into the Mesan security apparatus. In general, the authorities ignored the activities of the sutlers (which, accordingly, were not taxed), and in return, the sutlers were expected to help defuse tensions in the slave community—and to inform the authorities if they saw something in danger of getting out of hand. In fairness to them, one of the reasons seccies played the informant role as often as they did stemmed less from the rewards they received for it than their recognition that any sort of organized slave revolt on Mesa would be not simply totally futile but guaranteed to produce stupendous numbers of dead slaves. For all that they were frequently venal, it was still true that seccies identified more closely with their still enslaved brethren than they did with the rest of Mesa.

It was that large class of seccies and the inherently complex and disorganized life they led that would be the key to open Mesa to Cachat and Zilwicki, if they decided to go. Hugh knew none of the details, and didn't want to, but he was certain that the Ballroom had connections with many seccies on Mesa. Given the amount of traffic going in and out of the Mesa System, it really wouldn't be that hard for Cachat and Zilwicki to disembark openly—as members of a freighter crew, perhaps—and then quietly vanish into seccy society. As long as they watched their steps—and the two were experts at this work—there really wasn't much chance they'd be spotted by Mesa's security agencies.

As long as they didn't *do* anything, that is. But the moment any alarms were triggered, the gloves would come off and Mesa's ruthless and brutal security forces would come down on the seccy ghettos like a hammer. The real trick would be getting *off* the planet and making their escape afterward.

Hence the tramp freighter and its Butry clan crew. They'd have absolutely no connection to Cachat and Zilwicki at all, so far as anyone on Mesa would be able to determine. Even if the security forces went so far as to do a DNA analysis of the crew—quite possible, actually—they'd not find anything to arouse their suspicions.

Hugh started rubbing his chin again.

Jeremy recognized the gesture, of course. He'd known Hugh since a frightened and bewildered five-year-old boy who'd just lost his entire family came off a Beowulfan warship and was greeted by a Ballroom contingent who took him and the few other survivors under their wing.

"I knew you'd see the light of day," he said cheerfully.

Hugh smiled. "I'm still not available as a consort."

"Oh, come on. One date. Surely a fearless commando—gorilla commando, at that—won't shy away from such a paltry thing. The girl's barely twenty years of age, Hugh. What could be the danger?"

Hugh brought up his memories of the queen from their one brief encounter. A plain-looking girl, really. But Hugh wasn't impressed by such things. He'd been struck by her eyes.

"Don't play the fool, Jeremy. You know the answer perfectly well, or you wouldn't have made her your queen in the first place."

CHAPTER TWENTY-THREE

"What's on your mind?" Harper S. Ferry asked when Judson Van Hale came into his office. The former Sphinx Forestry Service ranger was frowning and the treecat perched on his shoulder seemed unusually somber as well. "You're looking disgruntled this morning."

Van Hale gave him a quick smile, but there wasn't any humor in it. "Whatever happened to the background check you were going to do on Ronald Allen?"

"Ronald *who*?"

"He was one of the ex-slave immigrants who arrived here about two months ago. Genghis thought his mental—'taste,' he calls it—was a little wrong. I brought the matter to your attention and you were going to do a more thorough background check."

"Yeah, I remember now. Hm. Good question, actually. I'd forgotten about it. Let me see what Records has to say." Harper began keying entries into his computer. "Spell the name, would you? The last name, I mean."

"Allen. A-L-L-E-N, not A-L-L-A-N." Judson drew a memo pad from his pocket and thumbed the entry he'd pre-selected. "Here. This is what he looks like."

Harper glanced at the screen in Van Hale's hand and saw a tall man in a brown jumpsuit. Going by his appearance, he was probably one of what Manpower called its "general utility lines," which they designated either D or E. That was a fancy way of saying that they hadn't bothered to do much in the way of genetic engineering.

A screen came up on Harper's computer. After studying it for a few seconds, he hissed in a breath.

Judson could feel Genghis tensing on his shoulder. The treecat was picking up the emotional aura Harper was emanating as a result of whatever he'd seen on the screen. "What's the matter?" he asked.

"God damn all business-as-usual clerks," Harper said. "This should have been flagged and brought to my attention immediately."

He swiveled the screen so Judson could see it. The screen read:

```
Background search
Allen, Ronald
MANPOWER SLAVE IDENTITY NUMBER:
    D-17d-29547-2/5.
SCANNING ERROR
NUMBER  ALREADY REGISTERED
REGISTRATION DATE: MARCH 3, 1920
REGISTRATION IDENTITY: ZEIGER, TIMOTHY
RESUBMIT FOR SCANNING
```

"Oh, hell," Judson said. "Where's Zeiger? And what happened to Allen?"

Harper S. Ferry was working at the keyboard again. After a moment he said: "Zeiger'll be easy to find, thankfully. He's a resident of Beacon"—that was the name the ex-slaves had bestowed on Torch's capital city not long after the insurrection—"and, better still, he works for the Pharmaceutical Inspection Board. He's a clerk, too, not a field agent, so he ought to be right here." He gestured at one of the windows. "Well, just a few blocks away. We can be there in five minutes."

"And Allen?"

Harper keyed in some final words. "Oh, wonderful. He also works in the pharmaceutical industry, but he's a roustabout. He could be anywhere on the planet."

"Which company does he work for?"

"Havlicek Pharmaceutics. One of the Erewhonese firms."

"Well, that's a break. They'll have good personnel records, unlike most of the homegrown outfits—and you didn't hear me cast that aspersion upon our stalwart native entrepreneurs."

Harper chuckled, and pulled out his com unit. "I'll see if I can track down Allen's whereabouts, while I'm pulling up the scanning records. Meanwhile, trot over to the PIB and see what's up with Zeiger."

Judson headed for the door.

✧   ✧   ✧

He was back in half an hour, with a stocky, balding, middle-aged man in tow. "This is Timothy Zeiger. Tim, meet Harper S. Ferry. Harper, his number checks out."

Without being prompted, Zeiger stuck out his tongue. Ferry rose from his desk and leaned over. There, quite visible, was the number at issue: *D-17d-2547-2/5*.

Harper glanced at the treecat. "What does Genghis say?"

"He thinks Tim's kosher. A little apprehensive, of course, but that's to be expected. Mostly, he's just curious."

"I sure as hell am," said Zeiger. "What's this all about?"

Harper didn't answer him immediately. He'd resumed his seat and was studying the screen. "You're pretty well-established, aren't you? Married eighteen months ago—less than half a year after you arrived, congratulations—one child—"

"And another on the way," Zeiger interrupted.

Harper kept going. "You belong to Temple Ben Bezalel. Hipparchus Club, center bowler for the club's torqueball team, and you and your wife even belong to an amateur theater troupe."

"Yeah. So what? And I'm asking again—what's this all about?"

Harper leaned back in his seat and looked up at Van Hale. "What do you think, Judson?"

"Same as you." He hooked a thumb at Zeiger. "He checks out all across the board. What about Ronald Allen?"

Ferry scowled. "He smells worse and worse the more I study him. He seems to have made no serious attachments since he got here. And he has no regular address."

"Being fair, most roustabouts don't. And he hasn't been here that long."

"True. Still . . ."

Zeiger was obviously on the verge of exploding. Harper raised a calming hand and said, "What this is all about, Tim, is that somebody else was registered with your genetic marker number. Which, so far as anyone knows, doesn't ever happen. At least, I've never heard of Manpower duplicating numbers."

"There wouldn't be much point in it, anyway," Judson said, shaking his head. "If we assume for the moment that there's a covert operation involved. You'd run too much risk of the duplication being spotted, it would seem to me. Here on Torch, anyway. We've never kept quiet the fact that we require all ex-slaves to register when they arrive."

Zeiger had an odd look on his face. Whatever emotions were stirring in his head were enough to perk Genghis' interest. The treecat was looking at him intently.

"Uh . . . maybe not," he said.

"What do you mean?"

"The way I got freed was something of a fluke. A Havenite warship intercepted a slaver convoy—this was about thirty-five years ago—"

"Convoy?" Judson was a little startled.

Ferry nodded. "It's not unheard of. Usually slaver ships operate solo, but there are some exceptions. So what happened, Tim?"

"Well, the Havenites sprang the trap a little too early. Most of the convoy was able to translate into hyper before they could be run down. The ship I was on was the last one and the Havenites destroyed it, just a couple of minutes before the slave ship ahead of it made the transition."

Harper pursed his lips. "So . . . they'd have seen your ship blow up, is that what you're saying?"

"Yeah. And according to the Havenites who rescued me, it was pretty spectacular. They were astonished to discover any survivors. There was just me and a girl and the two slaver crewmen who grabbed her and dragged her into a lifeboat. I scrambled in just before they closed the hatch. They were mad enough to beat me a little, but not much, since they were mostly desperate to get free. I guess we left the ship just in time."

For an instant, his heavyset face got savage. "The Havenites pitched the two slavers into space less than an hour after they rounded us up. Without skinsuits. So me and the girl wound up being the only survivors."

The expression on his face lightened. "Her name was Barbara Patten. The one she took, I mean, after we were freed. Patten was the name of one of the Havenite crewmen. She wound up marrying him a year or so later, I heard. But I haven't had any contact with her in a long time now. Nice girl."

Harper and Judson looked at each other. "The proverbial hell's bells," muttered Ferry. "The slavers would have had records of their cargo, so they'd assume that Tim here just vanished. Perfect way to disguise an identity, without running the risk of faking a number entirely."

Zeiger was now frowning. "I don't get it. If this other guy has the same number on his tongue . . . The way you guys check those numbers, there's no way to fake them with cosmetics. They had to have been *grown*."

"You're absolutely right," Harper said grimly, rising from the desk. "Tim, don't leave the city till you hear from us again. Judson, I found Allen's current whereabouts. He's in a camp not more than a three hour flight from here. What say we sign out an air car and go talk to him?"

"*After* we pay a visit to the armory," said Van Hale. On his shoulder, Genghis growled approvingly.

✧   ✧   ✧

God damn Jeremy. Hugh Arai's thought was simultaneously irritated and amused. Since the very beginning of this second audience he was having with Queen Berry, he hadn't been able to stop thinking of her as a woman instead of a monarch. Which, of course, was exactly the effect Jeremy had aimed for. The notorious terrorist was also a shrewd psychologist.

The effect was pronounced, too. Hugh was discovering that the more time he spent in the presence of Berry, the more attractive she became. In his earlier audience with the queen, he'd had a hard time to keep from laughing at the all-too-evident way the three Butry boys had been smitten by the young monarch. Especially so, after Ruth blurted it out openly. Now, he was getting worried his own tongue might be starting to hang out.

Figuratively speaking, of course. Hugh wasn't *that* far gone.

Still, the effect was striking. It had been a long time since Hugh had been this powerfully drawn to a woman.

That was her personality at work, he knew.

One thing being designed as marketable commodities did for genetic slaves was to make them automatically, one might almost say "painfully," aware of the difference between outside packaging and contents. Pleasure slaves, for example, were specifically genegineered to be physically attractive because physical beauty made them more valuable, brought a higher price. Heavy-labor units, like Hugh himself, on the other hand, were often downright grotesque, by the standards of most humans, because nobody gave a good goddamn what *they* looked like. After all, they were really just vaguely human-shaped pieces of disposable machinery, weren't they?

That left scars, whether the slaves wanted to admit it or not. Obviously, it was worse for some than for others, and the Beowulf medical community had worked with enough slaves over the centuries to be well aware of that fact. Hugh had undergone the standard psychological evaluations and therapy himself, although he'd actually gotten out light in that respect, compared to altogether too many liberated slaves. Still, the ultimate consequence was that, for better or worse, genetic slaves as a group were as well conditioned as any humans in history to ignore physical appearances and concentrate on the characters and personalities of the people they ran across.

The first impression most people would have of Berry Zilwicki was that she was a plain-looking girl. Attractive, overall, but only in the sense that any woman or man is attractive at that youthful age, assuming they are healthy and not significantly malformed in any way.

But Hugh had barely noticed her outward appearance at all. Instead, he'd focused from the outset on her personality. That was also somewhat superficial, of course, since personality and character overlapped but were hardly identical. Still . . .

If the human race held personality pageants the same way they did beauty pageants, Berry Zilwicki would surely be a finalist. Probably not a winner, because she just wasn't quite flashy enough. But a finalist, for sure—and given that Hugh wasn't partial to flashiness, that hardly made a difference.

God damn Jeremy.

Without realizing it, he must have muttered the words. Berry turned a friendly face toward him, smiling in that extraordinarily warm way she had. "What was that, Hugh? I didn't catch the words."

Hugh was tongue-tied. Odd, that, since he was normally a fluent liar when he needed to be. Something about those bright, clear, pale green eyes just made dissembling to her very difficult. It'd be like spitting in a mountain stream.

"He was cursing me," said Jeremy, who was sitting near the queen—and not that close to Hugh at all. But Jeremy had phenomenal hearing as well as eyesight. The secretary of war was trying not to smirk, and failing.

Berry glanced at him. "Oh, dear. You should really stop doing this, Jeremy. Being elbowed by the galaxy's most cold-blooded killer isn't actually the best way to get a man to overcome his hesitations about asking a queen out on a date."

She turned back to Hugh, her smile widening and getting warmer still. "Is it, Hugh?"

Hugh cleared his throat. "Actually, Berry . . . in my case, it probably is. But I agree with you as a general proposition."

"Well, good!" The smile was now almost blinding. "Where do you propose to take me, then? If I can make a recommendation, there's a very nice ice cream parlor less than a ten-minute walk from this office-pretending-to-be-a-palace. It's got several small tables in the back where we'd even have a chance of enjoying a private conversation."

She looked over at two very tough-looking women standing not far away. Her expression got considerably cooler. "Assuming, that is, we can keep Lara and Yana from sitting in our laps."

The woman on the left—he thought that one was Lara, but he wasn't sure—got a grin on her face. "Sit on your lap, maybe. No way I'm getting within arm's reach of that caveman."

"He is sort of cute, though, Lara," said the other woman. "Clean-shaven, even. He must have a really sharp stone ax."

Hugh took a deep breath. This was *really* not a good idea.

"Sure," he said.

✧   ✧   ✧

The Havlicek Pharmaceutics camp was larger than most such exploratory operations. That probably meant they'd found enough potential in the area to move toward setting up production facilities. The fact that they'd erected a permanent headquarters building instead of just using temporary habitats lent support to that theory as well.

Harper and Judson found the camp's director in an office on the first floor. His name was Earl Manning, according to the plaque on the open door.

"What can I do for you?" he asked as they came in. He didn't look up from the paper on his desk. The question was posed brusquely. Not impolitely, just in the way that a very busy man handles interruptions.

"We're looking for Ronald Allen," said Harper.

That got Manning to look up. "And who is 'we,' exactly?"

"Immigration Services." Harper pulled out his ID and laid it on the director's desk.

Manning actually examined the ID. With considerable care, too, more than was really warranted given the rarity of identity theft on Torch. Judson got the impression the camp director was one of those people whose instinctive response to government authority was to dig in his heels.

"Okay," he said sourly, after about ten seconds. He handed the ID back to Harper. "What's this about?"

Manning's attitude was triggering off an equivalent response from Ferry. "That's not actually any of your concern, Mr. Manning. Where's Allen?"

Manning started to bristle. Then he made a face and jerked a thumb at the window behind him. "You'll find him operating one of the extractors. On the south edge of the camp. If you don't know what he looks like—"

"We do know," said Harper. He turned and left the office. Judson followed.

Once in the corridor and after having walked most of the way to the outside door to the building, Harper muttered: "What an asshole."

Judson just smiled. He was quite sure that Manning had uttered—or at least thought—equivalent sentiments after Harper left his office.

Genghis bleeked his amusement, confirming Judson's guess.

Once they were outside, they consulted a map of the camp that was posted on the wall of the building. It was hand-drawn, insofar as the term meant much given modern drafting equipment.

"Close enough to walk," Harper pronounced. He headed south, tugging lightly on the grip of his pulser to make sure it would come easily out of the holster. Judson followed suit. For the first time, it registered clearly on him that they might be on the verge of a violent incident. Despite his intensive training and proficiency with weapons, Judson's work as a forest ranger back on Sphinx had been a lot closer to that of a guide and sometime emergency medical technician. SFR personnel *were* policemen, as well, and they took that part of their training seriously, but Judson had never actually found himself acting *as* a policeman.

Not yet, at least.

Harper S. Ferry didn't have a policeman's background either, of course. He had one that had been a lot more violent. Judson could only hope that the year and a half which had passed since Harper gave up his old profession had placed at least a patina of restraint on the man.

Something of his tension must have shown. Harper glanced at him and smiled. "Relax. I don't intend to shoot the guy. Just find out why he's got an identity number he's got no business having."

✧   ✧   ✧

It didn't take them more than ten minutes to reach the south edge of the camp and find Allen working on the extractor. The machine wasn't particularly big, but it was incredibly noisy.

Noisy enough that Allen never heard them coming. The first he knew of their presence was when Harper tapped him on the shoulder.

The man turned a control, placing the machine on idle and drastically reducing the noise. Then he turned his head and said: "What can I do for you?"

He was quite relaxed. Then his gaze moved past Harper and fell on Judson, with Genghis perched on his shoulder.

The treecat's ears suddenly flattened, and Judson could feel his claws tightening on his shoulder. There were protective pads there for precisely this purpose. Judson knew that Genghis was readying to launch an attack.

"Be careful—" he started to shout at Harper. But Harper must have spotted something in Allen's stance or perhaps his eyes, because he was already reaching for the pulser on his hip.

Allen shouted something incoherent and struck Harper with his fist. The blow indicated the immigrant had had some martial arts training, but was certainly no expert at hand-to-hand combat. Harper rolled with the punch, catching it on his arm instead of his rib cage.

Still, the blow knocked him down. Allen was a big man, and very strong.

A lot stronger than Van Hale, certainly. But between his own pulser and Genghis' formidable abilities as a fighter, Judson wasn't really worried.

Allen apparently reached the same conclusion. He turned and darted around the extractor, heading for the nearby forest.

He was fast as well as strong. Judson probably couldn't have caught up with him, and he was reluctant to just shoot the man down when they still didn't really know anything.

But Genghis solved that problem. The 'cat was off Judson's shoulder and onto the ground and racing in pursuit within two seconds.

It was no contest. Genghis caught up with Allen before the man had gotten even halfway to the tree line. He went straight for the big man's legs and brought him down in two strides.

Allen hit the ground hard, screeching. He tried to knock Genghis away but the 'cat's razor-sharp claws were more than a match for his fist. A human being in good condition and with really good martial art skills had at least a fair chance against a treecat in a fight, simply because of the size disparity. But it wouldn't be easy and the human would certainly come out of it badly injured.

Allen didn't even try. He wriggled around onto his stomach. Then, oddly, he just stared at the trees for a few seconds.

By then, Judson had reached him. "Hold still, Allen!" he commanded. "Genghis won't hurt you any further as long you don't—"

He saw Allen's jaws tighten. Then the man's eyes rolled up, he inhaled once, gasped, gasped again . . . and he was unconscious and dying. Judson didn't have any doubt of it. From his little screech, neither did Genghis.

"What in the name of . . ." He shook his head, not sure what to do. Normally, he'd have begun CPR treatment, even though he was pretty sure there was no way to save Allen's life at this point. But there was a nasty-looking greenish slime beginning to ooze out of Allen's mouth, which he was almost certain was the residue or side effect—or both—of some sort of powerful poison. Whatever the stuff was, Van Hale wasn't about to get close to it.

Harper came up, cradling his arm. "What happened?"

"He committed suicide." Judson felt a bit stunned. Everything had happened so fast. From the time Harper tapped Allen on the shoulder to the man's suicide, not more than thirty seconds could have passed. Probably less. Maybe a lot less.

Harper knelt down next to Allen's body, and rolled him onto his back. The former Ballroom killer was careful not to let his hands get anywhere near Allen's mouth.

"Fast-acting poison in a hollow tooth. What in the name of creation is an ex-slave immigrant doing with *that* kind of equipment?" He looked around, spotted a sturdy-looking stick within reach, and picked it up. Then, used the stick to pry open Allen's mouth so he could look at the man's tongue.

"And . . . that's a Manpower breeding mark, for sure and certain. No chance at all it's cosmetic."

He straightened up from the corpse and rocked back on his heels, now squatting instead of kneeling. "What the hell is going on, Judson?"

CHAPTER TWENTY-FOUR

It *was* a good ice cream parlor, in fact. But not as good as Muckerjee's Treats in Grendel, the largest city of Beowulf.

The planetary—and system—capital was the city of Columbia, of course, but Columbia, alas, was only Beowulf's *second* largest city. In fact, it had been the system's second largest city for right on five hundred T-years, now. There were moments when its population had surged, threatening to overtake Grendel at last, yet it never had. Whenever Columbia seemed on the brink of finally overtaking its rival, something always happened to give *Grendel* a sudden surge of its own. Indeed, the more conspiracy-minded Columbians had muttered for generations that it was all a plot by some secret conspiracy to maintain the status quo. There'd never been any actual proof of that, mind you, but by now it was enshrined in Beowulfan legend that Grendel would *always* be bigger, more commercial—flashier in general. And, while Hugh would never want to appear overly credulous where such paranoid accusations were concerned, he'd once been curious enough to do a little research of his own . . . in the course of which he had discovered that Grendel's zoning laws had, in fact, been modified to encourage accelerated growth on several . . . demographically significant occasions. And on very little notice—and with very little public debate—too.

There *were* those (although Hugh didn't *think* he counted himself among them) who went still further and asserted that the same nefarious population plotters had deliberately enticed the original owner of Muckerjee's Treats into locating her emporium in Grendel. The parlor was certainly regarded as one of the city's hallmark and legendary attractions, at any rate, and rumor had it that the city government had extended the current owners several very attractive tax breaks to keep it right where it was. And with good reason, too. No ice cream anywhere in the inhabited galaxy was as good as that to be found in Muckerjee's Treats. Such, at least, was the firm opinion of Hugh Arai and every single member of Beowulf's Biological Survey Corps except the notoriously contrarian W.G. Zefat—and it was perhaps no coincidence that Captain Zefat had been sent off on what was expected to be the longest survey mission in the history of the Corps.

For that matter, the ice cream made in the parlor favored by the queen of Torch—J. Quesenberry's Ice Cream and Pastries, it was called—wasn't really as good as the ice cream made in a number of parlors in Manticore or any one of the inhabited planets in Sol system. Still, it was awfully good, and it had the great advantage over all other ice cream parlors in the galaxy of being the only one currently inhabited by Berry Zilwicki.

After about one hour of conversation in the parlor, an idle remark made by Berry reminded Hugh that when he'd first met the queen he hadn't taken much notice of her appearance. *Healthy-looking, not otherwise striking,* had pretty much summed it up.

That seemed like the memories of early childhood, now. Vague, half-forgotten—most of all, amusingly childish. In the way these things happen, Hugh's fascination with the young woman had completely transformed her appearance. His view of it, at least, and what else did he care about?

This is still a really bad idea. He repeated that mantra for perhaps the twentieth time. With no more effect than the first nineteen self-reminders.

"Jeremy more-or-less raised you, then?"

Hugh shook his head. "No such luck, I'm afraid. And given his lifestyle at the time—wanted by just about every police force in the galaxy—there was no way he could have even if he'd wanted to. No, I spent the first few years after my rescue in a relocation camp on Aldib's second planet, Berstuk."

"I never heard of Berstuk. Or Aldib, for that matter."

"Aldib's a G9 star, whose official monicker is Delta Draconis. Despite being in the same constellation as Beowulf's star, it's not really that close. It's about seventy-five light years from Sol. As for Berstuk . . ."

Hugh's expression grew bleak. "It's named after the Wendish god of the forest. Who was a pretty evil character, apparently. Which I can well believe."

Berry tilted her head slightly. "Well-named because of the forest, or the evil?"

"Both. The planet's gravity is slightly above Earth-normal. There aren't many oceans and those are small, so the climate is a lot worse. What they call 'continental.' Not unlivable, but the summers are bad and the winters are terrible."

"I thought you were rescued by a Beowulf warship."

"I was. But . . ." Hugh shrugged. "All things considered, I'm fond of my adopted homeworld, and Beowulf's probably—no, scratch that, *definitely*—the most ferocious star nation in the galaxy when it comes to enforcing the Cherwell Convention. Still, Beowulf has its faults. One of them, in my opinion, is that it pretends the Solarian League is really a functional nation, not just a batch of self-satisfied, overly prosperous, basically self-centered, piles of shared interests tied together in an association of convenience."

Berry raised her eyebrows, and Hugh chuckled. The sound was not remarkably cheerful.

"Sorry. The thing is, the ship that took out the slaver I was aboard happened to be operating in the territorial space of a fellow League star system. No one was ever able to prove anyone in that system had anything to do with the nasty slave traders, of course, but the local government insisted that the poor, liberated slaves be handed over to it so that it could personally see to their needs. The skipper of the cruiser—Captain Jeremiah—was a good sort, but he didn't have any choice but to go along with the demands of the local, legally constituted authorities. So we got handed over."

"And?" Berry prompted when he paused.

"And it's a good thing Captain Jeremiah *was* a good sort, because he put in a call to Beowulf's local trade representative. In the League, 'trade representatives' do a lot of the same things 'commercial attachés' do for relationships between independent star nations, so they've got more clout than the title might suggest. And the Beowulf representative made a point out of informing the local government that Beowulf felt responsible for the slaves it had liberated and would be expecting regular reports on their well-being. Which is probably the only thing that kept us all from getting 'disappeared.' Unfortunately, it didn't keep those oh-so-concerned local authorities from dumping us with the Office of Frontier Security when it found out it couldn't just make us all—poof, go away." He grimaced. "So, we all wound up stuck on Berstuk. It took quite a while for even Beowulf to get us unstuck. Once it did, though, we were fast tracked for citizenship." This time, he smiled. "The truth is, it's not that easy to get Beowulfan citizenship. The professional associations have a lot of clout on Beowulf—too much, in my opinion—and getting citizenship can take a *long* time unless you've got highly desirable professional skills or money or something else they find especially valuable. It can be done, but there are a lot of hoops to jump through, and it takes a while. Except for liberated slaves. Whatever else I might think about Beowulf, it really and truly hates Manpower's guts. Which is one of the main reasons that liberated slaves get to jump the line over just about everybody else when it comes to getting citizenship."

"I knew some of that, thanks to Cathy and Daddy, even before Web and Jeremy got hold of me," Berry said. "So you got citizenship?"

"Yep. On the other hand, OFS isn't especially fond of Beowulf, either. It didn't exactly fall all over itself to cooperate with any expatriation requests. Even with the Anti-Slavery League pushing our case, Frontier Security was dragging its heels for all it was worth. Matter of fact, although Jeremy's never admitted it, I've always suspected that the mysterious demise of at least one sector commissioner had something to do with finally breaking that particular log jam." He shook his head. "Either way, though, it took six T-years to get it done, and I was already eleven, standard, before Beowulf managed to pry us back loose from Frontier Security."

"Oh. Why does that name, when you say it, seem to rhyme with Wicked Cesspool Demons of the Universe?"

Hugh smiled. "It's probably best to stay away from my opinion of the OFS. Or all the ice cream in this parlor might suddenly melt. Let's just say that growing up in an OFS relocation center—call it refugee camp, which is blunter but a lot more accurate—is not an ideal environment for a child. If Jeremy—excuse me, I meant to say if whoever my anonymous guardian angel was—hadn't been able to . . . expedite things in the end, I'm afraid to think what might have become of me."

The smile stayed on his face, but there wasn't much good humor left in it. "By the time I was eleven, I was a real thug. With an eleven-year-old's view of the world, but a body as big as that of most adult males. And I'm stronger than I look, too."

"Than you *look*?" Berry started to giggle, and covered her mouth with her hand. "Uh . . . Hugh. I hate to be the one to tell you this, but it's not actually an accident that my Amazons"—she nodded at the two ex-Scrags sitting at the next table—"call you either 'the gorilla' or 'the caveman.'"

"Well, yeah. That's been pretty much a constant my whole life. By now, I'm used to it. But to get back to the point, by the time Jeremy—personally—turned up to tell me Beowulf was finally going to haul us out of there, I had a bright career ahead of me as a criminal. I wasn't actually that happy to leave, to tell you the truth."

"I take it you changed your mind, eventually?"

Hugh laughed. "Took about three months. Trust me on this one, Berry. The surest and fastest way known to humanity I can think of to get gangster attitudes nipped in the bud is to have Jeremy X as a godfather. That man makes any gang boss or criminal mastermind in the universe look wishy-washy and sentimental, if he sets his mind to a project. Which, in my case, was what you might call 'the Reformation and Re-Education of Hugh Arai.'"

Berry laughed also. "I can believe that!" She reached across the table and gave Hugh's hand a squeeze. "I'm certainly glad he did."

Her voice got a little huskier with that last sentence. And the touch of her hand—it was the first time they'd had any physical contact—sent a spike down his spine.

This is SUCH a bad idea. But he brushed aside that shrilling inner voice of caution much as a moose might brush aside slender spruce branches. In rutting season. He probably had a sappy grin on his face, too.

There was a little commotion at the door. Turning his head, Hugh saw that one of the Ballroom militants—ex-Ballroom, officially, although Hugh had his doubts—was trying to push his way into the parlor. He was having a tough time of it, but not because of any opposition being put up by Berry's Amazons.

Rather to the contrary. Lara rose from her seat, arms spread wide. "Saburo, honey! I wasn't expecting to see you until next week!"

No, the real problem was simply the population density in the outer and larger public room of the ice cream parlor. Every seat at every table was taken, and every square foot in between was jammed tight with people.

That had happened within five minutes of their arrival at the parlor. Hugh had commented on it, at the time. "You weren't kidding when you said this place was popular, were you?"

Berry had looked uncomfortable. At the next table, Yana had laughed and said: "It's popular, all right. But it's only this popular when *she* comes in."

As a former security expert, Hugh was simultaneously pleased and appalled. On the one hand—what you might call, the strategic hand—the quite-evident immense public approval that Torch's queen enjoyed was her greatest protection. It was no accident, after all, that for a public figure to be unpopular was the single most important factor in assessing his or her risk of being assassinated.

On a tactical level, however, this expression of public approval was something of a nightmare. Hugh found himself automatically falling into old habits, continually scanning the crowd on the lookout for weapons or any sort of threatening moves.

"Hugh!" Berry had exclaimed irritably, after a little while. "Do you *always* have the habit of not looking at the person you're talking to?"

Guiltily, he'd remembered he was officially on a date with the queen, not acting as her bodyguard. Thereafter, he'd managed to keep his eyes and attention on Berry, for the most part—something which grew easier as the evening wore on. Still, there remained some part of him always on alert and periodically shrilling warnings.

Saburo finally gave up trying to force his way through the mob. "Forget it!" he said, exasperated. "Lara, tell Her Way Too Popular Majesty that something's come up. We need her at the palace. ASAP. That means 'as soon as possible,' not 'as soon as Her Diet Unconscious Majesty gets around to finishing her' . . . what is that thing, anyway? A banana split on steroids?"

The whole parlor erupted in laughter. As densely packed as the place was, the sound was almost deafening. Berry made a face and looked down at her ice cream confection. It *did* look something like a banana split on steroids, in fact, even though whatever that fruit was it certainly wasn't a banana. Hugh knew, because he'd had a real Earth banana once, when he visited the planet. Truth to tell, he hadn't much liked the thing. Too squishy. Like almost anyone brought up on Berstuk, he was accustomed to fruit that was dense, hard and not too sweet—more like what Earth's own inhabitants would have called nuts than fruit.

"I guess we'd better go," she said reluctantly.

Hugh studied the confection at issue. There was still more than half of it left. The ice cream dish he'd ordered had vanished within three minutes. Manpower's genetic engineers had designed his somatic type to be unusually strong even for his size. Although not to the same extreme as Thandi Palane, his metabolism was something of a furnace.

"We might be able to take the rest of it back," he said, sounding dubious even to himself.

"In *this* heat?" said Berry, smiling skeptically. "Not without portable refrigeration equipment. Which we don't have, even if there are any such units on the planet at all."

Yana had come up to the table. "Sure, there are plenty of them. But they're all out at the pharmaceutical sites. Why would anyone want the things here? A little stroll through the tropics is good for you." She studied the half-finished confection disapprovingly. "And why do you always order that dish, anyway? You never finish it."

"Because they won't make it half-sized for me, even though I've asked over and over. They claim if they don't serve me what they call a 'queen-sized' order, they'll look bad."

She gave Hugh a plaintive look. "Does that seem as silly to you as it does to me? Of course, most of this royal stuff is silly, in my opinion."

How to answer that? Hugh was cautious, even though on Torch *lèse majesté* couldn't be any worse than a misdemeanor.

"Well . . ."

"Of course it's not silly," said Yana. "They must sell half again as much ice cream here as they would otherwise. What *is* silly are customers who let themselves get swindled like that."

"You order queen-size dishes yourself," pointed out Berry.

"Sure. I finish them, too. Come on, Your Mousety. Even with me and Lara and Mr. Human Iceberg leading the way, it's going to be a tussle getting you out of here."

✧   ✧   ✧

In fact, extricating themselves from the back room of J. Quesen-berry's Ice Cream and Pastries and getting onto the street outside proved to be quite easy. In some mysterious manner that Hugh was sure violated at least one of the laws of thermodynamics, the patrons in the place managed to squeeze themselves aside, just enough to leave a lane for Berry and her companions to pass through.

That was further proof, if any was needed, of the queen's high level of public approval. But the experience practically had Hugh screaming. One of the basic principles of providing security to a public official was to keep a clear zone around them. That gave the security force at least a chance—a pretty good chance, in fact, if they were properly trained professionals—of spotting an emerging threat in time to deal with it.

From that standpoint, J. Quesenberry's Ice Cream and Pastries might as well have been named Death Trap. In that press, literally dozens of people could have murdered Berry with nothing more complicated or high-tech than a non-metallic poisoned needle. And there would have been no way Hugh or Lara or Yana—or any bodyguard this side of guardian angels—could have prevented it. They wouldn't have even spotted the threat until Berry was on her way down.

And already dead, not more than a few seconds afterward. Hugh knew at least three poisons that would kill a normal-sized person within five or ten seconds. Of course, they wouldn't actually *die* that quickly. Contrary to popular mythology that had been fed by way too many badly researched vid dramas, not even the deadliest poison could outrace the passage of oxygen and fluids through the human body. But it hardly mattered. With any one of those three poisons, the person's death was inevitable unless the antidote was administered almost simultaneously with the poison itself. One of them, in fact, a distant derivative of curare developed on Onamuji, had no known antidote at all. Luckily, it was unstable outside of a narrow temperature range and therefore not very practical as a real murder weapon.

Once they were out on the street, Hugh heaved a sigh of relief that was loud enough for Berry to hear it.

"Pretty bad, huh?"

Lara jeered at her. "You think those midgets in there could

have squeezed *his* lungs empty? Not a chance, girl. I was following him—much to my pleasure—and it was like following a walrus through a pack of penguins. Plenty of room. No, he's obviously a security type—I can spot 'em a mile away—and he's sighing with relief that the security threat level to Your Average Heightness just dropped from Screaming Scarlet to Fire Engine Red."

Berry gave Hugh a reproachful look. "Is that true? Did you just accept my invitation—well, technically, you were the one who asked me out on a date even though like usual the girl had to do most of the work—because you were watching out for my security?" A trace of shrillness entered her voice. "*Did Jeremy put you up to this?*"

Hugh had always been an adherent to the ancient saw that honesty was the best policy. As a rule, at least. And he'd already figured out that, with Berry Zilwicki, honesty would always be the best policy.

"The answer is yes, no, and he tried but I declined."

Berry got a little cross-eyed as she parsed that reply. "Okay. I think." She took his elbow and began leading him back toward the palace. Managing, somehow, to make it seem as if he'd politely offered her his arm and he'd accepted.

Which he hadn't, in fact. His real inclination was to keep both hands free and clear, in case some threat materialized . . .

"Gah," he said.

"What does that mean?"

"It means Jeremy's right. You *are* a security expert's nightmare."

"You tell her, Hugh!" came Yana's approving voice from behind them.

"Yeah," chimed in Lara. "You are the walrus."

CHAPTER TWENTY-FIVE

Once they arrived back at the palace, they found a small delegation waiting to meet them. Jeremy X was there, along with Thandi
Palane, Princess Ruth, and two men Hugh didn't know. One of
them had a treecat perched on his shoulder.

"Should we meet in the audience chamber?" Berry suggested.

Jeremy shook his head. "The security precautions there are sub-
standard, as I've told you a gazillion times." Sternly: "And this time,
damnation, you *will* listen to me. We'll meet in the operations
room. It's the only place in the palace that's really secure."

Berry didn't argue the point. In fact, she almost—not quite—
looked a bit chastened.

The two Amazons and Saburo politely detached themselves.
Jeremy led the rest of the group to an elevator, which was just
large enough for all of them to fit into it. The elevator took them
down . . .

A long, long, long way. Wherever they were headed, Hugh
realized, it had to be a place specially constructed for a specific
purpose, and almost certainly by Manpower. They were going far
deeper than could be explained by any normal architecture, and
there hadn't been enough time since the foundation of Torch—not
with everything else to be done—for the new nation to have
completed such a project.

Hugh's spirits picked up. That was old training at work. The
simplest and still surest way to make a room secure from any spying apparatus was to bury it deeply in the earth. Judging from the
time it was taking the elevator to get there, and Hugh's estimate of

their speed, this room must be at least a thousand meters below the surface, and probably closer to two thousand. About the only particles that would penetrate to that depth, at least reliably, were neutrinos. To the best of Hugh's knowledge, not even Manticore had managed to build detection equipment that used neutrinos.

Sound detection was far easier, of course, since depth actually provided some benefits. But that was easy to block.

Jeremy must have sensed Hugh's curiosity. "Manpower built this buried chamber to cover its most secure computers—read 'really deep dark and secret, burn-before-reading record archives.' Which, of course, meants they were also their most incriminating records, as well as the most sensitive. And then the incompetent clown charged with destroying the evidence neglected to punch in the instructions in the proper sequence during the rebellion. Probably because he was shitting his pants. So the chamber computers locked down instead of slagging the molycircs and everything stored in them. And then he couldn't get them to unlock and let him back in because—apparently—he either never had the access code for that little problem in the first place or (more likely, my opinion) he simply forgot what the hell it was. Probably because he was shitting his pants. Then he just ran away—see prior explanation—and apparently got killed in the general mayhem. We're not positive, because it took us—Princess Ruth, that is—almost two days to unseal the chamber. By then, few of the bodies anywhere in the headquarters area had enough left for good physical identification. And the DNA records were mostly destroyed because the slaves who stormed the record office reduced the library files to teeny, tiny, thoroughly stomped upon *and* incinerated chunks of circuitry. Along with the technicians and clerks who'd maintained those records."

Berry grimaced.

But Jeremy just smiled. Thinly, but it was a smile. Whatever else might be preying on his conscience, the massacre of so many of Manpower's management and employees during the rebellion was obviously not one of them.

Hugh didn't blame him in the least. He'd seen some of the vids taken at the time himself, and had just shrugged them off. Yes, some of what had happened here had been hideous—but there was a good reason Manpower's slaves called most of its employees "the scorpions."

Hugh's parents and all of his siblings had been shoved into space unprotected and died horrible deaths, just so a slaver crew might claim they'd had no cargo. Hugh wasn't any more likely to lose sleep over the butchery of anyone connected with Manpower than he was to lose sleep over the extermination of dangerous bacteria. So far as he was concerned, anyone who voluntarily joined Manpower forfeited any right to be considered a human being any longer.

That didn't mean he had approved of the Ballroom's tactics. Some he had; most he hadn't. As a rule, Hugh had been inclined toward Web Du Havel's view of the matter. But, as with Du Havel, for him the issue was purely one of tactical effectiveness. By any reasonable moral standard, anyone connected to Manpower deserved any fate meted out to them. Such, at least, was Hugh Arai's opinion—which he'd held rock solid since the age of five.

The elevator came to a stop.

"How deep—"

"One thousand, eight hundred and forty-two meters," Berry said. "I asked myself, the first time. The place still gives me the creeps."

From the elevator, it was a short walk down a wide corridor—there was plenty of room there for additional computer systems, if they were needed, although it was currently empty—and then into a circular and very spacious chamber. Looking around at the equipment lining much of the wall space, Hugh recognized them as security-proofing devices.

State of the art, too. Much of the equipment had been made on Manticore, he was pretty sure.

At the very center of the chamber was a large and circular table. Torus-shaped, rather. Keeping an actual "center" in a table with that great a diameter would have been pointless and sometimes even awkward. Instead, the open center had a robot standing idle, ready to move papers and material around, and Hugh could see where a portion of the table could be slid aside to allow a person to enter that central space.

In short, it was a state-of-the-art conference table that had probably been designed and built somewhere in the Republic of Haven. The table itself was made of wood—or possibly a wood veneer—and Hugh thought he recognized it as one of the very expensive hardwoods produced on Tahlmann.

Jeremy had been leading the way, but once they reached the chamber Berry took charge. Young she might be, and generally disinclined toward the trappings of royalty, but it was already clear to Hugh that when she wanted to be, the queen was quite capable of taking control of things.

"Please, everyone, take a seat. Judson and Harper, since I presume your presence here means you're the ones making the report, I'd recommend you take those two seats over there." She pointed to two seats on either side of some discretely recessed and subdued equipment. Hugh recognized it as the control center for sophisticated displays.

That equipment, judging from what he could see of it, had been made on Erewhon. Combined with the origins of most of the other equipment present—all the lighting equipment was obviously Solarian, probably made somewhere in Maya Sector—this chamber was a testimony in itself to the material support Torch had gotten from its many powerful sponsors.

Once they were all seated, Berry gestured toward the two men Hugh wasn't familiar with. "Hugh, since you've never met them, let me introduce Harper S. Ferry and Judson Van Hale. They both work for Immigration Services. Harper's a former member of the Audubon Ballroom; Judson's parents were both genetic slaves although he was born free on Sphinx and was a forest ranger before coming here."

That explained the treecat. Hugh nodded at both of them, and they nodded back.

"As for Hugh, he's a member of Beowulf's Biological Survey Corps—"

That news heightened Ferry's interest, quite obviously. As was true of many people in the Audubon Ballroom, he was aware that the BSC was not the innocuous outfit its name suggested. Just as obviously, it didn't mean anything to Van Hale.

"—who came here for reasons I don't think I'm at liberty to discuss in front of the two of you"—she smiled at them—"unless the nature of your report changes things."

"Which it certainly will," said Jeremy. "But, at least for the moment, Harper and Judson don't need to know the ins and outs of it. I'll simply add that I've known Hugh since he was five years old. He claims me as some sort of godfather, a notion which is preposterous on the face of it. Still, I'll vouch for him."

He turned toward Berry. "May I?"

"Please do."

The war secretary leaned forward on the desk. "This morning, alerted by some peculiarities, these two agents began an investigation. Everything unfolded very quickly, and by mid-afternoon a man was dead at one of our pharmaceutical camps and our brand new star nation—this is my opinion, at any rate—finds itself confronted by a new and serious threat. More precisely, has *discovered* a serious threat. I doubt very much if it's actually new. That's one of things we need to find out."

By then, he had everyone's attention. He turned toward Van Hale and Ferry. "Take it from there, please."

Harper S. Ferry cleared his throat. "I'm afraid we don't have any visual records beyond the basics, so a lot of this is going to be verbal. A little over two months ago, on February ninth, Genghis here"—he nodded toward the treecat on Van Hale's shoulder—"detected an unusual emotional aura coming from one of the newly arrived immigrants. A man by the name of Ronald Allen."

"It wasn't really *that* unusual," Judson interrupted. "Allen was certainly uneasy, especially when he caught sight of Genghis. But a lot of immigrants are nervous when they arrive, and treecats often cause uneasiness in people. It was mostly just a matter of Genghis feeling that the 'mind glow' tasted a little . . . odd."

Everyone at the table looked at the treecat; who, for his part, returned their scrutiny with an appearance of indifference. It might be better to say, casual insouciance.

Which, it probably was. Everyone in the room was very familiar with treecats and their abilities.

Van Hale continued. "It was enough for me to bring the matter to Harper's attention, and he set an inquiry into motion."

"Nothing special," said Harper. "Just the sort of routine double-check we launch any time there's anything that appears to be possibly amiss. Still, it's my fault that I forgot the matter and didn't follow up on it. And, unfortunately, the clerk who handled the inquiry didn't notify me immediately when an anomaly turned up. Instead, she just launched a routine double-check herself."

"Strip her damn hide off, when you get the chance," Jeremy growled.

"Don't think I'm not tempted. But I won't, beyond making

sure she understands her mistake, because the responsibility was ultimately mine." Harper made a face. "By the time Judson reminded me of the case—which was just this morning—weeks had gone by. Allen had gotten a job as a roustabout with one of the pharmaceutical companies—they're almost always hiring, with the boom we're having—and wasn't residing in the capital any longer."

"What was the anomaly?" asked the queen.

"As I believe you know, Your Majesty—"

"We're in private, here," she reminded him just a bit tartly. "Please call me Berry."

"Ah . . . Berry. As I think you know, we scan every ex-slave immigrant's tongue marker as soon as they arrive. Partly as a security device, but mostly as a health measure. A lot of Manpower's genetic lines are subject to medical problems, some of which are severe. Many of those conditions are susceptible to preventive or ameliorative treatment. But it's often the case that the person in question isn't even aware of their medical problem. By doing the automatic scans, we give our medical services a leg up."

She nodded. "Yes, I knew that. But what was the anomaly?"

"Ronald Allen's number turned out to be a duplicate. Another immigrant named Tim Zeiger, who'd arrived a year earlier, has the same number."

Berry looked puzzled. "But . . . how is that kind of mistake possible?"

"It's not," Jeremy said flatly. "Those bar codes are genetically programmed into the slave at fertilization, Berry, and the process used to assign them is about as close to fool-proof as human endeavors get. This isn't the kind of situation where 'mistakes' happen."

"Then how . . ." The young queen's face, pale by nature, turned even paler. "Oh . . . my . . . God. That means Manpower had to have deliberately violated their own procedures. And the only reason they would have done *that* was in order to . . ."

She looked at Jeremy, seeming in that moment to be even younger than she was. "They've been penetrating the Ballroom, Jeremy."

"All too true. *And* Torch, now. This Ronald Allen never claimed to be a Ballroom member, nor do we have any indication that he's ever joined."

For a moment, Jeremy's expression lightened. "Mind you, it's still possible he had. For reasons I presume are obvious, it's never been the Ballroom's custom to maintain precise and readily accessible membership records."

A nervous little titter went around the table. But it was over very quickly.

"Sending in counter-agents to penetrate revolutionary regimes is a tactic at least as old as the Tsarist Okhrana," Jeremy went on after a moment, "and that's because, properly done, it's as effective as hell. But, of course, there are always those little problems, as well, aren't there? Like *this* one."

He nodded to Harper, who worked briefly at the display controls, and a hologram sprang up in the open center of the table. It was a crude hologram, with peculiar lacunae in the imagery. Hugh recognized what he was seeing immediately. As was true of police officials most places in the modern universe—or even people whose jobs involved at least some policing functions—Harper S. Ferry and Judson Van Hale had been legally required to carry vid-recording equipment at all times and turned on whenever they were functioning in an official capacity. That was partly for the purpose of protecting suspects from possible police misconduct, but mostly because such records had proven time and again to assist the police themselves.

The crudity and sometime raggedness of this particular hologram was caused by the fact that it was a computer composite of only two vid-recorders—both of them located on the officers' shoulders, from the apparent height of the viewpoints, and both of which had been subject to violent motions during the critical last period.

Still, the record was clear enough. Whatever motives or incentives might have been driving the man named Ronald Allen, they'd been powerful enough to lead him to commit suicide, after only a moment's thought. Even though he'd only seen it second-hand, Hugh knew he'd never forget that image of Allen staring into the trees for two or three seconds, before he clenched down on his poison tooth. A man taking one last brief look at the world, before he deliberately and consciously ended his own life. Hugh wouldn't be surprised if either Harper or Judson—maybe both—would need some psychological treatment in the near future. That sort of vivid and gut-wrenching image—never mind that Harper was a hardened Ballroom killer and the man who died worked for Manpower—was exactly the sort of thing that could trigger post-traumatic stress disorder.

The final image was of a dead man's mouth, pried open with a stick to show the bar code on his tongue. There was something particularly horrifying and gruesome about the sight, and the expression of everyone sitting around the table was a bit hag-gard when it finally faded. In fact, Berry's complexion was almost completely white when Jeremy spoke again, harshly.

"There's no way known for that kind of genetic tongue-marker to be faked cosmetically," he said, his voice flat and hard. "Not against the kind of scanning we do, at least. There's no way to remove it that isn't both difficult and damned expensive—Manpower made sure of that, the bastards—and the thing will grow back even if you simply amputate the tongue and use regen to grow it back again. Trust me, we've already determined that *both* the codes in this instance are as genuine as genuine can be. Duplicates, yes; fakes, no."

"But why?" Berry asked in the tone of someone just as happy to have something to distract her from the memory of a dead man's poison-frothed tongue. "Why bother to use a *duplicated* number? After all, Manpower designs the numbers in the first place. Why not just use new numbers altogether, set aside for the purpose?"

Jeremy shook his head. "The process used to assign and imprint numbers isn't all that complicated, really, Berry—not for someone who's designing complete human genotypes! Trust me, we know how it works—and from too many independent sources—to doubt that Manpower can, and does, make *damned* certain there aren't going to be any *accidentally* duplicated numbers. They've got a lot of reasons to want to be sure of that, including their own security concerns and the need to be able to positively and absolutely identify any individual slave's specific batch in case some genetic anomaly turns up and they need to track down anyone else who may have it. Keeping the numbers straight—both before and after a slave is decanted—isn't a minor consideration, given that they produce slaves at so many different breeding sites, and they've put a lot of effort into developing procedures to do just that.

"If they started screwing around with those procedures, they might poke a hole in them they don't want. Oh, they could set aside the occasional batch number. In fact, I think they probably do, if they need lots of them. But they'd have to set aside the *entire* batch each time, given their procedures, so I doubt they do it very often. If they did, the bar codes would have to 'clump,' and there'd always be the chance—probably a pretty good one, actually—that somebody might notice an association between batch mates doing suspicious things. It might not be too likely in any single agent's case, but statistics play no favorites. Sooner or later, somebody would be likely to notice the clumping—or, for that matter, just notice an age spread, or a genetic variation, or any number of little differences batch mates shouldn't have. And if that happened, then those agents would be sitting ducks. Manpower might as well have their tongues marked *shoot me now.*"

He shook his head again. "And Manpower knows it, don't think they don't. No, there's a good reason they'd use duplicate numbers, especially from different batch numbers—whenever they could be certain the numbers in question were available, at least. Among other things, that would give them a lot more potential age varia-tions, not to mention letting them randomize batch numbers to avoid that particular association. And how much safer could it be to reuse a given number than in a case where they knew the legitimate 'recipient' was already dead? Which, in this case, they did—or thought they did—since the aforesaid legitimate recipient was aboard a ship they knew had blown the hell up. It's really a pure fluke that we found out."

Hugh had already reached that conclusion himself, but he had a rather more burning question on his mind.

"How?" he asked simply. He and Jeremy looked at one another in silent understanding, their expressions grim, and Berry frowned at the two of them.

"'How' what?" she demanded after a moment.

"How can you use a person bred to be a genetic slave—and with no way to ever disguise the fact—as a counter-agent?" Jeremy asked in reply. "How do you do that without running the constant and tremendous risk that he or she will turn on you—and a turned agent is far worse than having no agent at all. Anybody who's familiar with the ABCs of espionage and counterespionage knows *that* much."

Ruth interjected. "Counterespionage is to espionage what epis-temology is to philosophy, Berry. The most fundamental branch. *How* do you know what you know? If you can't answer that, you can't answer anything." She flashed a quick, nervous smile. "Sorry. I know that sounds pedantic. But it's true."

Hugh had only a fuzzy sense of the meaning of the term "epistemology," but he understood the gist of the princess's comments, and agreed with her. Manpower could obviously *breed* such a counter-agent. That would be no more difficult, biologically speaking, than breeding any other slave. And although it would be a nuisance—but no more than that—they could easily enough duplicate a number.

But, as Jeremy had just asked, how could they possibly be sure of retaining the agent's loyalty, once they sent him out?

Hugh could think of ways Manpower might *try* to retain that loyalty, to be sure. Threatening hostages would probably be the one with the greatest likelihood of success; sometimes the crudest methods really did work best. But keeping people close to the agent hostage and threatening to harm them wouldn't work as well in this sort of situation as it might in others. In the very nature of their origins and upbringing, Manpower's slaves didn't *have* people close to them. Except for the sort of adopted relations that Hugh himself had gotten, of course. He, of all people, was unlikely to ever underestimate how precious that sort of "relationship" could become . . . yet every slave knew in his bones that those bonds were fragile. They existed only on the sufferance of others, and they were *always* subject to being torn apart by those same others—and always *would* be . . . so long as the institution of slavery itself survived. When an agent ended up confronting the sort of gut-wrenching stress inherent in betraying comrades dedicated to the overthrow of the monstrous evil threaning to do just that, "reliability" went straight out the airlock.

In fact, that was true of just about every method Hugh could think of, in a case like this, and Ruth's basic point sat at the center of everything: a turned agent was the great disaster every intelligence agency did everything in its power to avoid. Unless the people Manpower had in charge of its counterespionage against the Ballroom were complete fools—and there was no evidence that they were, and plenty of evidence that they weren't—there was no chance they'd take this sort of risk.

And if they had *been inclined to, it would have bitten them on the ass a* long *time ago*, he thought grimly.

There was a a long, still moment of silence as the question lay ugly and naked among them. Then Ruth inhaled audibly.

"Manpower isn't what it seems," she said. "It just *can't* be. We already suspected as much, and this is still more evidence—and powerful evidence at that. There is no way a mere corporation, no matter how evil and shrewd and influential and powerful, could have created the man we all just saw dying. Not the way he died. One or two, maybe. With the right psych programming, the right threats and bribes. *Maybe.* But there's no way—*no way*—they could create *enough* of him to justify sending him to Torch for what had to be no more than a routine penetration. We've put this man's life here on-planet under an electron microscope, and he did nothing—nothing at all—except the sort of things a simple, white-bread information probe would have required. No corporation, not even the biggest transtellar, could have enough of these sorts of people to waste one of them on something that routine. They just *couldn't.* Something else is going on."

"But . . . what?" asked Berry.

"That's what we have to find out," said Jeremy. "And, finally, we're going to put the needed resources into it."

Ruth looked very cheery. "Me, for starters. Jeremy's asked me to . . . well, coordinate it, anyway. I'm not really heading it up, exactly. God, is this fun or what?"

Berry stared at her. "You think this is *fun?* I think it's pretty horrible."

"So do I," said Palane forcefully.

"Well, sure. One of you was born and raised in the warrens of Chicago, in the proverbial desp'rate straits. And the other was born and raised in the serf hellhole of Ndebele, which isn't exactly desp'rate straits but is about as miserable as anything this side of . . . of . . ."

"Dante's third level of Hell," Hugh offered.

"Who's Dante?" asked Berry.

"He must be referring to Khalid Dante, the OFS security chief for Carina Sector," said Ruth. "Nasty piece of work, by all accounts. But the point I was getting to is that *I* was born and raised in the comfort and security of the royal house of Winton, so *I* know the truth, which is that the ultimate horror is boredom."

She sat back in her seat, looking very self-satisfied.

Berry looked at Palane. "She's gone barking mad on us."

Palane smiled. "So? She was *always* barking mad, and you know it. Which only makes her an even better choice, when you come down to it. Who *better* to set on Manpower?"

CHAPTER TWENTY-SIX

"I think that just about does it, Jordin," Richard Wix observed. He was obviously trying to keep his voice properly blasé—or, at least, professionally detached—but he wasn't doing a particularly good job of it, and Jordin Kare chuckled.

"You do, do you?" he inquired.

"We've got the locus' central focus nailed, we've got the tidal stresses, and we've got the entry vector," Wix replied.

"Which is all well and good, Doctor," Captain Zachary put in, "except for that other little problem."

"We've been over that and over that," Wix said, as patiently as he could (which, truth to tell, wasn't all *that* patiently). "I don't see any way a gravitic kick that weak is going to have any significant impact on efforts to transit. We compensate for kicks like that every day, Captain."

"No, TJ, we don't, actually," Kare said. Wix glowered at him, but Kare only shrugged. "I'll grant you that we routinely compensate for kicks of its *magnitude*. For that matter, we've got a kick several times this strong on the Manticore-Basilisk transit, and it's never been a problem. But you know as well as I do we've never seen one like this—one whose strength *and* repetition rate vary this sharply *and* unpredictably." He shook his head. "If you can show me what's causing it—a model that explains it, one that lets you predict what it's going to do for, say, a twenty-four-hour duration—then I'll agree with you that it's a matter of routine compensation. But you can't do that, can you?"

"No," Wix admitted after a moment. "I don't think it's powerful

249

enough, even at the strongest reading we've recorded, to seriously threaten a ship transiting the terminus, though."

"I agree with you." Kare nodded. "That's not really my point, though. My point is that we're looking at something we've never seen before: a kick—and let's not forget, TJ, that what we call a 'kick' could just as accurately be called a 'spike'—that doesn't seem to be associated in any way with the routine stress patterns of the locus."

"Exactly how significant is that?" Zachary asked. Kare cocked an eyebrow at her, and she shrugged. "I'm nowhere near the theoretician the two of you are, of course, but it looks to me like Dr. Wix does have a point about the relative strength of the kick, or 'spike,' or whatever we want to call it. There's no way anything that weak is going to pose any kind of threat to *Harvest Joy*'s hyper generator or alpha nodes, so I don't see its significantly impacting our transit, either. Obviously, something about it bothers you a lot more than that, though."

"What bothers me is that there's not another single instance anywhere in the literature of a gravitic spike like this one that wasn't somehow connected to the observable patterns of the locus associated with it," Kare said, his expression thoughtful. "People tend to think of wormhole termini as big, fixed doorways in space, and in gross terms, I don't suppose there's anything wrong with that visualization. But what they actually are are fixed *points* in space where intense gravity waves impinge on one another. On the gravitic level, they're areas of immense stress. It's a very tightly *focused* stress, one in which enormous forces are concentrated and counterbalanced so finely that they appear, on the macro level, to be stable. But it's a stability which results only from keeping enormous amounts of *instability* perfectly balanced against one another.

"That's always been the really tricky point about surveying and charting wormholes, of course. Nobody could possibly build a ship tough enough to survive even momentarily if it tried to power its way through that interface of balanced instabilities by brute force. Instead, we have to chart them, much like I suppose oceanographers chart currents and winds, to determine the precise vectors which let ships . . . well, 'shoot the rapids,' as a friend of mine likes to put it."

He paused until Zachary nodded, and to the captain's credit, he noticed, there was no apparent impatience in her nod. He flashed her a quick smile.

"I know none of that came as any great surprise to you, Captain," he told her. "But restating it may help to put my current concerns into context. You see, every other 'kick' or 'spike' we've ever encountered has been linked directly to a stress, or an eddy, in those patterns of focused instability. In fact, more often than not, when we find a kick, it leads us to a stress pattern we might not have noticed otherwise. In this case, though, it appears to be totally unrelated to *any* of the stress patterns in this terminus. It comes and goes on its own periodicity and with its own frequency shifts, completely irrespective of anything we've been able to observe or measure from this locus. I'm not saying it doesn't *have* a regular periodicity; I'm simply saying we haven't been able to determine what that periodicity may *be*, and we haven't been able to find any aspect of the terminus which is associated with it. It's almost . . . almost as if what we're observing here doesn't really have anything to do with the terminus at all."

Wix snorted. Kare looked at him, and the younger hyperphysicist shook his head at him.

"Oh, I can't disagree with anything you just said, Jordin. But whatever else this may be, it's clearly a hyper wall interface spike, and the only two things we've ever seen produce wall interface spikes are hyperdrive alpha translations and wormhole termini. One way or another, it's associated with a terminus!"

"Maybe." Kare said. Wix arched a skeptical eyebrow, and Kare grimaced. "All right, it's definitely associated with a terminus. Unfortunately, we haven't been able to establish how it's associated with *this* terminus, have we?"

"Well, no." Wix frowned as he made the admission, then shrugged. "It's almost like it's coming from somewhere else," he said.

"But what I seem to be hearing both of you saying, is that even in a worst-case scenario, based on what we know at this point, *Harvest Joy* could safely transit?" Zachary asked.

"Pretty much," Kare admitted after a moment.

"Then I think it's time we talked to Queen Berry and the Prime Minister," she said.

✧   ✧   ✧

"So, let me see if I have this straight," Berry Zilwicki said. "We know enough, we think, to send *Harvest Joy* through the wormhole—sorry, through the *terminus*—but we've got this 'kick' thingy, and we don't know what's causing it. And because we don't, Dr. Kare," she nodded courteously to the Manticoran, "is worried that we may be dealing with something no one's ever seen before."

"That's pretty much it, Your Majesty," Kare agreed. "It's not the *strength* of the kick that worries me; it's the fact that we can't explain what's causing it. The hyper-physicist in me is intrigued as hell by the discovery of a new phenomenon. This is the kind of thing we look for all the time, you understand. But the surveyor in me is more than a little unhappy because of the hyper-physicist in me's inability to explain what's going on before I go venturing off into the unknown."

"But you don't see any physical danger to the ship in making the transit?" Web Du Havel asked.

"Probably not," Kare said "Almost certainly not, in fact. But given that we're dealing with something I ought to be able to explain and can't, I can't make any sort of categorical guarantee. I'm perfectly willing to make the transit aboard her, you understand, and I'm not exactly in the habit of sticking my neck out unless I'm pretty sure I'm going to be able to pull it back in safely afterward. But the bottom line is that we're dealing with an uncertainty factor no one's ever dealt with before."

"What about getting back again?" Thandi Palane asked. Everyone looked at her, and she shrugged, hazel eyes intent. "If there's anyone in the galaxy who knows less about surveying wormholes than I do, I've never met her," she said. "On the other hand, I've been doing my best to bone up on the subject, and I've been watching those of you who do know what you're doing for the last three T-months. It occurs to me that you've been paying a lot of attention to charting the patterns, and what I'm wondering about is whether or not you think this 'kick' is enough that we should be worrying about how well we'll be able to chart the patterns from the other side for the return trip."

"I don't see any reason it should make the charting exercise significantly more difficult from the other end," Kare replied. "Despite my own concern over the kick's unpredictability, it didn't keep us from getting a quick fix on the terminus's basic patterns. I don't see anything about it to suggest that it's going to significantly scramble patterns at the other end of the bridge, and having made transit once, *Harvest Joy*'s sensors will have given us a huge head start on analyzing them, anyway. I suppose it's theoretically possible we'd have a problem, but it seems extraordinarily unlikely."

"Forgive me, Doctor," Palane said with one of her dazzling smiles, "but 'extraordinarily unlikely' doesn't exactly sound like 'no way in hell' to me. And I can't help thinking the Star Kingdom might just be a little ticked off with us if we absentmindedly misplaced their best hyper-physicists by feeding them to some kind of rogue terminus."

"That's probably true," Du Havel agreed with a chuckle. "And that doesn't even consider the kind of PR effect it could have on the summit between Manticore and Haven."

The others around the conference table nodded, although in Wix's case it was obviously a nod of acknowledgment, not agreement. Eloise Pritchart's acceptance of Torch as the site for her summit meeting with Elizabeth Winton had reached the Torch System two days ago, and no one in that room was unaware of the monumental possibilities direct, face-to-face negotiations between the two warring heads of state presented. Wix, though, clearly failed to see the connection Du Havel was making, and the prime minister shrugged.

"I never said it would be a *logical* effect, Dr. Wix," he said. "Human beings, however, don't always proceed on the basis of logic. For that matter, I think they almost *never* proceed on the basis of logic, when you come down to it. If nothing else, the fact that we'd managed to 'misplace,' as Thandi puts it, an entire survey team just three months before the summit would probably put something of a damper on the festivities. I imagine some people might even take it as an omen for the summit's ultimate chances of success, and the last thing anyone needs at this point is any sort of self-fulfilling prophecy of doom and gloom."

"I could live with that, Web," Palane said dryly. "I'd just as soon not piss Queen Elizabeth off at us, though."

"Worst-case scenario, Your Majesty," Captain Zachary said, "is that we can't survey the other end at all. Or that we can't chart it well enough to come back through it, anyway. In that case, we're looking at having to come home the long way around, via a regular hyper-space route."

"Would that be likely to pose any significant problems or risks?" Du Havel asked.

"Mr. Prime Minister, there's no way anyone could make this process risk free, whatever you do," Wix pointed out. "We could have dropped a decimal point in our analysis of the terminus. Over the last couple of hundred years, we've actually turned up a terminus no one has ever successfully transited. Just one. That's an absurdly tiny percentage of the total, but it *has* happened. Frankly, though, the possibility of something that unlikely happening would be a lot greater than the possibility that *Harvest Joy* couldn't get home again—eventually—from the other end of the bridge, wherever it is."

"That's true, Mr. Prime Minister," Zachary agreed. "The longest wormhole leg anyone's ever charted is right on nine hundred light-years long in normal-space terms. The average is a lot shorter than that, and transits of more than three or four hundred light-years are rare. *Harvest Joy,* on the other hand, has a four-month unrefueled endurance. That gives us a cruising radius of eight hundred light-years before we'd have to re-bunker, and that figure is based on our having to make the entire trip under impeller drive. As soon as we could get into a grav wave, our endurance would go up hugely, so we'd have to go a hell of a lot farther directly away from any settled area of the galaxy before we wouldn't be able to get home *eventually*."

"Well, that's a relief," Du Havel said.

"So are we prepared to authorize the transit?" Kare asked.

"I think . . . yes," the prime minister replied after a thoughtful moment, and glanced at the queen. "Finding out where that terminus connects to is going to have too many economic and strategic implications for us to even think about delaying over something as . . . esoteric as this 'kick,' I think."

"I agree." Queen Berry nodded, but she also frowned. "Before we do, though, is there any reason *you* have to go along, Dr. Kare?"

"I beg your pardon, Your Majesty?"

"I asked if there was any reason you, personally, would have to go along," the queen repeated.

"Well, no . . . not really, I suppose," Kare said slowly. "It's my project, though, Your Majesty. If we're going to send anyone through, then I ought to be going along, as well. Sort of like the captain going along with the rest of his ship."

"With all due respect, Jordin," Zachary said with a chuckle, "that's not really the best example you could have come up with.

It wouldn't be like a captain going along with the rest of her ship; it would be like an admiral going along with *one* of the ships under her command. You might want to consider which one of us would actually be in command."

"Well, you would, of course, Josepha!" Kare said quickly.

"And that's *my* point," Berry said. "From what you're saying, it sounds to me like the return charting ought to be pretty straightforward. They aren't going to need you or Dr. Wix to do it, at any rate, right?"

"Right," Kare acknowledged with manifest unwillingness. "But—"

"But I'm afraid that means you're staying home, Doctor." There was understanding, and more than a little compassion, in the teenaged monarch's voice, yet that voice was also firm. "I know we're almost certainly worrying about nothing. And I know how much I always hated it when Daddy told me I couldn't do something I really wanted to do. Especially when I knew that he knew I wasn't *really* going to get into trouble if I did it. And I know you're going to be really pissed off if I don't let you go along with Captain Zachary. Despite which, I'm not going to."

"Your Majesty—" Kare began, but Berry shook her head.

"Doctor," she said with a very slight yet undeniably impish smile, "you're grounded."

CHAPTER TWENTY-SEVEN

"Ready to proceed, Ma'am," Commander Samuel Lim, HMS *Harvest Joy*'s executive officer reported crisply.

"Thank you, Sam," Captain Josepha Zachary acknowledged, and glanced one last time around her bridge.

Although she'd managed to hang on to *Harvest Joy*, she had an entirely different complement of officers from the one she'd had for the exploration of the Lynx Terminus. They were just as good a bunch, she thought, but there was a subtle difference this time around. Last time, *everyone* had been a newbie as far as wormhole exploration was concerned; this time, she was the experienced "Old Lady" whose calm, confident demeanor everyone else was trying to duplicate.

The thought amused her more than a little, and she turned her attention to one of the half-dozen other veterans of the Lynx Terminus expedition who were back aboard *Harvest Joy* today. Dr. Michael William Hall was the third-ranking member of Dr. Kare's team, in terms of seniority, which made him the most senior scientist present, given Queen Berry's edict. Hall's shaved scalp gleamed as if it had been waxed, and with his swarthy complexion, broad shoulders, and generally muscular physique he looked far more like the stereotype of a rugby player (which he was) than of an extraordinarily well-qualified hyper-physicist (which he also was). At the moment, she suspected, Hall was finding it a bit difficult to restrain his own half-triumphant and half-sympathetic smile as he reflected upon what must be going through Jordin Kare and Richard Wix's minds about now. It was truly amazing how stubborn Berry Zilwicki could be when she set her mind to it, Zachary reflected.

Or maybe not so amazing at all, given the stories about what she survived in Old Chicago before the Zilwickis came along, she thought much more grimly, then shook that thought aside.

"If you're ready, Doctor?" she asked out loud, arching one eyebrow.

"We're ready, Captain," Hall confirmed for the remainder of his team. He was the only one actually on the bridge; the others were assembled under Dr. Linda Hronek, the survey expedition's fourth ranking scientist, in the wardroom which had been transformed temporarily into the science team's command post.

Lt. Gordon Keller, *Harvest Joy*'s tactical officer, had made himself even more than normally useful helping them set up their equipment. Which was saying quite a bit, since Lt. Keller was *always* useful to have around. He was definitely on the young side for a cruiser's tactical officer, but *Harvest Joy*'s combat days were well behind her now. Zachary and Keller kept her people well trained and well rehearsed—she *was* a Queen's ship, however long in the tooth she might be growing, and the possibility that she might yet be called to action always existed, however slight it might have become—but she'd sacrificed a quarter of her armament when she was converted for service with the Astrophysics Investigation Agency.

At the moment, Keller was on the command deck, with his weapons crews closed up, but his attention—like everyone else's—was on the astrogation plot, and Zachary had no doubt that his extra efforts on the survey team's behalf had been his own way of getting his hands at least a little dirty. Missiles and energy weapons might not have anything to contribute to exploring a wormhole, but at least he could tell himself truthfully that *he'd* contributed.

"Well, if everyone's all set, I suppose we should get started," Zachary said calmly now, and glanced at Lt. Karen Evans, her astrogator.

"The transit vectors are locked in?" Zachary knew the answer to the question already, of course, but there were rules to follow, and those rules existed for very good reasons.

"Yes, Ma'am." If Evans felt any irritation at being asked a question she'd already answered for the XO, her response showed no trace of it.

"Very well." Zachary turned to her helmsman. "Ten gravities, Senior Chief."

"Ten gravities on Astro's programmed heading, aye, aye, Ma'am,"

Senior Chief Coxswain Hartneady acknowledged, and Zachary looked down at the com display by her left knee as *Harvest Joy* began to creep slowly towards the terminus.

"Prepare to rig foresail for transit, Mr. Hammarberg," she told the face looking back at her from the com.

"Aye, aye, Ma'am," Lt. Commander Jonas Hammarberg replied formally. "Standing by to rig foresail on your mark."

"Threshold in two-zero seconds," Evans reported.

"On your toes, Senior Chief," Zachary murmured.

"Aye, Ma'am," Hartneady replied, never taking his eyes from his own displays as *Harvest Joy* edged into the terminus. The survey ship was tracking directly down the path Evans had programmed. If everything went the way it was supposed to go, she'd go right on doing that. If things decided *not* to go the way they were supposed to go, however, James Hartneady might find himself extraordinarily busy sometime in the next few seconds.

"Threshold!" Evans said sharply.

"Rig foresail for transit," Zachary ordered.

"Rigging foresail, aye," Hammarberg responded instantly.

Harvest Joy's impeller wedge fell abruptly to half strength as her forward beta nodes shut down. At the same moment, her forward alpha nodes reconfigured, dropping their own share of the cruiser's normal-space impeller wedge to project a Warshawski sail's circular disk of focused gravitational energy, instead. The sail was perpendicular to *Harvest Joy*'s long axis, and over three hundred kilometers in diameter.

"Stand by after hypersail," Zachary said, watching the flickering numerals in the Engineering window opened in one corner of her own maneuvering plot as the cruiser continued to creep forward under her after impellers alone.

"Standing by aft hypersail, aye," Hammarberg replied, and she knew he was watching the same flashing numbers climb steadily higher on his own displays as the foresail moved deeper into the terminus. They weren't climbing anywhere near as quickly as they could have been, given the absurdly low speed with which anyone but a madwoman approached a first-transit through an uncharted terminus, of course, but—

The numbers suddenly stopped flashing. They went on climbing, but their steadiness told Zachary the foresail was drawing enough power from the terminus' grav waves to provide movement.

"Rig aftersail," she said crisply.

"Rigging aftersail, aye," Hammarberg said, just as crisply, and *Harvest Joy* shivered as her impeller wedge disappeared entirely and her after hypersail spread its wings at the far end of her hull.

Senior Chief Hartneady's hands moved smoothly through the tricky maneuver, and Zachary felt her stomach trying to turn over as the cruiser slid into the terminus' interface with equal smoothness.

The inevitable queasiness of crossing the hyper wall was briefer but substantially more intense in a wormhole transit, and she ignored it with the practice of several decades' experience, never looking away from her maneuvering display. She watched it narrowly, eyes focused, and then it flashed again.

No one had ever been able to measure the duration of a wormhole transit. Not from the inside of one, at any rate, and no chronometer aboard *Harvest Joy* managed to measure this one, either. For however long that fleeting interval was, though, the cruiser simply ceased to exist. One instant she was sixty-four light-minutes from the star called Torch; the next she was somewhere else, and Zachary felt herself swallowing in relief as her nausea vanished.

Harvest Joy's Warshawski sails radiated the brilliant blue flash of transit energy as she continued to slide forward out of the far side of the terminus under momentum alone, and Zachary nodded in satisfaction.

"Transit complete," Hartneady reported.

"Thank you, Senior Chief," Zachary acknowledged. Her gaze was back on the sail interface readout again, watching the numbers spiral downward as her ship moved further forward.

"Engineering, reconfigure to—"

An alarm shrilled with shocking suddenness, and Zachary's head whipped around towards the *tactical* display.

"Unknown starships!" The professionalism of merciless training flattened the stunned disbelief in Lieutenant Keller's voice without making his report one bit less jarring. "*Two* unknown starships, bearing zero-zero-five by zero-seven-niner, range one-zero-three thous—"

Twelve battlecruiser-grade grasers, fired at a range of just over a third of a light-second, arrived before he could complete his final sentence, and HMS *Harvest Joy*, Josepha Zachary, and every man and woman aboard her ship disappeared in a single cataclysmic ball of incandescent fury.

CHAPTER TWENTY-EIGHT

"But what could have happened to them?" asked Berry Zilwicki. The young queen's face was creased with worry.

Dr. Jordin Kare's face showed concern also. But he was doing his best to maintain a calm composure. "There could be any number of reasons they're not back yet, Your Majesty. I know TJ and I both emphasized how unlikely it was, but, frankly, the most probable explanation is that *this* time, for one reason or another, they didn't manage to chart the gravitic stresses accurately enough on their way through. *Harvest Joy*'s instrumentation is damn good, but if they *didn't* get a good read when they make transit, it could take months for them to nail things down with sufficient accuracy for a return transit without additional support."

"For that matter, assuming they did fail to get a good map on their way through, they may have come out someplace close enough to Torch for Mike and Linda—I mean Dr. Hall and Dr. Hronek—to figure it'd take longer to do the survey than to come home the long way round, through hyper, and head back with better support," Dr. Wix interjected.

"In either of those cases," continued Kare, "then they've already begun returning through hyperspace. But that could take them some time, before they get back."

"How much time?" asked Berry.

Both physicists shrugged simultaneously. "There's simply no way to know," said Kare.

Berry shook her head. "Sorry, I said that stupidly. What I

260

should have asked is what's the probable range of time, given past experience?"

Wix ran fingers through his long and thick blond hair. "At the short end, a few days. That'd be unlikely, though. At the other extreme . . . Well, the longest recorded voyage—well-documented, anyway—through hyperspace for a wormhole survey ship was a little under four months."

"One hundred and thirteen days, to be precise," said Kare. "That was the Solarian survey ship *Tempest* back in . . . what? 1843, TJ?"

Wix nodded, and Berry made a face. "Four months!"

Kare's look of concern was replaced by one of reassurance. A good attempt at it, anyway. "It's not as bad as it sounds. For one thing, there's not much danger involved. Like Captain Zachary said before they ever headed out, survey ships are designed with the possibility in mind that this might happen. They've got plenty of endurance and life support."

"Absolutely," Wix agreed with an emphatic nod. "The real thing to worry about on a trip that long is boredom, Your Majesty. It's not that big a ship, you know."

Their attempt at reassurance didn't help. Berry grimaced, as she imagined being trapped in such a vest-pocket world for almost four months.

"But of course survey ships are designed with that in mind also," Kare added, a bit hurriedly. "I can assure you, Your Majesty—I speak from personal experience here—that a survey ship has as much in the way of stored entertainment as even a big city. Well . . . not live entertainment, of course. But there's about all you could ask for in the way of reading material, vids, games, music, you name it."

"Sure is," said Wix. "I once took the opportunity on a long survey voyage—almost certainly the once-in-a-lifetime-opportunity—to watch the entirety of *The Adventures of Fung Ho*."

Berry's eyes widened. *The Adventures of Fung Ho* had been the longest-running fictional vid series in human history—aside from soap operas, of course—with forty-seven continuous seasons.

"*All* of it? That's—" She had a knack for math, and did the calculations quickly. "That's over a thousand hours of viewing time. A thousand and thirty-four, to be precise, except that I think there were a couple of years when they had shortened seasons."

Wix nodded. "Three seasons, actually. In 1794, due to an actors' strike, where they lost almost a third of the season. In 1802, from a writer's strike—but that only lasted for a few weeks. And the biggest loss, over half the season in 1809, when Lugh came under severe bombardment and just about all activity on the planet had to be suspended for the duration of the emergency."

Lugh was the third planet of the star Tau Ceti, and was the location where most of the episodes in *The Adventures of Fung Ho* had been recorded. The planet was popular for a large number of vid series, especially those involving adventure, due to its flamboyant scenery and even more flamboyant biota. Unfortunately, the Tau Ceti system also had over ten times as much dust as did Sol's system and that of most inhabited solar systems. That massive debris disk meant the planet was subject to more in the way of impact events than all but a handful of other planets with permanent human settlements. The danger of bolides shaped everything about Lugh's culture, from the structure of its system defense force down to the fact that those same bolides were a regular feature in the adventure vids produced there.

Berry shook her head slightly as she continued with her calculations. A thousand hours of viewing time translated into eighty-three consecutive days, assuming you sat and watched for twelve hours a day.

"Gah," she said. "*All* of it?"

"He cheated," said Kare. "He skimmed through all the episodes involving E.A. Hattlestad and Sonya Sipes."

"That has *got* to be the silliest sub-plot ever invented by the human race," groused Wix, "even allowing for the fact that it's supposed to be romance."

Berry chose not to argue the matter. She'd seen a large number of the episodes of the *Fung Ho* series herself—although certainly not all of it, nor even close—and had been rather partial to the romance between Hattlestad and Sipes. As much of it as she'd seen, at least. Granted, the premises were pretty extreme, starting with the size disparity between Hattlestad—who was practically a homunculus—and the eight-foot-tall giantess Sipes. But so were the premises of the entire series, when you got right down to it. That wasn't surprising, given that *Fung Ho* had been inspired by the adventures of Baron Münchausen. Add asteroids, alien tempters and temptresses (whose temptations usually succeeded, Fung Ho being Fung Ho), and energy weapons.

"Still," she said, "I'm impressed. Or appalled, I'm not sure which."

Kare and Wix both chuckled. "To be honest," said Wix, "after it was all over and I thought about it, I was a lot closer to being appalled than impressed, myself. The series is addictive, but speaking objectively it's about as ludicrous an exercise in fiction as you can find in the record."

Kare's smile faded. "But to get back to the point, Your Majesty, I think it's much too early to start really worrying about what happened to the *Harvest Joy*. Yes, there are some explanations that involve real disasters. But they're not that likely."

"Well, okay," said Berry. She cocked her head. "I'm presuming that until you know more, you have no intentions of sending another survey ship through the wormhole." That was a statement, not a question. Beneath the pleasant tone, there was the hint that Berry—*Queen* Berry, when push came to shove—would not permit any such foolishness.

Kare shook his head. "Oh, no. Even if we had another survey ship with an experienced captain and crew at our disposal—"

"Which we certainly *don't*," Wix said forcefully.

"—we wouldn't do it, anyway. There's a standard procedure to be followed in cases like this. Stripping away the jargon, the gist of it is: remeasure, recalculate, and refigure everything, before you so much as breathe heavily on that wormhole."

Berry nodded. "Okay. We'll just wait then. For now, at least."

The very muscular woman named Lara appeared in the entrance to the small salon where Berry had been meeting with the two scientists. Jordin and Wix weren't quite sure what her formal duties were. She seemed to serve the queen as a combination bodyguard, personal handler and court jester.

"The delegation from the pharmaceutical companies has now been waiting for twenty-five minutes," she said. "You're late, not them."

The physicists, accustomed to the court of Manticore, were startled. Even now, after having spent two and half months on Torch, they still weren't really acclimatized to the planet's sometimes odd customs. It was inconceivable that anyone, much less a mere bodyguard, would speak that bluntly—no, rudely—to Queen Elizabeth. And if they did, there'd be hell to pay.

But Queen Berry seemed to think it was simply amusing. "Lara, weren't you paying attention in your sessions on royal protocol?"

"Slept right through the silly business. Are you coming, or do you want me to dream up some more excuses?"

"No, no, I'll come. We're done here." She gave Kare and Wix a smile and a semi-apologetic nod of the head. "Sorry, but I'm afraid I've got to leave now. Please let me know immediately if anything further turns up."

After she left, Wix let out his breath slowly. "Well," he said, "it *is* the most likely explanation."

Kare made a face. He had not, in fact, lied to the queen. As Wix had just stated, the most likely explanation *was* that the *Harvest Joy* couldn't return through the wormhole, for whatever reason, and was now slowly making its way back to Torch via hyperspace.

But . . .

It wasn't the *only* possible explanation. He'd been honest enough when he stressed how uncommon it was—these days, at least—for ships to be lost during wormhole surveys. Statistically, the odds *were* very much against anything of the sort having happened to *Harvest Joy*. On the other hand, though, there was a reason he'd deliberately avoided getting into any details concerning the disasters that could happen to survey ships. However *unlikely* they might be, they could happen, and some of them were . . . gruesome. The fate of the *Dublin* and her crew was still something no one involved in survey work wanted to contemplate or talk about, even a century and a half later.

And there *was* that one wormhole no one had ever come back from . . . at all.

"Yes, it is," he said. "The most likely explanation, by far."

"Where's Ruth?" Berry asked plaintively, once they were in the corridor that led—eventually—to the ballroom where the trade delegation was waiting.

"Saburo says she's running late, girl," Lara said, shrugging with the casual informality which was such a quintessential part of her. "Even later than you are."

The ex-Scrag was still about as civilized as a wolf, and she had a few problems grasping the finer points of court etiquette. Which, to tell the truth, suited Berry just fine. Usually, at least.

"If I've got to do this," the queen said firmly, "Ruth has to do it with me."

"Berry," Lara said, "Kaja said she'll be here, and Saburo and Ruth are already on their way. We can go ahead and start."

"No." They'd reached an intersection of corridors that was wide enough that someone had seen fit to place a couple of armchairs in it. Berry flounced—that really was the only verb that fit—over to one of them and plunked down in it. "I'm the Queen," she said snippily, "and I want my intelligence advisor there when I talk to these people."

"But your father isn't even on Torch," Lara pointed out with a grin. Thandi Palane's "Amazons" had actually developed senses of humor, and all of them were deeply fond of their commander's "little sister." Which was why they took such pleasure in teasing her.

"You *know* what I mean!" Berry shot back, rolling her eyes in exasperation. But there was a twinkle in those eyes, and Lara chuckled as she saw it.

"Yes," she admitted. "But tell me, why do you need Ruth? It's only a gaggle of merchants and businessmen." She wrinkled her nose in the tolerant contempt of a wolf for the sheep a bountiful nature had created solely to feed it. "Nothing to worry about in *that* bunch, girl!"

"Except for the fact that I might screw up and sell them Torch for a handful of glass beads!"

Lara looked at her, obviously puzzled, and Berry sighed. Lara and the other Amazons truly were trying hard, but it was going to take years to even begin closing the myriad gaps in their social skills and general background knowledge.

"Never mind, Lara," the teenaged queen said after a moment. "It wasn't really all that funny a joke, anyway. But what I meant is that with Web tied up with Governor Barregos' representative, I need someone a little more devious to help hold my hand when I slip into the shark tank with these people. I need someone to advise me about what they really want, not just what they *say* they want."

"Make it plain anyone who cheats you gets a broken neck." Lara shrugged. "You may lose one or two, early, but the rest will know better. Want Saburo and me to handle it for you?"

She sounded almost eager, and Berry laughed. She often suspected Saburo X still didn't understand exactly how it had happened, but after a brief, wary, half-terrified, *extremely* . . . direct "courtship," he wasn't complaining. On the face of it, his and Lara's was one of the most unlikely pairings in history—the ex-genetic-slave terrorist, madly in love with the ex-Scrag who'd worked directly for Manpower before she walked away from her own murderous past—and yet, undeniably, it worked.

"There *is* a certain charming simplicity to the idea of broken necks," Berry conceded, after a moment. "Unfortunately, that's not how it's done. I haven't been a queen for long, but I do know that much."

"Pity," Lara said, and glanced at her chrono. "Now they've been waiting over half an hour," she remarked.

"Oh, all right," Berry said. "I'll go—I'll go!" She shook her head and made a face. "You'd think a queen would at least be able to get away with *something* when her father is half a dozen star systems away!"

CHAPTER TWENTY-NINE

Harper S. Ferry stood in the throne room, arms crossed, watching the thirty-odd people standing about. He knew he didn't cut a particularly military figure, but that was fine with him. In fact, the ex-slaves of Torch had a certain fetish for *not* looking spit and polish. They were the galaxy's outcast mongrels, and they wanted no one—including themselves—to forget that.

Which didn't mean they took their responsibilities lightly.

Judson Van Hale walked casually across the throne room, angling a bit closer to Harper, with Genghis riding his shoulder.

"This is a lively bunch," Judson murmured disgustedly out of the corner of his mouth as he stopped beside Harper. "Genghis is downright bored."

He reached up and caressed the cream-and-gray treecat, and the 'cat purred and pressed his head against Judson's hand.

"Boring is good," Harper replied quietly. "Exciting is bad."

"Aren't they running late?" Judson asked after a moment, and Harper shrugged.

"I don't have anyplace else I need to be today," he said. "And if Berry's running true to form, she's dragging her heels, waiting for Ruth. And Thandi, if she can get her here."

"Why *aren't* they here?"

"They're going over something to do with security for the summit, and according to the net," Harper tapped his personal com, "Thandi's sending Ruth on ahead while she finishes up." He shrugged again. "I'm not sure exactly what it is she's working on. Probably something about setting up liaison with Cachat."

"Oh, yeah. '*Liaison*,'" Judson said, rolling his eyes, and Harper slapped him lightly on the back of the head.

"No disrespectful thoughts about the Great Kaja, friend! Not unless you want her Amazons performing a double orchidectomy on you without anesthesia."

Judson grinned, and Genghis bleeked a laugh.

"Who's that guy over there?" Harper asked after a moment. "The fellow by the main entrance."

"The one in the dark blue jacket?"

"That's the one."

"Name's Tyler," Judson said. He punched a brief code into his memo pad and looked down at the display. "He's with New Age Pharmaceutical. It's one of the Beowulf consortiums. Why?"

"I don't know," Harper said thoughtfully. "Is Genghis picking up any sort of vibes from him?"

Both humans looked at the treecat, who raised a true hand in the thumb-folded, two-finger sign for the letter "N" and nodded it up and down. Judson looked back at Harper and shrugged.

"Guess not. Want us to stroll a bit closer and check him out again?"

"I don't know," Harper said again. "It's just—" He paused. "It's probably nothing," he went on after a moment. "It's just that he's the only one I see who's brought along a briefcase."

"Hm?"

Judson frowned, surveying the rest of the crowd.

"You're right," he acknowledged. "Odd, I suppose. I thought this was supposed to be primarily a 'social occasion.' Just a chance for them to meet Queen Berry as a group, before the individual negotiating sessions."

"That's what I thought, too," Harper agreed. He thought about it for a moment longer, then keyed a combination into his com.

"Yes, Harper?" a voice replied.

"The guy with the briefcase, Zack. You checked it out?"

"Ran the sniffer over it and had him open it," Zack assured him. "Nothing in it but a microcomputer and a couple of perfume dispensers."

"Perfume?" Harper repeated.

"Yeah. I picked up some organic traces from them, but they were all consistent with cosmetics. Not even a flicker of red on the sniffer. I asked him about them, too, and he said they were gifts from New Age for the girls. I mean, Queen Berry and Princess Ruth."

"Had they been pre-cleared?" Harper asked.

"Don't think so. He said they were supposed to be surprises."

"Thanks, Zack. I'll get back to you."

Harper switched off the com and looked at Judson. Judson looked back, and the ex-Ballroom assassin frowned.

"I don't like surprises," he said flatly.

"Well, Berry and Ruth might," Judson countered.

"Fine. Surprise *them* all you want, but not their security. We're supposed to know about this kind of crap ahead of time."

"I know." Judson tugged at the lobe of his left ear, thinking. "It's almost certainly nothing, you know. Genghis would be picking up something from him by now if he had anything . . . unpleasant in mind."

"Maybe. But let's you and I sashay over that way and have a word with Mr. Tyler," Harper said.

William Henry Tyler stood in the throne room, waiting patiently with the rest of the crowd, and rubbed idly at his right temple. He felt a bit . . . odd. Not ill, really. He didn't even have a headache. In fact, if anything, he felt just a bit euphoric, although he couldn't think why.

He shrugged and checked his chrono. "Queen Berry"—he smiled slightly at the thought of the Torch monarch's preposterous youth; she was younger than the younger of Tyler's own two daughters—was obviously running late. Which, he supposed, was the prerogative of a head of state, even if she was only seventeen.

He glanced down at his brief case and felt a brief, mild stir of surprise. It vanished instantly, in a stronger surge of that inexplicable euphoria. He'd actually been a bit startled when the security man asked him what was in the case. For just an instant, it had been as if he'd never seen it before, but then, of course, he'd remembered the gifts for Queen Berry and Prince Ruth. That had been a really smart idea on Marketing's part, he conceded. Every young woman he'd ever met had liked expensive perfume, whether she was willing to admit it or not.

He relaxed again, humming softly, at peace with the universe.

"All right, see? I'm here," Berry said, and Lara laughed.

"And so graceful you are, too," the Amazon said. "You who keep trying to 'civilize' us!"

"Actually," Berry said, reaching out to pat the older woman on the forearm, "I've decided I like you all just the way you are. My very own wolfpack. Well, Thandi's, but I'm sure she'll lend you to me if I ask. Just do me a favor and try not to get any blood on the furniture. Oh, and let's keep the orgies out of sight, too, at least when Daddy's around. Deal?"

"Deal, Little Kaja. I'll explain to Saburo about the orgies," Lara said, and it was perhaps an indication of the effect Berry Zilwicki had on the people about her that an ex-Scrag didn't even question the deep surge of affection she felt for her teenage monarch.

✧   ✧   ✧

A slight stir went through the throne room as someone noticed the queen and her lean, muscular bodyguard entering through the side door. The two of them moved across the enormous room, which had once been the ballroom of the planetary governor when Torch had been named Verdant Vista. The men and women who'd come to meet the Queen of Torch were a little surprised by how very young she looked in person, and heads turned to watch her, although nobody was crass enough to start sidling in her direction until she'd seated herself in the undecorated powered chair which served her for a throne.

Harper S. Ferry and Judson Van Hale were still ten meters from the New Age Pharmaceutical representative when Tyler looked up and saw Berry. Unlike any of the other commercial representatives in the room, he took a step towards her the moment he saw her, and Genghis's head snapped up in the same instant.

The 'cat reared high, ears flattened and fangs bared in the sudden, tearing-canvas ripple of a treecat's war cry, and vaulted abruptly from his person's shoulder towards Tyler.

Tyler's head whipped around, and Harper felt a sudden stab of outright terror as he saw the terrible, fixed glare of the other man's eyes. There was something . . . insane about them, and Harper was suddenly reaching for the panic button on his gun belt.

The pharmaceutical representative saw the oncoming 'cat, and his free hand flashed across to the briefcase he was carrying. The briefcase with the "perfume" of which no one at New Age Pharmaceutical had ever heard . . . and which Tyler didn't even remember taking from the man who'd squirted that odd mist in his face on Smoking Frog.

Genghis almost reached him in time. He launched himself from the floor in a snarling, hissing charge that hit Tyler's moving forearm perhaps a tenth of a second too late.

Tyler pressed the concealed button. The explosive charges in the two massively pressurized canisters of "perfume" in the briefcase exploded expelling the binary neurotoxin which they had contained under several thousand atmospheres of pressure. Separated, its components had been innocuous, easily mistaken for perfume; combined, they were incredibly lethal, and they mingled and spread, whipping outward from Tyler under immense pressure even as the briefcase blew apart with a sharp, percussive crack.

Genghis stiffened, jerked once, and hit the floor a fraction of a second before Tyler, left hand mangled by the explosion of the briefcase, collapsed beside him. Harper's finger completed its movement to the panic button, and then the deadly cloud swept over him and Judson, as well. Their spines arched, their mouths opened in silent agony, and then they went down as a cyclone of death spread outward.

Lara and Berry did their best to maintain suitably grave expressions, despite their mutual amusement, as they walked towards Berry's chair. They were about halfway there when the sudden, high-pitched snarl of an enraged treecat ripped through the throne room.

They spun towards the sound, and saw a cream-and-gray blur streaking through the crowd. For an instant, Berry had no idea at all what was happening. But if Lara wasn't especially well socialized, she still had the acute senses, heightened musculature, and lightning reflexes of the Scrag she had been born.

She didn't know what had set Genghis off, but every instinct she had screamed "*Threat!*" And if she wouldn't have had a clue which fork to use at a formal dinner, she knew *exactly* what to do about that.

She continued her turn, right arm reaching out, snaking around Berry's waist like a python, and snatched the girl up. By the time Genghis was two leaps from Tyler, Lara was already sprinting towards the door through which they'd entered the throne room.

She heard the sharp crack of the exploding briefcase behind her just as the door opened again, and she saw Saburo and Ruth Winton through it. From the corner of her eye, she also saw the outrider of death scything towards her as the bodies collapsed in spasming agony, like ripples spreading from a stone hurled into a placid pool. The neurotoxin was racing outward faster than she could run; she didn't know what it was, but she knew it was invisible death . . . and that she could not outdistance it.

"*Saburo!*" she screamed, and snatched Berry bodily off the floor. She spun on her heel once, like a discus thrower, and suddenly Berry went arcing headfirst through the air. She flew straight at Saburo X, like a javelin, and his arms opened reflexively.

"The door!" Lara screamed, skittering to her knees as she over-balanced from throwing Berry. "Close the door! *Run!*"

Berry hit Saburo in the chest. His left arm closed about her, holding her tight, and his eyes met Lara's as her knees hit the floor. Brown eyes stared deep into blue, meeting with the sudden, stark knowledge neither of them could evade.

"I love you!" he cried . . . and his right hand hit the button to close the door.

CHAPTER THIRTY

"It's getting harder, Jack." Herlander Simões leaned back in the visitor's chair in Jack McBryde's kitchen and shook his head. "You'd think it would either stop hurting, or that I'd get used to it, or that I'd just go ahead and give up." He bared his teeth in a bitter mockery of a smile. "I always used to think I was a fairly smart fellow, but obviously I was wrong. If I really were so damned smart, I'd have managed to do *one* of those things by now!"

"I wish I could tell you some magic formula, Herlander." McBryde flicked the top off another bottle of beer and slid it across to his guest. "And, I'll be honest with you, there are times I just want to kick you right in the ass." There was at least a little humor in his own smile, and he shook his head. "I don't know whether I'm more pissed off with you for the way you keep right on putting yourself through this or for the way it's twisting up your entire life, not just your work."

"I know."

Simões accepted the new beer and took a long pull from the bottle. Then he set it down on the table top, folding his hands around it so that his thumbs and forefingers were a loose circle about the base. He stared down at his cuticles for several seconds, his worn face set in a pensive expression.

"I know," he repeated, looking up at McBryde at last. "I've been trying to get past my own anger, the way you suggested. Sometimes, I think I'm making progress, too. But something always seems to come along."

"Are you still watching those holos at night?" McBryde's voice had gone very gentle, and Simões' shoulders seemed to hunch without actually moving a millimeter. He looked back down at the beer bottle, his hazel eyes like shutters, and nodded once.

"*Herlander*," McBryde said softly. Simões looked up at him, and McBryde shook his own head. "You're just killing yourself doing that. You know it as well as I do."

"Maybe." Simões inhaled deeply. "No, not maybe—yes. I know it. You know it. For that matter, my *official* therapist knows it. But I just . . . can't, Jack. It's like as long as I look at the HD every so often she isn't *really* gone."

"But she *is* gone, Herlander." McBryde's voice was as merciless as it was gentle. "And so is Harriet. And so is your entire damned life, if this succeeds in sucking you down."

"Sometimes I think that might not be such a bad thing," Simões admitted quietly.

"*Herlander!*" This time McBryde's voice was sharp, and Simões looked up again.

It was odd, McBryde thought, as their eyes met. Under normal circumstances, having one of the scientists whose security he was responsible for overseeing as a guest in his apartment—as someone who had turned into something remarkably like a personal friend—would have broken every rule of the Alignment's security services. In fact, it *did* break every one of them . . . except for the fact that Isabel Bardasano's personal orders were still in effect.

He'd had his reservations when he first received those orders, and in some ways, he had even more reservations now. For one thing, his relationship with Simões really had turned into something which truly did resemble friendship, and he knew that hadn't been a good thing, in oh so many ways. Turning someone who was a solid mass of emotional anguish into a friend was one of the best recipes for destroying one's own peace of mind he could think of. Empathizing with what had been done to Herlander Simões and his daughter was even worse, given what it did to his own anger quotient . . . and the mental byroads it had been leading him along. And leaving all of that aside, he was only too well aware that his objectivity—the *professional* objectivity it was his sworn duty to maintain where Simões was concerned—had been completely destroyed. What had begun as obedience to orders, as a mere dutiful effort to keep an important scientific asset functional, had segued into something very different.

Simões was equally aware of that. It was odd, but in some ways the fact that McBryde had begun from a purely pragmatic effort to salvage Simões' utility to the Gamma Center had actually made it easier for the hyper-physicist to open up with him. McBryde was the only person who hadn't started out concerned only for Simões' "own good," and that had let Simões lower his guard where the security man was concerned. There were times when McBryde wondered if there hadn't been at least a trace of self-destructiveness in Simões' attitude towards him—if a tiny part of the scientist hadn't been actually hoping that he would say or do or reveal something which would force McBryde to yank him from the Center.

But regardless of the exact nature of the tangled emotions, attitudes, motives, and hopes, Jack McBryde was the one person in the entire galaxy with whom Herlander Simões was prepared to be totally honest. He was also the only person who could take Simões to task for something like the scientist's self-flagellating habit of watching the recorded imagery of Francesca night after night without triggering Simões' instant, self-defensive anger.

"Let's be honest here, Jack," the scientist said now, smiling crookedly. "Sooner or later you're going to decide it's time to pull me. I know as well as you do that my efficiency is still dropping. And I'm not exactly what someone might call the life of the party when it comes to the rest of the team's morale, now am I? It's not even *actively* destructive, anymore. Not really. It's just this slow, grinding, wearing away. I'm so frigging *tired*, Jack. There's a big part of me that just wants to stop. Just wants it to be *over*. But there's another part of me that *can't* stop, because if I do, Frankie's just gone forever, and those bastards will just go ahead and forget about her. Sweep her under the rug."

His voice had hardened with the last two sentences, and his hands locked around the beer bottle, squeezing it. *Throttling* it, really, McBryde thought, and wondered if he should try to distract Simões from his anger.

He knew he really ought to be consulting with the scientist's assigned therapist. He should have been offering his information to her, and asking her advice on how he could most constructively respond to Simões. Unfortunately, he couldn't. To his surprise, part of the reason he couldn't was because it would have been a betrayal of Simões' confidence. Despite what he'd said to the other man at their very first meeting about respecting his privacy, he'd never actually violated it, and he suspected that Simões knew it.

The other reason was more disturbing, when he allowed himself to confront it (which he did as seldom as possible). He was afraid. Afraid that in discussing Simões' mindset and anger, he might reveal altogether too much about certain thoughts of his own . . . especially to a trained Alignment therapist who was already thinking in terms of the potential security risk her patient might present.

Should I try and pull him up out of the anger, or just let him vent? He needs to let some of that pressure out, but it doesn't just go away when he does, does it? McBryde shook his head mentally. *Of course it doesn't. It's like letting the pressure* out *only lets more oxygen* in. *Only makes the fire burn hotter in the end.*

"You're still pounding away at Fabre and the rest, aren't you?" he asked out loud.

"You're the security guy," Simões riposted with just a flash of anger directed at him. "You're already reading all my mail, aren't you?"

"Well, yes," McBryde admitted.

"Then you know, don't you?" Simões challenged.

"The question was what's known as a conversational gambit," McBryde said just a bit flatly. "A way of edging into a point that needs to be discussed with at least a modicum of tact, Herlander."

"Oh." Simões' eyes fell for a moment, then he shrugged. "Well, in that case, yeah. I'm still . . . letting them know how I feel."

"Somehow I suspect they've already got at least a vague idea about that," McBryde said dryly, and Simões surprised both of them with a chuckle. A *harsh* chuckle, but still a chuckle.

Despite that, it wasn't really a laughing matter. Simões hadn't—quite—degenerated to the point of issuing actual threats in his twice-a-week e-mails to Martina Fabre, but the degree of anger—of hatred, to use an honest word for it—in those messages was distressingly clear. In fact, McBryde had quietly advised Fabre to take a few additional security precautions of her own. Had the man sending those messages been one whit less important to the Alignment's military research efforts, he might very well already have been arrested. He certainly would have been put under precautionary surveillance . . . except, of course, that in this case he already *was* under precautionary surveillance.

It was like watching a slow-motion holo of an avalanche, McBryde thought. And in many ways, Simões' sheer brilliance and the mental agility, focus, and stubbornness which had made him one of the Alignment's star researchers only made it worse. Whether he wanted to or not (and McBryde had come to the conclusion that he actually did want to), the hyper-physicist was actively applying that same focused refusal to quit to his campaign to make Fabre and the members of the Long-Range Planning Board fully aware of the searing depth of his hatred and resentment. In some ways, that campaign was all that was keeping the rest of his life afloat, the only thing giving him the momentum—and the will—to go on facing the wasteland the rest of his life had become.

Yet not even that was enough to halt the grinding collapse of who and what he had once been. It wasn't happening overnight. It wasn't *merciful* enough to happen overnight. But despite all of the effort being mounted to salvage Herlander Simões—or, at least, the asset he represented—the scientist continued his slow, steady, inexorable collapse. They'd managed to slow it down, and his therapist credited McBryde with the lion's share of that accomplishment, yet nothing seemed able to arrest it.

I don't think anything can arrest it, McBryde thought somberly. *I think it's his own impotence driving it. I have read those e-mails, so I know exactly what he's been saying to Fabre, and if I were her, I'd have already demanded that he be placed in preventive custody. As a member of the LRPB, she'd get it if she asked for it, too. I wonder why she hasn't? I suppose it's at least possible she feels sorry for him. That she genuinely does feel responsible for having created the circumstances that ripped his life apart. But there's so much anger inside him, so much need to punish someone—someone besides himself, or in addition to himself, maybe—for what happened to his daughter. One of these days, he really is going to work himself around to the point of trying to kill her, or someone else on the Board, or anyone he can punish for what happened to Francesca. And that's going to be the end.*

When that day ultimately came, McBryde knew, it would be his job to stop Simões, and the awareness gnawed at him. Gnawed at his sympathy, and at his own doubts.

Because the truth is that Bardasano's actually right about how quickly we're finally coming up on Prometheus, he thought. *I never really expected it to happen in my own lifetime, which was pretty stupid, given how young I am, and how much I knew about what was going on inside the "onion." But we've been working towards that moment for so long that, emotionally, I never really realized I might be one of the ones to see it. Now I know I will be . . . and Herlander's kicked every one of those doubts I didn't really know I had fully awake, hasn't he?*

How many more Herlanders is the Board going to create? How many people—and just because they're "normals" doesn't keep them from being people, *damn it!—are going to find themselves in his position? Hell, how many billions or trillions of people are we going to end up killing just so that the Long-Range Planning Board can steer the entire human race into the uplands of genetic superiority? And how willing are we really going to be to accept Leonard Detweiler's challenge to improve every single member of the human race to our own pinnacle of achievement? Are we really going to do it? There'll have to be at least some beta lines, of course. And probably at least a few gamma lines. Obviously we won't be able to do without those, now will we? We'll find plenty of reasons for that, and some of them will probably even be valid! But what about Manpower's slaves? What about all those "normals" out there? Are we really going to treat them as our equals . . . aside, of course, from the unfortunate necessity of dictating what children they're allowed to have? Assuming, of course, that their chromosomes offer sufficient promise for them to be allowed to* have *children at all? And if we don't treat them as our equals—and you really know we damned well won't, Jack—are the children we allow them to have really going to end up our equals? Or will they be sentenced forever to never climb above the gamma level? And who the hell are we to tell an entire galaxy that it has to do things* our *way? Isn't that the very thing we've been so pissed off over at Beowulf for so long? Because the sanctimonious bastards insisted that we couldn't do things* our *way? For telling us what to do, because that's what it comes down to in the end, however high the motivations we impute to ourselves.*

He looked down into his own bottle of beer for several seconds, then shook himself and looked back up at Simões.

"You know, Herlander," he said conversationally, "it's going to be those letters to Fabre that finally yank the rug out from under you. You do realize that, don't you?"

"Yeah." Simões shrugged. "I'm not going to just give her a pass on it, though, Jack. Maybe I can't do anything to stop her from doing it to some other Frankie, and maybe I can't do anything to . . . get even with the system. Hell, I accept that I can't! But I can at least make damned sure she knows how pissed off I am, and why. And telling her's the only relief I'm likely to find, now isn't it?"

"I happen to know that there are no surveillance devices in this kitchen." McBryde leaned back in his own chair, and his tone was almost whimsical. "At the same time, you might want to consider the wisdom of telling someone who works for Security for a living that you want 'to get even with the system.' That's what we call in the trade becoming an active threat."

"And you don't already know I feel that way?" Simões actually smiled at him. "For that matter, you're the only person I can say it to knowing that someone isn't going to *report* it to Security! Besides, you're supposed to be keeping me on the rails as long as you can, so I figure you're not going to turn me in as a security risk—which would undoubtedly come as a huge surprise to your superiors, I *don't* think—as long as you can keep on getting at least some work out of me for the Center."

"You know it's not as cut and dried as that anymore, don't you, Herlander?" McBryde asked quietly, and the hyper-physicist's eyes flicked up for a moment, meeting his.

"Yeah," Simões said after a moment, his own voice quiet. "Yeah, I know that, Jack. And"—he smiled again, but this time it was a smile fit to break a statue's heart—"isn't it a hell of a galaxy when the only true friend I've got left is the man who's ultimately going to have to turn me in as an unacceptable security risk?"

CHAPTER THIRTY-ONE

"I think we should talk to Admiral Harrington," said Victor Cachat. "As soon as possible, too—which means going to see her where she is right now, not spending the time it would take to set up a meeting on neutral ground."

Anton Zilwicki stared at him. So did Thandi Palane.

So did Queen Berry and Jeremy X and Web Du Havel and Princess Ruth.

"And they say *I'm* barking mad!" exclaimed Ruth. "Victor, that's *impossible*."

"Harrington's reported to be at Trevor's Star," said Zilwicki. "In command of Eighth Fleet, to be precise. What do you think the chances are that she'll agree to let a Havenite secret agent on board her flagship?"

"Fairly good, actually, if everything I've learned about her is accurate," replied Victor. "I'm more concerned with figuring out how I can protect Haven from having information forced out of me if she decides to get hardnosed."

He gave Zilwicki a look that might be called "injured" if Cachat had been someone else. "I will point out that *I'd* be the only one taking any real risks, not you and certainly not Admiral Harrington. But that's easy enough to handle."

"How?" asked Berry. She glanced apologetically at Ruth. "Not that I think the Manticorans would violate their word to allow you safe passage, assuming they gave it in the first place. But you really don't have any way to be certain, and once they got their hands on you..."

Zilwicki sighed. Palane looked as if she couldn't decide between just being very unhappy or being furious with Victor.

"Are you kidding? We're dealing with Mad Dog Cachat here, Berry," Thandi said. Her tone of voice was not one you'd expect from a woman describing the love of her life. It had a greater resemblance to a file peeling off metal. "He'll handle it the same way that presumed Manpower agent Ronald Allen handled it. Suicide."

Cachat didn't say anything. But it was obvious from the look on his face that Thandi had guessed correctly.

"Victor!" Berry protested.

But Anton knew how hard it was to talk Victor Cachat out of a course of action once he'd decided upon it. And the truth was, Anton wasn't inclined to do so anyway. It was less than a day since they'd returned to Torch and learned about the assassination attempt on Berry that had happened three days earlier. Anton Zilwicki was as furious as he'd ever been in his life—and Cachat's proposal had the great emotional virtue of being something concrete they could *do*—and do it *now*.

Besides, leaving emotional issues aside, there were a number of attractive aspects to Victor's proposal. If they could get Honor Harrington to agree to meet with them—a very big "if," of course—they'd have opened a line of communication with the one top Manticoran leader who, from what Anton could determine, was skeptical of the established wisdom in the Star Kingdom when it came to Haven.

Of course, even if Anton was right, it was still a stretch to think she'd agree to let a known Havenite agent—who, if he wasn't precisely an "assassin," was certainly a close cousin to one—into her physical presence. Given that she herself had been the target of an assassination attempt less than six T-months earlier.

On the other hand . . .

By now, Anton and Victor had gotten to the point where, at least when it came to professional matters, they could almost read each other's minds. So Zilwicki wasn't surprised when Victor said, "Anton, it'll be the very openness of our approach that's most likely to lead Harrington to agree. Whatever I'm up to, she'll know I'm not skulking about—and unlike the assassination attempt on her, I'd be coming at her directly. Which, given her level of protection—not to mention her own reputation as a hand-to-hand fighter—is hardly a real danger."

He spread his hands and looked down upon himself, smiling

as beatifically as Victor Cachat could manage. Which, admittedly, would have left any saint appalled. "I mean, look at me. Is this the physique of a deadly assassin? Unarmed assassin, at that, since she'll be perfectly capable of detecting any weapons and insisting I remove them."

Zilwicki made a face. "Anybody know a good dental technician? He'll also have to be immediately available—*and* be familiar with archaic dental practices like tooth extraction."

Berry frowned. "Why do you need a dental technician?"

"He's actually suggesting that *I* do, Berry. So I can get a poisoned hollow tooth installed. Which is just silly." Victor clucked his tongue chidingly. "I have to tell you, Anton, that in this technological area Haven is way ahead of Manticore. And apparently Manpower, as well."

Thandi Palane was squinting at him. "Victor, are you telling me that you routinely carry around suiciding devices?" Her tone of voice was short of absolute zero, but could have made ice cubes in an instant. "If so, I am not pleased. And wouldn't be, even if we didn't share a bed every night."

Cachat gave her a quick, reassuring smile. "No, no, of course not. I'll have to get it from our station on Erewhon. But we'll need to pass through Erewhon en route to Trevor's Star, anyway."

✧   ✧   ✧

On their way out of the palace to start making their preparations, Anton murmured, "Nice save, Victor."

Cachat might have looked a bit embarrassed. If so, though, it was only an itsy-bitsy teeny-weeny bit of embarrassment.

"Look, I'm not crazy. *Of course* I don't carry the thing into bed. In fact, I don't keep it anywhere in the bedroom. But . . . what would be the point of having a suicide device in another star system? Naturally, I carry the thing with me at all times. I've done so for years."

Zilwicki didn't shake his head, but he was sorely tempted. There were times when Victor seemed like an alien from a far away galaxy with an emotional structure not even remotely akin to that of human beings. It was obvious Cachat thought it was perfectly reasonable—normal practice for any competent secret agent—to carry around a suicide device at all times. He'd no more think of venturing out without one than another man would go without putting on shoes.

In point of fact, no intelligence agency other than that of

Haven followed such a practice—and, although he wasn't positive, Anton was pretty sure not even the Havenites did so routinely. Not even when Saint-Just had been running the show. Suicide devices would only be provided to agents on rare occasions, for missions that were especially sensitive. They wouldn't be passed around like so many throat lozenges!

Once again, if Anton needed the reminder, Victor Cachat was demonstrating that he was Victor Cachat.

"One of a kind," he muttered.

"What was that?"

"Never mind, Victor."

✧   ✧   ✧

Hugh ran his fingers through his hair. That was a gesture he normally only did when he was exasperated. Which . . .

He was and he wasn't. It was all rather confusing—and Hugh Arai hated being confused.

"I still don't see why you're so insistent—"

"Cut it out, Hugh!" snapped Jeremy X. "You know perfectly well why I'm twisting your arm as hard as I can. First, because you're the best."

"Oh, that's nonsense! There are plenty of security people in the galaxy better than I am."

Jeremy's beady gaze really had to be seen to be believed.

"Well . . . all right, fine. There aren't all that many and while I think it's ridiculous to claim I'm 'the best,' it's probably true . . ."

His voice trailed off. Web Du Havel finished the sentence: "That nobody is any better than you."

Hugh gave the prime minister of Torch a rather unfriendly look. "Meaning no offense, Web, but when did *you* become an expert on security?"

Du Havel just grinned. "I'm not and never claimed to be. But I don't have to, since"—here he indicated Jeremy with a thumb—"I've got as my war secretary a man who proved, year after year after year, that he could thwart just about any security system in existence. So I figure I can take his word for it, when it comes to such matters."

That was . . . hard to argue with.

Jeremy waited just long enough to make sure Hugh had conceded the point. Concession by stubborn silence, perhaps—but concession it was, and they both knew it.

"The second reason's just as important," he continued. "Normally, we'd lean on the Ballroom for anything like this. But with what we know now, from the Ronald Allen incident, we can't do that. I doubt if Manpower has been able to get very many agents to penetrate the Ballroom or Torch government offices—but it seems almost certain that however many such agents there are, all of them will have assassinating the queen as one of their top priorities."

He paused, waiting for Hugh—forcing Hugh, rather—to agree or disagree.

Since the answer was obvious, Hugh nodded. "No argument there. And your conclusion is . . . ?"

"Obvious, it seems to me. We need to pull together a security team that's completely outside the Ballroom and doesn't depend on using genetic ex-slaves."

Hugh saw a possible beam of light.

"Well, in that case, I need to remind you *I'm* a genetic ex-slave, so that would seem—"

"Cut it out!" That was as close to a roar as Hugh had ever seen coming from Jeremy. The man's normal and preferred style was whimsical, not ferocious.

Jeremy glared at him. "*You* don't count, and the reason's obvious—and you know it. I can vouch for you since the age of five, and if *I* can't be trusted we're all screwed anyway since I'm the be-damned Secretary of War! Let's not go crazy, here. But even with you in charge, I still want the rest of the team to be from Beowulf."

Even while he'd been raising his objections, Hugh's mind had been chewing on the problem. On a second track, so to speak. He hadn't needed Jeremy to explain to him the advantages of using a security team that had no preexisting ties to Torch or the Ballroom. That had been obvious, from the outset. And the solution to *that* problem was just as obvious—if it could be done at all.

"The best way to handle it would simply be to have the BSC assign me and my team to Torch."

Jeremy nodded. "Finally! The lad's thinking clearly."

Web Du Havel looked from one to the other. "I didn't have the impression BSC teams specialized in security."

Hugh and Jeremy smiled simultaneously. "Well, they don't.

As such," said Jeremy. "It's rather like my own expertise on the subject. What you might call, developed from the inside out. Or the outside, in."

Web rolled his eyes. "In other words, you don't have a clue about security procedures except how to get around them."

"Pretty much," said Hugh. "Leaving me aside—I do have a lot of security training and experience—the skills of my team are what you might call those of the OpForce. But that's plenty good enough, Web. And since they're completely out of the loop in terms of Torch or the Ballroom—and I can vouch for each and every one of them—we don't have to worry that we've been penetrated."

"That still leaves the problem that whatever method is being used in these latest assassinations and assassination attempts might be able to circumvent everything."

Hugh shook his head. "I don't believe in magic, Jeremy, and neither do you. I think Manpower's behind all this, myself, although I'd admit that may just be my preexisting bias. Still, whatever the method is, it smacks of some sort of biological technique. Except for Beowulf—and not even Beowulf, in some areas—Manpower has the greatest biological expertise in the galaxy. But regardless of who's behind it, that means it *can* be thwarted, once we figure out how they're doing it. Whoever 'they are.' And in the meantime . . ."

His tone got very grim. "I can think of at least one method that'll provide Berry with security even while we're in the dark. She won't like it, though."

Web looked a bit alarmed. "If it involves cloistering her, Hugh, you may as well forget it. Even as comparatively amenable as she is right now, because of the death of Lara and the others, there's no way Berry will agree to living like a recluse."

"That's not what I was thinking of—although whether she likes it or not, she's going to have to be sequestered a large part of the time. That doesn't mean she won't be able to move around at all, just . . . Call it security by extreme ruthlessness. But I know Berry well enough already to know she'll have a hard time accepting the procedures I'd set up."

Somewhere in the course of the last minute or so, Hugh realized he'd made up his mind. He found it simultaneously intriguing and disturbing that the key factor had been nothing more sophisticated than an intense desire to keep a certain Berry Zilwicki alive.

Perhaps because the thought was unsettling, he went back to glaring at Jeremy. "Of course, this is almost certainly a moot point, since I can't think of any reason the BSC would agree to any of this. Detaching an entire combat team to serve a foreign nation, for an unspecified but probably long stretch of time? You're dreaming, Jeremy."

Now it was Jeremy and Du Havel who smiled simultaneously. "Why don't you let us worry about that," said Web. "Perhaps we can manage something."

❖   ❖   ❖

"Sure," said Princess Ruth. "Do you want me to make the recording for my parents as well as my aunt? I'd recommend including my mom and dad. Aunt Elizabeth would get peeved if anyone said it right out loud, but the truth is that my father can usually wheedle anything out of her. And since any security measures that protect Berry are likely to spill over onto me, he'll probably wheedle pretty good."

Web and Jeremy looked at each other. "Whatever you think, Ruth. You're the expert here."

"Okay, then." Ruth pursed her lips. "Now . . . I've got to figure out what would work best. Teary-eyed or sternly-insistent-just-short-of-filial-disrespect. Is 'filial' the right word, when you're a daughter?"

❖   ❖   ❖

"Why are you so certain Manticore can bring enough influence to bear on Beowulf?" Jeremy asked later.

"There are at least four reasons I can think of," replied Web. "The simplest of which is that even though you've spent a lot of time around Beowulfers, I don't think you really grasp the depth and relentlessness of the enmity Beowulf's elite has for Manpower. For them, in some ways even more than for ex-slaves like ourselves, this war is profoundly personal. A grudge match, you might say."

"That all happened centuries ago, Web. Over half a millennium. Who can hold a personal grudge *that* long? I don't think I could even do it, and I'm a well-known fanatic."

Web chuckled. "There are at least eight projects on Beowulf that I know of which are studying evolutionary effects, every one of which was started within five years of the first settlement of the planet—almost one thousand, eight hundred years ago. At a certain level of dedication, biologists aren't really sane."

He shook his head. "But leave that aside. One of the other reasons is that Manticore can bring a lot of pressure to bear on Beowulf. Call it influence, rather. And vice versa, of course. The relations between those two star nations are a lot closer than most people realize."

Jeremy still looked a bit dubious. But he didn't pursue the matter any further. This, after all, was Web Du Havel's area of expertise.

CHAPTER THIRTY-TWO

The warship which emerged from the Trevor's Star terminus of the Manticore Wormhole Junction did not show a Manticoran transponder code. Nor did it show a Grayson or an Andermani code. Nonetheless, it was allowed transit, for the code it did display was that of the Kingdom of Torch.

To call the vessel a "warship," was, perhaps, to be overly generous. It was, in fact, a frigate—a tiny class which no major naval power had built in over fifty T-years. But this was a very modern ship, less than three T-years old, and it was Manticoran built, by the Hauptman Cartel, for the Anti-Slavery League.

Which, as everyone understood perfectly well, actually meant it had been built for the Audubon Ballroom, before its lapse into respectability. And this particular frigate—TNS *Pottawatomie Creek*—was rather famous, one might almost have said notorious, as the personal transport of one Anton Zilwicki, late of Her Manticoran Majesty's Navy.

Everyone in the Star Kingdom knew about the attempt to murder Zilwicki's daughter, and given Manticore's current bloody-minded mood, no one was inclined to present any problems when *Pottawatomie Creek* requested permission to approach HMS *Imperator* and send across a couple of visitors.

❖   ❖   ❖

"Your Grace, Captain Zilwicki and . . . guest," Commander George Reynolds announced.

Honor turned from her contemplation of the nearest drifting units of her command, one eyebrow rising, as she tasted the peculiar

288

edge in Reynolds' emotions. She'd decided to meet with Zilwicki as informally as possible, which was why she'd had Reynolds greet him and escort him to the relatively small observation dome just aft of *Imperator*'s forward hammerhead. The panoramic view was spectacular, but it was symbolically outside her own quarters or the official precincts of Flag Bridge.

Now, however, that odd ripple in Reynolds' mind-glow made her wonder if perhaps Zilwicki wouldn't be just as glad as she was to keep this an "unofficial" visit. Reynolds, the son of a liberated genetic slave, was an enthusiastic supporter of the great experiment in Congo, not to mention a personal admirer of Anton Zilwicki and Catherine Montaigne. He'd worked remarkably well with Zilwicki immediately prior to Honor's deployment to the Marsh System, and he'd been delighted when she asked him to meet Zilwicki's cutter. Now, however, he seemed almost . . . apprehensive. That wasn't exactly the right word, but it came close, and she caught Nimitz's matching flicker of interest as the 'cat sat up to his full height on the back of the chair where she'd parked him.

"Captain," she said, holding out her hand.

"Your Grace." Zilwicki's voice was as deep as ever, but it was also a bit more abrupt. Clipped. And as she turned her attention fully to him, she tasted the seething anger his apparently calm exterior disguised.

"I was very sorry to hear about what happened on Torch," Honor said quietly. "But I'm delighted Berry and Ruth got out unscathed."

"'Unscathed' is an interesting word, Your Grace," Zilwicki rumbled in a voice like crumbling Gryphon granite. "Berry wasn't hurt, not physically, but I don't think 'unscathed' really describes what happened. She blames herself. She knows she shouldn't, and she's one of the sanest people I know, but she blames herself. Not so much for Lara's death, or for all the other people who died, but for having gotten out herself. And, I think, perhaps, for the *way* Lara died."

"I'm sorry to hear that," Honor repeated. She grimaced. "Survivor's guilt is something I've had to deal with a time or two myself."

"She'll work through it, Your Grace," the angry father said. "As I said, she's one of the sanest people in existence. But this one's going to leave scars, and I hope she'll draw the right lessons from it, not the wrong ones."

"So do I, Captain," Honor said sincerely.

"And speaking of drawing the right lessons—or, perhaps I ought to say *conclusions*," he said, "I need to talk to you about what happened."

"I'd be grateful for any insight you can give me. But shouldn't you be talking to Admiral Givens, or perhaps to the SIS?"

"I'm not certain any of the official intelligence organs are ready to hear what I've got to say. And I know they're not ready to listen to . . . my fellow investigator, here."

Honor turned her attention openly and fully to Zilwicki's companion as the captain gestured at him. He was a very young man, she realized. Not particularly distinguished in any way, physically. Of average height—possibly even a little shorter than that—with a build which was no more than wiry, almost callow-looking beside Zilwicki's massively impressive musculature. The hair was dark, the complexion also on the swarthy side, and the eyes were merely brown.

But as she gazed at him and reached out to sample his emotions, she realized *this* young man was anything but "undistinguished."

In her time, Honor Alexander-Harrington had known quite a few dangerous people. Zilwicki was a case in point, as, in his own lethal way, was young Spencer Hawke, standing alertly to watch her back even here. But this young man had the clear, clean uncluttered taste of a sword. In fact, his mind-glow was as close to that of a treecat as Honor had ever tasted in a human being. Certainly not evil, but . . . direct. *Very* direct. For treecats, enemies came in two categories: those who'd been suitably dealt with, and those who were still alive. This unremarkable-looking young man's mind-glow was exactly the same, in that regard. There was not a single trace of malice in it. In many ways, it was clear and cool, like a pool of deep, still water. But somewhere in the depths of that pool, Leviathan lurked.

Over the decades, Honor had come to know herself. Not perfectly, but better than most people ever did. She'd faced the wolf inside herself, the aptness to violence, the temper chained by discipline and channeled into protecting the weak, rather than preying upon them. She saw that aspect of herself reflected in the mirrored surface of this young man's still water, and realized, with an inner shiver, that he was even more apt to violence than she was. Not because he craved it one bit more than she did, but because of his focus. His purpose.

He wasn't simply Leviathan; this man was also Juggernaut. Dedicated every bit as much as she to protecting the people and the things about which he cared, and far more ruthless. She could readily sacrifice herself for the things in which she believed; this man could sacrifice *anything* in their name. Not for personal power. Not for profit. But because his beliefs, and the integrity with which he held them, were too strong for anything else.

But although he was as clean of purpose as a meat-ax, he was no crippled psychopath or fanatic. He would bleed for what he sacrificed. He would simply do it anyway, because he'd looked himself and his soul in the eye and accepted what he found there.

"May I assume, Captain," she said calmly, "that this young man's political associations, shall we say, might make him ever so slightly *persona non grata* with those official intelligence organs?"

"Oh, I think you might say that, Your Grace." Zilwicki smiled with very little humor. "Duchess Harrington, allow me to introduce you to Special Officer Victor Cachat of the Havenite Federal Intelligence Service."

Cachat watched her calmly, but she felt the tension ratcheting up behind his expressionless façade. Those "merely brown" eyes were much deeper and darker than she'd first thought, she observed, and they made an admirable mask for whatever was going on behind them.

"Officer Cachat," she repeated in an almost lilting voice. "I've heard some rather remarkable things about you. Including the part you played in Erewhon's recent . . . change of allegiance."

"I hope you don't expect me to say I'm sorry about that, Duchess Harrington." Cachat's voice was as outwardly calm as his eyes, despite a somewhat heightened prickle of apprehension.

"No, of course I don't."

She smiled and stepped back a half-pace, feeling the way Hawke had tightened internally behind her at the announcement of Cachat's identity, before she waved at the dome's comfortable chairs.

"Sit down, gentlemen. And then, Captain Zilwicki, perhaps you can explain to me exactly what you're doing here in company with one of the most notorious secret agents—if that's not an oxymoron—in the employ of the sinister Republic of Haven. I'm sure it will be fascinating."

Zilwicki and Cachat glanced at one another. It was a brief thing, more sensed than seen, and then they seated themselves in unison. Honor took a facing chair, and Nimitz flowed down into her lap as Hawke moved slightly to the side. She felt Cachat's awareness of the way in which Hawke's move cleared his sidearm and put Honor herself out of his line of fire. The Havenite gave no outward sign he'd noticed, but he was actually rather amused by it, she noted.

"Which of you gentlemen would care to begin?" she asked calmly.

"I suppose I should," Zilwicki said. He gazed at her for a moment, then shrugged.

"First, Your Grace, I apologize for not clearing Victor's visit with your security people ahead of time. I rather suspected that they'd raise a few objections. Not to mention the fact that he *is* a Havenite operative."

"Yes, he is," Honor agreed. "And, Captain, I'm afraid I have to point out that you've brought the aforesaid Havenite agent into a secure area. This entire star system is a fleet anchorage, under martial law and closed to all unauthorized shipping. There's a great deal of highly confidential information floating around, including what could be picked up by simple visual observation. I trust neither of you will take this wrongly, but I really can't permit a 'Havenite operative' to go home and tell the Octagon what he's seen here."

"We considered that point, Your Grace," Zilwicki said, much more calmly than he actually felt, Honor observed. "I give you my personal word that Victor hasn't been allowed access to any of our sensor data, or even to *Pottawatomie Creek*'s bridge, since leaving Torch. Nor was he given any opportunity to make visual observations during the crossing from *Pottawatomie* to your vessel. This—" he raised one hand, waving it at the panoramic view from the observation dome "—is the first time he's actually had a look at anything which could be remotely construed as sensitive information."

"For what it's worth, Duchess," Cachat said, meeting her eyes steadily, his right hand resting lightly in his lap, "Captain Zilwicki is telling you the truth. And while I'll confess that I was very tempted to attempt to hack into *Pottawatomie Creek*'s information systems and steal the information I'd promised him I wouldn't, I was able to suppress the temptation quite easily. He and Princess Ruth are both accomplished hackers; I'm not. I have to rely on other people to do that for me, and none of those other people happen to be along this time. If I'd tried, I would have bungled it and gotten myself caught. In which case I would have gotten no information and destroyed a valuable professional relationship. For that matter, my knowledge of naval matters in general is . . . limited. I know a lot more than the average layman, but not enough to make any worthwhile observations. Certainly not relying on what I can see from the outside."

Honor leaned back slightly, gazing at him thoughtfully. It was obvious from his emotions that he had no idea she could actually taste him. And it was equally obvious he was telling the truth. Just as it was obvious he actually *expected* to be detained, probably jailed. And—

"Officer Cachat," she said, "I really wish you would deactivate whatever suicide device you have in your right hip pocket."

Cachat stiffened, eyes widening in the first sign of genuine shock he'd given, and Honor raised her right hand quickly as she heard the snapping whisper of Spencer Hawke's pulser coming out of its holster.

"Calmly, Spencer," she told the young man who had replaced Andrew LaFollet, never looking away from Cachat herself. "Calmly! Officer Cachat doesn't want to hurt anyone else. But I'd feel much more comfortable if you weren't quite so ready to kill *yourself*, Officer Cachat. It's rather hard to concentrate on what someone's telling you when you're wondering whether or not he's going to poison himself or blow both of you up at the end of the next sentence."

Cachat sat very, very still. Then he snorted—a harsh, abrupt sound, nonetheless edged with genuine humor—and looked at Zilwicki.

"I owe you a case of beer, Anton."

"Told you so." Zilwicki shrugged. "And now, Mr. Super Secret Agent, would you *please* turn that damned thing off? Ruth and Berry would both murder me if I let you kill yourself. And I don't even want to think about what Thandi would do to me!"

"Coward."

Cachat looked back at Honor, head cocked slightly to one side, then smiled a bit crookedly.

"I've heard a great deal about you, Duchess Harrington. We have extensive dossiers on you, and I know Admiral Theisman and Admiral Foraker both think highly of you. If you're prepared to give me your word—*your* word, not the word of a Manticoran aristocrat or an officer in the Manticoran Navy, but *Honor Harrington*'s word—that you won't detain me or attempt to force information out of me, I'll disarm my device."

"I suppose I really ought to point out to you that even if *I* give you my word, that doesn't guarantee someone else won't grab you if they figure out who you are."

"You're right." He thought for a moment longer, then shrugged. "Very well, give me *Steadholder* Harrington's word."

"Oh, very good, Officer Cachat!" Honor chuckled as Hawke stiffened in outrage. "You *have* studied my file, haven't you?"

"And the nature of Grayson's political structure," Cachat agreed. "It's got to be the most antiquated, unfair, elitist, theocratic, *aristocratic* leftover from the dustbin of history on this side of the explored galaxy. But a Grayson's word is inviolable, and a Grayson steadholder has the authority to grant protection to anyone, anywhere, under any circumstances."

"And if I do, I'm bound—both by tradition and honor and by law—to see to it you get it."

"Precisely . . . Steadholder Harrington."

"Very well, Officer Cachat. You have Steadholder Harrington's guarantee of your personal safety and return to *Pottawatomie Creek*. And, while I'm being so free with my guarantees, I'll also guarantee Eighth Fleet won't blow *Pottawatomie Creek* out of space as soon as you're 'safely' back aboard."

"Thank you," Cachat said, and reached into his pocket. He carefully extracted a small device and activated a virtual keyboard. His fingers twiddled for a moment, entering a complex code, and then he tossed the device to Zilwicki.

"I'm sure everyone will feel happier if you hang onto that, Anton."

"*Thandi* certainly will," Zilwicki replied, and slid the disarmed device into his own pocket.

"And now, Captain Zilwicki," Honor said, "I believe you were about to explain just what brings you and Officer Cachat to visit me?"

"Your Grace," Zilwicki's body seemed to incline towards Honor without actually moving, "we know Queen Elizabeth and her government hold the Republic of Haven responsible for the attempt on my daughter's life. And I trust you'll remember how my wife was killed, and that I have no more reason to love Haven than the next man. Rather less, in fact.

"Having said that, however, I have to tell you that I, personally, am completely satisfied Haven had nothing at all to do with the assassination attempt on Torch."

Honor gazed at Zilwicki for several seconds without speaking. Her expression was merely thoughtful, and then she leaned back and crossed her long legs.

"That's a very interesting assertion, Captain. And, I can tell, one you believe to be accurate. For that matter, interestingly enough, *Officer Cachat* believes it to be accurate. That, of course, doesn't necessarily make it true."

"No, Your Grace, it doesn't," Zilwicki said slowly, and Honor tasted both of her visitors' burning curiosity as to how she could be so confident—and accurately so—about what they believed.

"All right," she said. "Suppose you begin, Captain, by telling me why *you* believe it wasn't a Havenite operation?"

"First, because it would be a particularly stupid thing for the Republic to have done," Zilwicki said promptly. "Leaving aside the minor point that being caught would be disastrous for Haven's interstellar reputation, it was the one thing guaranteed to derail the summit conference *they'd* proposed. And coupled with Ambassador Webster's assassination, it would have been the equivalent of taking out pop-up ads in every 'fax in the galaxy that said 'Look, *we* did it! Aren't we nasty people?'"

The massive Gryphon highlander snorted like a particularly irate boar and shook his head.

"I've had some experience with the Havenite intelligence establishment, especially in the last couple of years. Its current management is a lot smarter than that. For that matter, not even Oscar Saint-Just would have been arrogant enough—and stupid enough—to try something like that!"

"Perhaps not. But, if you'll forgive me, all of that is based purely on your reconstruction of what people ought to have been smart enough to recognize. It's logical, I'll admit. But logic, especially when human beings are involved, is often no more than a way to go wrong with confidence. I'm sure you're familiar with the advice 'Never ascribe to malice what you can put down to incompetence.' Or, in this case perhaps, stupidity."

"Agreed," Zilwicki said. "However, there's also the fact that I'm rather deeply tapped into Havenite intelligence operations in and around Torch." He bobbed his head at Cachat, "The intelligence types operating there and in Erewhon are fully aware that they don't want to tangle with the Audubon Ballroom. Or, for that matter, with all due modesty, with *me*. And the Republic of Haven is fully aware of how Torch and the Ballroom would react if it turned out Haven was actually responsible for the murder of Berry, Ruth, and Thandi Palane. Believe me. If they'd wanted to avoid meeting with Elizabeth, they would simply have called the summit off. They wouldn't have tried to sabotage it this way. And if they *had* tried to sabotage it this way, Ruth, Jeremy, Thandi, and I would have known about it ahead of time."

"So you're telling me that in addition to your analysis of all the logical reasons for them not to have done it, your own security arrangements would have alerted you to any attempt on Haven's part?"

"I can't absolutely guarantee that, obviously. I believe it to have been true, however."

"I see."

Honor rubbed the tip of her nose thoughtfully, then shrugged.

"I'll accept the probability that you're correct. At the same time, don't forget that someone—presumably Haven—managed to get to my own flag lieutenant. ONI still hasn't been able to suggest how that might have been accomplished, and while I have the highest respect for you and your capabilities, Admiral Givens isn't exactly a slouch herself."

"Point taken, Your Grace. However, I have another reason to believe Haven wasn't involved. And given the . . . unusual acuity with which you appear to have assessed Victor and myself, you may be more prepared to accept that reason than I was afraid you would be."

"I see," Honor repeated, and turned her eyes to Cachat. "Very well, Officer Cachat. Since you're obviously Captain Zilwicki's additional reason, suppose you convince me, as well."

"Admiral," Cachat said, abandoning the aristocratic titles which, she knew, had been their own subtle statement of plebeian distrust, "I find you have a much more disturbing presence than I'd anticipated. Have you ever considered a career in intelligence?"

"No. And about that convincing?"

Cachat chuckled harshly, then shrugged.

"All right, Admiral. The most convincing piece of evidence Anton has is that if the Republic had ordered any such operation on Torch, it would have been *my* job to carry it out. I'm the FIS chief of station for Erewhon, Torch, and the Maya Sector."

He made the admission calmly, although Honor knew he was very unhappy to do so. With excellent reason, she thought. Knowing with certainty who the opposition's chief spy was would have to make your own spies' jobs a lot easier.

"There are reasons—reasons of a personal nature—why my superiors might have tried to cut me out of the loop for this particular operation," Cachat continued, and she tasted his painstaking determination to be honest. Not because he wouldn't have been quite prepared to lie if he'd believed it was his duty, but because he'd come to the conclusion that he simply couldn't lie successfully to *her*.

"Although it's true those reasons exist," he went on, "it's also true that I have personal contacts at a very high level who would have alerted me anyway. And with all due modesty, my own network would have warned me if anyone from Haven had invaded my turf.

"Because all of that's true, I can tell you that the chance of any Republican involvement in the attempt to assassinate Queen Berry is effectively nonexistent. The bottom line, Admiral, is that *we didn't do it.*"

"Then who did?" Honor challenged.

"Obviously, if it wasn't Haven, our suspicions are naturally going to light on Mesa," Zilwicki said. "Mesa, and Manpower, have plenty of reasons of their own to want Torch destabilized and Berry dead. The fact that the neurotoxin used in the attempt is of Solly origin also points towards the probability of Mesan involvement. At the same time, I'm painfully well aware that everyone in the official intelligence establishment is going to line up to point out to me that we're naturally prejudiced in favor of believing Mesa is behind any attack upon us. And, to be totally honest, they'd be right."

"Which doesn't change the fact that you really do believe it was Mesa," Honor observed.

"No, it doesn't."

"And do you have any evidence beyond the fact that the neurotoxin probably came from the League?"

"No," Zilwicki admitted. "Not at this time. We're pursuing a couple of avenues of investigation which we hope will provide us with that evidence, but we don't have it yet."

"Which, of course, is the reason for this rather dramatic visit to me."

"Admiral," Cachat said with the first smile she'd seen from him, "I *really* think you should consider a second career in intelligence."

"Thank you, Officer Cachat, but I believe I can exercise intelligence without having to become a spy."

She smiled back at him, then shrugged.

"All right, gentlemen. I'm inclined to believe you. And to agree with you, for that matter. It's never made sense to me that Haven would do something like attack Berry and Ruth. But, while *I* may believe you, I don't know how much good it's going to do. I'm certainly willing to present what you've told me to Admiral Givens, ONI, and Admiralty House. I don't think they're going to buy it, though. Not without some sort of corroborating evidence besides the promise—however sincere—of the senior Havenite spy in the area that he really, *really* didn't have anything to do with it. Call me silly, but somehow I don't think they're going to accept that you're an impartial, disinterested witness, Officer Cachat."

"I know that," Cachat replied. "And I'm not impartial, or disinterested. In fact, I have two very strong motives for telling you this. First, because I'm convinced that what happened in Torch doesn't represent my star nation's policy or desires, and that it's clearly not in the Republic's best interests. Because it isn't, I have a responsibility to do anything I can do mitigate the consequences of what's happened. That includes injecting any voice of sanity and reason I can into the Star Kingdom's decision-making process at the highest level I can reach. Which, at this moment, happens to be *you*, Admiral Harrington.

"Second, Anton and I are, as he said, pursuing our own investigation into this. His motives, I think, ought to be totally understandable and clear. My own reflect the fact that the Republic is being blamed for a crime it didn't commit. It's my duty to find out who did commit it, and to determine why he—or they—wanted to make it appear *we* did it. In addition, I have some personal motives, tied up with who might have been killed in the process, which also give me a very strong reason to want the people behind this. However, if our investigation prospers, we're going to need someone—at the highest level of the Star Kingdom's decision-making process we can reach—who's prepared to listen to whatever we find. We need, for want of a better term, a friend at court."

"So it really comes down to self-interest," Honor observed.

"Yes, it does," Cachat said frankly. "In intelligence matters, doesn't it always?"

"I suppose so."

Honor considered them both again, then nodded.

"Very well, Officer Cachat. For whatever it's worth, you have your friend at court. And just between the three of us, I hope to heaven you can turn up the evidence we need before several million people get killed."

May, 1921 PD

CHAPTER THIRTY-THREE

"Princess Ruth's not coming with us?" asked Brice Miller. He and his two friends Ed Hartman and James Lewis had distressed expressions on their faces.

Marti Garner shook her head, trying not to laugh. "No, that part of the plan had to be scrapped."

"Why?" asked Michael Alsobrook. If anything, his expression was even more woebegone. That was perhaps understandable, since he was about the same age as Ruth Winton, so whatever fantasies he'd been having fell into the *Very Unlikely* category rather than, as with the three fourteen-year-olds, into the delusional realm known as *You Have* Got *To Be Kidding*.

Marti heard a little choking sound to her left. Turning her head, she saw that Friede Butry had her attention riveted onto the screen showing their departure from Torch orbit—a subject which was really not all that interesting. Clearly enough, the clan matriarch was finding the romantic anguish of the male members of her party over the sudden and unexpected absence of the princess to be every bit as amusing as Marti did.

Before explaining, Garner considered the security issues involved. They didn't seem to be critical, however, since the only "secret" she'd be divulging was something that would be blindingly obvious to any observer very soon anyway.

"Well, the request Torch sent in that the Biological Survey Corps release our team for detached duty—"

Hearing another choking sound, she broke off and turned her head to the right. Haruka Takano seemed to be utterly fascinated with the data appearing on a different screen. Which was odd, on the face of it, since that data pertained to the ship's completely routine environmental processes.

"Is something amiss, Lt. Takano?"

He didn't take his eyes off the screen. "'Request,'" he mimicked. "Is that 'request' as in 'the gangster requests that you cough up your extortion payment'?"

From her own seat on the *Ouroborous'* command deck, Stephanie Henson spoke up. "You have a low and nasty mind, Haruka."

"You didn't complain about it last night."

"A low, nasty and *vulgar* mind."

"You didn't complain about that either."

"A low, nasty, vulgar and—"

"Enough!" laughed Marti. "To get back to your question, Michael, the delegation that arrived here from Beowulf to finalize our new assignment as Queen Berry's security detachment included several Manticorans. That's not surprising, of course, since Manticore would have initiated the process with Beowulf. One of them was no less a personage than Ruth's father, Michael Winton-Serisburg, the Queen of Manticore's younger brother."

Comprehension seemed to be dawning, judging from the winces on the faces of Alsobrook and the three youngsters.

"Yes, indeed," said Marti. "The prince—well, he's technically a duke these days, but he's still a prince, if you know what I mean. He's still Ruth's father, too, and—apparently knowing his own daughter quite well—he'd come for the specific and express purpose of making sure she did *not* engage in any risky endeavor like accompanying some scruffy albeit doughty vagabonds—that's you, no offense intended—on what seems to be on the face of it a most perilous enterprise."

"Because it *is* a most perilous enterprise," grumbled Ganny El, "and I should have held out for an annual stipend from Manticore as well as from Beowulf. Would have, too, if I'd known we'd make the House of Winton this jumpy."

Either Brice Miller's faith in the princess or his fantasies were stratospheric, because he piped up: "You watch! I bet Ruth figures out a way to sneak around him. She's really *smart*."

"I don't doubt that," said Garner. "But 'smart' can only take you so far, when you have a guard detachment of the Queen's Own Regiment watching you at all times. And don't kid yourself,

Brice. They may be Ruth's bodyguards, and they may have been with her for a year and a half now—but they'll take their orders from the Queen herself. Or the Queen's brother."

"Oh."

"Cheer up, boys," said Haruka. "There was never a chance they'd let her come, once they found out what she had in mind. A member of the royal family? She's already been taken hostage once—at least, the criminals thought they had her—and the first thing that would have crossed the minds of her family was that if they let her run loose, somebody else would do the same."

"But how did they know what she was planning to do?" asked Ed. "I'm sure the princess didn't tell them."

Garner discovered that the screen in front of her—who would have thought it, of engineering data?—was deeply engrossing. Judging from the sudden silence, a similar fascination had seized the other members of the crew.

"*You* did it!" accused Ruth. Her forefinger was shaking right under Hugh's nose. "Don't even try to deny it! *You're* the one who told them!"

Watching them, Berry couldn't help but be amused. Given the size disparity between Ruth and Hugh, the situation was a bit like a chipmunk—well, being fair, a pretty good sized dog—trying to chastise a bear.

Fortunately, Hugh was generally quite phlegmatic. That was one of the things—one of the many things—Berry liked about him. So he didn't snarl back at the Manticoran princess, nor huff and puff that he was being put upon.

"Why would I try to deny it?" he said calmly. "I readily agree that I'm guilty as charged. Which, in turn, simply means that unlike one person in this room—female, about one hundred and sixty-seven centimeters tall, weight somewhere in the range of sixty-five kilograms, of Masadan ancestry—I'm not crazy. Face it, Ruth. Whether you like it or not, your ability to operate as a field agent is now and will forevermore be tightly constrained by the fact that on the scale of 'Hostage, Value Thereof,' you rank ten out of ten. Or at the very least, nine point nine nine unto the two thousandth decimal point out of ten."

Her glare hadn't faded in the least. "It's *sixty* kilos, thank you very much. I exercise regularly."

He accepted the correction with a solemn nod.

Berry decided that Ruth's temper had probably crested and was now on the downslope. Time to intervene.

"I'm really glad you'll be staying here on Torch, Ruth. It'd be awfully lonely without you—"

She summoned her very best glare—which was pretty feeble, being honest—and bestowed it upon Hugh. "—given the living arrangements that this paranoiac insists I have to maintain from now on."

"Just for the duration of the emergency situation," Hugh said.

"'Duration of the emergency situation,'" Ruth jeered. "And what would that situation be, O Paranoid-in-Chief? The all out war to the death between Berry's star nation and Manpower, which has now been in existence for, oh, somewhere in the neighborhood of six hundred years. That one?"

Hugh chuckled. "Yes. That one."

"A life sentence, in other words," said Berry unhappily.

"Maybe not, Your Majesty. If we can—"

"Don't call me that!"

Hugh took a slow deep breath. "I don't have any choice, Berry—and that's the last time you'll hear me use your given name so long as I have this assignment." For a moment, he looked distinctly unhappy. "One of the basic rules concerning security work is that security agents need to keep their personal distance from the person or persons they're providing security for. In this case . . . that's not going to be easy for me. Informality would make it impossible."

Berry didn't know if she was delighted or chagrined to hear that. Probably both. "I'll kill Jeremy, I swear I will. The first guy who comes along since they put this stupid crown on my head who's not intimated by going out on a date with me—and he makes him my security chief!"

"You can't kill Jeremy," said Ruth. "Sorry, girl—but you were the one who specifically refused his offer to give you the right to exercise the death penalty once a year, at your whim and discretion." The princess beamed up at Hugh. "Been me, I would have taken it. And you'd be for the high jump, right about now."

"Fine. I can have him banished." Berry cocked her head, studying Hugh for a few seconds. "But it wouldn't do me any good, would it? You're one of those people with an overdeveloped sense of duty. Even with Jeremy gone, you'd keep soldiering on."

"Well. Yes. But to get back to what I was saying, the main reason for this admittedly extreme precaution"—he waved his hand, indicating the operations chamber buried far below the surface—"is because somebody is using some sort of assassination method that we don't understand yet. Once we learn how to counter it..."

He looked at the bed that had been crammed into the largest available space in the chamber. "Then you can start living somewhere else again."

Ruth's temper was now rapidly subsiding, as was usually true when she got angry. "Look on the bright side, Berry. At least the bathroom down here is up to snuff. State of the art, in fact."

"You'd better hope so," Berry said. "Seeing as how you'll be sharing it with me. There's room down here—barely—for another bed."

"Berry!"

The queen ignored her and looked up at her security chief. "I'm sure the Queen's Own would agree, aren't you?"

"They'll sing hosannas."

"Berry!"

✧   ✧   ✧

But Ruth's displeasure at being banished along with Berry to what she called The Netherworld—her Queen's Own guard detachment did indeed sing hosannas—lasted less than twenty hours. The next day Anton and Victor returned from their visit to Trevor's Star, just two hours after a courier ship brought a detailed report on the recent Battle of Monica.

However much Ruth might daydream of being a dashing field agent, the truth was that her great love was analysis. There was enough meat on the bones of that report concerning Monica to keep her down in the operations chamber for four days straight, not even coming up for meals but having them delivered. To her great pleasure, she'd discovered that the computer equipment in the chamber was every bit as state of the art as the toilet and bathing facilities.

Anton spent a great deal of his own time with her, although he did go up to the surface for meals—and, of course, he didn't sleep down there. There would hardly have been room for a third bed, anyway.

Victor Cachat divided his time during that four-day stretch

about evenly. Half of the time he spent with Thandi—a good part of that, in their bedroom—and the other half he spent helping Anton and Ruth analyze the data from Monica.

The decision that he and Anton would take the risk of trying to penetrate Mesa still hadn't been made yet. But that was just a formality, now. The information they were getting from the Monica reports were confirming all the suspicions they'd ever had.

✧   ✧   ✧

Princess Ruth brushed back her hair. "There's no doubt about it, any longer. Anton and I crunched those figures till they're flat as pancakes. So you can put your fears about any 'hall of mirrors' effect to rest, Jeremy. We weren't looking at images, we were looking at hard cold facts."

"What facts are you referring to in particular?" asked Web Du Havel. He was sitting next to Queen Berry at the conference table in the center of the operations chamber. Victor was sitting next to him, and Thandi and Anton more or less across from him. Jeremy X was standing. As was usually the case, Jeremy preferred to stand at business meetings rather than sit down.

"The data concerning Manpower's financial flows," said Ruth. "There's no way an operation as huge as the one mounted at Monica can keep its costs hidden. And here's what comes out of it. They dropped a bundle on this little fiasco—or someone did, anyway. Sort of. That many battlecruisers don't come cheap, you know, and I think some of the analysts back home in Landing are suffering sticker shock from just looking at the tonnage they threw at us. But—*but*, Jeremy—I think they're missing something."

"Indeed?" Jeremy gave her one of his patented quizzical smiles. "By all means, dazzle us once again with your legerdemain, O Princess!"

Ruth stuck out her tongue at him, then shrugged.

"I think I can make a pretty good case that they figured out how to cover their costs (assuming it all worked, of course) in such a way that they'd at least break even on the Monica project, especially with Technodyne thrown into the mix. If *Technodyne's* part of the deal was to provide the battlecruisers from the ships they were supposed to be scrapping, costs come way down . . . on an out-of-pocket basis, anyway. Oh, they still had to pay for all the munitions they were planning on using, not to mention getting the technicians they needed all the way out to Monica. So, yeah, there were some pretty hefty damn expenditures involved here. But hefty as they were, they weren't as hefty as it might look at first glance. And if you factor in the possible future revenues from the Lynx Terminus—which was clearly their long-term target—Manpower could still have wound up coming out of the whole thing smelling like a rose."

"GIGO," said Jeremy. "Garbage in, garbage out."

"I know what the acronym means, thank you," Ruth said crossly. "What's your point?"

Jeremy smiled at her. "Meaning no offense. Still, in the nature of things those figures you fed into your programs were just guesstimates. You have no access to the actual figures. You could be misreading the figures . . . including just how far Technodyne was willing to go to help subsidize this little venture."

"That's true," said Victor. "In fact, I'd accept a disparity of two-to-one or even three-to-one—conceivably even four-to-one—as a GIGO effect. But it would take something like a full order of magnitude to really alter our conclusions, Jeremy."

"He's right," Anton said. "Those guesstimates, as you call them, were produced by me and Ruth working independently of each other. Victor provided us with his own estimates, as well, although those were a lot less rigorous. We didn't match the results until all three of us were finished. Then Ruth crunched the numbers every way possible—using nothing but Victor's numbers, then nothing but mine, then nothing but hers, then every possible combination of the three. Not a single one of those calculations produced a result that was off by more than fifty percent from the numbers produced as an overall average. To hell with false modesty, Jeremy. You'd be hard pressed to find two intelligence agents anywhere in the galaxy who are better than Victor and I are at this business, and Ruth is as good an analyst as almost anyone in ONI."

Jeremy raised a hand pacifically. "I'm not disputing that," he said. "So what you're saying, in essence, is that there's no way you could be misreading the figures?"

"Oh, I'm sure we *are* misreading them," said Victor. "As you say, we have no direct access to Manpower's records. But we can't be misreading them enough. We just can't, Jeremy. Whatever the exact figures might be, we're close enough to be certain that Manpower's covert activities over the past period can't possibly be explained as the behavior of a business enterprise using any conceivable business model, no matter how ruthless and unrestrained by morality it might be."

"But you just said yourself that they'd at least break even—and might wind up making a fortune off the revenues from the Lynx Terminus."

Ruth got a very self-satisfied look on her face. "Yes—but that's not really the point. Oh, I'll bet the rest of the galaxy's busy looking at it exactly that way right this minute, but there are two other factors I think—Anton and I think—they should be looking at, instead."

"And those are?"

"First, no matter who fronted the cash—Manpower or Technodyne—the fact remains that very few corporations in history have ever thrown such huge resources into speculative endeavors as risky as the Monica project. Oh, there've probably been at least a few private venture operations with this kind of price tag, given the scale the big transtellars operate on. All those battlecruisers together didn't cost much more than a couple of superdreadnoughts all by themselves, after all, even if they had to pay full price for them. And when you stack that up against something like, say, TranStar of Terra's infrastructure project in Hiawatha, it starts looking downright picayune. But the risk factor in this case was way outside any standard operation. Especially one that was unsecured. TranStar got a huge chunk of its expenses guaranteed upfront by the League before it ever sent the first survey crew into Hiawatha, and that sure as hell didn't happen here! If everything had worked, they'd have made a fortune. But if anything went wrong—which, after all, it did—they were going to get exactly zilch back on whatever they put into the effort. That's what's so far outside the standard models."

"Corporations are intrinsically conservative when it comes to things like this, Jeremy," Anton put in. "That's why no long-term, really expensive projects that don't have a definite payoff within a reasonably short and specified time frame are ever undertaken by private corporations—*unless* they have solid government backing and some pretty hefty government guarantees."

"Yeah!" Ruth nodded energetically. "And that brings us to the *second* thing I think everybody should be considering here. If the primary goal was to kick the Star Kingdom off of Mesa's front step—and that's what everything seems to be indicating—then the possible payoff for grabbing the terminus was entirely secondary, right? I mean, we're postulating that profit wasn't the primary motive."

"Some people are, at any rate," Jeremy replied, then shrugged. "All right, and I'll grant you that all the internal evidence we've seen so far suggests the same thing. But that doesn't mean profit couldn't have been a really *important* secondary motive!"

"Sure. But they could've accomplished both of their objectives a lot more cheaply, Jeremy, and without doing something so likely to screw up their relations with the League. All they had to do was keep supplying people like that lunatic Nordbrandt, on Kornati, or even Westman, on Montana. If they'd done that, and managed to find a few other hotspots to keep stirred up, they could have kept us tied up dealing with 'local unrest' for *years*. And that's assuming it didn't make enough domestic stink back in Manticore to make us just decide it was all a bad idea in the first place and go home again. Might not have gotten us to let go of the terminus, but if it went on long enough, it'd probably have gotten OFS involved, and that was really more or less what they had in mind in the first place. Which doesn't even consider the fact that someone back in the League was eventually going to figure out where Monica's new navy came from. Subsidizing terrorists is one thing, as far as the League is concerned; handing *its* starships over to a bunch of neobarbs was way too likely to be something else entirely. So it's not just how much they were willing to put up against the possible gains, it's also that they had another, cheaper—and *safer*—alternative. And it was an alternative they damned well *knew* about, because they were pursuing it at the very same time!"

Jeremy still looked skeptical, but Du Havel was nodding. "They're right, Jeremy, as far as it goes—and if I needed to, and had the spare time, I could easily write a book showing how that pattern has been consistent throughout history. To go back to pre-Diaspora times, for instance, railroads and canals—even a lot of toll roads—weren't built unless the companies involved had gotten some sort of backing or incentives from whatever governments were in place at the time. That said, however, before we leap to any conclusions, we should remember Napoleon's dictum."

"Who's Napoleon?" asked Berry.

"Bernice Napoleon. She's the minister of system defense for Eta Cassiopeiae," said Ruth. For someone as young as she was, the Manticoran princess's knowledge of astropolitics was phenomenal.

"I think Web's referring to an ancient conqueror," said Zilwicki. "But the only dictum I can remember associated with him is something about an army marching on its stomach, which seems pretty irrelevant here."

"'Never ascribe to malice that which is adequately explained by incompetence,'" said Victor. "I first heard it from Kevin Usher. He practically dotes on the quip."

Ruth was looking puzzled again. "And what is that supposed to . . . Oh."

"Web is raising the possibility that Manpower's behavior might simply be the product of mismanagement," said Anton.

"Yeah, I figured it out," Ruth said. Her eyes got a bit unfocused. "You know . . . I could probably crunch those numbers, too. Even here on Torch, the data bank we've been able to compile is enormous. There should be enough in there for me to run models using figures from companies that went bankrupt."

"Don't bother," said Zilwicki. "I've run models close enough to those in the past. Even assuming the worst case variant—a private company run by a single individual with no internal restraints of any kind, which doesn't resemble Manpower at all—you still won't get numbers anything like this. These are the sort of outlays measured against possible gain that you only get from governments. And aggressive governments, at that. The sort led by your Alexander the Great types. Not bean-counters."

"Why in the world would you have taken the time to develop such models?" asked Cachat. "I can't think of any reason to do so."

Zilwicki clucked his tongue. "That's because you have the limited horizons and stunted vision of someone who's spent his whole life in the hall of mirrors. I didn't do it for intelligence reasons, Victor. I did it back in my yard dog days, so I'd have a gauge for businesses that submitted bids."

"And you're certain about this, Anton?" asked Web.

"Yes. There's simply no way to explain Manpower's recent behavior unless you introduce major non-commercial factors into the equation. The same's probably true for Jessyk and Technodyne, by the way, although we're not sure about that yet. But we don't think there's any question any longer that it's true about Manpower. Especially when you add this latest data concerning Monica to the information we already had. A corporation would no more behave like this than a corporate employee would behave like Ronald Allen."

Du Havel leaned forward, planted his hands on the table, puffed out his cheeks, and then blew out the air. "Well. I will be damned."

"We may all be," said Jeremy. "What do you think is happening then?"

"The simplest explanation," replied Victor, "is that the recent reverses suffered by Manpower and some other powerful Mesan corporations has driven the so-called Mesan 'government' to actually begin acting like one. If that hypothesis is true, then what we've actually been seeing are not Manpower operations but *Mesan* operations using Manpower as a cover."

Web cocked his head and looked at Cachat with a quizzical expression. "You don't seem too convinced by that explanation."

Victor shrugged. "It can't be ruled out. It's the simplest explanation, and the most famous of all dictums applies to intelligence work also."

"Oh, I know that one!" said Berry cheerily. "You're talking about Occam's Razor."

"Which is what?" asked Ruth, with some asperity. Her extensive knowledge of political and military matters did not extend to a solid grounding in the history of philosophy.

"I've forgotten the exact words," said Berry. "But the gist of it is that whenever you're presented with two or more possible answers to the same question, always pick the simplest answer. It's the one mostly likely to be correct."

Web, who was quite familiar with Occam's Razor, had sat silently through the exchange. When Berry finished, he said, "But you're skeptical, Victor."

"Yes. I am." Cachat nodded at Zilwicki. "So is Anton."

Du Havel now looked at Anton. "Why?"

Zilwicki scowled. It wasn't much of scowl, actually, but it didn't take much given Anton's blocky face for him to resemble a very peeved dwarf king. "It's a fuzzy matter, admittedly. But I just find it too hard to believe that a planetary 'government' with the history of Mesa's could suddenly start operating as smoothly and efficiently as they seem to have been doing."

"I think it's just about impossible to believe," said Victor. "That so-called 'government' on Mesa has a lot more in common with the board of directors of a company than it does with a normal government."

Du Havel thought about it. There was certainly a lot of truth to what Victor was saying. The political structure of Mesa was essentially that of a corporation in which all free citizens owned voting stock. Slaves, of course, were permanently barred from ever owning voting stock.

The CEO of Mesa was elected by the General Board of the star system. Membership on the board was split between the star system's major corporate entities and members elected by the free citizenry as a whole. The balance of power was unambiguously in the hands of the board members appointed by the major corporations, however. Elective members constituted only one-third of the General Board's total membership; the other two-thirds were appointed by the corporations on the basis of the percentage of the government's taxes which each corporation paid. Because Manpower was far and away the largest single corporation, and, indeed, provided almost sixteen percent of the government's total tax base, its appointees dominated the General Board and normally determined who would hold the office of CEO.

In addition to the appointments Manpower could make in its own right, it had carefully concealed (or, at least, carefully never mentioned) relationships with other major Mesan corporations, through which it controlled the appointment of still more members of the General Board. For example, the Jessyk Combine was officially an independent corporation which appointed 4.5% of the General Board's members, but those appointments were actually controlled by Manpower. If their suspicion that a similar relationship existed with Mesa Pharmaceuticals, that would give Manpower control of—or influence over, at least—another 9.5% of the General Board. Between just those three nominally independent corporations, the Directors of Manpower probably controlled thirty percent of the General Board of the star system outright.

Under the Mesan Constitution, the CEO had to be selected from among the members of the General Board, which virtually guaranteed that he would come out of the ranks of the corporate appointees. And he was, indeed, the chief executive officer of the star system, in fact, as well as name. He served at the pleasure of the General Board, and no CEO could hold office continuously for a period greater than ten T-years, but while he held office, his power was effectively unlimited, and all decisions of government policy were made in a top-down fashion from his office, through an executive branch staff answerable directly to him. His budgetary proposals had to be approved by the General Board, but they were usually confirmed without a great deal of debate. In fact, the (extremely rare) refusal by a General Board to endorse the current CEO's budget proposals was the equivalent of a vote of no confidence, and terminated that CEO's term of office immediately.

It was certainly not a political structure that lent itself to suppleness and risk taking. So far as that went, Du Havel agreed with Victor. On the other hand, he thought Cachat's egalitarian political philosophy sometimes blinded him—partially, at least—to certain realities.

Governments run along corporatist lines were actually fairly common in the galaxy, and Mesa was by no means the sole example. As originally established, for instance, the original Manticoran government had been set up in a very similar fashion. True, it had changed extensively over the centuries, but change was the one true constant of human institutions, when one came right down to it, and many another star nation had evolved *into* a corporatist form, rather than away from one.

And, done properly, they worked just as well as any other system. Which was to say, never perfectly, but often more than well enough to get by with.

Beowulf was a case in point, actually, since it also had a corporate political structure which mirrored its economic structure. The shareholders who owned all of the stock in the Corporation (which, in turn, owned the entire Beowulf System) elected a Board of Directors and corporate officers, who then ran the corporation and were responsible for providing necessary public services to the citizens of Beowulf. This structure had persisted, essentially unchanged, for the better part of five hundred T-years, and was retained in outer form even today, to some extent. Yet Beowulf's government was quite capable of behaving like a genuine national state, and not just a squabbling oligopoly.

That said, Du Havel thought Cachat was probably right. The key difference between Beowulf and Mesa was slavery. About seventy percent of Mesa's population were slaves. That crude and simple demographic reality placed its stamp on every aspect of Mesan society. True, the thirty percent of Mesa's population who were not slaves enjoyed a high degree of individual civil liberties and were quite well provided for by the various corporations for whom they worked in what amounted to a patron-client relationship. In no small part, though, that represented a payoff from the corporations to their clients as a way to help defuse any inclinations towards abolitionism.

That "payoff" mentality was probably unnecessary, since the notion of a Mesan Anti-Slavery League boggled the mind, but it was indicative of the fundamental paranoia which the institution of slavery bred in its slaveowner class. That paranoia also extended itself—with considerably greater justification—to suspicion of outside "troublemakers." While free Mesan citizens enjoyed relatively high degrees of civil liberty, there were specific areas in which those liberties were extremely restricted. The security organs of Mesa enjoyed virtually carte blanche authority in any matter impinging upon the institution of slavery, and they were ruthless in the extreme with any suspected abolitionist. The majority of Mesan citizens had no objection to this, since they, like their corporate overlords, lived in fear of the specter of servile rebellion and generally supported any measure they believed would make that rebellion less likely.

What all that meant, however, was that the formally democratic aspects of Mesa's governmental structure were basically just that—formalities. That was quite unlike the situation on Beowulf, where the population as a whole—that is to say, its *citizens*—had final control of the government.

While Web had been ruminating, the rest of the people in the room had kept silent. Partly out of personal respect, and partly for the practical reason that Du Havel was Torch's prime minister. If any decisions were to be made today, he'd have to be in favor of them.

"I don't fundamentally disagree with your assessment, Victor. Or yours, Anton. I could quibble here and there, but that's what they'd be. Quibbles."

"Right, then," said Jeremy. He took a seat next to Berry. The other people in the room recognized the signs—symptoms, you could almost say. Jeremy X was ready to start making decisions. "What do we do?"

"*We* don't do anything—if by 'we' you're including Torch or the Ballroom," Anton replied. "We've already agreed that Mesa's gotten agents here. So we have to start small and . . . call it 'quarantined.'"

"Who, exactly, is 'we,' then?" asked Du Havel.

"Initially, just three of us." Anton jabbed a thumb at his chest, and then pointed to Victor and Ruth. "Me. Him. Her. It's the only way we can be sure we're completely evading any Mesan double agents. And then, if and when we need backup, we'll use Ganny Butry and her people."

"And just how do you propose to get *into* Mesa?" Jeremy demanded. "Or I should say, vanish from sight once you do. There's no way you'll be able to do that without using at least some of the Ballroom's contacts on Mesa."

He cocked his head. "So. How exactly do you plan to get around that problem?"

"By using one member of the Ballroom as our liaison, and one only. Saburo. He knows a number of Ballroom contacts on Mesa and"—Zilwicki's jaws tightened—"given what happened to Lara, we figure he's as trustworthy as anyone this side of Whatever Saints Might Be."

Jeremy pondered the matter, for a moment, and then nodded. "Good plan, I think. I assume you'll leave Saburo behind, though, when you do the actual penetration?"

"Oh, yes," said Victor. "Trying to smuggle *him* into Mesa would be an order of magnitude harder than smuggling ourselves in. The one thing that Mesan police forces watch for like hawks is any attempt by ex-slaves to penetrate their security."

"True enough. For you and Anton, though, the real trick will be vanishing once you get onto the planet." He smiled. "And do please note that I'm not asking you how you plan to do that."

They smiled back. And said nothing.

Web didn't even try to figure out the espionage technicalities. He was far more intrigued by another issue. "Leave aside security," he said. "Am I the only one here who thinks it's downright weird that you propose to form an elite corps—no more than three of you; four, if you count Saburo—of secret agents, made up of Manticorans and Havenites?"

Berry grinned. "It *is* weird, isn't it? Given that they're officially at war with each other."

"Technically, I've got dual citizenship now," said Ruth stoutly. "So I figure I count as a citizen of Torch, not a Manticoran."

That claim was ... dubious. To begin with, while Torch recognized dual citizenship, the Star Kingdom didn't. Not for anyone, much less a member of its own royal house. Granted, under the circumstances, the Manticoran government had been willing to look the other way when Ruth took out Torch citizenship. Leaving that aside, nobody in their right mind—and certainly not Victor Cachat—doubted for a moment that Ruth would never act against Manticore's interests.

Cachat looked uncomfortable. Zilwicki, on the other hand, seemed quite relaxed. "We can chew on the legalities until the heat death of the universe. What matters, though, is that if we're right, then Manpower and Mesa are engaged in a lot deeper game than we thought they were. And whatever else may be true, the one thing that's sure and certain is that their intentions will be hostile in the extreme toward *both* Haven and Manticore."

Victor spoke up. "Which means that whatever we uncover, we're going to have to share it and—what's almost certainly going to be the biggest problem of all—convince both Haven and Manticore that our assessment is accurate. There will be no way to do that without both Anton and me being involved from beginning to end."

"I can see that," said Jeremy, nodding. "But . . . ah, I hate to remind another person of his duty, Victor, but I thought you were the head of Haven's intelligence not only here on Torch but also on Erewhon. 'Chief of Station,' I think it's called."

Victor looked uncomfortable again. "Well . . . yes. But there's a lot of latitude involved." More brightly: "And they've sent out a very competent subordinate. I'm sure she can handle things while I'm gone."

"And just how can you be so certain she's that good?"

"Oh, we've worked together before, Jeremy, on La Martine. She did a superb job of organizing the murder of a rogue StateSec officer, and handled the beating I gave her afterward just about as well." Seeing the stares, he added: "Well, I *had* to have her beaten. Only way to cover her tracks. I learned that from Kevin Usher, the time he beat me to a pulp in Chicago."

He rose from the table. "And now that we're settled on our course of action—even though most of you don't actually know what it is—I've got to start planning our entry into Mesa. Anton and Ruth still have a lot of data-crunching to do, but they don't really need my help. That sort of thing is, ah, not my forte."

Du Havel saw that Berry was now looking cross-eyed. It was hard not to laugh. He was quite sure he knew what the young queen was thinking.

Sure isn't. Victor Cachat's forte is mayhem.

CHAPTER THIRTY-FOUR

"Are you sure about this, Victor?" asked Jeremy. "It's a hell of a risky way for you to try to get onto Mesa."

He gave Victor's companion a glance that was not quite skeptical, but close. "And—meaning no offense, Yana—but adding you to this small team seems to me to increase the risk, not lower it."

The ex-Scrag Amazon gave the war secretary a cool smile in return. A bit hastily, he added: "Not because I doubt your loyalties, you understand. It's just . . ."

He chuckled softly. "I will say, Victor, if you pull this off you'll have raised the bar for *chutzpah* about a meter."

"Who Hutspa?" asked Berry.

"Miguel Jutspa," said Ruth. "Spelled with a 'J,' not an 'H.' He's a leader of the Renaissance League, one of Jessica Stein's close advisers."

Web Du Havel smiled. "I think Anton's actually using a Yiddish term, Ruth."

"What's—"

"Ancient dialect of German used by Jews. 'Chutzpah'—it actually starts with a 'ch'—means . . ." His eyes got a little unfocused. "There's no exact translation. It's a wonderful term, really. The closest would be brazen, brash—but with the connotation of breathtaking self-righteousness as well. A good illustration is the old joke about the man who murdered his parents for the inheritance and then, when caught and convicted, argued that he should get a light sentence because he'd been deprived of parental guidance. That's *chutzpah*."

316

Berry looked back and forth between Victor and Yana. "All right, I can see that. Victor and Yana go in as a couple, pretending to be among the very few survivors of the Manpower Incident on Terra—the only StateSec agent and one of the few Scrags who somehow managed to keep from getting slaughtered by the murderous alliance between the Ballroom, Kevin Usher—now the head of Haven's FIS—and a certain then-completely-unknown StateSec agent by the name of . . . Victor Cachat."

"Look at it this way," said Victor. "If anybody presses me, I can give them details about the episode that they've never heard, but which will ring absolutely true."

Anton laughed softly. "Since, in fact, there *were* no survivors of that StateSec unit—except you." He looked at Yana. "And it's almost certain that no one has an exact record of exactly which Scrags were killed in Chicago. Some did survive, after all. So why not you?"

Ruth looked a bit uncertain. "I don't know . . . It would seem to me that there's a risk there. If there were so few Scrag survivors of that incident—and there aren't all that many Scrags in the universe to begin with—isn't there a chance that one of the real survivors will know that Yana wasn't among them? Of course, that's assuming she runs into any such on Mesa, which is probably not likely. Still, it's a risk."

Yana shook her head. "You don't really understand how Scrag society works, Ruth. The level of what you might call internal belligerence is closer to that of predators than humans. It wouldn't be at all surprising if I'd gotten irritated with other Scrags and gone my own way. And, as it happens, I *did* spend a fair amount of time on Terra in my younger days, most of it in Chicago. A lot of Scrags do, though, so I'd hardly stand out."

She looked at Berry. And, for an instant, might have seemed a tiny bit embarrassed. "I even—just for a short time—had a fling with one of the Scrags who was involved—several years later, you understand, I was long gone by then—in your sister's kidnapping."

Berry put her hand over her mouth, stifling laughter. "Wait'll I tell Helen!"

"I'd just as soon you didn't. No reason to bother, anyway. That particular ex-boyfriend ranks close to the bottom on my long list of ex-boyfriends whose memory I hold in cheerful contempt."

She bestowed an approving look upon Victor. "Not that I'm holding a grudge, seeing as how Victor eventually blew the bastard apart with a flechette gun."

Victor smiled politely in return, the way someone smiles when they're thanked for having done a minor favor in times past. Held open a door in the rain, lent someone a small amount of money, butchered an ex-lover, that sort of thing.

"To get back to the point," he said, "unless someone very high up in Mesan security gets involved, there's really not much chance that anyone will see through the charade. In the nature of things, StateSec saw to it that there were no records of me readily available. No vids, no images, no DNA records, nothing. They were methodical about that to the point of mania, especially during the Saint-Just years. So unless I meet someone on Mesa who actually worked with me in StateSec, I'm not running that much risk. And the chance of that happening is quite low, because . . . well . . ."

"You didn't leave too many survivors," said Ruth sweetly.

"That's one way of putting it, I suppose."

Berry had been frowning. "Victor, what did you mean when you said 'unless someone very high up in Mesan security gets involved'?"

They'd been meeting, as usual, in the deeply-buried operations chamber which now also served as Berry and Ruth's living quarters. Looking at his adopted daughter, Anton had to suppress an urge to grin for perhaps the tenth time since the meeting had started. There was something just plain comical about the very young Queen of Torch officially presiding over a meeting . . . while sitting in a lotus position on top of her bed.

There wasn't much choice, though. The addition of Saburo and now Yana to the inner circle had crowded the seats at the conference table to the point where both Ruth and Berry found it more comfortable to perch on their beds—which wasn't hard, of course, since the *beds* were jammed up against the table.

As the operations center for which it had been designed, the buried chamber had seemed perfectly roomy. Now that it had to double much of the time as the effective seat of a planet's government, it no longer did.

"What he means," said Anton, "is that we have to assume that even given the incredibly low profile Victor's maintained over the years, Manpower—or whoever's really running the show on Mesa—will by now have gotten enough to be able to identify him. *If* one of their own top agents spots him. But the odds that they've spread that information widely, even among their own ranks, is low."

"Why?" asked Ruth. "I'd think that's the first thing they'd do."

Thandi Palane smiled, and shook her head. "That's because you've been an individualist your whole life, Ruth—even when your membership in the Winton dynasty enabled you to shoehorn yourself into a central position as an official spy."

Ruth frowned. "Which means . . . what?"

"It means you've had no experience with bureaucracies from the inside out," said Jeremy. "Neither had I, of course"—here he gave Web Du Havel a sour look—"until this inveterate paper-pusher finagled me into accepting a position in his administration. But I know the dynamic, since I often manipulated it myself to good effect. Any bureaucrat, especially a bureaucrat in a security or espionage agency, has what amounts to an automatic reflex to keep things a secret. That's because 'being in the know' is the currency by which such stalwarts trade favors and influence—and thereby their own advancement."

Ruth looked dubious. So did Berry. But both Anton and Victor were nodding their agreement.

"He's right, Ruth. Trust me on this—since I'm the one risking my life, after all."

"And mine," piped up Yana. "But I trust you completely. Sweetheart."

Thandi seemed to choke. The look she gave Yana was one part warning, and ten parts simple amusement.

Even the one part warning, Anton knew, was just a sort of subconscious reflex. He was sure that Palane wasn't really worried about Victor "straying" while he spent weeks or possibly even months in Yana's close company, even sharing a bed with her.

With another man, she might have worried. But one of Victor's cover stories for years had been the pretense he and Ginny Usher had put up of being secret lovers, cuckolding Ginny's older and foolish husband Kevin. They'd used that disguise often and sometimes for long stretches, and almost always shared the same bed.

Yana was an attractive enough woman, to be sure. But she wasn't remotely close to Ginny Usher, when it came to sheer beauty and sexiness. That was hardly surprising, since Yana's genome had been designed to be that of a soldier and Ginny's had been manipulated to be that of a pleasure slave. If Victor could manage to spend months in bed with Ginny Usher and do nothing, Thandi would be quite confident he could manage the same with Yana. The man's self-control bordered on the inhuman.

Except when it came to being teased by women. In that quirky area of the human psyche, Victor was often still as vulnerable as he'd been at the age of fourteen or fifteen. Anton had to suppress another urge to grin, seeing the way Victor actually *flushed* at Yana's wisecrack.

Hastily, Cachat pressed on. "The very fact that it's so hard to dig up anything on me means that if Mesa managed it—and we have to assume they did—the information will be kept tightly restricted to the upper echelons of their security forces. At least, until such time as they have reason to think I belong on their front burner—and I can't see any reason they'd do so. Not yet, anyway. Beyond that . . ."

He and Zilwicki exchanged glances. "This is something I've discussed extensively with Anton. Mesan society, no matter how tightly organized and no matter what secret cabal might actually be running the show, has *got* to have a huge and filthy underbelly. There's simply no way a society can operate on such brutal and elitist premises for so many centuries without creating such an underbelly—which it's very likely even Mesa's elite doesn't really know that much about. Partly because they can't, and partly because they don't want to."

Ruth still looked dubious. Berry, on the other hand, looked to Du Havel. She understood, better than Ruth did, that the truth when it came to such matters was more often found in historical patterns than in the minutiae of intelligence work.

"I agree with them," said Web. "In fact, if we had the time and you knew the math involved, I could demonstrate that Victor and Anton's assessment is certainly correct. The only real variable, in fact, is simply *how* correct it is. To put it another way, how big and how filthy is that underbelly? But that the underbelly will exist at all, is a given."

Seeing Ruth's still-skeptical expression, he added: "And I could positively bury you under a mountain of historical analogies. As an example, one of the two societies in history which originally produced the term 'totalitarian' was the ancient Soviet Union. When it collapsed, not much more than a century before the

Diaspora, it didn't take long at all for a highly-developed and very powerful gangster sub-culture to emerge. For a time, in fact, many analysts referred to the new government as a kleptocracy. The point being, that beneath the apparent surface—as hard and tightly policed as any in history—a very thuggish society had been gestating and developing."

He looked now at Victor and Anton, who were seated next to each other. "And that's what they're counting on. Anton as well as Victor, although his chosen entry route is a lot less flamboyant." Here, he smiled. "As you might expect. But both of them are counting on finding plenty of rot and corruption once they arrive on Mesa."

"In my case, simple greed," said Anton. He gestured with a thumb at Victor. "In his case, he's counting on the fact—fine, the assumption—that while Manpower has been using a lot of mercenaries, including StateSec renegades, they will almost certainly be keeping an arm's distance from them. They'll especially be keeping an arm's distance from the StateSec renegades, even the ones on Mesa itself. Which they can do because they're using the mercenary outfits as their 'cut-outs.'"

"*Especially* the ones on Mesa," said Victor. "We already discussed, yesterday, the information Rozsak's intelligence officer Watanapongse passed onto us. They're almost certain—and we agreed with that assessment—that Mesa is planning to launch a massive attack on Torch in the near future using mostly StateSec renegades as the shock troops. *And* that they're most likely planning to violate the Eridani Edict."

"Ah." The frown on Ruth's forehead cleared away. "Which means Mesa is going to want as much plausible deniability as possible when it comes to those StateSec renegades—including the ones on their own planet."

Victor nodded. "My guess, in fact, is that shortly before the attack happens, Mesa will launch a major purge of those StateSec people still on the planet. A few will be rounded up in case show trials are needed, but most of them—and certainly any who know anything—will be shot while resisting arrest or shot while attempting to escape or accidentally killed by a freak meteor strike."

"Don't forget lightning bolts and—a perennial favorite—air car accidents," added Anton cynically. "There'll be a rash of suicides, too, driven by remorse, and a statistically improbable number of drownings and accidental drug overdoses."

"In short," resumed Victor, "all Yana and I have to do is get past Mesan customs—easy enough, with our cover story—and then we can disappear into the mercenary underworld on Mesa. We'll have to get out before the hammer comes down, of course, but that's a given anyway."

"I'll be using more conventional means," said Anton. "A shady trade delegation, basically, whom everyone will assume is really there to develop some contacts with seccy sutlers. Which is another murky underworld, and one which"—he nodded to Saburo—"the Ballroom can provide me entry into."

He looked around the table. "And . . . that's the gist of it. I'm not going into the specific details, of course. There's no reason to."

"How soon do you plan to leave?" asked Ruth.

"I'll be leaving tomorrow," said Cachat. "Anton, in about a week."

Palane's face got pinched. This was probably the first she'd heard of Victor's specific timetable. The man could take "need to know" to extreme lengths, sometimes. That might be excellent secret agent practice—but it was also guaranteed to cause some harsh words being spoken once Thandi got him in private.

"How will you arrange to meet each other after you've gotten there?" asked Du Havel. Then he held up his hand. "Sorry, I don't really need to know that. I'm just curious."

Anton shrugged. "We couldn't tell you anyway, since we haven't figured it out ourselves. And won't. I'm just leaving it to Victor to find me. That's because while his cover story is riskier than mine, it has the advantage of giving him greater freedom of movement if it works. A lot of this is stuff we'll jury-rig as we go along."

A number of frowns appeared.

"Relax," said Victor. "We really are very good at this."

The next morning, after discussing a few last moment details, Victor said: "You'll let Harrington know, I assume."

"Yes. But not until I leave."

Victor nodded. "All right, then. I'll see you on Mesa, Anton. Yana, let's be off."

And off they went. As unsentimental partings went, this one couldn't have been improved upon by any creatures on their side of a spinal cord. It would have done crustaceans proud.

"Damn. You guys really *are* good," said Ruth.

CHAPTER THIRTY-FIVE

"You wanted to see me, Albrecht?"

Albrecht Detweiler turned from his contemplation of the familiar, sugar-white beaches beyond his luxurious office's windows as the dark-haired, boldly tattooed woman stepped through its door.

"Yes, I believe I did," he observed, and tilted one hand to indicate one of the chairs in front of his desk.

Isabel Bardasano obeyed the wordless command, sitting with a certain almost dangerous grace and crossing her legs as he walked back from the windows to his own chair. Her expression was attentive, and he reflected once again upon the lethality behind her . . . ornamented façade and toyed once more with the notion of telling her that a cross between the Bardasano and Detweiler genotypes was even then being evaluated by the Long-Range Planning Board. And, as he had before, he decided against sharing that particular tidbit. For now, at least.

"Well," he said, tipping back slightly in his chair, "I'd have to say that so far, at least, removing Webster—and, of course, Operation Rat Poison—seems to be working out quite well. Aside from whatever new weapons goody the Manties seem to have come up with."

"So far," she agreed, but there was the merest hint of a reservation in her tone, and his eyebrows arched.

"Something about it concerns you?"

"Yes, and no," she replied.

He waggled his fingers in a silent command to continue, and she shrugged.

"So far, and in the short term, it's had exactly the effect we wanted," she said. "I'm not talking about whatever they did at Lovat, you understand. That's outside my area of expertise, and I'm sure Benjamin and Daniel already have their people working on that full time. If either of them needs my help, I'm sure they'll tell me so, as well. But leaving that aside, it does look like we got what we wanted out of the assassinations. The Manties—or, at least, a sufficient majority of them—are convinced Haven was behind it; the summit's been derailed; and it looks as if we've managed to deepen Elizabeth's distrust of Pritchart even further. I'm just not entirely happy with the fact that we had to mount both operations in such a relatively tight time frame. I don't like improvisation, Albrecht. Careful analysis and thorough preparation have served us entirely too well for entirely too long for me to be happy flying by the seat of my pants, whatever the others on the Strategy Council may think."

"Point taken," Detweiler acknowledged. "Benjamin, Collin, and I have been discussing very much the same considerations. Unfortunately, we've come to the conclusion that we're going to have to do more and more of it, not less, as we move into the end game phase. You know that's always been part of our projections."

"Of course. That doesn't make me any happier when it's forced upon us, though. And I really don't want us to get into a make-it-up-as-we-go-along mindset just *because* we're moving into the end game. The two laws I try hardest to bear in mind are the law of unintended consequences and Murphy's, Albrecht. And, let's face it, there are some fairly significant potential unintended consequences to eliminating Webster and attacking 'Queen Berry.'"

"There usually are at least some of those," Detweiler pointed out. "Are there specific concerns in this case?"

"Actually, there *are* a couple of things that worry me," she admitted, and his eyes narrowed. He'd learned, over the years, to trust Bardasano's internal radar. She was wrong sometimes, but at least whenever she had reservations she was willing to go out on a limb and admit it, rather than pretending she thought everything was just fine. And if she was sometimes wrong, she was *right* far more often.

"Tell me."

"First and foremost," she responded, "I'm still worried about someone's figuring out how we're doing it and tracing it back to us. I know no one's come close to finding the proverbial smoking gun yet . . . so far as we know, at any rate. But the Manties are a lot better at bioscience than the Andermani or Haven. Worse, they've got ready access to Beowulf."

Detweiler's jaw tightened in an involuntary, almost Pavlovian response to that name. The automatic spike of anger it provoked was the next best thing to instinctual, and he reminded himself yet again of the dangers of allowing it to affect his thinking.

"I doubt even Beowulf will be able to put it together quickly," he said after a moment. "I don't doubt they could eventually, with enough data. They certainly have the capability, at any rate, but given how quickly the nanites break down, it's extremely unlikely they're going to have access to any of the cadavers in a short enough time frame to determine anything definitive. All of Everett's and Kyprianou's studies and simulations point in that direction. Obviously, it's a concern we have to bear in mind, but we can't allow that possibility to scare us into refusing to use a capability we need."

"I'm not saying we should, only pointing out a potential danger. And, to be frank, I'm less worried about some medical examiner's figuring it out forensically than I am about someone reaching the same conclusion—that it's a bioweapon and that we're the ones who developed it—by following up other avenues."

"What sort of 'other avenues'?" he asked, eyes narrowing once again.

"According to our current reports, Elizabeth herself and most of Grantville's government, not to mention the Manty in the street, are absolutely convinced it was Haven. Most of them seem to share Elizabeth's theory that for some unknown reason Pritchart decided her initial proposal for a summit had been a mistake. None of them have any convincing explanation for what that 'unknown reason' might have been, however. And some of them—particularly White Haven and Harrington—don't seem very convinced it was Haven at all. Since the High Ridge collapse, we no longer have enough penetration to absolutely confirm something like that, unfortunately, but the sources we still do have all point in that direction. Please bear in mind, of course, that it takes time for information from our best surviving sources to reach us. It's not like we can ask the newsies about these things the way we can clip stories about military operations like Lovat, for example. At this point, and even using dispatch boats with streak capability on the Beowulf conduit, we're still talking about very preliminary reports."

"Understood. Go on."

"What concerns me most," she continued with a slight shrug, "is that once Elizabeth's immediate response has had a little time to cool, White Haven and Harrington are still two of the people whose judgment she most trusts. I think both of them are too smart to push her too hard on this particular issue at this moment, but neither of them is especially susceptible to spouting the party line if they don't actually share it, either. And despite the way her political opponents sometimes caricature Elizabeth, she's a very smart woman in her own right. So if two people whose judgment she trusts are quietly but stubbornly convinced that there's more going on here than everyone else has assumed, she's just likely to be more open-minded where that possibility is concerned than even she realizes she is.

"What else concerns me is that there are two possible alternative scenarios for who was actually responsible for both attacks. One, of course, is that it was us—or, at least, Manpower. The second is that it was, in fact, a Havenite operation, but not one sanctioned by Pritchart or anyone in her administration. In other words, that it was mounted by a rogue element within the Republic which is opposed to ending the war.

"Of the two, the second is probably the more likely ... and the less dangerous from our perspective. Mind you, it would be bad enough if someone could convince Elizabeth and Grantville that Pritchart's offer had been genuine and that sinister and evil elements—possibly throwbacks to the bad old days of State Security—decided to sabotage it. Even if that turned around Elizabeth's position on a summit, it wouldn't lead anyone directly to us, though. And it's not going to happen overnight, either. My best guess is that even if someone suggested that theory to Elizabeth today—for that matter, someone may already have done just that—it would still take weeks, probably months, for it to reach the point of changing her mind. And now that they've resumed operations, the momentum of fresh casualties and infrastructure damage is going to be strongly against any effort to resurrect the original summit agreement even if she does change her mind.

"The first possibility, however, worries me more, although I'll admit it would appear to be a lower order probability, so far, at least. At the moment, the fact that they're convinced they're looking at a Havenite assassination technique is diverting attention from us and all of the reasons we might have for killing Webster or Berry Zilwicki. But if someone manages to demonstrate that there has to be an undetectable bio-nanite component to how the assassins are managing these 'adjustments,' the immediate corollary to that is going to be a matching suspicion that even if Haven is *using* the technique, it didn't *develop* the technique. The Republic simply doesn't have the capability to put something like this together for itself, and no one as smart as Patricia Givens is going to believe for a moment that it does. And that, Albrecht, is going to get that same smart person started thinking about who *did* develop it. It could have come from any of several places, but as soon as anyone starts thinking in that direction, the two names that are going to pop to the top of their list are Mesa and Beowulf, and I don't think anyone is going to think those sanctimonious bastards on Beowulf would be making something like this available. In which case Manpower's reputation is likely to bite us on the ass. And the fact that both the Manties' and the Havenites' intelligence services are aware of the fact that 'Manpower' has been recruiting ex-StateSec elements is likely to suggest the possibility of a connection between us and some *other* StateSec element, possibly hiding in the underbrush of the current Republic. Which is entirely too close to the truth to make me feel particularly happy.

"That could be bad enough. If they reach that point, however, they may very well be willing to go a step further. If we're supplying the technology to some rogue element in Haven, then what would keep us from using it ourselves? And if they ask themselves *that* question, then all of the motives we might have—all of the motives they already *know* about because of Manpower, even without the additional ones we actually do have—are going to spring to their attention."

Detweiler swung his chair gently from side to side for several seconds, considering what she'd said, then grimaced.

"I can't disagree with the downsides of either of your scenarios, Isabel. Still, I think it comes under the heading of what I said earlier—the fact that we can't allow worry about things which may never happen to prevent us from using necessary techniques where we have to. And as you've just pointed out, the probability of anyone deciding it was us—or, at least, that it was us acting for ourselves, rather than simply a case of Haven's contracting out the 'wet work' to a third-party—is low."

"Low isn't the same thing as nonexistent," Bardasano countered. "And something else that concerns me is that I have an unconfirmed report Zilwicki and Cachat visited Harrington aboard her flagship at Trevor's Star."

"Visited Harrington?" Detweiler said a bit more sharply, letting his chair come upright. "Why is this the first I'm hearing about this?"

"Because the report came in on the same streak boat that confirmed Elizabeth's cancellation of the summit," she said calmly. "I'm still working my way through everything that was downloaded from it, and the reason I requested this meeting, frankly, has to do with the possibility that the two of them actually did meet with her."

"At Trevor's Star?" Detweiler's tone was that of a man repeating what she'd said for emphasis, not dubiously or in denial, and she nodded.

"As I say, it's an unconfirmed report. I really don't know how much credibility to assign it at this point. But if it's accurate, Zilwicki took his frigate to Trevor's Star, with Cachat—a known Havenite spy, for God's sake!—on board, which would mean they were allowed transit through the wormhole—and into close proximity to Harrington's fleet units—despite the fact that the entire system's been declared a closed military area by Manticore, with 'Shoot on Sight' orders plastered all over the shipping channels and newsfaxes and nailed up on every flat surface of the Trevor's Star terminus' warehousing and service platforms. Not to mention the warning buoys posted all around the system perimeter for any through traffic stupid enough to head in-system from the terminus! And it would also appear that Harrington not only met with Cachat but allowed him to leave, afterward. Which suggests to me that she gave fairly strong credence to whatever it was they had to say to her. And, frankly, I can't think of anything the two of them might have to say to her that *we'd* like for her to hear."

Detweiler snorted harshly in agreement.

"You're right about that," he said. "On the other hand, I'm sure you have at least a theory about the specific reasons for their visit. So be a fly on her bulkhead and tell me what they probably said to her."

"My guess would be that the main point they wanted to make was that Cachat hadn't ordered Rat Poison. Or, at least, that neither he nor any of his operatives had carried it out. And if he was willing to confirm his own status as Trajan's man in Erewhon, the fact that he hadn't carried it out—assuming she believed him—would clearly be significant. And, unfortunately, there's every reason to think she *would* believe him if he spoke to her face to face."

Detweiler throttled another, possibly even sharper spike of anger. He knew what Bardasano was getting it. Wilhelm Trajan, Pritchart's handpicked director for the Republic's Foreign Intelligence Service, didn't have the positive genius for improvisational covert operations that Kevin Usher possessed, but Pritchart had decided she needed Usher for the Federal Investigation Agency. And whatever else might have been true about Trajan, his loyalty to the Constitution and Eloise Pritchart—in that order—was absolute. He'd been relentless in his efforts to purge FIS of any lingering StateSec elements, and there was no way in the world *he* would have mounted a rogue operation outside channels. Which meant the only way Rat Poison could have been mounted without Cachat knowing all about it would have been as a rogue operation originating at a much lower level and using an entirely different set of resources.

That was bad enough, but the real spark for his anger was Bardasano's indirect reference to the never-to-be-sufficiently-damned treecats of Sphinx. For such small, fuzzy, outwardly lovable creatures, they had managed to thoroughly screw over altogether too many covert operations—Havenite and Mesan alike—over the years. Especially in partnership with that bitch Harrington. If Cachat had gotten into voice range of Harrington, that accursed treecat of hers would know whether or not he was telling the truth.

"When did this conversation take place, according to your 'unconfirmed report'?"

"About a T-week after Elizabeth fired off her note. The report about it came from one of our more carefully protected sources, though, which means there was even more delay than usual in getting it to us. One of the reasons it's still unconfirmed is that there was barely time for it to catch the regular intel drop."

"So there was time for Harrington to go and repeat whatever they told her to Elizabeth or Grantville even before she headed out for Lovat, without our knowing anything about it."

"Yes." Bardasano shrugged. "Frankly, I don't think there's very much chance of Elizabeth or Grantville buying Haven's innocence, no matter what Cachat may have told Harrington. All he can tell them is that as far as *he* knows Haven didn't do it, after all, and even if they accept that he was telling her the truth insofar as he knew it, that wouldn't mean he was right. Even if he's convinced Harrington he truly believes Haven didn't do it, that's only his personal opinion . . . and it's damned hard to prove a negative without at least some outside evidence to back it up. So I strongly doubt that anything they may have said to her, or that she may have repeated to anyone else, is going to prevent the resumption of operations. And, as I said before, now that blood's started getting shed again, the war is going to take on its own momentum all over again, as well.

"What worries me quite a bit more than what Zilwicki and Cachat may have told Harrington, frankly, is that we don't know where they went after they *left* her. We've always known they're both competent operators, and they've shown an impressive ability to analyze any information they get their hands on. Admittedly, that's hurt us worse tactically than strategically so far, and there's no evidence—yet—that they've actually begun peeling the onion. But if Cachat is combining Haven's sources with what Zilwicki is getting from the Ballroom, I'd say they're more likely than anyone else to start putting inconvenient bits and pieces together. Especially after they start looking really closely at Rat Poison and how it could have happened if Haven didn't do it. Working on their own, they can't call on the organizational infrastructure Givens or Trajan have access to, but they've got plenty of ability, plenty of motivation, and entirely too many sources."

"And the last thing we need is for those Ballroom lunatics to realize we've been using them for the better part of a century and a half," Detweiler growled.

"I don't know if it's absolutely the *last* thing we need, but it would definitely be on my list of the top half-dozen or so things we'd really like not to happen," Bardasano said with a sour smile, and, despite himself, Detweiler chuckled harshly.

The gusto with which the Audubon Ballroom had gone after

Manpower and all its works had been one more element, albeit an unknowing and involuntary one, in camouflaging the Alignment's true activities and objectives. The fact that at least some of Manpower's senior executives were members of at least the Alignment's outer circle meant one or two of the Ballroom's assassinations had hurt them fairly badly over the years. Most of those slaughtered by the vengeful ex-slaves, however, were little more than readily dispensed with red herrings, an outer layer of "the onion" no one would really miss, and the bloody warfare between the "outlaw corporation" and its "terrorist" opposition had helped focus attention on the general mayhem and divert it *away* from what was really going on.

Yet useful as that had been, it had also been a two-edged sword. Since all but a very tiny percentage of Manpower's organization was unaware of any deeper hidden purpose, the chance that the *Ballroom* would become aware of it was slight. But the possibility had always existed, and no one who had watched the Ballroom penetrate Manpower's security time and time again would ever underestimate just how dangerous people like Jeremy X and his murderous henchmen could prove if they ever figured out what was truly going on and decided to change their target selection criteria. Or if they realized . . . certain other things about the Ballroom and who might be peeking inside its operations. And if Zilwicki and Cachat actually were moving towards putting things together . . .

"How likely do you really think it is that the two of them could pull enough together to compromise things at this stage?" he asked finally.

"I doubt anyone could possibly answer that question. Not in any meaningful way, at any rate," Bardasano admitted. "The possibility always exists, though, Albrecht. We've buried things as deeply as we can, we've put together cover organizations and fronts, and we've done everything we can to build in multiple layers of diversion. But the bottom line is that we've always relied most heavily on the fact that 'everyone knows' what Manpower is and what it wants. I'd have to say the odds are heavily against even Zilwicki and Cachat figuring out that what 'everyone knows' is a complete fabrication, especially after we've had so long to put everything in place. It *is* possible, however, and I think—as I've said—that if anyone *can* do it, the two of them would be the most likely to pull it off."

"And we don't know where they are at the moment?"

"It's a big galaxy," Bardasano pointed out. "We know where they *were* two T-weeks ago. I can mobilize our assets to look for them, and we could certainly use all of our Manpower sources for this one without rousing any particular suspicion. But you know as well as I do that what that really amounts to is waiting in place until they wander into our sights."

Detweiler grimaced again. Unfortunately, she was right, and he did know it.

"All right," he said, "I want them found. I recognize the limitations we're facing, but find them as quickly as you can. When you do, eliminate them."

"That's more easily said than done. As Manpower's attack on Montaigne's mansion demonstrates."

"That was Manpower, not us," Detweiler riposted, and it was Bardasano's turn to nod.

One of the problems with using Manpower as a mask was that too many of Manpower's executives had no more idea than the rest of the galaxy that anyone was using them. Which meant it was also necessary to give those same executives a loose rein in order to keep them unaware of that inconvenient little truth . . . which could produce operations like that fiasco in Chicago or the attack on Catherine Montaigne's mansion on Manticore. Fortunately, even operations which were utter disasters from Manpower's perspective seldom impinged directly on the *Alignment's* objectives. And the occasional Manpower catastrophe helped contribute to the galaxy at large's notion of Mesan clumsiness.

"If we find them, this time it won't be Manpower flailing around on its own," Detweiler continued grimly. "It will be us—*you*. And I want this given the highest priority, Isabel. In fact, the two of us need to sit down and discuss this with Benjamin. He's got at least a few spider units available now—he's been using them to train crews and conduct working-up exercises and systems evaluations. Given what you've just said, I think it might be worthwhile to deploy one of them to Verdant Vista. The entire galaxy knows about that damned frigate of Zilwicki's. I think it might be time to arrange a little untraceable accident for it."

Bardasano's eyes widened slightly, and she seemed for a moment to hover on the brink of a protest. But then she visibly thought better of it. Not, Detweiler felt confident, because she was afraid to argue the point if she thought he was wrong or that he was running unjustifiable risks. One of the things that made her so valuable was the fact that she'd never been a yes-woman. If she did disagree with him, she'd get around to telling him so before the operation was mounted. But she'd also take time to think about it first, to be certain in her own mind of what she thought before she engaged her mouth. Which was *another* of the things that made her so valuable to him.

And I don't doubt she'll talk it over with Benjamin, too, he thought sardonically. *If she has any reservations, she'll want to run them past him to get a second viewpoint on them. And, of course, so the two of them can double-team me more effectively if it turns out they agree with one another.*

Which was just fine with Albrecht Detweiler, when all was said and done. The one thing he wasn't was convinced of his own infallibility, after all.

CHAPTER THIRTY-SIX

"I can't tell you how much I'm looking forward to this, Hugh. The first time I've been out of that damn hole since the murder of Lara and all those other people."

They'd just emerged from the elevator leading down to the buried operations-center-doubling-as-royal-residence and were heading toward the front entrance. Impulsively, Berry slid her hand into her security chief's elbow. Then, feeling him get tense, she made a face and withdrew the hand.

"Sorry. Forgot. You have to keep your gun hand free—both of them, it seems—in case evil-doers leap out at us. And never mind the fact that no evil-doer smaller than a gorilla is likely to 'leap out' at you in the first place—and if they did, so what? I've seen you lift weights, Hugh. Any real world baddie with a functioning brain who wants to do me evil when you're around is going to try to blow me up or shoot me at long range or poison me or whatever—none of which scenarios leave any room for Dead-Eye Arai to go down with guns blazing."

Hugh couldn't help but chuckle. In purely cold-blooded and practical terms, Berry was almost certainly correct. Hugh *didn't* need to keep both his hands free. In fact, you could even make a case that by lending Berry his arm he was lowering the risk that the queen might hurt herself by tripping and falling.

But it didn't matter. The real problem was psychological, not practical. Even without any physical contact, Hugh was finding it very hard to maintain his emotional detachment. Harder, in fact, as time went by. He figured he needed every crutch he could get.

The queen's latest remark was just another nail in his emotional coffin, so to speak. And if the term "coffin" might strike another man as a ridiculous way to describe the fact that he was falling in love, that other man wasn't his would-be paramour's head of security. By now, Hugh silently cursed Jeremy X the moment he woke up, at least a dozen times during the course of each day—and his last thought before he fell asleep was to curse him yet again.

Since the murder of Lara and all those other people. To the best of Hugh's knowledge, Berry Zilwicki was the only person who described that now-notorious historical episode in that manner. For probably everyone else in the settled universe—and certainly every newscaster—the episode was known as *the attempted assassination of Queen Berry of Torch.*

Hugh thought of the incident that way himself. But Berry didn't. And never would. It might be better to say, was flatly incapable of it. There was a transparency in the way she saw the universe that passed through the many layers of positions and titles and posts and status that most people automatically and usually subconsciously laid over the other people they encountered.

It wasn't that Berry was disrespectful toward people of high social rank. She wasn't, unless that person had given her specific cause to be. It was simply that she had the ability to extend that respect to anyone, no matter how low their status might be, without even thinking about it.

She had survived, and Lara and many others had not. So, forever more, that incident would be defined for her by the people who'd suffered the most, not by their respective status. She'd taken the time and effort afterward to find out the name of every person who'd died, down to the servants, and send personal messages of condolence to their families. (If they had any. Many ex-slaves didn't.)

That quality made her someone who gathered friends faster than anyone Hugh had ever seen in his life, and drew the friends she already had still closer. Hugh didn't think any of Berry's other bodyguards were falling in love with her, the way he was. But by now they were all completely devoted to her.

And . . . if he'd gauged things correctly, Torch's populace as a whole had done exactly the same thing. They were about to find out. This would be Berry's first appearance in public since the assassination attempt.

He'd damn well better be right. Or Berry would skin him alive. She might do it anyway.

✧   ✧   ✧

The queen and her head of security emerged into the sunlight spilling onto the front entrance of the palace. Immediately, two things happened.

The huge crowd gathered to greet her exploded in cheers, and a dozen guards moved in and surrounded her.

A little over half of the guards were Beowulfers and the remainder were a mix of Ballroom people and Amazons, each and every one of whom had been carefully vetted. Vetted not only by Hugh himself, and Jeremy and Saburo, but by one of the members of the bodyguard that Ruth's father had brought with him.

His name was Barry Freeman, and he'd been the only member of that Queen's Own detachment partnered to a treecat. The treecat's name was Oliver Wendell Holmes, and he'd been present throughout the process whereby Hugh put together Berry's new security team.

Her first *real* security team, rather. Berry had insisted the unit be titled Lara's Own Regiment. "Regiment" was absurd at the moment, of course. But if the new star nation survived, it wouldn't always be.

Hugh wished desperately that Barry and Oliver were still here on Torch. He'd have felt a lot better if he'd known there was at least one treecat able to sense the emotions of the people who came within striking range of Berry. Unfortunately, treecats who'd taken human partners were few and far between. The only one they'd had on Torch had been Genghis. Hugh missed him and Judson Van Hale more with every passing day, and not just from the utility perspective. Neither Genghis nor Judson—nor Harper—had hesitated for a moment. If they had, Berry would have died and the overall death toll would have been immeasurably worse. For Hugh Arai, that made all three of them his brothers, and species be damned.

Yet there *was* a utility aspect to it, and Hugh had discussed the matter, at some length, with Winton-Serisburg and Freeman, the day before they left. They'd promised they'd do what they could when they got back to the Star Kingdom to see if some treecat-partnered Manticorans with the needed security experience and training could be freed up to serve for a time on Torch.

"But don't get your hopes too high," Freeman had said. "There just aren't that many of us anywhere, much less with the skills you need . . . and, to be honest, we have to use the ones we've got to keep an eye out for whatever the hell they're using for these assassinations closer to home." He'd looked almost apologetically at Winton-Serisburg. "Her Majesty, Baron Grantville, Earl White Haven, Baroness Mourncreek . . . there are still a *lot* of people someone with this kind of capability"—like most of the Queen's Own who'd been to Torch, he didn't seem quite as sold as the Star Kingdom's official intelligence analysts on the notion that the someone in question spoke with a Havenite accent—"would like to see dead. And keeping *them* alive is going to use up a huge chunk of our available supply of 'cats."

"Barry's right about that, and the pairings we do have are most likely to be found on Sphinx, probably working for the Forest Service," Michael had added. "But I'll raise it with my sister, Hugh, and we'll do what we can."

"Oh, good lord," said Berry, staring with dismay at her security guards. What would be upsetting her the most, Hugh knew, was not so much their presence as the fact that each and every one of them was armed with a pulse rifle—which they carried ready to fire. Lara's Own was making it as crystal clear as possible that they were prepared to shoot anyone instantly, on the slightest suspicion.

True, the crowd itself didn't seem to mind. In fact, an even bigger roar of approval went up the moment the security guards closed in around the queen. But from the expression on Berry's face and the added pallor of her complexion, she was aghast.

"Hugh . . ."

He set his jaws. "Your Majesty, this is how it is. This is how it'll stay, at least until Manpower goes down for the count. If you can't stand it, then you'll need to get a new security chief."

He wouldn't have been surprised if she fired him on the spot. He'd long since come to realize that while Berry always tried to accommodate people, she was very far removed from being meek or easily intimidated. But, instead, after a few seconds a little smile came to her face.

"Is this as hard for you as it is for me?" she asked quietly. "The truth is, I really *would* like to fire you—but for a way better reason than this." A little accompanying gesture indicated not only the guards around them but also, in some indefinable manner, the whole panoply of security measures Hugh had erected. "Way, way better."

He managed to keep his expression stern and alert. "Yes. It is. But there's nothing we can do about it now, so . . ."

He decided that insisting on keeping both his hands free, given that he was the only guard around who *wasn't* openly carrying a weapon, was just plain silly.

So, he extended his elbow. "May I offer you an arm, Your Majesty?"

"Why, yes. Thank you."

"And now, your ice cream awaits."

❖   ❖   ❖

From the look on her face when they arrived at J. Quesenberry's Ice Cream and Pastries, Berry found those arrangements even more appalling than the ferocious security contingent that surrounded her. The whole place was vacant, except for the employees.

"Hugh . . ."

"Your Majesty, this is how—"

"Oh, shut up," she said crossly.

"I will point out"—he swept his hand around—"that the management is hardly complaining."

That was . . . true enough, obviously. Since the whole city block had been closed off anyway, by other security guards, Quesenberry's staff had placed tables up and down the street. In the middle of the street as well as both sidewalks—anywhere they could find enough room to squeeze in another small round table and some chairs. They must have rented most of them. Apparently, they were expecting ten times as many customers as they'd gotten in the past, even on those days when Berry had shown up at the ice cream parlor.

"Well . . ." She heaved a sigh. "Okay, then. I guess."

She took his arm and more or less marched him inside. "But since you insist on getting rid of any other company, Mr. Arai, you'll have to provide me with all the scintillating conversation I need. And I warn you! If I catch your eyes roving about looking for Manpower agents hidden in the pastry bins, there'll be hell to pay."

❖   ❖   ❖

Berry only had to scold him twice. With the interior of the parlor completely deserted except for the two of them and one employee, and with Lara's Own standing guard at the entrance, Hugh found he could relax a bit.

Of the two times she caught him lapsing, one of them did indeed happen to be an excessive scrutiny of one of the pastry bins.

(You never knew. A small bomb might be buried under those fruit rolls.)

The other, and longer, lapse came when his suspicions fell on the one employee present. There were no good reasons for that suspicion, true. Not only was the employee slaving away at some new concoction Berry had decided to try; not only was she beaming her obvious approval of the queen's new security arrangements; not only was she probably the smallest and least threatening person in the employ of J. Quesenberry's Ice Cream and Pastries—the young woman stood less than one hundred and fifty centimeters and couldn't have weighed more than forty kilos—but she had one of Lara's Own watching her at all times, gun pointed almost right at her.

(You never knew. She might be one of the ninjas of legend and fable, even if she did seem to be basking in the unusual attention.)

Whether his conversation was scintillating or not, he did not know and never would. Mostly, he listened to Berry. He could do that for hours. She was one of those rare people who, in some uncanny way, made the phrase "idle conversation" something that denoted real pleasure rather than tedium. Maybe it was the way she was so obviously paying attention to the person she was talking to, even when she was doing most of the talking.

When they were readying to leave, she said, "This wasn't so bad, to my surprise. But I have to say I liked our first date better."

"This was not a date," Hugh said firmly. Sternly. With granite resolve. "For you, it was an outing. For me, a security assignment."

Berry smiled. There was something about that smile that Hugh decided he didn't dare think about it too much.

"How could I have missed that?" she murmured.

Damn the girl. Better still, damn Jeremy.

✧   ✧   ✧

Before they made their exit, Hugh gave the detachment from Lara's Own a five-minute warning to get the street cleared. Then he had to extend it to ten minutes, and then to fifteen. The crowd that filled every seat at every table out there—just as Quesenberry's owners had figured they would—was friendly and cooperative. But they saw no good reason not to finish their dishes in a leisurely manner, and even in the best of circumstances it took time to get that many people to move. What could he do? Order Lara's Own to open fire? Berry damn well *would* have him skinned alive.

When they were finally able to leave, he extended his arm once again.

"If I may, Your Majesty."

Berry nodded, placed her hand in the crook of his elbow, and they went out onto the street beyond.

On the way back to the palace, a few minutes later, Berry got that peculiar little smile back on her face. "Did I mention that I have the ability—not always, sure, but more often than sheer chance can allow—to foretell the future?"

"Ah . . . no, Your Majesty. You didn't."

"It's quite true. And I'm getting another of those premonitions."

"Which is what, Your Majesty?"

"The day will come, Hugh Arai, when you will pay dearly and bitterly for each and every one of these blasted 'Your Majesties.' Mark my words."

Hugh mused on the matter all the way back to the palace. By the time they arrived, he'd reached the tentative conclusion that as dire predictions went, that one had the potential of being quite delightful.

The conclusion, of course, triggered off Hugh's overly-developed sense of duty again. And, again, he heaped silent curses on Jeremy X.

CHAPTER THIRTY-SEVEN

"Yes, Jiri?"

Luiz Rozsak went right on methodically crushing gingersnaps for the eventual gravy as Commander Watanapongse appeared on his personal com. The rich, comforting smell of home-baked rye bread with caraway seeds was a subtle background incense for the stronger, more immediate scent of simmering sauerbraten, and, as usual, when he was occupied in the kitchen, Rozsak had set the com for holographic mode, which meant Watanapongse's head and shoulders seemed to sprout out of the counter before him while he worked.

"Sorry to disturb you, Luiz, but I thought you'd want to hear about this ASAP." The commander grimaced. "I think we've just managed to confirm what Laukkonen was talking about back in March."

"Laukkonen?"

Rozsak's fingers paused in their work, and he frowned slightly. There were enough things breaking loose in the Maya Sector and its immediate environs for even Luiz Rozsak to need a handful of seconds to sort through his orderly mental files. Then he nodded.

"Ajax," he said.

"Exactly." Watanapongse nodded as the single word told him Rozsak had found the required memory and called it up. "This isn't from him, and it isn't as clear cut and . . . concise, let's say, as what he had for us, either. But it's from two separate low-level sources in two different star systems. Neither of them happened to have any senior StateSec officers who owed them money, but between the two of them, they've reported the departure of three rogue ex-Peep warships from their areas. There's a lot of little stuff—minor crap, the kind of barroom and restaurant chatter where people let things slip—to suggest all three of them were headed for the same rendezvous somewhere, as well. Obviously, we can't confirm that positively at the moment, but we have been able to confirm that the ships in question all left in a fairly tight time window. One which would match pretty well with what Laukkonen gave us from Bottereau, the StateSec guy who owes him all that money."

"I'm not hearing anything about positively confirming their target," Rozsak observed, and Watanapongse twitched a slight smile at him.

"No, you're not," he agreed. "But as we agreed when we talked about Laukkonen's original report, it's hard for me to think of another target in our area Manpower would be interested in beating on."

"That assumes operations in our area are what's on their mind, though," Rozsak pointed out. "Given what seems to be going on out Talbott's way, they could be pulling in extra forces for *that* area."

"They could be." Watanapongse nodded. "On the other hand, given the scale of the operation Terekhov busted at Monica, all the StateSec holdouts combined wouldn't matter a fart in a skinsuit. If we can figure that out, then Manpower probably can, too, so why waste an asset that's only going to disappear like snow on a griddle when it gets run over by the reinforcements the Manties *have* to be sending that way?"

"Assuming the Manties have very much to send," Rozsak replied.

"You know, Luiz, you really do seem to get more enthusiastic about playing devil's advocate whenever I catch you in the kitchen. I thought cooking was supposed to be a *soothing* pastime."

"This *is* me being 'soothing'—or as close to it as I can get these days, anyway."

Rozsak smiled crookedly, finished crushing the gingersnaps, set them aside, and wiped his fingers on the hand towel draped around his neck. He stayed that way for several seconds, his smile gradually fading into a slight frown, then exhaled heavily.

"I don't suppose we've got anything new on what the Manties did to Giscard at Lovat?" he asked.

"Not really." Watanapongse shook his head, and Rozsak grimaced.

The assassination of James Webster in Old Chicago and the *attempted* assassination of Queen Berry on Torch had done exactly what he, Barregos, Watanapongse, and Edie Habib were convinced they'd been supposed to do: completely derail the proposed summit between Queen Elizabeth and President Pritchart on Torch. Elizabeth's reaction, Rozsak thought, had been almost as predictable as sunrise, particularly in light of the People's Republic of Haven's penchant for using assassination as a tool and the attempt on her own life which had been organized by Oscar Saint-Just. He had to admit that, in her place, he would have automatically been deeply suspicious of Haven, as well. Of course, he *wasn't* in her place. He didn't have her personal history—or the history of her star nation as a whole—with the *People's* Republic of Haven. And because he didn't, it seemed extremely unlikely to him that Pritchart would have gone about sabotaging her own proposed summit in such an elaborate and potentially disastrous fashion.

Of course, that may be in part because you know—now—just how "disastrous" it looks like turning out after the fact, Luiz, he pointed out to himself. *It's obvious Pritchart and Theisman didn't see whatever the hell it was Harrington used at Lovat coming any better than we did, so they couldn't have had any idea* before *the fact just how bad any fresh shooting was likely to be from their perspective. There is still the possibility that it was someone else in the Republic who wanted to sabotage the peace talks when it looked like outright military victory was comfortably in reach, too, I suppose. But still . . .*

"In the absence of any additional evidence one way or the other," he said out loud, "I think you and Edie are probably on the right track. God knows I'd love to know how even Manties managed to cram a two-way FTL link into something the size of a missile, but I don't see what else could account for Lovat."

"I'd be happier if we had something more concrete than secondhand reports about it," Watanapongse responded.

"We'd always be happier if we had *something* we don't have!" Rozsak snorted. "It's only the specific 'something' we have in mind that changes, isn't it?"

Watanapongse gave an answering snort of agreement, and the admiral shrugged.

"Well, since we *don't* have anything more concrete than sec-ondhand reports about Lovat, we can't begin to predict where that whole mess is going. And, since we don't have anyone inside Manpower's command and control loop, either, we can't be posi-tive exactly what target they're planning to hit. I think, though, that we're going to have to assume—provisionally, at least—that they *are* planning on going after Torch. If that attempt on Berry Zilwicki *was* a Manpower-organized hit, they may have been after more than one bird."

"Softening Torch up as well as getting the Manties and the Havenites shooting at each other again, you mean?"

"That's exactly what I mean," Rozsak acknowledged. "And 'soften-ing up Torch,' as you put it, would be a logical first step if they're planning on hitting it with a follow-up attack from space."

"Those poor bastards can't seem to catch a break, can they?" Watanapongse asked rhetorically. "First they lose their survey ship, a week later somebody tries to assassinate their queen, and now it's looking more and more like Manpower plans on hammering them from space, by proxy, at least."

"And the two navies most likely to be able to do something about it are busy shooting at each other again," Rozsak agreed. "Besides which, if I were a betting man—which, of course, we both know I'm not—" he and Watanapongse grinned at one another; Luiz Rozsak had never been interested in betting mere *money* "—I'd be willing to put a few credits on the probability that any instructions Manpower might give where Torch is concerned wouldn't contain the words 'Remember the Eridani Edict' anywhere."

"I'm pretty damn sure they wouldn't." Watanapongse's short-lived grin disappeared. "And with Manticore and Haven shooting at each other again, Erewhon's going to want to keep its own military assets closer to home, just in case."

"All right." Rozsak nodded to himself. "I think you're right about Erewhon, and even if you aren't, they're not the ones who have a treaty with Torch. We are. I want you and Edie to do a full staff appreciation on all of the intelligence information we've got about Manpower, outlaw StateSec ships, and anything else we can scrape up about the Manties' new targeting systems and known redeployment plans. I want to be able to brief Oravil on the entire situation, hopefully within the week."

✧   ✧   ✧

"Are you all right, Jack?" Steven Lathorous asked, and Jack McBryde looked up quickly from the memo he'd been studying.

The two of them sat in McBryde's Gamma Center office, going over routine paperwork as part of the current installment of their regularly scheduled three-times-a-week meetings. Lathorous was the Center's assistant security director, McBryde's senior subordinate, and they'd known one another literally since they joined Alignment Security as cadets. They worked well together, and, what was more, they were personal friends. Which gave the look in Lathorous' eyes—a sort of fusion of mingled perplexity and concern—additional weight in several ways.

"Am I 'all right' about what?" McBryde asked after a moment.

"If I knew what might be bothering you, I'd probably know whether or not it really *was* bothering you. As it happens, I don't 'know' anything of the sort, but, if I had to hazard a guess, I'd say it probably has something to do with our problem child hyper-physicist."

"Simões?"

"Unless you happen to know about *another* 'problem child hyper-physicist' you may have simply failed to call to my attention," Lathorous said dryly, and almost despite himself, McBryde chuckled.

"No, thank God." He shook his head. "But you're probably right. If I seem a little . . . distracted, it's probably because I am worrying about him."

"We're getting close to the end of his project, Jack," Lathorous pointed out in a considerably more serious tone.

"I know." McBryde made a waving-away motion with his right hand. "But even when we do, the man's still a valuable research asset."

"Yes, he is." Lathorous' dark eyes met McBryde's blue eyes very levelly. "That's not the main reason you're worrying about him, though."

McBryde gazed at him for a moment, thinking about how long they'd known one another. Their careers had brought them together and separated them again often enough over the years, and Lathorous had spent considerably longer in the field as a "shooter" than McBryde had. Unlike the McBryde genome, the Lathorous genome was a beta-line, but even without the sort of nonbiological implants some of the military and/or security-oriented beta and gamma lines often received, Lathorous was a decidedly lethal presence. McBryde was reasonably certain his old friend had been assigned to the Gamma Center specifically to provide the additional, relatively recent field experience he himself lacked.

And, despite their friendship, Lathorous was undoubtedly the most dangerous person in the entire Gamma Center where McBryde's own increasingly ambivalent feelings towards the Alignment in general—and the rapid approach of Prometheus, in particular—were concerned.

"No." McBryde sighed finally. "No, Steve, it's not just about his value. The man's already been hammered hard enough. I don't want to see him get hammered any more."

"Not a good attitude, Jack," Lathorous said quietly. "I'm not saying I *do* want to see him get beaten up on any more than he has to be, but we're supposed to maintain our professionalism where the people we're responsible for keeping an eye on are concerned. And we're especially not supposed to get too close to someone who's so likely to self-destruct."

"Wasn't *my* idea in the first place, Steve!" McBryde pointed out. "Bardasano personally stuck me with this one."

"A point of which I'm painfully well aware." Lathorous nodded, yet concern still hovered in his eyes. "But whoever's idea it was, it's been six months—almost seven—since the girl was terminated, and better than four months since Bardasano assigned him to you, and he's not getting better. In fact, we both know he's getting worse. He's going to crash, Jack. We can't—*you* can't—prevent that, however hard we try. All we can do is minimize collateral damage when it happens . . . and I don't want the effect it has on you to be part of the fallout."

"I appreciate that," McBryde said softly. "And I'm pretty sure I'm going to be okay," he added, lying as carefully as he ever had in his life. "I'm working on it, anyway."

Lathorous nodded again. He was obviously still less than happy about the situation, though. As much as McBryde appreciated his friend's concern, letting Lathorous pick up even a hint of what was really going on inside him was definitely contraindicated, so he twitched his hand at the memo he'd been looking at without really seeing.

"What do you make of this?" he asked.

"I think it's about damned time . . . and pretty damned silly,"

Lathorous replied with a sour chuckle. "Mind you, I'm sure I don't know *everything* about the full damage Zilwicki and Cachat have managed to do to Manpower—and us—over the years, but I know enough to think eliminating them would be a very good idea. That much I'm entirely in favor of. My only real problem with it, from an operational perspective, is that I'm pretty sure what really happened was that they finally did something that pissed Albrecht off. I mean, really *pissed* him off." He shook his head. "Putting out what amounts to a 'shoot-on-sight' order to *everyone* isn't exactly a calm, reasoned response. I mean, how likely is it that anybody here at the Center is going to stumble across them in our daily routine?"

His chuckle was the least bit sour, which, McBryde suspected, had something to do with the fact that Lathorous really missed fieldwork. He probably would have enjoyed pitting himself against the redoubtable Anton Zilwicki or Victor Cachat. Unfortunately (from his perspective), his assessment of how likely anyone in the Gamma Center was to encounter those particular targets was undoubtedly dead on the money. On the other hand . . .

"I think the theory is that finding them is going to be the next best thing to impossible," McBryde pointed out. "Until we can pin down their physical location with some degree of confidence again, all we can really do is hope that they wander into our sights somewhere along the line."

"Oh, I understand the theory just fine," Lathorous agreed. "And you're right—given the fact that we don't have a clue in hell where they are, this is probably the most effective way to go about it. Even if it doesn't have a snowflake's chance in hell of succeeding!"

"You just want to take them down yourself," McBryde teased.

"Well, it wouldn't look too bad in my résumé," Lathorous conceded with a chuckle. Then he sobered. "On the other hand, I've got to admit that their reputations would make me a little nervous unless I was in a position to completely control the situation."

"They *are* a capable pair of bastards," McBryde acknowledged.

He considered the memo again, then paged ahead to the next screen. He scanned the header on the new memo quickly, then grimaced.

"I see Lajos is bitching again," he said.

"Hard to blame him, really."

Lathorous' words were reasonable enough, even sympathetic, but his tone was anything else. He and Lajos Irvine had never gotten along particularly well, and McBryde suspected that at least part of it was Lathorous' yearning to be back in the field. He knew he wasn't going to get there anytime soon, and the fact that Irvine seemed to be agitating for the type of assignment Lathorous wasn't going to get only increased the irritation quotient.

"Actually, I agree with you," McBryde said out loud. "I'm probably as tired of his whining as anyone, but, let's face it, spending your time pretending to be—no, scratch that, actually *being*—a slave has got to be just about the least appealing assignment Security has."

"Better than getting his ass shot at in the field by those Ballroom yahoos."

There was a certain degree of feeling in Lathorous' response, due, no doubt, to the fact that his own last field assignment's cover had been as a mid-level Manpower executive, and the Audubon Ballroom had almost gotten lucky in his case.

"Agreed." McBryde nodded. "On the other hand, it's the poor bastards pulling Lajos' duty that keep that sort of thing from happening right here on Mesa on a regular basis, you know."

"Oh, I know. I know!" Lathorous shook his head. "And I promise I'll try to make nice to him."

McBryde looked at him for a moment, then shrugged.

"Look, Steve, I know you and Lajos don't exactly get along like a house on fire. How's about I take it over with him for a while? It's not like it would use up a lot of my time, and I could at least reduce your irritation factor a bit. Maybe a few weeks' vacation would actually make him easier for you to take. And, frankly, I could use something besides Simões to worry about."

Lathorous had begun an automatic refusal, but he paused at McBryde's final sentence. He hesitated visibly, then shrugged and gave his friend a slightly sheepish smile.

"If you really mean it, I'll take you up on it," he said. "I know I shouldn't get pissed off with him when he comes in to make his personal reports. And I even know you're right, that what he does is important. It's just something about his attitude. It gets right up my nose, even though I know it shouldn't. And I'm pretty sure he knows I'm getting pissed off with him, even if I try not to show it, and that only gets him even more pissed off. To be honest, I think it's taking the shine off of our joint professionalism, if you know what I mean."

"I know exactly what you mean," McBryde told him with a chuckle. "And don't expect me to take this over permanently, either! But I can at least give both of you a break from each other. After all, that's what an astute manager of personnel resources does, right?"

"Right," Lathorous said with a warm smile. "I know it's only cold, cynical calculation and manipulation on your part. But, anyway, thanks."

CHAPTER THIRTY-EIGHT

"What are the DNA results from the inspection of . . ." The Mesan System Guard officer looked back at her display for the name of the ship in question. "The *Hali Sowle*? They should have come back from the lab by now."

The SG was one of Mesa's (many) uniformed security forces, but it was far less punctilious than the majority of its fellows about things like military ritual and formal address.

"I don't know," said her junior partner. "Let me check." Gansükh Blomqvist pulled up a new screen at his own work station, checked for a list, and pulled up yet another screen. He then spent perhaps half a minute studying the data displayed.

When he was done, his face was creased by a smile that bordered on a leer. "They check out all right, E.D. But talk about motherfuckers! It seems as if everybody on that piece of crap is closely related. The one married couple—I kid you not—are uncle and niece."

E.D. Trimm shook her head, but made no wisecrack of her own. Unlike Blomqvist, who was newly hired, she'd been employed by the SG for almost four decades. Most of which time, she'd spent in orbit working on ship inspection. Since she'd married another resident of the huge space station eighteen years earlier, she rarely returned to the planet any longer, even on vacations.

Blomqvist thought a freighter crew made up of closely related individuals, especially when marriage was involved, was a subject of derision and wonder. He'd learn, soon enough. A high percentage of the crews of such freighters—"gypsies," they were called,

350

usually small in size and with no regular runs of any kind—were comprised of people related to each other. There were whole clans and tribes out there, working the fringes of the interstellar freight trade. Some of them were so large they even held periodic conclaves; where, among other things, marriages were contracted. There were some powerful incentives to keeping their businesses tightly held, after all.

Unlike her new partner, whom she'd already decided was a jackass, E.D. was not given to much in the way of prejudice—at least, so long as genetic slaves weren't involved. On that subject, she had the same attitudes as almost all freeborn Mesans.

But, unlike Blomqvist, who, despite the benefits of a good education, seemed remarkably incurious about the universe into which he'd been born, E.D. had actually absorbed what she'd learned as a student in one of Mesa's excellent colleges. Those colleges and universities, of course, were exclusively reserved for freeborn citizens. Mesa didn't forbid slaves to get an education, as many slave societies had done in past. They *couldn't,* given that even slaves in a modern work force needed to have an education. But the training given slaves was tightly restricted to whatever it was felt they needed to know.

She'd been particularly fond of ancient history, even if the subject had no relevance to her eventual employment.

"Why should tramp freighter crews sneer at the same practices that stood the dynasties of Europe in good stead?" she asked. "To this day, I think the Rothschilds still set the standard, when it comes to inbreeding."

Blomqvist frowned. "Who's Europe? And I thought the name of that dog breed was rottweiler."

"Never mind, Gansükh." She leaned over him, studying the screen. "Cargo . . . nothing unusual. Freight brokerage . . . okay, nothing odd there."

Blomqvist made a face. "I thought Pyramid Shipping Services was one of those outfits serving the seccy trade."

"It is. And your point being . . . ?"

He said nothing, but the sour look on his face remained. Normally, Trimm would have let it go. But she really was getting tired of Blomqvist's attitudes—and, looked at the right way, you could even argue she was just doing her job by straightening out the slob. Technically, she was Blomqvist's "senior partner," but in the real world she was his superior. And if he didn't realize that, he'd soon be getting a rude education.

"And what would you prefer?" she demanded. "That we insist the sutler trade be serviced by the Jessyk Combine? No—better yet! Maybe we should have Kwiatkowski and Adeyeme handle it."

Blomqvist grimaced. Kwiatkowski & Adeyeme Galactic Freight, one of the biggest shipping corporations operating out of Mesa, was notorious among System Guard officers for being a royal pain in the ass to deal with. Worse than Jessyk, even though they didn't have nearly as much influence with the General Board.

Still, they had enough. The quip among experienced customs agents was that any finding of an irregularity by a K&A freighter guaranteed at least fifteen hours of hearings—and, if people had still been using paper, the slaughter of a medium-sized forest. As it was, untold trillions of electrons would soon be subject to terminal ennui.

She straightened up. "Just take my word for it. Everyone's better off leaving the ragtag and bobtail seccy trade to the gypsies. Easier for everybody, especially us. The only important thing—check this for me too, if you would—is how long the *Hali Sowle* is requesting orbit space."

Blomqvist pulled up yet another screen. "Anywhere up to sixteen T-days, it looks like."

Trimm frowned. That was a little unusual. Not unheard of, by any means, but still out of the ordinary. Most gypsies wanted to be in and out of Mesan orbit as fast as possible. Not because the Mesan trade gave them any moral qualms, but simply because they weren't making money unless they were hauling freight somewhere.

"What reason do they give?" she asked.

"They say they're waiting for a shipment of jewelry coming from Ghatotkacha. That's a planet . . ." He squinted at the screen, trying to find the data.

"It's the second planet of Epsilon Virgo, over in Gupta Sector," said Trimm. The request for such a long orbital stay made sense, now. Gupta Sector was rather isolated and the only easy access to the big markets of the League was through the Visigoth Junction. Given the notorious fussiness of Visigoth's customs service, any freighter captain with half a brain who needed to spend idle time in orbit waiting for a shipment to arrive would choose to do so at the Mesan end of the terminus.

Gupta Sector was known for its jewelry, and jewelry was one of the high value freight items that a freighter would be willing to wait for. Provided . . .

"Send them a message, Gansükh. I want to see the financial details of their contract of carriage. Certified data only, mind you. We're not taking their word for it."

From the frown on his face, it was obvious that Blomqvist didn't understand why she wanted that information.

"For your continuing education, young man. The financial section of their contract of carriage should tell us who's *paying* for their lost time in orbit. The shipper of origin? Or it could even be the jewelers themselves. Or the final customer, or *their* broker. Or . . ."

His face cleared. "I get it. Or maybe they're eating the cost themselves. In which case . . ."

"In which case," E.D. said grimly, "we're sending a pinnace over there with orders to fire if they don't allow a squad of armored cops aboard to search that vessel stem to stern. There's no way a legitimate gypsy would agree to swallow the cost of spending that much time in orbit, twiddling their thumbs."

"What's a stem?" he asked, as he sent the instructions to the *Hali Sowle*. "I thought it was part of a plant. So why would it be connected to a starship?"

Since he couldn't see her face, she let her eyes roll. At least she'd only have to put up with the ignoramus for another three days before the shifts were restructured. If she got lucky, she might even be partnered next time with Steve Lund. Now, *there* was a man with whom you could have an intelligent conversation. He had a good sense of humor, too.

"Never mind, Gansükh. It's just a figure of speech."

She sometimes thought that for Gansükh Blomqvist, the whole damn universe outside of his immediate and narrow range of interests was a figure of speech. Oh, well. She reminded herself, not for the first time, that every hour she spent bored by Blomqvist's company piled up just as much in the way of pay, benefits and retirement credit as any other hour on the job.

"And there it is, Ganny," said Andrew Artlett admiringly. "Just like you predicted. How do you *know* these things, anyway?"

Friede Butry smiled, but gave no answer. That was because

the answer would have been heartbreaking for her. She knew the many things she did which almost none of her descendants and relatives did, for the simple reason that she'd had a full life prior to being stranded on Parmley Station—while most of them had spent their entire lives there.

For some considerable part of that pre-Station life, she and her husband had been very successful freight brokers. That was how they'd amassed their initial small fortune, which Michael Parmley had then parlayed into a much larger fortune playing the Centauri stock exchange—and then blown the whole thing trying to launch a freight company that could compete with the big boys in the lucrative Core trade.

She'd loved her husband, sure enough. But there hadn't been a day go by since his death decades earlier, that she hadn't cursed his shade. Michael Parmley hadn't had a malicious bone in his body—but he hadn't had a very responsible one either. An inveterate gambler, he'd lost three fortunes already before he completely bankrupted himself and his kin building the station.

And, in doing so, condemned at least one entire generation of his extended family to lives that were distorted by isolation and would surely end in early graves. Ganny knew full well—had known for years, now—that the day would inexorably come, assuming she survived herself, when she would be grieving at the death of her beloved great-nephew Andrew Artlett. He'd die of old age—while his great-aunt still had perhaps a century of life ahead of her.

"Never mind, Andrew. It's a long story. Make sure you send the financial records within ten minutes—but not too much before then. They won't expect a tramp freighter in orbit to be all that alert."

He nodded. "And how long do we stay?"

"Until the freighter from Gupta brings us the goods. If they time it right, they'll arrive two or three days before our deadline here in orbit runs out. It'll take less than a day for customs to check everything. Then we're on our way to Palmetto, just as our—completely legitimate—papers say we are. A quick swap of the jewels on Palmetto for a cargo of sutler goods, and we're back again. That shouldn't take more than two weeks. By then, we'll have established our bona fides with Mesan customs, and we should be able to get permission to stay in orbit for up to thirty T-days."

"And what if Anton and Victor need to make an escape during one of the stretches while we're gone?"

"Then they're shit out of luck. There's simply no way we can stay in orbit indefinitely, given our cover story. Not anywhere that has a functioning planetary government, much less Mesa. They're on the paranoid side here, and for damn good reason, as generally hated as they are." She shrugged. "But if those two characters are as good as they think they are—which is probably true—then they'll have enough sense to time whatever they might be doing that's likely to set off any alarms for one of the stretches we're in orbit. Of course, it's always possible they'll get caught by surprise by something unexpected. But that's the risk they run, in that business. Either way, I made sure we're covered in the contract. We get paid, no matter what happens."

She didn't see any reason to explain that the "contract" amounted to nothing more than a verbal agreement between herself, Web Du Havel and Jeremy X, and a representative of Beowulf's BSC. She knew, from a lifetime's experience, that she could trust the BSC and if she couldn't trust the Torch people there was nothing she could do about it anyway. But she couldn't see any way to make that clear to Artlett without undermining her years-long campaign to get her reckless great-nephew to stop trusting the fates so much.

Besides, the BSC would be footing most of the bill anyway. They'd agreed to pay the Butry clan an annual stipend for the use of the station. The stipend was more than enough to pay for the expense of providing every one of its members still young enough with prolong treatments—and with plenty left over to send them away for a regular education. The contribution of the Ballroom—technically, the Torch military and if you accepted that at face value you were a moron—was mostly going to be muscle. They'd be the ones who staffed the station, maintained the pretense it was still a slaver entrepot while actually using it as a combination stellar safe house and way station for covert operations—*and* treat themselves to shooting down the stray slaver ship that showed up from time to time.

It was over. Regardless of what happened to Ganny and the few members of her clan on the *Hali Sowle,* she'd finally managed to save the clan itself.

She heard the three boys squabbling over something, in a nearby compartment. The mess hall, from the sound of their voices. She couldn't quite make out the words. Ed and James were going at it and Brice seemed to be trying to act as peacemaker.

If they survived this expedition—and whatever other adventures their none-too-cautious souls got them into thereafter—all three of them would live for at least two centuries.

For the first time in years, Elfriede Margarete Butry discovered she was crying.

✧　　✧　　✧

"The financial data from the *Hali Sowle*'s contract of carriage checks out okay, E.D." Gansükh Blomqvist pointed at the screen in front of him.

She leaned over and looked. Sure enough, the logo and seal of the Banco de Madrid was prominently displayed.

"Okay, then." She went to her own work station and spent a minute or so keying in some instructions, before hitting the send button. The *Hali Sowle*'s legitimacy, heretofore provisional and temporary, was now established in the data banks of the Mesan System Guard. The next time they came through, if they ever did, the routine would go much more quickly.

She hadn't bothered to check the details of the data on Blomqvist's screen. There was no reason to waste the time. Faking that seal and logo was effectively impossible for anyone except maybe a handful of governments in the galaxy. It was certainly beyond the capability of a gypsy freighter.

✧　　✧　　✧

It was not, however, beyond the capability of the government of Erewhon—or any of its major families, even using their own private resources. Jeremy X had been quite right. The great families of Erewhon were still the galaxy's premier money-launderers.

When one of his subordinates brought the news to Walter Imbesi that everything had cleared for the *Hali Sowle* in the Mesa System, he simply nodded and went back to his business. The only reason he'd asked to be notified at all was because of the political sensitivity of the project. In purely financial terms, measured against the fortune of his family, it all amounted to chicken feed.

Still, even chicken feed was not to be sneered at. The Imbesis would very likely turn a small profit. The jewels were perfectly legitimate and there was a market for them, after all. Even the sutler trade on the reverse leg shouldn't do worse than break even.

CHAPTER THIRTY-NINE

"All right, Luiz, what do you and your minions have for me?"

Oravil Barregos sat in a chair at the head of the conference table in the high-security briefing room attached to Luiz Rozsak's personal office. Vegar Spangen was parked in another chair, against the briefing room's back wall, and Rozsak, Watanapongse, and Commander Habib sat facing the governor from the far end of the table.

"A lot," Rozsak said. He grimaced and nodded to Habib. "Edie?"

The admiral's chief of staff brushed a hand over her short-cropped, dark, reddish-brown hair, then straightened in her seat as she turned slightly to face Barregos fully.

"The general strategic situation's experienced what you might describe as a . . . 'significant shift,' Governor," she said. "Most immediately pressing from our perspective is what happened at Manticore last week." She shook her head, and even her normally unflappable expression showed more than a little lingering shock. "As near as we can tell, both sides got royally reamed. Manticore's Home Fleet is just plain gone, and it sounds like their Third Fleet got hit equally hard. We don't have any official confirmation of those numbers, of course, and all the information we've got on *Haven's* losses is secondhand, at best, via the Manties. Bottom line, though, is that it looks like the majority of Theisman's numerical superiority just got blown out from under him."

"That was my own impression," Barregos said quietly. He shook his head. "What in God's name did Theisman think he was *doing*?"

"He rolled the dice, Sir," Habib replied flatly. Barregos raised one eyebrow, and the chief of staff shrugged. "After what happened at Lovat, it was pretty obvious the Havenite fleet was going to be toast going up against whatever it was Harrington's Eighth Fleet used on Giscard. Our best guess"—she twitched her head sideways at Watanapongse—"is that Theisman already had the strike force he used at Manticore assembled under Tourville when he found out about Lovat. We're guessing he'd started putting it together as part of a contingency plan either before the summit talk was ever proposed, or when Elizabeth deep-sixed the idea, at the very latest. At any rate, he had the operation already planned before Lovat—he had to have had it ready, or he couldn't have gotten it off the ground so quickly. When Harrington hammered Giscard, Theisman and Pritchart must have figured their only real chance was to score a knockout before the Manties got the new targeting systems into general deployment. Even with everything ready to go, it took someone with one hell of a lot of nerve—not to mention pure gall—to go for all the marbles that way. I doubt very much that anyone in Manticore ever even dreamed they'd pull the trigger on something like this, but one thing Theisman's already demonstrated pretty damned conclusively is that he's got enough guts for any three or four normal people."

"And he came damned close to pulling it off, too, as far as we can tell," Rozsak put in. "We still don't have the details, of course, but it sounds like he had a pretty good ops plan. Unfortunately—from his perspective, at least—it also sounds like the Manties were further along in deploying the new hardware than he'd hoped. And, unless I miss my guess, Murphy put in his centicredit's worth, as well."

"Not to mention Duchess Harrington's minor contribution," Habib added.

"Not to mention that," Rozsak agreed with a nod.

"So both sides are basically neutralized, you're saying?"

"Not exactly, Governor," Habib replied. "For the moment, yes, both sides are pretty much at a standstill. Theisman's lost his major striking force, but at least he's got a lot of new construction currently working up to give him coverage in his rear areas, for whatever good it's going to do against the Manties' new fire control. Manticore and the Alliance, on the other hand, still have Eighth Fleet, but they don't have anything else left to cover

Manticore if they cut Harrington loose for additional offensive operations. They don't have as many new-build wallers already working up as Haven does, but they've got quite a few, and they've got a *bunch* of new construction getting ready to come out of the yards. After the Battle of Manticore, they may be a little short of experienced personnel for crews, but they're going to have a lot of hulls available shortly. Not as many as Haven has, even now, but a *lot* . . . and I think we have to assume all of their new wallers are going to have their new fire control. So while neither side has anything it can use to go after the other one *right now*, in another few months, Manticore is going to be in a position to reach right down Haven's throat and rip its lungs out."

Barregos grimaced at the chief of staff's choice of phrases, but he also nodded in understanding.

"What kind of implications does all this have for us, Luiz?" he asked.

"Edie and Jiri have a complete brief for you," Rozsak replied. "They'll be taking us step-by-step through our best current estimates of force levels and probable intentions. You want the short version first?"

Barregos nodded, and Rozsak shrugged.

"Basically, we're currently in a strategic vacuum. Nobody's got a lot of firepower to spare or to throw around, but as Edie says, once Manticore's new construction starts really coming forward, that's going to change. All of those 'minor distractions' the Manties are facing in Talbott are going to have a braking effect on their deployment postures, of course, but even so, I give Haven another six T-months—nine at the outside—before Harrington is sent off to turn the entire Haven System into one huge scrapyard. And unless Pritchart and Theisman are prepared to surrender, I think that's exactly what's going to happen. I sure as hell don't see them coming up with some kind of silver bullet in time to save them, anyway.

"In our immediate area, I've got a feeling Erewhon is going to be very carefully staying close to home until the situation between Manticore and Haven finally works itself out. I'm certain the Erewhonese were as taken by surprise by the direct attack on Manticore—and, for that matter, by whatever new toy Admiral Hemphill's come up with—as we were. I think they probably view the fact that Elizabeth was prepared to ask them to provide security for Torch when it looked like the summit was going to meet as a provisionally good sign. At the same time, though, they have to know Manticore generally is still pretty pissed off with them. I think they're going to want to make it as evident as they can that, despite any mutual *defense* treaties with the Republic, they're about as neutral as anyone can get and still be breathing where the current unpleasantness is concerned. Preliminary indications are that they're basically forting up at home, aside from routine commerce protection missions, and I'll be surprised if that changes.

"Which brings us to our other little problem area."

"Luiz, I always hate it when you use that particular phrase," Barregos said almost whimsically. "What knuckleduster is waiting for me this time?"

"Possibly not one at all," Rozsak replied.

"I hate that word 'possibly' almost as much as I hate 'little problem area.'" Barregos sat back in his chair. "Go ahead. Tell me the worst."

"It's not a case of 'worst,' but we are turning up significant—and, Jiri and I are both inclined to think, reliable—indications that Manpower is planning to mount an operation directly against Torch."

"It is?" Barregos abruptly sat back up, eyes narrowing.

"That's what it looks like," Rozsak said. "We're still working on trying to confirm the intelligence. Frankly, I don't think it's going to be possible to positively confirm it one way or the other, but if we're right, what's happened to the Manties and to the Republic is only going to make their job a lot easier. Especially if Erewhon's going to keep all of its heavy units home the way I expect it to. Unless, of course, someone *else* does something about it."

"The 'someone else' in question being the someone else who has a defensive treaty with the Kingdom of Torch, by any chance?" Barregos inquired.

"Pretty much," Rozsak replied.

"And what sort of position would we be in to do anything of the sort?"

"A lot better one than we would have been a year ago," Rozsak said frankly. "I'm not going to say we're anywhere near what I'd consider full readiness yet, of course. We've got significantly more capability than I really expected to have by this point, though. Which, of course, raises the interesting question of exactly how much of that capability we want to risk revealing by actually using it."

"Um."

Barregos frowned thoughtfully. He sat silently, obviously thinking hard, for several seconds, then refocused his attention on Rozsak.

"How much of the new stuff would we have to trot out if we wanted to defend Torch?"

"That depends on the exact force level Manpower would be able to commit against us." Rozsak shrugged. "I'm not trying to waffle; it's just that we don't know, at this point, exactly what kind of resources are involved from the other side. Before the Battle of Monica, I would have felt fairly confident we wouldn't be facing anything except the ex-StateSec ships we know they've recruited and probably another double handful or so of other pirates or mercs. Nothing bigger and nastier than two or three backgrounders, in other words, and mostly getting pretty long in the tooth, as well. As things stand now, I'm not prepared to rule out the possibility that they've got a few more Solarian Navy—or *ex*-SLN, at least—warships to make available to them. Against the level of opposition I'd have anticipated before Monica, I think we could probably do a pretty good job without bringing everything we have to the party. Against what we may actually be looking at, we'd probably need just about all of our new units."

"But, Governor," Watanapongse put in diffidently, "we need to bear in mind *where* we'd be using them. If we intervene to defend Torch, there's no way the Torches would be telling anyone anything about *how* we intervened if we asked them not to. And assuming this really would be a Manpower operation, the other side wouldn't have any powerful motive that we can see to make Old Chicago privy to whatever information might get back to it with the survivors."

"So you're saying you think letting the cat out of the bag in Torch would constitute an acceptable risk, Commander?" Barregos said.

"What he's saying, and I happen to agree with him, is that risking letting the cat out of the bag in Torch is a more acceptable risk than depriving ourselves of the firepower we might need to *win* in Torch," Rozsak said, and Barregos nodded.

"Before we start reaching any firm decisions, though," the admiral continued, "I think you should go ahead and hear Edie and Jiri's full brief."

"I think you're right," Barregos agreed, and Rozsak leaned back and waved one hand at his subordinates.

"That's your cue, Edie," he said.

CHAPTER FORTY

"He doesn't look like much," said Jurgen Dusek, after studying the holopics on his desk. But the man who was the acknowledged boss of the Neue Rostock seccy district of Mesa's capital city was simply making a comment, not a reproach. Triêu Chuanli was his top man. He wouldn't have brought this matter to Dusek's attention if he hadn't had good reason to do so. "What's the guy's name?"

"Daniel McRae. What he claims, anyway. He also claims to be another StateSec on the run. I couldn't tell you if that's true either, but he does have a Nouveau Paris accent. That's hard to fake."

"Did you send him to Cybille and her people?"

"Yeah. They spent hours with him. Cybille says his story checks out down the line and he's okay." Triêu made a face. "Well . . . 'okay' is not exactly the right word. She's says McRae's probably a psychopath. Most of those really hardcore StateSec guys were. But this one's pretty tightly wrapped, she figures. The fact that he was that close to Saint-Just means he can't just be a screwball. Whatever else he was, Saint-Just was thoroughly practical. He wouldn't have tolerated anyone around him who was so crazy he couldn't keep the lid on."

Jurgen Dusek nodded. Over the past few years, he'd become a lot more familiar with the history and inside practices of the former People's Republic of Haven's security forces than you'd expect anyone on Mesa would be. More familiar than he wanted to be, for that matter. But the business of brokering between StateSec mercenaries and the people who'd been hiring so many

362

of them had turned out to be a more profitable line of business than anything else he was engaged in.

Damn risky, though. Not because he was dealing with ex-StateSec toughs and thugs—Jurgen had been handling people like that since he was fourteen—but because of the people on the other end. Those still-very-murky individuals or organizations whose exact identity Dusek didn't know and didn't want to know. "Still-very-murky" suited him just fine. If everything worked out well, they'd stay nice and murky.

But that was the problem. There was always the danger, dealing with "murky people" on Mesa, that you'd eventually discover you'd climbed into bed with Manpower. Or, even worse, the *really* murky people whom Dusek sensed were lurking somewhere within Manpower, or behind it.

It wasn't that he had any moral objection to the idea of being tied to Manpower. Either today or at some point in his life, Jurgen Dusek had been a knee-breaker, a contract killer, a pimp, a drug dealer, a counterfeiter (of welfare chits, not money; nobody in their right mind tried to pass fake money on Mesa), a brothel-keeper—several brothels, in fact—a gambling overlord, a smuggler—the list went on and on. His capacity for accepting and taking advantage of immoral business opportunities was well-nigh infinite.

No, it was the damn *risk*. Getting involved too closely with Manpower had a history of turning into a nightmare for the person foolish enough to do it. At the very least, you wound up losing your independence and becoming just another one of their flunkies.

Risk or no risk, though, the mercenary business really was profitable. And if this new guy . . .

"She's *sure* he was part of Saint-Just's inner circle?"

"Absolutely and positively certain. She says McRae knows far too many things—details, specifics, not generalities—than anybody possibly could without having been right in the middle of things. In fact, she figures he probably knows more than she ever did, when it comes to field work. Cybille stresses that McRae would have been a very junior member of that inner circle. He wasn't any sort of high level StateSec official, or even mid-level like she was. But she says she recognizes the type. Saint-Just had the habit of cultivating young protégés for field work. People whose dedication and ruthlessness were . . . well, 'extreme' is the word she used. Coming from Cybille . . ."

Dusek grinned humorlessly. Cybille DuChamps had her own reputation for, ah, extreme behavior. For her to call anyone else a "psychopath" was pretty rich. It was literally worth your life to become her lover—and you didn't even get to enjoy the status for more than three or four months.

"All right, then. He's a lot more than just common muscle, in other words. We might be able to get quite a bit in the way of a commission from Luff, if he decides to take him on."

Triêu looked a bit skeptical. "I get the impression Luff's not all that keen on the really hardcore StateSec types."

"He's not. But that's just a matter of personal preference. Adrian Luff also has a very large military force he needs to keep in line. Somebody like Daniel McRae could prove very handy for him."

"Ah . . . you do know Luff's gone, boss?"

"Don't teach your grandmother how to suck eggs. Of course I know he's gone. And I don't know where he is, either, and while I could probably guess I'm nowhere near crazy enough to do so. But he left me with a contact person who stayed behind. Inez Cloutier. I'll get in touch with her and see if she's interested in pursuing the matter."

"Okay. I'll tell McRae to stick around for a while."

"Is he asking for anything right now? Money? Women? A place to stay?"

"He seems well enough set up." Chuanli smiled. "The only thing he says he wants—he's willing to pay for it, too—is a gun. And unless he's got the sex drive of a rabbit, I doubt he needs a woman. He's got a big blonde with him who's better looking than most of the girls we could provide him with."

"What's her story?"

"Scrag, believe it or not."

Jurgen's eyes widened. For a StateSec man to be coupled with a Scrag girlfriend was highly unusual. Offhand, in fact, Dusek couldn't think of a single case he knew of.

"How'd he manage *that*?"

"They were both on Terra during the Manpower Incident. Among the few who got out alive and intact. I guess they got hooked up there and they've stayed together ever since."

Not a casual girlfriend, if they'd been together that long. The Manpower Incident had happened years ago.

Dusek was silent for a minute or so, as he weighed the risks and benefits of providing the McRae fellow with a gun. On the pro side, the risk was minimal and selling McRae a gun would serve for a while to keep him on an informal payroll without actually having to pay him anything. On the con side, there *was* a risk, however small—and there was always the chance that McRae was just a nut case.

But, even if that were true, it just meant there'd be another killing in a district which already had the worst murder rate in the city. (The worst *official* murder rate. The actual murder rate was a lot worse.) Easy enough to handle.

What finally decided Dusek was the need to cross-check McRae yet again. If DuChamps' assessment was accurate—and Jurgen had little doubt that it was—then Daniel McRae had indeed been a legitimate (using the word loosely) member of Saint-Just's inner circle. But that didn't necessarily mean that he was up to snuff, personally. Every inner circle had its flakes. So far as Dusek knew, Saint-Just's sexual preferences had been a complete unknown. Maybe this guy McRae had just been his catamite.

"What's he want?"

"A Kettridge Model A-3."

That was an awfully small gun. Easy to hide and deadly enough, if you were a good shot. But most people wanted something quite a bit more powerful, especially mercs.

So, again, there was a possible problem. Maybe the guy *was* a real gunman. On the other hand, McRae could just be putting up a show and didn't want a man-sized gun that might tire him out, having to lug it around all the time.

"Okay, let him have it. But I want this guy tested, Chuanli. Tested *hard*. If I broker him to Luff as a top Saint-Just inner circle field op—what lowly crooks like you and me would call an enforcer—then I have to be sure I'm not passing on a creampuff. I don't want to lose Luff as a customer."

Triêu took a little time to ponder the problem. "He's got some rooms not far from the Rhodesian. I'll tell him some people who might want to hire him frequent the place, and he'd be smart to hang out there in the evening. Then I'll tell Jozef to have those three new guys of his show up and hit on the blonde. We'll see what happens."

"What if he doesn't bring her?"

Chuanli shrugged. "Figure out something else. But don't forget she's a Scrag, boss. How likely is it she'd let a man—any man—tell her she has to stay home knitting socks while he parties?"

Dusek chuckled. "True enough. You wouldn't catch *me* picking a Scrag for a girlfriend."

"Me neither. No, she'll be there. I figure the bigger problem is that she might decide to handle the matter herself."

       ❖   ❖   ❖

"You have any problem with the idea?" asked the owner of the restaurant.

Anton Zilwicki smiled. "You mean the degrading status of being a waiter in a greasy spoon joint?"

Steph Turner gave him a thin smile. "You hand a customer a greasy spoon and you're out the door. I don't care how many hosannas Saburo and his people pile on you. The last thing I need is to give the local authorities a reason to inspect the place. The one thing they do take half-seriously are health and sanitation regulations."

"Sorry, I was just trying to make a joke. No, I don't have any problems with the idea."

Turner nodded. "You ever worked as a waiter?"

"Not since I was a teenager. And then, not for long. I can't say I liked it much, and the pay was lousy."

"The pay's always bad in the restaurant business. Low profit margin. Been that way for at least five thousand years, near as I can determine. The only reason anybody's dumb enough to open up a restaurant—"

She shrugged. "First, a lot of people *can* do it. And, second, at least you're your own boss."

"I wasn't complaining," Anton said mildly. "When do I start?"

"Tomorrow morning. We open early, since half of our business is the breakfast trade, and we're mostly servicing people in manufacturing. They'll be starting early themselves, much earlier than office workers. So be here by four o'clock."

She watched him closely for a couple of seconds. The smile that followed actually had some warmth in it. "Nary a wince. Good for you. Of course, you won't really have to worry that much about getting up on time, since you're sleeping in one of the back rooms. I'll make sure you're up. Trust me on that."

"I wouldn't doubt you for a second," Anton said.

Turner shook her head. "I've gotta be crazy to do this. But . . . I owe Saburo. My life, not money, so it's not a debt I can shuffle off. But that's where my involvement ends, you understand? I'm not part of his . . . business."

Zilwicki nodded. "I understand."

Later, in the tiny room in the back of the building that Turner had provided him for sleeping quarters, Anton felt guiltier than he had in many years. He'd do his best to protect the woman and her teenage daughter, but the odds were that Steph Turner was going to pay a steep price for the help she was giving him. It might well wind up being a price as steep as her debt to Saburo. Her life itself.

Hopefully, it wouldn't come to that. Or, if it did, maybe he could smuggle Turner and her daughter off the planet with them.

But that was all in the future. Right now, Anton was just wondering how Victor was managing things. He'd have arrived on Mesa a couple of days sooner than Anton. Maybe as much as three or four days. Either way, though, Cachat would still be getting himself situated. Anton figured he had a few days to get into the rhythm of being a waiter again, before Victor tracked him down.

He smiled, as he started to unpack. "Hell, who knows? Maybe he hasn't even killed anybody yet."

CHAPTER FORTY-ONE

"So you're ready to call it 'official,' then?" Oravil Barregos asked.

"I'm not going to call *anything* we can't get better confirmation on than this 'official,'" Luiz Rozsak began in a significantly more sour tone of voice, only to pause as his voice was buried in a sudden roar of applause from the audience.

Neither of them had been speaking very loudly to begin with, since they were seated in the governor's box in Corterrael Coliseum on Vorva, the single moon of the planet Smoking Frog. The coliseum's enormous expanse opened before and below them, packed to old-fashioned standing room only as the annual System Festival got underway, and the clowns, acrobats, and jugglers of the Lebowski Circus were taking full advantage of Vorva's low natural gravity. It was one of the "Fabulous Lebowskis'" boasts that they used neither counter-grav nor even safety nets, and the spectacular quadruple somersault Aletha Lebowski had just executed between trapezes had the entire crowd on its feet.

"I'm not prepared to call anything 'official' at this point," Rozsak repeated, once the uproar had eased enough for Barregos to hear him. "Not when the best we've been able to come up with is corroborating rumors. With that proviso, though, I'd say it's 'official' enough for us to proceed on the assumption that it's reliable information. It's close enough for me to think we'd damned well better not act as if it *isn't* reliable intel, at any rate!"

As always, Vegar Spangen had the governor's portable anti-snooping system in operation. It was quite a good system, but nothing was infallible, and given the public venue, neither Rozsak nor

368

Barregos was being very specific, despite all the background noise. Now the governor frowned for a moment, then shrugged.

"Well, if that's your judgment, I'm not going to argue with it. Go ahead."

"Yes, Sir," Rozsak acknowledged with a bit more formality than usual, and the two men turned their own attention back to the Fabulous Lebowskis.

"Impressive," Rozsak observed two of Smoking Frog's planetary days later as he stood on the flag bridge of SLNS *Marksman* contemplating the icons on her master plot.

The *Marksman* class was unique among Solarian Navy light cruisers in that it *had* a flag bridge. Of course, the fact that *Marksman* and her sisters belonged to the Solarian *League* Navy was something of a technicality, Rozsak supposed. As was the fact that, at 286,750 tons, she was bigger than the majority of the League's *heavy* cruisers.

She was, in fact, the first of the Maya Sector's "emergency program" to emerge from the newly expanded Carlucci Industrial Group yards in Erewhon, and she and the seven sisters currently in formation about her represented the largest warships in the Maya Sector Frontier Fleet Detachment the SLN had seen fit to place under Rear Admiral Rozsak's command.

Which didn't make them the largest *ships* under his command, of course. And didn't mean the SLN knew they were actually "his," either. In point of fact, his nominal superiors back on Old Earth were under the odd impression that they were *Erewhonese* units the SLN was merely helping to man because the Republic of Erewhon found itself "temporarily" short of trained manpower. That sort of assistance was part of the Office of Frontier Security's standard operating procedure for gaining influence with independent star nations, so no one back on Old Earth had turned a hair when Rozsak reported that he was applying the tactic in Erewhon's case. It helped that Erewhon had applied the Royal Manticoran Navy's new standards of automation to its own new construction without bothering to mention that fact to the galaxy at large. The fact that an entire ship's company for one of the *Marksmans* was actually considerably smaller than the complement of one of the SLN's far smaller *Morrigan*-class light cruisers made it far easier to convince The Powers That Were back on Old Earth that all

Rozsak's people were doing was to "help fill in the holes" in otherwise Erewhonese crews.

For a few more seconds he gazed at the icons which had just completed their scheduled exercise, then turned to face Captain Dirk-Steven Kamstra, *Marksman*'s commander. Kamstra was of only moderate height, with brown hair, brown eyes, and a rather chunky physique. No one would have called him massively muscular, although he was considerably broader (and, undeniably, *thicker*) than Rozsak himself, and the uncharitable might have been inclined to describe his habitual expression as somewhat bovine. "Phlegmatic" might have been a better term, although it was sadly true that there was no glow of genius or superior intellect in those brown eyes.

Which was fortunate, in Luiz Rozsak's considered opinion, since it had caused so many people to completely overlook the incisive, sharply honed intelligence lurking behind that stolid, unimaginative-looking exterior. In point of fact, he knew the exterior in question had been developed specifically to hide what was going on behind it . . . including its owner's simmering hatred for what Frontier Security had done to Geronimo, his parents' homeworld. The fact that Kamstra had managed to attain officer's rank in the SLN despite having been born on what had become a Frontier Security protectorate planet six T-years before his own birth made him almost unique. The fact that he'd made it as high as captain (which was a recent promotion) had been made possible only by certain strategically placed patrons, prominent among whom were one Oravil Barregos and one Luiz Rozsak, and they would never have managed to pull it off if anyone in the Solarian League Navy's flag ranks had suspected for one moment how Dirk-Steven Kamstra had come to regard OFS and all its works.

The fact that no one ever had—or would, before it was too late, at least—was one huge reason why Dirk-Steven Kamstra was both the commanding officer of Light Cruiser Squadron 7036, SLN, and, after Edie Habib and Jiri Watanapongse, Rozsak's most trusted subordinate. He was also one of the very few people who knew exactly what Oravil Barregos and Luiz Rozsak had in mind for the Maya Sector's future. All of which, of course, explained why he held the command he currently held.

"Very impressive, Dirk-Steven," Rozsak said now.

"I'm pleased with them myself, Sir," Kamstra replied. "We've still got a few rough spots—couldn't be any other way, I suppose, given how much doctrine we're inventing as we go along—but, overall, I think they've done well." He glanced at the icons himself, then looked back at Rozsak. "It'd help if we could go ahead and exercise the entire force together instead of more or less hiding the new units off in a corner, as it were, of course."

"It looks like you might just get that opportunity," Rozsak said a bit less cheerfully. Kamstra's left eyebrow arched slightly, and Rozsak snorted in harsh amusement. "Let's go ahead and take this to your briefing room," he suggested.

"Of course, Sir." Kamstra inclined his head respectfully in the direction of the door which connected the bridge directly to the flag briefing room.

"Attention on deck!" the newly promoted Captain Edie Habib said crisply as Rozsak stepped through the door with Kamstra at his heels.

The people seated around the briefing room table rose quickly, standing as Rozsak made his way to the chair awaiting him at the table's head. Kamstra, as his senior officer in space, took the chair at the table's far end, waiting with the others until Rozsak had seated himself.

"Sit, sit," the rear admiral said, just a bit impatiently, and his subordinates did. It was all a bit more formal than usual, he reflected, but, then, circumstances weren't exactly usual, either.

He let his eyes circle the table. The officers present represented only a small percentage of the Maya Sector Frontier Fleet Detachment's ship commanders, but they were the most important ones. All of them understood what Barregos and Rozsak had been working towards for so long, and all of them would be critical to its accomplishment. And then, of course, there were Habib and Watanapongse.

Kamstra, as *Marksman*'s CO and the senior officer of Light Cruiser Squadron 7036, wore two official "hats." Three, really, since he normally acted as Rozsak's space-going deputy. In effect, he was the in-space commander of the Maya Sector Detachment, given Rozsak's heavy planet-side administrative duties. Tactically, he would function as Rozsak's flag captain if—as had become increasingly likely—the Detachment found itself committed to action. As such, he'd carried a huge share of the burden when it came to training and integrating the new-build units coming out of Erewhon over the past several months.

Commander David Carte, the CO of *Marksman*'s sister ship *Sharpshooter*, was also the commanding officer of Light Cruiser Division 7036.3, while Commander Laura Raycraft of the *Artillerist* commanded LCD 7036.2. Commander Iain Haldane commanded both the cruiser *Ranger* and also LCD 7036.1, to which *Marksman* was assigned, which got that job, at least, off of Kamstra's shoulders. Lieutenant Commander Jim Stahlin commanded the destroyer *Gustavus Adolphus*, while Lieutenant Commander Anne Guglik commanded *Gustavus Adolphus*' sister, *Hernando Cortés*. Like the *Marksmans*, the *Warrior*-class destroyers were something entirely new in (theoretically) Solarian service—twenty thousand tons larger and far more lethal than the SLN's standard *Rampart*-class. Unlike the *Marksmans*, they were also official units of the SLN, although no one outside the Maya Sector or the Republic of Erewhon realized just how big and powerful they actually were. Commander J.T. Cullingford, Commander Melanie Stensrud, and Commander Anne Warwick completed the ship commanders present, although none of them commanded what were technically warships (as far as anyone outside the Maya Sector or Erewhon knew, at any rate). What they did command was something considerably more dangerous—the first three of the *Masquerade*-class "freighters" delivered by CIG.

"All right," Rozsak said after they'd all settled back into their chairs, "it looks very much like what we thought was going to happen *is* going to happen. So in the next couple of days, all of us are going to be heading off to Torch 'for maneuvers.'"

No one said a word, and he was pleased to observe that their expressions were mostly alert and thoughtful, with nothing approaching consternation. Of course, it wasn't as if what he'd just said came as any great surprise to them, but it was also true that the step they were about to take would be about as close to irrevocable as actions came.

Not that all of them hadn't been heading for it for a very, very long time now.

"Edie"—he twitched his head briefly to his right, at Habib—"will be giving all of us the detailed appreciation and basic ops plan in a minute, but before she does, let me go ahead and—at the risk of being a bit redundant, under the circumstances—run over the high points." He smiled slightly. "Redundancy is one of the privileges which comes with my lordly flag rank, you all understand."

Most of them smiled, and Stahlin chuckled.

"Basically," Rozsak continued a bit more seriously, "life is getting more interesting out of our way. Given what happened to the Manties and the Havenites at the Battle of Manticore, neither of them is going to have any attention to spare for events in our neck of the woods, and Admiral McAvoy has confirmed to me that he's under orders to keep the Erewhonese Navy close to home."

He shrugged.

"We've shared our intelligence about what seems to be headed Torch's way with both the Torches and the Erewhonese. Jiri's impression—and mine—is that both of them consider the intel reliable, even though we protected one of our better sources from them. Given the fact that Thandi Palane only has a handful of frigates and McAvoy's under orders to stay home, though, there isn't a whole lot either of them can do with it. Under the circumstances—including the fact that we're the ones with the treaty with Torch—Governor Barregos has directed us to deal with it. That's where you people come in.

"I wish we didn't have to take the wraps off this early." He made the admission unflinchingly. "And, conversely, since we *do* have to take the wraps off, I wish we had more of the new hardware already trained up and ready to go. Unfortunately, however, in light of the Battle of Monica, we've been forced to substantially revise our estimate of the forces Manpower could make available to its proxies rather drastically upward. That means we can't count on holding what they *could* be throwing at Torch with nothing but the *War Harvests* and three *Morrigans*."

Most of his subordinates nodded soberly at that. The *War Harvest*-class represented the largest destroyer design in current SLN inventory. The fact that the Maya Sector had been assigned a full flotilla of them (although Destroyer Flotilla 3029, the flotilla in question, *was* one ship short of the eighteen it should theoretically have had) was an emblem of the Sector's economic importance. The three elderly *Morrigan*-class light cruisers which had been assigned to lead the flotilla's three squadrons, on the other hand, were an emblem of Frontier Security's . . . ambiguous feelings where Oravil Barregos was concerned. Although they'd been refitted with first-line electronics, they were very little larger than the destroyers they'd been assigned to work with—less than half the size of the *Marksmans*, in fact.

"If these people come in even with just the forces we already know have been recruited by Manpower," Rozsak continued, "they'd be in a damned good position to beat up on our 'official' ship list. If they come in with any substantial additional combat power, our people would be toast. And unlike that asshole Navarre, Manpower's 'proxies' won't have any official connection to Mesa. Our estimate is that that will make them a lot less likely to back down to keep the SLN from getting pissed off at Mesa—since Mesa can always say 'Who? *Us?* No, no, no. *We* didn't have a thing to do with all that mayhem and destruction!'" He shook his head. "They're headed for Torch to turn Torch into a smoking cinder, people . . . and it's going to be up to *you* to see to it that that doesn't happen."

He paused for a moment, letting them digest what he'd just said, then tipped his chair back slightly.

"Does anyone have any comments at this stage?" he invited.

There was silence for a moment while people glanced at one another, then Kamstra faced Rozsak up the length of the table.

"I don't think any of us have any questions about 'why,' Sir," he said. "I imagine there are a few little concerns about exactly '*how*,' though. And about hardware availability. So far, J.T. is the only one of our arsenal ship skippers who's actually had the opportunity to roll pods in an all-up live-fire exercise. We've spent a lot of hours in the simulators, of course, but that's not quite the same thing. And then there's the question of how many pods we'll have when the credit actually drops."

"Those are all valid concerns," Rozsak acknowledged, "and I think you'll find Edie and her people have dealt with them in their ops plan. Nobody's pretending we're delighted with the compromises we're going to be forced to adopt, but to paraphrase a pre-space politician by the name of Churchill, perfect operational conditions obtain only in Heaven . . . and admirals who insist on them before they'll take action seldom get there."

Someone—it wasn't Stahlin, this time—chuckled, and Rozsak grinned briefly.

"I know we've hit a few snags in the production pipeline," he went on, "but, especially since this intel on Torch came up, we've been pressing Carlucci—and McAvoy—on the pod numbers. Our best guess at this point is that by the time we reach Torch, we should find a couple of Carlucci freighters waiting for us with somewhere around fifteen hundred pods. That won't be quite enough for a complete load-out on all three of the *Masquerades*, and we'll probably be short on EW birds, but it'll still give us a hell of a lot more punch than anyone else is going to be expecting us to have. What it's *not* going to give us is a lot of ammunition to use up in those live-fire exercises you were talking about, Dirk-Steven. Exercises which, I hasten to add, I entirely agree we ought to be carrying out. Since these are going to be the six-pod rings, though, they aren't going to be reusable, so even if we had the replacement birds to load into them, we wouldn't be able to reload after the exercise."

Heads nodded soberly around the table.

The transitional ship types which had been produced for the Maya Sector in the Carlucci yards were experimental, in one sense, but used proven technological components, in another. The new *Warrior*-class destroyers were almost ten percent larger even than the *War Harvest*-class, yet they had twenty-five percent fewer missile tubes and forty percent fewer energy weapons in each broadside than the much smaller *Rampart*-class. That lesser throw weight had been emphasized in the various reports being sent back to Old Chicago, since it had helped to assuage any possible fears over the combat power of the ships Barregos was building for himself out in Maya. What *hadn't* been emphasized was that the energy weapons in question were all grasers (not the *Ramparts'* much lighter—and less powerful—*lasers*); that the ships carried almost twice the anti-missile defenses of a standard SLN destroyer, that they carried substantially more missiles per tube; and that the missiles in question were the same ones carried by the *Royal Manticoran Navy's* light units at the close of the First Havenite War. Nor had anyone mentioned the improvements in inertial compensator improvement which gave a *Warrior* a thirty percent acceleration advantage over Rozsak's *War Harvest*-class destroyers. It was probably as well for the blood pressure of various senior SLN officers that they were blissfully unaware of just how enormous an increase in combat power all of that represented.

The *Marksman*-class would have come as an even more unpleasant surprise, had anyone in the Sol System had the least idea of their actual specifications. In many ways, what the *Marksman* really represented was a slightly downsized prewar RMN *Star Knight*-class *heavy* cruiser with updated electronics, energy weapons, and missiles and a substantially *downsized* crew. Her compensator gave her an acceleration rate which, while inferior to a *Warrior*'s, was still twenty-eight percent better than a *War Harvest*'s, and she carried the Mark-17-E, the Erewhon-built version of the Manticoran Mark-14 missile then-Captain Michael Oversteegen had used to such good effect at the Battle of Refuge three T-years earlier. They weren't multidrive missiles; in fact, Manticore had abandoned further development on them when the Mark 16 dual-drive missile proved a practical concept for cruiser-sized tubes. But they were substantially longer ranged than anything in the Solarian inventory, and in the latest Erewhonese version, they mounted heavier laser heads (although with fewer lasing *rods*) than were carried by any Solarian combatant short of the wall of battle. They were also, unfortunately, much too large to be fired out of the *Warriors*' missile tubes, far less by any of the older, Solarian-built units under Rozsak's command, and the *Marksmans* carried only thirty of them for each of the six tubes in each broadside.

Had any SLN observer taken a good look at one of Rozsak's "light cruisers," he might have observed two interesting external peculiarities. First, their weapons seemed a bit asymmetrically arranged. Although they showed the very respectable (especially for a *light* cruiser) broadside armament of six missile tubes, five grasers, twelve counter missile tubes, and eight point defense stations, there was a peculiar gap in the middle of each broadside—one just about large enough to have accommodated two additional missile tubes. Second, they seemed to have an awful lot of additional planar arrays stuck in some odd-looking places.

The reason for the apparent peculiarity was that the ships had been designed with *eight* broadside missile tubes, not six. As built, however, two tubes in each broadside had been replaced by lots and lots of additional fire control. The compartments which had been intended to mount the missile tubes had then been sealed with solid plugs of armor—armor which, in fact, was substantially heavier than that which protected her actual weaponry. The peculiar plethora of arrays dotting her flanks provided the telemetry links for all that fire control, which gave them—despite the fact that they mounted only six tubes each—enough capability to simultaneously control *sixty* missiles in each broadside firing arc.

Ultimately, all of that massively redundant fire control would be removed and replaced with the missile tubes of the original "official" design. At the moment, however, they were half the key to Rozsak's entire strategy for covering the gap until the Maya Sector began to take delivery of a substantial force of Erewhon-built ships-of-the-wall of its very own.

The other half of the key was represented by the *Masquerades*—the ships which had received the unofficial type designation of "arsenal ship."

Based loosely on the Silesian-designed *Starhauler* "modular" merchant ship, the *Masquerade* massed a shade over two million tons. The original *Starhauler* design had featured a downsized standard, configurable internal cargo hull, surrounded by an outer shell of "container" spaces. The idea had been to produce a vessel which could transport individually loaded cargo modules which could be dropped off in transit without taking time for routine offloading procedures. On paper, it had offered many advantages although, in practice, it had proven less successful.

What Carlucci had done in designing the *Masquerade* as a similar "modular merchant ship" for the Maya Sector was to eliminate the internal cargo hold entirely. Instead, each ship had sixteen pod bays arranged along each side, and each bay had its own power and life-support connections, since part of the idea was that the ship could also be fitted with passenger-carrying pods or climate-controlled or refrigerated pods. That potential power demand also explained why a merchant ship had not one, but two fusion plants.

Commercially, the ship was a pure boondoggle, which, Rozsak had no doubt, would be painfully evident to anyone back on Old Earth who ever actually looked at it as a practical freight hauler. No one was doing that, of course, given the rationale for their construction which he and Barregos had crafted for Solarian consumption.

Militarily, the *Masquerade* was probably the best illustration of the principle of mounting sledgehammers in eggshells Luiz Rozsak had ever seen or imagined. In fact, it was really more of a case of mounting pile-drivers in soap bubbles, as far as he was concerned.

Each of the *Masquerade*'s pod bays just happened to be deep enough to mount three of the Erewhonese Space Navy's standard missile pods stacked end-to-end. It was considerably *wider* than a single missile pod, however, and CIG had been considerate enough to design a mounting for multiple pods. The initial design accommodated six pods in three rows of two pods each, but an improved design mounting only four pods each in a true "ring" arrangement was just entering production.

The original six-pod configuration offered a greater throw weight per "ring," but the pods it contained were stripped down, with very lightweight grav-drivers. They weren't *quite* intended as single-shot weapons, but they would require extensive refurbishing before they could be used a second time. The currently available pods also contained the Mark-17-E, not full-scale multi-drive missiles.

The four-pod version's component pods, on the other hand, were far more robust. They'd be reloadable and reusable without requiring enough additional maintenance to amount to something just short of actual rebuilding, and they'd have the independent endurance to be deployed for up to a week at a time. Even more significantly, their individually larger pods would be loaded with the Mark-19, the ESN's most recent MDM variant.

Given the fact that there were sixteen pod bays in each of a *Masquerade*'s broadsides, each arsenal ship carried up to ninety-six pods, which, with the six-pod ring, gave her a total of five hundred and seventy-six pods. That was more firepower than was carried by the vast majority of pod superdreadnoughts three times her size. Unfortunately, those missiles were *all* she carried. She was a *merchant* design, with zero armor, no integral point defense capability, no core hull, no life support redundancy, no military-grade lifepods, no integral firecontrol even for her own pods, and no integral electronic warfare capability. If a genuine warship—even a dinky little pre-Manticore LAC—ever got into weapons range of her, she (and her crew) would disappear quickly from the cosmos. Which was why she wasn't supposed to *get* into weapons range of anyone else. Instead, she was supposed to lie safely out of range of an opponent with no multidrive missiles, launching salvo after salvo of pods which would then be taken under control by the *Marksmans*, with all of those redundant telemetry links.

Eventually, her class would also be provided with specially designed "combat pods" which would contain things like counter-missile tubes, point defense stations, sidewall generators, additional life support, fire control, electronic warfare systems, and the like. Unfortunately, all the "combat pods" in the galaxy would never turn her into a proper warship which could hope to survive even minimal damage. Even more unfortunately at the moment, none of those specially designed combat pods were yet available for the only three *Masquerades* of which Maya had so far taken delivery.

"As I say, we're going to be short on expendable ammunition for at least another month or so," Rozsak continued. "It's not the missiles themselves; it's the pod rings. Carlucci is concentrating on getting as many of them produced as quickly as possible, even at the expense of pulling people and capacity off the combat pods, and he's moved the four-pod rings—and the Mark-19s for them—up in the production chute, as well. But it's probably going to be sometime late in October before CIG actually gets any of those new goodies delivered to us at Torch. In the meantime, we're just going to have to do the best we can with the simulators, and, frankly, I expect that to be pretty damned good, given the caliber of our people."

The praise implicit in his last sentence was even more gratifying to his subordinates because of the matter-of-fact tone in which it was delivered, and he smiled slightly as he recognized the pleasure in their expressions.

"Any other comments or questions?" he asked.

"I imagine there are probably a few more thoughts chasing around in people's heads, Sir," Kamstra replied. "On the other hand, as you just pointed out, Edie probably has answers for most of them already built into her ops plan. Considering which, I think we should go ahead and let her bring us all up to speed. I'm sure if there are any questions left afterward, she and Jiri will be able to dispose of them."

"And, of course, if disposing of them should prove to be beyond their merely mortal capabilities, *I* will be available to dispense wisdom from on high," Rozsak agreed benignly. This time, the response was a chorus of laughter, no mere chuckles, and he gave them all a much broader smile. Then he waved one hand in Habib's direction.

"The stage is yours, Edie."

CHAPTER FORTY-TWO

"Do you really think there's someone here who'd be interested in hiring us?" Yana's eyes, as she inspected the interior of the bar, were as skeptical as her tone of voice. "Talk about a dive."

"No, I don't. DuChamps wouldn't have spent that much time with me if they were just thinking of pawning me off in a routine transaction."

"Then why are we here?"

"A test, I figure. Dusek wants to see if I really have the credentials."

Sitting across from him at the small table in a corner, Yana continued her casual inspection of the place. So it would seem to any observer, at any rate. The fact that she spent at least a minute doing so would be understandable enough. Any woman as good-looking as she was would have a few trepidations about being in the place.

Victor had done some quiet checking after Triêu Chuanli had more-or-less ordered him to spend time at the Rhodesian Rendezvouz. He'd discovered, not to his surprise, that the place was notorious for being a hangout for mercenaries, even by the standards of notoriety that held sway in the worst seccy district of Mesa's capital city. It was one of those places where the police were said to always come in pairs—except no policeman had set foot in the Rhodesian Rendezvouz in over eight years. According to the stories he'd heard, the last one to do so had left in a body bag.

There'd been no repercussions, apparently. The cop had been new to the police force and trying a private shakedown of the bar. If the owner hadn't had his own people take care of the problem, the district's police captain probably would have done it for him.

Victor had spent years in districts similar to Neue Rostock. For a spy like himself, they were often good places to go to ground or set up an operation. There were some disadvantages to working with criminals, to be sure. But the one great offsetting advantage was that very few hardened criminals were burdened with anything in the way of idle patriotic impulses. As long as they got paid, they didn't care who you were or why you were doing whatever you were doing—which they didn't want to know, anyway.

Every planet with a large population had districts like this in their major cities. The Neue Rostock was by no means the worst Victor had run across. Two of the slum areas in Nouveau Paris, one of them less than a mile from where he'd been born, were just as rough or worse. And, everywhere, there were certain standard practices. Not quite formal rules, but very close. One of them was that any establishment—certainly one like the Rhodesian Rendezvouz—had to pay off the cops to stay in business. But the pay-offs were done in a proper and orderly manner, from the top down. Freelance policemen were not welcome and usually didn't last long.

The only thing out of the ordinary at all about Mesa was that the police were almost completely indifferent to what happened in the seccy slums. The cops left the maintenance of order in these districts to the bosses who ran them. As long as they got their baksheesh, they simply didn't care what happened there. And, being fair about it, the bosses probably maintained order at least as well as the police would have done, and the cut they took from every business was no worse than taxes would have been.

Still, it was a rough sort of order—at least, in a place like the Rhodesian.

"It'll be the three at the table on the south wall," Yana predicted. "The ones who came in a few minutes ago."

She spoke softly also; but, just as Victor had done, she relied on their scrambling equipment to protect them from being overheard by eavesdroppers. Nobody would think anything of that, either. Such equipment was pretty much *de rigueur* in a place like this. If there was any blind trust or milk of human kindness to be found on the premises, it'd be in the paws of a blind mouse hiding in a hole somewhere.

"I think you're right. They're avoiding looking at you. Half of the other men in the place haven't stopped ogling you since we came in."

Yana's cold smile appeared. "You sure you want to handle this? I can take care of it myself, you know."

"I don't doubt that. But I'm the one they want to find out about."

In point of fact, Yana was a bit nervous. Not because of the three men at that table. She ate alpha males for breakfast. What made her nervous was the man she was *with*.

Victor Cachat. Her friend Lara, not long before she died, had made the quip that *with Victor on your side, you don't need to make any bargains with the devil.*

It was true enough. She saw the men at the table push aside their chairs and come to their feet. All three were large, muscular, and obviously experienced when it came to physical confrontations. They were probably all mercenaries.

She sensed a very slight motion in Victor's right arm and knew that he'd slid the pistol all the way down his sleeve. He'd be holding it there, on his wrist, with just one finger. One quick motion—very well practiced in simulation chambers, Cachat being Cachat—and the gun would be in his hand.

As three more babes in the woods are about to find out.

Jurgen Dusek leaned forward to study the recording Chuanli had brought him. The three men were now within two meters of the couple at the corner table.

They were almost certainly carrying weapons. One of them was, for sure. Jurgen could see the pistol butt peeking out from under his jacket. Careless of him. But in practice there was no chance he'd get accosted by the police—not in Neue Rostock—and as long as he kept the weapon technically out of sight the barkeeps at the Rhodesian wouldn't make any objection.

All three men had that certain sort of smile on their faces that Jurgen recognized from long experience. Dangerous thugs, about to prove it once again, taking the first steps in a familiar dance. When the dance was over—clearly, they didn't expect it to take long—they'd have some new female company to enjoy and a punk would have learned his true place on the pecking order. Maybe he'd survive the experience, maybe he wouldn't.

Dusek now looked at the man still seated at the table. If McRae was carrying any weapon, it wasn't visible. There was no sign of the pistol that Thiêu had sold him. In fact, he seemed oblivious to the menacing trio approaching him. So far as Jurgen could tell, McRae hadn't noticed them at all. The good-looking blonde sitting across from him had spotted them coming, sure enough, but she didn't seem too twitchy either.

Chuanli had told him it was interesting.

"What's your name, sweetheart?" asked one of the three men, when they came up to the table.

The blonde glanced at him, shook her head, and pointed at McRae. "Ask him."

McRae didn't even glance at them. "She's my woman. Leave it at that." His tone of voice was that of a man thoroughly bored.

The man who'd made the initial advance began to bridle. "Listen, shithead, you—"

McRae somehow had the pistol in his hand. He brought it up, still seated, and shot the man in the chest. As he began to crumple, the Havenite rose, smoothly and easily, and shot him in the head. Twice. Then shot the man to his left, then the one to his right. Three shots each. The first center mass, then a double-tap to the head.

It all took maybe three seconds. Only one of his victims even got a hand on a gun, and he didn't succeed in pulling it out of its shoulder holster. When it was over, half the floor of the bar was covered in blood and brains and the other dozen or so patrons—all of them very tough people in their own right—were pale-faced with stunned surprise.

"Which word in 'she's my woman' does anybody in this bar have trouble understanding?" the gunman asked. He still sounded thoroughly bored.

"Jesus H. Christ," said Jurgen Dusek. "Run it again, Chuanli."

The crime boss watched the recording three times over. Each time looking to see . . . *anything* that would make that gunman seem like a human being. Or even a normal sociopath.

Nothing.

After watching the recording four times, though, Dusek understood what had happened. It wasn't that McRae was some sort of "fast gun." True, he'd figured out a way to get the pistol into his hand without anyone spotting it, and then he'd moved quickly and surely, with not a single wasted motion. But any man well trained, familiar with weapons and in good condition could have done the same.

No, the secret was mental. This guy was one of those very rare people who could kill at the proverbial drop of the hat. He hadn't needed the stages of emotional escalation that even hardened thugs required, as quickly as those stages might pass. With him, everything had been instantaneous. Recognition of threat, calculation that the threat was best handled ruthlessly, start the killing.

"Talk about a hardcase," he muttered. "No wonder Saint-Just tagged him. You talk to him afterward?"

"Yeah. I waited a bit, you understand. It took the barkeeps a while to clean everything up. The three guys he shot weren't any complication. The working arrangement they had with Jozef was just providing him with occasional muscle."

Jozef Ortega was no more sentimental than any under-boss. He worked for Jurgen anyway. Chuanli had been waiting nearby and had been called in by the barkeeps as soon as the fight was over. He could have been there in thirty or forty seconds, but he stretched it out to five minutes. McRae would probably figure out the whole thing had been a setup, but there was no reason to make it obvious. That might even be a little dangerous.

The rest would have been routine. Clean up the place, quietly threaten whatever patrons—probably none—might have an inclination to shoot their mouths off, and then pitch the three corpses into the garbage disintegrator of the restaurant next door. Dusek owned the restaurant as well as the Rhodesian, and he'd provided it with a top-of-the-line disintegrator. And then paid bribes to the police and the sanitation department to have all the recorders and detectors disabled. Nobody except the people involved would ever know what happened to those bodies.

"Give Jozef a payoff for lost services from his three guys. Ex-guys. Just to keep him from having hard feelings."

Chuanli nodded. "And McRae?"

"Is he willing to talk further? Or is he holding a grudge?"

"Yeah, sure. Cold-blooded killer be damned, boss. He probably figured out we set it all up, but it's not like he suffered any damages. He's got to eat like anyone else—not to mention keeping that big blonde happy. And for that he needs to get some work."

Dusek pursed his lips. The remaining issue that had to be considered was whether this McRae fellow was actually an agent for . . .

It wouldn't be any government agency or corporate security service. Not, at least, of any government or corporations Dusek was familiar with. This guy was just plain too murderous.

But that still left the Ballroom as a possibility. Not likely, but it couldn't be ruled out altogether. Dusek had no loyalty to Mesa, but he also wasn't a fool. This planet was his place of business—a very profitable one, too—and keeping that business up and running required him to avoid pissing off the powers-that-were.

A triple killing, when the dead men were thugs themselves and had no important patrons or allies, wouldn't concern the Mesan authorities. Not one that took place in this district. But if there was any Ballroom connection, the official indifference would end abruptly. Twice in his life, Jurgen had seen what happened when Mesa took off the gloves and really went after someone in the seccy districts. "Due process" and "reasonable force" were meaningless noises. They'd think nothing of leveling entire city blocks and butchering everyone in them, just to kill one person they were after.

That said . . .

Dusek figured he could probably ignore the problem, as long as Inez Cloutier hired McRae and got him off the planet quickly. It really *wasn't* likely, after all, that a former inner circle StateSec person would have anything to do with the Ballroom. True, the Havenites had always been opposed to genetic slavery. But so what? The one thing every former StateSec whom Dusek had ever encountered had in common was that they were mercenaries. And what did the Ballroom have to offer them?

"So what do you want to do with McRae?" asked Chuanli.

Dusek made his decision. "Just have somebody keep track of him. It doesn't have to be any sort of elaborate tailing operation, Chuanli. That costs real money. Just somebody keeping an eye on his lodgings. Letting us know when he leaves, when he comes back, his daily routine."

"Can't find out where he goes without tailing him, boss."

"Who the hell cares where he goes? We're not in the least bit interested in this guy, Chuanli. He's bad news. A full-bore psychopath—and good at it. The sooner he's off the planet, the better. We just want to turn a nice profit getting him off, that's all. For that, we don't need to know anything we don't know already. He's legitimately StateSec, was all that mattered. Good enough for this market."

CHAPTER FORTY-THREE

Jack McBryde sat in his comfortable office, watching the smart wall opposite his desk, and worried.

The wall was configured to show bird's-eye views from the ceiling-mounted security pickups scattered throughout the facility for which he held primary responsibility. From those views, an uninformed observer would never have guessed that the entire Gamma Center was buried under better than fifty meters of the planet Mesa's dirt and rock. Actually, it was buried under the foundations of one of the commercial-zoned towers which fringed the outskirts of Green Pines, as well. Its original construction had been handily concealed by all the other activity involved in building Green Pines in the first place, and it was far enough out from the residential district that it had no "full-time" neighbors to notice anything peculiar about it. Even better, perhaps, the fact that the tower above it was packed with specialty shops, financial offices, medical service providers, and better than a dozen various government and corporate offices provided ample cover for the comings and goings of the Center's seven hundred-odd scientists, engineers, and administrators and the security people responsible for keeping an eye on them.

The Alignment, however, had learned long ago that a troglodyte existence wasn't conducive to getting the very best out of creative people. That was why the Center's subterranean chambers boasted surprisingly high ceilings and large, airy rooms and offices. Corridors were broader than they had to be, with their smart walls configured to provide remarkably convincing illusions of open forest glades or—on the second floor—sundrenched, white-sugar beaches. The public areas' ceilings were likewise designed to give the impression that people inside them were actually outside, but the individual researchers' work spaces and offices were config- ured as the interior rooms they were, since quite a few people seemed to find it difficult to concentrate their full attention on the work at hand when they were "outside." On the other hand, the decision of exactly how to configure any team's work area was left up to the team's members, and the majority of them had opted for "windows" looking out on the same scenery their public corridors afforded. Better than half had added large "skylights" whose views of the sky matched the apparent time of day of the corridors which, in turn, were coordinated with the actual time of day outside the Center.

The result was a working environment which avoided the impression of being shut up inside a bunker (despite the fact that it was) and simultaneously kept the researchers' mental and physical clocks adjusted to the rest of Mesa's clocks when they finally got to head home at the end of work each day.

Unfortunately, that wasn't enough to keep all of them focused and productive, McBryde reflected gloomily, and tapped the vir- tual keyboard key which selected the view of Herlander Simões' team, brought it to the center of his office's wall, and zoomed in on the hyper-physicist.

In some ways, Simões actually looked better than he had during his first conversation with McBryde, almost six T-months before. He was taking more care with his grooming, now, at least, and as far as McBryde could tell, he was actually getting more sleep. But the bouts of depression were still there. They seemed to be less frequent, yet, according to his therapist they were even deeper and darker than they had been, and McBryde himself had noticed over the last several weeks that Simões' occasional bursts of furious temper—which had never been a part of his amiable, easy-going personality before his daughter's death—had grown increasingly violent.

He hadn't—yet—approached the point of actually laying hands on any of his colleagues, but his red-faced, vicious outbursts, often laden with intensely personal profanity, had thoroughly alienated his coworkers. Many of them had been his and his wife's close friends before Francesca's death, and some of those seemed to

be trying to maintain at least a degree of personal contact with
him, yet even they had retreated behind a protective barrier of
formality. The other members of his team, however, despite any
sympathy they might have felt, avoided him whenever it was
remotely possible. When they *couldn't* avoid him, they limited
themselves to the minimum possible number of words. It was
painfully obvious they'd written him off, and three of them were
at the point of making it clear they *didn't* sympathize with him.
The best McBryde could say about those three was that they'd at
least tried to avoid expressing their agreement with the Board's
decision in Francesca Simões' case where Herlander was likely
to overhear them. On the other hand, he doubted any of them
would be particularly heartbroken if he *did* happen to hear.

Their current project was nearing its conclusion, which was
both good and bad. The improvement to the "streak drive" likely
to result from their R&D would be a significant plus, of course.
And the fact that Simões had remained basically functional
throughout was a major plus, both personally and professionally,
for Jack McBryde. But the unfortunate truth was that despite his
past record, and despite his obvious ability, Herlander Simões
wasn't really uniquely important to the Alignment's research
efforts. He wasn't irreplaceable—not in the long term, whatever
the disruptive effect on dropping him from his team's current
projects might have been. And McBryde had no illusions about
what was going to happen to Simões, at least as far as his work
at the Center was concerned, as soon as those current projects
were all safely put to bed.

They're going to shit-can him, that's what's going to happen,
McBryde thought grimly. *Hard to blame them, really. He's turned
into such a basket case no one in his right mind would include him
in a new team if they could find anyone at all to use instead. He
sees it coming, too. I think that's one of the reasons his temper's
been even shorter-fused lately. But what the* hell *is going to happen
to him when he loses even his work?*

He grimaced as a still darker thought crossed his mind once
again. Given the fact that Simões was aware of the countdown
until he was removed from his current duties, the possibility that
his anger and despair might drive him to some self-destructive
(and ultimately futile) overt attempt at vengeance loomed large
on McBryde's list of Things to Worry About.

And what about you, *Jack?* He asked himself, gazing at the enlarged imagery of Herlander Simões working at his terminal, all alone in his self-created pocket of isolation. *You're not the basket case he is . . . yet, at least. But you're infected, too, aren't you? And Zack's starting to worry about you, isn't he? He doesn't know what's eating on you, but he knows* something's *gnawing away down inside there.*

McBryde leaned back in his chair, rubbing his closed eyes with the fingers of both hands, and a feeling of bleak despair flowed through him. There was more than a little anger in that despair, and much of that anger was directed at Herlander Simões. Intellectually, McBryde knew it was as irrational for him to be angry with Simões as it was for Simões to flash into a white-hot rage at some innocent remark from one of his coworkers. It wasn't as if the hyper-physicist had set out to destroy Jack McBryde's peace of mind. For that matter, Simões wasn't really even the one who'd done it. But what he *had* done was to become the factor which had crystallized McBryde's own . . . ambiguities into a grim self-admission.

As he'd watched Simões' centimeter-by-centimeter dissolution, what had happened to the hyper-physicist and his daughter had become a microcosm for all of his own doubts, all of his own concerns about the Mesan Alignment and its ultimate purposes. And that, McBryde thought, was because the Simões family's fate *was* a microcosm. Not even a Mesan alpha's mind could truly grasp—not on a fundamental, emotional level—the concept of centuries of time, of thousands of inhabited planets and literally uncounted trillions of human lives. The scale, the scope, was simply too huge. The mind retreated into the concept of "one, two, three, many"—a conceptualization which could be manipulated intellectually, factored into plans and strategies, but not truly *grasped*. Not inside, where a human being actually lived.

But Herlander, Harriet, and Francesca Simões represented a merely human-scale tragedy. It was one which *could* be grasped, could be understood. Something which could be experienced, at second hand, at least, and which, even worse, could *not* be ignored. Couldn't be labeled "Not My Business" and swept under a convenient mental carpet while one got on with one's own life.

Not by Jack McBryde, anyway.

And as he'd grappled with the emotionally draining task of

keeping Herlander Simões functional long enough for him to complete his work, the new set of lenses his empathy with the hyper-physicist had given McBryde kept mercilessly examining what the Alignment had become. Deep at the heart of him, he knew, he was still committed to the Detweiler vision he'd assimilated as a youngster. He still believed the galaxy-wide rejection of the notion of genetically uplifting the entire human race to become all that it could have been was deeply, fundamentally, and tragically wrong. It rejected so *much*, turned its back on so *many* possibilities, doomed so many people to be so much less than they might have been. He *believed* that, with every fiber of his being.

But, he admitted to himself now, letting himself truly face it for the first time, *what you* don't *believe anymore is that we have the right to force those who disagree with us to submit to our vision of their future. That's too much for you now, isn't it, Jack? And it's what the Board did to Francesca—and Herlander—that made it that way.*

No, that wasn't entirely fair, he thought. It wasn't just the tragedy of the Simões family. It was a lot of things, including the realization of how many billions of people the Alignment's strategy was inevitably going to kill along the way—the "collateral damage" the Alignment's master strategy was prepared to accept.

And it's the fact that you've finally realized that you, personally, are going to be directly responsible for bringing about those deaths, he thought despairingly.

He knew it was an unfair indictment, in many ways. He might be an alpha, but he was still only one tiny cog in the vast machine of the Mesan Alignment. His personal contribution to what was about to happen wasn't *unimportant*, but it *was* statistically insignificant. Yes, he'd contributed—efficiently, enthusiastically, and with a sense of satisfaction—to the wave of death about to sweep across the galaxy, yet his direct contribution to the killing would never even be noticed in the grand scheme of things, and it was supremely egotistical of him to think otherwise.

But that wasn't truly the point, was it? Not the point that was beginning to disturb his own sleep, at least. No, the point was that he *had* contributed to it. That he had ambled along, dedicated his own life to perfecting, protecting, and—ultimately—launching the Juggernaut of the Mesan Alignment. It had never even occurred to him *not* to, and that was what he truly found impossible to forgive himself. It wasn't even as if he'd confronted his doubts, his worries, and worked his way through them to a decision that the ultimate benefits to the race vastly outweighed the cost to the individual. He hadn't done even that much.

He tapped another brief command, and the close-up of Simões and his team disappeared from the smart wall. Another image replaced it—a file image of a single face, with huge brown eyes, an olive complexion, and the enormous, dimpled smile it had provided for its owner's father and his camera. He looked into those laughing eyes, at all the joy and all the love which had been stolen from them and from Francesca Simões' parents, and knew he should have confronted those questions. He'd never even met the little girl smiling at him from the center of his wall, and yet his heart twisted within him and his eyes burned as he gazed at her now.

She was only one child, only one person, he told himself. *How much can any single life really count in the battle for the ultimate fate of the entire human race? It's insane, Jack. There's no way to even rationally compare what happened to her and to her parents to all of the literally inconceivable advantages we can provide to all of the rest of humanity!*

It was true. He *knew* it was true. And yet, despite everything, he knew it was a truth that didn't really matter. Because, in the end, he was his parents' son, and he knew. Oh yes, he knew.

It's not about the advantages, about the "nobility" of our purpose—assuming the Board truly remembers what that purpose once was, he thought. *Those things still matter, but so does your soul, Jack. So does the moral responsibility. There's right, and there's wrong, and there's the choice between them, and that's part of the human race's heritage, too. And it's about the fact that if we're really right—if Leonard Detweiler was really right—about how the entire species can choose to improve and uplift itself, then why haven't we committed even a fraction of the resources we've committed to building the Alignment to convincing the rest of the galaxy of that? Maybe it wouldn't have been easy, especially after the Final War. And maybe it would have taken generations, centuries, to make any progress. But the Alignment's already invested all of those generations and all of those centuries in our grand and glorious vision . . . and it had abandoned the idea of convincing other people we were right in favor of killing however many of them it took to make them* admit *we were right almost before Leonard Detweiler's brain function ceased. For that matter, the way we've embraced and used Manpower and genetic slavery has actually* contributed *to the prejudice against "genies," damn it!*

Jack McBryde looked at that smiling face and saw the mirror of his own people's arrogance. Not the arrogance of which Leonard Detweiler had been accused, not the arrogance of believing a better, healthier, more capable, longer-lived human being was achievable. Not *that* arrogance, but another deeper, darker arrogance. The arrogance of fanaticism. Of the ability—of the willingness, even the eagerness—to *prove* to the rest of humanity that Detweiler had been right. To rub the rest of the galaxy's nose in the fact that, as Leonard Detweiler's descendents, *they* were right, too . . . and that everyone else was still wrong.

That in their own persons they already represented that better, more capable human being, which was proof of their own superiority and their own right to dictate humanity's future to every other poor, benighted, *inferior* "normal" in the universe. That they'd been right—*had* the right—to actually expand the genetic slave trade and all of the human misery it entailed not for profit, but simply as a cover, a distracting shield for the high and noble purpose which justified any means to which they might resort.

And to create, evaluate, and "cull" however many little girls had to be thrown away to accomplish that glorious purpose.

CHAPTER FORTY-FOUR

Captain Gowan Maddock of the Mesan Alignment Navy looked down at the ornate rings of braid around the cuffs of his Mesa *System* Navy uniform with remarkably scant favor. He'd always thought the MSN's uniform, with its hectares of braid and its tall caps whose visors dripped old-fashioned "scrambled eggs," looked more like something out of a bad operetta than anything any *real* navy would have tolerated. Of course, no one had ever *wanted* anyone to take the MSN seriously, had they? It was supposed to be a pretentious Lilliputian force with delusions of grandeur—exactly what the galaxy would have expected out of a star nation whose government was totally dominated by outlaw, profit-driven transstellars.

And, by the oddest turn of fate, that was precisely what the Mesa System Navy actually was. It would never have done to create a force whose professionalism might inadvertently have given itself away, after all. And so the Mesan *Alignment* Navy, which until very recently had boasted no more than a handful of carefully hidden destroyers and light cruisers, had been created as a completely separate organization. Unlike the comic opera pretensions and strutting of the "navy" everyone knew about, the MAN was a deadly serious, highly motivated, intensely professional service, and its austere uniforms were in deliberate contrast to those of the MSN.

And the ships we've already got could tear the ass right off the entire MSN without even breaking a sweat, Maddock reflected. *The ships we're going to have very shortly could do the same thing to just about anybody else, too.*

He took a deep and burning pride in that knowledge, and he looked forward to the rapidly approaching day when everyone else in the galaxy would know what he already knew. When the words "Mesan Navy" would be spoken with respect, even fear, instead of amused contempt.

But that day wasn't here yet, and aside from Commander Jessica Milliken, his own second-in-command, none of the other people filing into the briefing room aboard the battlecruiser *Leon Trotsky* knew the MAN existed. Which was why Maddock and Milliken wore the uniforms they did.

He waited while the newcomers took their places, standing behind their chairs as he stood behind his own, waiting. A few seconds ticked past, and then the briefing room door opened once again and Citizen Commodore Adrian Luff of the People's Navy in Exile strode through it, flanked by Citizen Commander Millicent Hartman, his chief of staff, and Captain Olivier Vergnier, *Leon Trotsky*'s commanding officer.

If I think my *uniform is stupid*, Maddock thought sourly, *what about the one* these *lunatics are wearing?*

It was a legitimate question, and one which had occurred to him more than once during the endless purgatory of his six-month assignment to his present duty. He'd experienced his share of idiocy during his occasional assignments to provide technical expertise to some operation being mounted by Manpower bureaucrats who knew no more about the truth of the Mesan Alignment than anyone else, but this one took the cake. It wasn't just Manpower loonies this time. Oh, no! *This* time he got to deal with an entire task force of people who were so far around the bend they wouldn't have been able to see it with a telescope . . . if it had ever so much as crossed their teeny-tiny minds to look back in the first place.

Luff marched to his chair at the head of the conference table and waited while Hartman and Vergnier stood behind their own. Then he seated himself, paused for two carefully counted heartbeats, and nodded regally to the lesser beings clustered about him.

"Be seated," he commanded, and Maddock made himself wait another half-second before he obeyed.

He and Milliken looked conspicuously out of place at that table in their black tunics and charcoal-gray trousers. True, the other uniforms around them sported almost as much braid as theirs did, but those other uniforms' tunics were red, and their trousers were black.

And no one else in the entire galaxy is crazy enough to wear them, either, he thought sourly, and shook his head mentally behind the expressionless façade of his eyes. *I wonder, do even* they *still genuinely believe there's a single chance in hell they'll ever return victoriously to Nouveau Paris and deal with the counter-revolutionary scum whose backstabbing treason brought down the people's paladins of the Committee of Public Safety?*

It seemed unlikely to Maddock that anyone could truly be that completely and totally out of touch with reality, but the People's Navy in Exile certainly acted the part. Even the names they'd assigned to the surplus *Indefatigable*-class battlecruisers Man-power had provided to them reflected that: *Leon Trotsky, George Washington, Marquis de Lafayette, Oliver Cromwell, Thomas Paine, Mao Tse-tung, Maximilien Robespierre . . .*

Well, I don't really care how far out to lunch they are, he reminded himself. *All I care about is that they do what they're supposed to do . . . and that I get the hell off this ship before the button gets punched on Wooden Horse.*

"First," Luff said as he surveyed the officers seated around the table, "let me say I'm extremely pleased with how well the most recent exercises have gone. I think I can say without fear of contradiction that this is the best trained, most proficient naval force with which I have ever been associated."

There were murmurs of satisfaction, and Maddock made himself nod in sober agreement with the commodore's assessment. And it was probably accurate, too, he reminded himself. Unlike at least a few of the People's Navy in *Exile's* ship commanders, Luff himself had never served in the original People's Navy of the People's Republic of Haven. He'd attained his pre-Thesiman rank of captain (the self-granted promotion to "commodore" had come later—purely, of course, as an administrative necessity when he organized the PNE) because of his loyalty and reliability. And his function had been not to fight actual battles but to make certain that no one in the regular navy entertained any thought of resisting the Committee of Public Safety's orders. He'd been the regime's enforcer, not a naval officer, and it was unlikely any members of the regular "naval forces" to which he had been attached during his StateSec career would have considered him one of their "associates," either.

Still, there was some valid basis for Luff's current satisfaction, the Mesan officer reminded himself. Especially given the fact that for all their pretension to the status of warriors of the revolution, the men and women in this briefing room had spent the last six T-years as little better than common, garden-variety pirates. It was amazing to Maddock that they'd managed to hang on to any shared sense of identity, and he supposed their identification of themselves as a "navy in exile," however ludicrous it might be, helped account for it. Well, the fact that Manpower had subsidized the PNE generously enough for them to hold their ships' companies together had something to do with it as well, he imagined.

The consequences of their degeneration into ten-a-credit brigands had been painfully evident when they gathered here to begin drilling for the Verdant Vista operation, though. They'd never been what Maddock would have considered real naval officers, but they'd become even sloppier and more incompetent than he'd expected. Integrating the mercenaries Manpower had been forced to retain to flesh out their crews—especially when the additional SLN units had been added to the PNE's order of battle—had made things even worse. Given the nature of this particular operation, Manpower had prudently avoided the more respectable mercenary outfits. In fact, the bulk of its new hires were basically common thieves, thugs, and murderers with a thin veneer of technical competence. Beating *them* into a semblance of efficiency had been a daunting task. It was fortunate Luff and his fellows had acquired so much experience in instilling terror-based discipline, he supposed, but even with the aid of Milliken and the other Manpower "advisers" provided by the "Mesa System Navy," it had taken every single day of the endless months spent orbiting this bleak, planetless red dwarf to get them ready.

But they really are ready, he told himself. However hard to believe that may be, they're actually ready to mount the operation. It's still probably a damned good thing they're only going up against a handful of frigates manned by a bunch of semiliterate runaway slaves with maybe a few Erewhonese cruisers in support, but I have to admit, they've worked up to a level of efficiency I never would have believed they'd get to.

"As all of you are aware," Luff continued gravely, "the execution date for Operation Ferret is almost upon us. This was our last exercise, which makes it particularly gratifying that it went so well."

He paused again, briefly, then cleared his throat.

"I'm sure we're all also aware that at least some of our personnel continue to cherish a few . . . reservations about the requirements of the ops plan. Under the circumstances, I suppose that's inevitable."

He glanced briefly at Maddock and Milliken from the corner of his eye, and Maddock blandly pretended not to notice.

"There are two points to bear in mind," the commodore went on after a moment. "First, from a purely pragmatic viewpoint, our obligation to our . . . benefactors requires us to carry out this operation. Not to put too fine a point on it, and without intending offense to anyone," this time he nodded openly to Maddock, "this operation is our payment for the ships and the support the PNE requires to finally mount an organized, sustained offensive against the counterrevolutionaries in Nouveau Paris. I realize that even with the additional hulls we've added to our force, the counterrevolutionaries will substantially outnumber us. However, I also realize, as I'm sure all of you do, that not *everyone* in Nouveau Paris and elsewhere in the People's Republic has forgotten everything the Committee of Public Safety stood for. There *are* people in the People's Republic, even in the current Navy, who sympathize with us and are only waiting for an example. For some leadership. We will provide that example and that leadership, and the ships and the advanced weapons with which our benefactors have already supplied us—and promise to continue to supply to us—are what will make that possible."

He gazed around the silent briefing room, and Maddock could almost hear his audience's thoughts. The PNE's "new" ships were effectively SLN castoffs, and he knew Luff and many of his ship commanders had reservations about them. And rightly so, he reflected, given how weak their missile defenses were. The MAN was equally aware of that weakness, although Maddock hadn't admitted anything of the sort to his ex-StateSec pupils, since neither the Solarian League Navy nor the official Mesan System Navy, had any concept of just how outclassed they truly were. The Alignment had seen to it that all of the new battlecruisers had Aegis, the SLN's most recent (and, in Maddock's considered opinion, hopelessly belated) bid to increase counter-missile salvo density, and it had upgraded all of the PNE ships' electronics to current first-line Solarian standards. It was clear from the State-Sec holdouts' reactions that they were impressed but not exactly overawed by the capabilities of their new fire control and EW systems, but it was equally clear they remained less than enthralled by the paucity of point defense clusters and counter-missile tubes. Maddock had been privately amused watching them upgrade the software of the vaunted Solarian League Navy's defensive systems. They'd made that their very first priority, and, amused or not, he had to admit that they'd probably enhanced their vessels' missile defenses' efficiency by somewhere around twenty-five percent.

They'd still be dogmeat going up against the Manties, and they know it, he reflected. *Fortunately, they're only planning on going up against Havenite hardware. We had to come up with a hell of a lot of ships to get them to sign on for this operation, anyway, of course. And the Cataphracts—let's not forget them! But Luff's probably right about what a swath they'd be able to cut through Theisman's light units.*

He suppressed a thin smile at that thought, since ultimately, they weren't going to have the chance to do anything of the sort.

Pity about the ships, he thought. *Of course, they're only SLN crap, which means they're all obsolescent—at best—against our own current hardware or the Manties. But at least we're about to get a chance to field test the Cataphracts and see how they work out against a live opponent. Too bad the opponent in question's going to be too outclassed to give us a more meaningful yardstick on their penetration capabilities.*

"However . . . distasteful some of us may find the discharge of that obligation to be," Luff told his officers, "Operation Ferret is nothing less than part of the price we must pay to liberate our homeland, and the overriding importance of that must outweigh any other consideration."

He paused yet again, gravely, letting his eyes circle the table, sweep the faces of his audience, then allowed those eyes to harden.

"Second," he resumed, his voice as hard as his eyes, "it would be as well to remember that these are not slaves being liberated from the hold of a slave ship somewhere. I'm sure Captain Maddock's and Commander Milliken's superiors are unlikely to be surprised by the fact that, despite our sincere gratitude for their support, we scarcely see eye to eye with them on the general issue of genetic slavery. In this instance, however, we aren't talking about liberating slaves or freeing the victims of someone else's mistreatment. We're talking about dealing with a terrorist organization. If any of your personnel are having trouble remembering that, I recommend you require your ships' companies to view the HD of the ghastly atrocities these people visited upon their prisoners following the 'liberation' of Verdant Vista. Remind them of that brutality and cruelty, and I think you'll find their reservations manageable."

He smiled very thinly, then turned his own attention to Maddock.

"And now, I understand, Captain Maddock has a few last-minute words for us. Captain?"

"Actually, Commodore," Maddock replied gravely, "I have very little to add to what you've already said. The only thing I'd really stress at this time is that it's important to remember Battle Fleet is only beginning to assess the Cataphract's capabilities. It still isn't operational with the SLN, and it won't be, for quite some time, given how . . . conservative we all know the Sollies are about adopting new hardware."

And especially given the fact that the SLN doesn't even have a clue it exists, I suppose, he added silently, and smiled at the exiled Havenites around the table.

"That's why we have no real body of doctrine for its employment. Our current estimates are that the . . . target will be covered by somewhere between a minimum of four and a maximum of ten of the new frigates the Manties have been supplying to the system. Our tech people's analyses suggest that they're probably pretty damned nasty for anything anyone else would call a 'frigate,' but they wouldn't pose any significant threat to your forces even without the Cataphract. It's also possible, however, that the Erewhonese Navy will have detailed a division of light cruisers or even heavy cruisers to back up those frigates. We don't really expect it, but it's clearly possible, given Erewhon's strong support for the . . . earlier incident in the system. If that *should* be the case, we're going to be confronting at least some Manty-grade hardware, which could make the entire operation substantially more expensive. With Cataphracts in the tubes, however, we anticipate that you should succeed with zero or at least negligible damage."

He paused, looking around the table, and reflected that everything he'd just told them had the highly unusual status of actually being the truth. Not the *whole* truth, perhaps, but still the truth.

"That's all I have, Sir," he said, nodding respectfully to Luff.

"I'm sure we'll all bear it in mind, Captain," Luff replied, then waved one hand at Citizen Commander Hartman.

"And now, Millicent, I believe you and the rest of the staff have a few points *you* wanted to make, as well?"

"Yes, Sir, we do." Hartman looked around the table. "First," she began, "there's the question of—"

CHAPTER FORTY-FIVE

"*Hali Sowle,* you are cleared to leave orbit." E.D. Trimm checked the screen again, more out of habit that anything else, just as a final precaution against the very remote possibility that an unauthorized flight—or possibly even a bolide, as statistical unlikely as that was—might have blundered into the freighter's projected course.

"*Hali Sowle,* signing off."

Just routine. By now, two weeks later, Trimm had only a vague memory of having done an additional check on the *Hali Sowle.* That was in the records, of course. But she was no more likely to check old records for no reason—the volume of traffic in and out of Mesa was truly enormous—than she would be to start going to work with a hop, skip and a jump rather than taking the perfectly functional tube.

Besides, this shift she'd had the good luck to be partnered with Steve Lund, and they'd been in the middle of a friendly argument about the latest fads in women's apparel when the call from the *Hali Sowle* had come in. As soon as the freighter starting moving, E.D. went back to the debate.

There were times she regretted Steve's sexual orientation. In some ways, he'd have made a better husband for her than the one she had. But it wasn't a perfect universe, after all.

❖   ❖   ❖

"Well, I'd say that went perfectly." Friede Butry sagged back in her seat a little. She'd been more tense than she'd needed to be, a phenomenon she ascribed to her advancing years. In her youth, she'd have thought nothing of taking risks far greater than this one had been.

"*À bientôt*, Anton and Victor. Good luck."

"What does that mean, Ganny? A ban-ban—" Brice Miller struggled with the unknown word. He was perched on one of the other seats on the freighter's command deck. Like everything else on the *Hali Sowle,* the seat—like Ganny's own—exhibited those characteristics which were euphemistically referred to as having seen better days.

"*Ah byan-toe.* It's French. It means 'see you later.' Well, more or less. Like most words in other languages, it doesn't translate perfectly neatly. Some people might translate it 'see you soon.'"

"How soon *will* we see them? And where did you learn to speak French?"

"Answering the questions in order, I have no idea when we'll see them again. Maybe never. But if you're asking what you *should* have been asking, we'll probably be back here in the Mesa system within ten days. Two weeks, at the outside, but I'd bet on the ten days. The variable is whether or not the Imbesi arrangements work as planned, and those people strike me as well organized. As for where I learned French . . ."

She pursed her lips, studying the astrogation screen. Looking at the screen, rather. Her mind was elsewhere.

"It's a long story, youngster."

"We got time. Tell me."

✧   ✧   ✧

"You've got cruddy tastes in clothes. Of course, I guess that's to be expected, growing up in Nouveau Paris."

"You should talk. Do you ever wear anything other than Scrag chic? Which seems to run entirely to leather."

"I look good in leather. Hey, that's an idea. Maybe we should try it."

"Don't be vulgar."

"I'm not vulgar, I'm bored. You are really lousy in bed."

"Of course I'm lousy in bed. I don't do anything. And that's hitting below the belt."

"Big deal. Far as I'd know, there's nothing down there anyway."

Anton heard a slight choking sound. At a guess, he thought Victor was trying to suppress a laugh. Fortunately, the momentary lapse was small enough that the scrambling equipment would disguise the slight break from what was supposed to be the body language of a couple having a quiet but rather fierce argument.

The equipment they had wasn't really *top* of the line. For that, they'd have needed Manticoran gear which could potentially cause trouble. But the stuff they'd obtained on the black market in Neue Rostock—Victor's contact Thiêu Chuanli was a veritable cornucopia of handy items—was plenty good enough for their purposes. The equipment not only protected against sound detection efforts, which any well-designed scrambling equipment would do, but it also produced just enough in the way of visual distortion to make lip-reading impossible and even interpreting body language all but impossible for any but a trained expert—and then, only if the people being interpreted were incapable of acting at all.

Victor Cachat, on the other hand, was a pretty decent actor. As you'd expect from a secret agent. And Yana had a natural flair for it.

They wouldn't have to keep it up for much longer, anyway. Anton was almost done. He kept his head down, concentrating on the personal com device in his hands. To any observer, the little not-so-dramatic scenario in the underground passageway would appear to consist of a couple having a quarrel, which their friend and companion was politely ignoring by taking care of some personal business while he waited for them to be done.

Unlike the scrambling equipment, the com device *was* top-of-the-line, cutting edge equipment. More precisely, it was bleeding edge equipment, specially designed for Anton by one of Manticore's top electronics firms, for a cost that was normally associated with the price of air cars, not personal handheld communication equipment.

Anton could afford it. Or, rather, Catherine Montaigne could afford it. Anton was stubborn about not relying on Cathy for his personal financial needs, but he didn't hesitate to tap into her enormous fortune when it came to his professional work.

"—you manage that, anyway?"

"Not my fault that you—"

Anton keyed in the final instructions. "We're just about done with the sandbox, kiddies," he murmured, loud enough for Victor and Yana to hear him.

That done, he slid the com into his pocket. He made no attempt to disguise the motion, or the device itself. He was just a man finishing some routine work. To anyone who examined it, the com unit would seem to be a perfectly normal if somewhat expensive item produced in the Solarian League. Only if someone really attempted to break into the device would they be able to discover otherwise—and, by then, the com unit's self-destruct mechanism would have been triggered and there'd be nothing to examine but a small pile of smoldering slag.

By the time he'd put away the com unit, Victor and Yana were embracing each other. Nothing passionate, just the sort of embrace with which a pair of lovers resolve a quarrel. Or, at any rate, end it for the moment.

"Okay," he said, almost as softly. "One more to go."

They walked off, the three of them side by side. There was plenty of room, since the underground passageway was more in the nature of a large open space. The area was primarily used for the storage of private vehicles.

"I'm sick of arguing with him," muttered Yana. "It's like trying to pick a fight with a rutabaga."

"Save it for the next stop, Yana," cautioned Anton.

"What's a rutabaga?" asked Victor.

✧　　✧　　✧

That night, in Anton's room—not the one he still maintained in the back of Turner's restaurant, but another one he'd obtained without using Saburo's contacts—he and Victor and Yana held another of the meetings they tried to hold at least every three days.

"It still seems like sorcery to me," Victor complained. "And spare me that tired old cliché about a sufficiently advanced technology being indistinguishable from magic. This is *not* all that advanced, damnation."

"Yes and no," said Anton. "The technology itself isn't especially advanced, true enough. State of the art is about the best you can say for it. But the specific programs that we developed are . . . I don't know if 'advanced' is the word I'd use. It's more like 'esoteric.' There just aren't very many people who work on this level of security programming, Victor. Sure, there are plenty of people who could have figured out how to bypass the security systems and implant false records, but so far as I know there are only two people in the whole galaxy who'd know how to prevent anyone from being able to detect that it was done afterward, even with a thorough investigation. One of them is named Anton Zilwicki and the other is Ruth Winton."

"Modest, isn't he?" said Yana. "At least he gave the woman some credit too."

Anton smiled. "In some ways, she's better at this that I am. The truth is, Ruth's reached the point where she's operating on a plane I don't even usually reach. I'm mostly acting as what you might call her crosscheck and rudder, these days. She's still prone to being over-confident."

Victor ran fingers through his hair. "And you're sure it'll work?"

"Yes. When we run—assuming we do, but we'd be fools not to count on it—we'll have left a completely false trail. Assuming you can get Carl Hansen and his people to take care of their end of the deal, so far as anyone on Mesa will ever be able to figure out, you and I and Yana exist only as scattered molecules."

Victor grunted. "The technical side of it's not a problem. That bomb will vaporize anything within two hundred meters. Whatever DNA traces they'd expect from a normal explosion will simply be too scattered to be usable, even with Mesan or Beowulfan techniques and equipment. The real problem is . . ."

He shook his head. "Let's just say that the people Saburo put us in contact with aren't as tightly wrapped as I'd like. They're not crazy, as such, but . . ."

"Fanatics," said Anton. "I do hope you notice that I didn't add any wisecrack such as 'and coming from Victor Cachat, that's saying something.'"

"Very funny. The problem is that tepid, wishy-washy people like you, whose commitment to anything beyond immediate personal matters is like mashed potatoes, just don't grasp all the fine distinctions between 'fanaticism' and 'fervor' and 'zeal.'"

Victor took a deep, slow breath. Not to control any anger—by now, the banter between him and Anton produced nothing more intense than occasional irritation—but to give himself time to try to figure out how to explain his concern.

"You just . . . don't really know, Anton. That's not a criticism, it's just an observation. From the time you were a kid, you lived in a world with wide horizons."

Zilwicki snorted. "Not usually the way the highlands of Gryphon are described!"

"Try growing up in a Dolist slum in Nouveau Paris. Trust me, Anton. The difference is huge. I'm not talking in terms of any scale of misery, mind you. I'm simply talking in terms of how narrow a view of the universe you're provided with. When I entered StateSec Academy, for all practical purposes I had no real knowledge of the universe beyond what I'd grown up with. Which wasn't much, believe me. That's . . ."

He paused for a moment. "I know a lot of people think I'm inclined toward zealotry. I suppose that's fair enough. What *has* changed, as the years have passed, is that my understanding of the universe has become . . . well, very large. So while I still retain the fundamental beliefs I had as a teenager, I can now put those beliefs in a much better context. I can, for instance, spend hours discussing politics with Web Du Havel—as I have, any number of times—listening to his basically conservative views without automatically dismissing those views as the self-serving prattle of an elitist."

Anton smiled. "Web just doesn't fit that pigeonhole, does he?"

"No, he doesn't. And while I still disagree with Web—for the most part, though by no means always—I do understand why he thinks the way he does. To put it another way, my view of things hasn't changed all that much, but it's no longer monochromatic. Does that make sense?"

Anton nodded. "Yes, it does."

"All right. If my view of the world was monochromatic, growing up in a Nouveau Paris slum under the Legislaturist regime, try to imagine just how little there is in the way of subtle shadings for a young man or woman who grew up here, as a seccy under the thumb of the Mesan regime."

Anton couldn't help but wince.

"Yeah," said Victor. "*That's* the problem, Anton. It's not that these kids are too fanatical. Frankly, I don't blame them one damn bit for their zeal and fervor. The problem is that they see everything in black and white. Forget the colors of the spectrum. They don't even recognize the color gray, much less any of its various shades."

A frown had been gathering on Yana's forehead, as she listened. "I don't get it, Victor. Why do you care in the first place? It's not as if you have any doubts any longer about their loyalties or dedication. Unless you've changed your mind over the last two days."

He shook his head. "It's not that I don't trust *them*. It's that I don't entirely trust their *judgment*. Let's not forget how close they've come already to compromising our mission. To put it mildly."

Anton leaned back in his chair at the kitchen table, and considered Victor's words. He understood what was concerning the

Havenite agent. The small group of young seccies with whom they'd established a relationship, using the liaisons provided by Saburo's contacts, had been very helpful. They provided Anton and Victor with natives who knew the area extremely well, especially Neue Rostock. And they could also provide Anton and Victor with the assistance they might need in the future, depending on the way things developed.

Furthermore, while they were young, and suffered from the haphazard education that all seccies received, they were very far from dull-witted or incapable. To Anton and Victor's surprise, for instance, when the group had been asked to provide them with a powerful explosive device, they'd proudly presented them a few days later with a low-yield nuclear device. Nothing jury-rigged either. The device was a standard construction type used in ter-raforming, designed and built by a well-known Solarian company. The best Anton and Victor had expected had been something chemical and homemade.

He chuckled. "That was quite a scene, wasn't it? Funny—well, sort of—now that it's over."

"Impressive," said Anton, gazing down on the nuclear demolition device. He was doing his best not to let his surprise show.

Enough of it must have shown, though, to cause the chests of the young firebrands gathered in the basement of a modest seccy home to swell with pride. Their informal leader Carl Hansen said: "A cousin of—well, never mind the details—told us he could get his hands on one of them."

Anton nodded. He didn't want to know the details, anyway. "How'd you disable the locator beacon?"

Hansen's face went blank. He and the other youngsters in the room—David Pritchard, Cary Condor and Karen Steve Williams— exchanged glances.

"What's a locator beacon?" asked Williams.

Victor leaned away from the device—fat lot of good that would do!—and whistled soundlessly. He looked even paler than usual. Anton was pretty sure his own face looked about the same.

Moving carefully—fat lot of good that would do!—he pulled the com out of his pocket. A quick scanning search of the nuclear device yielded the port he needed.

For something like this, Anton wanted a physical connection.

So he pulled out the rarely-used cable attachment and plugged it into the port.

"What are you doing?" asked Cory.

"He's going to disable—*try* to disable—the locator beacon," Cachat said tonelessly. "Hopefully, before anyone in charge finds out the device isn't where it's supposed to be."

A bit of irritation crept into his tone: "Did you honestly think Mesans—hell, anybody—let nuclear explosive devices roam around loose?"

"Please be quiet, everyone," said Anton. "This is . . . really quite tricky."

He heard Victor suck in a little air. Coming from him, that was the equivalent of someone else shrieking *My God—doom is almost certain!* Cachat knew what a genuine expert Zilwicki was when it came to these things. If *he* admitted it was . . . *really quite tricky* . . .

Complete silence proved to be too much for the youngsters. "You mean . . . they can figure out where the thing is?" whispered Pritchard.

"To within three meters, as a rule," said Victor. He was back to speaking tonelessly. "At which point they have several options, although they'll probably settle for one of the first two."

Pritchard's eyes—quite wide they were, at the moment—stared at him appealingly, and Victor shrugged.

"First, they can send out the elite commando unit to retrieve it, with lots of very big, very nasty, and *very* efficient guns. Plenty to"—he gave the basement a quick scan—"well, to give all the walls down here a nice even coating of new paint. The color known colloquially as BGB. Blood, guts and brains." He smiled ever so slightly at his *extremely* attentive young audience. It was not a pleasant expression. "Or, second, they can detonate the device. True, that second option's usually a bit extreme, but they might not really care a lot about that. Especially if they figure out who's *got* the damned thing."

"What part of 'this is really quite tricky' did I not make clear?" Anton said crossly.

Finally, blessedly, silence fell. And, perhaps three minutes later, Anton succeeded in disabling the beacon. In a perfect world, he'd have reprogrammed the beacon to simulate a legitimate location. But there were simply too many unknown factors to risk doing that, here. They'd just have to hope that no one had spotted the device "wandering" over the past period. If they hadn't, they wouldn't spot the missing device now until a complete physical inventory was made. Fortunately, that didn't usually happen more than once a year, even with devices as potentially dangerous as these. Modern locator beacons were so accurate, reliable and tamper-resistant that people usually just relied on a periodic check of the beacons themselves.

And, also, fortunately, most people tended to equate "tamper-resistant" with "tamper-proof." Being fair, there really weren't very many people in the galaxy who could have done what Anton had just done.

✧　　✧　　✧

On the positive side, the incident had solidified Anton and Victor's credentials with their local contacts faster and more surely than probably anything else would have done. But the same capability the youngsters had shown, when coupled to their ignorance of so many things and the narrow viewpoint Victor was describing . . .

Anton made a face. "You're worried they'll go off half-cocked."

Victor shrugged. "Not exactly. They're not fools, far from it. I'm mostly worried that, first, they'll slip on security. To really do counterespionage properly you need to be patient and methodical more than anything else. That's . . . not their strength. So I think they're more open to being penetrated than they think they are. Second, I'm worried that if things do start to come apart, they're more likely to react by helping the process than trying to dodge it, if you know what I mean. Especially some of them—like David Pritchard. Who was just assigned the task of handling the device, if we need it."

Anton grimaced again. He hadn't attended the last meeting of the group. ("The group" was the only name they had. In that, at least, showing more of a sense for security than they did in other ways.) The decision to put Pritchard in charge of the device must have been made there.

There wasn't anything *wrong* with David Pritchard, exactly. But Victor and Anton both sensed that the youngster had a level of quiet yet corrosive fury that might lead him off a cliff, in the right circumstances.

But . . .

There really wasn't anything they could do about it. It wasn't as if he and Victor had any real control of the group. Even its nominal leader, Carl Hansen, was no more than a first among equals.

"We'll just have to live with it. To be honest, Victor, I'm more worried at the moment about your situation with Inez Cloutier. Realistically, how much longer can you stall her?" He squinted a little. "You *have,* I trust, given up any idea of accepting employment?"

Victor sighed. "Yes, yes, yes. The voice of caution has prevailed. Although I hate to think what I'll be passing up."

For a moment, his expression had a trace of wistful sorrow. The sort of expression with which a normal and reasonable young man half-regrets his decision not to pursue a possible romantic involvement. On Victor Cachat's face, the expression signified his regret at not undertaking the harrowing risk of accepting employment with a rogue ex-StateSec military force, being dispatched to places unknown and with no way to get free that either he or Anton could figure out.

"You'd have to be crazy to even think about it," said Yana. "And keep in mind that assessment is coming from a former Scrag."

Victor smiled, then ran fingers through his hair again. "We've got a bit of luck, there. Cloutier got called off-planet yesterday. At a guess, she's got to go consult with whoever is running this operation. I'm almost certain now that that's Adrian Luff, by the way."

Anton nodded. He and Victor had tentatively come to that conclusion a few days earlier, based on what Victor had been able to find out in the course of his negotiations with Cloutier.

Adrian Luff...

That was mostly bad news, according to Victor. Zilwicki really had no opinion of his own. He'd recognized the name from his days working for Manticoran naval intelligence, but that was about it.

Cachat knew more about him, as you'd expect, although he'd never actually met the man. According to Victor, Luff wasn't an especially brutal or harsh man, certainly not by StateSec standards. He'd scarcely been what a professional Manticoran or Havenite naval officer would have thought of as a fleet commander, but at least he'd had a far better idea than most of his SS fellows about which end of the tube the missile came out of. And while no StateSec officer assigned to ride herd on the People's Navy was likely to be a total novice where brutality and discipline was concerned, Luff had understood that breaking a man's spirit wasn't the best way to produce a warrior when you needed one.

That might speak well of the man, but Anton would have been a lot happier if this rogue StateSec military force—which was a very powerful one; he and Victor had been able to learn that much for sure and certain—had as its commander someone like Emile Tresca. Tresca, at one time the commandant of StateSec's prison planet, had been notorious for his viciousness and sadism. On the other hand, nobody in their right mind would have put him in charge of a frigate, much less an entire fleet.

"When will she be back?"

Victor shrugged. "No way to know for sure, but I get the distinct feeling it won't be very soon. If I'm right and she was summoned to meet with Luff, this is just one more little indication that wherever Luff's assembling that fleet of his, it's not that close to Mesa."

"But probably quite close to Torch," Anton said grimly. "Victor . . . I have to raise this again. I think we need to consider whether we should leave now, and bring the news of this threat back to Torch. You know and I know that Luff's planning to ignore the Eridani Edict."

"That's not actually certain yet," Victor said mildly. "I get the sense that Luff's resistant to the idea. But . . . yes, it's clear enough from the sort of questions Cloutier asked me. Part of the reason they're being so cautious about hiring people for any sort of high-level positions, it seems pretty obvious, is because Luff and his people think there's a good chance they'll be galactic pariahs before too long."

He got up and began walking about, just to stretch a little. The kitchen in the apartment was too small for him to be able to walk more than three paces. Still, they'd been sitting for hours. Anton was tempted to get up himself and join him—except there wouldn't be room. The kitchen was excessively narrow as well as small.

"I've thought about it, Anton. But I still think it'd be a mistake—and, yes, I know I'll be cursing myself for the rest of my life if we get back and find that Torch is a cinder because everyone was caught by surprise. But, first, I don't think they will be.

There's simply no way for an operation of this size to be mounted without tripping some alarm wires somewhere. You have just as high an opinion of Rozsak's chief of intelligence as I do. I don't think there's much chance that Jiri Watanapongse hasn't figured out what's happening yet. Neither do you."

He paused in his pacing. "And that's really all that's involved, isn't it? Just bringing a warning? It's not as if either you or I would be any help on Torch, even if we got back in time to meet the attack. That'll be a naval brawl, pure and simple. And if neither Maya nor Erewhon comes to Torch's aid"—here, his expression got very bleak—"then about all that'll be left to do is wreak whatever vengeance we can."

He started pacing again. "On the other hand, if we stay here, we have a real chance of making a lot of progress on any number of fronts. Just for starters . . ."

Anton glanced at the clock on the wall. They'd been at it for almost three hours, and it was now clear they wouldn't be ending any time soon.

"Sit down, Victor," he said. "Give someone else a chance to stretch a little."

"Yeah," said Yana. "Me first."

CHAPTER FORTY-SIX

"Sit down, Lajos," Jack McBryde invited. "Take a load off. How does a cup of coffee sound?"

"Coffee sounds good," Lajos Irvine replied. He smiled as he said it, yet there was a slight—very slight, perhaps, but undeniable—edge to his response, and McBryde reminded himself not to grimace.

Irvine wore the traditional gray smock of a general laborer genetic slave. The smock's shoulder carried the stylized image of a cargo shuttle, which marked its wearer as a ground crewman at the Green Pines shuttle port, and the three chevrons above the shuttle marked him as a senior supervisor—in effect, a trustee. Irvine had the heavyset, muscular build to go with that smock, and if he'd cared to open his mouth and display it, his tongue carried the barcode of a slave, as well. In fact, physically, he *was* a slave—or, at least, clearly the product of a slave-bred genotype. Except, of course, for the fact that unlike real genetic slaves, he had the enhanced lifespan of a gamma line.

It was a fact which the Alignment's star lines seldom discussed, even among themselves, that genetically, they were much more closely related to Manpower's slaves than they were to the vast majority of humanity. For centuries, the slave lines had been the laboratories of the Long-Range Planning Board—the place where newly designed traits could be field-tested, tried out, and then either culled or incorporated into those same star lines and conserved. The LRPB had been careful to work from far behind the scenes, even (or, perhaps, especially) within the Manpower

413

hierarchy, but its access to Manpower's breeding programs had always been a major factor in its successes.

One consequence of that was that even the Alignment's alpha and beta lines shared a whole host of genetic markers with Manpower's slaves. None of those slaves had ever received the entire package of one of the star lines, of course, just as none of them had received prolong, yet there was an undeniably close relationship between them.

That relationship helped the Alignment's penetration of the slave community as a whole, too. Irvine was an example of that, given how little modification his basic genotype had required to suit him for his role. There were never as many deep-penetration agents of his type as Alignment Security might have wished, but that was the result of a conscious policy decision, not of any inherent limitation on the number of *potential* agents. There'd been the occasional discussion of increasing the numbers of agents like Lajos, especially as the Audubon Ballroom had grown in sophistication and audacity. There were those (and he knew Steven Lathorous was one of them) who believed the Ballroom's capabilities were reaching the point of genuinely threatening to uncover the truth of the Alignment's existence. The people who felt that way were most likely to press for the creation of additional deep-penetrators, yet however cogent their arguments might be, the considerations of the Alignment's "onion strategy" continued to preclude the possibility. The Alignment had always relied on misdirection, stealth—on not being noticed in the first place, rather than building the sort of rockhard firewalls which were likely to attract the very attention it sought so assiduously to avoid.

Ironically, the limited numbers of available deep-penetration agents was part of what had made them so successful for so long. Not even Manpower knew that some of its "slaves" were nothing of the sort. That had made life hard for quite a few of Irvine's predecessors and fellows. In fact, the conditions of their "slavery" had cost more than one of them his life along the way, despite everything the Alignment's penetration of Manpower's bureaucracy had been able to do to protect them. But it also meant their security was absolute. *No one* outside their controls and handlers even dreamed of their existence, and keeping things that way meant holding their total numbers down to something manageable. The Ballroom was aware of the dangers of counter-penetration of course. There'd always been some of that, just as there would always be human beings who could be bribed—or coerced by terror and threats against those they loved—to spy upon their fellows. At least some of the Alignment's agents had been identified as exactly that, over the years, and paid the price the Ballroom exacted from traitors. Yet all of them had died without anyone ever realizing who—and what—they actually were.

Which, to be honest, was one of the reasons McBryde and Lathorous found Irvine's constant efforts to escape his current assignment particularly irritating. McBryde could sympathize with the fact that living a slave's life wasn't going to be especially pleasant under any circumstances, but at least Irvine's present duties were downright cushy compared to what some of his fellows had suffered—or to what they were enduring at this very moment, for that matter.

McBryde gave himself a mental shake, climbed out of his chair, and personally poured the man a cup of coffee. Brooding on Irvine's unhappiness and how much less happy the man could have been wasn't going to accomplish much. Besides, in some ways it resonated too closely for comfort with his own unhappiness.

"So," he said, handing the cup across and parking himself on the edge of his desk with a deliberate air of informality, "is there anything going on out there I should know about?"

"I don't think so," Irvine replied. He took a sip of coffee, obviously savoring it as much because McBryde had fetched it for him as for its richness, then lowered the cup and grimaced.

"That batch of malcontents I reported to you and Lathorous a couple of months ago is still simmering away," he said. "Hansen's group. And I'm positive now that the Ballroom's managed to make at least peripheral contact with them."

"It has?"

McBryde's eyes narrowed, and he considered buzzing Steven Lathorous. His friend's more recent operational experience might be useful if Irvine was right. He started to reach for his com, but then stopped. Steve really loathed Irvine, he reminded himself, and he was already recording the interview. He could always show Steve the record, if it seemed necessary. For that matter, they could haul Irvine back in again if they needed to.

"I'm pretty sure it has," Irvine said in answer to his question.

"I know the theory is that it's better to keep an eye on known points of contact. I even agree with that, more or less. But I'd really like to have this particular group at least broken up, if not eliminated outright."

"Why?" McBryde asked, watching him intently.

Irvine was right about Alignment Security's basic policy. Not surprisingly, the Ballroom's efforts to penetrate Mesa were unceasing. It would have been amazing if they hadn't been, and given the percentage of the planetary population which consisted of genetic slaves, the opportunity for that sort of effort was obvious. Despite that, the Ballroom had never managed any high level penetration. Part of that, McBryde admitted less than totally happily, was because of the brutal efficiency of the official Mesan security apparatus. He was just as happy not to be associated with that apparatus himself, yet he had to admit that sheer brutality and terror could be effective ways of cowing potential rebels.

Those same techniques, however, also *produced* rebels, and those were the people the Ballroom looked for. They were also the people Alignment Security's deep-penetration agents looked for, as well, and once they'd been found, it was far more efficient and effective to watch them—to let them attract other potential rebels into identified little clusters. Eventually, of course, any given cluster would probably reach a point at which it was sufficiently large and sufficiently well organized to become a genuine threat, at which point it would have to be eliminated. Until that point was reached, though, it was better to know who to be watching than to eliminate them and start over from scratch again and again.

"Why do I think they should be broken up? Or why do I want them eliminated?" Irvine asked in response to his own question.

"Both."

"Well, I guess it's really the same reason for both. I'm starting to think they're better organized than I originally thought they were, and, like I say, they're obviously in at least loose contact with the Ballroom." He shrugged. "The fact that they're better organized makes me wonder what else I might have missed about them, who else might be in contact with them. And the fact that they've established at least some contact with the Ballroom suggests they might actually manage to pull off some kind of sabotage operation. Maybe even an assassination or two."

"Directed here? At the Center?" McBryde asked more sharply, and Irvine shook his head.

"Except for the fact that you're under a tower that might have one or two offices they'd consider targets, I don't think the Center's in any kind of danger. There's absolutely no indication anyone in the slave community even suspects the Center exists, much less that anyone might be planning an attack on it. Believe me, if I saw any sign of that, I'd be in here in a heartbeat! No, I'm thinking more about managing to pick off a Manpower executive, or maybe blow up a Manpower or Jessyk office . . . along with its staff."

McBryde relaxed a bit, but he also nodded in understanding. The Ballroom's successes against Manpower throughout the explored galaxy could scarcely be kept a secret from the slave population of Mesa. The number of those successes in the Mesa System itself was minuscule, however, and the authorities had managed to suppress knowledge even of some of the Ballroom's successful efforts. Alignment Security found itself in general agreement with the normal planetary security forces in that regard, too. Enheartening the spirit of rebellion among the planetary slave population by allowing successful attacks here in the home system wouldn't be in any one's interests.

"What makes you so positive they *are* in active contact with the Ballroom?" he asked after a moment. "It's not that I doubt your judgment," he added hastily, as Irvine's eyebrows lowered. "I just want a breakdown on the evidence so I'll have a better appreciation of the situation."

"Well," Irvine's expression eased, "there've been quite a few little things over the last few months. But the kicker, as far as I'm concerned, is that two new people have turned up. And neither of them is a sutler. In fact, neither of them is a seccy."

"Ringers from outside, you mean?" McBryde asked with a frown.

"I mean two people I've never seen before at all, hanging around with Carl Hansen and his group. One of them is working as a waiter in Steph Turner's restaurant."

"Who's she?"

Lajos waved his hand dismissively. "Just a woman who owns a small restaurant that caters to the seccy trade. Divorced, one kid, a teenage daughter. I've never mentioned her before, as I recall, since I don't think she's more than vaguely connected to the underground, if she's even connected at all."

McBryde nodded. Given the fact that slaves made up sixty percent of Mesa's population and seccies made up another ten percent, the anti-slavery underground was vast and extensive. For the most part, the underground concentrated on activities that were not directly threatening to the Mesan order: smuggling slaves out and contraband in; maintaining a network of social services that made up to a degree for the lack of such services provided by the government; and so forth. Only a small percentage of the underground's members had direct and close ties to the Ballroom or engaged in violent activities. If Lajos had been in the habit of reporting every seccy who had any connection at all to the underground or even the Ballroom, neither he nor Jack would ever be able to get any sleep. You had to be practical about these things.

"But it's the other one that mostly makes me twitchy. He's a Havenite. Claims to be a former StateSec agent, and seems to have the credentials for it."

McBryde frowned thoughtfully. "What would an ex-StateSec be doing hanging around with that group you're watching?"

"Good question. The waiter might just be another malcontent, although I'm almost sure he's not a seccy—or an ex-slave of any kind, for that matter. I haven't been able to get that close to him, so I haven't seen his tongue or gotten any DNA samples. But he's got a very pronounced and unusual phenotype, and it's nothing like any line we've ever developed. Not that I'm familiar with, anyway. But the StateSec guy . . ."

Lajos took a sip of his coffee. "For starters, there doesn't seem to be any question that he's legitimate. Meaning, his background is in fact what he claims it to be. I know for a fact that Cloutier is eager to pick him up—eager enough that she's been willing to dicker terms with the guy for some time now."

McBryde's eyebrows went up. Luff's top recruiting agent didn't handle run-of-the-mill hiring. Still, he couldn't recall any instance where Inez Cloutier had allowed a prospective contractor to dicker for more than a couple of days. Admittedly, Jack hadn't tried to keep entirely on top of that situation.

"In short," Lajos concluded, "one of them is definitely from outside the system and the other—the waiter, that is—could very well be. And regardless of their origins, I can't think of any legitimate reason either one of them would have any contact with Hansen's group. I'm thinking one or both is likely to be a Ballroom agent. Pulling them in and breaking them could give us an additional peek inside the Ballroom's plans where Mesa is concerned."

"Not all that likely, though," McBryde observed, and Irvine grunted in sour agreement.

They might have kept Ballroom agents from establishing any significant presence here on the planet, but Ballroom operatives seldom provided anything useful in the way of information, either. Partly because the Ballroom understood operational security at least as well as anyone else in the galaxy. It compartmentalized information tightly, and it applied the "need-to-know" rule ruthlessly. More than that, any of its operatives who possessed truly sensitive knowledge were also provided with the means for reliable self-termination. More than one of them had chosen surgically implanted explosive devices, which had taken their share of security personnel with them over the years.

"I didn't say it was likely," Irvine said. "I only said it *could* give us some extra information."

"Have you managed to pick up anything else about them? Anything more than just the fact that we don't know who they are, I mean?"

"Not a damned thing," Irvine admitted frankly. "I did get a few images of them, though. These are from the one and only time I ever spotted the two of them together in the same place. The StateSec guy seems to be having breakfast in the same restaurant where the waiter works. Here."

He reached into the neck of his smock and flipped across a chip folio. McBryde caught it, extracted the single chip inside it, and inserted it into his desk computer. It took a moment for the computer's internal security systems to decide the data on the chip was acceptable, and then a holo image of two men appeared above his desk.

He gazed at them curiously. Whatever the StateSec man's purpose might be, if Irvine's suspicion that the other one also came from outside the Mesa System had any validity, then the waiter wasn't a seccy at all, even though he was working for one. McBryde had always wondered what went on inside the heads of escaped genetic slaves who voluntarily walked straight back into the lion's den. Unlike some of his fellows, he'd always respected their courage, and of late he'd begun to understand the kind of personal outrage which motivated many of them far better than he'd ever understood it before. Still—

His thoughts slithered to a halt. Somehow—he never knew how—he managed to keep his eyes from widening or his jaw dropping, but it was hard.

It can't be, his brain insisted quietly. *Not here. Not even those two would be ballsy enough!*

Yet even as his brain insisted, he knew better. The one sitting at a table was a thoroughly unremarkable-looking, almost slightly built young fellow. If Jack hadn't been told he was a Havenite, he would have assumed that the man was descended from any of several general laborer lines. But the other . . . At a glance, you might assume the other was obviously descended from a *heavy* labor line. But Jack knew Irvine was right. This was no line ever developed by Manpower. The guy was simply much too short for that incredible physique. When Manpower developed a line specifically for muscular power, they made them big all around. It would have been foolish not to do so, as a practical matter, and probably even genetically difficult.

McBryde studied the images, concentrating on the waiter. The facial features were different, but that could be done any number of ways. The things that were much harder to disguise . . . The coloring, that massive neck, that tilt of the head, those incredibly broad shoulders, like some dwarven mountain king—or troll . . . those McBryde recognized. Recognized because he'd seen them so recently, in a broad-distribution, priority memo, and he wondered how Irvine could possibly *not* have recognized them.

Because he never got the memo, he realized almost instantly. *He's at too low a level, and it never would have occurred to anyone to look right here, on Mesa itself. The only reason Steve and I ever saw the memo was that it was distributed to everyone above Level Twelve, and Lajos isn't routinely cleared for anything above Level Three unless it's specifically related to his current assignment.*

"Well," he said out loud, "*I* don't recognize them." He chuckled. "On the other hand, I don't suppose they'd send anyone they expect us to be able to pick out of a lineup, now would they?"

McBryde killed the images. "I'll pass it around, Lajos, but don't get your hopes up." It was his turn to shrug. "I don't imagine we're going to get a direct hit on the imagery, even assuming these two were stupid enough to come in without at least trying to disguise themselves. And, frankly, I'm inclined to doubt that anyone higher up the chain is going to authorize taking out the entire group, either. In fact, if they are in contact with the Ballroom, the decision's probably going to be that that very fact makes keeping an eye on them and seeing what they do even more important."

"I know." Irvine sighed. "I can hope, though."

"Oh, we can *always* hope," McBryde agreed. "We can always hope."

CHAPTER FORTY-SEVEN

It's been too damned long since you were operational, Jack McBryde told himself nervously. *And you were never as good at this sort of thing as Steve is, anyway.*

The thought was unfortunately accurate, but there wasn't a lot he could do about it. Except, of course, to forget the entire insane idea and hand his suspicions over to Isabel Bardasano the way he was damned well supposed to.

But that wasn't going to happen. If it had been, he wouldn't be sitting here in a back corner of a so-called eatery of the sort which was still known as "a greasy spoon," nursing a spectacularly bad cup of coffee and watching flies buzz through the overhead clouds of sleep-weed smoke. That smoke was so thick he was frankly amazed the flies didn't simply nose dive out of it and smack into the tabletop in a drugged stupor.

He grimaced at the thought, but there was some truth to it. Enough, in fact, that he'd been careful to inhale the nanotech busy scavenging the stuff out of his own bloodstream as quickly as it got there. Sleep weed, also known as "old sleepy" and just plain "weed," was one of the Mesan slave labor force's intoxicants of choice. It was more addictive than alcohol (for most people, at least), yet it was also less expensive, and it didn't produce a hangover. With persistent use (and most of its users smoked it very heavily), it *did* produce some nasty respiratory problems, but that usually took several decades. Given the fact that very few genetic slaves lived much more than five or six decades, total, it was scarcely a pressing concern for the slaves who smoked it.

McBryde took another sip of tepid coffee, then followed that with another bite from the sugarcoated doughnut he'd ordered to go with it. About the only thing he could say for the doughnut was that it was better than the coffee and probably not *actively* poisonous. Or not, at least, sufficiently poisonous to pose a threat to an alpha's enhanced physiology.

He hoped. At least the silverware was clean.

"Need a refill?" an extraordinarily deep voice rumbled, and McBryde forced himself not to twitch.

He glanced up with exactly (or, at least, what he hoped like hell was exactly) the right degree of disinterest at the massively built "waiter." He'd been hoping that if he only drank enough of the diner's truly atrocious coffee, this particular waiter would eventually come close enough. Now that the moment had come, however, he felt his pulse speeding up. At the same time, a little to his surprise, he felt his professionalism kicking in, as well, including his trained ear. He'd heard recordings of this man's natural accent, and he was privately amazed by how well the other had managed to turn his normal buzz-saw burr into the guttural yet still far softer accent of the Mesan slave underclass.

"Sure," he said casually, hoping that his own accent was equally convincing. He held out his cup, watching the waiter top it off, then raised his other hand, index finger extended in a "wait a minute" gesture.

"Something else?" The waiter arched one eyebrow, his expression calm, and McBryde nodded. "What can I get you?" the other man asked, setting down the coffee pot to pull his battered order pad out of his pocket and key the screen.

"Something from off-world," McBryde said softly.

The waiter didn't even twitch. His shoulders didn't tense; his eyes didn't narrow; his expression didn't even flicker. He was good, McBryde thought, but, then, he'd already known that. Just as he knew that at this particular instant his own life hung by the proverbial thread.

"I think you're in the wrong place for that," the waiter replied in obvious amusement. "In this joint, we're lucky to get our hands on *local* produce that doesn't poison the customers!"

"Oh, I don't doubt that." McBryde snorted with an edge of what he was astonished to discover was genuine amusement. "On the other hand, I wasn't thinking about the menu . . . Captain Zilwicki."

"Then you're *really* in the wrong place," the waiter said calmly. It wasn't a calm McBryde found particularly reassuring, but he made himself smile and twitch the extended index finger in a cautionary sort of way.

"Actually, I'm not," keeping his own voice low enough to avoid being overheard yet loud enough—and steady enough—to project a confidence he was actually quite some way from feeling. "I came here to speak to you . . . or to Agent Cachat, if you'd prefer."

Anton Zilwicki's eyes narrowed—minutely—at last, and his right hand shifted ever so slightly on his order pad.

"Before you attempt to twist my head off like a bottle cap—probably with a degree of success I'd regret—" McBryde continued, "consider your situation. I'm sure you and Agent Cachat have several alternative escape strategies, and it's entirely possible that several of my fellow 'customers' would be delighted to help you slit my throat before taking your leisurely and well-planned leave. On the other hand, I wouldn't be sitting here running the risk of your doing exactly that if I hadn't taken a few precautions of my own, now would I? And if it should happen that I'm wired, then whoever's at the other end of the link already knows what's going on here, doesn't he? Which, presumably, means my backup—assuming, of course, that I was clever enough to arrange one—would undoubtedly arrive before my lifeless body hit the floor. So before either of us does anything the other one would regret, why don't you and I talk for a moment."

"While we waste enough time for your goons to close in, you mean?" Zilwicki inquired calmly.

"If my 'goons' were planning on closing in on you, Captain, I'd for damn sure have had them do it before I sat here in arm's length of you and blew the whistle on myself, now wouldn't I?"

"The thought had crossed my mind. So since we're being so civilized and all, just what is it you *do* want?"

"I want to talk," McBryde replied, expression and tone both suddenly dead serious. "I'd prefer to talk to both you and Agent Cachat simultaneously, but I'd be very surprised if the two of you were willing to run that sort of risk. I'd also like to talk to you now, if possible, but no matter how good your security is—and, by the way, it's actually pretty damned good—I don't think we need to be seen having a tête-à-tête right here in front of everybody."

Zilwicki considered him thoughtfully for a moment or two, then slid the order pad back into his pocket. To McBryde's considerable relief, when his hand came back out of the pocket it didn't bring a lethal weapon with it. On the other hand, Anton Zilwicki didn't exactly need *artificial* lethal instruments to deal with most problems likely to come his way.

"Two minutes," he said. "Drink some more coffee, then amble down the hallway. Outside the men's room, turn left. Take the 'Employees Only' door."

He nodded, turned, and walked calmly away.

McBryde pushed open the old-fashioned, unpowered swinging door and stepped through it. He'd fully expected to be looking down the muzzle of a pulser when he did, but instead he found himself in what clearly passed for a staff break room. At the moment, it was empty, aside from the single massively built man seated at its single battered table with a cup of coffee.

"Sit," Anton Zilwicki invited, pointing at the chair opposite him across the table. McBryde obeyed the one-word command, and Zilwicki slid a second cup of coffee across to him.

"This is better than the crap we have to serve out there," he said, this time making no effort to hide his Gryphon accent. "Of course, it could be laced with all sorts of deadly poisons. Would you like me to take a sip first?"

"Why?" McBryde smiled crookedly. "If I were going to poison me, I'd've taken the antidote first myself, then put the poison in *both* cups."

He accepted the coffee and—not without an internal qualm or two, despite his own words—sipped. It really was much better than the brew served to the diner's patrons.

Assuming of course that it *wasn't* poisoned, after all.

"All right," Zilwicki said, leaning back in a chair which creaked alarmingly under his weight, "now that we've both established our professionalism, suppose you tell me what it is you wanted to talk about."

"First, let me point out a couple of things," McBryde said. "As I already mentioned, if all I wanted was to get my hands on you and Cachat, I wouldn't need any elaborate tricks to pull that off. Or, rather, my chances of success would probably be higher just going straight after you and the diner in a brute force kind of way. Or, for that matter, waiting until you return to your quarters this evening and pouncing then. In other words, it will save both of us a lot of time and wasted effort if we just start out assuming that I really do want to *talk*, and that I'm not baiting some kind of incredibly devious trap by coming here."

"Speaking purely theoretically, I can more or less accept that," Zilwicki replied. "Of course, there's no telling what kind of devious strategy—other than getting your hands on me and my associates, that is—you might have in mind."

"Of course," McBryde acknowledged. "And, as it happens, I do have a strategy in mind. I don't know that I'd call it 'devious,' but I do rather suspect that it's going to come as a surprise to you."

"I'm not especially fond of surprises." There was an undeniable note of warning in Zilwicki's deep voice, McBryde noticed.

"This one might be the exception to your rule, Captain," he replied calmly. "You see, I want to defect."

CHAPTER FORTY-EIGHT

"Well, I guess that's about the best we're going to be able to do," Luiz Rozsak said. He leaned back in his chair to arch his spine and rubbed his eyes with the thumb and forefinger of his left hand while his right hand cradled his coffee cup. "It's not perfect, but then again, nothing ever is, is it?"

He lowered his left hand to grin crookedly at Edie Habib, Dirk-Steven Kamstra, Laura Raycraft, David Carte, J.T. Cullingford, Melanie Stensrud, and Anne Warwick.

"I believe this is the point where my loyal minions are supposed to say 'Nothing except your brilliant battle plans, Sir!'"

"Well, Admiral," Habib replied for the others, "given our keen awareness of the aforesaid brilliance, we realize full well that, despite our best efforts to conceal it—so as to avoid embarrassing you, you understand—you must already be aware of the veneration, awe, and near idolatrous reverence with which we regard our fearless leader."

A chorus of chuckles ran around the table in Kamstra's flag bridge briefing room, and, for just a moment, Rozsak's grin would have looked quite at home on any urchin's face. And not just because he was amused, either. It was also a beaming smile (or as close to one as he ever permitted himself to come) of pure delight. He treasured those chuckles—and their proof of his subordinates' confidence and morale—like a miser might cherish diamonds or rubies.

Especially since every one of them knew that, in almost every way that counted, any defense of the Torch System they might mount would represent their own personal Rubicon. They might—*might*—get away with no one back on Old Earth noticing anything *this* time, but that wouldn't really matter in the longer term.

He took a sip of coffee, then let himself come back upright and regarded all of them with a considerably more serious expression.

"I genuinely do think this is the best we're going to be able to nail things down," he said. "If any one has any reservations at all—or if there's something you think we should revisit—this is the time to bring it up."

The others looked at one another, and then all of the ship commanders looked at Habib. Several eyebrows were raised, as if inviting the chief of staff to bring up anything *they* might have forgotten, but she only looked back and shook her head. Then she turned to Rozsak.

"I'm not saying something *won't* come up during the exercises, Sir. With that proviso and sheet anchor, though, I'd have to say I agree with your assessment. It's *not* perfect, but the tactical problem's got too many nasty pointy things growing out of it for 'perfect.' We've done our best to disaster-proof things, though, and I think it'll get the job done."

She was right about the thorniness of the situation, Rozsak reflected. It wasn't that any single one of his objectives here in Torch was all that complicated. It was simply that some of them were fundamentally incompatible.

First and foremost, there was the need to protect the planet itself. And it was entirely too likely—indeed, a virtual certainty as far as he, Habib, and Watanapongse were concerned—that the StateSec outlaws Manpower had recruited had no interest at all in putting "boots on the ground."

Manpower didn't want its ex-slaves back, especially after they'd enjoyed such a taste of freedom and vengeance. No, what Manpower *wanted* was to see Torch erased from the face of the galaxy, preferably in a way which would thoroughly discourage any future, similarly uppity thoughts on the part of its property. And the Eridani Edict's prohibition of deliberate, genocidal attacks on planetary populations was aimed at star nations—which knew the Solarian League Navy would come to call on them if they violated its restrictions. Since Manpower *wasn't* a star nation, and there was no legal mechanism for the Solarian League Navy to go after a non-Solarian *corporation*, the Edict was a moot point as far as it was concerned. And since its mercenaries represented a force which no longer *had* a star nation to call its own, the actual officers and crews carrying out the operations wouldn't be particularly concerned by the Edict, either. All of which meant the attackers would probably settle for pasting the planet with a few "accidental" cee-fractional missile strikes. A half-dozen hundred-ton missiles hitting the planet at sixty percent or so of light-speed should pretty much pasteurize its ecosystem and anyone living in it. Forty-gigaton-range fireballs tended to have that effect.

Which, in turn, meant providing enough missile defense close to the planet to keep that from happening.

Rozsak's second objective was, while accomplishing the first one, to suffer as few casualties of his own as possible. That meant using his range and maneuver advantages to the full. Unfortunately, units placed to provide missile defense around the planet would be effectively anchored to Torch. They wouldn't be *able* to maneuver freely without exposing the planet.

His third objective was to accomplish the first two without revealing his new weapons' capabilities to anyone outside the Torch System. Frankly, he didn't want *anyone* else to find out about them, even the Torches. That wasn't going to happen, of course, but it was particularly important to keep anyone in the Solarian League from finding out if at all possible.

Fourth, the best way to accomplish that third objective, was to see to it that no one who might be interested in sharing his discoveries with people Rozsak didn't want finding out about them just yet—which was to say, no one at all from the attacking force—escaped.

Individually, each problem was relatively straightforward; in combination, they demanded a tricky judgment of capabilities, possibilities, and threats. And, try as they might, neither he nor any of his staff had been able to come up with a solution to their problems which didn't violate the principle of concentration of force. To make this work was going to require the *division* of his forces, and that was a notion Luiz Rozsak hated with every tactician's bone in his body.

But, he reflected, *as that old proverb Oravil is fond of quoting says, "Needs must when the Devil drives." And the Devil is sure as hell driving* this *one.*

"I think you're right, Edie," he said out loud, then turned to

Commander Raycraft and Commander Stensrud. "Still, Laura, you and Melanie are the ones who're going to have the toughest job if anything goes wrong with the interception. I wish we had the four-pod rings aboard *Charade*. I'd feel a lot more comfortable if we could just go ahead and deploy the pods and pull Melanie back out of the inner system."

Raycraft and Stensrud nodded in unison. The lightweight pods in *Charade*'s bays were simply too stripped down for any sort of extensive independent deployment. They required too much external power supply, just for starters, and the people who'd designed them had deliberately accepted limited—very limited—operational lifetimes for their onboard systems. All of which meant Stensrud couldn't simply stack the things in Torch orbit and then get her ship the hell out of the way.

"I can't say I'm particularly enthralled by the limitations myself, Sir," Raycraft acknowledged. "On the other hand, I'll have a lot more missile defense than you will. And if your jaw of the nutcracker does what it's supposed to, it probably won't matter a lot."

"I know." Rozsak snorted in amusement. "The problem is that I've never been all that enthralled"—he used her own verb deliberately—"by operational planning that includes words like 'probably won't.'"

Someone else chuckled in matching amusement, but then the admiral set his coffee cup firmly aside with an air of finality.

"All right. I think we have a plan. Now let's see how it works out as an exercise. Edie, I want you and Dirk-Steven to set that up ASAP. We don't know how long we have before the bad guys come calling, but it's always best to err on the side of pessimism in a case like this. That means we're not going to be able to spend a lot of time actually working on this in real space, so get the sims loaded to everybody. Hopefully, we'll be able to have at least one run through with everything short of live-fire exercises from the *Masquerades*, so be ready to tweak the simulations on the basis of anything we discover in the process."

"Yes, Sir," Edie Habib replied in a rather more formal than usual tone. "A lot of this is going to come straight out of the playbook we've been working on," she continued, "so I think we can probably set up the exercise pretty quickly. We can probably be ready to go by... what?" She arched an eyebrow at Kamstra as she spoke. "Tomorrow morning, Dirk-Steven?"

"Better make it afternoon," Kamstra advised after a moment's thought. "I've noticed Murphy tends to turn up during the planning process, as well."

"A cogent thought," Habib agreed, and turned back to Rozsak. "Make that tomorrow afternoon, Sir. Right after lunch."

"Good," Rozsak said. "In that case, I think we can adjourn."

✧   ✧   ✧

"So how bad is it?" Friede Butry leaned over, peering into the space uncovered by a removed cover plate. The inside of that space was filled with a lot of equipment whose precise purpose she understood only vaguely.

Andrew Artlett straightened up from the piece of machinery he'd been working on, squatted on his heels, and started wiping his hands with a rag. That was rather silly, really. The interior of a hyper generator—even one for a ship as small as a mere million tons—needed to be kept clean at all times. In fact, Andrew had washed his hands before starting to work on it as thoroughly as a surgeon washes his hands before undertaking an operation.

But old habits died hard. Andrew always thought of himself as what he called a "jackleg mechanic," and such stalwart and doughty souls by definition always had dirty hands that needed to be wiped clean.

"Pretty damn bad, Ganny. It could go out at any time."

"Why?" Butry glared at the housing. "Those damned things are supposed to be the next best thing to indestructible!"

"Well, they are . . . mostly," Andrew acknowledged. "Unfortunately, even a hyper generator has some moving parts, and this one"—he tapped a badly worn-looking rotorlike device longer than his arm—"is one of them. Worse, it's an *important* one of them. In fact, it's the stabilizer for the primary stage. If it goes down, you've got no hyper control at all, Ganny. Zip. And this sucker ought to have been changed out in a routine overhaul at least a hundred thousand hours ago. We really need to replace it, before we try to make another jump."

"It can't just be fixed?"

"Fixed? How?" He pointed a finger at the rotor's shaft. Even Ganny, whose many fields of expertise and knowledge did not include matters mechanical, could see that it was badly worn.

"I'd have to remove it, first. That could be done, although it'd take a while. That's the easy part. Then I'd have to add metal to it, using welding equipment we don't have, so I'd have to design and build the welding equipment which I could probably do with the odds and ends we have on this rustbucket of a so-called starship but you're looking at weeks of work, Ganny. Might be as much as two or three months. Then I'd have to turn it back down to specs using metal-shaping equipment which we *also* don't have. The so-called 'machine shop' on this piece of crap is a joke and you can tell that cheapskate Walter Imbesi I said so. There's no way on God's green earth I could possibly build a modern computerized machining center. And even if I could, who'd design the program? You're probably the closest we've got to a real programmer and . . ."

He cocked an inquisitive eye up at her. Ganny shook her head. "I'm not really that good a programmer and what little skill I do have runs entirely toward financial stuff. There's no way I could design a program to do what you want, Andrew."

He nodded. "What I figured. So that means I'd have to build an old-style lathe."

"A . . . *what*?"

He grinned. "And you claim to be the old-timer here! A 'lathe' is an antique piece of equipment, Ganny, used to cut metal. More or less contemporaneous, I think, to ox-drawn plows. Still, it'd do the trick although it'd take a lot longer than modern equipment. Fortunately, we've got a pretty good suite of measuring instruments so I could probably manage to get the shaft back to specs using a micrometer."

"A . . . *what*?"

"A micrometer's an ancient type of measuring tool, Ganny. Definitely contemporaneous to ox-drawn plows. Well, yardsticks anyway."

"What's a 'yardstick'?" piped up Ed Hartman. He and his two buddies had been watching the process with great interest from close up. As close up as Andrew would let them come, anyway. He was deeply suspicious of their claims to being crispy clean.

"A stick to measure a yard, what d'you think?"

"So what's a 'yard'?" asked Brice Miller.

Artlett scowled. "Ganny, is this a consultation over critical repair issues or a remedial history class?"

She smiled, and made shooing motions at the three teenagers. "Give your uncle some breathing room, kids. I'll explain to you what a yard is later."

She looked back down at Andrew. "And how long would it take to make this . . . 'lathe,' you called it?"

"At least as long as it took me to make the welding equipment. Even though it'll have to be a primitive as they come, since I've got no way to make a lead screw. Fortunately I can probably jury-rig an electromagnetic actuator of some kind."

"What's a 'lead'—never mind. Again, in other words, you're talking about weeks."

"Might even be months. There's really no way to know ahead of time. The bottom line is this, Ganny. Unless we replace the worn out parts now, this equipment is likely to go out completely once we put any real stress on it. At that point, we're dead in the water. We'd still have power, so it wouldn't be immediately life-threatening. We could probably survive for at least a year. But we'd just be drifting in space until I could fix it. And, like I said, that could take anywhere up to half a year."

She nodded. "All right, then. I'll just have to tap into what funds we've got. Write up what you need, Andrew, and I'll transmit it down to the surface as soon as we've been given customs clearance. That shouldn't take long. This is our third visit. The Mesans are being downright gracious now that they figure we're repeat business."

CHAPTER FORTY-NINE

Yana came into the kitchen, brushing a light sprinkling of snow off her shoulders. "I hope your plans for a fast getaway don't include antique wheeled ground vehicles squealing around corners. It's pretty slick out there. And the people who are out don't seem to know a damned thing about how to get around in it."

She shook her head in disgust, and Victor and Anton grinned. Despite the fact that Yana had spent most of her adult life in one city or another, she'd spent her girlhood on the planet of Kilimanjaro. Winters there weren't *quite* as long as on the Star Kingdom's Sphinx, but they were definitely in the same league. She was inclined to look down her nose at the weather complaints voiced by effete scions of milder planets, and her opinion of Torch's tropical and sub-tropical climate was normally summed up with a snort of magnificent contempt.

Her *special* scorn, however, was reserved for watching people who obviously had no idea what to do with snow trying to cope with it, and it was obvious her morning stroll had given her ample fuel for that response. Mesans, it would appear, were even more clueless than most—in her humble opinion, of course—when it came to dealing with frozen atmospheric water vapor.

Perhaps that was because the planet enjoyed mild and pleasant climatic conditions. Even the dead of winter, except in the polar regions, was no worse than a mild winter day on Haven. It didn't even begin to compare with the ferocious winter conditions of Zilwicki's native Gryphon, and the hypothermia of a

Sphinxian winter would have clear-cut the planetary population like one of Old Earth's Final War bioweapons.

Mesa's summers were probably tougher on human beings than its winters—but the summers weren't bad either. The planet's sun was a G2 star virtually identical to Sol, and Mesa itself was almost a twin of Earth. Not quite. The gravity was almost identical, but Mesa had slightly more land surface. That might have made the climate more extreme than Earth's, with less of the ameliorative effect of oceans. But Mesa was about forty light-seconds closer to the system primary and had a much smaller axial tilt—only nine degrees, in contrast to the home planet's twenty-three and a half. So the average temperature was somewhat higher and the seasonal variations quite a bit smaller.

On most of the planet's surface, in fact, winter never brought any snow at all. But the planet had taken the name of "Mesa" from the high, tableland mesa near the center of its largest continent where the survey party placed its initial base camp on the planetary surface. What eventually became the planet's capital city had developed there, for the same largely accidental reasons that most cities on most worlds came into existence. Being at a greater altitude than most of the planet, and with a definitely continental effect, the weather in the capital was probably worse than almost anywhere else on Mesa.

That wasn't saying much. In truth, Mesa was one of the most pleasant worlds Anton or Victor had ever visited. That made it even more disgusting that it had become the center for what both of them considered one of the foulest political systems ever produced by the human species—which had produced plenty of foul political systems, since the pharaoh Khufu erected his great pyramid with the use of slave labor more than six and half millennia in the past.

Anton and Victor now knew a lot more about the true nature of Mesa's political system than they had when they landed on the planet, or than any other Manticorans or Havenites still knew. Jack McBryde had been cagey about imparting information to them, in each of the secret meetings they'd had since the initial contact. He'd peeled off that data much like the onion he used to depict the centuries-old strategy of the shadowy conspiracy he'd introduced to them as "the Alignment." Being as sparing as possible, each time, in the hopes of bargaining for a better deal.

Still, he'd had to give them a lot already. It was just a crude fact of life that a person seeking to defect had less in the way of bargaining power than the people in a position to provide a new life for him or her. And neither Anton nor Victor was in any mood to be charitable.

It spoke well for Jack McBryde, true enough—even Victor would allow this much—that he'd come to understand and detest the system created over the centuries by what he called the Mesan Alignment. But it was still appalling that any man with his obvious intelligence—even genuine sensitivities—could have supported that system as long as he had, in such a central capacity, before he finally turned against it.

As Victor had quipped sarcastically after their third meeting with McBryde, paraphrasing a line from one of his favorite movies, it was as if an officer at one of the ancient Nazi death camps was suddenly to exclaim: "I am shocked—shocked!—to discover genocide at Auschwitz!" (Anton had understood the reference, but he'd had to explain it to Yana.)

That probably wasn't entirely fair. Anton pointed out that the initial impulses that eventually led to the Mesan Alignment had clearly been idealistic, which it was awfully hard to say of the vision of the ancient despot Hitler. This was hardly the first time in human history, after all, that a political movement (or religion, for that matter) had begun with the best of intentions and turned into something which its founders would never have imagined might be the horrible end result. He went so far as to point out—after clearing his throat—that Victor himself bore an uncanny resemblance to many of the members of the Bolshevik Cheka in the early years of the Russian revolution almost two centuries before the Diaspora.

Victor knew what Anton was referring to; and, after stiffening for a moment, had admitted (even with a slight smile) there was possibly a certain resemblance. In the years since he'd met Kevin and Ginny Usher, Cachat had become a genuine student of history.

"It's still not the same, Anton," he'd said. "If you know that much about ancient history, then you also know that within two decades of the original revolution the tyrant named Stalin had murdered almost all of those early revolutionaries and replaced them with his own lickspittles. Rob Pierre and especially Saint-Just tried to do the same thing with the Aprilists in our own revolution—and damn near succeeded.

"But we're talking centuries here, Anton, not decades. *Centuries* during the course of which these people committed the foulest crimes you can imagine, condemning generations of other people to slavery and brutality—and Jack McBryde finally starts choking on it, more than half a millennium after it began and after enjoying a long career himself at the trade?"

By the time he'd finished, Victor had been as outwardly angry as Anton had ever seen him.

"So . . . what?" he said. "Do you want to tell McBryde to take a flying leap into hellfire and be damned to him?"

That had been enough to crack Cachat's quiet fury. "Well . . . no, of course not." He even managed a chuckle. "I'm not crazy, after all. McBryde could be one of Shaitan's top underlings and I'd work with him under these circumstances, if he wanted to defect from Hell. Holding my nose, maybe, but I'd do it. We have far too much to gain—and that's not even counting these latest hints McBryde's been giving us."

Anton looked skeptical. "Do you really think he's got his hands on some sort of super-secret technical developments—assuming those developments exist at all?"

"I don't think McBryde himself knows diddly squat about starship design, which is what he's been hinting at. But if I'm interpreting some other remarks of his properly, he's got someone else with him. Someone whom he's kept out of sight from us up until now."

Anton stared at the wall, thinking about it. There *had* been the suggestion, in some of what McBryde had said in their last meeting the day before yesterday, that—if you interpreted it this way, and then tweaked it that way—it was not for nothing they called this trade a hall of mirrors—he wanted some form of transport off the planet that was more elaborate than a single person would need. Anton had been a little puzzled by it at the time, in fact. McBryde was a security specialist himself, so he knew perfectly well that the easiest and safest way to smuggle someone off a planet with security precautions as tight at Mesa's was to disguise them in some way or another as someone else. The more people you tried to do that for, the harder it got—and the increase in the risk was exponential, not linear.

Alternatively . . .

He sucked in a breath. "How many people then, do you think?"

"At a guess, just one," replied Victor. "McBryde doesn't have a wife or children—or significant other of any kind, so far as we've been able to determine. I get the feeling he's rather close to his family, but I'd be astonished if someone with his training and experience would do anything to compromise them. There's no possible way he could get *all* of them off the planet, parents and siblings both. And for all we know some of his brothers and sisters have children of their own."

Cachat leaned forward over the kitchen table, leaning his weight on his arms. "He's putting them all at a considerable risk already, it seems to me. Once he leaves, there'll be hell to pay, even if there's no indication that any of them knew what he was planning. If this were Haven under Pierre and Saint-Just, his family would probably all be executed anyway. But from everything we've been able to determine, this Mesan Alignment doesn't operate that crudely."

Anton considered Victor's argument, in his slow and methodical way. Cachat, who knew him very well by now, simply waited patiently. In fact, he took advantage of the pause to make a fresh pot of coffee and find out what Yana had learned. As she did every morning, the Amazon had gone out to check the astrogation records. Entries and exits from the system by all merchant and passenger ships—most military craft, too—were kept up to date and publicly available.

Checking those records on a daily basis was a perfectly legal activity, but it was always possible that someone might be monitoring them. So, Yana used a different method every day to search the data. Sometimes a public library, and never the same one twice in a row; sometimes the commercial shipping offices—there were lots of those in the city; and once she'd even gone down to the Extrasolar Commerce Authority itself and used their computers.

"The *Hali Sowle* just entered the system again," she said quietly, not wanting to disturb Anton's train of thought. She didn't know Zilwicki as well as Victor did, but she had a near-superstitious respect for the man's fabled ability to work his way through any problem.

Victor nodded. "Any word yet as to their permitted length of stay?"

She shook her head. "No, but it'll probably be on the records by tomorrow. No later than the day after that, for sure. I'll say this for Mesa. Their bureaucrats aren't slouches."

Victor chuckled. "And this is . . . praise?"

Hearing a slight noise behind them, Victor turned and saw that Anton had moved his chair back from the table a little.

"That didn't take as long as I thought." He held up the pot. "Fresh coffee?"

Zilwicki extended his cup. "There isn't really that much to figure. I think you're right, Victor—and I'm pretty sure McBryde will come out into the open with it at our next meeting. It'll be one more person that he wants us to smuggle out with him, and that person will be a scientist or technician of some kind who actually has the knowledge he's been hinting about."

"You don't think he's faking anything, in other words?"

"No." Slowly, Anton shook his blocky head. "Victor, unless I'm very badly mistaken, Jack McBryde is starting to get desperate and wants off the planet as soon as possible."

Victor frowned. "Why? He's essentially the head of security here. Well, one of them, anyway. But you'd be hard pressed to think of anyone who could disguise what he's doing as well as he could. Even if someone does spot him up to something questionable, he could almost certainly provide some sort of half-reasonable explanation. A good enough one, at least, to give him time to make his escape."

"I don't think it's his own situation that's pressing on him, Victor. I think—and I'll be the first to admit there's a lot of guesswork on my part—that it's this mysterious other person's situation that's driving most of the timetable here."

"Ah." Victor sat down and took a sip from his coffee, then thought about it for a couple of minutes, and then took another sip.

"I'm not about to second-guess you, Anton. So let's put everything on the table when we meet McBryde in two days. Tell him it's put-up-or-shut-up time, and offer the very big carrot of being able to get him and his Mysterious Other off the planet almost immediately."

He nodded toward Yana, who'd taken a seat at the table with her cup of coffee. "The *Hali Sowle*'s back."

Anton drew in a breath. "In other words, you think we should make our exit at the same time. Once the Butrys leave the system, none of our alternate means of escape is all that attractive."

"'All that attractive'?" Victor chuckled. "Anton, unless I miss my guess, the moment the Mesan Powers-That-Be find out Jack McBryde has stabbed them in the back, all hell will break loose. There isn't a chance worth talking about that any of those 'alternate means of escape'—which I could also call the rickety ladders with which to exit a burning skyscraper—will be anything other than a death trap. If he goes, we have to go with him."

"Well . . . true. Besides, I can't imagine we could find out much more by staying."

"Oh, we *could*. Even before McBryde approached us, we'd already discovered a fair amount and started to develop some promising leads. But I agree there's nothing we could find out if we stayed that comes close to what McBryde will provide us. Besides . . ."

He took another sip. "I was about to tell you. Inez Cloutier just got back yesterday—and she's got a definite offer from whoever the top dog is. Probably Adrian Luff, if we're right."

"Good offer?"

"Better than I'd imagined. There must be somebody out there who knows more about the workings of Saint-Just's field operations than I figured there'd be. I guess my, ah, reputation has preceded me."

"Not as Victor Cachat, I hope?"

"No. Well . . . probably not. Almost certainly not. It's always theoretically possible that they've figured out exactly who I am and are laying a clever trap. But they work closely with the Alignment, obviously—so if they've figured out who I am, why not just report me and let the Mesans right here do the wet work?" He shook his head. "No, they're probably figuring me for another one of Saint-Just's young troubleshooters. I wasn't the only one, by any means. There were at least a dozen others I knew of, and probably two or three times that many. Who knows? Now that Saint-Just's dead, probably no one. If there was ever a man who kept his own counsel, it was Oscar Saint-Just."

"So that's the bottom line. Take it or leave it."

Jack McBryde returned Victor Cachat's flat gaze with what he hoped was an imperturbable gaze of his own.

The fact that Cachat had made what amounted to the ultimatum was a signal in itself, Jack knew. As their negotiations had progressed, Zilwicki and Cachat had fallen into the familiar roles of "good cop/bad cop." McBryde recognized the routine, of course—which Cachat and Zilwicki would know perfectly well—but that didn't really make much difference. The routine was ancient because it was so effective.

All the more effective here, Jack thought wryly, when your option as the "good cop" was Anton Zilwicki! As part of any other pairing except with Victor Cachat, Zilwicki would have been playing the "bad cop."

Cachat was . . . unsettling. And would have been, even if McBryde hadn't known his reputation. There were times when those dark eyes seemed as black as the stellar void, and every bit as cold.

"All right. Here's what I want: passage off the planet for myself and a friend of mine. The friend is male, close to my age, and one of Mesa's top physicists specializing in ship propulsion. More precisely, he's an expert on a new type of ship drive that is completely unknown to anyone else in the universe."

There might have been a slight expression that came to Zilwicki in response to that statement. Hard to tell, on that blocky face. There was no expression at all on Cachat's.

"Go on," said Victor. "And what do you provide us, beyond this physicist of yours?"

In for a penny, in for a pound. Jack had once even looked up the etymology of that old saw. "What I give you is the following: First, the nature and plans of the Mesan Alignment for both Manticore and Haven. Which are, ah, about as inimical as you can imagine."

"Generalities only go so far, McBryde."

"Let me finish. And, second, I can tell you how—in layman's terms; I don't have the background to understand the technical aspects of it myself—the Mesan Alignment asassinated Ambassador Webster, got Colonel Gregor Hofschulte to attempt to assassinate Crown Prince Huan, and got a Lieutenant Meares to attempt to assasinate Honor Harrington and William Henry Tyler to attack your own step-daughter Berry, Anton. Among other attacks. Trust me, there are more of them—and more successful ops—than you people even guess yet. Including"—He looked squarely at Cachat—"the one which . . . inspired, shall we say, one Yves Grosclaude to kill *himself*, if that means anything to you."

For the first time since he'd met Victor Cachat, an actual expression came to the Havenite's face. It was a very faint expression, true, but between that little frown and the slight pallor, Jack knew the reference had registered.

Zilwicki was frowning at Cachat. "Does that mean anything to you?"

"Yes," Victor said softly. "Something Kevin's suspected—" He shook his head. "I'm afraid I can't talk about it, Anton. This is one of those places where the interests of my star nation and yours probably aren't the same."

Anton nodded, and looked back at McBryde.

"Okay. And what do you want in exchange? Keep in mind, Jack, that because of the—ah—unusual nature of this partnership between Victor and me, neither one of us can offer you asylum in our own systems. Eventually, I imagine you'll probably wind up on Erewhon, or somewhere in Maya Sector. For the time being, though, you'll be sequestered on Torch and I can pretty well guarantee that one of the very first people who'll be talking to you is Jeremy X. He's not likely to be friendly, either."

A slight smile came to Zilwicki's face. "There won't be any physical stuff, though—you know, beatings, torture, that sort of thing—and you won't even be subject to poor living conditions. My daughter will see to that; and would, even without me talking to her. But there won't be anything fancy or luxurious. Not for several years, at a guess."

Jack wasn't surprised by any of that. And . . . didn't care. Not any longer.

"It's a deal," he said. He took a chip out of his vest pocket and slid it across the table. "Here. I made this up as a sort of . . . good will gesture, I suppose you'd call it. It doesn't have any technical stuff on the assassination technique itself. As I say, the best understanding I have of it myself is only what you might call an informed layman's grasp. Basically, though, it's a new approach to medical nanotech, only this one's virus-based and *does* replicate on its own."

He saw the surprise—and alarm—in all three of his listeners' eyes, and shrugged.

"I don't know how they arranged it, but everything I've seen from the operational side stresses that they're confident they've built in a control mechanism to keep it from getting away from them. And that they need a DNA sample of the intended 'host' before they can design the weapon for a given mission."

"And what does it *do*?" Anton asked almost softly.

"It basically builds its own dispersed architecture, bio-based computer," McBryde replied levelly. "It taps into its host's neural system, but it's totally passive until the host encounters whatever triggering event was preprogrammed into it. At that point, it . . . takes over." He waved one hand vaguely, clearly frustrated by his inability to describe the process more clearly. "As I understand it, it can only be programmed to carry out fairly simple, short term operations. It *does* have some limited AI function, apparently, but not very much. And it can't override the host's own efforts to reassert control of his voluntary muscles indefinitely. No longer than four or five minutes, apparently."

"Which is long enough, obviously," Victor said grimly. He regarded McBryde for several silent seconds, then tapped the chip on the table between them. "And this is?"

"Well, let's just say that when I started thinking about how well I could explain this thing to you, I realized the answer was 'Not Too Damned Well,'" McBryde replied with a slight smile. "So it occurred to me it might be as well for me to provide any supporting evidence I could. That"—he indicated the chip—"is the best version of that supporting evidence I was able to get my hands on without tripping too many internal lines. It's the report of the field agent who supervised the Webster assassination. It includes names, places, and dates . . . and also describes the hack of the bank records he used to implicate the Havenite ambassador's driver. Plus the elimination of the hacker who carried it out. I imagine there's more than enough in there that can be corroborated from the Old Earth investigation, once you know where to look."

"I imagine there is," Anton agreed. He picked up the chip and tossed it into the air, then caught it and tucked it into a pocket. McBryde was almost certainly correct about that, he thought, and glanced at Cachat, one eyebrow arched. The Havenite nodded ever so slightly, and Anton looked back at McBryde.

"The day after tomorrow suit you?"

Jack shook his head. "I can't. Well, *I* could, but it'll take at least another day to get Herlander ready and, besides, I can put the extra time to good use by covering our tracks on the way out." He smiled thinly. "Of course, I imagine you've already done the same—and please note that I'm not asking what or how—so I figure between your schemes and mine not even Bardasano will be able to figure out how we got off the planet."

CHAPTER FIFTY

"I hate waiting for the sound of a second shoe's hitting the floor,"
Admiral Osiris Trajan grumbled. None of his three dinner guests
responded. First, because he hadn't directed the comment specifically to one of them, but, secondly, because they'd both been
with the admiral long enough to recognize a rhetorical statement
when they heard one.

Apparently, though, it wasn't quite as rhetorical this time as
they'd thought it was, and he looked across the table at the
auburn-haired, gray-green-eyed woman in the captain's uniform
sitting opposite him.

"How about you, Addie?" he asked. "Are you feeling a bit less
than perfectly cheerful about this whole thing?"

"Ours not to reason why, Sir," Captain Adelaide Granger, the
commanding officer of Trajan's dreadnought flagship, replied with
a wry grin. She wiped her lips with her snow-white napkin and
arched one eyebrow quizzically at the admiral. "Might I respectfully inquire what has aroused the Admiral's ire at this particular
moment?" she asked.

Trajan gave something which sounded suspiciously like a snort
and wagged his head at his flag captain.

"You'll come to no good end, Addie," he warned her. "Trust
me, you're not irreplaceable, you know."

"No, Sir," she agreed equitably. "But—again, with the utmost
respect—given the Admiral's own . . . foibles, finding a replacement
and beating her into shape would probably take longer than the
Admiral would care to invest in the project."

This time, the other two officers seated at the table noted with relief, there was no doubt about Trajan's amusement. All three of his subordinates admired and respected Trajan—he wouldn't have been selected as Task Force Four's commanding officer if he hadn't been widely regarded as one of the Mannerheim System-Defense Force's two or three best flag officers. Normally, he was also an excellent boss. But there was no denying that he had his moods, and frustration tended to make him more than a little . . . prickly. Fortunately, Captain Granger had been something of a personal protégé of his for quite some time, and she'd developed a deft touch for defusing any serious irritation on his part. That would have been enough to make her presence welcome to Trajan's staff even if she hadn't been such a clearly superior officer in her own right.

"You're probably right about that," Trajan agreed with his flag captain now, and tossed his own crumpled napkin onto the table beside his empty plate. "About how long it would take, that is, of course," he added. "That bit about 'foibles' is scarcely applicable in my own case, however."

"Of course not, Sir," Granger said gravely. "I must have misspoken somehow."

"That happens sometimes to lesser mortals, or so I hear," Trajan observed, and it was Granger's turn to chuckle.

"Nonetheless," Trajan went on a moment later, in a considerably more serious tone, "I'm not happy about this entire op. I never have been, and I haven't gotten any happier in the last four or five T-months, either."

There was no doubt in any of his listeners' minds what operation he was speaking about. Task Force Four had no direct involvement in it—for which all of them were privately grateful—but they'd been briefed on "Operation Ferret". . . and about its objectives, given its implications for the MSDF's future operations.

"I don't think anyone's really happy about the notion of relying on Luff and his collection of paranoiacs, Sir," Commander Niklas Hasselberg said now. Trajan looked at his fair-haired chief of staff, and Hasselberg shrugged. "Sometimes deniability comes at a price in reliability, Sir."

"I realize that, Niklas," Trajan said. "In this particular instance, though, I'm not really convinced deniability is an important enough reason to rely on them. For that matter, I'm not really convinced the operation itself is a wonderful idea—or even necessary, at this point. Especially when we've gone to so much effort to keep this end of the bridge so completely black for so long."

"My understanding is that the decision was made at the highest levels, Sir," Commander Ildikó Nyborg, Trajan's operations officer, pointed out in a diplomatic tone, and Trajan snorted yet again, this time harshly.

"It was certainly that," he agreed.

All three of his subordinates understood. Although Hasselberg was the only other person present who knew the identity of the actual individual behind that decision, all of them represented star-line genomes. Star-lines were a minority in the MSDF's officer corps as a whole, of course, but they were heavily concentrated in the more senior ranks, and for duties as sensitive as their own current assignment there'd been some judicious personnel shuffling. As a result of which, Task Force Four's command structure was undeniably top-heavy in alpha-lines, beta-lines, and gamma-lines.

Which meant that, unlike the majority of their fellow officers, they knew the Mannerheim System-Defense Force was actually an adjunct of the Mesan Alignment Navy no one else knew even existed. So the term "higher up" had a very different meaning for them than it would have had for any of those non-Mesan officers.

"I'm not saying the Verdant Vista terminus isn't important, because it is," Trajan continued. "And I realize that using obvious Manpower proxies is about as deniable as it gets, given who's in charge of the system these days. From that perspective, I don't have any qualms about Ferret. The problem is that I think the operation itself is unnecessary. Worse, it's a complication we don't need. We could put a force through the bridge any time we wanted to that would be more than big enough to overwhelm anything the 'Kingdom of Torch' could possibly put in our way. We don't really have to take the system to exercise effective control of the terminus, and if it were my call, we'd go ahead and wait until we actually needed to use the thing. In which case we wouldn't have to rely on Luff's rejects at all."

There was silence for a moment. Osiris Trajan had a well-deserved reputation for openness with subordinates he trusted. "Everybody knows everything" about any current operation, at least at the level of his own staff, was practically a mantra of his, because he regarded it as the only way to get their best thoughts—and prevent competent people from making ignorance-based mistakes. But his comments about the operation against Torch were unusually blunt, even for him, given the fact that TF 4 wasn't even assigned to the MSDF covering force on the other end of the Verdant Vista wormhole bridge.

Captain Granger cocked her head to one side, clearly considering what he'd said. She stayed that way for two or three seconds, then shrugged.

"From a purely military perspective, I agree with you completely, Sir. And I suppose it's always possible someone somewhere's gotten her nose out of joint over what happened in Verdant Vista when we lost control of the system in the first place. I think, though, that the operative factor here, in many ways, is a concern about what the Manties may eventually figure out about the wormhole bridge."

"They aren't going to figure out anything about it that's going to do them any good, Addie," Trajan countered. "Besides, they've already figured out just about anything that could be deduced from their end, or they never would have gotten their survey ship through to SGC-902 in the first place. For all the good that did them."

He grimaced, and so did Granger and Nyborg. Hasselberg, on the other hand, only shrugged.

"I admit that was . . . unpleasant, Sir," the chief of staff said. "It was clearly within policy and Commodore Ganneau's instructions, though."

"I'm fully aware of both those points, Niklas." Trajan's voice was considerably frostier than normally came Hasselberg's direction. "I'm also aware, however, that it was a single cruiser—and one that was the next best thing to totally obsolescent, at that—and Ganneau had an entire battlecruiser squadron sitting there, with two of them already at action stations and knowing exactly where anything from the other end had to come out. Do you really think a Manty skipper would have been stupid enough to fight with eight battlecruisers sitting there ready to turn his ship into plasma? Ganneau had the option of ordering him to surrender; he just refused to take it."

"I'm not defending his decision, Sir," Hasselberg pointed out.

"I'm saying what he did was covered. And it probably wouldn't hurt to remember who his sister-in-law is."

Trajan frowned at the reminder. It was just like Hasselberg to bring it up, though, he reflected. The man was as tough-minded—not to say ornery—as they came. And he definitely believed in calling a spade a shovel, even if it wasn't very diplomatic to remind his admiral that Commodore Jérôme Ganneau's wife, Assuntina, was the youngest sister of Fleet Admiral Chiara Otis, the Mannerheim System-Defense Force's chief of naval operations.

Diplomatic or not, it was also an indication of just how much Hasselberg trusted the other officers seated around the table. It was highly unlikely that his observation would have evoked any anger from Fleet Admiral Otis, but that wasn't really the point.

"He may be Admiral Otis' brother-in-law," Captain Granger said, "but that's not who's watching his ass for him, Niklas."

"Of course not, Ma'am," Hasselberg agreed. "But Admiral Kafkaloudes is. And, unfortunately, that's almost the same thing."

"I think we should probably turn this conversation in another direction," Trajan said calmly. The others looked at him, and he shrugged. "Oh, I don't disagree with anything that's been said. On the other hand, there's not much point in discussing something everyone already agrees about, and discussing the CNO's and her chief of staff's—or her chief of staff's, at least—little . . . foibles"—he smiled quickly at Granger as he used her own earlier terminology—"even among friends is neither productive, diplomatic, wise, nor supportive of good discipline."

Granger looked back at him for a moment, gray-green eyes stubborn. Then she inhaled deeply, nodded, and sat back in her chair, reaching for her wine glass.

The truth, Trajan thought, was that Kafkaloudes' empire-building tendencies were well known throughout the MSDF. In fact, they were so well known that Fleet Admiral Otis' willingness to put up with them was widely regarded as her single true weakness. She was smart, competent, experienced, and dedicated to her duty, yet it was impossible for Trajan to believe she was unaware of Kafkaloudes' vendettas against anyone who ever made the mistake of rousing his ire. And it was an ire which roused with remarkable ease.

The problem was that, personality shortcomings aside, he really was very good at his job. And, to give the devil his due, part of his job clearly was to protect Otis, because in protecting her, he also protected her effectiveness. That was why Granger and Hasselberg were almost certainly correct where Ganneau was concerned. Otis might not protect him just because he was her brother-in-law—in fact, Trajan, who knew the fleet admiral quite well, was pretty damn sure she wouldn't—but she didn't have to. The commodore could rely on Kafkaloudes to quietly suppress any personal criticism of him. After all, it wouldn't do to have that criticism splash on the CNO! Or that, at any rate, was how Kafkaloudes could be counted upon to see things.

And Hasselberg had a perfectly valid point about Ganneau's actions. They were covered by his orders, even though Trajan knew Ganneau had been expected to use his own discretion about employing lethal force. And there were arguments in favor of exactly what the commodore had done. Trajan might not like them very much, but he couldn't deny their existence. The reason Ganneau's squadron had drawn the duty of watching the Alignment's end of the Verdant Vista Bridge in the first place was that judicious personnel assignments similar to those which had been tweaked in Task Force Four's favor had led—purely coincidentally, of course—to the Sixth Battlecruiser Squadron's being exclusively officered and manned by what happened to be Mesan star-lines. None of them were going to mention what had happened to anyone else, but if a Manticoran survey vessel had been brought in by vessels of the Mannerheim System-Defense Force . . .

All of that's true enough, Trajan thought, *but they wouldn't have had to be brought into Mannerheim in the first place. The Alignment could've squirreled them away somewhere. Hell, we've managed to "squirrel away" the entire frigging Darius System for two hundred damned years! But Ganneau didn't want to mess with the "inconvenience," so he just casually went ahead and blew away an entire ship full of people, instead.*

"Leaving aside any discussions of our senior officers," Hasselberg said after a moment, "there's still your own point, Admiral. The Manties can't possibly realize what they're dealing with from their end of the bridge."

He glanced at the smart wall bulkhead of Trajan's dining cabin as he spoke, and the others followed his gaze to it. The wall was configured at the moment to show not the Felix System, where Vivienne and the rest of TF 4 were currently conducting "routine training exercises," but what lay at the other end of the Verdant Vista Wormhole Bridge.

It was centered on a single star which looked slightly brighter than any of the others in their field of view. In fact, the only reason for its apparent brightness was that it had been considerably closer to the recording pickup than any of the others. It was actually only a lowly M8 dwarf, without a single planet to its name. Or, rather, to its number, for it had never achieved the dignity of the name all its own. It was simply SGC-902-36-G, a dim little star just this side of a "brown dwarf," of absolutely no particular interest to anyone and over forty light-years from the nearest inhabited star system.

It was also, however, home to a never before observed hyperspace phenomenon: a pair of wormhole termini, less than two light-minutes from one another and less than ten light-minutes from SGC-902-36-G itself. In fact, they were precisely 9.24 light-minutes from the star, which put them exactly on its hyper limit, and made them the only wormhole termini in the explored galaxy which were less than thirty light-minutes from a star.

No one had ever encountered anything like it before, and even all these years after its discovery, the Mesan Alignment's hyperphysicists were still trying to come up with an explanation for how the "SGC-902-36-G Wormhole Anomaly" (also known as "The Twins") had happened when all generally accepted wormhole theory said it couldn't have. There were currently, Trajan had been told, at least six competing "main" hypotheses.

Obviously, no one had ever predicted that any such thing was possible. In fact, the Alignment had literally stumbled across it in the course of surveying the wormhole junction associated with the Felix System, where Trajan's task force was currently exercising. Not that the galaxy at large had any idea of that junction's existence, either. It had been discovered initially by a survey expedition backed by the "Jessyk Combine" and operating (very surreptitiously) out of Mannerheim under direct orders from the Alignment. Jessyk never shared survey information with anyone unless there was an excellent reason for it to do so, and in this case the Alignment had decided there was an excellent reason *not* to broadcast the Combine's discovery.

Felix was an uninhabited star system little more than ten light-years from Mannerheim. The dim K2-class star was brighter than

SGC-902-36-G, and it did have one marginally habitable planet, although that was about the best anyone was ever likely to say about it. The planet itself, which had never been assigned any better name than "Felix Beta," was a fairly miserable piece of real estate, with a gravity 1.4 times that of Old Earth, an axial inclination of thirty-one degrees, and a miserly hydrosphere of barely thirty-three percent. With an average orbital radius of right on six light-minutes, it was a cold, arid, dusty, windstorm-lashed, thoroughly wretched lump of dirt, but the Alignment had been considering it as a potential site for further development anyway, because of its proximity to Mannerheim.

The Republic of Mannerheim openly abhorred and despised the genetic slave trade and the outlaw Mesan transstellars which promoted it . . . which was one of the things that made it so valuable to the Mesan Alignment. The fact that Mannerheim's system-defense force was one of the most powerful of the entire Solarian League, and that there was absolutely nothing to associate it with Manpower or the Mesa System's government, didn't hurt, either. As such, it would have been handy, the Alignment had thought, to tuck its secret arsenal away someplace everyone knew was absolutely useless yet was simultaneously close enough to Mannerheim for the MSDF to keep a protective eye on it. Of course, there had been downsides to the proposition, the worst of which was that it would also have been close enough to Mannerheim for someone to innocently stumble across things the Alignment didn't want anyone stumbling over. The chance of someone actually doing that had been remote, to say the least, of course. When it came to concealing things, ten light-years might as well be ten thousand, unless there was something to prompt some busybody into making the trip in the first place.

What no one had expected—until the survey team the Alignment had sent to Felix under cover of the Jessyk expedition completed a thorough analysis of the system primary's emissions—was that there would have been plenty of reason to make the trip, if only anyone had known that Felix was associated with a major worm-hole junction. Not on anything like the scale of the Manticoran Wormhole Junction, perhaps, but still considerably larger than most, with no less than four secondary termini.

They led to several interesting places (including the Darius System, which actually had been chosen as the site for the MAN's arsenal), and the Alignment had kept the Felix Junction's existence as "black" as they had the entire colony in Darius.

In fact, although the Alignment had known about it for better than two T-centuries, the MSDF had first become aware of it less than ten years ago. Officially, at least; many of the senior MSDF officers who knew about the Alignment had also known about the Felix Junction from the very beginning. As far as the bulk of the MSDF was concerned, however, Mannerheim had discovered the junction only eight and a half T-years ago, and the decision had been taken to keep its existence a secret because it had only two secondary termini . . . and because the Republic intended to make sure that when its existence became generally known, it was also firmly established as belonging to Mannerheim.

Fortuitously, from the Alignment's perspective, establishing that ownership was going to be complicated and (even better) time-consuming. Useless as the Felix System had turned out to be, colonization rights to it had been purchased by a Solarian corporation better than five hundred T-years ago. Since then, they had passed through the hands of at least a dozen levels of speculators—always trading downward, once the newest owner discovered how difficult it would have been to attract colonists to the system when there were so many other, more attractive potential destinations. By now, there were actually four separate corporations which claimed ownership, and none of them were likely to relinquish their claims without seeking at least some compensation to write off against their bad debt.

If Mannerheim suddenly showed an interest in the system, someone was going to wonder why. Aside from the Jessyk survey (which had been poaching on someone else's property, not that one would have expected that consideration to weigh heavily with Jessyk, of course), no one had ever bothered to update the original survey of the system. But if Mannerheim started offering to acquire the colonization rights, that was almost inevitably going to change, since the contending "owners" would certainly suspect (correctly) that Mannerheim knew something about it that they didn't. So they'd go and take a look for themselves, in the course of which they would discover the junction for themselves. At which point all manner of litigation, claims, counterclaims, and demands for immense compensation would come frothing to the surface.

So Mannerheim had the perfect cover for keeping the junction's existence under wraps while it very carefully and quietly, through a web of agents and arm's-length associations, sought to acquire ownership of Felix for itself without anyone's noticing. Those members of the MSDF who were not themselves Mesans but who were aware of the Felix Junction's existence knew exactly why they were supposed to keep their mouths shut about it. And they didn't know that the "official" survey information which had been shared with them didn't include the Darius Terminus . . . or the SGC-902-36-G Terminus.

"To be honest, Sir," Captain Granger's voice was very serious, almost somber, "that's only part of the reason for my own reservations about this operation. We're not planning on moving in on Verdant Vista, anyway. Not until we need a back door into the Haven Quadrant, at any rate, and we've waited around for two hundred years without doing that. I know that's probably going to change in the not too distant future, but the decision about when to finally use it is going to lie with us, and not anyone else, as long as no one figures out what's going on, at least. And we're all pretty much in agreement that the Manties aren't really likely to be able to do that. I'm damned sure they're not going to keep feeding survey ships into a terminus nothing ever comes back from, at any rate! So there's no need for the attack or any of its . . . collateral damage."

What you mean, Addie, is there's no need to kill everything—and everybody—on the planet, Trajan thought, more than a bit grimly. *And if I had the guts to openly admit it, that's really what's bothering* me *about it, too. We don't have to kill all those people just to use a wormhole terminus that happens to be associated with their star. At this point, there's no way in the galaxy they could possibly put together a force of their own that we couldn't blow out of the way without even working up a sweat. Once we do that, who cares who "owns" the planet? For that matter, we could take it away from them any time we wanted to. Or, at least, if they flatly refused to surrender, we'd be legally justified in sending down the troops or even bombarding them until they saw reason.*

He knew the arguments in favor of the operation. Even agreed that the concerns behind them were well taken. The fact that the "Kingdom of Torch" didn't have a navy now didn't mean it couldn't acquire one. Or, for that matter, even borrow one. There was that treaty Cassetti had negotiated with it, for example. And the Republic of Erewhon had shown clearly enough where its sympathies lay. So, yes, it was always possible a genuine military threat could evolve in Verdant Vista.

From that perspective, it could be argued that creating a situation in which no one lived in Verdant Vista anymore was the most economical way to protect the secret. And the advantage Verdant Vista would offer when the Alignment's military operations inevitably intruded into the Haven Quadrant were huge. A direct wormhole connection to the quadrant from the Alignment's primary military base? Any commander in history would have killed for that kind of an advantage!

But would he have killed an entire planetary population to get it? Or, for that matter, to fend off a "threat" to it that would probably never materialize anyway? One he'd have plenty of time to factor into his plans later if it did look like materializing, come to that? Trajan asked himself. *That's what sticks in your craw, Addie . . . and in mine. And it's the reason we're both so damned pissed off with Ganneau, too, isn't it? Because what he did to that Manty survey cruiser is exactly what "Manpower" is planning on doing to the entire damned star system.*

Of course it was, and that was the reason he should never have started this conversation in the first place. Task Force Four wasn't going to be involved in it, anyway—not unless something went more massively wrong than Trajan could imagine, at any rate. And dragging his most trusted subordinates into this sort of moral morass with him wasn't what a good commanding officer was supposed to do.

If you can't stand the heat, get out of the kitchen, Osiris, he told himself grimly. *Either send in your resignation because it's so morally repugnant to you, or else keep your mouth shut instead of contributing to your subordinates' possible uncertainty.*

"I take your point, Addie," he said out loud. "And I don't disagree with you. But as you just pointed out," he looked across the table, holding her eyes levelly, his own silently warning, "the actual execution order came from someplace way above my pay grade. So there's not really much point in our kicking it around, is there?"

"No, Sir," she replied after a moment, and he smiled at her.

"In that case, let's kick something else around," he said much more briskly. "In particular, there's that new simulation I understand you and Ildikó have been tinkering with. Tell me about what you've got in mind."

"Well, Sir," his flag captain glanced at Commander Nyborg, then back to Trajan, "it occurred to us that it might not be a bad idea for us to begin at least playing around with a 'notional dual-drive missile.' I don't want to make it anything too close to current MAN hardware capabilities, but I do think it would be a good idea to start stretching our tac officers' minds in that direction. So, what Ildikó and I were thinking is that we'd take the position that at least some of the reports about current Manty capabilities may have a stronger basis in fact than the SLN is prepared to admit. On that basis, we could then sketch out the capabilities of something approaching current MAN hardware."

She paused and nodded to Nyborg, clearly inviting the operations officer to jump in, and the commander leaned slightly forward in her chair, her feminine yet undeniably square and sturdy face, alight with interest.

You're relieved we've stopped talking about what's about to happen in Verdant Vista, aren't you, Ildikó? Trajan thought, and knew it was true.

"What the captain is suggesting here, Sir," Nyborg said, "is that coming up with this 'notional missile'—that was her idea, Sir, but I think it was a damned good one—will start our tac people thinking in terms of the offensive potentials of that kind of weapon . . . which will also start making them fully aware of the threat potentials. Frankly, it's our ability to stop or seriously degrade, at least, Manty missile strikes that concerns us the most, so starting an open consideration of ways to do that strikes us as making a lot of sense."

"I can't argue with that," Trajan told her. "So tell me about this 'notional missile.'"

"Well, Sir," Nyborg said, "what we started with was—"

CHAPTER FIFTY-ONE

"So, Jack . . . how much longer do you think it'll be till the Center hands me my severance pay?"

"Not long, actually," McBryde admitted.

He leaned back in his own chair, taking his beer stein with him, and shook his head. He and Herlander Simões sat in his kitchen once again, as they'd sat so often over the past months. The fact that they'd been just about due for one of their regular conversations when he paid his visit to Turner's diner had had more than a little to do with his timing.

"That's about what I figured." Simões managed a twisted smile. "I don't suppose you have any idea what they might plan on doing with me after that, do you?"

"No. To be honest, though, I don't think it's going to be very pleasant, Herlander." He grimaced. "All those e-mails of yours to Dr. Fabre aren't exactly likely to weigh in your favor, you know. To be frank, *I've* been worrying a little bit about you over the last couple of weeks. We both know your time at the Center's getting short. I figure that's one reason your temper's been even worse than usual lately, to be honest. And I've also been wondering just how tempted you've been to try something to get even."

"Get even with who?" Simões laughed harshly. "The Alignment? You think they'd even *notice* anything I could do at this point? And I'm pretty sure Fabre's security wouldn't let me anywhere *near* her. Or any of the rest of the LRPB, for that matter! And"—his voice softened ever so slightly—"I'm not going to do anything

456

to 'get even' with the Center, Jack. Not when I know how that would have to splash on you."

"Thank you," McBryde said softly.

He took a swallow of beer, giving his guest a moment or two, then leaned forward.

"Thank you," he repeated, "but, be honest with me, Herlander. You *do* want to get even, don't you?"

Simões looked at him silently for several seconds. Then his nostrils flared, and his face took on a strange, hard expression—a *focused* expression, harsh with hatred.

"In a heartbeat, Jack," he admitted, and it was almost as if he found it a relief to say the words out loud, even to McBryde, the man—the friend, as well as keeper—whose job it was to keep him from achieving exactly that. "Oh, in a *heartbeat*. But even if I wanted to, how could I? It's not like I'm in a position to accomplish anything on the grand scale. And, to be honest, I could spend the rest of my life 'getting even' and never come close to what those bastards deserve."

He looked McBryde straight in the eye, letting him see the anger, the hatred, the concentrated bitterness, and McBryde nodded slowly.

"That's what I thought," he said quietly. "But tell me this, Herlander. If I were to show you a way you *could* get even, or make a down payment, at least, would you be interested?"

Simões' eyes narrowed. McBryde wasn't surprised. Even now, after the months they'd known one another, despite the fact that Jack McBryde was probably closer to Herlander Simões' soul than anyone else in the universe, there had to be that instant suspicion. Was this the Alignment's final betrayal? The "friend" completing Simões' destruction by luring him into an overtly treasonous statement?

McBryde understood that, and he made himself sit calmly, looking back at the other man, waiting while Simões' highly competent brain followed that same logic chain to its conclusion. There was no need for McBryde to "lure" him into anything—there'd been more than enough past conversations to provide all the evidence Alignment Security needed to lock him away for the next several decades, at the very least.

The seconds trickled past, tensely, slowly, and then Herlander Simões drew a deep breath.

"Yes," he said, his voice even softer than McBryde's had been. "Yes, I'd be interested. Why?"

✧　✧　✧

Lajos Irvine's eyebrows almost disappeared into his hairline when he played back the imagery from his bug and recognized the "stranger" at the diner's table. His surprise was heightened by the fact that this was a bug he'd put in place weeks ago and this recording was now fairly dated. He didn't check these records regularly, since he didn't want to visit the diner often enough to be recognized.

What the hell . . . ?

He realized he was sitting there, frozen in astonishment, and gave himself an impatient shake. It still didn't make any sense to him, but he triggered the fast forward, watching the take from the bug, and there was no question what he was seeing.

What the fuck is Jack McBryde *doing sitting around drinking coffee in a dive like Turner's? That's so far outside his bailiwick it's not even funny. And if he's going to run an op on* my *turf, why the hell didn't he* tell *me he was?*

He frowned, tipping back in the battered armchair in the tiny kitchen of the cramped apartment to which his trustee's status entitled him, and thought hard. McBryde wasn't like that asshole Lathorous. Oh, he had some of the same star line's "my shit doesn't stink" attitude, but he had it under better control. And he'd at least always tried to look like he respected the unglamorous and thoroughly unpleasant duty of deep-penetration agents like Irvine. And he *had* suggested he'd be keeping his own eye on the situation Irvine had reported to him. He was far enough up the seniority tree that he could do it just about any way he wanted to, too, but still . . .

He's been an office puke for years now, Irvine reflected. *It shows, too. He's so far out of practice he didn't even come up with a disguise that would have fooled anyone. And it never occurred to me to mention to him I'd left bugs in the place.*

Irvine grimaced and reminded himself to be fair.

No, it didn't fool me, that's true, but, then again, I know him. I doubt anyone in that restaurant has ever met Mr. Jack McBryde, Secret Agent at Large. In fact, the only people who would *recognize him would be other Security types. But in that case,* his eyes narrowed, *why worry about a disguise at all? As far as I know, he's never been operational here on Mesa, so who the hell is he disguising himself* against?

Irvine sat thinking for several more seconds, then leaned forward and replayed the imagery from the very beginning. It wouldn't have been obvious to most people, but Irvine wasn't "most people." He was a highly trained intelligence officer, and his frown deepened again as he realized McBryde was there for the express purpose of speaking with the waiter. And, Irvine decided, both of them were working very hard at pretending that he hadn't. They were doing a damned good job of it, too. If anything had been needed to convince Irvine that the big seccy really was an operator himself, watching him "not talking" to McBryde would have supplied it.

And McBryde was doing exactly the same thing back, although not quite as well. Probably because he was rusty from so many years sitting behind a desk. But why was he bothering? What the hell were they talking about? It had to be some kind of infiltration operation, but what the hell did McBryde think he was doing, pulling that kind of stunt on his own? And why hadn't he even bothered to get more background out of Irvine? Or at least alert Irvine so that he'd have had some kind of backup if this bizarre effort of his went belly-up?

It wasn't just stupid, it was *dangerous*, and something about it was ringing bells somewhere deep inside Lajos Irvine's brain. Obviously, McBryde was senior enough to him that there was absolutely no reason the other man should have bothered to get Irvine's *permission*. He had the authority to initiate investigations whenever and wherever he chose, if he thought there was any threat to the Gamma Center's security. But—

Irvine's train of thought stuttered abruptly, and he sat suddenly bolt upright in his chair.

No, he told himself. *That's just too fucking off the wall even for you, Lajos! The man's the frigging head of security for the Gamma Center, for crying out loud! He's a Level Fourteen, damn it, and Bardasano's only a Sixteen, herself!*

Yes, he is, a small, quiet voice said in the back of his brain. *And there could be all kinds of perfectly legitimate reasons for him to be doing this. The fact that you can't remotely begin to imagine what one of them might be doesn't mean they don't exist. But what if that's because he* doesn't *have a reason—a legitimate one, at least?*

The thought sent an icy shudder down Lajos Irvine's spine. It was preposterous, and he knew it. But if McBryde *was* up to something, his general knowledge and—especially!—his assignment as the Center's security chief put him in a position to do a terrifying amount of damage. And he was the Center's security *chief*, so who'd question anything he might choose to do?

Oh, shit. I do not need this. I really, really do not need this. If he is up to something, then God only knows how much damage he's already done. But if he's not up to something and I start punching alarm buttons, he's not going to like it very much. And he's going to be in a hell of a position to make me wish I'd never opened my mouth. Besides which, whose alarm buttons do I punch? Not his, that's for damned sure! And that bastard Lathorous is not only a major pain in the ass in his own right, but he and McBryde go way back. Taking this to him wouldn't be the most career-enhancing move I can think of, either. But if I don't take it to someone and there's anything at all to it . . .

He sat staring at the frozen imagery, and his brain raced.

✦   ✦   ✦

"Tomorrow? So soon?" Herlander's tone of voice was more that of a man puzzled than one distraught. By now, the estrangement between Simões and everyone he knew except Jack was essentially complete. The only thing he really cared about any longer, besides his anger and desire for vengeance, was the memory of his daughter—and he could take that wherever he went.

"Tomorrow's Saturday," McBryde explained. "I've already been told to have one last interview with you, in order to settle everything before you go off to Siberia."

Simões frowned. "Where's Siberia?"

"Sorry. It's just an old reference. It means a long exile, Herlander, and under very tough conditions. In your case, it's probably going to mean a long stint of 'rehab' and a series of shit assignments where they can sit on you and be sure you don't fuck anything up looking for some sort of revenge. You're too valuable to just get rid of entirely, but it's going to be a cold day in hell before anyone really trusts you again, and you know it."

Simões looked at him for a moment, then nodded.

"Okay, I can't argue with any of that. But why is tomorrow significant?"

"I already told Bardasano that it'd be best to have our last meeting on a Saturday. There won't be a lot of people around in the Gamma Center, so I said it'd be more relaxing for you. Make it easier for me to get whatever final wrapup information you might be able to provide." He shrugged. "I was planning to stall until next Saturday—maybe even the one after that—but given the new developments we should do it right away."

Herlander took a deep breath. "Okay. What should I do?"

"Early tomorrow morning, go to this address." He slid a piece of paper across the table. "Memorize it and destroy the note. Someone will be there to take you to the rendezvous with the people who'll be taking us off the planet. I'll meet you there later, after I finish some last business at the Gamma Center."

"What bus—? Oh. You'll be laying false leads."

Jack smiled. "That's one way to put it."

Anton looked around the table. "Is everyone clear on what needs to happen?"

Carl Hansen gave his three subordinates a quick glance. "Yes, I think so. David, you've got the trickiest assignment. Any questions?"

David Pritchard shook his head. "No, it's straightforward enough. After whoever-it-is-whose-name-remains-unknown leaves this 'Gamma Center' place—which I'll be told by a signal from Karen—I park the air car in the lot of the sports stadium next door and walk away, giving myself plenty of time to get clear. Cary will trigger the device we've already planted in the old Buenaventura tower as soon as word comes from Carl that he's on his way to the spaceport with whoever-it-is. Then I blow mine."

"It probably won't even scratch the 'Center,'" Hansen said, "given how deep it's buried. But it should do some major damage to Suvorov Tower." Like the other members of his group, Hansen had only the vaguest notion, even now, of what the Gamma Center truly was, but he didn't have to know *what* it was as long as he knew it was important to the authorities he hated with every fiber of his being. "Suvorov's right on top of it," he continued, "so the scorpions're bound to assume the Center's the real target of whatever is happening."

Pritchard had a sour look on his face. "I still don't understand why we're taking so much effort to keep the casualties down. That part of the city, the only seccies around will be servants and janitors."

"Which is exactly why we're doing it this way, David." Karen Steve Williams was making no effort to hide her unfriendliness. "Those servants and janitors are our people too, you know, even if you don't care about them. As it is, we'll be killing a few of them. But at least this way—and it'll help a lot that it's on a Saturday—it shouldn't be too bad."

Cary Condor nodded. "I agree with Karen. David, try to hold the bloodlust to a reasonable minimum, will you? It'd be a different story if you could park the air car in Suvorov's own garage—"

"Better still, park it right in the middle of Pine Valley Park," Pritchard said savagely. Pine Valley was the park at the exact center of Green Pines, and Green Pines was inhabited only by freeborn citizens—and wealthy and very well-connected ones, at that. The Gamma Center's hidden location was well inside the Green Pines city limits, but it was on the commercial side of the city.

"Yeah, sure, that'd be great—except there's no way you're parking an air car in or near either place and getting out safely. Not with the security they've got. The parking lot of the sports stadium is as close as we can realistically get."

Pritchard was not happy with the arrangement. Even a nuclear device—as small as the one he had, anyway—wasn't going to do that much damage to a buried, hardened installation. Not when it was set off out in the open, in an empty parking lot, more than a kilometer from its target, anyway.

But . . . he supposed it was better than nothing. And he knew there was no point in continuing the argument any longer.

"Yeah, yeah, fine. I understand the plan."

Victor and Yana finished their final walk-through of the escape passageway. It had originally been built to be one of the conduits for the city's underground transport network. About a century earlier, the city had discontinued most of that network, but had seen no reason to demolish what existed. In fact, they'd spent some money shoring it up and making sure it was stable. The expense of tearing apart buildings which had been erected on top of the areas in order to do a proper job of filling in the conduits would have been far greater. So would the repair cost of having parts of the city collapse if those old underground passageways started corroding.

Since then, the abandoned passageways had been put to different uses by different people. Not surprisingly, the city had a large population of indigents, including a number of people who were not sane. Many of them lived down there. Criminals used the passageways for any number of purposes—and paid off the police to keep them from inspecting too often or too carefully. Merchants used them to store perishable goods, under what amounted to dirt-cheap climate controlled conditions. And, finally, the passageways were used by the underground, smuggling escaped slaves to freedom.

This particular passageway could be reached from a hidden entry in the basement of one of the tenements not far from Steph Turner's restaurant. The passageway ran for fully two kilometers thereafter under the city's streets. They'd use the next-to-last exit, which would put them within easy walking distance of the delivery van that would take them into the spaceport itself. By the time they reached the van, Carl Hansen and the two Mesan defectors should already have arrived. All of them except Carl and Victor—Carl as the driver; Victor as his helper—would be hidden in the crates in the van's interior. Unless the security guards at the spaceport insisted on physically searching the van, including breaking into the crates, everything should work fine. Among the many items Victor had obtained from the ever-helpful Triêu Chuanli had been shipping containers that were not only environmentally sealed but even had equipment designed to block the sort of instrumental inspection that security guards were usually satisfied with.

It wasn't likely at all that these guards would insist on a physical search. That area of the spaceport was given over to shipments to and from the smaller and less reputable freighters in orbit. It was taken for granted that a certain amount of smuggling was being carried out. Carl's bribes should be enough to do the trick.

If not . . . Well, Victor was there. With the same Kettridge Model A-3 tucked up his sleeve. There was at least a chance—not a bad one, either—that he could kill all the guards before they could send out a warning. From there, they might be able to make it to the *Hali Sowle*'s tender and get into low orbit before anyone really knew what had happened. There were so many such tenders coming and leaving that unless the authorities spotted which one they were in, they might be able to get aboard the *Hali Sowle* undetected.

Hopefully, of course, it wouldn't come to that.

"Well, that's it," Yana said. "Victor, I have to say it's been a real pleasure sleeping with you night after night after night in the sure and certain knowledge that I would get no thrills whatsoever."

"Oh, stop whining. If I *had* given you any thrills—and Thandi found out—you'd get the thrill of a lifetime."

Yana grinned. "A very short lifetime."

"They don't call her Great Kaja for nothing."

On his way back from the safe house where he'd had the meeting with Hansen's group, using a different underground passageway, Anton decided to wrestle with his conscience. There wasn't any time left. He'd either pin the damn thing down or he'd have to concede defeat—which would mean reopening those parts of the plan with Victor that he wasn't happy about.

His pangs of conscience centered on the fact that they'd be using nuclear devices. He'd never been comfortable with that. Initially, he'd argued that they could substitute fuel-air bombs, which could do just as much damage as small nuclear explosives. He'd given up that argument when their local contacts insisted they didn't have the resources to build homemade bombs of that type—which, of course, was an obvious . . . prevarication. True, unlike nuclear devices, there was no civilian use for fuel-air bombs that made the alternative of just buying them on the black market feasible, but that wasn't really the point, either. *He* could have whipped up a suitable fuel-air bomb for them in two or three hours using commercially available hydrogen, a portable cooking unit, and a cheap timer, and he knew they knew it. Which meant that the real reason they "didn't have the resources" was because they wanted to make a statement, and he had serious reservations about making the statement in question.

Partly, of course, it had been his hope and expectation at the time that this sort of "flamboyant" (to put it mildly) escape method would never be necessary anyway. There'd been no way, of course, to predict or even envision the sort of espionage treasure trove that Jack McBryde and his companion represented.

Anton knew that, as a purely practical proposition, his reluctance to use nuclear devices was pointless. You could even argue—as Victor certainly would—that it was downright silly. The human race had long since developed methods of mass destruction that were more devastating than any nuclear device ever built. The former StateSec mercenaries who'd soon be trying to destroy Torch on Mesa's behalf wouldn't be using nuclear weapons. It would take far too many of them, and why bother anyway? They'd be using missiles, of course, but they'd be using them as kinetic weapons. Accelerated to seventy or eighty percent of light-speed, they'd do the trick as thoroughly as any "dinosaur killer" in galactic history, but it wouldn't be because of any nuclear warheads! For that matter, a few large bolides—nothing fancier than rocks or even ice balls—could have done the job just fine, if the attackers had only had the time to accelerate them to seventy or eighty thousand KPS, which was barely a crawl by the standards of an impeller-drive civilization. It would simply be faster and simpler to use missiles than piss around with rocks and ice cubes.

That said, for a lot of people in the modern universe—and Anton happened to be one of them—nuclear weapons carried a lingering ancient horror. They had been the first weapons of mass destruction developed and used by human beings against each other. For that reason, perhaps, they still had a particular aura about them.

Of course, that was exactly the reason Hansen and his group— certainly David Pritchard—were so determined to use nuclear explosives. Not only were they in the grip of a ferocious anger going back centuries, but the knowledge which Anton and Victor had given them that Mesa planned to destroy Torch had given that fury a tremendous boost. Stripped to its raw and bleeding essentials, the attitude of Hansen's people could be summed up as: *So the scorpions want to play rough, do they? No problem. Rough it is.*

They knew that setting off nuclear devices on Mesa itself would constitute a massive—indeed, qualitative—increase in the already-murderous intensity of the struggle between slaves and their creators. The plans of those slavemasters to violate the Eridani Edict would do the same, of course. But, at least once, it would be slaves who struck the first such blow.

Zilwicki had real doubts about the wisdom of that course of action. Even Victor did, if not to the same degree as Anton. But there was a momentum to this fight that, at certain places and times—and he suspected this was one of them—overrode all caution.

For a moment, hearing a slight rustling noise to his left, Anton stopped and turned toward it. That was just a reflex action on his part, making clear to anyone who contemplated attacking him that such a course of action would be most unwise.

Perhaps it was inevitable. Perhaps even beneficial. Anton had no hope that the people behind this "Mesan Alignment" scheme could be brought to see reason. Just the information McBryde had already given them made it obvious that, for all their intellect and acuity, they'd abandoned reason centuries ago. But maybe they could be intimidated, in the same crude manner that Anton was even now intimidating whoever lurked in that darkness to the side of the passageway.

Probably not. Almost certainly not. But was it still worth a try?

What decided him in the end, though, was none of that. It was nothing more sophisticated than the impulses driving Hansen and Pritchard and their people. These Mesan Alignment people and their Manpower stooges were, after all, the same swine who had kidnapped one of his daughters, tried to murder another, tried to murder his wife—him too, of course, but he held no grudge about that—and were now trying to murder his daughter *again*.

To hell with it. Let them burn.

They'd already decided Anton would spend this last night in Victor and Yana's safe house. That posed a slight risk, but less than adding an additional complication to their actions on the morrow by requiring yet another rendezvous.

His two companions were there when he arrived, sitting at the same kitchen table where they'd spent so many hours already.

"You're looking pensive," said Victor. "Is something troubling you, Anton?"

He draped the jacket he'd been wearing to fend off the chill over one of the seats. "No," he said.

Late that night, Lajos came to his decision. Much as he hated to take the risk, he didn't see where he had any choice. He'd have to tell Bardasano.

Tomorrow, early in the morning. It'd take a fair amount of persuasion before he could get past Bardasano's aides, since he was not one of the people she had any regular contact with. Trying to do it at night was probably impossible.

Tomorrow would be soon enough, anyway. It wasn't as if Jack was going anywhere.

CHAPTER FIFTY-TWO

Jack McBryde felt a curious brittle, singing hollowness swirling around inside him as he offered his retinal pattern to the scanner and slid his hand through the biometric security sensors as he'd done so many times before. Even now, it was almost impossible for him to believe—really believe—that this was the last time he would ever do it.

"Good morning, Chief McBryde," the uniformed sergeant behind the sensors said with a smile. "Didn't expect to see you here today. Sure as hell, not this early."

"*I* didn't expect to see me here today, either," McBryde replied with carefully metered wry humor. "That was before I realized how far behind I am, though." He rolled his eyes. "Turns out there are a few little details that need to be tied up for my quarterly reports."

"Ouch." The sergeant chuckled sympathetically. Unlike some of his peers, Jack McBryde was popular with his subordinates, and part of that was because he didn't go around ripping people's heads off because he thought he was some sort of tin god.

"Well, I'd better get to it," McBryde sighed, then shook his head. "Oh, by the way, I'm expecting Dr. Simões. Send him straight along to my office when he gets here, okay?"

"Yes, Sir."

The sergeant's sympathetic humor vanished. By now, everyone in the Center knew about Simões. They knew how long and hard McBryde had fought to keep him functional ... and they also knew the security chief had finally lost the battle. The sergeant

467

very much doubted that McBryde was looking forward to what would almost certainly be his final interview with the embittered scientist.

"Thanks."

McBryde nodded, then headed for his office.

❖　　　❖　　　❖

Lajos Irvine showed up at Steph Turner's diner at eight in the morning, as Bardasano had instructed him to do, feeling distinctly unhappy with this assignment. His unhappiness stemmed from two factors.

First, he disliked—intensely—getting orders that were vague to the point of being oatmeal.

Check out the diner and see if you can spot anything suspicious. Let me know right away on my private com if anything turns up. While you're doing that, I'll be putting McBryde through the wringer to find out what the hell he thinks he's doing.

Wonderful. And Bardasano was supposed to be some sort of star-line genius! She might as well have told him to hang out at the playground and tell her if he spotted any of the kids acting in an unruly manner. What—*specifically*—did she want him to look for? Who knew?

Something about McBryde's activities must have rattled her more than he'd thought they would. Oh, having it come at her cold probably accounted for some of that, and Irvine supposed having a peon of his own lowly rank crash her security just as she was sitting down to breakfast probably hadn't helped. Maybe she just wasn't a morning person?

His lips quirked slightly at the thought, even now, but the temptation to smile faded quickly. At least some confusion had to be inevitable when a junior agent jumped the queue the way he had, but this struck him as more than just the inevitable bureaucratic confusion of something the size and complexity of Alignment Security. By all accounts he'd ever heard, Bardasano was normally as sharp as a razor, yet no impartial observer would have reached that conclusion based on the instructions she'd given *him*.

The second source of his unhappiness, and an even greater one, was shuffling along the street about a hundred meters behind him. In addition to giving him vague instructions, Bardasano had also insisted on saddling Lajos with what she called "backup." Three people from one of her "special units"—whatever the hell that meant—who'd be there to provide him with whatever force he might need.

Wonderful. Irvine was a *spy*, not some sort of stupid HD "action hero." He collected information, was what he did. If Bardasano wanted him to do his job, he'd be able to do it a lot better working on his own with no backup at all—much less "backup" whose fieldcraft was so rusty that probably the mutts in the street knew the three clowns following him were official muscle. And if, on the contrary, she wanted to crack down on whoever was at the diner this morning, then why the hell did she insist on dragging Lajos into the business at all?

He wasn't even carrying a weapon. If for no other reason, because he was legally as well as genetically a seccy, and seccies were forbidden to possess firearms of any kind. Even having a knife whose blade was longer than six centimeters would get you arrested, if you were found with it.

Lajos made a silent vow that in the unlikely event violence did break out in Turner's place, his contribution to the cause of righteousness was going to be to duck under a table. Let Bardasano's "specialists" deal with it. They were the kind of people who swaggered to the bathroom.

Herlander Simões eyed the young man in front of him uncertainly. He'd probably never been this close to a seccy in his entire life, he realized. Even by the standards of star-lines raised in privilege, he'd led a cloistered life.

And now he was putting that life in the hands of one.

No, two. A big, tough-looking blonde woman emerged from the back of the van. She didn't look much like a seccy, though.

"Get in," she said. "I'll help you get tucked away in your crate."

The woman climbed into the crate with him. The crate itself hadn't been sealed yet.

"Now we wait," she said. "I'm Yana."

Jack would really have preferred to take care of all of this yesterday, yet he hadn't quite dared. In some ways, it might not be necessary at all, but he wasn't prepared to settle for "might not" at this point. There was too much data in his computer files, too much information about Simões, too much that might point an alert investigator in the right direction before Zilwicki and Cachat could get them off-planet and out of the system.

Even more important than wiping away any fingerprints he might inadvertently have left, though, was the need to create a diversion. He and Simões were both going to be missed, probably before they could get off-planet, and certainly before they could get out-system. McBryde was pretty sure he'd figured out which of the non-Mesan ships currently in the star system was Zilwicki and Cachat's chariot, and if he could figure it out, so could someone else. So, since they were going to be missed anyway, setting up a suitable school or two of red herrings seemed in order. And the best place to do that was from right here, in his office.

Jack was also pretty sure that Zilwicki and Cachat had their own plans for diversions, although he had no idea what they might be. Probably crude violence, since they didn't have the sort of cybernetic access he did. He hadn't asked, and if he had they probably wouldn't have told him—just as, if he'd been asked, he would have kept his own plans private. He hadn't even told Herlander what he planned to do.

He settled into place at his desk and entered his personal access code. The display winked to life, and, despite himself, he smiled as he pulled the chip from his pocket and snapped it into place.

Lajos had been seated for over two minutes and been handed a menu by the time his three backup people came into the diner. At least they could follow simple instructions. He figured enough time had elapsed that no one would connect his entrance with theirs. Turner's diner was busy this time of the day.

Most of the tables were taken, but there was an open booth against the wall across the restaurant from Irvine's table. Bardasano's three "specialists" slid into the seats.

Lajos had to fight not to wince. This went beyond rusty tradecraft. Hadn't these clowns gotten any training at all? Just for starters, the trio consisted of two men and a woman—and the woman was sitting across from the two men. That was probably a reflection of some pecking order of their own. But that gender configuration, although certainly not unheard of, was unusual enough to draw the attention of anyone who was really a professional at this business.

And . . . sure enough. From beneath lowered eyebrows, he saw

the burly waiter turn away from the trio—he'd been about to
bring them menus—and glance in the direction of the other guy
Lajos was certain was a Ballroom agent.

That one was sitting on a stool at the front counter. Lajos
couldn't see him without turning his head a little. He decided to
risk it, since it wasn't likely—

He'd never been more astonished in his life. The guy was off
the stool already and his hand—

Gun!

Irvine ducked under the table. By the time he got all the way
down, the whole thing was over. In a state of shock, on his knees,
he stared at the carnage across the room.

Anton knew what would happen the moment the three newcomers settled into their seats. Victor would have spotted them when
they came in, just as instantly and surely as Zilwicki had. And
he'd have drawn the same conclusion. One agent might simply be
a spy. Three, especially acting in such obvious unison, meant the
hammer was on its way down. Something had blown. Somehow,
somewhere—who knew?—but it had definitely blown.

Cachat's philosophy in that situation was to shoot the hand
holding the hammer before they got it all the way up. He'd only
been waiting for that inevitable psychological moment when even
the most experienced and hardened commando feels the comfort
of his or her weight settling into a seat, and relaxes just that tiny
little bit.

Giving Victor Cachat that "tiny little bit" was like giving a great
white shark a "tiny little bite."

Anton didn't even try to join in. He was as far out of Cachat's
league here as the Havenite was when it came to manipulating
security software. He'd just get in his way. What he *did* do was
activate the jamming device he carried with him. If the three
people who'd come in had recorders, none of them would now
operate.

Victor took out the woman first. From the seating pattern
they'd assumed in the booth, she was probably the leader. Two
shots to the head, without a center mass preliminary. That was
useful against someone on their feet, especially with a small gun
like the Kettridge, but more likely to be a waste of time with
someone seated at a table.

Then he double-tapped both of the men. Then he took several strides across the room and shot all three of them again. One shot each, taking just an extra split second to aim and make sure the shots were fatal. That was probably unnecessary, since they were almost certainly dead anyway. But Cachat was a firm adherent to the principle that if it was worth doing, it was worth doing well.

He then went to stand at the door. That both prevented anyone from leaving and gave him a clear view of everyone in the diner so that—

"Anyone who tries to use a personal com—so much as takes one in hand—I will shoot dead. Just sit still. None of you still alive are at risk."

That wasn't entirely true, of course. By the time Victor started to point to the man under the table, Anton was already there. He reached under, grabbed him by the collar, and hauled him out.

"I'm afraid you're a suspicious sort of fellow," he said mildly. "You ducked a bit too soon."

Jack had actually prepared the chip several days ago, but there were too many random security checks of the Center's electronic systems for him to have risked downloading his handiwork any sooner than he absolutely had to. When the time came, though, all hell was going to be out for noon as the carefully sequenced messages—and computer-controlled acts of sabotage—raced outward. They'd start right here in the Center, invading computer memories, reducing critical molecular circuitry to slag, and then moving on to invade the Long-Range Planning Board's systems. He doubted they'd get very deep, but he could be wrong. He and Simões had combined the hyper-physicist's expertise and McBryde's knowledge of the security systems when they'd set up the attacks, so there was at least a significant chance they'd manage to do some real damage before their electronic minions were defeated. In the meantime, the master execution programs would be bootstrapping themselves about from one high security system to another and generally wreaking all the havoc they could. Coming from so deep inside, they were almost certain to cause far more chaos and confusion—not to mention damage—than any of the cybersecurity types' worst nightmares had ever envisioned.

And while all that was going on, his own frantic messages would be being dumped to the system, feverishly seeking to alert his superiors to Simões' berserk efforts to punish the Alignment for everything it had done to his daughter and to him. They'd been very carefully crafted to create the impression that McBryde was in personal pursuit of Simões . . . and that the two of them were headed directly for Mendel, where Simões intended a suicide run on the capital itself.

That would be the final touch, the perfect cover for their escape, because that fearless protector of the Alignment, Jack McBryde, would stop the madman who'd become his friend by ramming his explosive-laden air car in midair short of the city's airspace. It would be a very large, very noisy explosion, and any wreckage would be distributed (harmlessly) over large areas of wooded countryside just outside Mendel. Eventually, it would become evident to the crash investigators that there were no human remains strewn about with it, but given how pulverized the wreckage was going to be, it would probably take them a while to reach that conclusion. By which time—

His com pinged suddenly, and he twitched in his chair as he recognized the priority of the signal. His heart seemed to explode inside his chest for a moment, but then he shook himself. There were all kinds of reasons someone might be reaching for him on a priority basis, given his duties, he reminded himself, and hit the acceptance key.

"Yes?"

"Jack, it's Steve." Steven Lathorous' image appeared on the display as he spoke. His dark eyes were even darker than usual, and his expression was deeply worried.

"What is it, Steve?" McBryde asked, concern deepening his own voice as his friend's obvious distress registered.

"What the *fuck* have you been doing?" Lathorous half-blurted.

"Me?" Somehow McBryde put genuine surprise into his voice. He looked at Lathorous for a moment, then grimaced. "What do you mean, what have *I* been doing?"

"I just got off a really strange com conversation," Lathorous said. "One with Bardasano."

"Bardasano?" That name was enough to justify showing at least a little concern, a corner of McBryde's brain told him with lunatic calm, and he let his grimace turn into a frown of mingled confusion and apprehension. "A conversation about *what*?"

"About *you*, dummy!" Lathorous shook his head. "When you offered to take Irvine off my back, it never occurred to me that you'd try to mount some kind of idiot investigation of your own! I mean, you're one of my best friends, Jack, and I think you're one of the smartest people I know, but you haven't worked in the *field* in years. I may not *like* the son of a bitch, but if you felt like someone else just had to look into Irvine's reports, you should've brought it to *me*."

"Oh, *hell*," McBryde muttered while his brain raced frantically. "I didn't want to bother you," he went on improvising on the fly. "It didn't seem all that complicated. Besides, I figured I could use the change of pace. Get away from worrying about Simões and all the rest of the crap here at the Center."

"Oh, yeah? Well, let me tell you, buddy, you're gonna need a better story than 'I got bored pushing chips around' for this one. Unless I miss my guess, Bardasano's on her way to the Center right now to personally rip you a new one for screwing around with procedure this way. I don't think she's feeling very *amused*, Jack."

"Shit," McBryde said. Then he gave himself a shake. "Thanks, Steve. I appreciate the heads-up, and I hope none of this splashes on you."

Lathorous snorted. "The hell with splashing on *me*, you just get started now on figuring out how to spin this the best way you can when she stalks into your office with blood in her eye."

"Best advice I've heard yet," McBryde replied with a somewhat forced smile. "Thanks again. Now I'd better go get started on that spinning, I guess. Clear, Steve."

"Clear," Lathorous replied, and the com blanked.

"Steph, shut up." Anton met the restaurant owner's glare stolidly. "There's no point yelling at me. I'm sorry it came to this, but it did. You have no choice. You either come with us, bringing your daughter, or you'll be dead within a week. So will Nancy."

She sagged a little. "Dammit, I *told* you I had no part—and didn't want any part—of Saburo's business."

"We're not actually Ballroom. But that's no help to you, because from the standpoint of the people running this planet, we're a lot worse. They *will* kill you, Steph. You and Nancy both—after squeezing you dry even though there's nothing to squeeze. They'll never believe you weren't involved."

Despairingly, her eyes looked around the kitchen. "But . . . this is all I *have*. Everything in the world."

Anton smiled. "Well, as far as that goes, you're in luck. Winning the lottery sort of luck. I'm stinking rich, Steph. My wife is, rather. But Cathy's been donating to good causes since she was a kid. She won't blink at setting you up with a restaurant way better than this one."

"You sure?"

"Yeah, I'm sure. Now can we *please* get moving?" He looked at the teenage girl standing wide-eyed against one of the stoves. "We haven't got time for any packing, Nancy. So if there's anything you or your mother desperately need to take with you, it'll have to be something from this kitchen."

Steph took a ladle, which she claimed was her "lucky ladle." Her daughter Nancy, exhibiting a great deal more in the way of practicality or fighting spirit or both, took the biggest knife she could find. In her small hand, it almost looked like a sword.

CHAPTER FIFTY-THREE

McBryde sat staring at the empty display for two or three heart-beats, and his earlier swirling hollowness was suddenly very still, very calm. He knew what he had to do.

His hands went back to the computer keyboard, and he called up one of the sequences he'd just installed. It wasn't in the order he'd planned on activating it, but it ought to do the trick, and he bared his teeth as the central computer's memory was adjusted to show that Herlander Simões had entered his office with him. Information on the personnel movements in and out of the Center was automatically copied to an off-site stand-alone system. He could have reached the off-site system from his personal terminal here in the Center if he'd wanted to erase the information in it, but that was the last thing he wanted, because that stand-alone system was what was going to cover Simões' escape . . . he hoped. He felt a sudden, deep pang of sorrow as he thought about the sergeant down at the entrance foyer, but he couldn't warn the man without undoing Simões' cover. Besides, despite the weekend, the sergeant wasn't the only other person in the complex with him, and there wasn't anything he could do about any of them now.

✧   ✧   ✧

This was proving to be an interesting experience, actually. Curiosity was one of Herlander's most prominent traits, and he now realized that he could possibly use that trait to keep his fear under control.

A climate controlled crate—with top-of-the-line air scrub-bers and what looked like an emergency backup air tank—that

476

appeared, from the outside, as if it was carrying nothing more delicate than heavy machinery.

It was lit inside, too. Very dimly, but it was still light. He'd expected to make the whole trip in darkness, which he hadn't been looking forward to at all.

The woman looked at her timepiece, for perhaps the hundredth time. "They should be here soon," she muttered. "Well. Maybe another half hour."

Herlander's eyes, moving around with interest, were arrested by a panel in one of the corners of the crate.

Good God. Is that scrambling *equipment? Where did they get this stuff?*

Jack thought about sending a final message to Zachariah, or his parents, or his sisters, but not very hard. Much as he wished he could have explained his reasoning to them, he'd already decided he couldn't risk that. Security was going to be looking at all of them very closely, and their best protection was going to be the fact that he'd never said a single word to any of them about what he planned. Given Security's facilities, it wouldn't take very long to establish that none of them had had a clue or been involved in any way in his actions. And, despite the revulsion he'd come to feel for the Alignment and all it stood for, it did not punish people for someone else's actions. There'd be a stigma, of course, and they'd all be watched carefully, at least for a while, but no one would hold them responsible for what *he* had done. Sending them any final messages might undermine that immunity, however. Worse, it might start them thinking in the same direction he had, bring them onto the same collision path with the Alignment and everyone around them, and he simply couldn't risk that.

Especially not in light of what he was actually going to do now.

When Anton came back out of the kitchen, Victor still had everyone in the diner completely subdued. That included a new person whom Anton didn't recognize. She must have had the bad luck to walk in a short while ago.

It also included the man Anton had dragged out from under the table. He was kneeling not far from Victor, with his hands clasped behind his back.

Again, Anton grabbed him by the collar and hauled him to his feet. "You're coming with us, fella."

As he headed toward the rear exit, he heard Victor saying to the people held captive: "Here's how it is. We have associates standing guard outside both doors, front and back. Anyone who tries to leave within five minutes will be shot. No warning, no discussion, you will simply be dead. Once five minutes are up"—he pointed to the far wall—"according to that time display, you can leave the diner. Go anywhere you want. My own advice, take it or leave it, is that you'd be wise to pretend you were never here. This place has no recording or security equipment, except whatever these corpses brought with them, and we took care of that. So you can probably get away with it."

He started walking across the room toward the back exit. "Or you can report the incident to the authorities, who will certainly treat you with the respect traditionally given to seccies. It's your choice."

Half a minute later, he and Anton and the two women and their captive were in the escape passageway.

There, they stopped. Anton shoved the captive against the wall and stepped back. Victor stepped forward, the gun in his hand.

Lajos Irvine was petrified. He was about to die, and he knew it. There was no mercy at all in those black eyes and the gun hand was as steady as a bar of steel.

A few seconds passed. Maybe five, although it seemed like fifty.

"I'm just not positive," said the black-eyed man.

"It's your call," said the waiter.

The black-eyed man stepped back. "He needs to be out for at least four hours."

"Not a problem." The waiter came to stand right in front of Lajos. He looked as wide as the sea.

"I'd say this was going to hurt me more than it hurts you, but that'd be ridiculous."

The sledgehammer fist didn't hurt at all, oddly enough. Or, if did, Lajos could never remember.

✧　　✧　　✧

From the beginning, Jack McBryde had realized that simply defecting wasn't enough—not in light of all he'd contributed to the Alignment first. That was the real reason he'd chosen to attack the Center's secure data network and every other computer system he could reach. There were backups, of course, but there was at least a chance of inflicting significant damage on the Alignment's most secure data systems, and that was definitely worth trying.

Only now he wasn't going to have that opportunity. There wasn't going to be enough time. Which meant there was only one way he could hope to take out a meaningful chunk of truly significant data, and since it was painfully clear to him that he wasn't going to be getting off Mesa after all . . .

He tapped a combination into his personal com. It was a one-time, untraceable combination—one he'd set up through his own security connections, even as he'd hoped he'd never need it. It buzzed only once, and then Herlander Simões's voice answered. McBryde could hear the tension in it, the recognition that he wouldn't have been calling on this combination unless something had gone seriously wrong.

"Yes?" Simões said.

"Eggshell," McBryde replied, and heard an audible inhalation as the emergency codeword registered.

"I—" Simões began, then stopped. There was the harsh sound of someone clearing his throat. "Understood. Thanks. I . . . won't forget."

"Good." McBryde wanted to say something more himself, but there wasn't time, and there wasn't much he *could* have said, anyway. Except—"Be well. Clear."

Feeling stunned, Herlander keyed off his com.

"What does that mean?" asked Yana.

"It means he's been . . . he's going to . . ." He burst into tears. "He's the only friend I *have*."

They were practically running down the passageway, now. Anton wasn't happy about that at all. First, it broke every rule of tradecraft. Secondly, there was a genuine risk of tripping over something in the dim light. And there were plenty of "somethings" to trip over, too. The floor of the passageway was littered with debris. Unlike some of these underground tunnels, this one was little-used. That was a good part of the reason they'd selected it, of course. But all they needed at this point was for someone to get injured in a fall.

They simply had no choice. The incident in the diner had not only delayed them, it had also made clear that something had gone wrong. What that something might be, they still had no idea. But whatever time they might have, it was running out.

Jack killed the circuit connecting him to Simões and began punching more keys. It was a long, complicated sequence this time—one carefully designed so that no one would ever enter it by accident—and he felt his stomach knotting with tension as the security fences went down, one by one, each seeking and demanding its own confirmation. He was probably the only person on the entire planet who had all of the required security codes, and even he wasn't supposed to have *all* of them. It was supposed to be a "two-man" rule situation, but McBryde had always recognized that if they were actually needed, there might not be time to get the designated "second man" online before it was too late.

I never realized how long this took, a corner of his mind thought distantly as he entered yet another in the queue of required commands and codes. *If I had, I would have suggested streamlining things. How does anyone expect to have the time to go through all this rigmarole in a genuine emergency situation? It's stupid, that's what—*

The mental sentence broke off in mid-thought as a boldly tattooed woman and three of her personal aides appeared in the field of view of the pickup he had focused on the Center's main entrance. He watched the uniformed sergeant springing to his feet as he recognized Isabel Bardasano and swore softly.

There's still time, he told himself. *It takes a good six minutes to get to my office from there, even using the high-speed lift. And I think I can probably slow things down at least a bit . . .*

"Thank God," said Carl Hansen, as Victor and Anton came out of the tenement. Then, seeing the two women with them, he frowned. "Who're they?"

"Never mind right now. They're coming with us. Something's gone wrong."

Yana emerged from the back of the van. "No kidding something's gone wrong." She hooked a thumb over her shoulder. "Our passenger in there got a call a little while ago from He Who Is Not To Be Named. He's been found out, he's trapped in the center, and . . ."

Victor nodded. "He'll suicide. Good man."

Yana's grin was purely feral. "Oh, he's not going out alone, Victor. Not by a long shot."

That was one of the few times in his life Anton ever saw Victor Cachat's eyebrows raise in surprise. It would have been worth a chuckle except they had too much to figure out and decide.

"If he's going to blow the Gamma Center, we should alert Cary to wait and blow the Buenaventura at the same time. If we're lucky, the Mesans will think the acts were coordinated ahead of time."

He was a bit relieved at the prospect of setting off the device hidden in the basement of the Buenaventura this early on a Saturday morning. The tower itself was abandoned, and situated in an old industrial area that was mostly vacant. There were bound to be some casualties, but at least they'd be kept to a minimum.

Unfortunately, from Anton's viewpoint, they couldn't simply abort the explosion. Destroying the Buenaventura was the key to their faked escape records—which they now probably needed more than ever.

There was no longer any point, however, in setting off the explosion at the sports stadium. First, because David Pritchard might very well get killed when McBryde detonated the nearby Gamma Center. Secondly, what was the point anyway? David's bomb couldn't possibly do as much damage as McBryde's measures would.

Carl was keying the new instructions to Cary. "Okay, that's done," he said a short while later. "What's next?"

"Send instructions to Karen and David. Tell them to get the hell out and go to ground. If they go into hiding now, I think they've still got a decent chance of eluding the manhunt that's about to come down. Which is going to be one hell of a manhunt."

Hansen's face seemed to get a bit drawn, but he typed out the instructions quickly and surely.

"What about me, Anton?" he asked quietly.

"You'll have to come with us, Carl. There's no way around it now."

Hansen shook his head. "No. I'm not leaving my people on Mesa in the lurch."

Anton set his jaws. "Carl, if you wait to run until we've launched for the *Hali Sowle*, there is almost no chance you won't be spotted."

"I understand that. But I'm not changing my mind."

"Leave it, Anton," said Victor. "He's full-grown and it's his choice—and it's the same choice I'd make, in his position." He started climbing into the passenger seat in the front of the van. "Now, let's get going."

After driving for perhaps three minutes, in the direction of the spaceport, Carl pulled out his com to see if there'd been any reply to his messages. He didn't expect there would be, since there was really nothing to say and each transmission carried a slight risk of being intercepted.

Sure enough, there was nothing from Cary or Karen. But from David Pritchard . . .

"Oh, hell and damnation," he sighed.

"What's the matter?" asked Victor.

Carl handed him the com. "Read it for yourself."

Victor looked at the screen.

FUCK YOU
COWARDS
FUCK YOU

"He's lost it."

"Big time," said Carl.

It was obvious Bardasano didn't have a clue how deep Jack's own internal rot had truly spread. If she had, she'd have come in with sirens screaming, three battalions of security troops, and enough heavy weapons to suppress a full-bore slave rebellion. And she would have used her own security overrides to completely shut down the Center, too. From her expression, she really was more than a little pissed off over his shenanigans—what she *thought* were his shenanigans, at any rate—but she wasn't moving with anything like the urgency she would have shown if she'd even suspected what was really going on. Which was why Jack McBryde still had control of the Center's computers and internal security systems.

On the other hand, she's got the ultimate override access authority for every security system on the damned planet, he reminded himself. *She can always take that control away from me if something convinces her that's a good idea.*

Which was true enough, but entering her own authorization codes would take at least a little time, and in the meanwhile . . .

He watched Bardasano and her aides pile into the lift car while he kept his other eye focused on his computer display.

Only three more entries to go, he thought, and punched up a separate subsystem.

You know, Jack, he told himself almost whimsically, *you were just thinking about inflicting "significant damage," weren't you? And Bardasano's the most effective security type the Alignment's had in decades. So I guess this comes under the heading of serendipity.*

His forefinger came down on a single macro, and he watched over the lift car's internal pickup as Bardasano's head snapped up in astonishment. The lift car stopped, alarms began to wail all over the Center, and Jack McBryde bared his teeth in a smile. Security doors slammed shut throughout the Center, and "fire alarms" started screaming in the commercial tower above it. There probably still wouldn't be time for Suvorov to be completely evacuated—and for all of the evacuees to get far enough clear—but the casualty count had just been materially decreased, and that was good.

The main computers cycled through another level of commands and asked for the next one. He entered it, then sat back, waiting, watching over the lift car pickup as Bardasano snatched out her personal minicomp and started entering commands of her own.

I guess this is where I find out whether it's going to take her as long as I thought it was or not, he reflected, and opened his desk drawer.

He took out the pulser, checked the charge indicator, and made sure there was a dart in the chamber. If it turned out she could invade the system more quickly than he'd thought she could, he was going to have to settle for a much less spectacular goodbye.

❖   ❖   ❖

David Pritchard was shrieking with rage as his air car approached the sports stadium.

"I am *sick* of you spineless bastards! You hear me? Sick to fucking death of your whining and puling and whimpering—fuck

❖   ❖   ❖

Bardasano was still punching keys when McBryde's computer accepted the last authorization code he'd entered and asked

for one more. This one had to be given orally, with voiceprint authentication.

"Scorched Earth," he said very carefully.

"Scorched Earth acknowledged," an emotionless computer voice said. "All sequences successfully entered and acknowledged. Execution enabled. Do you wish to proceed, Chief McBryde?"

Jack McBryde looked at the people in the lift car one final time.

Good luck, Herlander, he thought softly at the tormented man who had become his friend. *Give them hell for me . . . and Francesca.*

Then he cleared his throat.

"Execute Scorched Earth," Jack McBryde said calmly.

CHAPTER FIFTY-FOUR

Luckily for the inhabitants of the city, Gamma Center was deeply buried. No part of the Center proper was less than fifty meters underground; most of it was considerably deeper than that—and the nuclear device triggered off by Scorched Earth had been deliberately positioned at the very base of the huge subterranean complex.

The people who'd guided the Mesan Alignment for centuries and had built Gamma Center were far removed from the half-crazed ancient despots whose response to disaster was often to burn their cities down around them. Scorched Earth was not a suicide program in the normal sense of the term—although, if triggered, it would certainly kill everyone in the Center at the time.

But its purpose was rational, not emotional—and certainly not hysterical. Scorched Earth was not designed to kill people, much less to kill people outside the Center who just happened to be living in the city. That would happen, but only as a byproduct. No, the sole and single function of Scorched Earth was to destroy the Center itself, so completely and thoroughly that no enemy could possibly glean anything from its ruins.

The bomb amounted to a shaped charge on a gigantic scale. It was specifically designed to cause maximum damage to the Center itself—and minimal damage to anything beyond.

It worked as planned, too. Unfortunately, "minimal damage" when done by a fifty kiloton nuclear device, no matter how well planned and executed, is only "minimal" by the peculiar standards of people who design and build nuclear weapons.

By anyone else's standards, Scorched Earth was a holocaust.

✧   ✧   ✧

The explosion wasn't triggered until almost three seconds after McBryde spoke the final words, and during those three seconds, the sabotage programs from his chip had time to upload themselves out of the Center's computers. Not many of them, compared to his original plans, but one hell of a lot more than any of the Alignment's cybersecurity teams had ever imagined might come at them from *inside* their primary firewalls. Or might carry with them so many perfectly valid access and authorization codes.

Once the first tier of the network started going down, watchdog systems sprang into action, of course, but not quickly enough to prevent some fairly awesome destruction. Very few of the major subsystems escaped altogether unscathed.

The military was much less severely affected, for several reasons. First, because by the very nature of things the military preferred standalone systems wherever possible. Second, because Alignment Security was very carefully partitioned off from the official Mesan secret services and the star system's official military forces, which meant access points were strictly limited. Third, because in the case of the military, the gateways which existed were under the control of the admirals of the clandestine Mesan Alignment Navy, and without much more time to work with, McBryde's cybernetic saboteurs were unable to wiggle their way through. Fourth, because McBryde had possessed nowhere near as much access to the MAN's authorization codes. And, fifth, because there simply wasn't time for his programs to get through before the Gama Center—and its computers—ceased to exist.

But there were far more links from Alignment Security's primary net to most of the other, openly maintained civilian intelligence agencies, and *those* were under the control of the Alignment, not the agencies which didn't even know they'd been penetrated. Indeed, they were specifically set up to allow Alignment Security to sneak in and out of the "official" databanks tracelessly—to co-opt those banks' data without anyone outside Alignment Security's ever being the wiser. The people who had designed the system had always realized that all those backdoors hopelessly compromised the official agencies' security, but since the *Alignment* was the one doing the compromising, they hadn't lost much sleep over the thought.

As it happened, it still took precious time for McBryde's programs to squirm through, yet they got through much more *quickly* than they had in the military's case. Not only that, but he'd prioritized his attacks carefully.

Only one attack fully succeeded, even so, but it was the one upon which he'd lavished the most care and effort, and he wasn't taking any chances on simply *erasing* the data he was after. Oh, no. *His* attack came equipped with the specific security codes for the computers in question, triggering the command sequence which reformatted their molecular circuitry itself. Turned those computers' memories into solid, inert chunks of crystalline alloy from which Saint Peter himself could not have recovered one single scrap of data. And because the man who'd prepared that attack came from so high inside Security itself, he'd known where all the *backups* were maintained . . . and how to reach them, too.

In that one successful attack, over ninety percent of all Mesan records concerning the Ballroom—those of the "official" agencies and the Alignment's alike—simply vanished. And since Mesa still considered Torch an extension of the Ballroom, all the Alignment's data on Torch went with it.

All gone, except for whatever scraps survived in partial form in other locales. No doubt there were enough of those scraps to reconstitute much of that data in the fullness of time, yet it was a task which would take literally years . . . and never be anything remotely like complete.

The day after Scorched Earth, Jeremy X himself could have walked openly down the streets of any Mesan city, giving DNA samples at every corner, without anyone being the wiser, unless he was spotted by one of the very few Mesans who'd encountered him personally and survived the experience.

Among the *other* cybernetic systems which were damaged were those of Mesan customs. The damage was . . . odd, and seemingly quirky.

E.D. Trimm stared at the main screen in her operations center, unable to believe what she was seeing. All the many *ships* were still shown. They could still track any of them, whether approaching or leaving or in orbit. Presumably, if they scrambled furiously, they could open up manual lines of communications if any of the ships was in danger of colliding with another.

But the rest of the information was lost. Gone. Vanished.

"*Which ship is which?*" she half-wailed.

"I can still figure out tonnages," said Gansükh Blomqvist. "I . . . think."

"Oh, wonderful. My day is complete."

David Pritchard's air car was caught in the blast and blown wildly off course. He barely managed to avoid a wreck. Rather, the automatic pilot did. David's air car skills were pretty rudimentary, as was true of most seccies.

When his head cleared he saw that he'd overflown the stadium. He looked back, and despite his fury, his eyes widened as he saw the shattered wreckage of what had been Suvorov Tower. The structures of counter-grav civilizations were tough almost beyond belief, and Suvorov had been the better part of a kilometer tall, yet so broad that it looked almost squat. Now it looked like the broken, smoke-and-flame-spewing fang of some hell-spawned monster. The towers on either side were heavily afire, their façades badly shattered, yet they'd coffer-dammed much of the blast effect. Suvorov might be a total loss, and several square blocks of Green Pines' commercial district had been savagely mangled, but—as the people who had planted that charge had planned—the residential portions of the city were untouched.

"Warning. Warning," the autopilot squawked. "Unsustainable damage. Cannot remain airborne longer than five minutes. Land immediately."

Pritchard stared at Suvorov for a moment, then whipped his head around. Pine Valley Park was now clearly visible ahead of him, the dark-blue waters of its central lake dotted with model sailboats.

"Manual control," he commanded.

Ganny Butry's clan, including Ganny, didn't put much stock in the so-called "wisdom of age" except when the phrase was applied to Ganny herself. So the pilot of the shuttle that waited for Anton and Victor on the tarmac was Sarah Armstrong, all of twenty-two years of age—and her copilot was Brice Miller, eight years younger than she was.

Why were they the pilots? Because they were the best Ganny had at the moment. Simple as that. A lot of things were simple for the clan, probably because they were often too ignorant to know better.

"I don't think that's a good idea," said Brice dubiously. He watched as Anton and Victor and Yana and a man he didn't know and two women he'd never seen before but one of whom was already of great interest because she was about his own age continued to unload one of the crates. They were unceremoniously dumping everything it held into a refuse bin that Yana had brought up from one of the nearby maintenance centers. (The mechanics hadn't objected. Partly because Yana gave them her biggest smile but mostly because she gave them an even bigger bribe.)

"Got no choice," grunted Anton, lifting out a piece of equipment only he could have picked up unassisted. "Got to make room for Steph and Nancy."

The big piece of equipment went into the bin. Brice thought there was something familiar-looking about it, but couldn't remember why at the moment.

Most of his mind was elsewhere. *She must be the Nancy one.*

Sarah was practically dancing back and forth with anxiety. In her case, though, not because of the cargo they were jettisoning.

"Hurry it *up*, folks," she hissed. "If we lift off more than thirty seconds behind schedule, customs will have a fit. You could sharpen sticks in their assholes, each and every one. I think they send them all to obsessive-compulsive disorder school for advanced training."

Anton heaved another piece of gear into the bin.

"Why can't we just ride in the shuttle?" asked the younger of the two women. She seemed bright-eyed, alert and curious. That, combined with the big knife in her hand, made her thoroughly fascinating. She was sort of pretty, too.

Brice screwed up his courage. "No room except in the bays. And they're not pressurized. You'd die, outside of the crates."

The girl looked at him. "Who're you?"

"Brice. Brice Miller. I'm the copilot."

"The copilot, huh? How old are you?"

"Uh . . . almost fifteen. Next month."

"I'm Nancy. Nancy Becker. I turned fifteen four months ago. So I'm older than you." Having established that critical point of status, however, the girl's expression became quite warm. "Already a copilot. That's really cool."

Brice still thought dumping the contents of that crate was

probably a bad idea. But he didn't care any longer. Not in the least, littlest, tiniest, teeniest bit.

The crate now emptied, it and its twin were hoisted into the cargo bay with the lift that Sarah had already rented. (For considerably more than she could have gotten it with a bribe—but she was only twenty-two. Still young and naïve.)

"Climb in, all of you!" she said, heading for the shuttle's cabin. "We can still make our schedule. Barely. Brice, seal them in."

The crates were segregated by sex. Zilwicki, Cachat and the man Brice didn't know in one. Yana and the two new women in the other. The crate inhabited by the men was crammed full. The one inhabited by the women was . . . not.

"There's still room for you," said Nancy.

Brice summoned every ounce of duty and discipline he could muster. "Sorry. Can't. I'm the copilot. But I'll be seeing you soon anyway. Uh, all of you."

It didn't take long to seal the crates. Then, seal the bay. Nonetheless, by the time he climbed into his seat in the cabin, Sarah was yelling.

"—fault if we get arrested!" The shuttle began to lift. "And don't expect me to bail you out!"

Sarah could be dense, sometimes. Brice was pretty damn sure that if Mesan customs—much less police—arrested them and discovered they were smuggling superspies and who-knew-what-else off the planet, making bail would be the least of their problems.

"What happened?" demanded Albrecht Detweiler as his son Collin's face appeared the small display.

"We don't know yet, Father," Collin replied. "Gamma Center's gone, but we still have no idea why it happened. The 'how' is clear enough, of course. Some way or another, Scorched Earth got triggered. Beyond that . . ."

With most communications systems in the vicinity of Green Pines disabled, Collin and Albrecht were relying on their personal com equipment. Collin's wife and children had left some time earlier for the family get-together that would soon be taking place at his parents' villa. That villa was incredibly luxurious and incredibly secure—only a relative handful of people even knew it existed, and still fewer knew who lived there. Unfortunately, it was also the better part of eight hundred kilometers from the capital, which made it an inconvenient commute even by air car. The circuitous (and constantly varied) routing Albrecht's security staff demanded only made that worse, so Collin had sent Alexis and the kids ahead while he dealt with a handful of last minute details of the sort his job threw up only too routinely. There was no point having them kick their heels here in Green Pines rather than splashing around in the surf with grandparents determined to spoil them rotten, after all.

But those same routine tasks were the reason he'd been at home when the disaster happened. Since "home" was the penthouse on one of the high-rent residential towers that fronted Pine Valley Park, he had an excellent view of the wreckage which had once been Suvorov Tower and the Gamma Center. Now he stood gazing out through the crystoplast wall of the dining room, shaking his head slowly, as he continued his report to his father.

"... was another explosion in one of the old industrial areas, about twelve kilometers away, just about simultaneously."

"Nuclear?"

"Apparently so, Father. At least, we've gotten reports of high radiation readings from the first responders in the area."

He noticed an air car approaching from the west. Its approach looked damned shaky, even at this distance, a corner of his mind noted. Not that it was especially surprising. It might well have taken damage from the explosion, and even if it hadn't, the pilot was undoubtedly badly rattled. From his approach angle, he must have been almost on the fringes of the blast itself ... no wonder he was making for the park's parking apron. In his place, *Collin* would certainly want to put his car on the ground as quickly as possible!

Those were just idle thoughts, however. The *focus* of his mind was elsewhere.

✧   ✧   ✧

David Pritchard managed to land the air car on the parking apron without wrecking it. But the landing was about as rough as any landing an air car could survive without suffering significant damage.

He could see a pair of city cops turning toward him, and he snarled. They weren't even security legbreakers—just two of those pretty, duded up, glorified nannies who took care of the kinds of people who lived in Green Pines. The kind of people David

Pritchard hated from the very bottom of his soul. The kind of people he could see beyond the cops, laughing and talking while their kids played in the park, enjoying the morning sun. They were turning now, those happy faces, staring at the huge plume of smoke rising to the west. He could see their owners gesticulating at the rising cloud, could almost *hear* their babbling curiosity.

From the look on the cops' faces—concern, mostly—he realized the men must assume that he himself was a scorpion in good steading. Someone whose vehicle had been damaged by the blast, perhaps, and who'd had to set it down wherever he could and as quickly as he could.

He scanned the area, for a few seconds. There was no way to escape, in the time he'd have.

So be it. He'd expected as much. He pulled out the device's control unit and began keying in new timing instructions.

✧   ✧   ✧

"—may as well leave and come here, Collin. The first responders are already blanketing the area—the same at the other location—and what seems to be an army of security people has gotten there also. You won't be able to add anything important from Green Pines."

"On my way then, Father." Collin tucked away his com unit and headed for the door to the corridor beyond. He didn't bother to stop for a jacket, since the weather was so pleasant today.

✧   ✧   ✧

"Hey!" one of the cops shouted suddenly. "That guy's a seccy! He doesn't belong here!"

He and his partner both paused for a moment in disbelief. Sure enough. And now that they looked at it from close up, they could see that a lot of dents and nicks in the air car were vintage wear and tear, not anything produced by the rough landing.

Any seccy intruding into Pine Valley would have had a hard enough day under any circumstances. On *this* day, with their coms screaming about nuclear explosions and the evidence of those same explosions rising before their very eyes...

One of them reached for his pulser.

✧   ✧   ✧

David figured six seconds was enough time. But after he keyed the final code, he discovered he had nothing to say. No final words, no speech. His fury was simply too great.

So, the last sight two Green Pines City Police had was of a face distorted with rage, screaming something they couldn't hear because the seccy was still inside the cockpit.

One of them was something of a lip reader, though. So he figured out that what the seccy was shouting was just "Fuck you!" repeated again and again.

As he waited for the elevator, Collin called Albrecht again. "Father, have you heard anything from Benj—"

At that proximity, the radiation from the blast barely had time to penetrate the protective glass that formed the penthouse's walls on three sides before the hydrodynamic front arrived. As tough as they were, those windows had never been designed—nor could they have been—to withstand that sort of overpressure. They disintegrated into thousands of slivers which would have ripped Collin Detweiler apart if he'd still been standing there. As it was, everything inside the penthouse from the furniture down to the bedding was turned into shreds and the shreds themselves ignited by the thermal pulse.

Ceramacrete was incredibly strong, however—and the buildings at Green Pines had been designed with the possibility in mind that they might be subject to attack from terrorists. The ceramacrete towers in Nouveau Paris which surrounded the Octagon had managed to survive its destruction during Esther McQueen's coup attempt—and that blast had been far more powerful than the one set off in Green Pines.

Collin Detweiler's tower was far enough from ground zero to be well outside the fireball. Moreover, the interior walls protected him from the effects of radiation as well as keeping the fires in the outer apartments from spreading into the inner corridors and elevator shafts.

So, he was still alive when the rescue teams arrived. Battered into a pulp by the effects of the blast, with multiple broken bones and contusions and lacerations seemingly covering his entire body. Barely alive, but alive—and given modern emergency medical techniques, that was enough to ensure his survival.

"You did WHAT?" shrieked Andrew Artlett, less than two minutes after the shuttle began disgorging its contents in one of the cargo bays of the Hali Sowle.

"There goes another one, E.D. What do you want me to do?"

Helplessly, Trimm stared at the screen. Yet another ship was leaving orbit. That was hardly unusual, in and of itself, given the traffic that came in and out of the Mesan system. But there were now at least twice as many ships leaving as there normally would have been.

Whatever had happened down on the surface of the planet to have caused this chaos, it had obviously spooked a lot of ship captains.

She still had no idea which ship was which. But—for once—that jackass Blomqvist had proved to be useful. His jury-rigged system for gauging ship tonnages seemed to be working pretty well. So at least E.D. could separate the big boys from the flotsam and jetsam.

"What's their mass?"

He studied the screen for a few seconds. "I make it about a million tons. Give or take a quarter of a million, you understand."

Trimm waved her hand. "Doesn't matter. It's a small fry. No point in worrying about it with everything else on our plate. I'm not sending out what few pinnaces we have available to check anything smaller than four million tons."

Less than an hour after they made their upward alpha translation, Andrew Artlett was completely and totally vindicated.

Mainly because they'd just made an unscheduled—and *most* unpleasant—*downward* translation.

"Congratulations, you stupid goofballs. The hyper generator is now officially defunct. We're *damned* lucky it lasted long enough for the failsafes to throw us back into n-space before the stabilizer went. Of course, that was *all* the good luck we got issued. You may have noticed that the damned rotor shaft is snapped? Not warped, not bent, not deformed—*snapped?* Which doesn't even mention the collateral damage the thing did when it went! And—thanks to a pair of frigging cowboys I could name—the parts we need to *fix* it are in a garbage *bin* somewhere down on the surface of *Mesa!*"

His volume had risen steadily through the course of his explanation. That might have had something to do with how long he'd spent throwing up after the violent nausea of the totally unexpected crash translation. Or, of course, it *might* have stemmed from some other concern, Brice supposed.

Most likely not, though.

Victor Cachat didn't seem disturbed, however. Neither did Anton Zilwicki.

"Trust us, will you, Andrew?" Victor said. "Nothing that can happen to us now is remotely as bad as what would have happened had we not gotten off Mesa in time."

Andrew was still glaring. "It's going to take *months* to get that generator working again!"

Zilwicki shrugged. "I admit that's unfortunate—but mostly because I'm worried what's going to happen before we can finally get our news back home. Just drifting in space for a few months by itself—we've got power, right? Plenty of food and water, too—is no big deal. That's why they invented chess and card games and such."

Andrew didn't stay mad for long. He was no stranger to hard and tedious labor and a damn good card player. But what overrode all those issues was that if Zilwicki and Cachat hadn't dumped the spare parts a certain Steph Turner wouldn't be on board the ship.

Given the right circumstances—especially the right company—there was actually a lot to be said in favor of drifting through space for months.

Brice would certainly have agreed with that proposition. He'd been worried, at first, that he'd have to engage in a constant emotional wrestling match with Ed and James. But within two days, Nancy somehow made it clear that if she was going to get interested in any of them, it was going to be Brice. At that point, being reasonably good sports and excellent friends, Ed and James stepped aside.

Why did she have that preference? Brice had no idea. Maybe girls climbing into crates got imprinted like ducks climbing out of eggs. At the age of ten, he'd understood girls just fine. Five years later, everything about them was a mystery.

CHAPTER FIFTY-FIVE

"Alpha translation in twelve minutes, Citizen Commodore," Citizen Commander Hartman reported.

"Thank you, Millicent," Citizen Commodore Adrian Luff said with deliberate calm. He glanced around the flag bridge of his new flagship, inhaled a deep, unobtrusive breath of satisfaction at the disciplined efficiency of his personnel, and then looked at the "adviser" standing courteously beside his command chair.

Captain Maddock looked like his own calm, professional self—despite what Luff had always thought of as the truly ridiculous uniform of the Mesa System Navy. There were times Luff was actually tempted to like Maddock, but the moments were few and far between. However courteous the Mesan might be, and Luff was willing to admit the captain took pains to be as courteous as possible, no officer of the People's Navy in Exile could ever forget what Maddock really represented.

Their keeper. Their paymasters' agent. The "technical adviser" whose real function was to make certain the PNE was prepared to do exactly what it was told, when it was told to, and where it was told to do it. And the fact that their paymasters were something as loathsome as Manpower only made what he symbolized even worse. The Mesan captain was the living reminder of every single nasty little accommodation Luff had been forced to make, all of the sordid lengths to which he and his people had been forced to go in their crusade to maintain something which could someday hope to oppose the counterrevolutionaries who had toppled the People's Republic.

There were times, especially late at night, when he found it difficult to sleep, when Adrian Luff had found himself wondering if that "someday" would ever come. Now he knew it would. Although no one—including himself—would have argued for a moment that the odds weren't still enormously against the PNE's ultimate victory (or even its survival), at least they had a chance now. However poor and tattered it might be, it was a *chance*, and he told himself—again—fiercely that buying that chance was worth even what they were about to do at Manpower's orders.

He glanced at the master plot whose icons showed the ships of his fleet, translating steadily down the alpha bands as they rode one of hyper-space's gravity waves towards the normal-space wall. There were more—lots more—of those icons than there had been, including a solid core of battlecruisers. The ten ex-*Indefatigables* were smaller than the four *Warlord-C*-class ships, like his own *Bernard Montgomery*, which had remained loyal to the Revolution, and they were woefully underprovided—by Haven Quadrant standards, at least—with active antimissile defenses. But he had to admit that their basic electronics fit was better than anything the People's Republic had ever had, even though the software driving those electronics had required considerable tweaking. And they had a healthy number of broadside tubes, although the standard Solarian anti-ship missiles, frankly, were pieces of junk.

On the other hand, from his Mesan contacts, he knew the SLN was in the process of upgrading all of its standard anti-ship missiles, and he had to admit that the Cataphracts in his battlecruisers' magazines were better than anything the People's Navy—or State Security—had ever been able to provide him with. They weren't as good as the multidrive missiles the damned Manties had introduced (and which Theisman and his never-to-be-sufficiently-damned counterrevolutionaries had since developed), but they offered a far greater capability than the *PNE* had ever before possessed, and they could be launched internally, rather than requiring pods.

His eight heavy cruisers were all *Mars-D*-class ships which had escaped the counterrevolutionaries, but five of his light cruisers—all of them, actually, except for the *Jacinthe*, *Félicie* and *Véronique*—were Solarian *Bridgeport*-class ships, essentially little more than upsized *War Harvest*-class destroyers. The *Bridgeports* had three more energy mounts per broadside and substantially more magazine space than the *War Harvests*, but they had the same number of tubes and were even more woefully underequipped than the *Indefatigables*, proportionally, with active missile defense.

All sixteen of his destroyers were *War Harvests*, and seven of their captains weren't exactly what he'd call reliable. StateSec's naval forces had been heavily weighted towards heavy cruisers and battlecruisers, and most of the rest of the SS's units had been ships-of-the-wall. Their real function had been to ensure the reliability of the regular People's Navy ships with which they had been stationed (which was why most of them had been destroyed in action when the regular Navy's ships deserted in such droves to the counterrevolutionaries), and that had put a heavy emphasis on firepower and size. Which meant, of course, that very few StateSec warships had been mere light cruisers or destroyers. He'd really have preferred to promote internally to provide commanding officers for *all* of the destroyers with which Manpower had provided the People's Navy in Exile, but it had been far more important to provide solidly Havenite complements for his heavier units first, and adding so many *Indefatigables* to his force mix had eaten up qualified officers at an alarming rate. In fact, he'd been forced to promote quite a few enlisted personnel to officer's rank just to do that much.

Providing similarly solid officer complements for the destroyers had been impossible, so he'd had no choice but to rely on more of the mercenaries (there was no point using any other term to describe them) with which Manpower had supplied him. He'd chosen his nine Havenite destroyer skippers as much for toughness of mind as capability, but although he hadn't discussed it with anyone outside his own staff and flag captain, he had serious doubts about how many of those ships the PNE was going to be able to hang onto after Operation Ferret. It was much more likely, in his opinion, that the mercenary-officered light units were going to mysteriously disappear—with or without their captains' approval—and set up in the piracy business for themselves, especially since the mercenaries would want to disassociate themselves as thoroughly as possible from those responsible for Operation Ferret. There wasn't anything he could do about that, though, and if it happened, it happened. It wasn't exactly as if the ships in question were going to be an enormous loss to his heavy combat power, although he *would* deeply regret losing the commerce-raiding platforms they represented once it was time to begin actual, sustained operations against the counterrevolutionary regime.

But that's for the future, he reminded himself grimly. *First we have this . . . other thing we have to accomplish.*

He glanced at Maddock again, jaw muscle clenching slightly at the thought of what he was about to do, then turned back to Hartman.

"Have Yvonne send the message, Millicent," he said.

✧   ✧   ✧

"General message to all units from the flagship, Citizen Commander," Citizen Lieutenant Adolf Lafontaine said.

Arsène Bottereau looked up, raising one hand to pause his three-way conversation with Citizen Lieutenant Commander Rachel Barthumé, *Jacinthe's* XO, and Citizen Lieutenant George Bacon, her tactical officer.

"Put it on the main display, Adolf," Bottereau instructed, and watched as Adrian Luff's stern-faced image appeared.

"In just a few moments, we will execute Operation Ferret," the commodore said without any of his usual formal (actually, Bottereau usually thought of them as "pompous") opening remarks. "I know all of you are prepared for what will shortly be required of us. I also know some among us continue to feel certain reservations about it. I sympathize with you, but it's time to put those reservations aside. We are committed, citizens, not just to this operation but to the eventual final liberation of the entire People's Republic. In a very real sense, what we are about to do today has been forced upon us by the unspeakable treachery of the enemies of the People who betrayed all they were sworn to uphold and protect. In order to visit the retribution those criminals so richly deserve upon them, we must first possess the means, and *that* is the real reason we are here today."

He gazed at them from displays scattered throughout the task force, and his eyes were hard.

"We *will* carry out this operation," he said flatly. "We will discharge our obligations to the benefactors who have supplied us with so many ships, so many weapons. And when we carry out this operation, it will be the first step in a journey which will return us one day to Nouveau Paris itself as the guardians of the Revolution to which all of us swore our own allegiance and loyalty so many years ago. We *will* redeem those oaths, citizens, and those vile traitors who have betrayed everything the People's Republic fought so long to achieve *will* regret their contemptible actions.

"Luff, clear."

Someone cleared her throat discreetly, and Luiz Rozsak looked up from his dinner conversation with Edie Habib. A very fair-haired, fair-skinned, blue-eyed, and extraordinarily youthful-looking lieutenant stood in the open dining cabin door.

"Yes, Karen?"

"Sorry to disturb you, Sir," Lieutenant Karen Georgos said politely, "but we've just received a priority message from *Nat Turner*. She reports the arrival of an unidentified force, headed in-system on a least-time approach to Torch, at zero-seven-four-three, local. They made their translation just about a light-second short of the hyper limit at five hundred KPS. Rate of acceleration is three-point-eight-three-niner KPS-squared. *Turner*'s CIC identifies the bogeys as four *Warlord*-class battlecruisers, ten *Indefatigable*-class battlecruisers, eight *Mars*-class heavy cruisers, eight light cruisers, and sixteen destroyers. Five of the light cruisers appear to be *Bridgeports*, and *Turner* is calling all of the destroyers *War Harvests*."

Karen Georgos was the youngest member of Rozsak's staff, but she was remarkably levelheaded, despite her youth, and her voice was very calm as she delivered her report.

Rozsak glanced at the bulkhead-mounted chrono. It was late evening, by shipboard time (which, by ancient tradition, was kept set to Greenwich Mean Time aboard all units of the Solarian League Navy), but one of its multiple displays was set to Torch planetary time, and his mind did the math automatically. If the bogeys had made their alpha translation at 7:43, local, then they'd been in normal-space for almost four minutes now. They'd still be a minute or so short of the hyper limit—no one wanted to hit a hyper limit *too* closely, especially when that limit lay inside a gravity wave, like the Torch System's, which made things even more complicated than usual for an astrogator.

He reached out to activate the terminal built into his dining table, but—

"I make it right on two hundred minutes from his alpha translation to the planet, if he's going for a zero-zero, Boss," Edie Habib said before he actually touched it. She was looking at the display of her minicomp, her expression thoughtful. "Call it a hundred and forty minutes for a straight flyby." She looked up at Rozsak. "*Turner* did a good job getting us the data this quickly."

Rozsak nodded. He'd been impressed by the Royal Torch Navy from the outset. It had been obvious to him, as his units exercised with it, that quite a few members of its officer corps had come from professional naval backgrounds before immigrating to Torch. Several of them spoke with pronounced Beowulf accents, and at least three of the frigates' skippers had clearly been born and raised—and trained—on Manticore, although all of them appeared to be descended from genetic slaves. The RTN might be tiny, but with that hard kernel of professionalism as a starting point, and with the ruthless training schedule Thandi Palane had insisted upon, its crews were as good as any he'd ever seen. He wasn't surprised by how promptly *Nat Turner* had been able to identify the invaders' ship classes, but as Habib had said, the frigate had done an outstanding job to get the information to him so rapidly.

Now it's time I do something with it, he thought.

"Well, they're here," he said, and turned to his other dinner guest. "Dirk-Steven, I think we'd better get underway. Given the numbers, it looks like Alpha Two's our best bet."

"Yes, Sir," Commodore Kamstra acknowledged, and began speaking quietly into his personal com as Rozsak returned his attention to Georgos.

"Thank you, Karen," he said. "I assume that's for me?"

"Yes, Sir," she replied, laying the memo board in his outstretched hand.

"We'll see you on Flag Bridge in a few minutes," Rozsak continued. "Go ahead and rout out the rest of our people and get them assembled there, please."

"Of course, Sir." Georgos braced briefly to attention, then disappeared, and Rozsak smiled across the table at Habib.

"Is it my imagination, or has Karen gotten even younger since we got to Torch?"

"It's just having Thandi back in reach again, Boss." Habib smiled. "I knew they'd been buddies, but I hadn't realized how badly Karen had missed her."

"I know—neither had I," Rozsak agreed, but his tone was more absent than it had been, and his attention was on the memo board's display.

"Alpha Two's been activated, Sir," Kamstra reported, then pushed back from the table. "With your permission, I'll head for the command deck now."

"Of course, Dirk-Steven." Rozsak looked up, meeting his flag captain's eyes levelly. "Please go ahead and send *Turner* a 'well-done' for getting this to us so quickly, too. I should've remembered to have Karen do that for me."

"I'll see to it, Sir." Kamstra gave his superior a respectful nod, smiled briefly at Habib, and headed for the dining cabin door.

"Sounds like Manpower's really loaded these bastards up with firepower, Boss," Habib commented, bringing Rozsak's attention back to her. She was gazing down at the memo board herself, her expression thoughtful. "*Ten* ex-SLN battlecruisers?" She shook her head and looked up at him with a tart smile. "They don't exactly believe in subtle, do they?"

"Edie, they're planning an *Eridani Edict* violation, whatever they want to call it. Compared to that, what's a dozen or so *Indefatigables* one way or the other?"

"Point," Habib conceded.

"Well." Rozsak looked at his half-full wine glass thoughtfully for a moment, then shrugged and drained it. "Let's be getting to the flag deck."

✧   ✧   ✧

"All right, people, they're here," Rear Admiral Luiz Rozsak said six minutes later, smiling thinly at his staff on SLNS *Marksman*'s flag bridge. "Unfortunately, we hadn't counted on quite how many people they were bringing to the party," he observed.

"I can't say I'm too happy about those emission signatures, either, Sir," Lieutenant Commander Thomas Szklenski said from his quadrant of the outsized com screen which tied Flag Bridge to Auxiliary Control. As in the Royal Manticoran Navy, *Marksman*'s Erewhonese designers had placed the emergency command deck as far from the cruiser's normal bridge as they possibly could and still keep it inside the armored protection of her core hull. As *Marksman*'s executive officer, AuxCon was Szklenski's battle station, and his brown eyes were narrow as he contemplated the tactical plot in front of him. "*Ten* Solarian battlecruisers?"

He shook his own head as he unwittingly echoed Habib's earlier remark. "Where the hell did they get their hands on *those*?"

"At least they're all *Indefatigables*, not *Nevadas*," Lieutenant Robert Womack pointed out from his own com display. Womack, the cruiser's tactical officer, was with Commodore Kamstra on *Marksman*'s command deck.

"True, Robert," Rozsak acknowledged. "On the other hand, I don't think we can afford to assume Manpower just picked these things up in a boneyard somewhere. From all the reports we've seen, the units they supplied to Monica had first-line electronics on board. I don't think there's any reason to hope *these* units don't."

"No, Sir," Habib agreed, gazing down at the plot. "At the same time though," she looked up again, "the *Indefatigables'* missile defenses are going to be a lot weaker than what those four *War-lords* will be able to manage."

"Oh, *thank* you, Edie!" Rozsak said, shaking his head at her with a much broader smile. "It's such a comfort to know I can always count on you to find the silver lining in even the darkest cloud."

"You're welcome, Sir," Habib replied from behind a perfect poker face, and Rozsak waved a finger under her nose.

"You *can* be replaced, you know," he warned her, and she nodded.

"I realize that, Sir," she said gravely.

"Good!"

Rozsak gave his finger one more wave, then turned his attention back to Lieutenant Womack. The lieutenant, like most of the other officers physically or electronically present, was smiling at the byplay between the admiral and his chief of staff. That was a good sign, Rozsak thought, especially given the tactical plot's current display.

I've been telling everyone we had to assume they'd been heavily reinforced, but I never figured on there being this *many of them,* he told himself. *At least I picked the right threat axis . . . assuming, of course, that they haven't given these bastards even more ships than we've already seen to come sneaking in from somewhere else!* He suppressed an urge to shake his head as his own eyes went back to the plot. *On the other hand, let's not get* too *carried away here, Luiz. They're already using a sledgehammer to crack a peanut, given the resistance they undoubtedly expect. Given their firepower advantage, there's no point in their trying to fool around with some kind of fancy misdirection.*

"Commander Habib almost certainly has a point about their active defenses, Robert," he said out loud. "But I think we're going to have to assume these people have the Aegis upgrade. I know—I know!" He half-raised one hand. "The units at Monica *didn't* have Aegis. Well, they didn't have Halo, either, and I think we're going to have to assume these people have that, too. If they don't, there's no harm done. If they do have them, though, and we assume they don't, things could get uglier than they have to. So, assuming they do, tell me what you think that means for targeting priorities."

"Yes, Sir."

Womack frowned in obvious thought for several seconds, his eyes looking off-screen, where they were no doubt considering the command deck's repeater plot. Rozsak waited patiently. The one hole he had not yet filled in his own staff was Operations. He needed to do something about that, and he intended to, although he didn't expect Dirk-Steven Kamstra to be especially delighted when the commodore found out who Rozsak had in mind for the position. Despite his youth, Robert Womack had thoroughly demonstrated both his competence and his levelheadedness, and Rozsak had been impressed by his performance since they'd arrived here in Torch. He had every intention of stealing Womack from Kamstra as soon as the current operation was over. What mattered at the moment, though, was that in the course of the task force's exercises, the lieutenant had demonstrated a better grasp of the Mark-17-E missile's capabilities—and limitations—than Rozsak himself had, in some ways.

"Judging from our own exercises, and the data we've amassed on our new birds' capabilities, Sir," Womack said after a moment, "and bearing in mind that we know exactly how Halo works, which means we know how to allow for it, we can probably expect it to degrade our targeting and fire control by about . . . say, fifteen percent. It might be a little worse than that; it might be a little better than that. A lot's going to depend on operator proficiency, and there's no way we can know about that one way or the other ahead of time.

"At the same time, we're starting from a significantly better probability of hit percentage, thanks to the Erewhonese upgrades, so we still ought to have a significant advantage in terms of accuracy over anything they've got. And I doubt very much that the Havenite-built ships have Halo, at all. I could be wrong, but the onboard side of the system would have to have been squeezed in somewhere, and there's not room for that without taking something else fairly big out to compensate.

"To be honest, I think Aegis would be a bigger problem for us, at least where the *Indefatigables* are concerned. If they've got it, they're going to be able to thicken up their missile defenses quite a bit. They're still going to be weaker in point defense clusters than the Havenite units, but they'll be able to kill more of our birds in the outer and middle defense zones. Of course, the downside for them is that they're going to have standard SLN counter-missiles in the tubes—and the canisters—and they aren't as good as ours. And using Aegis is going to decrease their shipkiller throw weight, as well."

He paused, head slightly cocked, as if considering what he'd just said, then shrugged.

"Bottom line, Sir, is that the combination of Halo and Aegis will probably give us a per-missile hit probability against an *Indefatigable* that's only thirty-five or forty percent better than against a *Warlord*. Assuming the people on board the ships are fully familiar with their systems and trained to Frontier Fleet standards, that is."

Rozsak felt his lips twitch slightly at Womack's qualifying last sentence. "Frontier Fleet standards" implied a degree of contempt for Frontier Fleet's *Battle* Fleet colleagues which was unfortunately (or fortunately, depending upon one's viewpoint) fully justified. Probably because Battle Fleet spent all of its training time firing simulated missiles at simulated defenses all under the command of officers who not only never *had* seen combat but almost certainly expected that they never *would* see it. And in an environment where umpires and simulation managers knew better than to make potential enemies out of future senior officers by grading their results too critically. Luiz Rozsak was familiar with Frontier Fleet's own version of the Solarian League's institutional arrogance from direct, personal experience, but he fully shared Womack's estimate of Battle Fleet's capabilities. In fact, it was one of the things he and Oravil Barregos were counting on, when he came right down to it.

"All right," he said. "That's about what I expected. The bad news is that it's going to take lots of missiles to kill these people—probably a lot *more* missiles than we'd estimated. The good news is that we've *got* 'lots of missiles' to do it with. Lieutenant Wu," he looked at the com image of Lieutenant Richard Wu, *Marksman's* astrogator, "how long to normal-space?"

"We'll be making our translation in seventy-five seconds, Admiral." Wu's voice was remarkably calm, given the translation conditions Alpha Two called for.

"N-space velocity after translation?"

"Two-point-five thousand KPS, Sir," Wu replied, and more than one face grimaced.

Rozsak's wasn't one of them, but he understood perfectly. Crash hyper translations were never excessively pleasant, and crossing the alpha wall into normal-space fast enough to carry that much velocity across the interface would be even more unpleasant than normal. And they'd be able to manage it in such a short time window only because Torch lay in a gravity wave, which made enormously higher rates of acceleration possible.

On the other hand, it also made minor errors in astrogation into potentially catastrophic ones, he reflected.

"Well, Richard," he said, smiling at the astrogator, "let's all hope you've got your sums right."

CHAPTER FIFTY-SIX

"Hyper translation!" Citizen Commander Pierre Stravinsky announced suddenly, his voice sharp.

Citizen Commodore Luff's head snapped around, eyes narrowing, but Stravinsky didn't even notice. The ops officer was leaning forward, staring intently at his display. A handful of seconds ticked by, then Stravinsky looked up, meeting Luff's gaze.

"They're directly astern of us, Citizen Commodore," he said. "Range right on twelve million kilometers—sixteen point sources. All we've got so far are the impeller signatures, but they're accelerating after us at four-point-seven-five KPS-squared."

Luff frowned, then looked at Citizen Commander Hartman and raised his eyebrows.

"Hard to say, Citizen Commodore," she said in response to the unspoken question. "It could be anybody. But whoever it is, they're obviously responding to us. They must have had a picket out beyond the limit, monitoring their sensor platforms." She shrugged. "Now whoever it was has come back with friends."

"But what sort of friends?" Luff murmured, half to himself, and glanced at Captain Maddock.

The Mesan only shrugged in turn—which, Luff had to admit, was about all anyone could have done at this point. At twelve million kilometers, it was going to take the better part of forty seconds for any light-speed emissions from the suddenly appearing bogeys to reach them. On the other hand, Hartman clearly had a point about how those bogeys happened to be there, and that suggested several very unhappy possibilities to the citizen

507

commodore. First, it suggested that someone had known, or at least strongly suspected, that an attack like this one was coming. People didn't "just happen" to set up this sort of elaborate response unless they thought they might need one, and responses didn't come in this quickly unless the people behind them were poised and ready. Second, if these bogies had been summoned by a system picket which had detected and identified them before going for help, then, unlike Luff, they ought to have a very good notion of what was on the other side. Which suggested that they thought they had the firepower to do something about it. . . .

Don't leap to any conclusions, Adrian, he reminded himself. *At that acceleration rate, there can't be anything back there bigger than a battlecruiser—not unless it's got a Manty compensator, and the Manties are too busy closer to home to be worrying about us at a time like this. But if they've got an accurate count on us, then they know they're outnumbered by three-to-one. So if they don't have anything heavier than a battlecruiser, they have to be lunatics.*

Or desperate.

The citizen commodore grimaced unhappily at that thought. Given that these bogeys clearly *had* been waiting in hyper, then somehow word of the attack must have leaked after all. And if some warning of the attack had leaked, then the defenders might know—or have guessed—Operation Ferret's true objective. In which case, the people accelerating after them might well be desperate enough to pursue the PNE no matter *how* outnumbered they were.

If that were my *planet, if that were* my *family down there on it,* I'd *be going after anybody who planned on doing what we plan on doing whether I really thought I could stop them or not,* he thought grimly.

On the other hand, he might just be wrong about whether or not the Manties could have shaken a task group loose for something like this, especially if they'd had enough warning to know it was coming.

"Time for us to get back across the limit, Astro?"

"Just a moment, Citizen Commodore," Citizen Lieutenant Commander Philippine Christiansen replied. She punched numbers quickly, then looked back at him. "Approximately thirty-nine minutes assuming current acceleration, Citizen Commodore. Twenty-one minutes if we go to maximum military power."

"And how long for these bogeys to reach missile range of the hyper limit, Citizen Commander Stravinsky?" Luff asked.

"Assuming they maintain their acceleration profile and that their missiles have a powered range of seven-point-five million kilometers from rest, approximately . . . seventeen minutes, Citizen Commodore."

Luff grunted. He strongly suspected that whoever that was back there had undershot his planned translation point. Unless he had multidrive missiles, he was a good four million-plus kilometers outside his own missile range at the moment, and that had to represent an astrogation error. Luff rather doubted that he'd wanted to arrive at a range where he couldn't immediately engage the people attacking Torch, after all. But if he'd undershot, he hadn't undershot by a large enough margin for Luff to change his mind, reverse acceleration, kill his current velocity, and then get back across the hyper limit and disappear into the alpha bands before he could be engaged.

Of course, any engaging would take place at very long-range, he reflected. *They probably couldn't score a whole lot of hits before we hypered out, no matter what they've got back there.*

He glanced once more at Maddock, this time unobtrusively, out of the corner of one eye. The Mesan captain had to know why Luff had asked Christiansen those two questions, but if he was concerned about the citizen commodore's possible decision, no sign of it showed in his expression. Which could mean confidence on his part, or simply that he knew *Luff* knew what would happen to any hope of further support from Manpower if he blew this mission off. Or, for that matter, it could even mean Maddock would be simply *delighted* if the PNE scampered off to safety, taking his own personal skin along with it.

Part of Luff wanted to do exactly that. There was always the distinct possibility that the people chasing him truly were confident of their ability to deal with him if they caught him. And if they were, they might be right.

Of course, they might be wrong, *too*, he told himself. *Especially if they don't know about the Cataphracts. But be honest with yourself, Adrian. What you're really thinking is that this could offer you an excuse not to do something you don't want to do, anyway.*

"Citizen Commodore, we're getting some tonnage estimates from CIC," Stravinsky said.

"What kind of estimates?"

"According to CIC, it looks like eight units in the hundred and twenty-five-ton range, six in the two hundred and eighty-five hundred-ton range, and two at around two million tons, Citizen Commodore."

"And they're *all* pulling four-point-seven-five KPS-squared?" Hartman asked just a bit sharply.

"Yes, Citizen Commander," Stravinsky replied, and Hartman grimaced.

"It seems the Erewhonese are here after all, Citizen Commodore," she said, turning back to Luff. "Nothing that size could pull that much accel without an improved compensator."

"Excuse me, Citizen Commodore," Citizen Lieutenant Yvonne Kamerling, Luff's staff communications officer, said. Luff frowned reflexively at the interruption, but he smoothed the expression quickly. He knew Kamerling wouldn't have broken in on him and Hartman at a moment like this if she hadn't believed it was important.

"What is it, Yvonne?"

"Sir, we're beginning to pick up grav pulses. Whoever that is behind us is using an FTL com to talk to someone further in-system."

"Manties?" Luff asked rather more sharply than he'd intended to as visions of great big, nasty multidrive missiles flickered through his brain.

"I don't think so, Citizen Commodore," Kamerling replied. "The pulse rate and the modulation are both wrong. It's a bit more sophisticated than we were seeing out of the Manties during the final phases of the last war, but based on our current intel, it's a lot *less* sophisticated than anything we'd expect to see out of them now."

"I see."

Kamerling was probably right, Luff thought. It made sense, anyway. Then again . . .

"How confident is CIC about those tonnage estimates?" he asked Stravinsky. The ops officer looked at him, and the citizen commodore waved a hand. "I'm thinking about those reports on the Manties' new battlecruiser class. Two million tons is too small to be a waller, even a dreadnought, but isn't that new battlecruiser of theirs supposed to mass right around that much?"

"The *Nikes* actually come in at around two and a half million, Citizen Commodore," Captain Maddock said before Stravinsky could respond. Luff transferred his gaze to the Mesan, who shrugged. "That intelligence has been pretty conclusively confirmed, according to our sources," he said. "And I think your CIC crews are too good to underestimate a mass reading by twenty percent at this short a range."

"Captain Maddock has a point, Citizen Commodore," Hartman said. "Coupled with what Yvonne's just told us about their communications, it's got to be the Erewhonese."

"But Erewhon doesn't have anything anywhere near that tonnage range," Luff pointed out.

"They don't have any *warships* in that tonnage range, Citizen Commodore," Hartman replied grimly. "What they *could* have back there, though, is a couple of smallish freighters with mil-spec compensators and cargo holds packed full of missile pods."

Luff felt his stomach muscles tighten. Their "benefactors'" latest intelligence reports all insisted that Erewhon's multidrive missile capability was extremely limited compared to that of Manticore. Or, for that matter, of the counterrevolutionaries in Nouveau Paris, at this point. But even with the original, first-generation Manty MDMs they would outrange anything he had. Except—

"If they had MDMs, they'd already be shooting at us," he heard his own voice say calmly. "Twelve million kilometers is less than a quarter of the powered range they're supposed to have."

"Agreed, Citizen Commodore," Hartman said. "But everything we've seen suggests the real problem is that they've got more range than they have fire control capability. If they're chasing us with a pair of missile freighters, then those six heavy cruisers are probably planning on acting as forward fire control platforms. They'll try to bring them in close enough to improve their hit probabilities—probably *just* to the edge of single-drive missile range—while they keep the freighters far enough back to be outside our own range of them when they roll the pods."

"That makes a lot of sense, Citizen Commodore," Stravinsky said. "Assuming they are Erewhonese—and given what Yvonne's just said about their FTL com, I think the Citizen Commander's right about that—I agree they *could* be firing on us now, if our two bigger bogies *are* freighters and they are carrying MDMs. But Citizen Commander Hartman's also absolutely right about the accuracy penalty they'd pay at this range. *Manties* might not worry about that, if there's anything to the scraps we've heard about the Battle of Lovat, but Erewhon's accuracy at extended MDM range is going to be extremely poor. At the same time, they brought a lot more velocity over the alpha wall with them than we did, and they've got the acceleration edge on us—or, at least, their heavy cruisers do—so they must figure they can bring us into the range they want before we get into our own powered envelope of the planet. They may have lots of missiles, but why waste a bunch of them at this kind of range when they don't have to?"

Luff felt himself nodding slowly in agreement with his subordinates' logic. Given the Erewhonese Navy's capabilities, it made perfect sense. In fact, it was probably what he'd be doing. And it explained why sixteen ships were chasing forty-eight. It didn't matter how outnumbered they were if their weapons could reach their enemies and their enemies' weapons *couldn't* reach them.

Of course, he thought coldly, *there's a tiny flaw in their logic. They don't know—*

"Citizen Commodore, we have an incoming transmission," Kamerling said, and Luff turned back towards her. "It's from a Rear Admiral Rozsak."

Luff's eyes widened abruptly, and he heard a hiss of indrawn breath from Hartman. Rozsak? It *couldn't* be—not with those observed acceleration rates! And yet...

"Who is it addressed to, Yvonne?" he asked.

"To *you*, Citizen Commodore," she replied. "Not by name, but— With your permission, Citizen Commodore?"

She indicated the secondary com display at his command station, and he nodded. A moment later, the face of a man Luff had never met, but recognized instantly, appeared on the display.

"This is Rear Admiral Luiz Rozsak, Solarian League Navy." The voice was cold, hard. "I wish to speak to the senior officer of the State Security forces currently planning to attack the sovereign planet of Torch."

Luff felt an icy hand squeeze his heart as a crawl from CIC across the bottom of his display confirmed that, according to *Leon Trotsky*'s intelligence base, the image he was looking at and the voice he was listening to truly did belong to the senior Solarian naval officer in the region. Who obviously knew who they were.

No, he thought a heartbeat later. *No, he knows* what *we are—or* he thinks *he does, anyway—but* not *who* we *are. The* Warlords and the Mars-Cs *would make him pretty sure we're State Security, even if he'd never had any idea at all what was coming. Besides, if he knew names and faces, he'd be using them now—asking for me* by name. *He'd know exactly how badly that would shake the nerve of any CO in my position.*

He felt a flicker of relief at the thought, even though he knew it was irrational. If it wasn't the Erewhonese back there, if it really *was* the Solarian League Navy, the consequences for all of the PNE's plans and hopes could be catastrophic.

The Haven Quadrant was hundreds of light-years from the League, and the SLN's total disinterest in the Manticore-Haven conflict had been obvious for years. As far as the man-in-the-street's view of things was concerned, Solarian public opinion since the resumption of hostilities had tended to favor Haven over Manticore, and at the moment, given the confrontation between the League's interests and Manticore in the Talbott Cluster, there was little doubt that Solarian antipathy towards the Star Kingdom had hardened significantly. But all of that could—*would*—change in a heartbeat in the wake of an Eridani Edict violation. The Edict was the single element of Solarian foreign policy which enjoyed near-universal acceptance and support from all of the League's citizens. If Havenite units violated it . . .

But we aren't *"Havenite units" anymore. That's the entire reason Manpower wanted to use us in the first place. We're deniable. Even if they do know we're Havenite, even ex-State Security, no one in the League is going to go after the People's Republic for anything we do.*

Which, unfortunately, wouldn't do a single thing to mitigate the consequences for the *PNE.* The Eridani Edict carried no specific injunction to go after non-state violators with the full fury of the Solarian League Navy, but Adrian Luff nourished no illusions. The Solarian League wouldn't give a damn about attacks on Havenite shipping, or the Havenite navy. And Luff could slaughter his one-time fellow citizens in whatever numbers he chose without arousing the least Solarian ire . . . as long as he did it without resorting to the actions the Eridani Edict outlawed.

But if the PNE crossed this line, and if the League knew it had, that indifference would vanish. At the very least, he and his people would become pariahs, with every man's hand turned against them. Luff had learned a great deal, over his years of exile, about the astonishing depth of the Solarian League's basic, all-encompassing inefficiency. It was actually worse than the pre-Pierre People's Republic had ever been, in some ways. But, by the same token, he'd gained a bone-deep awareness of the League's sheer, stupendous size and power. If it decided the People's Navy in Exile needed to be hunted down, sooner or later, the PNE *would* be run to earth and destroyed.

But if we don't *do this, we lose the only real outside support we've been able to find. And what happens to our morale, our cohesion, if that happens? For that matter, if Rozsak really knows who we are, really knows we were* prepared *to do this, then we're tainted in Solly eyes, no matter what happens!*

"Accept his com request," he heard himself say. "No visual, and run the outgoing audio through the computers."

✧   ✧   ✧

"We have a response, Sir. Sort of, anyway," Karen Georgos announced.

"Took them long enough," Edie Habib half-muttered, and Rozsak gave her a half-smile.

"There's a forty-second transmission delay," he pointed out. "They didn't dither as long as I expected them to, actually."

Habib snorted softly, and Rozsak looked at Georgos.

"Put it through, Karen."

"Yes, Sir. Coming up now," the com officer replied, and the display in front of Rozsak went abruptly blank.

"What can I do for you, Admiral Rozsak?" a voice inquired. It was smoothly modulated, without any readily discernible accent, and Rozsak raised one eyebrow at Georgos before keying his own pickup.

"Computer generated?" he asked . . . quite unnecessarily, he was certain.

"Yes, Sir." She shrugged. "I can't guarantee it without a complete analysis, but it sounds to me like they're using our own hardware and techniques. Somebody at the other end is talking to the Nightingale, and the AI's generating a completely synthesized voice. There's no way anyone would be able to determine anything about the actual speaker's voice from this."

"That's what I thought," he said.

He'd have done exactly the same thing, if he'd found himself in the place of whoever was at the other end of that com link. In fact, he *had* used the Nightingale on occasions when deniability was more useful in the Solarian League's view of things. But if he wasn't surprised by that, he *was* slightly surprised by how irritating he found it.

Mostly that's because Karen's right—he's using our own tech against us. Which makes being pissed off with him even sillier, given what we're planning to do with "our own tech" in the increasingly less distant future.

He brushed that thought aside, squared his shoulders, looked directly into his own pickup, and brought it online.

"You can immediately break off your attack on the planet Torch," he said flatly. "I remind you that the Solarian League has signed a mutual defense treaty with the Kingdom of Torch. Any attack on Torch will be deemed an attack upon Solarian territory, and any violation of the Eridani Edict's anti-genocide protocols will lead to your summary destruction."

There was a forty-second delay as his words sped across to the PNE flagship. Then, forty seconds after that, his blank com display spoke again.

"I appreciate your position, Admiral," it said. "Unfortunately, I'm not in a position to comply with your demands. Not to mention the fact that you don't seem to have the means to accomplish our 'summary destruction' at this particular moment."

At least he's not trying to pretend this is only some kind of "friendly port visit," Rozsak thought.

"I don't?" He smiled thinly. "You might want to remember that appearances can be deceiving. And even if that isn't the case, the *Solarian League Navy* as a whole definitely does have the means."

"True," the anonymous voice acknowledged eighty seconds later. "But for the rest of the SLN to accomplish that it will have to be able to *find* us. And I think—Admiral Rozsak, was it?—that it might behoove you to consider the potential consequences for your current forces. You may find this difficult to believe, but I would prefer not having to kill anyone who doesn't have to die today."

Despite the artificiality of the voice, Rozsak thought he could actually hear an edge of sincerity in that final sentence.

And isn't it big of him to offer to allow us to run away so he "only" has to kill the four or five million people on Torch?

"That's very kind of you," he said out loud, his voice cold. "If, however, you do not break off your attack run on Torch, I *will* engage you, and if that happens, quite a few people are going to get killed today. You may believe you have a sufficient advantage to defeat my own forces with minimal casualties. I assure you, if you do think that's the case, that you're wrong. And I also hereby inform you that your violation of the Torch hyper limit with an unidentified military force is considered a deliberate hostile act by the Kingdom of Torch and by the Solarian League. I officially instruct you at this time to change course immediately and leave the Torch System on a least-time course. If you do not comply with those instructions, deadly force *will* be used against you."

"—*will* be used against you."

Adrian Luff looked around his flag bridge. Most of his personnel had their eyes focused upon their own displays, their own command consoles, but he knew where their *ears* were focused. And from the body language around him, from the expressions and partial expressions he could see, he knew the majority of them were thinking exactly what he was thinking—that here was the opportunity to break off. The excuse they could offer to their "Manpower" masters.

And, at the same time, they were also thinking—again, like him—that the PNE's *Warlords* and *Mars* were too distinctive to simply fade away into the background of other pirate and mercenary warships wandering about the galaxy. If the emission signatures of those ships got back to the SLN, got circulated throughout the League and all of the minor, independent star nations, they'd be easy to identify. So whatever degree of *personal* anonymity he and his crews, as individuals, might be able to maintain, as a *group*, they would be marked men and women. There might not be a star nation against which the Eridani Edict could be enforced in this case, but that wouldn't prevent anyone from classifying them as pirates...and under acknowledged interstellar law, the punishment for piracy was death.

But we've come too far, he thought harshly. *We've clawed our way too far back towards who we used to be, what we used to stand for. And without Manpower's support, we'll never have the logistics base to be anything* but *pirates. Murderers and* scum—ten-a-credit hired killers, not "defenders of the Revolution." If we walk away from this mission, we lose that.

A corner of his brain tasted the bitter, bitter irony of the decision he confronted. In order to restore the soul of the Revolution, to redeem his own star nation once again, he faced an action which would stain his own soul forever. And, he discovered, despite the Revolution's official atheism, he *did* have a soul, or something that *thought* it was a soul, anyway. A soul that didn't want to do this . . . yet saw no option to doing it which wasn't even worse.

And for all I know, that's not really Luiz Rozsak back there, at all, he told himself. *We're not the only people with the Nightingale or its equivalent, after all, and Millicent and Yvonne have to be right about where the* ships *came from, anyway. They're not Manties, they're not Theisman's, and they sure as* hell *aren't Sollies, whoever may be claiming to be in command of them—not with those acceleration curves and FTL com capability. That only leaves the Erewhonese. Given the fact that Erewhon is in bed with the Torches, it'd make sense for them to have decided to protect Torch, if they got a sniff of the operation. But they could still have expected us to be a lot weaker than we are. They may have figured that six of their cruisers could take the force they* thought *was coming, using their missile pods. If they did, and if they're having second thoughts now, this could be a bluff. They could be waving the future threat of the SLN at us to convince us to break off when Rozsak isn't actually within fifty light-years of Torch.*

And given our intel about their relationship with Barregos and Rozsak, Rozsak really could *be back there, too, Adrian. The fact that those are Erewhonese ships doesn't mean they couldn't have Solly "advisors" aboard. Don't forget that while you're trying to rationalize your way through all this. And that treaty he's talking about really exists, too, so it's entirely possible Rozsak is aboard one of those Erewhonese cruisers, even if there's not another single Solly in sight, in order to formally bring the League into all this.*

The thoughts flashed through his brain, and even as they did, he knew there wasn't much point to them. Not really. He was committed, and he'd committed all of his people along with him. The day they'd accepted these ships from Manpower, pinned all their hopes for restoring the Revolution on Manpower's material support, they'd also accepted this mission. And unless there was enough firepower out there to actually stop them, they had no choice but to carry it out.

"I appreciate the warning, Admiral Rozsak," he heard himself say, "but I'm afraid I'm going to have to ignore it. In return, though, I warn *you* that any use of force against this task group will be met in kind."

He pressed a stud on the arm of his command chair, shutting down his pickup, and turned back to his staff.

"All right," he said with a thin smile, "despite Admiral Rozsak's having identified himself for us, I think you and Yvonne are essentially right about who these people are, Millicent. And I think you're right about the hardware available to them and what it is they're planning to do to us. So, since we can't run away from them even if we wanted to, I think we should just go ahead and do exactly what they expect us to."

CHAPTER FIFTY-SEVEN

"It's confirmed, Ma'am—Alpha Two," Lieutenant Cornelia Rensi said.

"Thank you, Cornelia," Commander Raycraft acknowledged, then turned to her "staff." Actually, aside from Lieutenant Commander Michael Dobbs, who'd been added to *Artillerist's* complement expressly to act as Light Cruiser Division 7036.2's *chief* of staff, Acting-Commodore Laura Raycraft's staff officers were identical to Commander Laura Raycraft's ship's officers. That was the main reason she'd chosen, unlike Luiz Rozsak, who had ensconced himself on *Marksman's* flag bridge, to fight her ship and lead her division from *Artillerist's* command deck.

"Not much of a surprise, Ma'am, is it?" Dobbs said now, and she shook her head.

Like Dobbs, she'd always anticipated that Alpha Two was the most likely of the scenarios Luiz Rozsak and his officers had worked out. In fact, she'd felt it was *so* likely that she'd lobbied hard in favor of concentrating the entire task group in hyperspace. She knew Rozsak had been tempted to agree with her, but she'd also known he wasn't going to. As he'd pointed out to her, somebody had to be in a position to cover the inner system just in case it should happen they'd guessed wrong after all and the Peep mercenaries came in on more than one bearing. Which was how her own ship and *Archer* happened to be sitting here in orbit as the flagship of "Anvil Force," along with Commander Melanie Stensrud's *Charade* and Lieutenant Commander Hjálmar Snorrason's four *Warrior*-class destroyers: *Genghis Kahn*, *Napoleon*,

Alexander the Great, and *Julius Caesar.* They were accompanied by Commander Maria Le Fossi's three light cruisers and the seventeen ships of Destroyer Flotilla 2960—not to mention eight frigates of the Royal Torch Navy—but those other ships were there for slightly different reasons.

It was a lot of hulls, even though her own light cruiser division had been chosen because it had one less ship than either of Light Cruiser Squadron 7036's other two divisions. In fact, Anvil Force almost certainly had more ships than it was going to need. But since Anvil Force's true primary mission was to prevent any long-range missiles from getting through to Torch, redundancy had become a beautiful thing.

And if those people are prepared to go to maximum-rate fire, or if it turns out they're carrying full loads of pods tractored to their hulls, we may just turn out not to be all that "redundant" after all, she reflected grimly.

There was no evidence, aside from the weapons Technodyne had provided for the Republic of Monica that anyone outside the Haven Quadrant had been experimenting with pods. Even the Technodyne pods had been pure system defense weapons, never designed for offensive deployment a la Manticore or Haven, and all of Jiri Watanapongse's sources insisted that the SLN still dismissed the entire concept as the primitive, ineffectual thing it had been decades ago. But StateSec refugees who'd deserted after the Royal Manticoran Navy's ferociously successful Operation Buttercup brought the First Havenite War to a screeching halt would have a very different attitude towards them, and it was at least possible they'd managed to communicate that attitude to their Manpower sponsors. And if the thought of Manpower's putting advanced weaponry into production was ridiculous, so was the thought of Manpower's being able to make literally dozens of ex-SLN battlecruisers available to proxies like the Republic of Monica . . . or a lunatic fleet of StateSec holdouts.

So, yes, it *was* possible, however unlikely, that these people had missile pods of their own. And if they could generate enough saturation to overload the defenders' missile defenses . . .

They'd only have to get lucky with a handful of them, at relativistic speeds, she reminded herself.

"I have to say," Dobbs continued, "that I really kind of wish we'd gone with Alpha One instead of Alpha Two." She glanced at him, and he grimaced. "I understand the logic, Ma'am. I just don't like sitting around on my hands while someone else does all the heavy lifting."

"I can't say I don't feel at least a little the same," Raycraft admitted. Alpha One would have turned Anvil Force into a true anvil, with the light cruisers and Hjálmar Snorrason's destroyers advancing from Torch to catch the attackers between themselves and Rozsak's Hammer Force. "On the other hand, the Admiral was right. Alpha One probably *would* be a case of gilding the lily. If he can't do the job with six of the *Marksmans*, we probably couldn't do it with eight, either. Besides, I imagine there'll be time to go to Alpha *Three*, if it comes to it. And if it doesn't, then not giving ourselves away with active impeller signatures strikes me as a pretty good notion."

"Oh, I agree, Ma'am," Dobbs told her mildly, and she snorted once, then turned back to Siegel.

"How long until the Admiral has Hammer Force in position?" she asked.

"It looks like they came up about two million klicks short on their planned translation, Ma'am," Siegel replied, and Raycraft nodded. She already noticed that Lieutenant Wu's astrogation had been a little off, and she wasn't surprised. In fact, she was all in favor of coming up *short* in a situation like this one, herself. "Assuming constant accelerations across the board, though," Siegel continued, "Hammer Force will close to the specified range in about fifty-eight minutes. At that point, the enemy will be just under a hundred and twelve million kilometers—call it six-point-two light-minutes—from Torch."

Raycraft nodded again, then turned to the com image of Lieutenant Richard McKenzie, *Artillerist*'s chief engineer.

"Stand ready on the wedge, Richard. We may want it in an hour or so."

✧   ✧   ✧

"Velocities have equalized, Citizen Commodore," Citizen Lieutenant Commander Pierre Stravinsky said quietly, and Adrian Luff glanced at the master plot again.

There'd been no further communication with Admiral Rozsak, assuming it really was Admiral Rozsak behind them, although that didn't necessarily strike him as a good sign. Not that anything the other man might have said was going to cause him to rethink his own plans and options at this point. He'd decided what he was going to do, and he wasn't going to start second-guessing himself at this late point.

The range between his ships and their pursuers had opened while the bogeys made up their initial velocity disadvantage. With an acceleration advantage of just under one kilometer per second, that had taken 9.75 minutes. The range between them had risen to just over 13.3 million kilometers during that time; now that velocities had equalized at 7,886 KPS, the range had begun to drop once again. From here on, their pursuers would steadily eat away the distance between them.

He looked up and beckoned for Citizen Commander Hartman to join him. She stepped up on his left side, gazing at the plot with him, and he waved one hand at its icons.

"They're still almost eleven million kilometers short of the hyper limit," he observed, "so I suppose it's remotely possible they really don't have MDMs over there and they're trying to run a bluff on us. They could still be hoping our nerve will crack and we'll break off . . . and planning on hypering back out instead of coming across the limit after us and getting into standard missile range, if we don't. Just between you and me," his tone was dry enough to evaporate the Frontenac Estuary back home in Nouveau Paris, "I'd really like to think that's what's happening here. Unfortunately, what I think is really happening is exactly what you and Stravinsky suggested from the outset. Those are Erewhonese ships, whoever's aboard them, and those two big bastards *are* mil-spec freighters loaded with missile pods. The question I've been turning over in my mind for the last five or six minutes is how close they're going to want to get before they start rolling pods at us. May I assume you've been devoting some thought to the same problem?"

"Yes, Citizen Commodore." Hartman gave him a smile of her own, although hers showed a bit more of the tips of her teeth. "As a matter of fact, Pierre and I have been kicking that around, and we've consulted with Citizen Captain Vergnier and Citizen Commander Laurent, as well."

"And have the four of you reached a consensus?"

"We're all agreed on what they're going to try to do," Hartman replied. "We're still a little divided over the exact range they're looking for, though. Obviously, they're planning to close to a range lower than twelve million kilometers, or they would have fired before the range began to open. That being the case, they're clearly trying to get their fire control close enough to give them a reasonable hit percentage, exactly as Pierre suggested, which makes a lot of sense, if those six cruisers are the only fire control platforms they plan on using. Personally, I think they want to come as close as they can while staying out of our range, so I'm figuring eight million klicks. That would put them a half million kilometers outside standard missile range, and they've obviously got the acceleration advantage to hold the range at that point if they choose to.

"Pierre agrees with me, but he thinks they'll shoot for nine million klicks in order to give themselves a little more wiggle room after our birds go ballistic. Citizen Captain Vergnier and Citizen Commander Laurent argue that with two freighters full of missile pods, they'll probably be willing to start wasting ammunition sooner than that, so they're both thinking in terms of something more like *ten* million klicks."

Luff nodded thoughtfully.

"I think I'm inclined to agree with Stravinsky," he said. "If it weren't for the fact that they *have* got those two ammo ships back there, I'd agree with you and shave it a little closer, because that extra five hundred thousand kilometers is going to cost them a little accuracy. But Olivier and Citizen Commander Laurent have a point about how much ammunition they've got to burn. And the fact that it looks like they're bringing the ammo ships in with them suggests to me that they probably would like at least a little more time and distance for evasive maneuvers after our birds' drives go down."

"You and Pierre may well be right, Citizen Commodore." Hartman shrugged. "The important thing, though, is that they *are* bringing the ammo ships in. They've still got time to drop them off well back from the firing line, but I think if they were going to do that, they already would have. At their current velocity, they're committed to crossing the hyper limit now—assuming they want to stay in n-space where they can roll pods after us, at any rate—and with the observed range of even early generation MDMs, they wouldn't have to've gotten even this close to bring us under fire. The fire control ships, yes, but not the ammo carriers."

"Agreed." The citizen commodore grimaced. "I suppose it's

something of a judgment call. Leave them well back, but essentially unprotected if it should happen we've got somebody still waiting in hyper to pounce, or bring them along with you, where your fire control ships and destroyers can keep an eye on them but they still don't have to come quite into our missiles' envelope."

"I'm pretty sure that's exactly what they're thinking, Citizen Commodore. And, in their position, I'd have done the same thing. Less because I'd be afraid the other side actually had left somebody in hyper 'to pounce,' as you put it than because, with that kind of range advantage over the *known* threat, there wouldn't be any reason not to protect myself against the possibility of an unknown one sneaking in on me, however remote that might be."

"Exactly. Of course," Luff bared his teeth, "it'd be a pity if it turned out they were protecting themselves against the wrong 'known threat.'"

"Yes, Citizen Commodore." Hartman returned his predatory smile. "That *would* be a pity, wouldn't it?"

✧   ✧   ✧

"About another ten minutes, Sir," Edie Habib observed quietly, and Rozsak nodded.

They'd been in pursuit of the StateSec renegades for over half an hour, and they'd cut the range back to just barely more than the twelve million kilometers at which they'd begun the chase. Their overtake velocity was over fifteen hundred kilometers per second, and there was no way the enemy could escape them now.

"We'll reduce acceleration to three-point-seven-five KPS-squared at eleven million kilometers," he decided. "No point closing any faster than we have to."

"Yes, Sir," Habib replied, but her tone was a bit odd, and when he glanced at her, he realized she'd been gazing at his own profile with a slightly quizzical look.

"What?" he asked.

"I was just wondering what it is you didn't go ahead and say just now."

"'Didn't go ahead and say'?" It was his turn to give her a quizzical look. "What makes you think there's *anything* I didn't go ahead and say?"

"Boss, I've known you a long time," she said, and he chuckled.

"Yes, you have," he agreed. Then he shrugged. "Mostly, I was just thinking about Snorrason."

"Wondering if I was right all along, were you?" she asked with an arched eyebrow, and he grinned.

He'd waffled back and forth, with uncharacteristic ambivalence, over the question of where he should deploy Hjálmar Snorrason's four destroyers. After the *Marksmans*, the big *Warrior*-class destroyers were the most capable antimissile ships he had, in the area-defense role, at least. The Royal Torch Navy's frigates had turned out to be remarkably capable (for such small units) of looking after themselves in a missile-heavy environment, but they simply weren't big enough and didn't have enough counter-missile magazine capacity to be effective in the sustained area-defense role. He'd been tempted to tack Snorrason's ships onto Hammer Force, as Habib had suggested, just in case they'd found themselves forced into the enemy's missile envelope after all. But he'd decided in the end that protecting Torch was more important. It was extraordinarily unlikely that any of the ex-Peep attackers were going to get close enough to hit the planet with anything short of dead, easily picked off missiles which had long since gone ballistic. The consequences if it turned out that airy assumption was in error might well prove catastrophic, however, and providing against that eventuality took precedence over the equally remote possibility of Hammer Force straying into the enemy's missile envelope.

"No." Rozsak shook his head. "I never thought you were *wrong* about it, Edie." He turned away from the plot and smiled wryly at Habib. "In fact, the reason I was so ambivalent about it was because it really is a coin-toss kind of decision." He shrugged. "In the end, it's all about defending the planet, though, and I'm not going to second-guess my decision about Snorrason at this point. It's just . . ." He grimaced. "It's just that I've got this itch I can't quite seem to scratch."

"What sort of 'itch,' Boss?" Habib's expression was much more intent than it had been.

Luiz Rozsak was an intensely logical man, she thought. Despite the easy-going attitude which had been known to deceive friends, as well as adversaries, he was anything but casual or impulsive. His brain weighed factors and possibilities with an assayer's precision, and he was usually at least two or three moves ahead of anyone else in the game. Yet there were times when a sort of instinct-level process seemed to kick in. When he did make decisions on what might seem to others like mere impulses or whims. Personally, Habib had come to the conclusion long ago that his "whims" were actually their own version of logic, but logic that went on below the conscious level, so deep even he stood outside it as it operated on facts or observations his conscious mind didn't realize he possessed.

"If I knew what sort of itch it was, then I'd know how to scratch it," he pointed out now.

"If I can help you figure out what's itching, I'll be glad to lend a hand," she said. He looked at her, and she shrugged. "You've gotten an occasional wild hair that didn't go anywhere, Boss, but not all that damned often."

"Maybe." It was his turn to shrug. "And maybe," he lowered his voice a bit more, "it's opening-night nerves, too. This game's just a bit bigger-league than any I've played in before, you know."

Habib started to laugh, but she stopped herself before the reaction reached the surface. She'd stood at Rozsak's shoulder through all manner of operations—against pirates, against smugglers, against slavers, terrorists, rebels, desperate patriots striking back against Frontier Security. No matter the operation, no matter the cost or the objective, he'd never once lost control of the situation or himself.

Yet even though all of that was true, she realized, this would be his first true *battle*. The first time naval forces under his command had actually met an adversary with many times his own tonnage of warships and hundreds of times as many personnel. And, she reflected grimly, the price if he failed would be unspeakable.

Many of the people who thought they knew Luiz Rozsak might have expected him to take that possibility in stride. And, in some ways, they would have been right, too. Edie Habib never doubted that whatever happened to the planet of Torch, Rozsak would never waver in the pursuit of his "Sepoy Option." But Habib probably knew him better than anyone else in the universe, including Oravil Barregos. And because she did, she knew the thing he would never, ever admit—not even to her. Probably not even to *himself*.

She knew what had truly driven him to craft the "Sepoy Option" so many years before. She knew what hid beneath the cynicism and the amoral pursuit of power he let other people see. Knew what truly gave him the magnetism that bound people as diverse as Edie Habib, Jiri Watanapongse, and Kao Huang to him.

And what would never, ever let him forgive himself if some-how the StateSec renegades in front of him got through to the planet of Torch.

If he's feeling a little . . . antsy, it sure as hell shouldn't be sur-prising, she thought.

"Well," she said out loud, "maybe it *is* your biggest game so far, Boss. But your record in the minors strikes me as pretty damned good. *I* think you're ready for the majors."

"Why," he smiled at her, "so do I. Which, oddly enough, doesn't seem to make me totally immune to butterflies, after all."

❖   ❖   ❖

"Message from Admiral Rozsak, Ma'am," Lieutenant Rensi reported. "Hammer Force will be reducing acceleration in"—the communications officer glanced at the time display—"four and a half minutes."

"Thank you, Cornelia," Laura Raycraft said, and glanced at Lieutenant Commander Dobbs. "Do you think they'll decide to surrender after all when they find out about the Mark-17-Es?" she asked quietly.

"I don't know, Ma'am," Dobbs replied. "But if it was *me*, I'd sure as hell fall all over myself surrendering!" He shook his head. "Of course, if it *was* me, I'd've broken off and headed for home the minute the admiral came out of hyper. This is a busted op if I've ever seen one. Even if they manage to take out the planet, *somebody's* going to be left to pass on their ship IDs to the Navy and everybody else out this way."

"The same thought occurred to me," Raycraft agreed. "And if I were them, I'd be damned worried about multidrive missiles. I know we've identified ourselves as Solarian, but they have to have figured out that these are Erewhon-built ships, and in their shoes, I'd be figuring that meant those two 'freighters' behind the admiral were probably stuffed with MDMs. Of course, we *are* talking about StateSec types, and nobody with the brains to pour piss out of a boot would still be dreaming about 'restoring the Revolution' in Nouveau Paris. Anybody who's that far out of touch with reality obviously isn't very good at threat analysis to begin with."

"And maybe they're figuring on taking the time to hunt down anybody or anything that might be able to pass their emissions signatures on to anyone else, too," Dobbs said more darkly. Ray-craft raised an eyebrow at him, and he shrugged. "If they don't think they're looking at MDMs, Ma'am, then they have to think they've got an overwhelming advantage in weight of metal. Against what they've seen so far, assuming equal missile ranges, they probably *could* mop up everything we've got and then take their time making sure they've also destroyed anyone with a record of their emissions. If they managed that, there wouldn't be any evidence to prove who'd done it . . . which is what they've been planning on all along, isn't it?"

"You may be right about that. No," Raycraft shook her head, "I'm sure you *are* right about it. Unfortunately for them, they don't *have* equal missile ranges, now do they?"

Adrian Luff watched his own plot, and despite the impending clash, despite his own lingering revulsion at the mission he'd been assigned, he felt oddly . . . calm.

He and his ships were committed. They had been, from the moment Luiz Rozsak's force turned up behind them, and they knew it. Luff's initial attack plan had gone disastrously awry the instant those ships translated out of hyper, and everyone aboard all of his ships knew that, as well, just as they knew he'd refused to break off even when challenged in the name of the mighty Solarian League. Yet there was surprisingly little evidence of panic aboard *Leon Trotsky* and the other ships of the PNE. StateSec secret policemen they might once have been, uniformed enforcers of a brutal regime who'd become little more than common pirates since the fall of the People's Republic, yet they were more than that, as well.

However foolish the rest of the universe might think they were to dream of restoring the People's Republic and the Committee of Public Safety, it was a dream to which they had genuinely committed their lives. It was what bound them together, and in the binding they had found strength. The long months of preparation for a mission virtually none of them wanted to carry out had forged them back into a unit, an organized force, and in the forging they'd gained a temper they had never known before. Even some of the mercenaries Manpower had recruited to fill out their ranks had been forged into that same sense of unity, of purpose. Singly, they might still be the lunatic holdouts, the renegades, the agents of brutality the galaxy considered all of them to be, but together, they truly *were* the People's Navy in Exile.

They had that now, and Luff wasn't giving it up. Whatever the cost, whatever the consequences, they would be the People's Navy in Exile, or they would be nothing at all.

As Gowan Maddock sat on Adrian Luff's flag bridge, watching the kilometers between the citizen commodore's ships and their enemies dwindle steadily away, he realized just how badly he (and the rest of the Mesan Alignment) had underestimated these people. Oh, they were still lunatics—crackpots! But they were lunatics who refused to panic. Crackpots who'd accepted that they were probably going to die in pursuit of their lunacy, yet refused to relinquish the madness which empowered them.

He sat in his own command chair, watching Luff engage in a deadly version of the ancient Old Earth game of "chicken," and knew that in their quixotic quest, the men and women of the People's Navy in Exile had become something far greater—something far tougher and much more dangerous—than he'd ever admitted to himself before.

"Coming up on the specified deceleration point in thirty-five seconds, Sir," Lieutenant Womack said quietly.

"Thank you, Robert," Luiz Rozsak replied, his own eyes intent as he watched the master plot.

Masquerade and *Kabuki* had fallen back a bit, placing themselves behind Kamstra's cruisers and their destroyers. The range between *Marksman* and the enemy battlecruisers had fallen to the specified eleven million kilometers, and as he'd pointed out to Habib, there was no point closing the rest of the way to their chosen firing point too rapidly. Even at the *Masquerades'* maximum deceleration rate, it would have taken them over three minutes simply to decelerate to zero relative to the enemy, and that was assuming the other side kept running at its own current acceleration. Slowing their own overtake acceleration by one kilometer per second squared meant it would take them an additional thirteen minutes to enter his chosen engagement range . . . and that their overtake velocity would be down to less than 500 KPS when he did. If he needed to, he could hold that range forever—or open it still further, for that matter—even with his arsenal ships and even if the other side went to a zero compensator margin trying to catch him.

"The enemy's reduced acceleration, Citizen Commodore!" Citizen Lieutenant Commander Stravinsky said suddenly. "It's dropped a full kilometer per second squared!"

Luff looked quickly up from the plot at the ops officer's announcement, then turned to Hartman.

"I don't think they'd be killing any of their acceleration if they weren't pretty close to where they wanted to be," he said quietly.

"No, Citizen Commodore," she agreed, eyes meeting his, and he nodded. Then he turned back to Stravinsky.

"Open fire, Citizen Lieutenant Commander!" he said crisply.

CHAPTER FIFTY-EIGHT

"Missile launch!"

Commander Raycraft's head jerked around in astonishment. That *couldn't* be right! Hammer Force was still *eleven million* kilometers from the enemy!

"Many missiles, multiple launches!" Travis Siegel said. "Estimate three hundred ninety-plus—repeat, three-zero-niner-plus!"

"What the hell—?" Raycraft heard Commander Dobbs's muttered question, although the corner of her mind which was paying attention to such things felt confident he'd never meant to say it aloud. On the other hand, exactly the same question was burning through her own brain as she stared at the plot.

It was ridiculous. Hammer Force was at least three million kilometers outside the powered envelope of even a Javelin or Trebuchet shipkiller, and firing missiles that would go ballistic, unable to pursue evading targets, that far short of their intended victims was stupid! A useless waste of ammunition! They couldn't *possibly* think they could—

Oh, yes, they could, a tiny voice told her. *We've got Mark-17-Es in the pods—what if they've got something of their own over there? Something we didn't know about any more than they knew about the Mark-17?*

She remembered her own earlier thoughts about the possibility of missile pods on the other side. Escaped StateSec crews would also have known all about the existence of multidrive missiles. For that matter, *Manpower* had certainly known about them since shortly after their first use, and the fact that the SLN still hadn't done anything about it didn't mean everyone else was equally blind. So, yes, they could have a surprise of their own.

She looked at the acceleration numbers coming up on the plot. So far, they looked exactly like the profile of a Javelin anti-ship missile set for a three-minute, maximum-range burn, and she wanted to believe that was what they actually were. But that tiny voice told her they weren't. That not even a bunch of StateSec lunatics would have opened fire at this range unless they genuinely believed they could hit their targets.

"Missile launch!" Lieutenant Womack's report interrupted Rozsak's side conversation with Edie Habib. "CIC estimates four *hundred* missiles inbound, Sir!"

Rozsak's eyes whipped to the main plot, and for just a moment, he could only stare at the icons in disbelief. As he saw the missile vectors stretching out from the battlecruisers he'd pursued deeper and deeper into the Torch System for the last forty-seven minutes, they seemed just as pointless—just as foolish—as they seemed to every one of his junior officers. But then his face hardened into granite. Much as a part of his mind wanted to regard this as a panic reaction, an act of desperation as the enemy saw Alpha Two closing upon him, he knew it wasn't. His mind raced through exactly the same analysis Laura Raycraft had just considered, and for just a moment, even his formidable control wavered.

But it was only for a moment, and his voice didn't even quaver as he turned back to Kamstra's com image.

"Open fire," he said flatly.

Unlike the Solarian League Navy, the Mesan Alignment had no reservations at all about the missile ranges being reported by observers of the renewed conflict between Manticore and the Republic of Haven. They'd not only realized those reports were accurate, but figured out what the Manticorans and Havenites must have done to produce them.

Unfortunately, deducing what someone else had done wasn't the same thing as figuring out how to do it for oneself. Downsizing missile drive components without reducing their already limited lifetimes still further was a significant technological challenge—one the Alignment was working hard to overcome, but hadn't managed to pull off yet.

So they'd taken another approach as an intermediate step. The Cataphract was a rather basic concept, actually—they'd simply grafted what amounted to an entire counter-missile drive unit onto the end of a standard shipkiller. Coming up with an arrangement which let them cram that much impeller power *and* a worthwhile laser head into something they could fit onto the end of a standard missile had demanded quite a bit of ingenuity (and not a few basic compromises), but it had been a far easier task than duplicating a full scale multidrive missile would have been.

There were drawbacks, of course; there always were, and especially so in what had to be a compromise solution.

The weapon carried only half as many lasing rods as a standard laser head. Worse, the Cataphract was twenty percent longer than a standard missile of any given weight, which meant it would no longer fit into launch tubes which had been designed to handle the single-drive missile upon which it was based. The Cataphract-C, built around the SLN's Trebuchet capital missile, could be fired only out of one of the missile pods the MAN hadn't seen fit to offer Citizen Commodore Luff. The Cataphract-B, based on the Javelin missile intended for the League's battlecruisers and heavy cruisers, could be fired from a standard superdreadnought missile tube, but not by an *Indefatigable* or a *Warlord-C*. But Luff's battlecruisers *could* fire the Cataphract-A, based on the Spatha, the SLN's new-model destroyer and light cruiser shipkiller. His *Mars-Cs* could have, as well, but only the battlecruisers had been supplied with the new weapon, and even they carried only enough of them for a dozen full broadsides.

Compared to standard missiles of their size, their warheads were light, and the onboard seekers, ECM, and penetration aids which could be stuffed into such a size-restricted terminal bus were limited. But the weapon had a powered range from rest of almost 16.6 million kilometers, nobody had ever even imagined that it might exist . . . and Luff's fourteen battlecruisers mounted over eight hundred broadside missile tubes.

Luiz Rozsak cursed himself with silent passion as he watched four hundred and two missiles hurtle towards his command. By the standards of the recent, ferocious confrontations between the Star Kingdom of Manticore and the Republic of Haven, it was a puny effort, and he knew it. But the Manties and the Havenites clashed with entire fleets of superdreadnoughts; *he* had only six cruisers and eight destroyers with which to face it.

You were so damned confident you had the fucking range advantage, weren't you? a cold, hating voice demanded harshly. *You were so frigging* brilliant—*so goddamned,* stupidly *overconfident—that it never even* occurred *to you that someone else could be just as frigging smart as* you *are!*

It was vicious, that voice, filled with bitter awareness of the price his people were about to pay—the price *Torch* might be about to pay—for his overconfidence. But it was also buried deep, pushed down below the surface to clear his brain as he faced the cataclysm to come.

The flight time for Luff's missile salvo was two hundred and twelve seconds. That meant it would be over three and a half minutes before the first PNE laser head reached attack range, and Luiz Rozsak's brain whirred steadily.

"Defense plan X-Ray-Charlie-Three," he heard his voice saying. "Fire plan Delta-Zulu-Niner. *Warlords* are primaries."

"Defense X-Ray-Charlie-Three, aye," Robert Womack acknowledged. "Fire plan Delta-Zulu-Niner, aye. *Warlords* are alpha-priority targets!"

Hammer Force's formation began to shift. There wouldn't be time for it to make a great deal of difference before that first enormous salvo arrived, but defensive fire plans and responsibilities shifted far more rapidly—and radically—as X-Ray-Charlie-Three went into effect. And, at the same moment, Hammer Force's two arsenal ships started spitting rings of missile pods into space in massive, twelve-second spasms.

Rozsak would have preferred to launch them even more rapidly—to get all of them out of their suddenly imperiled pod bays. They would have fallen steadily astern at Hammer Force's still mounting velocity, and they would have been vulnerable to proximity kills, but that would still have been better than what his tightly knotted stomach muscles knew was about to happen.

Unfortunately, they didn't have the endurance. They were still the original, lightweight pods, and they had to launch their missiles almost instantly. He couldn't hold them back, and twelve seconds was about the tightest window for effective fire control he could manage, especially since his cruisers were going to have to take the missiles under control in successive waves.

The good news—such as there was and what there was of it—was that the minimum cycle time on a Flight VII *Indefatigable*-class battlecruiser's SL-13 shipboard launchers was thirty-five seconds. The earlier *Indefatigables*, with the older SL-11-b had the same theoretical cycle rate, but their feed queues were infamous for breaking down if they were pushed much above one launch every forty-five seconds. And as he watched the seconds ticking down, he realized at least some of those ex-Solarian ships had to be Flight V or Flight VI. Thirty-five seconds came and went, and still no second salvo had launched. It had to come any time now, though, and—

There! The second salvo had finally launched, but three of Rozsak's missile waves were already slicing downrange, and more were punching steadily out of *Masquerade* and *Kabuki*.

Adrian Luff's lips skinned back from his teeth as his first salvo went slamming back at his pursuers. He had no illusions about what multidrive missiles with their enormous laser heads would do to his battlecruisers, but he'd gotten at least several seconds' head start on the bastards, and they'd been coming straight up his wake for the better part of an hour. There'd been plenty of time for Stravinsky and the tactical officers aboard each of the PNE's battlecruisers to mark their targets, track them, run constantly updated firing solutions on them.

Of course, the long range was going to work against their targeting solutions. There was no help for that, and he had no doubt that accuracy was going to be poor, to say the least. But those were only *heavy* cruisers behind him, not battlecruisers. If he could get his initial salvos in among them, rip up their control systems, knock back their fire control . . .

"Enemy missile launch!" Stravinsky announced, and Luff's jaw muscles tightened. They'd been quicker off the mark than he'd expected, and MDMs had high acceleration rates. If Gowan Maddock's intelligence reports were accurate, they'd be quicker than his Cataphracts' primary drives, even over relatively short ranges, and—

"Estimate three hundred and sixty inbound," Stravinsky continued. "Acceleration rate four-five-one KPS-squared. Time of flight, two-one-seven seconds. Missile Defense is tracking and Halo is active."

Luff's eyes narrowed. That acceleration was lower than he'd expected—in fact, it was lower than his own birds' primary drives, far less the final sprint drive! That meant his flight time was going to be *lower* than theirs, not higher!

"Second wave launch!"

Damn! They were punching the damned things out at twelve-second intervals! At that rate, they'd be putting better than three salvos into space for every one he sent back at them! That was close to three missiles for each of his.

"Maximum rate fire," he said harshly.

"Maximum rate fire, aye, Citizen Commodore."

Luff sensed Millicent Hartman looking at him and looked up from the plot to meet her gaze.

"Better we risk jamming the tubes than let them pound us any harder than we have to," he told her.

Hundreds of missiles sliced through space towards one another, each of them a suicidal cybernetic agent of destruction, and their intended targets' defenses roused, dueling with their onboard sensors. Electronic warfare systems tried to blind them while others tried to trick them with false targets, and their own penetration aids did the same thing for the anti-missile targeting systems trying to lock them up. Mighty computers aboard the ships which had launched them—or, in Hammer Force's case, taken them under control after someone *else* launched them—monitored their telemetry links, adding their own enormous computational power to the titanic struggle. The defensive systems had more power, better AIs, and the advantage of human intuition, but starships were far bigger and far more brilliant target beacons. To offset that, the offensive telemetry links got progressively more arthritic as the attack missiles neared their targets. Exactly when to cut the control links and leave the shipkillers to their own rudimentary devices was always a judgment call, and at the next best thing to thirty-seven light-seconds' range, even the best light-speed fire control fell further and further behind the curve.

By the time Adrian Luff's first missile wave reached attack range of Hammer Force, the PNE had sent six more on its heels . . . and the Solarian ships had put seventeen salvos of their own into space.

Luff's face was expressionless as he watched that incredible thicket of missiles coming at him. Their icons dusted the plot, and it was already evident that the other side's EW was better than his. Not as much better as the People's Navy had become gallingly accustomed to against the Manties, perhaps, but still at least marginally better.

Still more hostile missile traces appeared in the plot with deadly, metronome precision, and his eyes narrowed.

"Targeting change," he said flatly. "Go for the cruisers."

"First salvo is already committed, Citizen Commodore," Citizen Lieutenant Commander Stravinsky replied. "Retargeting second salvo now."

Luff nodded, his eyes never leaving the plot. He hadn't counted on how rapidly they'd be rolling those waves of pods. He'd hoped he could kill the ammunition platforms before they got very many missiles into space, cut the hostile fire off at the source. Unfortunately, he no longer had time for that. Taking out the freighters would still be worthwhile, but with so many shipkillers already headed his way, it was more imperative that he beat down the enemy's fire control, first.

Luff's first salvo roared in on Hammer Force.

The cruisers and destroyers shuddered with the sawtoothed vibration of counter-missile launchers in rapid fire. They didn't have the massive armor, the multiply redundant control systems, of ships-of-the-wall, but they'd been designed and engineered specifically to face a massive missile threat. Luiz Rozsak had never anticipated exposing them to a storm like the one racing towards them—not without many more consorts to share the defensive load—but he and the Erewhonese designers working with him had visualized the missile environment far more accurately than the Solarian designers of Luff's *Indefatigables*.

X-Ray-Charlie Three was still coming fully online. There hadn't been time to complete the redeployment it envisioned, but the cruisers responsible for managing Hammer Force's defensive fire in the outer defense zone were up and tracking. Counter-missiles raced outward, using their hugely overpowered impeller wedges to sweep holes in the incoming fire. But the sudden burst of speed from the Cataphracts' second-stage "sprint drive" had taken Rozsak's tactical officers by surprise. None of the fire control solutions had allowed for it, and kill percentages in the outer zone were less than half of what they ought to have been. Far too many of the first salvo's shipkillers broke past the outer intercept zone, and more counter-missiles erupted from the destroyers tasked to back up the cruisers as they raced into the middle intercept zone.

Laser clusters trained around, tracking, waiting for the incoming fire to enter their own range, then spat rods of coherent lightning to meet them. Fireballs glared and flashed, and despite the "sprint mode" surprise, Hammer Force killed one hundred and thirty-seven of the attacking missiles.

Two hundred and sixty-five got through.

SLNS *Rifleman* twisted in anguish as X-ray lasers punched through her sidewall. They ripped deep, despite her cruiser-weight armor. Transfer energy shattered plating, ripped open compartments, blotted away offensive and defensive weapons—and the men and women who manned them. Her sidewalls blunted the onslaught; they couldn't possibly *stop* it, and for all her toughness, she was only a cruiser.

Her wedge fluctuated as a laser slammed into her forward impeller room. Power spikes surged through her systems, and she reeled off course as her forward nodes went down. Her acceleration fell drastically, and then another laser stabbed deep into her vitals.

Her compensator failed, and even with her forward nodes down, she was still pulling over two hundred gravities.

There were no survivors.

Pain ripped through Luiz Rozsak as he watched *Rifleman* die, but there was no time to grieve. More hits slammed in, and *Rifleman*'s sister ship *Ranger* staggered. Her impeller strength fell, over half her starboard broadside was turned into some mangled junk, but she held her place in the formation, and Lieutenant Commander Haldane was already rolling ship, bringing her port broadside to bear.

The destroyers of Lieutenant Commander Stahlin's Division 3029.2 were all on the cruisers' engaged flank when the wave of destruction swept across them. Rozsak doubted that they'd even been targeted, but his formation shift had taken them between the incoming missiles and Hammer Force's cruisers. He hadn't planned it that way, but the effect was to turn them into living missile decoys, and the *Warriors'* sheer size worked against them. The missiles raining down on them were in autonomous control, this far from the ships which had launched them, and they were nearsighted and narrow-minded without their telemetry links. Those which had lost their original targets as a result of the formation shift looked around for new ones, and a *Warrior*-class ship was more than big enough to satisfy the targeting criteria of AIs which had been told to go and kill cruisers.

Francisco Pizarro and *Cyrus* stumbled out of formation as furious lasers hammered them like brimstone lightning. *Pizarro* broke up seconds later, while *Cyrus* coasted onward, wedge down, life pods spilling from her flanks. Her sister ship *Simón Bolivar*, in Anne Guglik's Division 3029.3, staggered as she took half a dozen hits of her own, then turned away, rolling ship, fighting to bring her un-mangled broadside's counter-missile tubes and point defense clusters to bear.

And SLNS *Kabuki* shuddered as a pair of lasers slammed into her.

Only two of them. That was all that got past her defenders, all that got through to her, and she was two million tons of starship. Yet she was also totally unarmored, without any of a warship's armor, or internal bulkheads, or built-in survival features. Rozsak had accepted that when he conceived the class, because he'd had no choice, and now he remembered his own earlier thought about pile-drivers and soap bubbles.

The hits blew completely through that unarmored hull. They ripped massive holes straight through the heart of her, smashing missile bays, snapping structural members, shattering her fabric with contemptuous ease. Her secondary reactor went into emergency shutdown, and four of her alpha nodes exploded. Only the fact that she'd been built with mil-spec impeller rooms' massive circuit breakers saved her from instant destruction, and data codes indicating critical structural damage appeared under her icon.

Then it was over . . . for another forty-five seconds.

Adrian Luff knew his first wave of missiles had just ripped into the enemy formation. He'd seen their impeller signatures vanishing from his FTL gravitic detectors as they were picked off by defenders or reached the ends of their runs and detonated, and those same gravitics told him three of the enemy starships' wedges had also disappeared. But that was all the information he had, and it would be another half-minute before his light-speed sensors could tell him how much more damage they might have done.

In the meantime, he had other things to worry about.

Leon Trotsky's counter-missiles began to launch. The big ship's active antimissile defenses were far weaker than they ought to be for something her size, but the Aegis system which had been added to them went some way towards repairing that weakness. It was scarcely what Luff would have called a sophisticated solution, but there was a certain brutal elegance to the concept. Simply rip out a couple of broadside launchers, use the space they'd previously occupied for additional counter-missile fire control, and then use two of the remaining launchers to toss out canisters of defensive missiles. Even under optimal conditions, Aegis cost the ship which mounted it at least four offensive tubes per broadside. Normally, Luff would have considered it an equitable deal, given *Trotsky*'s original feeble defenses; now, he missed those shipkillers badly.

And I'm going to miss them even more *badly in just a few minutes*, he told himself harshly.

The Halo EW platforms deployed around the ship wove their protective cocoon, as well. He hadn't been especially impressed by Halo when his Manpower backers first showed it to him. The platforms were far less effective than the Manticoran tethered decoys the People's Navy had confronted over the years. But he'd changed his mind—provisionally, at least—once he saw them in action against his own ships' targeting capability in exercises. Yes, individually each platform was only marginally more effective than the ones which had equipped the PNE's ships when they initially fled the counterrevolutionaries. But Halo didn't depend on single platforms. It depended on multiple platforms—five of them in each broadside, for an *Indefatigable,* more for ships-of-the-wall—to generate multiple false targets and provide remote jammer nodes in carefully integrated defensive plans. And since they were small enough to be carried in substantial numbers, they could be quickly replenished as they eroded—as planned—under incoming fire.

I hope to hell they work as well against these people as they did against us in those exercises! he thought grimly.

✧　　✧　　✧

Luiz Rozsak's first salvo arrived on target, three hundred and sixty strong. But sixty of those missiles had gone to local control five seconds before they should have when *Rifleman's* telemetry links were taken brutally off-line at the source. The Erewhonese-built Mark-17-E's onboard seekers and AI were better than those of most navies, yet they fell immeasurably short of the capabilities of the Royal Manticoran Navy's new Apollo. They did their best, but most of them wasted themselves for minimal return, spreading out, scattering themselves among four different targets. Only two of them got through to their intended prey at all, and the damage they inflicted was scarcely crippling.

It was a very different story for their fellows.

Delta-Zulu-Niner was about as subtle as a battle ax. Luiz Rozsak was up against battlecruisers, and powerful as the Mark-17-E was, no one was going to confuse it with a true capital missile. It was more powerful than most battlecruisers carried, but at the cost of carrying fewer lasing rods. That meant fewer potential hits per missile, and those individual hits weren't going to do the sort of damage an all-up MDM could do, either. In fact, no one really knew exactly how well the Mark-17 was going to perform against targets with battlecruiser-range armor, and so Delta-Zulu-Niner concentrated all three hundred of the missiles that stayed under shipboard control until their planned handoff points on just two targets.

One hundred and fifty missiles hurtled in on the battlecruiser *Alexander Suvorov,* and she heaved and twisted as the first few laser heads punched through her counter-missiles and her point defense clusters, through the fire being thrown up by her consorts, through the blinding efforts of her onboard EW. More laser heads followed them, howling in at over 100,000 KPS in a solid wave of destruction. The big *Warlord*-class battlecruiser's active defenses were far stronger than *Leon Trotsky's,* and her armor was thicker and better placed, but there were simply too many threats coming in too quickly, too tightly sequenced, for her to stop them. Even *her* armor cratered, then splintered, then ripped apart as laser after laser gouged deeper and deeper.

Point defense clusters went suddenly dead. Her emission signature flickered and flared as primary tracking and targeting systems were blown out of existence and secondaries came up in their place. Three beta nodes went down, then an alpha, and despite the redundancy built into her overpowered drive systems, her acceleration faltered. She staggered, bleeding atmosphere in clear proof of internal hull breaching, and then, abruptly, she blew apart in an expanding ball of fury.

Four seconds later, PNES *Bernard Montgomery*, Adrian Luff's old command, followed her into destruction.

✧   ✧   ✧

Luff gritted his teeth as *Bernard Montgomery* blew up.

They're going for the Warlords *first. They're trying to kill our most effective missile-defense platforms.*

They were, and their laser heads were far more powerful than he would have believed anything smaller than a capital ship missile could mount. Worse, their fire was immeasurably heavier than he'd imagined six heavy cruisers could possibly control. No ships that size should have that many control links!

But *these* ships obviously did, and something icy ran down his spine as one of Stravinsky's secondary displays posted the percentage of hits which had gotten through to the two battlecruisers. Saturation explained a lot of it, but the defenses still should have stopped a lot more than they did. The incoming missiles clearly carried extraordinarily good penetration EW . . . and the people behind them clearly knew *exactly* what they were doing.

But EW or no, whatever those damned things are, they aren't *MDMs,* he thought. *Bad as they are, they're not doing enough damage per hit for capital laser heads . . . and isn't* that *a comfort when there are so damned many of the bastards? I was right to shift priority to their cruisers. I just hope to hell I shifted soon enough!*

His eyes went back to the main plot as the second wave of Hammer Force's missiles came slamming in twelve seconds after the first.

✧   ✧   ✧

Rozsak's second salvo concentrated its fury on the battlecruisers *Napoleon Bonaparte* and *Charlemagne*.

The PNE's missile defense officers had better data than they'd had against the previous wave, but twelve seconds wasn't enough time for them to apply it to their fire solutions, crank it into their EW profiles, adjust their formation and their thinking. Worse, the loss of *Bernard Montgomery* and *Alexander Suvorov* had punched holes into their defensive fire assignments.

Computer overrides reassigned responsibilities, spreading the load among the dead battlecruisers' consorts, and tactical officers aboard Luff's other ships responded with swift efficiency. Yet they were still off-balance, still *reacting*, when three hundred fresh missiles exploded into their faces.

Citizen Captain Hervé Bostwick watched his plot on PNE *Charlemagne*'s command deck as the vortex of destruction ripped straight through the task group's defenses towards his command. *Charlemagne* was one of the big *Warlord*-class battlecruisers whose crew had fled the triumphant counterrevoutionaries, and Bostwick had been in command ever since. After so long together, he sometimes thought he knew every man and woman aboard her personally, by face and name, and now he could almost physically feel his officers' and ratings' fear—especially in the wake of how unbelievably quickly *Montgomery* and *Suvorov* had been wiped away. He felt it, yet the voices in the tactical net were crisp, clear, and Bostwick remembered the carefully hidden contempt he'd seen behind the eyes of many an officer of the old People's Navy—the contempt of professional warriors for mere secret policemen and enforcers. Contempt for the sloppy training and poor combat efficiency of State Security's warships. He remembered his own resentment of that contempt, but that wasn't what he felt now. Tension and spikes of terror might crackle in the depths of his people's voices, yet hard-won training and discipline beat that down, thrust them aside. His people were doing their jobs as well as any "professionals" in any navy in the galaxy, and despite his own undeniable fear, what Bostwick felt most of all was pride.

"Threat axis red-one-zero!" his missile-defense officer snapped. "Battery Three, take it!"

"Battery Three, red-one-zero, aye!" one of his assistants responded, punching commands into his own console. "Engaging!"

Point Defense Three retargeted the laser clusters guarding *Charlemagne*'s port quarter, training around to meet the wave of missiles roaring in at thirty percent of the speed of light through the zone *Bernard Montgomery* should have been covering. Laser clusters went to continuous rapid fire, but they simply didn't have enough emitters to stop that many missiles coming in that quickly.

Charlemagne quivered as the first bomb-pumped laser clawed at her armored flanks. Then another ripped home, and another, dozens of them in a tsunami of destruction, slamming into her on top of one another, so quickly it was impossible for any human sense—or even *Charlemagne*'s computers—to isolate any single blow.

"Direct hit on Missile-Three!"

"Heavy casualties in Impeller-Two!"

"Graser-One and Graser-Three out of the net—no response, Citizen Commander!"

"Gravitic-Five destroyed! Lidar-Three's gone, too!"

"Core hull breach, Frame Three-Seven-Four! Pressure dropping—I think we've got a jammed blast door! Initiating damage control!"

"Direct hit, Boat Bay-Two! I show red board on the entire bay—no response from Boat Bay damage control parties!"

Bostwick heard the wave of damage reports rolling over the net as entire quadrants of the damage control schematic flared scarlet. *Charlemagne* was hurt, badly. It would take months in dock to repair the damage he could already see. Yet she was still intact, still in the fight, and her people were already bringing up backup systems, rushing repair parties towards her injuries.

"Third salvo impact in five seconds," his tactical officer announced, still focused on his own responsibilities, his own duties. "Defensive fire plan Bravo-Hotel. I want—"

"*Skipper!*" The voice in his earbug belonged to Citizen Commander Christy Hargraves, his senior engineer, and in all the years she'd served with him, he'd never heard that note of raw urgency in her voice before. "*We're losing containment on Fusion-Tw—*"

Adrian Luff's expression was bleak as *Charlemagne*'s icon disappeared from his plot. *Napoleon Bonaparte*, which had once been SLNS *Indurate*, was marginally luckier than the *Warlord*. She continued onward, rolling slowly on her axis, shedding bits and pieces of hull and clutches of life pods, yet at least her people were getting off. She might even have been salvageable, but she was clearly a mission-kill, completely out of the fight.

There must really be Solly attack officers back there. They sure as hell don't seem very distracted by the Halo platforms, anyway!

The thought rolled through a corner of the citizen commodore's brain without ever reaching its surface, and even as he watched the lurid damage codes flashing under *Bonaparte*'s plot icon, Rozsak's *third* wave of missiles came howling in.

✧   ✧   ✧

Luiz Rozsak seemed to feel himself flowing even more deeply down into his command chair as the second massive missile salvo plowed straight down Hammer Force's throat.

They came rocketing in, and if many of them had clearly had their telemetry links shot out from under them, far more of them hadn't. His missile-defense officers had had longer than their PNE counterparts to digest—and apply—the lessons they'd learned from Luff's first salvo, and it showed. They knew about the shipkillers' final "sprint mode" now. They were allowing for it, and their long-range counter-missile fire was far more effective . . . but it was also coming from fewer launchers, and there were fewer point defense clusters to back them up.

He winced internally as SLNS *Gunner's* back broke strewing the cruiser's shattered hull—and her crew—across unforgiving vacuum. In the same cataclysmic instant, her sister, *Sniper*, took at least five hits that sent her lurching out of formation before she somehow managed to recover. *Cyrus* took three more hits of her own and quietly broke up; her sister *Frederick II* died in a far more spectacular flash which momentarily rivaled the brilliance of Torch, itself.

And then the missile storm closed on *Kabuki*.

He didn't know how many missiles got through to her. There couldn't have been very many . . . not that it mattered. Her merchant hull was straw in the furnace as the bomb-pumped lasers broke her bones and spat out the splinters. She disintegrated into torn and tattered wreckage, spreading outward from the center of what once had been a two million-ton starship . . . and its crew.

Two thirds of his cruisers were damaged or destroyed, half his destroyers—and *Kabuki*—were gone, and it was only the second salvo.

"Fire Plan Charlie-Zulu-Omega," he said flatly.

CHAPTER FIFTY-NINE

Adrian Luff felt a small stir of satisfaction as the light-speed damage estimates from his first salvo finally came up on Stravinsky's status boards.

They'd damaged or destroyed a quarter of the enemy force, including what looked like it had to be major damage to one of the ammunition ships. By now, his second salvo was arriving on target, as well, and he'd seen four more impeller wedges—including what CIC thought was one of the ammunition ships—vanish from his plot.

Yet any satisfaction he felt had to be weighed against the loss of almost half his own battlecruisers. Hammer Force's third salvo had destroyed PNE *Sun Tzu* and reduced PNE *Oliver Cromwell* to a staggering wreck. Six ships was barely twelve percent of his own total force, but they represented a far larger percentage of his total *tonnage*. And, infinitely worse, they were *all* battlecruisers . . . and only the battlecruisers had Cataphracts or the fire control to handle them.

It's a race, he thought again, grimly. *It's a damned race to see which of us runs out of platforms first.*

✧   ✧   ✧

Luiz Rozsak's fourth salvo came slicing in.

His two undamaged cruisers could still handle sixty missiles each, but *Ranger* and *Sniper*, combined, could handle only sixty more. Hammer Force split its hundred and eighty shipkillers into two ninety-missile salvos and sent them ripping in on the battlecruiser *Isoroku Yamamoto*, Luff's last *Warlord*, and the limping wreck of the *Oliver Cromwell*.

There were fewer missiles in each salvo, and Luff's missile-defense officers had learned a great deal more about the Mark-17-E, but there was only so much they could do. They needed time to reorganize, to restore their formation, and there *was* no time. There were only the incoming waves of missiles, screaming into their teeth at the rate of five every minute. Their individual effectiveness might be eroding as more and more of those missiles came in without benefit of shipboard control, but they were still *coming*, and the defenders had to treat each of them as its own individual threat.

Isoroku Yamamoto slid out of her slot in the formation as her after impeller ring died completely. More laser heads shattered her midships armor, destroying control systems, wiping out half her starboard point defense and all but three of her starboard long-range telemetry arrays. She began to drop gradually astern, rolling to present her less damaged port broadside to the enemy while damage control parties fought frantically to get her after impellers back on line.

Oliver Cromwell took only a dozen more hits, yet they were enough. Her single remaining fusion plant went off-line, and she fell behind as her crew raced to abandon ship while there was still time.

Less than one minute had passed since Hammer Force's first laser head detonated, and seven of Luff's fourteen battlecruisers had already been destroyed or crippled.

Rozsak's *fifth* salvo came screaming in twelve seconds later.

Our turn. It's our turn, now.

The thought flashed through Adrian Luff's mind as he saw the attack pattern develop on the plot. The deadly ruby diamond chips of incoming missiles swerved, coalescing suddenly out of chaos into a precisely targeted, tightly coordinated hammer. They drove straight through the PNE's harrowed defenses, numbers melting like snow in the furnace of defensive fire, yet somehow sweeping onward.

Luff's brain whirred like another computer, thinking too quickly, too furiously, for his own sudden stab of terror to register.

"Message to Citizen Commodore Konidis," he heard his own voice saying crisply, decisively. "If we lose communication, he's to continue with the mission as per our original orders."

"Yes, Citizen Com—"

The arrival of Luiz Rozsak's missile storm interrupted Citizen Lieutenant Kamerling's acknowledgment.

There was no way for Hammer Force's tactical officers to identify the PNE's flagship. That was all that had spared *Leon Trotsky* in their initial salvos. But probability plays no favorites. Eventually, the uncaring odds catch up with everyone, and Luff had been correct. This time it was, indeed, *Trotsky*'s turn.

A hundred and eighty missiles hurled themselves at her and her division mate, *Mao Tse-tung*, and there was no stopping them. Or no stopping *enough* of them, anyway. They'd been lost in the clutter of autonomously-guided missiles until the very last instant, and they came down like a battle ax.

The battlecruiser heaved indescribably, writhing at the heart of a hellish latticework of bomb-pumped lasers. Entire sections of her heavily armored hull disintegrated, and raw craters blasted into her, ripping their way through deck after deck, seeking her vitals. Power surges cascaded through her systems, the heavily armored control capsules of on-mount personnel blew apart, and damage alarms screamed like tortured souls.

No mere human being could have kept track of the incredible damage which rained down on Adrian Luff's flagship. It took less than two seconds from the first hit to the last, and the carnage and devastation in its wake was impossible for the brutally shaken survivors to truly grasp. Yet even in the heart of that furnace, men and women clung to their training and their duty.

"Direct hit, Tracking Seven!"

"Direct hit, Graser Five!"

"Point Defense Niner and Ten in local control!"

"Missile Twenty-Three out of the net!"

"Fusion One, emergency shutdown!"

"CIC, direct hit! I can't get anyone on the com, Citizen Commander!"

The damage control reports poured in, a mounting litany of destruction and death. The master plot went dead as the Combat Information Center dropped out of the circuit, and it *stayed* dead as the auxiliaries which should have taken over to drive it died under hits of their own.

"Direct hit, Impeller Two!"

Leon Trotsky's acceleration faltered.

"Missile Defense Four is down, Citizen Commander! No response from on-mount personnel!"

"Dir—"

Adrian Luff, Millicent Hartman, Pierre Stravinsky, and every other man and woman on *Leon Trotsky*'s flag bridge died instantly as the trailer—the lonely, orphaned, autonomously-controlled missile no one had noticed in time—slipped through the flagship's shattered defenses like a dagger.

Trotsky and *Mao Tse-tung* staggered onward, too hideously maimed to do more than defend themselves feebly, and Hammer Force's sixth salvo went streaking in on PNES *George Washington* and PNS *Ho Chi Minh*.

✧　　✧　　✧

Citizen Commodore Santander Konidis stared at his plot, white-faced.

Citizen Commodore Luff's flagship was still there—barely—but there was no way to misread the lurid damage codes under her icon. Even if Luff was still somehow, impossibly, alive over there, his communications were clearly out. Which meant Santander Konidis was now the senior surviving officer of the People's Navy in Exile.

What there was of it.

He shook himself and made himself look up from his plot and meet his chief of staff's eyes.

"Pass the word to all units," he said harshly. "I'm assuming command."

"Yes, Citizen Commodore!" Citizen Commander Gino Sanchez responded immediately, and Konidis gave him a tight smile. He'd never really liked Sanchez—the man was too brutal when it came to shipboard discipline, and he had an undeniable tendency to browbeat and terrorize junior officers—but there wasn't a gram of quitter anywhere in him, and at the moment, Konidis found him remarkably reassuring.

Then the citizen commodore returned his attention to his plot, and any reassurance Sanchez might have engendered disappeared as *George Washington* and *Ho Chi Minh* staggered out of the missile holocaust.

Washington's tactical links were still up, although Sanchez would be astonished if even half her offensive and defensive weapons remained effective. *Ho Chi Minh*, on the other hand, was completely out of the net—another clear mission-kill.

My God, I'm down to three *effective battlecruisers—and that's counting* Washington *as effective!*

It didn't seem possible. Surely *six* heavy cruisers couldn't have mangled the PNE's *battle*cruisers this way!

It's those goddammed pods. *They just keep pouring them on, and they're ripping us to pieces!*

Adrian Luff's third salvo came down on Hammer Force like a guillotine.

SLNS *Sniper* blew up as fresh hits blasted through her defenses, adding catastrophically to her earlier damage.

There were no life pods.

David Carte's *Sharpshooter* lurched off course as half the beta nodes in her forward ring went down. More hits slammed into her like the hammers of hell, yet somehow she hauled back on course, maintaining her heading, her surviving missile defenses still in operation.

More missiles pounded down on the destroyer *William the Conqueror*. Her desperate point defense stopped twenty-seven laser heads short of detonation range; eleven others got through, and *Conqueror* blew up as spectacularly as *Sniper* . . . and with just as few survivors.

And then, with a sort of horrible inevitability, five laser heads got past the tattered defensive umbrella of Luiz Rozsak's two surviving cruisers and his three remaining destroyers. Bomb-pumped lasers ripped out yet again, enveloping SLNS *Masquerade*'s unarmored hull in a spider web of lightning, and suddenly Rozsak had no more arsenal ships.

Citizen Commodore Konidis grinned savagely. *Chao Kung Ming's* master plot was less detailed than *Leon Trotsky's* had been, but it was good enough for him to know the impeller signature of the enemy's second ammunition ship had just disappeared. Without light-speed confirmation, he couldn't be positive that it had actually been *destroyed*. If it hadn't, it could probably roll another three or four pod waves before the PNE's next salvo arrived to finish it off, but either way, its end was in sight.

I just hope to hell ours isn't, too, he thought grimly as Hammer Force's seventh salvo came rumbling in.

Luiz Rozsak was down to three cruisers, two of them badly mangled, and four destroyers, one of *them* crippled. That was all he had left, and the missile waves which had already been launched were the only ones he was going to get.

There were three hundred sixty missiles in each of those waves, but all three of his remaining cruisers between them could manage only a third of them, and that wasn't going to be good enough.

Which was why he'd ordered Charlie-Zulu-Omega. They'd trained for the possibility, but they'd never tried it in action. As far as Rozsak knew, *no one* had, and he would never have attempted it against an intact missile defense. But Hammer Force had already torn great, bleeding wounds in the StateSec renegades' anti-missile defenses. It might just work . . . and it wasn't as if he had a lot of options.

There wasn't time to implement Charlie-Zulu-Omega before his next two waves arrived, but the one after that would be different.

Santander Konidis felt his shoulders tightening as the seventh enemy salvo came slashing into the PNE. It was like watching storm-driven surf, he thought. Like watching wave after wave pound forward, driving itself up over the beach, ripping at the sand dunes behind it.

"Impact in five seconds!"

Citizen Lieutenant Commander Rachel Malenkov's soprano was higher and shriller than usual. Not that Citizen Commander Jarko Laurent blamed her. With *Leon Trotsky*'s command deck completely cut out of the brutally wounded ship's internal communications net, she'd inherited command of what was left of *Trotsky*'s tactical department . . . exactly as Laurent had inherited command of the entire ship from Citizen Captain Vergnier.

Not that either one of us is going to have to worry about it much longer.

"—ponse from Missile-Seventeen!"

He heard the litany of damage reports still coming in, still being faithfully attended to by the people fighting his ship's desperate wounds.

"Negative response Search and Rescue Bravo-Three-Alpha-Niner! Negative res—"

I wish there was going to be time to tell them how proud of them I am, he thought, as two fresh salvos coalesced out of the onrushing mass of shipkiller missiles. Obviously, they'd hammered the other side's control platforms into scrap. Too bad that hadn't been enough to stop what was about to happen.

Citizen Commodore Konidis felt a surge of hope as he watched the same pattern emerge.

For the first time, the enemy's targeting had gone after the wrong prey. The hammer of destruction came crashing down on what was left of *Mao Tse-tung* and *Leon Trotsky*, and neither one of them was contributing a thing to the PNE's offensive fire.

I shouldn't feel grateful *for what's about to happen.*

The thought flared through his brain, yet he *was* grateful, and rightfully so. None of his heavy cruisers carried Cataphracts, nor did any of them have the computer codes to control the long-ranged weapons. There'd been no reason they should—not with fourteen *battlecruisers* to launch and control them. But if he lost his final battlecruisers, he'd lose any ability to engage the enemy at all. And so, guilty as he felt, a part of him rejoiced to see that enemy wasting his own precious missiles on targets which could no longer hurt him.

Sixty Mark-17-Es ripped their way through *Leon Trotsky*'s enfeebled defenses, while another sixty slashed toward *Mao Tse-tung*. The PNE's tactical officers did their best, but too many of their platforms had already been destroyed. There was too much confusion, too many holes, too many units scrambling to reprioritize as those metronome brimstone combers smashed over them.

Despite everything, they managed to stop almost two thirds of the incoming fire. Unfortunately, *Trotsky* and *Mao Tse-tung* were already too badly hurt. Their side walls were down, their armor was already breached and broken, and their own close-in defenses had been virtually silenced.

Mao Tse-tung disappeared in a spectacular explosion. *Leon Trotsky* simply broke her back and disintegrated.

Santander Konidis watched their icons vanish from the plot.

It was at least possible there'd been a handful of survivors from the flagship, he thought; none of those still aboard *Mao Tse-tung* could possibly have gotten off.

He glanced at the time display in the corner of his plot. It didn't seem possible. Less than five minutes—*five minutes!*—had elapsed since Citizen Commodore Luff's order to open fire. How could so many ships have been destroyed, so many people killed, in only five minutes?!

The display ticked steadily onward, and Hammer Force's eighth wave of missiles came howling in.

Citizen Captain Noémie Beausoleil's face was haggard. Smoke hung in the air of *Napoleon Bonaparte*'s command deck, hovering below the overhead because damage control had shut off the ventilation trunks which might have sucked it away. She couldn't smell it with her helmet sealed, but she could see it, just as she could see its crimson highlights as it reflected the damage control schematics.

She didn't know how the battlecruiser had hung together this long, and she had absolutely no illusions about what was going to happen the next time somebody shot at her. In fact, it looked like—

"*Incoming!*" her tactical officer barked suddenly. "One hundred-plus! Attack range in seven seconds!"

Beausoleil's eyes snapped back to the tactical plot. CIC was gone, but enough of *Bonaparte*'s tactical department was still up, still doing its job, for her to know it was no mistake.

"Abandon ship." She heard her own voice, impossibly calm, coming up over the priority command circuit before she even realized she'd hit the button. "Abandon ship. All hands, abandon ship. Aban—"

She was still repeating the order when the missiles struck.

Konidis knew he should have felt more pain as *Napoleon Bonaparte* blew up. Worse than that, he knew he *would* feel that pain—every gram of it—if he himself survived this day. Yet for now, right this second, what he felt was something quite different. He'd lost only a single ship this time, and, once again, one which had already been mission-killed.

Luiz Rozsak's ninth salvo rumbled down on the PNE, and this time, there'd been time for Charlie-Zulu-Omega to be implemented.

Rozsak was wrong, in at least one respect; he *wasn't* the first tactician to come up with the same idea. Admiral Shannon Foraker had beaten him to it, although Rozsak could certainly be excused for being unaware of the fact.

He had three times as many missiles as he had control links, even with his surviving destroyers tied in. Given the toughness of their targets, and the defensive capability the enemy still possessed, sixty-missile salvos weren't going to be enough. Especially not when the missiles already in the pipeline were all he was going to get. Which was why *Marksman* was no longer controlling sixty missiles; she was controlling a *hundred and eighty*, and her wounded sisters, *Ranger* and *Sharpshooter*, were controlling another hundred and eighty.

The only way they could do it was by rotating each of their available command links through three separate missiles, and the *degree* of control they could exercise was significantly diminished. But "diminished" control was enormously better than no control at all.

✧   ✧   ✧

"What the—?"

Santander Konidis bit off the question as all three hundred and sixty missiles in Hammer Force's ninth wave suddenly reacted as one. The abrupt shift took all of his remaining missile defense officers by surprise, and dozens of counter-missiles wasted themselves on missiles whose totally unexpected course changes took them out of the CMs' envelope.

Half the mighty salvo went screaming in on PNES *Marquis de Lafayette*, and the already badly damaged battlecruiser vanished in a bubble of hell-bright brilliance. That was terrible enough, but the *other* half crashed through the desperate defensive laser fire of *Lafayette*'s so far undamaged sister, PNES *Thomas Paine*.

It took longer, this time. The incoming fire wasn't as finely focused, as finely controlled. More of the missiles came in staggered, not concentrated into a single devastating moment of simultaneous destruction.

Not that it mattered.

Konidis watched the battlecruiser vanish from his plot, as so many others already had, and his mouth was tight.

He had exactly one battlecruiser left, Citizen Captain Kalyca Sakellaris' *Maximilien Robespierre*. Oh, the hulks which had once been *George Washington* and *Ho Chi Minh* continued to stagger along in formation with her, somehow, but they were as thoroughly out of the battle as any of their consorts which had already ceased to exist.

His eyes went back to the main plot, where the impeller signatures of six hostile starships continued to burn. The PNE's fourth salvo would reach those distant signatures in another five seconds, and *Thomas Paine* hadn't been destroyed until she and *Robespierre* had already cut their telemetry links.

It's the last salvo that's going to go in before they take Robespierre *out,* he thought coldly. *They've already cut their control links to their* next *wave, too—probably to the next two* waves, *given how tightly sequenced they are. Nothing we can do is going to affect what* those *missiles do, and there's no way they're going to miss targeting* Robespierre. *So it all comes down to this. Either we take them out this time, or they've got—*he glanced at a plot sidebar*—another fifteen salvos already coming down on us.*

CHAPTER SIXTY

"Here it comes."

Luiz Rozsak was positive Edie Habib didn't realize she'd spoken out loud. For that matter, he could hardly have legitimately called that single, softly murmured sentence speaking "out loud," he supposed.

The pristine, undamaged neatness of SLNS *Marksman*'s flag bridge was a bizarre counterpoint to what had happened to the rest of Dirk-Steven Kamstra's cruiser squadron. Flag Bridge still had that new-air-car smell, still looked like the flag bridge of a modern, lethal fighting force, despite the carnage which had ravaged LCS 7036.

There should be smoke, he thought. *There should be the smell of blood, screams. There shouldn't be this . . . this antiseptic order. We should be* feeling *what's happened to the rest of the squadron.*

Shut up, stupid, he told himself. *Talk about misplaced survivor's guilt!* He shook his head, surprised to feel a slight, biting smile twisting his lips. *Before you start wallowing in that kind of crap, wait and see if you're going to survive after all!*

"Attack range in ten seconds," Robert Womack said quietly. "Eight seconds. Seven sec— Status change!"

It was scarcely unexpected, and Rozsak watched with something very like detached calm as sixty missiles suddenly separated themselves from their companions—more than half of them in obedience to the directions of tactical officers who were already dead by the time the shipkillers obeyed their instructions—and came streaking directly in on *Sharpshooter* and *Marksman*.

The ECM on this salvo was better than it had been on any of the others. Obviously, the people who'd launched it had gone right on refining their data, updating their penetration profiles, even as they and their consorts were disintegrating under Hammer Force's relentless fire. Worse, only *Marksman*'s missile defenses were anything like intact.

It was too late for counter-missiles—they'd been largely wasted, killing other missiles. No one had been able to identify the actual attack birds until they identified *themselves* by suddenly lunging for their targets, and their autonomously controlled fellows—over three hundred of them—had camouflaged them, hidden them, absorbed the fire which ought to have killed them.

Now point defense clusters blazed desperately, but there was too little response time. Over half of them got through, and Luiz Rozsak's command chair shock frame hammered him viciously as SLNS *Marksman*'s immunity came to an end at last.

✧   ✧   ✧

"Oh, my God," Lieutenant Commander Jim Stahlin whispered.

It wasn't an imprecation; it was a prayer from the heart as the shipkillers came screaming in.

Hernando Cortés seemed to run into some invisible barrier in space. The big *Warrior*-class destroyer simply disintegrated, and Stahlin watched sickly as the badly damaged *Simón Bolívar* broke in two. His own *Gustavus Adolphus,* somehow miraculously still undamaged, and her division mate, *Charlemagne*—which most definitely was *not* undamaged—were suddenly Hammer Force's only surviving destroyers.

And they hadn't even been the primary targets.

✧   ✧   ✧

"Direct hit on Impeller One!"

"Captain, we've lost helm control!"

"Direct hit Missile-One. Missile-Three and Five out of the net!"

"Counter-Missile-Niner out of the net! Counter-Missile-Eleven reports heavy casualties!"

"Sir, we've lost five betas out of the forward ring!"

"Heavy damage aft! Hull breach, Frames One-Zero-One-Five through One-Zero-Two-Zero! We have pressure drop, decks three and four!"

Luiz Rozsak heard the damage reports over his com link to Dirk-Steven Kamstra's bridge. He *felt* the damage in his own flesh, his own bones, as his flagship shuddered and bucked and heaved, flexing and twisting with the indescribable shock as bomb-pumped lasers transferred terajoules of energy to her hull.

And even as the energy blasted into *Marksman*, he saw SLNS *Sharpshooter* disappear from his plot forever.

✧   ✧   ✧

Santander Konidis snarled in triumph as half the enemy impeller signatures were blotted away. But even as he snarled, Hammer Force's tenth missile salvo howled down on the People's Navy in Exile.

Three hundred and sixty Mark-17-E missiles hurtled straight into *Maximilien Robespierre*'s teeth. It was scarcely a surprise. Everyone had known exactly who those missiles would target, but they'd had only twelve seconds to react to the knowledge. Every counter-missile that could be brought to bear, every point defense cluster which could possibly reach that wave of destruction, blazed desperately. Scores of missiles were intercepted by counter-missiles. Over seventy more were torn apart by close-in laser fire.

It wasn't enough.

✧   ✧   ✧

"That's the last of them, Sir," Robert Womack said wearily ninety-eight seconds later.

Luiz Rozsak nodded, equally wearily, and glanced at the time display in the corner of his plot.

Five hundred and twelve seconds. Less than nine minutes. That was how long it had taken, from the enemy's initial missile launch to the attack of Hammer Force's final wave of missiles.

How could less than nine minutes leave him so exhausted? With so much sick regret?

He looked at the tally boards, wincing internally as he saw the names of all the ships Hammer Force had lost, and saw the answer. SLNS *Gunner*, *Rifleman*, *Sharpshooter*, *Sniper*, *Francisco Pizarro*, *Simón Bolívar*, *Hernando Cortés*, *Frederick II*, *William the Conqueror*, *Kabuki*, *Masquerade*...

Of the sixteen ships he'd taken into combat, only four survived— Dirk-Steven Kamstra's *Marksman*, her sister, *Ranger*, and the destroyers *Gustavus Adolphus* and *Charlemagne*. Somehow, and he couldn't pretend to understand how, Jim Stahlin's *Gustavus Adolphus* was totally untouched. *Charlemagne* and *Ranger*, on the other hand, were little more than still barely mobile hulks, and *Marksman* wasn't much better.

But then his eyes moved to the enemy's losses, and they hardened into dark brown agates.

Fourteen battlecruisers, three heavy cruisers, and two light cruisers. The light cruisers had been almost accidents, killed by the autonomous missiles of Hammer Force's last nine salvos. *Marksman* and *Ranger*, even with *Gustavus Adolphus'* support and even rotating telemetry links, had been able to control barely ninety missiles, which had been only a quarter of the total in each of the salvos which had been launched before *Kabuki*'s and *Masquerade*'s destruction. There'd been no more effective fire coming from the enemy to distract his tactical officers after *Maximilien Robespierre*'s elimination, but less than a hundred missiles had been too little too batter through the PNE's tattered defenses if they'd been spread between multiple targets. So he'd concentrated on taking out the big *Mars*-class heavy cruisers and letting the rest of the shipkillers go wherever they went under their onboard AIs' direction. To be honest, he was surprised they'd achieved as much as they had.

Now, however, Hammer Force had spent its bolt. Aside from the Mark-17s in the surviving magazines of *Marksman* and *Ranger*, the remaining enemy ships were far outside Rozsak's range, and between them *Marksman* and *Ranger* had only nineteen operable launchers. There was no point wasting such minuscule salvos against the PNE's surviving twenty-seven units.

"All right, Dirk-Steven," he said, turning back to the com which linked him to *Marksman*'s bridge. "It's out of our hands now. Let's see about killing our velocity and heading back to pick up survivors."

"How bad is our damage, Irénée?"

Santander Konidis hoped his voice sounded a lot crisper and more confident than he felt.

"Actually, Citizen Commodore, we got off pretty lightly," Citizen Captain Irénée Egert, PNES *Chao Kung Ming*'s commanding officer, replied. "We're down a couple of point defense clusters, and I've lost two launchers out of the port broadside. Aside from that and the primary gravitic array, it's all pretty much cosmetic."

Konidis managed not to snort, although it was difficult. Egert had a point about the minor nature of *Chao Kung Ming*'s damage.

Unfortunately, the heavy cruiser was only one unit of a force which had been unbelievably mauled.

Worse, we've been identified, Konidis thought grimly. *They knew we were State Security before anybody even opened fire, and there must be thousands of life pods headed for the planet right now. Our life pods. If they make planetfall and the people inside them get captured, they'll talk, sooner or later, whether they want to or not. And when they do, there won't be any question in any one's mind about who we are. For that matter, I'm sure that bastard Theisman and that traitorous bitch Pritchart would be delighted to make positive identifications from our personnel files back home. And once the Sollies start spreading our ships' emission signatures around . . .*

He kept his face expressionless, but his thoughts were grim as he considered the decision which had become his and the unpalatable options available to him.

We can break off without attacking the planet. We can take our losses and run, and no one will ever be able to prove we had an Eridani Edict violation in mind when we arrived. For that matter, Torch has formally declared war on Mesa. That would make us legitimate mercenaries in Mesan service, if that was what we wanted to claim . . . and if we don't violate the Edict. So, in theory, at least, our survivors should become prisoners of war if they do make it to the planet, which would put them under the Deneb Accords' protection.

In theory.

He tipped back in his command chair, thinking hard.

The problem was that he couldn't quite convince himself that a planet of ex-slaves, whose government contained quite a few theoretically retired members of the Audubon Ballroom, were going to just forgive and forget. If Rear Admiral Rozsak knew why the PNE had come to Torch, it was extraordinarily unlikely that the Torches didn't know it, too. Which suggested to Santander Konidis that they weren't going to be extraordinarily concerned about how the rest of the galaxy might regard the "welcome" they extended to the people who'd been about to genocide their home world.

If we go ahead and take out the planet, we can hang around to pick up our life pods afterward. What's left of Rozsak's force isn't going to want to tangle with us, now that it's lost its ammunition ships. And I've still got eleven cruisers and sixteen destroyers. I don't care if the entire frigging "Royal Torch Navy" is waiting in orbit around the planet, they aren't going to be able to stand up to that without Rozsak's magic missiles to back them up! But if we do hit the planet, Rozsak's surviving ships are never going to let us get into range to take them out, too. And that means he'll get away clean with his sensor data . . . and the entire galaxy will know who did it.

He glanced at Jessica Milliken from the corner of one eye. Given the fact that both Citizen Commodore Luff and Captain Maddock were almost certainly equally dead, Commander Milliken was now the senior Mesan representative present. She looked just as shocked by what had happened to the PNE as the Havenite officers and ratings around her, but she still represented the price the PNE would pay if Konidis *didn't* attack the planet.

Manpower never backed us because it liked us, he thought harshly. *It backed us because we represented a useful tool. If we don't hit Torch, that usefulness disappears, as far as it's concerned, and without Manpower, we lose any future logistical support.*

Without some source of support, just repairing his surviving ships' damages would be out of the question. Any sort of sustained action against the counterrevolutionaries in Nouveau Paris would become impossible, unless they wanted to be seen as nothing more than common pirates. And if that happened, then everything they'd already done—the price they'd already paid—would have been for nothing.

But it'll be for nothing, anyway, if we do do this, he realized. *The only reason Luff agreed to the operation in the first place was because it was supposed to be* anonymous. *No one was supposed to know it was us. Thanks to Rozsak, though, everyone will know, and no one in the People's Republic is going to rally to "defenders of the revolution" they know violated the Eridani Edict for a bunch of genetic slavers.*

He glanced at Citizen Commander Sanchez. His chief of staff was involved in an intense four-way conversation with Citizen Commander Charles-Henri Underwood, *Chao Kung Ming*'s executive officer; Citizen Lieutenant Commander César Hübner, the heavy cruiser's tactical officer; and Citizen Lieutenant Commander Jason Petit, Konidis' staff operations officer. There was no question, no doubt, in Sanchez's intent expression, the citizen commodore thought resentfully. The chief of staff, unlike Konidis himself, had never entertained any doubts about Operation Ferret's justification. For him, it was a simple matter of buying the support the Revolution required, and that automatically validated anything that might be required of them.

I don't want to do this, the citizen commander admitted to himself. *I've* never *wanted to do it. And now—*

"Commander Milliken," he heard himself say.

"Yes, Citizen Commodore?"

"It seems to me," Konidis said, "that the current situation lies far outside any possibility that was envisioned when this operation was planned."

He paused. The blond-haired commander who had become the only official Mesan representative to the PNE in the same moment Konidis became its commander only looked back at him, her blue eyes and expression politely attentive.

"Completely disregarding the losses we've sustained," he went on, "it's evident that the enemy knows who we are and why we're here. They also know about Manpower's . . . sponsorship. If we proceed as originally planned, the consequences for the People's Navy in Exile will be extreme. By the same token, however, given the losses we've already inflicted on them, it strikes me as . . . unlikely, to say the least, that the Solarian League Navy is going to adopt a sympathetic attitude towards the Mesa System in general if it becomes known that a Mesa-based transstellar was behind everything that's happened here today. Would you agree with that assessment?"

Milliken said nothing for several seconds. Then she shrugged very slightly.

"Citizen Commodore, I think just about anyone would have to admit that what you've said so far is self-evident."

Her voice was noncommittal, but Konidis felt a stir of hope, anyway. At least she hadn't started out by trying to argue with him.

"As I see it, we have two options," he told her. "First, we can go ahead and carry out the operation, then try to pick up all of our surviving personnel before leaving the system. Assuming we succeed in doing that—and that we've got sufficient shipboard life support for it—there won't be any prisoners for anyone to interrogate. Despite that, though, I feel confident there are going to be enough recoverable bodies for conclusive DNA identification if someone checks back with Nouveau Paris for matches against our personnel files. Which would mean that Rozsak's basic analysis of who we are and where we came from—and, therefore, who we came here *for*—would be clearly validated, as far as the galaxy at large is concerned. My understanding of our initial operational plan was that Manpower wanted to avoid that. That anonymity was a primary operational objective."

He paused again, and, once more, she simply looked at him, waiting.

"Our second option is to abandon the direct attack on Torch," he said. "We have more than sufficient firepower to overwhelm anything Torch—I mean, Verdant Vista—has left. We could take out any warships they might have in orbit as we overfly the planet, then come back and take our time destroying their orbital infrastructure. Given the fact that the system's current regime has declared war on both Manpower and Mesa, that would be completely legal within the constraints of the accepted rules of war. We'd still have to worry about how the Solarian League might choose to react to what's happened to Rozsak's ships, but, legally speaking, Mesa and Manpower could make a strong argument that our actions were justifiable in light of Rozsak's announced intention to attack *us* if we didn't break off our completely legitimate operation against Verdant Vista."

Again, he paused. Again, she said nothing, and he grasped the dilemma by its horns.

"It's my thought that the first option would be disastrous for the People's Navy in Exile, and probably equally disastrous for Manpower and, quite possibly, the Mesa System itself. The second option would fail to accomplish our full operational objectives, but it would still inflict massive damage on the current Verdant Vista regime. It's even possible that we'd catch a significant portion of the regime's government aboard the space station. For that matter"—he allowed himself a slight smile, although he was far from feeling amused—"orbital debris is going to fall *somewhere* if we take out their station. It would be a pity if it happened to fall on any major population centers as a result of any . . . encouragement we might give it, but that sort of collateral damage would *not* constitute a violation of the Edict.

"Given all of that, I believe the second option is by far the better of the two. We'll go ahead and finish off their 'navy' and all of their orbital infrastructure and industry, but I'm not going to commit a clear violation of the Eridani Edict when it's bound to come back against not just me and my people but against Manpower and Mesa, as well."

Jessica Milliken gazed back at the Havenite with merely thoughtful eyes while her brain went into overdrive. Every word he'd just said was unarguably accurate. Of course, he didn't know about Wooden Horse, so he wasn't aware of just how little anyone in the Mesa System was going to care about what happened to the "People's Navy in Exile." Which didn't change the fact that he was absolutely right that Manpower's deniability had clearly been badly damaged. That wasn't the same thing as saying the *Alignment's* deniability had been damaged, but bringing the League's official displeasure down on Mesa, especially at this particular time, didn't exactly come under the heading of what her superiors would consider a good thing.

She thought about it for several seconds, and found herself wishing fervently that Gowan Maddock were here to take the responsibility off her shoulders. He wasn't, though. *She* had to make the call.

And, really, she reflected, *it's not my call to make after all. For that matter, it wouldn't be* Gowan's, *if he were here. I can't make Konidis do anything he doesn't choose to do, and Gowan couldn't, either.*

"Citizen Commodore," she said, "I can't argue with anything you've just said. I'm sure my own superiors, as well as Manpower, would have been much happier if our original intelligence estimates and planning had held up. Obviously, they haven't, and your people's losses have already been far, far greater than anyone could possibly have anticipated. And you're right about the fact that the current regime has declared war on us, as well, and about that declaration's implications under interstellar law and the rules of war. So, under the circumstances, I agree with you that the second option you've described is far and away the better of the two."

"I'm glad you agree." Konidis suspected he hadn't quite managed to keep his relief out of his voice, but he didn't much care, either. He wasn't going to become a genocidal mass murderer, after all. Not today. And, he discovered, for right now at least, the enormous relief of that fact outweighed the potential consequences for the PNE's future.

But it's not like I'm completely willing to just forgive and forget, he thought more grimly. *We may have just lost the entire future of the Revolution along with Citizen Commodore Luff, and if we have, I want some of our own back.* His eyes flicked to the master astrogation plot, where the planet Torch drew steadily nearer. *I'm glad we won't be bombarding the planet, but I think I'm even gladder that these people won't* know *that. That they'll come out and fight where I can get at them instead of just running away.*

"Citizen Commander Sanchez," he said, raising his voice to attract the chief of staff's attention. "We have some planning to do."

"Of course, Citizen Commodore."

"Ludivine," Konidis continued, turning to Citizen Lieutenant Ludivine Grimault, his staff communications officer, "I'm going to want a com conference with all of our squadron and divisional commanders. Get that set up ASAP, please."

"At once, Citizen Commodore."

Unlike Sanchez, who still seemed totally focused on the task in hand, Grimault was clearly relieved to have something to do, and Konidis smiled briefly at her. Then he turned back to Sanchez and his com link to Citizen Captain Egert.

"There's been a change of plans," he told them both. "We're not going to hit the planet directly."

Egert's eyebrows rose, but he thought he saw the reflection of his own relief in her eyes. Sanchez, on the other hand, frowned . . . predictably, Konidis supposed.

"We're not just going to go home, though," he continued grimly. "We owe these people, and we're going to take out every ship, every space station, every resource extraction center, and every communications and power collection array they have. We're going to completely trash their extra-atmosphere infrastructure, and if we've got time, we're going to take out any infrastructure they have on the *planet* with precision strikes, as well. We're not going to be committing any Eridani Edict violations now that the bastards know who we are, but we're going to do absolutely the next best thing. And, frankly," he bared his teeth, "after what's already happened to us, I'm going to enjoy every minute of it."

Sanchez still seemed less than delighted at Konidis' decision to abandon what had been the primary mission objective from the outset, but his expression showed his complete agreement with the citizen commodore's last sentence. For that matter, Egert nodded emphatically, as well.

"All right," the citizen commodore went on briskly, "first, I think we—"

"Excuse me, Citizen Commodore."

Konidis frowned at the interruption and turned his head.

"What is it, Jason?" he asked rather more sharply than he normally spoke to his ops officer.

"I'm sorry to interrupt, Citizen Commodore." Something about Citizen Lieutenant Commander Petit's expression sent a sudden icicle down Konidis' spine. "I'm sorry to interrupt," Petit repeated, "but CIC's just picked up three fresh impeller signatures breaking planetary orbit."

"And?" Konidis asked when Petit paused. The planet was still well over a hundred million kilometers away, far outside any range he would have had to worry about even if he'd still had Cataphracts in his magazines.

"And CIC has tentatively identified them, Citizen Commodore," the operations officer said quietly. "They make it two more of those Erewhonese cruisers . . . and another ammunition ship."

It took Santander Konidis almost five seconds to realize he was staring numbly at Petit, and the silence on PNES *Chao Kung Ming's* flag bridge was absolute.

PART III

*Late 1921 and 1922 Post-Diaspora
(4023 and 4024, Christian Era)*

Leonard Detweiler, the CEO and majority stockholder of the Detweiler Consortium, a Beowulf-based pharmaceutical and biosciences corporation, found himself with a great deal of money and not a great deal of sympathy with the Beowulf bioethics code which had emerged following Old Earth's Final War and Beowulf's leading role in repairs to the brutally ravaged mother world. Almost five hundred years had passed since that war, and Detweiler believed it was long past time that mankind got over its "Frankenstein fear" (as he described it) of genetic modification of human beings. It simply made sense, he believed, to impose reason, logic, and long-term planning on the random chaos and wastefulness of natural evolutionary selection. And, as he pointed out, for almost fifteen hundred years, mankind's Diaspora to the stars had already been taking the human genotype into environments which were naturally mutagenic on a scale which had never been imagined on pre-space Old Earth. In effect, he argued, simply transporting human beings into such radically different environments was going to induce significant genetic variation, so there was no point in worshiping some semi-mythic "pure human genotype."

Since all that was true, Detweiler further argued, it only made sense to genetically modify colonists for the environments which were going to cause their descendants to mutate anyway. And it was only a small step further to argue that if it made sense to genetically modify human beings for environments in which they would have to live, it also made sense to genetically modify them to better suit them to the environments in which they would have to *work*.

> From Anthony Rogovich, *The Detweilers: A Family Biography.* (Unpublished and unfinished manuscript, found among Rogovich's papers after his suicide.)

November, 1921 PD

CHAPTER SIXTY-ONE

Queen Berry looked a little bewildered by the flag bridge of the *Chao Kung Ming.* The *Spartacus,* rather, as the government of *Torch* had decided to rename her.

"Let me get this straight. You manage *battles* from here?"

"I can assure you, Your Majesty, that after you've spent some time in one of these"—Admiral Rozsak swept his hand around—"all of this actually makes sense, instead of seeming like a gazillion flashing lights and weird-looking icons. With experience, for instance, this"—here he pointed to the tactical plot—"is a most handy gadget. And quite easy to interpret, believe it or not."

Berry study the gadget in question, very dubiously. "It looks like a vid I saw once. A documentary about deep-sea luminous fish, looking really bizarre and moving around completely at random, so far as I could tell."

He chuckled. "I know it's a bit much, at first sight. I was nineteen years old the first time I came onto a flag bridge—that was the old *Prince Igor*—and I almost walked into the tactical plot, I was so confused. One of the worst ass-reamings I ever got followed, if you'll pardon the crude expression."

Berry smiled, but the smile faded away soon.

"You're sure about this, Luiz?"

She spoke informally because in the weeks since what had come to be called the Battle of Torch, a quiet but profound sea change had swept through the small number of Torch's leaders who knew the truth about the Stein assassination and the events

569

that had followed on *The Wages of Sin* and elsewhere. A change in the way they looked at Rear Admiral Luiz Rozsak.

Before the battle, they'd considered Rozsak an ally, true enough. But it had been purely an alliance of convenience and not one of them had personally trusted the admiral. *No farther than I could throw him—when I was a toddler,* was the way Jeremy had put it. Indeed, not only had they not trusted Rozsak, they'd been deeply suspicious of him.

Today, it was still unlikely (to say the least) that anyone was going to confuse the admiral with a saint. But it was impossible to match the previous assessment of Rozsak as a man driven solely, entirely and exclusively by his own ambition with the admiral who'd led the defense of Torch at such an incredible cost to his own forces and risk to his own life.

A man driven by a fierce ambition, yes. *Solely* by ambition, however . . . No. That, it was no longer possible to believe.

At that, the growing warmth of Torch's inner circle toward the admiral was a candle, however, compared to the enthusiastic embrace with which Torch's population had greeted the Mayan survivors of the battle. Any officer or enlisted person in the fleet who went down to the planet—and there none who didn't, except for those still too badly injured to make the trip—swore then and thereafter that there was not, never had been, and never would be a shore leave better than the one they enjoyed on Torch in the weeks that followed the battle.

No one on Torch doubted that those Mayan fighting men and women had saved the planet's population from complete destruction. Not once the StateSec officers who survived the battle and the ones who surrendered afterward started talking.

And they started talking very quickly, and they talked and talked and talked. Their immediate fear had been that Torch would hand them over to the Republic of Haven. Then Jeremy X and Saburo started interrogating, and within two days it was the profound hope of every StateSec officer that they *would* be turned over to the Haven navy.

Jeremy X's notions concerning "the laws of war" and the proper rules governing the treatment of POWs would have met with the approval of Attila the Hun. And while Berry Zilwicki might have squelched Jeremy, she wasn't going to squelch Saburo.

He started every interrogation by placing a holopic between himself and the person being interrogated. "Her name was Lara. And her ghost really, really, really wants you to tell me everything you know. Or her ghost is going to get really, really, really peeved."

So, within a few days, they knew everything—at least, everything that had been known by Santander Konidis and the other surviving officers. But that was enough to know the three critical items.

First, that Manpower had surely been behind the whole plot. Second, that the Mesa *System* Navy had played a major part in providing training and logistical support. And, third, and beyond any faintest shadow of a doubt, that Manpower had planned and ordered a complete violation of the Eridani Edict.

Thereafter, however—quite to the surprise of Konidis and his subordinates—all threats and mistreatment had stopped. Within a month, all of the StateSec survivors had been relocated onto an island and provided with the wherewithal to set up reasonably comfortable if austere living quarters, along with a sufficient food supply brought in once a week under heavy guard.

The armed forces of Torch placed no guards on the island itself, and didn't even maintain a naval patrol beyond a small number of vessels. But the more adventurous of the StateSec forces who experimented with the possibility of trying to escape by sea soon gave it up. It turned out that the lifeforms in Torch's warm oceans were every bit as exuberant as the ones in its tropical rain forests. Especially the predator that looked like a ten-meter long cross between a lobster and a manta ray, and whose dietary preferences seemed to exclude rocks but absolutely nothing else.

That measure had been taken at Rozsak's request.

"I'd really be much happier if I knew that none of those survivors was in a position to tell anyone—and that includes Haven—exactly what happened here and what weaponry I possessed and what tactics I used."

"Certainly, Admiral," Web Du Havel had said. "But . . . ah . . . that still leaves the population of Torch itself. Which, at last count, numbers a little over four and a quarter million people and grows—this is immigration alone—by almost fifteen thousand people every T-week."

Rozsak had shrugged. "It's not a perfect world. But the State

Sec survivors would have an incentive to talk—spill their guts, rather, once Haven gets hold of them—and your people don't. In fact, from what I've heard, you've launched a very effective public campaign to establish and maintain tight security."

"Yes, we have," Hugh had said.

Berry had glanced at him, smiled—and then made a face. "I still think 'loose lips sink ships' is a corny slogan."

"It is. It also works." There were some subjects concerning which Hugh Arai had no shame whatsoever. "How long do you want us to hold them, Admiral?"

"To be honest, I don't know. There are still too many variables involved in the equation for us to know yet what'll be happening. If it's a financial strain to maintain the prisoners, I can talk to Governor Barregos and see if—"

Du Havel had waved that aside. "Don't worry about it. The one thing Torch is *not,* is poor, even with having to provide initial support for most immigrants, who usually arrive with nothing much more than the clothes they're wearing. But the support doesn't normally last long, because the job market is booming. Plenty of pharmaceutical companies have been quite happy to come here and replace Manpower's operations with their own."

Web had exchanged looks with Jeremy and Berry and Thandi Palane.

"Consider it done, Admiral," Palane had said then, with one of her simultaneously dazzling and ferocious smiles. "We'll keep 'em on ice for as long as you want."

✧   ✧   ✧

"Are you sure, Luiz?" Berry repeated now. "You paid a terrible price for this ship, and the others."

For a moment, Rozsak's face looked a bit drawn. "Yes, we did. But there are some very good reasons why it'd be better if the surviving StateSec ships were pressed into Torch service rather than Mayan service."

"Such as?" Berry asked.

He looked at her for a moment, then shrugged.

"Trust me, it's not a case of misplaced gallantry on my part, Your Majesty!" He snorted in obvious amusement, then sobered. "The truth is, that they'd be white elephants as far as we're concerned. There are . . . reasons we'd just as soon not have anyone from Old Earth poking around in Maya, Berry, and if we start taking ex-Havenite ships into service, someone's likely to do just that."

"And they're *not* likely to when word of the battle gets there? Or were you thinking you could get away with just not mentioning it?" Berry knew she looked skeptical. "We're willing to keep *our* mouths shut, Luiz, but don't forget all of those pharmaceutical companies. I imagine we're going to have newsies out here from the League sometime real soon now, and there's no way we're going to be able to keep the fact that there was a battle here in the system under wraps when that happens! Weapons and actual losses are one thing, but . . ."

She gave a little shrug, and he nodded.

"Understood. But we're going to tell the galaxy it was the *Erewhon* Navy that did the real fighting. *Our* ships were limited to the flotilla everyone knows about, watching the planet against any missiles that might have come your way. And we don't plan on advertising how heavy our losses were, either." It was his turn to shrug, with a flicker of pain in his eyes. "We can't keep the rest of the galaxy from knowing we lost *some* people out here, but all our official reports are going to indicate that the people we lost were acting as cadre to help fill out the *Erewhonese* crews. The only people who could tell anyone different are stuck on your island, and no newsie—or League flunky—is going to get to them there, now are they?"

"No, they're not," Berry agreed with a certain flat steeliness. Then she drew a breath and nodded.

"Okay, then. If you're sure." When she looked around the flag bridge this time, she seemed a little less bewildered. "I still can't figure out most of what's happening here. But I know Thandi's happy about getting this ship—it's a heavy cruiser, right?—and the rest of them."

She smiled. "Well . . . 'happy' isn't quite the right term. 'Ecstatic' might be better. Or 'beside herself with joy.' Or 'delirious.'"

Rozsak smiled also. "I'm hardly surprised. She'll have a fleet that goes almost overnight from having a frigate as its flagship to—yes, it's a heavy cruiser, Your Majesty."

"Please, Luiz. Call me Berry."

✧   ✧   ✧

She returned from the *Spartacus* in a pensive mood. Visiting that ship had driven something home to her in a way that the inconvenience of living in what amounted to a bunker had not. Life—even with prolong—was simply too damn short to dilly-dally around the fundamentals.

So, when she returned to the palace, her first words were to Saburo.

"You're promoted, starting immediately. Now please leave Hugh and me alone, for a bit."

Saburo nodded, and left the room.

Hugh's face had no expression at all. As the months had gone by, Berry had learned that he was very good at that. It was one of the things she planned to change.

"Have I displeased you, Your Majesty?"

"Not hardly. I just can't deal with this any longer. I want your resignation. Now."

Hugh didn't hesitate for more than perhaps a second. "As you wish, Your Majesty. I resign as your chief of security."

"Don't call me that. My name is Berry and you damn well don't have any excuse any longer not to use it."

He bowed, slightly, and then extended his elbow. "All right, Berry. In that case, may I escort you to J. Quesenberry's?"

The smile that came to her face then was the same gleaming smile that had captivated Hugh Arai since the first time he'd seen it. But it was as if a star had become a supernova.

"Ice cream would be nice. Later. Right now, I'd be much happier if you'd take me to bed."

CHAPTER SIXTY-TWO

"So you've finished your analysis?" Albrecht Detweiler asked after his son had settled—still a bit cautiously—into the indicated chair.

"Such as it is, and what there is of it," Collin Detweiler replied, easing his left arm down. "There are still a lot of holes, you understand, Father." He shrugged. "There's no way we're ever going to close all of them."

"Nobody with a working brain would expect otherwise," Collin's brother, Benjamin, put in. "I've been pointing that out to you for—what? Two or three weeks, now?"

"Something like that," Collin acknowledged with a smile that mingled humor, resignation, and lingering discomfort.

"And did your brother also point out to you—as, now that I think about it, I believe your *father* has—that you could have delegated more of this? You damned near *died,* Collin, and regen"—Albrecht looked pointedly at his son's still distinctly undersized left arm—"takes time. And it also, in case you hadn't noticed, is just a teeny-tiny bit hard on the system."

"Touché, Father. Touché!" Collin replied after a moment. "And, yes, Ben did make both of those points to me, as well. It's just . . . well . . ."

Albrecht regarded his son with fond exasperation. All of his "sons" were overachievers, and none of them really ever wanted to take time off. He practically had to stand over them with a stick to make them, in fact. That attitude seemed to be hardwired into the Detweiler genotype, and it was a good thing, in a lot of

575

ways. But as he'd just pointed out to Collin (with massive under-statement), the regeneration therapies placed enormous demands upon the body. Even with the quality of medical care a Detweiler could expect and the natural resiliency of an alpha-line's enhanced constitution, simply regrowing an entire arm would have been a massive drain on Collin's energy. When that "minor" requirement was added to all of the other physical repairs Collin had required, some of his physicians had been genuinely concerned about how hard he'd been pushing himself.

Albrecht had seriously considered ordering him to hand the investigation over to someone else, but he'd decided against it in the end. Partly that was because he knew how important it was to Collin on a personal level, for a lot of reasons. Partly it was because even operating in pain and a chronic state of fatigue, Collin—with Benjamin's assistance—was still better at this sort of thing than almost anyone else Albrecht could have thought of. And partly—even mostly, if he was going to be honest—it was because the chaos and confusion left in the wake of the massive destruction hadn't left anyone else he could both have handed the task over to *and* trusted completely.

"All right," he said out loud now, half-smiling and half-glowering at Collin. "You couldn't hand it over to someone else because you're too OCD to stand letting someone else do it. We all understand that. I think it's a family trait." He heard Benjamin snort, and his smile broadened. Then it faded just a bit. "And we all understand this hit pretty damned close to home for you, Collin, in a lot of ways. I won't pretend I really like how hard you've been driving yourself, but—"

He shrugged, and Collin nodded in understanding.

"Well, that said," his father went on, "I take it you've decided Jack McBryde really was a traitor?"

"Yes," Colin sighed. "I have to admit, part of me resisted that conclusion. But I'm afraid it's almost certain that he was."

"Only 'almost'?" Benjamin asked with a sort of gentle skepticism. Collin looked at him, and Benjamin arched one eyebrow.

"Only almost," Collin repeated with a rather firmer emphasis. "Given the complete loss of so many of our records and the fragmentary—and contradictory, sometimes—nature of what survived, almost any conclusion we could possibly reach is going to be tentative, and especially where motivations are concerned.

But I take your point, Ben, and I won't pretend it was an easy conclusion for me to accept."

"But you do accept it now?" his father asked quietly.

"Yes." Collin rubbed his face briefly with his good hand. "Despite the scattered records we found that would seem to indicate Jack was making a desperate, last-minute effort to thwart some kind of conspiracy, there's simply not any way to account for those recordings Irvine made at the diner except to assume he was guilty. Certainly not once we confirmed that the waiter he was meeting with was Anton Zilwicki. And then there's this."

He drew a personal memo pad from his pocket, laid it on the corner of his father's desk so he could manipulate it one-handed, and keyed the power button.

"I'm afraid the visual quality isn't what we'd like, given the limits of the original recording," he half-apologized. "The only reason we've got this much is because the owners of the Buenaventura Tower didn't want seccy squatters moving in. But it's enough for our purposes."

He touched a key, and a small holographic image appeared above the pad. It showed a passageway of some sort. The lighting was quite dim, but after a moment, three people came into view, crossing hurriedly toward a door some distance away.

"We ran this recording through every cross check," Collins said. "The man on the left is definitely Anton Zilwicki, within a ninety-nine-point-nine percent probability. Outside the world of statistics, that means 'for damned sure and certain.' There's simply no question about it. That phenotype of his is obviously hard to disguise, and everything else matches. Not the face, of course . . . although it *does* match the face of the waiter in Irvine's recording."

"And the other man is . . . ?"

"Yes, Father." Collin nodded. "It's Victor Cachat. To be precise, it's Victor Cachat within an eighty-seven-point-five percent probability. We don't have anywhere near as much imagery on him as we had on Zilwicki, thanks to that documentary the Manties did on him a while back. That gave us a lot smaller comparison sample for Cachat, so the analysts' confidence level is considerably lower. I think they're just throwing out sheet anchors, though. For myself, I'm entirely confident it's Cachat."

"The woman?" Benjamin asked, and this time Collin shook his head.

"As far as her specific identity is concerned, we don't know, and it's almost certain that we never will. But her general identity is clear enough—ninety-nine-point-five percent probable, anyway. She's a Scrag, presumably one of that group of female Scrags who defected to Torch."

"She'd be a minor player, then."

"Yes. Zilwicki and Cachat were the critical ones."

"And you're certain they are dead?" Albrecht was frowning at the image, which was rerunning in a continuous loop. "No chance that recording was faked?"

"We don't see how it could have been, Father. Mind you, in this line of work we never deal in dead—you should pardon the expression—certainties. But at this point, the practical distinction between 'certain' and 'extremely probable' gets thin enough you just have to take it as a given. Nobody would ever get anything done if we insisted on one hundred percent verification of every single fact."

He settled back in his chair again, easing his regrowing arm once more, and crossed his legs.

"We ran those images through every comparative program we've got. What I can tell you, as a result, is that these are genuine images of genuine people in exactly the place they seem to be. The analyses we've run compare movements to background on an almost microscopic level. That's one reason it took so long. Those people"—he pointed at the still replaying imagery—"actually did exactly what it looks like they're doing against exactly the background we're seeing."

"So this is definitely a recording of *these* people going through *that* passageway?" Benjamin asked.

"Right."

"But I notice you didn't say anything about *when* they did it," Albrecht pointed out.

"No, I didn't. That's where the 'never deal in dead certainties' I mentioned above comes in. There's a possibility—a very *tiny* possibility—that they could have recorded this ahead of time and then substituted that recording for the live imagery from the tower's owners' security system. But given the security protocols which would have to be circumvented, pulling it off—and especially pulling it off without getting *caught* at it—would be . . . extremely difficult, shall we say."

Albrecht rubbed his jaw thoughtfully.

"By all accounts, Zilwicki is very good at that sort of thing," he pointed out.

"Yes, and the accounts are accurate, too. But pulling off something like you're suggesting would have meant meant getting into that bizarre virtual world where hackers have been jousting for over two thousand T-years." Collin made a "brushing away" gesture with his working hand. "Any security protocols can be circumvented, Father . . . and any program to circumvent security protocols can be detected. Then that detection can be circumvented, but the circumvention can be detected, and so on. It goes on literally forever. In the end, it comes down to the simple question of 'Are our cyberneticists as good as their cyberneticists?'"

Collin shrugged.

"I can't rule out the possibility that Zilwicki is—was—better at this than any—or, for that, matter *all* of—our people are. Frankly, it seems vanishingly unlikely that one man, no matter how good he may be, is going to be better than an entire planet's worth of competing cyberneticists. Still, I'll grant the possibility. But no matter how good he may have been, he was still playing in our front yard. If we'd been playing on *his* territory, I'd feel a lot less comfortable with our conclusions, but could Anton Zilwicki, using only the equipment and software he was able to smuggle onto Mesa—or obtain on the black market once he got here—get around the best protocols we've ever been able to create, with all the advantages of operating on our own home planet, and do it so seamlessly that we can't find a single trace of it?"

He shook his head.

"Yes, it's *theoretically* possible, but, in the real world, I really don't think it's likely at all." He pointed at the tiny, moving figures of the recorded imagery once more. "I think we're looking at what really happened and *when* it happened. Anton Zilwicki and Victor Cachat and an unknown female were passing through the parking facilities of what used to be the Buenaventura Tower when someone set off a two-point-five kiloton nuclear device. The center of the explosion was about thirty meters from what you're seeing right this minute."

"Which, of course, explains the absence of any DNA traces." Benjamin made a face. "They were simply vaporized."

"Oh, there were plenty of DNA traces in the area." Collin chuckled harshly. "Even in that location, and even at that time on a Saturday morning, there had to be somebody around. Buenaventura's been standing empty long enough, and it's far enough out into that industrial belt between the city proper and the spaceport, that traffic was thankfully light. In fact, that's almost certainly the reason Zilwicki and Cachat had chosen that particular route for their escape. Despite that, our best estimate from our pattern analysis of all of the tower's security recordings from the last couple of months or so is that there were probably at least thirty or forty people in the immediate vicinity. We've recovered over twenty complete and partial bodies, some of them pretty well incinerated, but we're positive there are quite a few we'll never know about.

"But the truth is that even if they hadn't been, for all practical purposes, right at the center of the fireball, we still wouldn't have gotten much from DNA analysis. Cachat is—was—a Havenite, born in Nouveau Paris itself, and StateSec did a pretty fanatical job of eliminating any medical records that might ever have existed when Saint-Just tapped him for special duties. No way we could get our hands on a sample we *knew* was his DNA. We'd have a better chance of getting a sample of Zilwicki's DNA, but he was from Gryphon. Nouveau Paris' population is an incredible stew, from everywhere, and Gryphon's population's genetic makeup isn't particularly distinct, either, so we couldn't even narrow an otherwise unidentified trace to either planet. We might have had a chance of identifying the Scrag—generically, at least—but even then only if she'd been a lot farther from the hypocenter. Ground zero, I should say. Technically, 'hypocenter' applies only to air bursts."

"All right," said Albrecht. "I'm persuaded . . . mostly." It was obvious to both his sons that the qualifier was pure spinal reflex on his part. "Now the question is: who set off the bomb?" Albrecht nodded at the hologram. "None of these people look to me like they were planning on committing suicide." He shook his head. "They were obviously *going* somewhere, and they were obviously in a hurry, even if they weren't exactly fleeing for their lives in panic. If they'd meant to kill themselves, then why go anywhere? And if they'd had even a clue a nuclear charge was about to go off less than fifty meters away, then I'd think they would have been going elsewhere a hell of a lot *faster* than they actually were!"

"We don't think they did it, Father. The possibility can't be ruled out, but we can't see any motivation they might've had to suicide. And as you say"—he nodded at the hologram himself—"that's definitely not the body language of people about to kill themselves, either."

"If not them, then who?" Benjamin asked.

"I doubt if we'll ever know, for sure," Collin replied. "Our best guess, after chewing on it for quite some time, is that *Jack* killed them."

"McBryde?" Albrecht frowned. "But why . . . Oh. You think he thought—correctly or otherwise—that Cachat and Zilwicki had doublecrossed him?"

"That's one explanation, yes—and the one that's favored by most of my team. This scenario is that Jack was trying to defect with Simões but the negotiations broke down. Probably because Cachat and Zilwicki decided they'd already gotten enough from him to make leaving Mesa worthwhile and that smuggling him and Simões off-planet wasn't worth the risk."

"And McBryde suspected they might try that, and had laid that device ahead of time. And used a nuclear device—talk about overkill!—because he figured it would help eliminate anything that might be traced back to him." Again, Albrecht rubbed his jaw. "But how would he get them to be there at the right time?"

"Who knows? Keep in mind that he didn't have to finagle them into being there at any specific, preset time. Someone with Jack's training and experience could easily have set up a method of remote detonation, and there are several ways he could have known what escape route they'd be taking, even if he couldn't predict ahead of time when they'd be going through it. So he could have set the charge purely as an insurance policy. Then, once he knew he was going to execute Scorched Earth, he could have linked that detonation to the one in the tower. They happened almost simultaneously, after all."

"In other words, he took his revenge before he checked out himself."

"Or at the same time, you could say." Collin raised his right hand. "Father, the truth is that, given the havoc Jack wreaked on our computer systems and records, and the fact that Lajos Irvine is the only one of the central players who survived, we'll *never* know all of what happened, or exactly the reason why. All I can give you is the best assessment my people could come up with after a very long, thorough, exhaustive analysis."

He leaned forward and switched off the memo pad.

"What we think most likely happened is that two separate sequences of events crossed each other. Jack, trying to defect with Simões, decided he was being doublecrossed. So, he planned to destroy Cachat and Zilwicki in a manner that would eliminate any trace of them, any evidence that could connect him to them. He'd figure we'd assume the Buenaventura explosion was an act of terrorism by the Audubon Ballroom. Don't forget, he had a perfectly reasonable explanation for being in Gamma Center that day, with Simões. It had been on his calendar for at least two weeks. In fact, he'd specifically memoed Isabel about it."

"And the surviving Gamma Center records confirm that's where the two of them were?" Benjamin's tone made the question a statement, and Collin nodded.

"Exactly. And, before you ask, Father, no, I can't be absolutely certain that the records which show Simões was there also weren't somehow faked. It wouldn't have been as hard for Jack to successfully fake those records as it would've been for Zilwicki to do the same thing at the Buenaventura, but why should he have? There's no way he himself wasn't present when he destroyed the Gamma Center. That much we know for certain, because Scorched Earth *had* to be triggered by someone inside the facility. It can't—couldn't—be done by remote control."

He scowled.

"In fact, it wasn't supposed to be possible for Scorched Earth to be triggered by any single person, either, no matter where they were. Trust me, some people have already . . . heard from me about *that* one. Jack figured out a way to circumvent the two-man protocols, and nobody was supposed to be able to do that."

"So you're assuming McBryde didn't find out about the doublecross until he and Simões had already met in his office," Albert said.

"Yes, and that's where the second sequence of events comes into play. What Jack overlooked—probably because he'd been out of the field long enough for his fieldcraft to get rusty—was the possibility that Irvine might have set up his own surveillance equipment and spotted him meeting Zilwicki. Irvine didn't recognize Zilwicki *as* Zilwicki because we hadn't spread that information far enough down the chain for him to have any idea what Zilwicki actually looked like. But he did understand that something fishy was going on, so he alerted Isabel. He got through to her on the same morning Jack's negotiations with Zilwicki and Cachat collapsed, and she went down to the Gamma Center to find out just what the hell Jack was up to."

"In other words, it was just really bad timing from McBryde's point of view," Albert mused. "He'd probably have gotten away with killing Cachat and Zilwicki, and he must've had plans for dealing with Simões, too, in the event that his defection fell through. But then Isabel showed up out of the blue, and he realized the wheels had come *completely* off. There was no way he was going to get away with it, and he knew what the penalty would be, so he committed suicide and took out Cachat and Zilwicki at the same time."

"That's the consensus," Collin confirmed. But Benjamin, who'd been studying his brother closely through the previous explanation, cocked his head.

"Why do I get the feeling you don't agree with that consensus, Collin? Or not fully, at least?"

"Hard to keep secrets between us, isn't it?" Collin gave him a wry smile. "You get that feeling because it's true. I think there's another explanation, one that's more likely, given the principals. But I'll also add that no one else on my team agrees with me, and it's possible I'm being sentimental."

His father had been studying him carefully, as well. Now Albrecht leaned forward slightly, propping one elbow on his desk.

"You think McBryde had a last-minute change of heart," he said softly.

"Not . . . exactly." Collin frowned. "The thing is, I *knew* Jack McBryde. We worked together for years, and one of Jack's best qualities was that he wasn't vindictive in the least. In fact, probably less vindictive than almost anyone I can imagine. That's one of the reasons he was so popular with his subordinates. Jack would discipline people, when it was necessary. Sometimes even harshly. But never more harshly than was necessary, and *never* out of anger. I've seen him mad, plenty of times, but it never came out in the way he treated other people. On the other hand . . ."

"He was squeamish."

"Yes, Father." Collin sighed. "It was his biggest weakness, frankly.

In fact, it was the reason I had him assigned to Gamma Center originally. Or, rather, the reason I had his permanent file quietly tagged 'not for field ops' and moved him over to the security side in the first place."

"I don't see where you're going with this," Benjamin said with a slight frown.

"I do," Albrecht said. "Why would an overly softhearted person with no history of vindictiveness or vengefulness kill—how many people was it, Collin?"

"As I say, we're figuring a minimum of thirty or forty for the Buenaventura explosion. Personally, I think it was probably close to twice that many, if you count the unregistered seccies who were probably caught in it, as well. We can add another sixty for the Gamma Center—even on a Saturday—even before we count Isabel, her team, and Jack himself."

"But that's not really the point," his father said, looking back at Benjamin. "The people inside the Center were unavoidable collateral damage once he decided on Scorched Earth. But we're talking about a minimum of more than three dozen people—quite possibly a lot more—in a separate explosion he didn't *have* to set off." Albrecht raised an eyebrow. "Now do you see? Some compulsion had to drive McBryde to overcome his scruples. And if it wasn't vengeance, what was it? What Collin is suggesting is that once it became clear to McBryde that his plans to defect had been aborted and he was going to die, he saw to it that Zilwicki and Cachat died also—and before they got off-planet with whatever he might have given them. As a last act of . . . what would you call it, Collin? Patriotism seems a little silly."

"More like . . . atonement, I think. Keep in mind that I can't *prove* any of this, Father. It's just my gut feeling. And, as I said, no one else on my team agrees with me."

"Practically speaking, though, it doesn't really matter which explanation actually applies, does it?" Albrecht asked gently, almost compassionately.

"No, Sir. It doesn't," Collin agreed a bit softly.

"And the Park explosion?"

"That one's still something of a puzzle," Collin confessed, and his eyes darkened once more. "I don't like admitting that, either, given how many of my neighbors were killed. The current casualty total for that one is around eight *thousand*, though, and I'm damned sure Jack McBryde didn't have anything to do with *that*! At the same time, I don't think I believe somebody would just 'coincidentally' pick that particular day to set off a nuclear charge in a completely separate, spontaneous terrorist incident."

"So you think they're related?"

"Father, I'm sure they *have* to be related somehow. We just don't know how. And we don't know—and will never know—who actually detonated the damned thing. We've got the feed transmitted from those two cops' HD cams, but neither camera ever had a good angle on the driver's face, so there's no way we can tell if whoever it was was ever in our files. Or, perhaps, I should say in our *surviving* files." His smile could have curdled milk. "It's possible—even probable—he was Ballroom affiliated, but we can't prove that. I'm inclined to think he was a seccy, not a slave, but that's really as far as I am prepared to go."

He shrugged, much more lightly—obviously—than he actually felt.

"What I don't understand, even assuming he was Ballroom connected, is *why*. I'm assuming that, with Zilwicki's own Ballroom connections, he was receiving support from assets of theirs here on Mesa, as well. We keep them pruned far enough back that they don't have a truly effective presence—or we *think* we do, at any rate; what happened with Jack could prove we've been a little over sanguine in that respect. But even pruned back, they've always had *some* contacts among the seccies, and I think we have to take it for a given that Zilwicki had tapped into them for assistance once he got here. So my first hypotheses was that this was intended as a diversion for his and Cachat's escape. And," his eyes hardened and his voice went grim, "it would have made one hell of a diversion. Eight thousand dead and another sixty-three hundred badly injured?" He shook his head. "It had every emergency responder in the city—and from Mendel, too, for that matter!—racing in one direction, and you couldn't have asked for a better diversion than that.

"But when I really considered it, I realized it wasn't Zilwicki's style. He could have achieved the same diversionary effect with an explosion that wouldn't have killed a fraction of as many people as this bomb killed. Not only that, but we know from his record that he had a soft spot a kilometer-wide where *kids* were concerned. Just look at the two he carted home with him from Old

Chicago!" Collin shook his head again, harder. "No way would *that* man have signed off on detonating a nuke in the middle of a frigging *park* on a Saturday morning. Cachat, now—*he* was cold enough he could have done it if he decided he had no choice, but I don't see even him going along with something like this purely for the sake of a diversion."

"Do you have any theory at all that might explain it?"

"The best one I've been able to come up with, and it's no more than my own personal hypothesis, you understand, is that some Ballroom associate or sympathizer here on Mesa who was at least peripherally aware of Zilwicki and Cachat's presence, did it on his own. Given the fact that we know from Irvine that they clearly had an emergency fall-back plan—the one that, unfortunately for them, took them too close to Jack's little surprise at Buenaventura—I think they may have intended for the Park Valley nuke to go off somewhere else, somewhere with a lot less people around. Somewhere it would have made a diversion but not killed so many people. But once Jack took them out at Buenaventura, whoever was in charge . . . changed his mind. In other words, the charge itself probably was part of Zilwicki and Cachat's escape plan, but I doubt very much that its *location* was."

Albrecht leaned back in his chair, folded his hands across his chest, and spent the next several minutes looking out the window at white beaches and dark blue water while he thought it all through.

"Well," he said finally, grimacing a little. "I'd be happier if there weren't so many loose ends. But"—he brought his eyes back to his two sons—"the bottom line is that the one thing that does seem to be definitely established is that all four of the really dangerous people involved are dead. McBryde himself, Simões, Cachat, and Zilwicki. And, of course," his eyes hardened slightly, "the one ultimately responsible for this debacle."

Collin faced his father squarely.

"I assume you mean Isabel," he said. His father gave a small nod, and Collin grimaced. "I think that's an unfair assessment, Father. Quite unfair, in fact. I don't think *anyone* could have foreseen that *Jack McBryde* was going to turn traitor. I can tell you that *I* didn't finally accept the truth for almost two full days, and I had the advantage of a lot of data Isabel never got a chance to see. She reacted as quickly as anyone could have asked when she found out he was behaving . . . erratically. And, in my opinion, she acted appropriately, given what she could have known or understood at the time. There'd been absolutely no earlier indication that Jack, of all people, could have become a security risk. And don't forget, we didn't identify Zilwicki from Irvine's bugs' imagery until after the smoke had cleared. There's no evidence that Isabel imagined for one moment that Jack had been talking to *Anton Zilwicki*. Or that she had any reason to suspect anything of the sort, for that matter! All she knew at that point was that one of our most senior security officers, with a faultless record, in charge of one of the three most important installations on Mesa itself, had apparently decided to follow up Irvine's reports on his own.

"After the fact, knowing what we know now, it's obvious to us that she should've ordered his immediate arrest and launched a full bore investigation. But that's being wise after the fact, Father. No, it didn't immediately cross her mind that he was planning on betraying the entire Alignment, and maybe it should have. But given what she knew, she reacted immediately, and, frankly, she did exactly what I would have done in her place.

"The truth is, Father, that if Isabel were still alive and you were proposing to punish her, I'd be pointing out that by any logic and reason, you ought to be punishing *me* at the same time."

For a moment, father and son locked gazes. Then Albrecht looked away. A little smile came to his face, and he *might* have murmured, "Like father, like son," but neither Collin nor Benjamin knew for sure.

When his gaze came back, though, it was still hard, still purposeful.

"Am I right in assuming that you don't propose to punish McBryde's family?" he asked.

"No. We have no reason to think any of them were involved. None. Oh, we've questioned them, of course, *thoroughly*, and it's obvious they're deeply distraught and grieving. Defensive, too. I think they're in denial, to some extent, but I also think that's inevitable. What I haven't seen is any evidence that any of them knew a thing about Jack's plans. And, frankly, I'm positive Jack would never have involved them. Not in something like this, whatever his own motives may have been, he'd never have put his parents, Zachariah, or his sisters at risk. Not in a million years."

"Lathorous?"

"Steve doesn't seem to have been involved either, except by accident. And even then, only tangentially. It's true he was Jack's friend, but so are a lot of people." Collin grimaced. "Hell, Father, *I* liked Jack McBryde—a lot. Most people did."

"So you propose no punishment?"

"I'll give him a reprimand of some sort. But even that won't be very severe. Enough to make him walk on eggshells for a couple of years, but not enough to wreck his career."

"And Irvine?"

"You know, Father," Collin smiled crookedly, "he's actually the one bright spot in all this. He was completely loyal, start to finish, he was smart enough to realize *something* was happening that shouldn't have been, even if he didn't have a clue what that 'something' really was, and he's the only one involved who did his job properly."

"So your thoughts are—?"

"Well, he wants a field assignment, but, frankly, I don't think that's going to be possible any time soon." Collin shook his head. "He knows too much about what happened—especially now, after all the interrogations. We can't put him out, use him for a deep-penetration agent, with all of that rattling around inside his head. By the same token, his genotype doesn't really lend itself well to any other assignment. So, what I've been thinking, is that we might bring him all the way inside."

"*All* the way?" Albrecht's surprise was obvious, and Collin shrugged.

"I think it makes sense, Father. We can run him through the standard briefing program, see how he reacts. He's already halfway inside the onion, and as I just said, he's demonstrated loyalty *and* intelligence—and initiative, for that. If he can handle what's really going on, I think he could be very useful to us in Darius now that we're in the final runup to Prometheus."

"Um." Albrecht considered for several moments, then nodded. "All right, I can see that. Go ahead."

"Of course. And now," Collin pushed himself up out of his chair, "if you'll excuse me, there's a memorial being planned for all the people killed at Pine Valley Park. They'll be unveiling the sketch for it in a public meeting where the Children's Pavilion used to be this afternoon, and"—his face tightened with something that had absolutely no relationship to the physical discomfort of his still healing body—"I promised the kids we'd go."

CHAPTER SIXTY-THREE

Brice brought the cab to a halt at the very apex of Andrew's Curve. "Well, here we are."

Nancy Becker got up from the seat and went to stand with her face almost pressed against the observation window. That wasn't as foolish as it seemed, because that was a real window, not a vid screen. Allowing for the various protective shields, she was looking at the vista beyond with her own eyes, not something relayed electronically.

Brice had thought she'd like that. He'd timed the trip so that they'd be in shade when they arrived. Ameta, along with its various moons (the smallest and certainly the most recent of which was Parmley Station), revolved around an F5 subgiant star, which was half again as massive as Old Earth's sun, had twice the diameter, and was almost eight times more luminous. Had the roller coaster cab been perched in direct sunlight, Brice would have had no choice but to use the vid screens. Even with the protective shields—which were cut-rate quality, forget state of the art—it would have been too risky to look at the vista directly.

But they'd be able to do so for at least two hours before the station's revolution around Ameta brought this portion of it back out of the shade.

Brice came to stand next to her. Ameta was on full display, with all of its cloud bands and rings. There seemed to be every shade of blue and green there, along with enough white bands to set them off perfectly. As a bonus—this was rather unusual—the moon Hainuwele was just peeking around the curve of the giant planet below. Most of the time, Brice wasn't fond of the moon. It was close enough to Ameta to be subject to pronounced tidal heating, and its blotchy red, yellow and orange surface was usually sick-looking. In its current location, however, it was far enough away for the ugly details to be unnoticeable. At that distance, its bright colors made a striking contrast to the much cooler shades of its mother planet.

Even Yamato's Nebula was on its best behavior at the moment. It was as if the entire sidereal universe had decided to give its full support to Brice's bold and risky endeavor. He knew that was a fantasy, of course. But it *ought* to be true.

"It's beautiful," Nancy said softly.

"Told you," said Brice. Then, spent a minute or so silently berating himself for being less suave than any human male since the extinction of *Homo erectus*.

But he did not concede defeat. Quaked, but did not lose heart. He'd been planning this campaign for *months*, and had warned himself over and over that there would be setbacks. Most of them caused by his clumsy tongue.

This was the first time the two of them had ever been alone, since they met on the tarmac of the spaceport. The months they'd spent since their escape from Mesa drifting on the *Hali Sowle* had been the equivalent of months spent in the most densely populated apartment in creation. You'd *think* that a freighter massing slightly over a million tons would have enormous empty reaches, but . . . it didn't. Or, rather, it *did* . . . but it was a working commercial vessel, nothing more. Despite the capaciousness of its huge cargo holds, the living quarters were small and Spartan. Neither Ganny nor Uncle Andrew would have reacted kindly if Brice had proposed that time be taken from the repair work needed to get the ship's drive working again to turn some of the freight compartments into additional living quarters so that he might have a chance to spend some time alone with Nancy, either. It was best not to even think how Zilwicki or Cachat would have reacted to that suggestion, and, just to complete the unfairness of the universe, there'd been the minor fact that every square meter of every cargo hold was covered by the bridge security and monitoring cameras. So even though there were all those vast stretches of space, Brice had been gloomily certain that any effort on his part to inveigle Nancy out into them would have been instantly discovered. Even if it would never have happened to anyone else, it would definitely—inevitably!—have happened to *him*. At which point his supposed best friends and the loving members of his family, with that dubious quality which supposedly served them—ha!—as a sense of humor would have made his life a living hell.

To be sure, had Brice and Nancy *already* established a clear relationship, they could have figured out a thousand ways to elude the informal chaperonage provided by Ganny and Nancy's mother . . . and those damned cameras! But that was precisely the task at hand. And while there were undoubtedly some fifteen-year-old boys somewhere in the galaxy who'd have the sheer nerve to try to start a romance by immediately proposing that the two of them disappear somewhere so they could . . .

Well. Brice was not one of them. His isolated upbringing as a member of the Butry clan had made him very self-confident in some situations, but very shy in others.

This was one of the others.

Nancy's head turned, her attention drawn by the sight of a shuttle heading toward the *Hali Sowle*.

"How soon are they going to be leaving, do you know?"

Brice shook his head. "I haven't heard anything definite yet. Uncle Andrew says they're still waiting for the proper replacement parts to arrive." He laughed suddenly. "I think he's a bit pissed off that they don't trust *his* repairs to get them there, but *I* sure don't blame them. 'Course part of the reason he's pissed is because he already *had* all the parts he needed, before we dumped 'em out to squeeze you and your mom in. Way he sees it, it was all their fault to start with, so they don't have any business turning their noses up at his custom-built parts."

Nancy returned his grin, and he shrugged.

"Anyway, the guys on the *Custis*"—EMS *Custis* was the Erewhonese repair ship which had been at the station as part of the ongoing work to turn Parmley Station into something that still looked like a decrepit and mostly abandoned amusement park but was actually quite a powerful fortress—"agreed to make a quick hop to get replacements for us. I think their skipper probably works for the people we got *Hali Sowle* from in the first place. Anyway, *he* obviously thinks we should use real parts to fix the hyper generator."

"How about us? How soon will we be going to Beowulf?" Nancy asked.

"I'm not sure about that either. I know Ganny wants us to go as soon as possible. Well, given the space available and where we are in the rotation."

That had been part of the deal. Every member of the clan still young enough was being transported to Beowulf in order to begin prolong treatments. The order in which they'd go was determined by their age. Those like Sarah Armstrong and Michael Alsobrook who were getting close to the limit would be sent first, of course. Brice and Ed and James were not at the top of the list, but he figured they'd be going pretty soon.

Best of all, Nancy would be going with them. It was too late for her mother Steph to undergo prolong, but not for Nancy herself.

Zilwicki had been as good as his word. Better, actually. The expense of paying for a complete suite of prolong treatments for her daughter was going to be at least as high as the expense of setting up Steph Turner in a new restaurant. But Anton hadn't blinked. "I'll cover the cost if Beowulf gets sticky about it."

From something Cachat had said, though, Brice thought Beowulf would probably just handle Nancy's treatments as part of the general arrangement they'd made with Ganny. When Brice had once expressed his concern over the issue to Victor, the Havenite had gotten a very cold smile on his face.

"I wouldn't lose any sleep over it, Brice. It's going to be a while yet—there are some other people we have to talk to first, for several reasons—but unless I miss my guess, you're going to see the rage of Beowulf unleashed in the universe sometime pretty damned soon now. They're not going to quibble over the cost of an extra prolong treatment while they're sinking a fortune into forging the weapons to finally take down Grendel. Which they surely will, once they learn the monster has a mother after all."

The last part of that hadn't meant anything to Brice, but the gist of it was clear enough.

Nancy went back to looking at Ameta. "It's so beautiful."

The moment had come. He was sure of it. Months of planning—he'd even practiced in a mirror—enabled him to slide his arm around Nancy's waist with no more clumsiness than a walrus calf taking its first waddle across the ice.

He held his breath, waiting for an explosion.

But she said nothing. Just continued to look at Ameta's glory, with a smile on her face. And about a minute later, nestled her head onto his shoulder.

Brice was utterly thrilled. This was, for sure and certain, the greatest exploit in his life. The greatest thus far, rather—in a life that would now last for centuries.

"I'm going to Torch, Andrew," Steph Turner said. "That's just the way it is." She leaned back from the table in the clan's mess hall on the station, setting her shoulders stubbornly. "And quit trying to claim you're doing anything but guessing. Me, I don't see any way this place is ever going to sustain enough of a clientele to keep a restaurant going."

His own shoulders were set almost as stubbornly as hers. Not quite.

"I don't know if I can get any work on Torch," he whined.

"Are you kidding? It won't be all that long, you numbskull, before the whole damn galaxy knows that Andrew Artlett is the mechanical wizard—the jackleg mechanic of all time—who got the *Hali Sowle* through on its desperate mission. Your problem won't be finding work, it'll be dodging Mesan assassination squads."

She got that twisted little smile on her face that Andrew found just as hard to resist now as he had the first time he'd seen it, less than a day after the *Hali Sowle* left orbit from Mesa. "And what better place to stay safe from those bastards than a Ballroom planet?"

"Well..."

"Make up your mind. I'm going to Torch. Are you coming with me or not?"

"I guess."

"I think the Republic owes us a stipend too, Victor. 'Course, I don't expect one as big as Beowulf's, much less as big as the one I figure I'll be squeezing out of the Star Kingdom." Friede Butry gave Victor Cachat a twisted smile of her own. "I realize you Havenites are the poor cousins in this part of the galaxy."

"I told you, you're just wasting your time. Sure, I'll put in a word for you. Be glad to. But after that, it'll work its way up the ladder until—don't hold your breath—it finally reaches Those Who

Decide Such Things." Cachat shrugged. "After that . . . ? You've been around a lot longer than I have, Ganny. You know what bureaucrats are like."

She said nothing for a few seconds. Just studied him with an intensity Victor didn't understand and even found a little disturbing.

Then she said: "I forget sometimes, the way you're still a babe in the woods when it comes to certain things."

"What does that mean?"

"Victor Cachat, your days of being on the bottom rungs of the ladder—or of the totem pole, if that means anything to you—are coming to an end. In about as spectacular a manner as you could imagine. A few weeks from now—sure as hell, a few months from now—a 'word put in' by Victor Cachat will be putting fleets into motion. Or whatever the flamboyantly notorious galactic super secret agent equivalent of that is, anyway. So I figure you're good for the stipend—to which I will point out that you just agreed."

After a while, the frown on Victor's face faded. But by then, his complexion was beginning to get pale.

Ganny chuckled. "Didn't think of that, did you? I found out yesterday from one of the BSC people that Anton Zilwicki appeared in a widely broadcast vid documentary a while back. So you've got some catching up to do. And since he's already nailed down the monicker of 'Cap'n Zilwicki, Scourge of the Spaceways,' you'll need to come up with something different. For the documentaries they'll be doing about you, I mean. My own recommendation would be either 'Black Victor' or 'Cachat, Slaver's Bane.'"

"I'm a *spy*."

Ganny shook her head sympathetically. "No, Victor Cachat. You *were* a spy."

CAST OF CHARACTERS

Allfrey, Philip	Brigadier General, Oravil Barregos' senior Gendarmerie officer.
Alsobrook, Michael	Member of the Butry clan on Parmley Station.
Arai, Hugh	Beowulf's Biological Survey Corps, CO BSCS *Ouroboros;* also commander of the ship's commando force; later chief of security for Queen Berry of Torch.
Armstrong, Sarah	Member of the Butry clan on Parmley Station.
Artlett, Andrew	Great-nephew of Ganny Butry; uncle of Brice Miller.
Bardasano, Isabel	Senior operative and second in command Mesan Alignment Security.
Barregos, Oravil	Maya Sector Governor.
Beausoleil, Noémie	Citizen Captain, People's Navy in Exile (People's Navy in Exile); CO, PNES *Napoleon Bonaparte.*
Blomqvist, Gansükh	Officer, Mesan System Guard; junior inspector, customs operations.
Bostwick, Hervé P.	Citizen Captain, People's Navy in Exile; CO, PNES *Charlemagne.*
Brosnan, Gail	Maya Sector Lieutenant Governor.

Butry, Elfriede
Margarete
Also known as "Ganny" or "Ganny El;" matriarch of the extended family (essentially a small clan) that officially owns and partially controls Parmley Station, the largely defunct amusement park in orbit around the giant ringed planet Ameta.

Carte, David
Commander, Solarian League Navy (Solarian League Navy); CO, CL(L) SLNS *Sharpshooter*. Also CO CL Division 7036.3.

Chapman, Alexander
Erewhonese admiral.

Christiansen, Philippine
Citizen Lieutenant Commander, People's Navy in Exile; astrogation officer, PNES *Leon Trotsky*.

Clarke, Donald
Oravil Barregos' senior economic adviser.

Cullingford, J.T.
Commander, Solarian League Navy; CO, arsenal ship SLNS *Masquerade*.

Detweiler, Albrecht
Head of the Detweiler family and Chief Executive Officer of the Mesan Alignment.

Detweiler, Benjamin
Son/clone of Albrecht; effectively Secretary of War of the Mesan Alignment.

Detweiler, Collin
Son/clone of Albrecht; Director, Mesan Alignment Security.

Dobbs, Michael
Lieutenant Commander, Solarian League Navy; Laura Raycraft's chief of staff.

Du Havel, W.E.B. ("Web")
Prime Minister of the Kingdom of Torch.

Egert, Irénée
Citizen Captain, People's Navy in Exile; CO, PNES *Chao Kung Ming*.

Evans, Karen
Lieutenant, Royal Manticoran Navy (Royal Manticoran Navy); astrogator of the HMS *Harvest Joy*.

Foley, Jennifer
Cousin of Brice Miller.

Frank, Jeremy
Mayan official; senior aide for Governor Barregos.

Garner, Marlene ("Marti")	Executive officer, BSCS *Ouroboros;* also a member of Arai's commando team and later a member of the Biological Survey Corps team detached to serve as security detail for Queen Berry.
Georgos, Karen	Lieutenant, Solarian League Navy; Rear Admiral Luiz Rozsak's staff communications officer.
Granger, Adelaide	Captain, Mannerheim System-Defense Force; the commanding officer of Admiral Osiris Trajan's flagship.
Grimault, Ludivine	Citizen Lieutenant; Konidis' staff communications officer.
Guglik, Anne	Lieutenant Commander, Solarian League Navy; CO, DD SLNS *Hernando Cortés.* Also CO DD Division 3029.3.
Habib, Edie	Commander, Solarian League Navy; Rozsak's chief of staff, essentially Rozsak's permanent executive officer and more often referred to as "XO" than as chief of staff.
Haldane, Iain	Commander, Solarian League Navy; CO CL(L) *Ranger.* Also CO CL Division 7036.1.
Hall, Michael William	Manticoran hyper-physicist assigned to Congo Wormhole survey expedition.
Hammarberg, Jonas	Lieutenant Commander, Royal Manticoran Navy; officer on HMS *Harvest Joy.*
Hargraves, Christy	Citizen Commander, People's Navy in Exile; senior engineer, PNES *Charlemagne.*
Hartman, Ed	Cousin of Brice Miller.
Hartman, Millicent	Citizen Commander, People's Navy in Exile; Luff's chief of staff.
Hartneady, James	Senior Chief Coxswain, HMS *Harvest Joy.*
Hasselberg, Niklas	Commander, Mannerheim System-Defense Force; Admiral Osiris Trajan's chief of staff.

Henson, Stephanie — Officer, BSCS *Ouroboros;* also a member of Arai's commando team and later a member of the Biological Survey Corps team detached to serve as security detail for Queen Berry.

Horton, Glenn — Erewhonese admiral.

Hronek, Linda — Manticoran hyper-physicist assigned to Congo Wormhole expedition.

Hübner, César — Citizen Lieutenant Commander, People's Navy in Exile; TO, PNES *Chao Kung Ming.*

Imbesi, Walter — Head of the Imbesi family; unofficially, one of the four people in the quadrumvirate that effectively rules Erewhon.

Irvine, Lajos — Undercover agent for Jack McBryde.

Jeremy X — Secretary of War of the Kingdom of Torch; formerly head of the Audubon Ballroom, the ex-slave guerrilla force considered by some people to be a terrorist organization.

Kamerling, Yvonne — Citizen Lieutenant, People's Navy in Exile; Luff's staff communications officer.

Kamstra, Dirk-Steven — Commodore, Solarian League Navy; CO, Light Cruiser Squadron 7036 and CL(L) SLNS *Marksman.* Kamstra is wearing two official "hats" (CO LCS 7036 and CO *Marksman*), and his "acting rank" is closer to that of commodore or even rear admiral; he's Rozsak's senior officer "afloat," effectively his task force commander.

Kao Huang — Lieutenant Colonel, Solarian Marines; Rozsak's senior ground combat advisor/deputy.

Kare, Jordin — Manticoran hyper-physicist assigned to Congo Wormhole expedition.

Keller, Gordon — Lieutenant, Royal Manticoran Navy; HMS *Harvest Joy*'s tactical officer.

Konidis, Santander	Citizen Commodore, People's Navy in Exile; later commanding officer, Operation Ferret.
Lara	Former Scrag, now one of Palane's "Amazons;" informally part of Berry's security team.
Lathorous, Steven	Jack McBryde's second-in-command, assistant chief of security, Gamma Center.
Laukkonen, Santeri	A fence and arms merchant for criminals (including pirates) in the Ajax System. He is also one of Luis Rozsak's (or, rather, Jiri Watanapongse's) informants.
Laurent, Jarko	Citizen Commander, People's Navy in Exile; succeeds as CO of PNES *Leon Trotsky*.
Laursen, Jimmi	Commander, Solarian League Navy; CO, arsenal ship SLNS *Kabuki*.
Le Fossi, Maria	Commander, Solarian League Navy; CO, CL SLNS *Freya*. Also CO DD Flotilla 2960.
Lewis, James	Cousin of Brice Miller.
Lim, Samuel	Commander, Royal Manticoran Navy; HMS *Harvest Joy*'s executive officer.
Luff, Adrian	Citizen Commodore, People's Navy in Exile; commanding officer, Operation Ferret.
Lund, Steve	Officer, Mesan System Guard; senior inspector, customs operations.
Maddock, Gowan	Captain, Mesan Alignment Navy; ostensibly Manpower's liaison with the People's Navy in Exile, covered as an officer in the Mesa *System* Navy.
Magilen, Julie	Barregos' personal secretary/office manager.
Malenkov, Rachel	Citizen Lieutenant Commander, People's Navy in Exile; succeeds as TO of PNES *Leon Trotsky*.

Manson, Jerry   Lieutenant, Solarian League Navy; an intelligence officer on Rozsak's staff.

McBryde, Jack   Chief of Security, Mesan Alignment's Gamma Center.

McBryde, Zachariah   Brother of Jack McBryde.

McKenzie, Richard   Lieutenant, Solarian League Navy; SLNS *Artillerist*'s chief engineer.

Miller, Brice   Nephew of Andrew Artlett.

Milliken, Jessica   Commander, Mesan Alignment Navy; Gowan Maddock's second-in-command; ostensibly one of Manpower's liaisons with the People's Navy in Exile, covered as an officer in the Mesa *System* Navy.

Montaigne, Catherine   Leading figure in the Liberal Party of Manticore; common-law wife of Anton Zilwicki; longtime and close friend of Web Du Havel and Jeremy X.

Nyborg, Ildikó   Commander, Mannerheim System-Defense Force; Trajan's operations officer.

Palane, Thandi   Commanding officer of the armed forces of the Kingdom of Torch.

Petit, Jason   Citizen Lieutenant Commander, People's Navy in Exile; Commodore Santander Konidis' staff operations officer.

Raycraft, Laura   Commander Solarian League Navy; CO, CL(L) SLNS *Artillerist*. Also CO CL Div 7036.2.

Rensi, Cornelia   Lieutenant, Solarian League Navy; *Artillerist*'s communications officer.

Rozsak, Luiz   Rear Admiral, Solarian League Navy; Governor Barregos' top military officer.

Saburo X   Former member of Audubon Ballroom; later head of Queen Berry's security force.

Sakellaris, Kalyca   Citizen Captain, People's Navy in Exile; CO, PNES *Maximilien Robespierre*.

Sànchez, Gino — Citizen Commander, People's Navy in Exile; Konidis' chief of staff.

Siegel, Travis — Lieutenant, Solarian League Navy; *Artillerist*'s tactical officer.

Simões, Francesca — Clone child of Harriet and Herlander Simões, placed with them by the Mesan Alignment Long-Range Planning Board.

Simões, Harriet — Mesan Alignment scientist assigned to Gamma Center, wife of Herlander, mother of Francesca.

Simões, Herlander — Mesan Alignment scientist assigned to Gamma Center, husband of Harriet, father of Francesca.

Snorrason, Hjálmar — Lieutenant Commander, Solarian League Navy; CO, DD SLNS *Napoleon*. Also CO DD Division 3029.1.

Spangen, Vegar — Barregos' personal bodyguard; commander of the governor's security detail.

Stahlin, Jim — Lieutenant Commander, Solarian League Navy; CO, DD SLNS *Gustavus Adolphus*. Also CO DD Division 3029.2.

Stensrud, Melanie — Commander, Solarian League Navy; CO, arsenal ship SLNS *Charade*.

Stravinsky, Pierre — Citizen Commander, People's Navy in Exile; operations officer, PNES *Leon Trotsky*.

Szklenski, Ted — Lieutenant Commander, Solarian League Navy; XO, SLNS *Marksman*.

Takano, Haruka — Intelligence officer, BSCS *Ouroboros;* also a member of Arai's commando team and later a member of the Biological Survey Corps team detached to serve as security detail for Queen Berry.

Taub, Andrew (Andy) — Cousin of Brice Miller.

Trajan, Osiris — Admiral, Mannerheim System-Defense Force (Mannerheim System-Defense Force); commanding officer, Task Force Four.

Trimm, E.D.	Officer, Mesan System Guard; senior inspector, customs operations.
Underwood, Charles-Henri	Citizen Commander, People's Navy in Exile; XO, PNES *Chao Kung Ming*.
Vergnier, Olivier	Citizen Captain, People's Navy in Exile; CO, PNES *Leon Trotsky*.
Watanapongse, Jiri	Lieutenant Commander, Solarian League Navy; Rozsak's staff intelligence officer.
Winton, Ruth	Manticoran princess; close friend of Berry Zilwicki; assistant director of Torch intelligence service.
Wise, Richard	Barregos' senior civilian spy.
Wix, Richard	Manticoran hyper-physicist assigned to Congo Wormhole survey expedition.
Womack, Robert	Lieutenant, Solarian League Navy; TO, SLNS *Marksman*.
Wu, Richard	Lieutenant, Solarian League Navy—astrogator, SLNS *Marksman*.
Yana	Former Scrag, now one of Palane's "Amazons;" detached to work with Victor Cachat in the mission to Mesa.
Zachary, Josepha	Captain, Royal Manticoran Navy; CO of the survey vessel HMS *Harvest Joy*.
Zilwicki, Anton	Head of Torch intelligence, although he is still a citizen of the Star Kingdom of Manticore; formerly an officer in the Manticoran armed forces; common-law husband of Catherine Montaigne; father of Helen Zilwicki and adoptive father of Berry and Lars Zilwicki.
Zilwicki, Berry	Queen of Torch; adopted daughter of Anton Zilwicki.
Zilwicki, Lars	Brother of Berry.